Noble

&

A Distant Land

Noble Outlaw
&
A Distant Land

St. Martin's Paperbacks

These are works of fiction. All of the characters, organizations, and events portrayed in them are either products of the author's imagination or are used fictitiously.

Published in the United States by St. Martin's Paperbacks, an imprint of St. Martin's Publishing Group.

NOBLE OUTLAW / A DISTANT LAND

Noble Outlaw copyright © 1975 by Matt Braun.
A Distant Land copyright © 1988 by Matthew Braun.

For information address St. Martin's Publishing Group, 120 Broadway, New York, NY 10271.

www.stmartins.com

ISBN: 978-1-250-21469-0

Our books may be purchased in bulk for promotional, educational, or business use. Please contact your local bookseller or the Macmillan Corporate and Premium Sales Department at 1-800-221-7945, ext. 5442, or by e-mail at MacmillanSpecialMarkets@macmillan.com.

Printed in the United States of America

Noble Outlaw St. Martin's Paperbacks edition / September 1996
A Distant Land St. Martin's Paperbacks edition / July 2005

10 9 8 7 6 5 4 3 2 1

Noble Outlaw

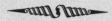

A sliver of fire seared Wes' side and in the same instant he heard the deep roar of a shotgun. Acting out of sheer reflex, he jerked the Navy and placed five shots in the precise spot he had seen the muzzle flash. There was a momentary lull while everyone stood rooted in their tracks, then the stablehand lurched out of a dark passageway between two buildings. The shotgun fell from his hand, and he teetered there like a tree rocking in the wind. His legs gave way all of a sudden, as if chopped from beneath him, and he pitched facedown in the street.

Hardin felt something warm and sticky soaking his shirt front, and without realizing it, his knees buckled and he found himself sitting in the road. From a great distance he heard the raspy croak of his own voice.

"Can you beat that? The sonovabitch hit me."

To
Nancy Gordon Hart
Friends for all seasons, all time

Book One
1868–1871

CHAPTER 1

1

The boy sat beneath a tall pecan tree beside the creek bank. Overhead the leaves rustled in a gentle summer breeze and somewhere in the distance a lone crow cawed in warning. Splintered shafts of sunlight, fading slowly into dusk, filtered through the pecan grove and sent sparkles of gold dancing along the stream. Across the water, beyond another stand of trees, lay a lush meadow, brilliant with bluebonnets and scarlet buckeyes. But the boy saw none of this. Nor had he heard the sentinel crow raise its strident call. He was concentrating on the gun.

Working with meticulous care, he measured powder from a flask into the pistol chambers. It was a weapon that had seen much abuse, worn and scarred, a veteran of untold battles in the late war. Yet it was serviceable and fired true, and the boy counted it his most prized possession. The man who sold it to him, a gimp-legged survivor of Shiloh and Vicksburg and other bloodbaths, had instructed him briefly in its use. According to the former Confederate, once a sergeant in Nathan Forrest's cavalry, it was the finest sidearm to emerge from the war. A Navy Colt with an octagonal barrel bored for .36 caliber. Light and well-balanced, quick to draw, yet powerful enough to down any man struck squarely in the vitals.

Sometimes, when he came to the pecan grove to practice, the boy stargazed a bit, conjuring up gory battlegrounds and

bluebelly Yankees. In his mind's eye he saw them fall before
the leaden jolt of his little gun like hay under a scythe. The
Navy bucked and spat, belching orangey streaks of flame,
and the whimpering Northerners toppled over in neat, win-
nowed rows. It was a pleasurable pastime, this killing of
Yankees, and if he thought on it hard enough he could even
visualize himself as having been there. Behind the gun, pulling the trigger, cutting them down with precision and unerring aim. He liked to imagine the cavalry engagements, the
thunderous charge of horsemen, and the deadly Navy sweeping the field with a sharp, barking sting. At times, if he really
put his mind to it, he was one of them. Astride a fiery stallion. Out in front, where the fighting was the thickest. And
always the little Navy was in his hand drilling holes that
spurted bright crimsoned fountains and left the earth puddled
with blood.

Seating a ball in the last cylinder, he tamped it down hard
with the loading lever. Then he hauled out caps and pressed
them snugly in place on the nipples at the back. The Navy
was ready to fire.

The boy stood and walked to the edge of the creek bank.
Each evening, when the work was done, he came here to
practice. Over the past month, since buying the pistol, he had
taught himself to use it with considerable skill. Sometimes it
was difficult to sneak away from the farm and his father's
watchful eye, but seldom a day passed that he didn't manage
to fire at least twenty or thirty rounds. At first he had used
the trees for targets, notching out an X with his knife for a
mark. As he grew accustomed to the Navy, and gained a feel
for its balance, he steadily became more accurate. Under
twenty paces he found that he no longer needed sights. The
gun became an extension of his arm, much as a pointed finger, and in three out of five shots he could place the slug
within a handspan of the mark. Along the creek some half-
dozen tree trunks were now pitted and scarred where he had
fired on them from varying angles. Within the past week he
had added a new twist to the game, stretching himself for a

more finely attuned sense of aim, and every evening his last full load was reserved for this sterner test.

Grasping a stoppered bottle, he lofted it in a shallow arc upstream. The bottle sank in a small silvery splash, then popped to the surface and came bobbing downstream as the current caught hold. He held the gun at his side, waiting, eyes fixed on the tossing bubble of glass. As it passed an overhanging limb his arm swept upward and locked shoulder-high. The Navy jumped with a sharp crack and a geyser of water erupted inches behind the bottle. Thumbing the hammer, he triggered two quick shots, missing by an even wider margin. Then he steadied himself, swinging the barrel in a smooth, unhurried arc, and fired again as the bottle passed directly to his front. Glass shards leaped skyward in a watery explosion and the back half of the bottle disappeared. The front half settled deeper, tilting upright, and for a moment part of the neck and the cork stopper bobbed nearly motionless in the stream. Deliberately, sighting along the barrel with both eyes, he feathered off the last round. One edge of the cork shredded as the slug skimmed past and thunked into the water. An instant later the bottle upended and sank from sight.

Standing there, the boy grunted to himself with a mixture of disgust and pride. He had rushed the first three shots, ignoring everything he had learned about the deliberation needed for accuracy. Hurry had caused him to waste lead, and had the bottle been a Yankee he might never have got the fourth shot off. It was a lesson he would tuck away and remember. There was a fine borderline between fast and sudden, and the man who rushed merely hurried his departure to hell.

Still, he had hit the cork. Something he'd never before pulled off. That last shot was the most near perfect he had yet made. Unhurried, with just the right blend of target and barrel centered in his eyes, and the silky touch of a butterfly on the trigger. It was a hell of a shot, and he had every right to gloat a little bit.

Except for one thing.

Instead of his last shot it should have been his first. When he could wing the necks off bottles first crack out of the box then he'd have something to crow about. Until that day rolled around, though, he still had a lot of powder to burn.

Dusk was fast approaching and he set such thoughts aside for another time. It would never do to be late for supper, and he had a good half-mile run back to the farm. Quickly, he disassembled the pistol and scrubbed it thoroughly with lye soap and a thin wire brush he'd bought in town. Then he dried it, wiped the parts with a greasy rag, and put it back together. Satisfied that it was free of grit and burnt powder, he wrapped the Navy in an oilskin cloth, and along with his loading gear, stuck it in a tanned cowhide bag. After drawing the thongs tight, he crammed it beneath the stump of a dead tree that had been struck by lightning three summers back. The summer the war ended.

Brushing twigs and leaves into the stump hole, he removed all sign from the hiding spot, then took off in a dogtrot toward home.

Less than ten minutes later he skidded to a halt behind the barn and started drawing deep breaths as he crossed the yard. When he entered the kitchen he had his wind back and a look of youthful innocence plastered across his face. It was a look he had cultivated since childhood, and around the Hardin household it came in uncommonly handy.

His mother turned from the stove and inspected him critically for a moment. Then she blew a wisp of damp hair from her forehead and nodded toward the front of the house.

"Your father wants to see you in the parlor."

"Aw cripes, Ma, I haven't done nothin'. What's he want now?"

"Don't try and wheedle me, John Wesley. You just march in there and find out for yourself." She brushed at the stray lock of hair and went back to the stove, muttering to herself. "Lord save us, I mortally never saw a boy so set on getting himself into meanness. Never in all my born days."

The youngster watched her slam lids and bang pots for a

minute, then abruptly decided he would get no help in that direction. The only thing left was to face the music, and he headed for the parlor wondering what hymn his old man would dust off this time.

James Hardin was exactly where the boy expected to find him. Seated in his rocker with a Bible laid out across his knees. Though a farmer by necessity, he was a preacher in his spare time and all day on Sundays, a man who had heard the calling and ministered to a flock of Bible-thumping Texans in the little town of Mount Calm. Most of the time his face was set in an astringent expression, as if his jaws had been broken and wired shut. Yet in his off moments, when he wasn't thinking so hard on the Lord's business, he could display a rare gift for understanding and forgiveness. This clearly wasn't one of those moments, though. Nor did he look in any mood to forgive his second-born, the one he'd named after the founder of the Church. The rocker squeaked to a halt and he stabbed with a bony finger at a chair on the opposite side of the fireplace.

"Sit down, Wes. I have something to ask you."

He waited while the boy crossed the room and took a seat. At times like this he wondered where he'd gone wrong. How a man could raise two sons as different as day and night. Joe, his eldest, was a fine upstanding Christian. Already had his own farm and a family that brought pride to the Hardin name. But Wes seemed cast from a different mold entirely. At fifteen he was the unchallenged hellion of Mount Calm. Big for his age, so large that his father hadn't tried to whip him in over a year, he was forever starting fistfights at school. And there were reports that he had recently shown a remarkable interest in a certain girl. All of which embarrassed the old man as a preacher and disturbed him as a father. Yet not nearly so much as he was at this very moment. Particularly if what he suspected was actually true.

Fixing the boy with a stern look, he demanded, "You have a gun, don't you?"

"A gun! Where'd you get an idea like that, Pa?"

"None of your tomfoolery, now. I followed you today and

lost your tracks in the woods. But on the way back I heard gunfire from the direction of the creek. It was you, wasn't it?''

The boy's ears reddened and his tone was hotly defensive. ''Well, cripes a'mighty, Pa, what if it was? Everybody else has got a gun. Why shouldn't I have one?''

''It's the Devil's handiwork. An instrument of death and damnation.'' There was a harried sharpness in the old man's words. ''Do you want your soul to burn in eternal perdition?''

''C'mon, Pa. God's not gonna send me to hell for shootin' up a few trees.''

'' 'He that diggeth a pit shall fall into it.' Ecclesiastes. Chapter Ten, verse eight.''

The youngster deliberated an instant and then brightened. '' 'The words of the wise are as goads.' Ecclesiastes. Chapter Twelve, verse eleven.''

''That's blasphemy, Wes. Blasphemy!'' James Hardin's voice shook with indignation. ''You will go fetch that gun and bring it back to me. Before supper. Is that understood?''

''Pa, I'll sure give 'er a try. You bet'cha I will. But if I'm not back by the time you get done eatin', don't start to worryin' over it. Tell you the truth, I'm not real hungry anyhow.''

The boy came to his feet and headed toward the kitchen, then changed his mind and went out the front door. When the latch clicked shut the old man wearily knuckled his brow and uttered a long sigh. After a while his eyes drifted to the Bible and his lips began to move in silent invocation.

2

Wes Hardin rode into his uncle's farm outside Livingston three days later. After a night of bickering over the gun, interspersed with threats of hellfire and damnation, he at last finagled his way around the old man. While his father never suspected that he had been flimflammed, it was actually the boy who planted the thought and nurtured it along. Perhaps Mount Calm, with all its temptations, was a bad influence. If he spent the summer working on Uncle Barnett's farm it might just get him started on the straight and narrow. The elder Hardin had swallowed it hook, line, and sinker, and appeared relieved to have the headstrong youngster off his hands.

But if the old man breathed easier, Wes was positively glowing. For one of the few times in his life, he was out from under his father's thumb. Not unlike a spirited pony with its fetters removed, he felt wild and free as the wind. Upon leaving the house he had to restrain himself from jumping up in the air and clicking his heels, and it was all he could manage to hide the grin that threatened to spill over. Bursting with energy, the boy quickly put his newfound freedom to practical use.

He circled back to the creek and collected his gun.

Afterward, with the Navy stuck in his belt, he turned his horse east toward Livingston. With the gun loaded and resting comfortably against his belly, he felt a yard wide and ten feet tall. Riding along the public road, his own man at last, he could only marvel at the hullabaloo raised by his father. The way he had it figured, anybody who worked like a man ought to be treated like a man. Yet his father still thought of him as a child, and all too often acted as if he didn't have sense enough to come in out of the rain. Which was a damn poor way—leastways from where Wes stood—to treat somebody who was full-grown and able to think for himself.

That he had sprouted tall and lithely muscled, bigger than most men, wasn't something people had to be told. Already he was just a shade under six feet, with lean flanks and broad shoulders, and farm work had turned his body hard as nails. He moved with the effortless, catlike grace of an athlete, and those who went against him in a slugfest came away looking as if they had tangled with a buzzsaw. After whipping everyone in school, there wasn't a boy left in Mount Calm who cared to try him on for size.

The next step, logically enough, would have been to test

himself against grown men. Trading blows, feeling his fist crunch against meat and bone, was something he enjoyed, a rough-and-tumble sport in which he took considerable zest and went out of his way to promote. Yet the men of Mount Calm, pool hall loafers and regulars at the town's one saloon, evidenced no great rush to butt heads with this young bull. Something about the square jaw and the wild look to his pale gray eyes gave them pause. They merely watched as he swaggered about town, waiting expectantly for somebody to knock the chip off his shoulder. But none of them felt the urge personally to test his grit. Though unspoken, there was common agreement on the subject.

It wouldn't do for a man to get tromped by an overgrown boy.

None of this fazed Wes one way or the other. He liked to fight and would gladly accommodate anyone looking for trouble. But he rarely started it. Contrary to what the townspeople thought, he wasn't spoiling to hand out lumps and bruises. Nor did he throw his weight around or act the part of a bully. He was simply a cocky kid, with a hair-trigger temper and a sledgehammer in each fist. Trouble sought him out like iron filings drawn to a magnet. Other boys took offense at his devil-may-care manner, and seemed gripped by some curious compulsion to taunt him over the line. In all the years he had attended the Mount Calm school, he'd never started a fight. Yet it was only after he had thrashed every boy in school, and some of them twice, that they had really had enough.

This was another of those things his father had never understood, or accepted as truth. Fighting was wrong, a sin according to the Gospel. He laid the blame on Wes, branding him a hotheaded troublemaker, and had taken him to the woodshed more than once to quell his pugnacious spirit. Within the last year, though, the boy had shown signs of rebelling. No longer would he meekly submit to the beatings, and considering his size, the trips to the woodshed had ceased. Instead, Reverend Hardin counseled him to turn the other cheek and reflect on the teachings of the Lord God Jehovah.

Wes found the advice impractical, if not downright foolish. The way he saw it, turning the other cheek merely got a fellow two black eyes instead of one.

The three-day ride to Livingston gave him time to ponder, among other things, the wisdom of his father's religious zeal. It was a difficult life, being a preacher's son, particularly with the added burden of having been named after the founder of the Methodist sect. People expected too much of him, like goodness and mercy and turning the other cheek. While he was his father's son, he just wasn't built that way. Only a simpering pisswillie let another fellow walk over him, and he'd roast in hell before he showed the white feather. Anybody who pushed him would get pushed back, and the rougher they shoved the better he liked it.

Now, there was this big rhubarb about the gun. Thou shalt not kill! Vengeance is mine, saith the Lord! His father had trotted out Scripture like a pitchman selling snake oil off the tailgate of a wagon. But so far as the boy could see, the whole windy sermon had been little more than a contradiction in terms. The meek might inherit the earth, but if they did, it was strictly an accident of nature. Like a tent show freak or a two-headed calf. However humble and righteous they were, God sure as hell didn't give them much help along the way.

The truth of that was plain to see in the way the war ended. If the Confederates had had more guns and less God it would have been a different story. That God hadn't waved his magic wand and made the South victorious ought to have been clear to everybody. But it appeared to be a message that was lost on the meek and humble servants of the Lord.

Since the summer of '65 the Union Army of Occupation had ruled Texas with an iron hand, conquerors in the harshest sense of the word. Carpetbaggers had swarmed in from the North, hovering over the land like vultures drawn to ripe meat. Next came the scalawags, southern-born turncoats, swearing allegiance to the Union in return for a license to rob their neighbors and kin. Between them they held every public office of importance across the state, and their dictates were enforced by the bayonets of federal troops.

Worse yet, Union commanders held the power of life and death over the people. Their word was law, without appeal or mitigation. The verdict of a military tribunal could send a man to prison for defaming the flag. Or hang him for some trifling offense that became heinous only when committed by a Southerner. It was a land where all men were held equal before the law—guilty whatever the charge—just so long as they were, white and native-born.

Not unlike the seven tribes in the Old Testament, the Confederate states had been shunted aside by their God, left to the questionable mercy of a conqueror who believed that an eye for an eye was but the first step along the road to retribution. Yet there were still men, Reverend James Hardin among them, who abhorred the use of guns and counseled the virtue of meek submission.

It confused Wes not so much as it annoyed him. A man should fight whatever the odds, especially if he was in the right. To back off and hide behind the good book was just plain foolish. The Lord worked in mysterious ways, well enough, but that didn't include wet-nursing dimdots and fainthearts. Leastways if He was to be judged on past performances, it appeared the Lord always threw the game to the side that carried the stoutest club.

Shortly before sundown of his third day on the road Wes neared the farm of his uncle. Suddenly he felt a surge of excitement come over him and his irksome ruminations were quickly forgotten. Barnett Hardin was a great bear of a man, ham-fisted and loud and uncommonly profane. Not at all like his preacher brother. The boy had always admired him, finding it easy to overlook any minor flaws of character, and the summer ahead promised grand things. As he rode into the yard and piled off his horse there was a booming shout from the barn. A moment later his uncle appeared and lumbered toward him like a boar grizzly walking upright.

"Gawdamn my soul, is that you, Wes?" Barnett Hardin smote him across the back and almost wrenched his shoulder out of the socket shaking hands. "Jesus Pesus Christ! You're growed up, boy. Damn me if you're not."

Wes grinned and turned the color of ox blood. "Well, I still got a ways to go."

"Horseapples! I'll bet you could give me a good tussle right now. How much you weigh? Two hunnert? Little more, mebbe?"

"Aw, quit your joshin'. I'm nowhere near that. Hundred and seventy at the outside. And I don't want to wrestle you, neither."

"The hell you say. Them that eats has got to fight for their supper around here." The older man cocked one eyebrow, inspecting the pistol, and rapped him in the belly. "See you got yourself a peashooter. Figger you was gonna meet up with some robbers, did you?"

"That's sorta why I'm here." Wes touched the Navy and suddenly wished he'd hidden it in his saddlebags. "Pa and me had it out 'cause I got myself a gun and he sent me over to spend the summer with you. Guess he had some idea you'd get me straightened out. Likely he's already got a letter posted with all the particulars."

"Why, Christ A'mighty,'course he does, boy. When it gets here we'll have ourselves a high old time readin' all that hellfire and brimstone talk he writes. Oughta be a barrel of laughs."

"You mean it's awright? I can keep the gun."

"Shore you can. Just so you don't shoot your toes off." The boy's look of relief brought a rumbling chuckle. "Listen, Wes, a gun ain't no worse than the fella behind it. That's a lesson I learned in the war. A man that can't be trusted is just as dangerous without a gun as he is with one. You tuck that away and keep it in mind."

"I will for a fact. You bet'cha I will. Makes sense too."

"Let's get ourselves some supper and then I'm gonna let you try puttin' a knot in my tail. Hunnert-seventy, you say? Damn, we gotta get you fattened up, boy."

Barnett Hardin clapped a paw over his shoulder and steered him toward the house. As they went through the door Wes smiled to himself and wondered how it would come out.

He'd never wrestled a real live gorilla before.

3

Along about sundown Wes unhitched the team from the traces and led them toward the barn. It had been a brutally hot day and he was glad to see it done with. Barnett Hardin played no favorites when it came to work and he demanded as much of the boy as any field hand. Not that Wes minded. He had worked hard ever since he was old enough to spit, and a little sweat was good for the joints. Kept them well oiled. However much was asked of him by his uncle, he gave it willingly. He was being treated like a man for the first time in his life and he meant to earn his keep. But there was one part of the bargain he hadn't counted on, and it was fast wearing him down to the nubbin.

After supper every night his uncle insisted they lock horns in a free-for-all wrestling match. Wes hadn't minded the first night, or even the second, but a solid week of such nonsense had left him half crippled. He was so sore he could scarcely walk, black and blue from stem to gudgeon, and once or twice he felt as if his spine had come unsnapped. The worst part of it was, he hadn't once thrown the old devil. Taking hold of Barnett Hardin wasn't much different from trying to stuff hot butter in a wildcat's ear. Whichever way a man twisted that mountain of flesh was all over him, grappling and heaving until he was dumped. Slammed to earth with close to three hundred pounds pulverizing him like sandstone in a rockcrusher.

Still, sore as he was, he didn't exactly begrudge his uncle the somewhat one-sided brawls. It took a little longer each evening to pin him, and along the way he got in some pretty good licks of his own. In a way it was sort of educational, despite the fact that he was giving away better than five stone in weight. The tricks he picked up might come in real handy someday, and when it got right down to cases, he had nothing whatever to be ashamed of. Anybody who could last ten minutes with that old woolly-booger had earned the right to strut his stuff.

That was the problem in a nutshell. Barnett Hardin was starved for rough-and-tumble, the no-holds-barred fracas that country folk thrived on as entertainment. Over the years he had cracked his neighbors' skulls and wrenched their backs with childlike gusto, and there wasn't a man in Polk County who dared risk his limbs by stepping into the circle. They had simply admitted to themselves and each other that he couldn't be beaten, and afterward avoided his offers to wrestle as if he had an advanced case of leprosy.

This left Barnett Hardin high and dry, not unlike a beached whale. None of his neighbors would sacrifice themselves to his lust for head-thumping, and most even went out of their way to sidestep his bone-crushing handshake. A few years back he looked around one day and suddenly discovered that he was fresh out of playmates. The only alternative, and it was really little more than a passing thought, was to wrestle his field hands. Lots of them were strong enough to give him a good tussle, and since their emancipation, not a few would have relished the idea of putting a couple of knots on his head. Trouble was, a white man, particularly a landholder, couldn't lower himself to butt heads with a common black. Maybe they were free, liberated from bondage by the Union juggernaut, but they were still niggers. Nothing changed that in Texas. Not Abe Lincoln or U.S. Grant or Jesus Christ resurrected and riding a broomstick.

Things being what they were, Barnett Hardin looked on Wes as something heaven-sent, a prayer answered. Like a captive participant, a gladiator-in-residence of sorts, the boy had no choice but to join in the fun and games. For all his rough ways, though, the older man was hardly an ogre. He handled Wes with brute gentleness, much the same as a sow bear cuffing her cubs, and took care never to inflict any lasting injuries. Right at the moment the strapping youngster was the only opponent he had, and he wasn't about to spoil the game with an excess display of strength. Yet he took certain pride in his roughhouse skills, and it never occurred to him to fake a fall. If the boy whipped him it would be done fair and square. Otherwise sport would become farce, and the arena a stage upon which he alone played the fool.

Wes had only a mild awareness of most of this, and even if he'd understood it fully, it would have done little for his lumps and bruises. He was stiff and sore and felt as though he'd come off second best in a skirmish with a meat grinder. As he led the team of horses into the barn it came to him that he was dreading suppertime. Somewhat ruefully, he was forced to admit that his uncle hadn't been joshing after all. Visitors to the Hardin farm really did have to fight for their supper.

After the horses were stalled, he grained and hayed them, then lugged in water from the well. All the time he was working he kept his eye on the milking stalls. Barnett Hardin's pride and joy was five butterball milk cows, and the small herd was the sole responsibility of a Negro freedman who went by the name of Mage. For the past week Wes had tried to make friends with the black man, only to find himself rebuffed with short answers and unintelligible grunts. Slowly he caught on that his uncle purposely kept Mage working around the barn, off away from the other field hands. The man was a troublemaker, what white folks called uppity, and was best left to his own company. Unlike most former slaves, Mage took little solace from his newly won freedom. He worked grudgingly, and seemed to resent every drop of sweat shed on behalf of a white landowner.

Wes simply quit talking to him after the first couple of days. It was like trying to make friends with a mean dog. But he kept an eye on the man all the same. Anybody who was that stiff-necked and surly wasn't to be trusted, and some sixth sense warned him to watch his step. Mage was broad as a singletree, with a girth to match Barnett Hardin himself, and he considered the barn his own personal bailiwick. Under the circumstances, it was best to ignore him and leave him to his cows. From the little the boy had observed, they were the only friends he had anyway.

With the horses stalled for the night, Wes suddenly became aware of the rumble in his own belly. Supper and then a brief flurry with his uncle. Afterward, like the livestock, he could call it a night and get some rest himself. That's how he'd come to think of it, and as he passed the milking stalls, his mind turned to the evening's chief sporting event. Somehow he had to figure a way to outsmart his uncle. It was a surefire cinch he couldn't outwrestle a mountain of blubber, and the situation seemed to call for new tactics all the way round. Something shrewd and crafty.

Pondering on it, he awoke with a start as the stall door slammed open in his face. Mage backed out carrying a bucket of milk in each hand and, too late, the boy tried to swerve aside. They collided head-on and the black man lurched backward, sloshing milk over the barn floor.

"You blind or sumthin'?" he demanded churlishly. "Watch wheah you goin'!"

The words brought a rush of anger flooding over Wes, and with it the realization that this was no accident. It was intentional.

"Boy, you are some kind of stupid, and you don't fool me for a minute. Anybody put your brains in a jaybird he'd fly backward."

Mage squinted hard, his muddy eyes flecked and smoky. "Who you callin' *boy*, white trash?"

"You"—the youngster's temper exploded—"you sorry sonovabitch!"

The black man backhanded him without warning and the whole left side of his head went numb. The blow brought a brassy taste to his mouth and flashing lights swirled before his eyes. Then he pulled himself together, set his jaw at a determined angle, and waded in. Mage uncorked a looping haymaker that would have demolished a stone privy, but it whistled harmlessly through the air. Crouching low, Wes ducked and let go two splintering punches on his chin.

Nothing happened. The black man just stood there, unfazed, blinking his eyes. For a moment Wes couldn't believe it. Never before had anybody stayed on his feet when he gave him the double whammy. There was something spooky about it, and all too suddenly, he realized he was in way over his head. This black glob of bone and gristle was about to tear his wings off. Squash him like a fly.

Barnett Hardin materialized out of nowhere and slammed Mage up against the wall with a crash that shook the entire barn. He rammed his forearm up under the black man's chin and bore down hard on the windpipe. Mage thrashed and sputtered, gasping for air, and his eyes bulged out of their sockets. Hardin held him pinned, nostrils flared with rage, and his words crackled like spitting grease.

"Lemme tell you somethin', coon! Touch that boy again and I'll peel your hide down to the bone. You hear me talkin'?"

Mage bobbed his head, unable to speak, hanging limp against the wall. After a moment Hardin released his hold and stepped back, jerking his thumb toward the door.

"Get your ass on over to the cabins. And don't lemme hear of you bellyachin' to anybody about this. Not unless you want another dose of the same."

The black man clutched at his throat, sucking wind, and shot Wes a look of raw hatred. Then he seemed to wilt before Hardin's glare and scuttled through the door without a word. Still rubbing gingerly at his windpipe, he crossed the yard and headed toward a row of cabins in the distance. He didn't look back and his pace slackened only after he had passed the main house.

Barnett Hardin watched after him for a long while in silence. At last, he turned to face the boy and his gaze was somber, troubled.

"Son, I hate to say it, but I think it'd be best if you went on back to your daddy's place."

"You mean I gotta leave?" Wes gawked at him in disbelief. "Just because I swapped punches with a burrhead?"

"I don't like it any better'n you, but that's how she shapes up."

"But I didn't do nothin'. It was him that started it. I just give him back what he dished out."

"Mebbe so, but there's more to it than that." The older man kneaded the back of his neck with a thorny paw, then went on lamely. "Ever' so often the Freedman's Bureau holds a meetin' in town and Mage is always up there shoutin' louder'n anybody else. Just as sure as God squats he's gonna raise a holy stink about this. Bright and early the next mornin' I'll have a bunch of pettifoggin' Yankees out here askin' damnfool questions that ain't got no answers."

He faltered and gave the boy a sheepish look. "Times bein' what they are, it'd be better for me if you wasn't here. That way them carpetbaggers won't have nothin' to get their hooks into and I can waltz 'em around till they run out of wind. See what I'm gettin' at?"

Wes shrugged and glanced away. "Yeah, I guess so. It's just that I don't like runnin'. Specially when I haven't done nothin'."

"None of us do. But sometimes a man ain't got no choice."

Barnett Hardin threw an arm over his shoulder and led him toward the door. As they came outside he stopped and watched Mage disappear into a rickety cabin in the colored quarters. After a moment he hawked and spat, eyes rimmed with disgust.

"We're livin' in sorry times, boy. And gettin' sorrier ever' day."

4

Bright golden streamers arched skyward as sunrise broke across the land. Somewhere in the distance a meadowlark greeted the day, and perched on top a fence, a speckled rooster with a great comb flapped his wings and crowed defiantly. It was the time when life awakened and stirred, and all about the farm there was a calliope of grunts and snorts and bawling moans.

Wes led his horse from the barn, saddlebags strapped behind the cantle and a sack of oats tied to the saddle horn. He had been up since false dawn, somehow anxious to be gone from this place, and he was ready to travel. Though he had hoped to avoid last-minute goodbyes, he was a moment late in taking the stirrup. The front door opened and his uncle stepped out of the house, walking toward him in that peculiar, shambling gait.

"Gawd A'mighty, boy, what's your rush?" Barnett Hardin halted a couple of paces off and gave him a quizzical frown. "There ain't no need to go tearin' out of here like your pants was on fire."

"Nothin' holding me now, I guess." The youngster's tone was flat and short, and he found it difficult to meet the older man's gaze. "Thought I'd put some distance behind me before it turns off hot."

"Yeah, I s'pose it is better ridin' early like this." Hardin glanced eastward, studying the ball of fire slowly cresting the earth's rim. "Looks like it's gonna be another scorcher."

Wes just stood there, groping for words, feeling awkward and uncomfortable. This wasn't the way he wanted it between them. Stiff and formal, like strangers making small talk. But the thoughts rattling around in his head could hardly be spoken aloud. Not to his own kin.

The silence deepened and presently his uncle shot him a sidewise look, clearly unsettled by the boy's attitude. "Y'know, Wes, part of growin' up is knowin' when to pull in your horns. There's days the odds don't favor a man. Them that's got any sense learns to swallow their pride and wait for a better time to do the fightin'."

"I never run from nothin' in my life."

"You will, son. Sooner or later we all do. Life's got a way of breakin' a man to halter, and them that can't accept it are in for some hard licks."

Again the boy fell silent, staring at the ground. They stood

that way for a while and finally Barnett stuck out his hand.
"Tell your pa I sent my best. And try not to be too hard on
us old folks, boy. Mortals are mighty puny creatures when
it comes down to cases. I reckon that's something you'll have
to learn the hard way, just like the rest of us.''

Wes gave his hand a couple of shakes and let go. Then
he swung aboard his horse and reined it out of the yard at a
brisk lope. Despite himself he looked back, and quickly
wished he hadn't. Hardin was still standing there, like a tree
taken root, and his wife had come to the door. They both
waved but the boy couldn't bring himself to wave back. He
jerked his head around and gigged the horse with his heels.

After rounding a curve, where the road meandered through
a grove of trees, he slowed the horse to a walk. He was glad
his aunt hadn't showed up till the very last. Bessie Hardin
was wholly unlike her husband, without his thick skin and
hard ways. Last night had been bad enough, sitting there in
growing silence while she tried to smooth over the strained
feelings. They had no children of their own and she had
taken it hard, his being forced to leave. Thinking back on it,
he was sorry he couldn't have made it easier for her. But
there were times when a fellow simply couldn't get his jaws
unlocked, and the way things were, maybe it was best for all
concerned that he'd kept his mouth shut.

As far back as he could remember, he had looked up to
Barnett Hardin. Idolized him for his bearish strength and
booming laugh and blasphemous disregard for all that was
holy. The very things his own father wasn't, and never would
be. Had anyone told him Barnett Hardin could be made to
haul water, back off from a fight, he would have laughed
himself hoarse. Such a thing wasn't possible with a man who
had stood off Indians and built a farm for himself from raw
wilderness, the Hardin who had come through the war
decked out with honors and a chest full of ribbons. Yet,
possible or not, it was true. The toughest man he'd ever
known had shown the white feather. Just because a burrhead
might sic a bunch of carpetbaggers on him.

It was enough to make a buzzard puke. A grown man, and

a Hardin at that, who'd learned to squat every time a Yankee yelled frog. Just the idea of it set his stomach to churning as though he'd swallowed a jar of butterflies.

Suddenly the boy's horse spooked, plunging sideways, and for an instant it was all he could do to stay in the saddle. He hauled up short on the reins, sawing cruelly at the bit, and managed to work his mount back onto the road. Then, hardly able to credit his eyes, he saw what had turned the horse skittery.

Mage was standing in the tree line on the opposite side of the road.

The black man had a gnarled oak limb in his right hand, and there was a peculiar glint in his eye. Without a word he moved out of the trees and onto the road. His purpose was clear and the club alone was explanation enough. He meant to brain himself a white boy, even the score for yesterday's humiliation. As the gap closed, he darted forward in a sudden, bounding leap, waving his arms and howling like a banshee.

Arrghhh!

The horse reared and Wes clutched at the saddle horn to hold his seat. For the merest fraction of a second he considered riding off, leaving the black man to eat dust and choke on his own curses. Then it was too late. Mage jumped clear of the flailing hooves and swung the club in a whistling arc. The blow caught Wes in the left side and his ribs buckled in a shower of fiery sparks that numbed him clean to the shoulder. Hardly before he realized what was happening, he felt himself falling, sledged out of his saddle by the impact of the stout limb. The ground came up to meet him in a rush, and air exploded from his lungs as his battered ribs absorbed the shock.

Mage swatted the horse on the rump, and as it broke away, he stepped forward. Just for a moment he stood there, towering over the youngster, slowly thumping the club against the palm of his free hand. Then his mouth split in a wide, pearly grin.

"Well now, what you say, *boy?* Ready to meet yo' Maker?"

Wes pulled the Navy in a single motion and shot him three times. It was done without thought, a reflex action, and the black man appeared as surprised as the boy. Bright red dots, side by side, blossomed at his beltline, and the third slug caught him just below the brisket. He reeled backward in a limp, nerveless dance, and then, as if his legs had been chopped from beneath him, he collapsed and sat down heavily in the road.

They stared at each other for what seemed a long time. Neither of them said anything, almost as though it had gone beyond mere words and must now be resolved in an older way. At last, gathering himself with a supreme effort, Mage came to his knees and commenced pushing himself erect with the club as a support. Wes raised the pistol, thumbing the hammer back to full cock, and very carefully shot him between the eyes. The black man's skull blew apart in a misty spray of bone and gelled brains, and he toppled over backward into the dust. His hand twitched spastically, grasping the club in a death grip, then he lay still.

The boy just sat there, staring at the body. He felt nothing. Neither remorse nor anger. Instead, he was gripped by a queer fascination at how easy it was to kill. His hand was steady, his mind clear, and he remembered every detail from the moment he pulled the gun to the last shot. It was hardly any different from drilling lead into a tree, or bursting bottles. Except the slug made an unusual sound when it struck bone and meat. Sort of a mushy splat. Like thunking rocks into a muddy creek bank.

But there was something else, now that he thought on it. Perhaps it was easy to kill but men damn sure didn't let go of life without a struggle. Not if this burrhead was any example, they didn't. Two slugs in the gut and a third in the chest and he'd still had plenty of starch left over. Apparently some men took a powerful lot of killing before they were dead. More than he had suspected, or would have believed

if he hadn't seen it for himself. Only after the sorry bastard
had been drilled through the head did he finally give up the
ghost.

It was a point worth remembering, and he filed it away
for future reference. A gut shot, or centering a man in the
chest, was easiest. But there was a strong chance it wouldn't
put them down for good. Next time he'd have to shoot a lot
straighter. The heart or the head. First crack out of the box.
The thought gave him a bad moment, and his nerves jangled
a little as he glanced over at the body. If the black scutter
had been using a gun instead of a club it might have been a
different story. Four shots to ring the gong was three too
many.

Uncoiling, he climbed painfully to his feet and walked off
toward his horse. By the time the flies settled over that hunk
of meat in the road, he had a hunch he'd better be long gone
from Polk County.

Not long after sundown, two days later, Wes reined to a
halt in the yard of his brother's farm outside Prairie Hill. He
felt surprisingly good considering he'd ridden better than a
hundred miles with a bucket of coals simmering in his rib
cage. All the same, he wasn't sure he could have stood another hour of jouncing around in the saddle. Just then, having
solid earth under his feet sounded real inviting.

He dismounted, took three steps toward the house, and fell
flat on his face.

5

Joe Hardin wasn't a paragon of virtue, for he'd sowed
some wild oats in his time, but that was before he settled
down. Since then he had taken to religion as though every
day was a brand-new revival meeting, and in a remarkably
short period of time, he'd become a Christian with his boots
firmly planted on the road to salvation. Upstanding, honest,
forthright, and straitlaced as a whalebone corset. He had seen

the light, and his conversion, in no small part, was brought about by the inducements of his wife, Ruby May. She was a buxom, good-natured, apple-cheeked girl who knew how to ying Joe's yang in all the right ways. Together, though they were still in their early twenties, they had built themselves a farm, whelped three kids, and maneuvered Joe into the post of deacon at the Prairie Hill Methodist Church.

They were prosperous, in a hardscrabble sort of way, reliable as a horse wearing blinders, and possessed of a faith that could have withstood an acid bath. Reverend James Hardin thought they were about the slickest thing ever to come down the pike, and every now and then, they had to admit that he was pretty close to right. The Good Lord had provided them with a bountiful life, and with a little judicious tugging in the right spots, they had become one of the leading families in their community. Like his father, Joe's neighbors thought he was something on a stick, and he meant to cultivate their support for all it was worth. Someday, the Lord willing, of course, he might just wind up one of the big augurs in Prairie Hill. With God on his side, Joe had more visions than a Comanche witch doctor. And none of them small pickings, either.

As Ruby May was quick to point out, Joe Hardin aimed high.

It was understandable, then, that Joe greeted his younger brother with something less than open arms. While Mount Calm was ten miles up the road, the people of Prairie Hill had heard an earful about Wes Hardin. Bad news travels best, and what with Methodists being a close-knit bunch, Reverend Hardin's flock had spread the word about his wild and unruly son. Local gossips were hard put to explain how the eldest son had come out so righteous and the youngest a practicing heathen, and for his part, Joe tried to ignore the whole affair. Like a cat scratching dirt over its mess, he figured to bury the stink beneath a layer of good works and flawless conduct.

Yet, when he let himself think about it, generally after

Ruby May was asleep, he couldn't help but envy Wes just the least little bit. In a manner of speaking, the kid had life by the balls.

Joe had discovered sometime back that the straight and narrow was a tedious path. Fun and games—especially wine, women, and song—were strictly forbidden. That Wes had charted a different course for himself struck Joe as sinful and wicked, but not without certain redeeming qualities. In his secret moments, he found himself wishing he had sown a few more wild oats before shouldering the old rugged cross.

Still, his backsliding was but a thing of the moment, fleeting and soon smothered in righteous thoughts. When he entered the house after a hard day in the fields, he decided to have it out with Wes. The boy had been here four days now, and despite Joe's incessant badgering, he had explained nothing of his condition or his reason for leaving Uncle Barnett's place. His one slip, stated with considerable gloom, was the request that their father be kept in the dark about his return, which in itself was highly suspect.

It was time for some talk. Straight from the shoulder.

Wes was seated in a rocker, watching Ruby May prepare supper. His ribs were bound tightly, and any sudden movement brought a wince of pain, but he was on the mend. Two days in bed, at Ruby May's insistence, had done wonders for a couple of cracked ribs. As the door opened, he glanced around and smiled warmly at Joe.

"Evenin', Brother. How goes the battle?"

"Well enough, I reckon."

Joe hung his hat on a peg, crossed the room to where Ruby May fluttered around a scorching stove, and gave her a quick peck on the cheek. Not to be distracted, she went right on with her cooking. After a moment he turned, came back, and took a chair across from the boy. Outside, the children were whooping and hollering, but he seemed unaware of the racket. Settling back, he gave Wes a dour look.

"I think it's time you spilled the beans."

"Cripes, you gonna start harpin' on that again?"

"Now I'm just gonna say this once, and you'd better listen

good.'' Ruby May paused at the harsh tone and darted a glance at her husband. His face was flushed and his knuckles turned white where he gripped the chair. ''You come to my house all stove up and we took you in. But everything's a big dark secret and you won't say nothin'. I got a family to think about and that entitles me to some answers. If you're in trouble I'll do my best to help you, but you stay clammed up and you're not welcome here no more. That's all I've got to say.''

Wes shifted uncomfortably in his chair, stung by the anger in his brother's words. He'd always resented Joe, thinking of him as a mama's boy, forever buttering up their folks to make himself look good. Like it or not, though, he was forced to admit that Joe had a point. This was his house and it was only fair that he called the shots under his own roof. That didn't mean Wes had to like it. But circumstances being what they were, he was obliged to supply some answers. Pony up or get out, which was a mighty slim choice.

Still, Joe had asked for it, and it might be fun to watch him squirm. Wes set the rocker in motion and smiled as though he had a mouthful of feathers.

''I killed a man.''

''Oh, my God.'' Ruby May dropped her stirring spoon and clapped her hands over her mouth.

Joe sort of recoiled, as though he'd been slapped in the face, and his eyes bugged out. ''Killed a man? What man? Where?''

''One of Uncle Barnett's hired help. A burrhead. He come at me with a club and I shot him.''

''Well, where was Uncle Barnett? What'd he say?''

''I dunno. It happened down the road from his place, and since I was leavin' anyway, I just kept on makin' tracks.''

''Whoa, back up a minute. How come you was leavin'? You was supposed to stay there the whole summer.''

Wes quickly sketched the story for them, starting with the fight in the barn. As he talked, it became apparent that he had no remorse whatever about killing the black man. But his remarks about Barnett Hardin were sharp and biting. The disillusionment had festered, gnawing on his insides, and he made no bones as to how he felt. When he finished, Joe scowled and shook his head with mild disgust.

"You've got a lot to learn, bubber. In case you don't know it, Uncle Barnett has never swore an oath of allegiance to the Union. He's what the Yankees call an un-reconstructed Rebel. He can't vote or hold public office, and if them carpetbaggers took a notion, they could steal that farm out from under him quicker'n you can say scat. Now that don't mean nothin' to you, naturally. But if you'd broke your back for twenty years scratchin' and grubbin' you might be whistlin' the same tune."

The boy blanched, eyes round as saucers. "Judas Priest. He never said nothin'. Not a word."

"He wouldn't. That's his way. But that's water under the bridge. We've got something more important to talk about." Joe scooted up on the edge of his chair, talking intensely, as Ruby May came to stand at his shoulder. "Wes, you've killed a colored man. That doesn't seem to faze you even a little bit, but you'd better get the cobwebs out and start thinkin'. We're livin' under military law, and next to shootin' a Yankee, the worst crime you can commit is to kill a tarbaby. You get yourself caught and that's all she wrote. They'll hang you deader'n a doornail."

"It was self-defense!" Wes blurted hotly. "How do you think I got these busted ribs?"

"That don't mean a hill of beans. They'll stretch your neck anyway. I'm tellin' you, the Army plays for keeps."

"He's right, Wes." Ruby May's face was pale and she couldn't seem to keep her hands still. "They hang men every day down at Austin for lots less."

The youngster blinked and suddenly lost his cocky look. "Maybe they won't know it was me. I mean, there was nobody around and I got out of there plenty quick."

"They'll find out," Joe countered. "Once they start talkin' to Uncle Barnett's hands they'll put two and two together."

"That sort of puts me between a rock and a hard place, don't it?"

"Well, you was right in stayin' away from Pa's place. That's the first spot they'll look. Now we've got to figure out someplace where you can get lost for a year or so. Give it time to blow over."

"How about China?" Wes grinned weakly. "That's pretty far off."

"You think you're jokin', but that's about what I had in mind. I was figurin' maybe Mexico would turn the trick."

"Mexico! Holy cow, there's nothin' down there but a bunch of greasers. Besides, I don't like their food. Tried it once and it like to melted my teeth."

"Better tortillas and peppers," Ruby May observed, "than a noose around your neck."

Wes started to answer but they suddenly heard a commotion out front. A wagon rattled into the yard and the children began jabbering at someone. Joe hurried to the door, waving the boy back, and stepped outside. Peering through the window, Ruby May and Wes saw Joe talking to Jack Oliphant, who owned a farm down the road. The conversation was short and clearly of a serious nature. Moments later Oliphant climbed into his wagon and Joe rushed back toward the house. When he came through the door his jaw was set in a grim line.

"Oliphant says there's four soldiers in town askin' questions about me. He overheard 'em in the store and beat it out here to warn me."

"They're on to me, just like you said." Wes puzzled over it a minute, then nodded. "Yup, that's it. Probably checked Pa's place first and figured they'd look here next."

"C'mon, bubber, we gotta get you out of here." Joe headed for the door but suddenly turned into the bedroom. A moment later he emerged with a double-barreled shotgun. Frowning, he thrust the greener and a bag of shells into the youngster's hands. "I don't hold with killin', but there weren't no Yankees when the good book was written. Just promise me you won't use it unless they get you backed into a corner.''

"You got my word on it, Brother. Cross my heart.''

Joe hustled him out of the house with Ruby May wringing her hands and screeching for the children to get inside. Within minutes they had a saddle slapped on his horse and paused for a last handshake. Wes tried to thank him but Joe would have none of it. He boosted the boy up, popped the horse across the rump, and let go an earsplitting Rebel yell. The horse took off as though he had been shot out of a cannon, and as they rounded the corner of the barn headed south, Wes glanced back over his shoulder. But instead of waving he swallowed hard and urged his mount into a headlong gallop.

Four bluecoats had just ridden into Joe Hardin's yard.

Shortly before sunset, Wes booted his horse across a shallow stream and dismounted in a thick stand of cottonwoods on the far side. There was no way he could outrun the soldiers, that was obvious now. They had been gaining on him steadily, with a good two hours of daylight left, they would overtake him long before dark. It was stand and fight or be run to earth. Which seemed more likely with each passing minute. His side hurt so bad he could scarcely breathe, and he would never have held on till dark anyhow. Better to have it done with here, on ground of his own choosing, where he had the advantage of surprise.

Walking to the forward edge of the tree line, he stopped behind a huge cottonwood and cocked both hammers on the shotgun. The wait was shorter than he had expected. When he heard hooves splashing in water he stepped clear of the tree, raising the shotgun to his shoulder. The soldiers were in single file, sweaty and cursing, suspecting nothing. He pulled the first trigger and the lead trooper was snatched from his horse as if struck by a thunderbolt. Then the second barrel roared and the man next in line somersaulted backward into the stream. The youngster flung the shotgun aside, jerked the Navy Colt, and hammered two slugs into the third trooper as he clawed frantically at his holstered pistol. The soldier at the rear was gone, pounding back across the prairie, before the boy could get off another shot.

Wes stood there for a long while, staring down at his handiwork. It was queer, unreal somehow, like a bad dream. In the space of a week he had killed four men. With hardly any effort at all. But he sensed that it wouldn't end here. After gunning down a black and three Union troopers, every bluebelly in Texas would be dogging his trail. The race had only started, and second best was a one-way trip to the gallows. Stuffing the pistol in his belt, he retrieved the shotgun and headed back through the trees. Barnett Hardin had been right.

Things were getting sorrier all the time.

CHAPTER 2

1

A long, dreary winter passed uneventfully and spring came once again to the land. After his brief spate of killing the summer before, Wes had somehow managed to stay out of trouble. This in itself was a remarkable feat for a boy who attracted misfortune the way horse dung draws flies. But the more striking accomplishment, by far, was that he had also managed to elude Yankee justice. Perhaps the only thing that saved him was a masquerade of sorts, cloaking himself in a highly unlikely disguise.

Wes Hardin had become a schoolteacher.

The irony of it was inescapable, and in guarded moments, Wes felt like the leading character in an outlandish farce. That he had pulled it off seemed a bizarre joke on everyone involved. All the more so since he had become something of a celebrity in the little town of Pisga.

The summer before he had stayed on the run for close to a month after ambushing the Union troopers. Seldom did he spend more than one night in the same spot, gradually working his way west, toward the remote backcountry of the great Texas plains. The thought of fleeing to Mexico, as Joe had suggested, was discarded out of hand. Texas was his home, a land peopled with his own kind, and he couldn't bring himself to leave it. Of equal significance, it was a big country, stretching from sunrise to sunset for close to a thousand miles. He figured that a lone boy, especially one who kept his wits about him, wouldn't have any trouble getting lost in the far-flung wilderness to the west.

Somewhere on the Brazos his mother had kin, and that became his immediate goal. If the Yankees came after him then he would simply pull another disappearing act. Yet, curiously enough, he found the western reaches of the Brazos a perfect sanctuary. Comanches and Kiowas were a constant threat, but Yankee patrols seldom ventured that far from outlying army posts.

In time, it became apparent that the Union forces were not hounding his trail. While he expected pursuit of some kind, absolutely nothing happened, almost as if his name had been mislaid by the authorities in Austin. As days turned into weeks, it slowly came clear that he hadn't reckoned with the truculent nature of his fellow Texans. Under Reconstruction politics hundreds of men had been declared outlaws, and certain parts of Texas were in what amounted to a state of armed insurrection. The Army of Occupation faced a monumental task policing its rebellious wards, and was kept busy merely trying to stop the flames of discontent from spreading. Shootouts between Federal troops and wanted men were so commonplace that they hardly warranted newspaper coverage. Unlike other Confederate states, Texas had not accepted the yoke of oppression with either manners or grace. Fiercely independent, nearly impossible to intimidate, the Texans fought back with every means at hand. And in the general turmoil, a hot-tempered kid who had seemingly vanished from the face of the earth was soon forgotten. The Army had its hands full merely catching the dumb ones.

Through his kinfolks on the Brazos, Wes began an exchange of letters with his parents in early July. Reverend James Hardin was mortified that his youngest son had fallen prey to Satan's wiles, but expressed hope that the boy's soul might yet be salvaged. Then, toward the latter part of the summer, Wes received an astounding piece of news. With the help of a fellow minister in Pisga, his father had secured for him the position of schoolteacher. Pisga was a small town, hardly more than a backcountry crossroads, without the funds to attract a highly educated man. Despite the youngster's age and his lack of experience, the townspeople were delighted when he arrived a week before the fall term began.

Wes discovered the reason for their high spirits only after school officially opened. The children, most of them from surrounding farms, were a diabolic lot. They had scared their last teacher into an early retirement, and considered it a personal affront that the town fathers had hired a replacement with such ease. But if adults and children alike took Wes for an easy mark, they were in for a rude awakening. He knew every trick in the hellraiser's handbook, having invented many of them himself, and the problems of higher education in Pisga were solved in a most elemental fashion.

The school bully, a lard-faced lout who at seventeen was still struggling to escape the fifth grade, unwittingly volunteered himself as an object lesson. On the second morning of the new term Wes thrashed him within an inch of his life, and offered to give his father a dose of the same if there were any objections. There were none. Peace reigned at the Pisga country school, and by whatever means, the parents were elated that discipline had been asserted.

Throughout the winter Wes taught his converts everything he knew, which was considerably more than they had learned in the past. In the process he became something of a hero to the kids and a much-sought-after guest in the homes around town, especially those with grown daughters. People found it difficult to believe that he was scarcely older than many of his students. The last year had matured him greatly—after killing four men he tended to act and think beyond his years—and he now found himself more comfortable in the company of men several years his senior. The townspeople of Pisga were both bemused and intrigued by the enigma they saw before them. A schoolteacher who carried a gun. A boy who handled himself like a man. A rough-and-tumble scrapper of considerable skill who went out of his way to avoid trouble.

It was a puzzle.

Perhaps the most baffled of the lot was Neal Bowen, owner of Pisga's most imposing structure, the general store. Wes had taken a shine to his daughter, Jane, and since Christmas had been courting her on a steady basis. Bowen tended to worry a lot anyway, always looking on the dark side of things, and the young schoolmaster left him vaguely uneasy. Not that he had any reason for his suspicions. The boy didn't drink or smoke. Nor did he gamble or frequent the pool hall. He attended church every Sunday, sang hymns in a loud, husky baritone, and could quote Scripture like a preacher. But Bowen's wariness persisted all the same. A man without visible vices was generally a man with things to hide. Even if the man was a boy.

Wes had two things working for him, though. He had charmed Elizabeth Bowen, the old man's wife, into thinking he was a gentleman and a scholar. A fine catch for their daughter. Someone to be gaffed fast and led to the altar before his eyes strayed to greener pastures.

The other thing in his favor was Jane Bowen. Though she was young Hardin's age, hardly anybody would call her a girl. She had blossomed early and ripened fast. Anything in Pisga that wore pants had his eye on her, and under normal circumstances she would have been married off inside a year. But things ceased being normal a couple of months after Wes came to town. Every time they were within sight of one another it was as if her eyes were fastened on something sweet and sticky.

Between mother and daughter, Neal Bowen didn't have a prayer. He was outflanked at every turn, and generally put to rout with a barrage of female chatter.

That was the way it stood the night Wes came to supper. It wasn't the first time he'd been invited to share their table, but it was a very special night. School had let out for the summer that day, and feminine intuition was working overtime. The prize catch hadn't yet proposed, and both the Bowen women were nervous wrecks for fear he would ride out of Pisga and never look back. Jane was especially skittish, and with good reason. Her young gentleman caller had

taught her much in the past few months, and having lost her
virtue, she was not about to lose her man. Not without a last-
ditch fight.

Jane looked so ravishing that Wes couldn't do justice to
the spread laid out in his honor. Her dark hair was piled up
in a fancy twist on top of her head, glinting with auburn
flecks of rust from the lamplight, and her eyes sparkled with
an animation that seemed to devour him bit by bit. She had
chosen a fluffy blue dress, his favorite color, and by sheer
coincidence, it displayed the firm roundness of her breasts
with stunning effect. Wes needed little imagination about the
rest of her. What he couldn't see was vivid in his mind's
eye, and he had a hunch that dessert might turn out to be
extra special.

Toward the end of the meal Elizabeth Bowen finally
popped the question that had preoccupied her thoughts for
the past week. "Wes, now that school is out, what are your
plans for the summer?" Before he could reply, she hurried
on. "I'm sure Mr. Bowen could arrange something for you
at the store."

Neal Bowen gave her a dour look, but he shouldn't have
bothered. Wes wasn't about to get himself snookered into
becoming a ribbon clerk. "Well, ma'am, I've given that a
lot of thought, and understand, I'm not sayin' anything
against storekeepin'. It's just that I had my mind set in another direction. I've got a cousin that's been workin' steady
for a big rancher and I figured he might be able to get me
on for the summer."

"A drover?" Elizabeth Bowen was appalled by the idea.

Jane looked crushed and the old man could scarcely hide
his grin. There was an awkward silence and then Wes went
on to explain that he needed some fresh air and sunshine. A
tonic of sorts, to get him in shape for another winter in the
one-room schoolhouse. The women perked up at that, and
later, when he asked Jane to go for a walk, she gave him a
bright little nod.

Outside, they walked toward a cottonwood grove north of
town. They had a special place there, secluded and private,

where they often met beside a small creek. Neither of them said much as they strolled along, arm in arm, but Jane snuggled close as they approached the trees. After he spread his coat on the ground, and they were seated near the stream, he tried to kiss her. She pulled back, elusive but not out of reach, and gave him an inquisitive, sideways glance.

"Wes, did you really mean it? What you said about coming back in the fall."

" 'Course I did. Only I'll be back lots of times before school starts. Cripes, Richland's not more'n a good ride from here."

"Richland?"

"Sure. Didn't I tell you? That's where I'll be workin'. The Richland Bottoms."

Her smile went smoky and warm, like an autumn sunset, and she cuddled back in his arms. "Oh, sugar, you make me the happiest girl alive. I just feel like dancing on air."

He brushed her lips with a soft kiss and his voice went husky. "Sure you wouldn't feel like somethin' a little more vigorous?"

"Why, Wes Hardin! You're a wicked, sinful man." Her mouth crinkled in a teasing smile and she lay back on the ground. "The way you read a girl's mind is a caution. Honestly, it's just not fair."

They fell back on the coat, a tangle of arms and legs, smothering one another with kisses. Along the creek the crickets quit chirruping, as if waiting, and after a while a soft, hungry moan joined with the sound of rushing water. The moon filtered down through the trees, bathing them in streamered light, and the moan became more urgent, demanding.

The crickets listened quietly, and then, satisfied, went back to their nightly serenade.

2

Working cattle wasn't the picnic Wes had envisioned. The days were long, hot, and dusty. Sleep was a sometimes thing, and the grub, while filling, was strong on heartburn and short on savory. The pay was considerably more than he had earned as a schoolteacher, but astride a cow pony, thirty a month and found came the hard way. He was battered and bruised, and generally collapsed on his bunk at night as if he'd been wrestling a pack of bears since sunrise.

All the same, Wes took to the life like a speckled pup with a bowl of cream. Simp Dixon, a distant cousin on his father's side, hadn't told him it would be easy. Quite the contrary, Dixon had been at some pains to convince him that it was a tough and sometimes hazardous job. But never dull, and in its own thorny way, a barrel of laughs. Wes found that true enough. After sixteen hours in the saddle, sporting an assortment of aches and pains, a man went out of his way to laugh. Invented things to raise a chuckle around the bunkhouse. Otherwise he could never have faced another gray dawn and the chance to do it all over again.

The first month had been the hardest. Though Wes could sit a horse well enough, he had never been aboard the hurricane deck of a cow pony. Mostly they were of mustang stock, small and quick-footed and fiery-tempered. Like all cowhands, he was given his own string of ponies the day he signed on with the Slash O spread. Much to the delight of the other hands, he discovered that no amount of breaking ever fully tamed a wild horse. Shortly after dawn the wrangler would drive the remuda in and the next hour was something on the order of a three-ring circus. Saddling a snorting, flailing bundle of dynamite was only the first step. Some of the horses had to be blindfolded or tied down just to get the bridle on and the cinch snugged tight. Then the real fun commenced. Early in the morning ponies were frisky and full of devilment, and the kinks had to be ironed out before they could be used to work cows. The older hands took immense pleasure in watching a greenhorn test out his string, not unlike curious onlookers drawn to the scene of a natural disaster. They generally ganged around, grinning and expectant, offering Wes free advice on the quirky ways of mustang stock. More often than not they were rewarded with a humdinger performance.

By rough count, Wes was bucked off forty-three times the first week. Apparently that was the barrel of laughs Simp Dixon had told him about, and the second week was only slightly less hilarious. He ate dust twenty-six times in topping off a string of twelve ponies. But he kept climbing back on, goaded by a bulldog determination to stick, and toward the end of the month the others quit joshing him so much. Among themselves, they agreed he had the grit to make a good hand. Time and hard knocks would turn the trick.

Wes found out quickly enough that hard knocks were easy to come by in a cow camp. Longhorns were wilder than the mustang ponies, and if anything, more dangerous. Where a pony would stomp a man all in good fun, a longhorn meant business. Pushed too hard, or cornered in the brush, a mossyhorn would turn and fight like a Bengal tiger fresh off a patch of locoweed. The first time the youngster roped an outlaw steer he discovered that the hardest part of catching a longhorn was in letting go. As a breed they were cantankerous, short-fused, and born man-haters, which was what kept the job from getting dull. Every day was sort of the first day of a man's life, and if he got careless it could easily become his last.

But Wes stuck, observing and learning as he went along. While he had joined the spring roundup late, there were still enough cows to go around. Tom Hardesty, owner of the Slash O, planned on sending four herds up the trail to Abilene that summer. Some eight thousand longhorns had to be caught and trail-branded in the course of a few short months. Between this and branding calves, every man on the place had all the work he could handle. By the time the spring gather was finished Wes was carrying his own weight, making up with spirit and persistence what he lacked in skill. While Hardesty passed him over for a spot on one of the trail crews, he didn't feel slighted. He was making good money, enjoying himself, and had put on better than ten pounds of whipcord muscle. It was a good life, carefree and unfettered, and with each passing day it exerted a stronger hold on him. So much so that it caused him no end of trouble back in Pisga.

Three times since signing on with the Slash O he had made a lightning trip to see Jane Bowen. Much to her father's undisguised glee, and Jane's dismay, he looked more like a cowhand and less like a schoolteacher with each visit. Their last night together, some two weeks back, had been nothing short of catastrophic. Jane had burst into tears, convinced he was dallying with her affections, and wound up calling him a fiddle-footed saddle tramp. Wes eased her fears before riding out the next morning, but secretly he was rather pleased with himself. He had the best of both worlds. A ripsnorter of a job and a pretty girl clutching at his shirttail. It was a dandy life, and for the moment, suited him just right.

Late one afternoon, riding back to the Slash O compound with Simp Dixon, he found himself lecturing on precisely that subject. That was the way people talked to his cousin anyhow, as if enlightening a backward child. Simp's real name was Jack, but nobody had used it since he was a kid. In the family they joked about it, dusting off an old saw and revamping it to fit the boy. Simple's not the same as stupid, except where Simp is concerned.

Yet, for all his slowness, Simp wasn't a man to cross. He was dangerous as a bee-stung bear, and had proved it by killing a couple of men in saloon-room shoot-outs. One of the deceased happened to be a soldier, and like Wes, Simp was wanted by the Union Army. With ferretlike cunning, some sort of instinctual urge for survival, he had lost himself on the vastness of the Slash O spread. The only time he went to town was when he needed a woman so bad his teeth hurt, and that was about once every six months. In the way of a simple man, he had simple needs, but people were still careful that he never caught them laughing at him.

Being kin, Wes was allowed liberties denied others. It was apparent in the worldly tone he took with Simp on the topic of women.

"Y'see, the way to handle a female is to keep her guessin'. Never let her get set so she can start workin' them female tricks on you. They're slick that way, and if you don't stay a step ahead of 'em, they'll punch your ticket real fast."

Simp thought it over for a while and finally screwed up his face in a quizzical frown. "I don't get it. Why d'ya have to stay a step ahead of 'em?"

" 'Cause they're all the time chasin' you. Tryin' to get a wedding ring through your nose."

"I ain't sayin' you're wrong, but that don't exactly hold water. Now you take me, fer instance. I don't never recollect no female chasin' me. Fact is, it's always been the other way around. I can't hardly name you a time I didn't wind up payin' fer it. 'Cept fer ol' Mollie Pritchard back home, and she just give it away to anybody."

Wes took a closer look at his cousin and had to admit that he had a point. Simp was a wiry feist of a man, with a crooked nose and scraggly yellow teeth. Nothing much to look at and even less to smell. The only time he took a bath was when it rained, and even then, he'd never been known to shed his long johns. Wes thought about it a moment longer and then had to hold back a chuckle. He had forgotten the cardinal rule. For Simp, things had to be kept simple.

"Well, Simp, it's like this. Y'know how a cow'll let three or four bulls come up and sniff her before she finally gives in? That's the way women are. Scatterbrained and fickle as all get-out. I guess you just haven't nosed the right woman yet."

"Balls o' fire!" Simp's eyes lit up like soapy agates. "You mean when I find me the right one and give 'er a good sniff she'll start chasin' me like this gal is doin' you?"

"Damn bet'cha, that's what I mean. She'll run right up your back and throw a half-hitch on you. Quicker'n scat."

"Keeerist! I sure wish I knowed where she was. I'd go

coldnose 'er so fast it'd make your head swim."

Wes started to laugh, but the sound died in his throat as they came over a low rise. The Slash O compound was less than a quarter mile off and what he saw froze his blood. Five Union soldiers sat their horses near the bunkhouse and a sixth was talking with Tom Hardesty in front of the main house. The youngster reined his pony in sharply and Simp followed suit. They just sat there gawking, too startled to speak, and at last Simp whistled under his breath.

"Guess I went tomcattin' in town once too often."

The youngster stiffened as the soldiers swung their mounts out of the yard and headed up the rise. "Hardesty's sicced 'em on us."

"That bastard'd sell his mother if it was a Yankee talkin'."

"What about it? Think we can outrun 'em?"

"After we worked the ass off these horses all day? They'd catch us 'fore we hit the river." Simp wheeled his pony around and spurred hard. "C'mon! Let 'em think we're makin' a run fer it."

The boys disappeared over the rise at a gallop as the soldiers pounded toward them. On the back slope Simp suddenly yanked his pony to a halt and spun about, facing the crest of the hill. He jerked his pistol and motioned back the way they had come.

"When them bluebellies top that rise, open up on 'em. Only chance we got is to get 'em before they get us."

Simp wasn't overly bright, but Wes had to give him credit for a wolflike cunning. It was the best chance open to them, and under the circumstances, likely to be the only one they would get. Then, quite suddenly, the time for thinking was past. They heard the thud of hooves and the Yankees came boiling over the hill.

Within a heartbeat both boys cut loose and it was as if the soldiers had been enveloped in a swarm of hornets. Three troopers were flung from the saddle in the opening blast and another man's horse bolted straight out across the prairie. Before the remaining troopers could get untracked slugs were

frying the air around their ears. One man doubled over and
tumbled to the ground, and the second crested the rise raking
his horse in headlong flight. For a moment the boys just sat
there, hardly able to believe they had pulled it off. Less than
ten seconds had elapsed from first shot to last, and between
them they had killed four men.

Wes came out of the trance an instant before Simp, but
they were both of the same mind. The fighting was done
with, at least for now. It was time to run. To put miles between themselves and the Slash O, and find a new hole.
Someplace where Yankees were scarce and men on the
dodge were made welcome. A far place. Long gone.

Hunched low over their ponies, they rode west toward the
Richland Bottoms.

3

Fort Griffin was a star-spangled oasis in the middle of
nowhere. The last stop between the rolling prairies of west
Texas and the vast, uncharted wilderness of the Staked
Plains. Some politicians considered it the forerunner of settlements that would one day dot the great buffalo ranges west
of the fort. But for those who had seen it, there was nothing
civilized about this remote way station. It was raw and crude,
a small slice of hell fashioned in man's own image.

The fort was situated on a hill overlooking the Clear Fork
of the Brazos, and below, along the riverbank, was what had
once been a grungy frontier outpost. Just that spring, though,
the village had suddenly come of age, transformed in an explosive burst of energy into a regular little metropolis. It was
called The Flats, and as a commercial enterprise, it was devoted almost exclusively to man's gamier pursuits in life.

Over the past winter word had gone out that Griffin was
to be the scene of the next buffalo slaughter. Within months,
from every corner of the plains, the race was on. Scenting
fast money on the freshening winds, the flotsam of humanity
descended on the Clear Fork of the Brazos. They all came—

hide hunters, gamblers, cutthroats, and harlots alike—
spurred on by greed and the chance for a quick kill. The lure
was as old as man himself, and in keeping with the nature
of the beast, the entertainment was lusty and uncomplicated.

Sprawled out across the flats at the foot of the hill, the
town had shot up at a dizzying pace as the horde swarmed
into this new mecca of fast women and easy money. Mer-
chants and tradesmen and slick-talking speculators vied with
the sporting crowd for choice locations, and whole caravans
of lumber were freighted west as row upon row of buildings
sprang up overnight. Where before there had been only a
store and a saloon, there were now three grand emporiums
and a half-dozen new watering holes. The tent hotel of earlier
times had given way to a two-story frame structure, and
along the river stood a clutch of bawdy houses to rival anything west of Kansas City.

The town's single street was a regular beehive of activity.
Mule skinners cursed and shouted, cracking their whips from
atop huge Studebaker freighters, as they jockeyed for position before the stores with an unending stream of hide wagons. Hitch racks in front of every building were jammed with
horses and every corner was crowded with knots of men out
to see the elephant. Hunters, cowhands, and soldiers turned
the boardwalks into a rowdy jostling match as they made
their way from one dive to the next. Dance halls and saloons
shook with the strident chords of rinky-dink pianos and the
sprightly wail of an occasional fiddle. Louder still, drowning
out all else, came the raucous babble of men busily engaged
in sampling the local firewater. Women stood in the doorway
of every dive, decked out in gaudy dresses and paint-smeared
faces, and their laughter racketed along the street in shrill
invitation to anything that wore pants.

It was a carnival come to life. Squalling, blustery, a vol-
atile mix of popskull whiskey, loose women, and a small
army of men flinging their money to the winds. A place
where a man could lose himself in the riotous crowd, simply
vanish in a sea of faces that all looked the same.

Which was precisely what Wes Hardin had done.

After the one-sided shoot-out at the Slash O, he and Simp Dixon spent a couple of weeks dodging army patrols and finally decided to split up. Together, with their descriptions plastered over half of Texas, they drew too much attention. Separately, they stood a better chance of moving about unnoticed, or so it had seemed at the time. Less than a week later Wes heard that Dixon had been cornered and killed while attempting a midnight visit with his family. Though the boy hadn't seen his own parents in more than a year, any thought of sneaking into Mount Calm quickly went by the boards. He headed west, toward the Brazos, where there were fewer towns and a scarcity of Yankees.

While news traveled slowly on the outer fringes of civilization, he learned a short time later that Union troops had ceased to pose a threat. Instead, he had a new enemy, and from all reports, one even more relentless and vengeful than the occupation forces.

Earlier in the year a Republican carpetbagger, E. J. Davis, had taken office as governor. Within six months, through manipulation and outright intimidation, he had gained control of the legislature. Having won his office through fraud and voting laws which disenfranchised all former Confederates, Davis immediately took steps to quell the unruly Texans. In late June he engineered a bill authorizing a State Police force, and on July 1 it became law. With his own personal janissaries, Davis was now the law in Texas, responsible for maintaining order among a conquered people who refused to knuckle under. As an object lesson to the masses, he published a wanted list which outlawed nearly two thousand men. One of the names on the list, charged with the murder of seven men, was John Wesley Hardin.

The State Police swarmed across central and eastern Texas. Though commanded by white officers, their ranks were comprised mainly of freed blacks and northern rogues, men owned body and soul by the carpetbagger machine. They ransacked houses, arrested scores of men without warrant, and quickly became known for their brutal methods. Within a fortnight close to a dozen prisoners had been killed while attempting to escape. Those newspaper editors who hadn't yet lost their backbone found it curious that in each case the prisoner had been shot in the back. While unarmed. It made for interesting speculation.

Wes Hardin speculated only briefly. The handwriting was on the wall, and he saw his own name there in bold, black letters. Drifting steadily westward, where the State Police had not yet ventured, he rode into Griffin in late July. The Flats was a haven for wanted men, a remote frontier way station where law officers simply didn't exist. The Army was concerned more with Comanches and Kiowas than with white fugitives, and what little law the town got was strictly hit-and-miss. It was every man for himself, and in a very real sense, Judge Colt proved to be the Court of Last Resort.

Soon after he hit Griffin the youngster joined forces with John Collins. They met in a saloon-room-brawl, standing back to back for mutual protection, and afterward, over drinks, discovered that each had something the other wanted. Collins was a gambler by profession, but what he won at the tables had lately been lost in racing horses. Though he owned a blooded stallion, he lacked a skilled rider, and the boy seemed to fit the ticket perfectly. For his part, Wes aspired to bigger and better things. The little he'd seen of the sporting crowd left him goggle-eyed. Men won and lost more in a single night than he could earn in an entire year as a cowhand. He saw it as an act of Providence that he and John Collins had been thrown together. The gambler would teach him all there was to know about the vagaries of poker and faro and chuck-a-luck, and in time he visualized himself as a full-fledged member of the fraternity. A true high roller.

Oddly enough, the partnership worked from the very outset. Collins was a loner by nature, quiet and reserved, a man who stayed alive through cold calculation of those he met across a gaming table. He dressed immaculately, went clean-shaven, and despite his chunky appearance, had the deft touch of a magician in his hands. This, along with a derringer that could materialize out of thin air, had won him the respect of the sporting crowd. But never before had he teamed up with another man, honest or otherwise. Wes was the first, and only after the boy had won a race astride the stallion did Collins fully accept him as a confederate.

That night Wes got his opening lesson in the ancient art of legerdemain. After supper they retired to Collins' hotel room and the gambler began a step-by-step demonstration of why the hand is quicker than the eye. He shuffled, allowed the boy to cut the deck, and then dealt a hand of five-card stud. Wes had learned the rudiments of poker in the Slash O bunkhouse, but he was mildly puzzled by Collins' performance. Obviously something was being taught here, and though he watched attentively, he saw nothing out of the ordinary.

Collins' face was impassive, a blank. "How would you bet your hand?"

Wes had a pair of queens and the gambler had an ace high showing. Still in a bit of a quandary, the youngster shrugged. "I'd bet the limit. Odds are you haven't got nothin' to go with that ace."

A slight smile ticced the corner of Collins' mouth. He flipped his hole card and exposed a second ace. "Kid, there's about a hundred different ways to cheat a man with a deck of cards. I just used three of them on you."

The boy gave him a level gaze. "Don't call me kid."

Collins regarded him thoughtfully for a moment, then nodded. "Fair enough. But that doesn't change anything. You were still suckered and you didn't catch it."

"I'm used to playin' with honest people."

"Then you'd better steer clear of saloons and gaming dives."

"Meanin' nobody plays straight."

"Let me put it to you this way. Whether you're straight or crooked is up to you. But if you try gamblin' without being able to tell the difference, you'll lose your ass in a hurry. That's what separates the men from the boys. Knowing how to spot the tricks."

"Which one are you"—Wes eyed him closely—"straight or crooked?"

"You'll figure that out for yourself when you get good

enough.'' Collins riffled the deck, never bothering to look at
the cards. ''Time for school. I'll show you what I did a
minute ago, and when you get to where you can catch me
most of the time, we'll go on to the slicker stuff.''

In slow motion, his hands moving with the languid grace
of a sleek cat, Collins began the lesson. First he shuffled and
asked Wes to cut. Then, with sleight of hand so simple it
was audacious, he collected the deck and switched it back
into the original order. Next he demonstrated dealing seconds, deftly slipping the top card aside just enough to
squeeze out the card below. Lastly, employing various fingers in distinct and separate movements, he showed the
youngster how to deal from the bottom of the deck. Finished,
he set the cards aside and the enigmatic smile returned.

''That's what I did. Think you could spot it at regular
speed?''

''Christ A'mighty.'' The words were awed, almost rev-
erent. ''I barely saw you do it just now.''

''Then you'd better watch close and practice like hell.''
Collins' stony mask cracked long enough for a small grin to
peek through. ''That is, if you're still of a mind to be a
gamblin' man.''

''You damn bet'cha I am. Just keep dealin' till I get the
hang of it. Way you work them pasteboards, I'm likin' this
game better all the time.''

Collins let the mask fall back in place and began shuffling.
His hands caressed the cards with the soft, fluttering touch
of a butterfly, and after the cut, he dealt another hand of
stud. Only this time he made the sucker bet all the more
enticing.

Kings for the boy and aces for himself.

4

They rode into Towash like a couple of errant knights
returned with the Holy Grail. Collins wore the customary
garb of a gambler, undertaker black with a downy white shirt

and a diamond stickpin, which was only a cut above the attire he generally affected when Lady Luck set him astraddle a winning streak. But his partner bore only scant resemblance to the young bumpkin he had taken under wing some six months past. Wes was decked out in a candy-striped shirt and knee-high *vaquero* boots, with jangly roweled spurs that sparkled in the wintry sunlight. Around his waist was a silvery concho belt and cinched over his hips was a gun belt that would have done justice to the most fearsome Mexican *bandido*. The sombrero he sported was merely frosting on the cake.

With a monkey and a bass drum, they could have drawn a crowd.

All of this was not without some little forethought on Collins' part. Whenever they hit a new town the contrast was certain to start talk. A professional gambler and a spiffy kid. It was a combination that aroused considerable curiosity, and had much the same effect as a candle on a flock of moths. Most folks figured them for a pair of sharpers, and rightly so. But human nature being what it is, the rubes couldn't resist trying them on for size. Win, lose, or draw, it was sure to be worth the price of admission.

The partnership of Collins & Hardin had prospered exceedingly since they joined forces at Fort Griffin. The youngster proved to be an apt pupil, practicing diligently and soaking up the tricks of the trade like a fresh sponge. Gifted with strong, supple hands, he soon acquired the knack of manipulating a deck of cards, and if so disposed, could make the pasteboards all but sit up and bark. Collins was at first amazed by the boy's dexterity and nimble wits, and in no small degree, gratified by his protégé's thirst to learn. Before long he felt like a master imparting the wisdom of the ages, and in the youngster's deft performance he saw something of himself made to live again.

Oddly enough, Wes discovered that the older man was a rarity among his breed, an honest gambler. Except in a crooked game. When Collins found himself head to head with a tinhorn he had no compunctions whatever about turning the tables. And the startling part was that he could out-slick the slipperiest sharper around. But given his choice, he preferred an honest game. Strategy, a working knowledge of the odds, and a good bluff, he explained to Wes, made gambling a higher form of science. Cheating was a crutch, a device employed by dullards who lacked either the wits or the savvy to hold their own with a true high roller. Yet there was a time for all things. If some penny-ante cardsharp tried to improve the odds, a man had a moral obligation to trim his wick. The money was not to be sneezed at, naturally, but that was purely secondary. The important thing was to beat a tinhorn at his own game. Leave him busted and bruised, if not wiser. A believer, of sorts, in the follies of a sparrow trying to fly high in the company of chicken hawks.

Wes listened and learned, absorbing in months the cagey gambits accumulated by Collins in a lifetime of courting the fickle lady. But it was a fair exchange, for in the process he pulled his own weight where it counted most. Astride the back of the blood bay stallion, Steeldust.

Collins had won the horse in a poker game, and quickly taken a fancy to the sport of kings. West of the Mississippi, though, the sport had been altered somewhat. Cow ponies weren't much on the long stretch, but they were chain lightning over the short haul. Over a period of time the distance had been reduced to accommodate the quick-starting, tough-bottomed little fire-eaters commonly used on cattle spreads. Instead of a grueling mile, the race had become more of a sprint, something on the order of a quarter mile. While the run was over and done with hardly before it began, this in no way diminished the ardor of those addicted to fleet ponies and fast money. A race was a major event, and in the far-flung towns of west Texas, men leaped at the chance to bet their favorite.

From Fort Griffin, Collins had taken the youngster on a six months' odyssey of the gambler's circuit. West along the Pecos, then south to the Rio Grande, and at last, a wide swing north toward the more settled areas. In that time Wes had been exposed to every gaming dodge in the book, and aside from the real artists, he could hold his own in pretty fast company. Though they seldom played at the same table, except to team up in a crooked game, the boy could even give Collins a stiff way to go. Still, his greatest contribution to the partnership had been aboard Steeldust. Which was what brought them to Towash. The stallion had gained a certain fame throughout west Texas, losing only once in the last several months, and there were towns standing in line to match their local champion against this explosive bay.

Christmas Day in Towash had become something of a tradition. A day to make a man's sporting blood run hot, and even more than the Fourth of July, a day when everybody cut the wolf loose. The lure was the Boles Racetrack, a hard-packed quarter mile that had felt the drumming hooves of many great horses. People came from as far as Dallas and San Antonio, and they brought with them some of the finest horseflesh in the Lone Star State. If not the most important race in Texas, it was one of the wildest. In a mad rush of betting, men wagered every dollar they possessed, and when the lust took hold extra hard, some went so far as to mortgage their farms and next year's crops. Short of a wife's virtue, anything was negotiable in Towash on Christmas Day.

Collins timed their arrival perfectly. Soon enough to enter Steeldust in the race, but with only a couple of hours to spare. The sporting crowd scarcely had time to look the stallion over, which was precisely as the gambler had planned it. The favorite was a roan stud, called Big Red, from over around Nacogdoches, and despite Steeldust's growing reputation, the odds held firm to the very last. With Wes doing the betting—to all appearances a slick-eared kid decked out to look like Sudden Death from Bitter Creek—they were able to get down better than two thousand dollars before starting time. Collins sort of hung around in the background, observing, immensely pleased with himself and his young partner. Unless he had miscalculated, Santy Claus was about to make it a Merry Christmas they would long remember.

The first groans went up when Wes shucked out of his spurs and fancy gun belt and climbed aboard Steeldust.

Everybody was struck by a sudden notion that things weren't as they appeared. Like maybe the kid had sunk the gaff and was about to land himself a barrelful of suckers. Though the weather was brisk and windy, several men found themselves sweating freely, and their qualms were lessened not at all when the starter fired his pistol.

Big Red broke to the front, taking a lead of a length and a half. But he held it for less than a furlong. Steeldust suddenly exploded from the pack, churning at the hard-packed earth, and yard by yard the gap began to close. Then they were nose to nose, the blood bay and the great roan, and an agonized roar went up from the crowd as Steeldust edged ahead. Big Red came on valiantly, narrowing the lead to inches, and for a moment it appeared that the favorite might yet pull it off. Seemingly without effort they had made it a two-horse race, and they thundered along side by side, some thirty yards separating them from their nearest rival. With the finish line in sight, locked in a dead heat, Wes played his joker at last. Bending low, he slammed his heels into the stallion's ribs.

Steeldust rocketed forward as if he'd been shot out of a cannon. The bay hated nothing worse than to be spurred, but it was a fury the boy had learned to harness. Now, enraged by the insult, Steeldust simply ran off and left Big Red. Driving hard, with Wes scrunched down tight against his neck, the stallion crossed the finish line six lengths in front of the Nacogdoches roan.

The crowd was curiously silent as the youngster slowed Steeldust and turned him, trotting back down the track. While there was some sullen muttering to be heard, most of the onlookers were rankled not so much with the boy and the horse as with their own gullibility. They hadn't been horn-swoggled, for Steeldust was a name known to all. But they had swallowed the bait, in the form of a big roan stud, and they were finding it damnedly hard to digest.

Two hardcases, men Collins had never seen before, couldn't get it down at all. When he and Wes finally worked their way through the crowd to the stakeholder, the strangers were standing nearby. As Collins collected their winnings, one of the men spoke up in a disgruntled voice, loud enough to make sure that everyone within earshot heard clearly.

"Mister, that was real slick. Lettin' that kid suck ever'body in. You two must've had plenty of practice."

Collins turned his head just far enough to rivet the loud-mouth with a quizzical frown. "You accusing me of something, friend?"

The stranger held his gaze for a moment, then snorted. "Well, Jesus Christ! Don't get your nose out of joint. I was just sayin' you work good together."

"Much obliged." Collins pocketed the money and turned away with Wes at his side. "Bet on Steeldust next time. He's surefire."

"Hey, looky here, you don't seem like a man to take a feller's poke and run. How about givin' me and my sidekick a chance to get some of it back?"

Collins stopped and again fixed him with a curious look. "What'd you have in mind?"

"Nothin' much." The stranger shrugged, almost too casually. "Maybe a little poker. Leastways if you're partial to the game."

The gambler studied both men for a moment, then nodded. "Matter of fact, I am. You know Dire's Store?"

"Sure. That's the one right in the middle of town."

"There's a back room with a card table. We'll meet you there after supper."

Collins walked off and Wes fell in beside him. The strangers exchanged sly looks and suddenly broke out grinning. Heads together they turned and marched off in the opposite direction.

The game was less than an hour old when Collins' hunch proved correct. The men were tinhorns, and inept tinhorns at that. Jim Bradly, the loudmouth, had a thick brushy beard and smiled a lot, like an amiable cockleburr. His partner, Hamp Davis, was sad-faced and skinny as a hound dog, and spoke only when a grunt wouldn't suffice. Somewhere he'd lost one ear, and the empty spot made him seem even more forlorn. But for all the contrasts in look and manner, they shared the same affliction. Neither man could cheat worth a damn.

Wes and the gambler were slowly trimming them, feeding one another good hands and bumping the pot with sucker raises. But the youngster's temper was steadily getting the better of him. The two sharpers were so clumsy he felt humiliated merely to be in the same game with them. Finally, when Davis awkwardly palmed an ace, Wes slammed his fist down on the table.

"The next sonovabitch that sneaks a card, I'm gonna shoot his other ear off. Savvy?"

Davis put on his best hangdog look, but Bradly demanded churlishly, "You sayin' we're cheatin'?"

Wes raked him with a cold glare. "What I'm sayin' is that the both of you don't know beans from buckshot about what you're tryin' to do. Why don't you just give it up and we'll call it quits?"

Bradly hawked, clearing his throat, vaguely unsettled by the boy's cocksure tone. After a moment he glanced over at Collins. "Mister, you better put that rooster to crowin' on some other roof."

"He's old enough to wipe his own nose," Collins said evenly. "Unless you figured to do it for him."

There was a long silence, and at last, Bradly slumped back in his chair. "Shit. We're wastin' time. Play cards."

Wes grinned. "Funny, how it's always the loser shoutin' for somebody to deal."

"Sonny, you keep askin' for it," Bradly rasped, "and you're gonna get it."

The youngster smirked and ran his fingers through the stack of coins in front of him. "Looks to me like I've already got it."

Bradly muttered something under his breath and snatched his cards from the table. Without a flicker, Davis fumbled the ace back into the deck and grunted to himself. He still couldn't believe the kid had caught on. Not so quickly anyhow.

Shortly before midnight it was done. Collins and the boy walked from Dire's Store with every nickel the tinhorns had between them. Crossing the street, headed toward a saloon, the gambler chuckled and slewed a sidewise glance at Wes.

"You shouldn't let a pair like that get your goat. Spoils the fun of watchin' them fry in their own fat."

Before the youngster could answer a slug whistled past him and the sharp crack of a pistol echoed up the street. Behind them, Bradly jumped off the boardwalk and rushed forward, cursing as he triggered another shot. But his aim was as bad as his poker. The ball sailed harmlessly by and shattered the saloon window.

Wes spun, crouching low, and drilled him square in the chest. Bradly stumbled to a halt, planting a slug in the earth at his feet, then toppled forward like a felled tree. The boy calmly shot him in the head and looked up just as Davis scampered back into the store. Holstering the Navy, Wes turned and strolled away as if he hadn't a care in the world.

Dumbfounded, Collins just stood there a moment, staring at the body. Then his lips moved, mouthing words heard only by himself and the dead man.

"Mother of God. Ain't he a sudden little bastard?"

5

Pisga appeared unchanged. Seated astride a grullo gelding, Wes studied the town as a soldier might reconnoiter an enemy stronghold. From a distance, atop a small knoll west of the business district, he saw nothing out of the ordinary. The night wind was chill and the dim twinkle of lamplight below gave him a warm feeling down in the pit of his belly. But it was a fleeting sensation, put to rout by a gritty wariness that chided such foolish notions. There was no safe place. There were only places less dangerous than others.

Still, he couldn't ignore the gut feeling about Pisga. A good feeling. Unless the State Police were better bloodhounds than the Yankee Army, this was one place they wouldn't have nosed out. Aside from his family, he'd never told a living soul about Jane Bowen and his winter as a schoolteacher. Not even John Collins knew about it, though in the end, he'd felt obligated to tell the gambler most everything else.

It saddened him in a queer sort of way. Not having a partner any longer. But Collins had been right, and wholly justified in the stand he took. A gambling man, one who rode the circuit regular as clockwork, couldn't afford trouble with the State Police. Sheriffs and town marshals could be bought off, or wheedled into looking the other way. But a man who valued his hide didn't monkey with the governor's hired mercenaries. After Wes spilled the beans, admitting that his name was on the now infamous wanted list, Collins had wasted little time in dissolving the partnership. The gambler did so reluctantly, swilling himself blind drunk in the process, for he had grown fond of the boy. What with him being a confirmed loner, that was no small honor in itself. Yet, drunk or sober, he hadn't wavered.

The killing in Towash would eventually find its way to the wrong ears. The youngster's name would be linked with his own, and before long the State Police would show up looking for both of them. It was a risk he couldn't afford to take. Much as he liked the boy, and needed him aboard Steeldust, the odds dictated only one choice. They had to go their separate ways.

They parted outside Towash the morning after Christmas. Wes felt no bitterness toward the gambler. Nor could he fault the man. Collins had taught him a trade. Educated him in tricks that remained a mystery to all but the most skilled high rollers. And perhaps the last lesson had been the most profound of all. Only a fool buys chips in another man's fight. In that there was a kernel of wisdom, one he wouldn't soon forget.

But never had he felt so alone, or at a loss for what came

next. He had the clothes on his back, close to a thousand dollars in gold, and a grullo gelding. That and a pair of hands trained to earn him an easy living.

Yet, of all he possessed, it was the gelding he prized most just at that moment. He had bought the grullo from a *vaquero* down on the border, after busting the man in a monte game. Dusky blue in color, with a sound bottom and strong lungs, the horse was built to last. Times before, when he'd been on the dodge, Wes had learned that endurance was what counted. A wanted man, with the law on his tail, was a goner unless he had something underneath him that wouldn't quit. The grullo was no quitter, and in that he found comfort. So long as the State Police didn't take him by surprise, he had a fair chance of pulling through.

With no real destination in mind, he had ridden aimlessly for a couple of days and awoke one morning with a sudden yearning to see Jane Bowen. Nearly seven months had passed since his last visit, and by now, like as not, she was married off to some ribbon clerk with a bright future. But he still wanted to see her, and like a bear overcome with a taste for honey, he headed east into the hornet's nest. Where the State Police swarmed in droves, and carpetbagger law still ruled the land.

Now, two days after New Year's, he brought the grullo down off the knoll and rode into Pisga. Skirting the business district, he swung north around town and approached the Bowen house from the back. After tying the gelding in a stand of live oaks, he stuck to the shadows and worked his way around to the front porch. When he yanked the pull bell it suddenly came to him that he reeked with sweat and a week's accumulation of grime. It was too late to back off, though. If she was still here, not yet married off, she'd have to take him as he was. Or not at all.

The door opened and Jane gave a small, stifled cry. Her hand flew to her mouth and she gaped at him in bemused wonderment. Several moments passed before she found her voice, and even then it came in a near whisper.

"Wes?"

"It's me, in the flesh." His stomach churned, and flipped

over in a full somersault, but he flashed a cocky grin. "Big as life and twice as ornery."

"You've changed." Her eyes took in the fancy duds and the gun belt, and she seemed to shrink back. "Or maybe it's the clothes."

He doffed the sombrero and shuffled his feet. The jingle-bobs on the big, roweled spurs chimed softly, and all of a sudden he felt very out of place. Like a kid playing the tough hombre and botching it all to hell.

"I was just passing through. Thought I'd stop by and say hello." Edging away, he smiled weakly and started to turn. "Nice seein' you again. Didn't mean to bust in on you so sudden like."

"Wes Hardin!" Her crisp tone stopped him cold. "You come into this house. Right this instant!"

Grabbing his hand, the girl tugged him through the door and into the parlor. Neal Bowen froze halfway out of his chair, and his wife sat immobile, her face drained of color. Then the old man sank back in his rocker and pinned the youngster with a glacial stare. Jane wasn't exactly radiant, but she managed a brave smile and dragged Wes a couple of steps closer.

"Mama! Daddy! Look who's here. It's Wes."

That much they could see for themselves, and the sight clearly wasn't to their liking. They gave his *charro* getup a hard once-over and frowned as if somebody had just broken wind. After a long, turgid silence, Bowen finally grumped out a few words.

"Well, Hardin, how are things in Mexico?"

Wes turned the color of beet juice, acutely aware of his peculiar garb. "Tolerable, I guess. Met some nice people down that way."

"You should have stayed. Or isn't the law after you any-more?"

"Law?" the boy echoed hollowly.

"I'll be frank with you, Hardin." The merchant's tone was clipped and stiff. "We accepted you into our home and you deceived us. You were wanted by the law then, and doubtless you're wanted by the law now. I have no use for a man who wantonly takes the lives of other men, and even less use for a liar.''

"Daddy!" Jane cried. "That's not fair. Give Wes a chance to explain."

"Explain what? That he's a liar and a killer, and from the looks of him, half greaser." Bowen stabbed out with a bony finger. "You're not welcome in this house, Hardin. And I'll thank you to leave my daughter alone. She'll have no truck with the likes of you. Do I make myself clear?"

The youngster's hackles pricked up as though he'd heard a new verse in an old sermon, and for an instant, he glared back in baffled fury. Then his temper came unhinged.

"Lemme tell you somethin', old man. I've been listenin' to that sanctimonious hogwash all my life. You high-and-mighty hypocrites sit back on your perch and play God judgin' people like me. And it don't even matter that maybe I had to shoot to save my own skin. All you can do is get puffed up with righteousness and start shoutin' *burn the sinner!* Well, Mr. High and Mighty, I'm here to tell you—just lookin' at you makes me sick to my stomach.''

Bowen flushed and sputtered something unintelligible, but Wes cut him off. "Don't say nothin', you hear me! Don't even open your mouth. I'm gonna walk out of here and I'm not comin' back. But you say one more word and you'll wind up eatin' with store-bought choppers.''

The boy spun on his heel and stormed out of the house. Jane hesitated a moment, almost mesmerized by the raw terror on her father's face, then turned and darted through the door. She caught Wes as he barreled around the corner of the house and clutched desperately at his sleeve.

"Wes! Please, Wes. Don't leave like this.''

"Like what?" He jerked his arm loose and stalked off into the darkness. "You want me to go back in there and apologize? Tell him what a swell feller he is for showin' me the gate?''

"You know that isn't what I mean. I defended you, didn't I? Answer me, Wes, didn't I?''

Something in her voice stopped him, a tiny cry of helplessness, and his anger simmered down as fast as it had boiled over. Sheepishly, he turned back and gave her a crooked grin. "Yeah, I guess you did, at that. I was so mad I plumb forgot."

She came into his arms and their lips met in a hungry yearning too long denied. When they parted, at last, she peppered his face with wet, sticky kisses. "Oh, Wes, I love you so much. Honestly, I do. Late at night I lie awake thinking about you and I break out in goose bumps all over. It's shameless, but I can't help it. I won't ever love anybody but you."

"Then let's get married. Tonight." He lifted her chin, searching her face intently. "We'll get some preacher out of bed and just put all this behind us. Ride off and never look back."

Her eyes went misty, the color of damp violets, and she shook her head. "I can't."

"What do you mean, can't?"

"I want to. It's all I've ever wanted. Since the first day we met. But I just can't till you clear yourself with the law. Don't you understand? I couldn't live that way. Always on the run. Never knowing from one minute to the next if you'll get killed—or have to kill somebody else."

"No, I don't understand. You're startin' to sound like your pa."

"That's not true"—she stamped her foot with tart annoyance—"and you know it very well."

"Well, by Jesus Christ, it's all I keep hearin'. And it's enough to gag a dog off a gut wagon." He crammed the sombrero on his head. "Tell you what. You and your goose bumps think it over, and if I get the chance, I might just stop by next time I'm in town."

Wheeling around, grinding his teeth in a burst of temper, he strode off toward the live oaks. Jane stood rooted, speechless, unable to move or call out. After what seemed a lifetime, she heard the faint thud of hoofbeats and a moment later the night went still. Then her knees went shaky and she began to cry. Very slowly she lowered herself to the ground and buried her face in her hands. But it helped not at all.

The flinty soil consumed her tears and nothing changed.

CHAPTER 3

1

Like a young hawk gaining its wings, a remarkable change had come over Wes Hardin. Those who knew him best merely nodded wisely and observed that strange things often happened to a boy when he turned seventeen. Others, especially those meeting him for the first time, found it difficult, if not impossible, to believe that he wasn't older. But there was no mistaking the steady look in his eye and his assured manner in dealing with the vagaries of life. Whatever the reason, the boy had set aside boyish ways. Tall and resolute, square-jawed with a brushy mustache covering his upper lip, he spoke and acted with the bearing of what he had become. A man.

Yet, if Wes Hardin had been a defiant boy, he had matured into a dangerous man. Within the crucible of death and gunsmoke and Yankee injustice had been fired a confirmed fatalist. Time and eight dead men had numbed him to the sight of death, hardened him to the act of killing. However unnatural, the outgrowth was an utter contempt for those who opposed him and a blind disregard for the consequences to himself. What others took to be rashness, or an excess of courage, was neither of those things. It was simply a complete and immutable absence of fear.

Though still headstrong and short-fused, Wes had learned to control his temper. Where before he had exploded with the suddenness of a firecracker, he now harnessed his anger to better effect. Cool and detached, calculated in a deadly sort of way, he appeared devoid of nerves in a tight situation. Here again, it was not a matter of icy bravery. Instead, it hinged on a single imponderable. He feared nothing that walked, talked, or crawled, and the offspring was a steely audacity that left other men vaguely uneasy in his presence.

Carpetbagger justice was in no small part the moving force behind his stoic outlook on life. The State Police had hounded him relentlessly, dogging his tracks from town to town across the state. Early in the spring, while visiting his parents for the first time in more than a year, he had narrowly escaped capture. Perhaps more than anything else, it was the thought of his family in jeopardy, badgered and ruthlessly questioned by black officers, which brought about the transformation. Where in the past he had run from the dreaded State Police, avoiding confrontation, he now took no steps whatever to elude them. He went where he wanted, when he wanted, supremely untroubled by the possibility that he might be caught.

This process of growth and maturity had revealed itself in other ways as well. Looking back, he was able to understand Jane's reluctance to take him on his own terms. In time, he even came to accept her deep-seated apprehension, and saw himself as something of a lout for the way he had acted. Certainly there was no place for a wife and family in the life he led, and in truth, that was what Jane had tried to tell him. While some six months had passed, he hadn't worked up the nerve to visit Pisga again, but he had written her several letters as he drifted from town to town. Whether she still waited for him, or had, after all, married some ribbon clerk, was an uncertainty that rode with him constantly. But it was something he accepted as inevitable, at least for the moment. Until Texas changed, and Yankee rule ended, he would remain what a topsy-turvy world had made him. A man outside the law.

Still, with all its assorted miseries, life hadn't been unkind to him. Cards and horse racing kept him well supplied with funds. Women found him easy on the eyes, yet he was free to come and go as he chose. Within the sporting crowd he was respected more than most, both as a gambler and a man ever willing to toe the mark. All in all, whenever he paused to reflect on it, he had no room for complaint. Things weren't exactly perfect, but they could have been a hell of a lot worse.

Along the way, he had even acquired a new partner. Upon skipping out of Mount Calm a step ahead of the State Police, he had taken refuge with the Barrickman clan, distant relatives on his mother's side of the family. There he had renewed a boyhood friendship with his cousin. Alec Barrickman. After a week of swapping tall tales, Alec decided the fast life sounded better than farming, and when Wes rode out, he tagged along. Here, too, the change in the young outlaw was evident. Though Alec was a couple of years older, there was never any question as to who called the shots. Wes figured he'd served his apprenticeship, and anyone who sided with him now would have to settle for second fiddle. That or nothing. Unless somebody put a shotgun on him, he had taken orders for the last time in his life.

Barrickman was a gangling, rawboned sort of fellow, with more spunk than savvy. Towheaded, with a wide gap between his front teeth and a quid of tobacco stuffed in his cheek, there was something of the hayseed about him. But he was bright enough, and early on it became apparent that they made a good team. With his country-boy smile and china-blue eyes, people right away took Barrickman for a natural born sucker. Wes taught him a few tricks, mostly how to boost a pot when dealt a loaded hand, and a steady stream of tinhorns were left scratching their heads over the young sodbuster's astounding luck. All the same, the senior partner saw to it that his cousin stayed out of straight games. Barrickman had an unnerving habit of drawing to inside straights and trying to bluff on a busted flush, which tended to whittle down the profits at an alarming rate.

Toward the middle of June, Hardin & Company drifted into the town of Horn Hill. There was a circus running full blast, drawing crowds from several counties, and the place swarmed with pigeons ripe for the plucking. Wes hadn't killed anybody since the Towash shoot-out, and as near as he could tell, the State Police had lost his scent. This, combined with the carnival mood of the town, made him a little less wary than usual. Barrickman was horny as a goat anyway, so he promised the junior member of the firm that part of their time would be devoted to the ladies of Horn Hill.

All the same, business came first.

That afternoon Barrickman went into what, by now, had become their standard routine. Wandering into a saloon, he flashed a fistful of double eagles and quick as a wink found himself engaged in conversation with a couple of sharpers. As it always did, the discussion ultimately worked around to the game of poker, and the young bumpkin allowed himself to be steered to the table. Magically, a deck of cards appeared, and by the third drink, things were off and running. Standing at the bar, Wes waited until another farmer had taken a seat in the game and then ambled over. The tinhorns sized him up as yet a third mark and invited him to take a chair. Their smug looks made it all the easier. Moments ago they were matching one another for drinks and suddenly— magi-presto—they had stumbled into a field of clover.

It took Wes only one turn as dealer to figure out the play. They were using strippers, and rather crudely shaved at that. In his hands the cards began performing wonders, and queer as it seemed, the young hayseed across from him started raking in some dandy pots. Wes worked on the premise that a man with larceny in his heart was the biggest sucker of all. But the kill had to be made fast, before the sharper suspected that someone had outslicked him at his own game.

The end came less than a half hour after Wes joined the game. He dealt one tinhorn a full house and the other four deuces. Alec Barrickman, after drawing three cards, wound up with his old standby, four nines. The farmer dropped out when the raising began, and by showdown time, the two sharpers had bumped the pot with all they had, pinky rings included. Gleefully, all wide-eyed innocence and boyish smiles, Barrickman dragged in the pot with his thorny paws.

The tinhorns just sat there, clicking their teeth like a couple of rabid skunks. In the parlance of the sporting world, they had been gaffed on their own play.

After leaving the card sharps to lick their wounds, Wes deposited Barrickman in a pool hall, where he couldn't get himself into any mischief. Then the young outlaw went looking for a straight game. He found it in the Bella Union Saloon, and about three hours later came out wishing he hadn't bothered. Lady Luck had dumped all over his head, handing him a steady run of second-best, and he had dropped better than a hundred dollars. Still, not once had he violated the cardinal rule as laid down by John Collins. Unless the other fellow cheated first a man played whatever he was dealt. There was always another day, and more often than not, the fickle lady smiled on those who kept the faith.

Barrickman wasn't even remotely interested in the details. He was tired of cards and sick to death of pool. What he wanted most was a greased pole, and after the debacle at the Bella Union, Wes had to admit he could use a little diversion himself. In high spirits, certain they would hit pay dirt of a different sort, the youngsters set out in the direction of the circus.

More quickly than they expected, good things began to happen. A brace of apple-cheeked farm girls had eluded their parents, and with only the mildest coaxing, the party shortly became a foursome. Arm in arm, the girls squealing and the boys licking their chops, they struck off down the midway to see the sights. As in most small-time carnivals, the tent barkers were the best part of the show. The bearded lady turned out to be a scraggly old crone with a face full of fuzz and the world's strongest man almost had a stroke lifting a midget pony. But it was fun, and the girls' squeals were growing louder, which the young gamblers took as a good sign, so nobody was overly disappointed that the freaks didn't live up to the barker's spiel.

After watching a fire-eater singe his tonsils, the foursome sailed back onto the midway laughing and snuggling closer with every step. Wes figured a few more shows ought to turn the trick and he steered them toward a tent proclaiming the eighth wonder of the world.

Whatever the colossus was, they never got to see it. A fight broke out behind them and a circus roustabout burst out of nowhere on the dead run. He scattered the foursome with a rough shove and lumbered on toward the fight. Wes's reaction was sheer reflex. Rushing back, he grabbed the man's shoulder and spun him around.

"Mister, somebody ought to learn you some manners. There's a couple of ladies back there that's got an apology comin' to 'em."

"Out of the way, rube. Less you want your face smashed."

"Smash and be damned! I'm kind of a smasher myself."

Somehow it wasn't the youngster's day. Sparkling lights danced before his eyes and the next thing he knew, he was flat on his back. Instinct alone saved him. As the roustabout tugged at a gun in his waistband, Wes cleared leather and stitched three slugs straight up his front. The last one caught the circus tough just below the hairline and his skull blew apart in a frothy pink gore. Wes was on his feet and running before the man hit the ground. Somewhere in the background he heard the girls shrieking at the top of their lungs and a murderous outcry from the crowd. Then he was around a tent and going strong. Barrickman loped up beside him, panting hard, and threw him a wild-eyed look.

"Gawd A'mighty! You play for keeps, don't you?"

"Alec, lemme tell you somethin'. And don't you never forget it. Any man worth shootin' is worth killin'."

Wes cast a peek over his shoulder and saw a mob hard on their heels. Digging harder, he sprinted off, roaring in Barrickman's ear as he went past."

"Now, run, you horny sonovabitch! Run!"

2

After Horn Hill young Hardin became even bolder. Somehow tucking tail like a whipped dog didn't sit well on his stomach. Granted, to stand his ground and face the mob would have bordered on suicide. A stranger in a small town would have had less chance than a snowball in hell. Especially if the sheriff had taken a notion to consult his wanted circulars. They would have strung him up before he had time to take a deep breath. And Barrickman alongside him. Sort of a grand finale to their circus holiday.

People were like that. Nothing tickled their fancy quite so much as a good hanging. The longer a man danced on air, slowly choking with bulged eyeballs and swollen tongue, the better they liked it. It was a sight to be savored down to the tiniest detail, something that added spice to dull conversation on a cold winter night.

Yet, for all the ghoulish mood of the people, Wes was still irked at being forced to run. Discretion was the better part of valor—that was one of his father's favorite little gems—but in the last two years he had damned sure had his share of running. A double helping, and then some. Upon fleeing Horn Hill, quirting his horse into the pitch-black night, he decided it was the last time. He would run no more.

With Barrickman in tow, he turned east, straight into the jaws of the governor's meat grinder. It was a nervy act of defiance, an engraved invitation to the State Police. They would come after him, of that he was sure, for his name was known and word of his presence in east Texas wouldn't be long in reaching Austin. But it hardly seemed to matter. In fact, he welcomed it. Killing saloon toughs and circus roustabouts had somehow lost its zest. It was time to get down to serious business. Put the nutcracker to work on those who had hounded him and shamed his family—the carpet-baggers and their pack of hired cutthroats.

Late in July, Wes and Alec Barrickman rode into Evergreen. The young outlaw now had a price of one thousand dollars on his head, but he entered the town openly, with no attempt to conceal his identity. Reward dodgers bannering his name, with a charcoal sketch bearing a fair likeness, were tacked on the notice board outside the sheriff's office. As he rode by, it gave him a moment of perverse amusement. The circulars showed a youthful, clean-shaven face, without a sign of his cookie-duster mustache.

On impulse, he reined in and dismounted. Scrounging around in his saddlebags, he found a stub pencil and walked to the notice board. Wetting the pencil on the tip of his tongue, he carefully blacked in a brushy mustache on the sketch. Stepping back, he studied his handiwork for a moment and then grunted, better satisfied with the likeness. Chuckling to himself, he swung aboard the grullo and reined back into the street.

Barrickman had sat spellbound through the entire performance, and now he gave the youngster a look of popeyed disbelief. "Wes, I'll swear to Christ, you got more balls 'n a bulldog. That or you ain't playin' with all your marbles."

"Well now, Alec, suppose you gimme the straight goods"—Wes smiled, thoroughly delighted with himself—"which one you figure it is?"

Barrickman wasn't that thick. However casual, the question called for a bit of diplomacy. "My pap used to tell about a feller that hunted bears with a switch. Folks always allowed as how he was strong on guts, and smart too,'cause he never once tangled with anything he couldn't handle."

Wes burst out laughing and heeled the grullo. "Quit your fibbin' and c'mon. Let's go see what's happenin' at the races."

Saturday was race day in Evergreen and the sporting crowd generally flocked in for the occasion. Wes figured to get down a few wagers on the ponies, and afterward, scare up a poker game in one of the dives along Main Street. Since Horn Hill he'd gone through a long dry spell, playing hide-and-seek with the fickle lady. Luckily, the youngsters had stumbled across enough card slicks to keep them in funds, and he still had close to five hundred dollars in his saddle-bags. Today he felt good, though, and he had a hunch the tide had changed. Any gambler worth his salt knew the feeling, and being a superstitious lot, they followed the oldest adage in the profession.

Get a hunch, bet a hunch.

Which was precisely what Wes did. But the ponies he liked apparently weren't listening. One faltered on the get-away, four in a row came in a strong second, and the sixth went berserk, pitching his rider ten yards short of the finish line. All in all, it was a bleak afternoon. The young gambler had dropped better than three hundred dollars and unless something changed fast, he was seriously considering another line of work. That or scouting up a voodoo witch doctor and buying himself a whole string of juju charms. Headed uptown from the racetrack, he had the distinct premonition that if he plucked a rose it would vanish in a puff of smoke and leave him holding a fresh horse turd.

Barrickman said little or nothing as they prowled the dives along Main Street. He had learned some time back that with Wes in a foul mood a man did well just to keep his mouth shut. Shortly before sundown, though, they wandered into the Acme Saloon and Gaming Parlor and Wes seemed to perk up the least bit. This was clearly the local hangout for the sporting crowd. There were faro layouts and chuck-a-luck along one wall and a whole row of poker tables on the opposite side. With the races over, the place had drawn a full crowd and the action was running heavy. Aside from that, the atmosphere alone told Wes they had found Evergreen's leading spot. Unlike saloons which catered to rowdy cowhands, a real gaming den was quiet as a church. Gamblers didn't like distractions or noise, complaining it broke their concentration, and a loudmouth ran the risk of getting his skull peeled with a bungstarter. Other than a murmured drone of conversation, the only sound here was the clink of gold coins and a random curse whenever a man's cards fell the wrong way.

The youngsters bellied up to the bar and ordered whiskey.

Wes was a sipper, generally nursing the same drink for a couple of hours. Rotgut impaired a man's reactions, not to mention clouding his judgment, and he had observed that hard drinkers usually finished last. At cards or in a fight. A sober man had the edge, and Wes sort of liked it that way. Besides, the stuff most joints served tasted like sheep dip anyhow. So there wasn't much sense in floating his gizzard just to be sociable. Better to keep the edge.

Wes turned, hooking his elbows over the counter, and made a slow survey of the action. There were chairs open at a couple of tables, and from the looks of things, the betting was light. Which, at the moment was just about his speed. Less than two hundred dollars damn sure wouldn't go far in a table stakes game. He was on the verge of giving it a whirl when a man seated at the nearest table climbed to his feet and strolled forward. The stranger halted a few steps off and leaned into the bar.

"Funny thing. I been watchin' you and I got a feelin' you're somebody I oughta know. Curious, ain't it?"

Wes uncoiled, freeing his gun hand. "You writin' a book or was you just born nosy?"

"Don't get your dander up, neighbor." The man extended his hand. "S'pose I go first. Name's Bill Longley."

Wes pumped the hand a couple of times and let go. He'd heard of Longley, and none of it good. Wanted for several murders, and according to reports, most of the victims bushwhacked. On top of that, he was a queer-looking bird. Tall, almost gaunt, with a lantern jaw and eyes deep-set under a ridged brow. His bony wrists dangled from the sleeves of a frayed hickory shirt and his feet were about the size of nail kegs. Taken at a glance, he made an unlikely-looking gambler and seemed built all wrong for gunfighting. Which might account for his reputation as a backshooter.

"Most folks call me Wes Hardin."

Longley nodded. "Yep, thought so. Seen the posters out on you. Guess it was the soup-strainer that throwed me." He paused, twisting his jaw in a crooked smile. "Workin' sorta close to home, ain't you? What with Austin bein' so handy,

I mean. Last I heard you was out west somewheres.''

The youngster shrugged, revealing nothing. ''Some folks might say you're kind of handy yourself.''

''Yeh, but I'm used to them nigger lawdogs. Eat 'em for breakfast.''

''That a fact? I'm sort of partial to dark meat myself.''

''Hey now, neighbor, you're talkin' my kinda talk.'' Longley jerked his thumb back toward the poker table. ''How'd you like to join a little game we got goin'? Be proud to have you sit in.''

Wes held back hard on a grin. It was like a wolf being asked to come play with sheep. Whatever else he was, Longley had the look of a born loser.

''Sure, why not? I got some time to kill. Might even get lucky and win a couple.''

The statement proved prophetic, in a way Longley and his friends could hardly believe. The young gambler hit a streak that was nothing short of stupefying. He caught straights and flushes and full houses, and three of a kind so often it was downright embarrassing. Once, defying the laws of poker and ordinary horse sense, he dragged down a pot on a jack high. Barrickman stayed at the bar, chuckling to himself as he swigged whiskey, certain beyond doubt that his cousin was goosing the odds with some slick tricks.

Similar thoughts occurred to the players themselves, but somehow the idea wouldn't hold water. Hardin didn't win just when he was dealing. He won damn near all the time, no matter who dealt. If they were being fleeced, the bastard was either a swami or a gypsy in disguise. Otherwise, it was pure outhouse luck.

And in that, they were right. Wes felt the lady riding his coattails, and he laid on strong. His luck had returned with a vengeance, and as a practical matter, it was like taking candy from babes. Everything he did was not so much right as faultless. Within an hour he had busted the four men flatter than flat. Dead broke.

Longley took it hardest, fancying himself the he-wolf of Evergreen and Jacinto County. But for all his fearsome reputation, he was a poor judge of character. More than money, he had lost face, and in a moment of rash bravado, he decided to sprinkle a little salt on the kid's tail. As Hardin pulled in the last pot, Longley shifted in his chair and dropped his hand below the table.

"Y'know, it's a funny thing. We heard them nigger police had sweet-talked some wanted men into playin' Judas goat. Spyin' on white folks and turnin' them in for the reward. What with you showin' up so sudden and all, I just been sittin' here wonderin' if maybe you got yourself a deal with them nigger-lovers in Austin."

Wes met his look with an icy smile. "Longley, you got about three seconds to back off. Then I'm gonna put a leak in your ticker."

A tomblike silence settled over the table and Longley swallowed nervously. Something in the kid's eyes told him he'd made a big mistake. If he so much as flicked an eyelash he was dead as a doornail. Evergreen's premier badman pasted a waxen smile on his face and made a game try at laughing.

"Why, hell, Hardin, I was just funnin'. Way you hauled our ashes I figured you owed us a little sport. No harm done."

"Much obliged, gents." The young gambler stood, stuffing the last of the coins in his vest pocket. "See you in church."

Hitching back his chair, he walked straight to the door and pushed through the batwings. Barrickman was only a step behind, and as they climbed aboard their horses, Wes grunted sardonically.

"That's rich. First man I ever really wanted to kill and the sorry shitheel lost his nerve. Alec, I tell you, there just ain't no justice."

Reining back, he spurred the grullo down Main Street past the sheriff's office. The reward dodger was exactly as he had left it, penciled mustache inky black in the gathering twilight.

3

Less than a week later Hardin & Company was dissolved. Unforeseen events conspired to end the partnership, and Wes reluctantly sent Barrickman back to the family farm. They parted outside the town of Kosse, in the dead of night, horses lathered from a long run. As he watched his cousin ride off, Wes was struck by the eerie feeling that life or fate, or perhaps some flaw in his own character, destined him to go it alone. Reflecting on it further, it came to him that maybe John Collins had been right after all. Some men simply weren't suited to lasting alliances with other men.

A lone wolf had only himself to worry about.

That was it in a nutshell. Responsibility. A sense of obligation to the man who rode beside him. The constant worry of being concerned about the other fellow's welfare. An infernal irritant that preyed on the mind like worms gnawing on rancid meat.

There were those seemingly born to such things. Men like his father, who saw themselves as the shepherd of the flock, their brother's keeper. They gloried in it, lived for nothing else, found their mission on earth in an everlasting vigil over their fellow man. Perhaps, at root, this was what separated Christian from heathen, sinner from saint. If so, then as his father had so often prophesied, he was doomed to the fires of eternal damnation. But if it was already ordained, if he was slated for hell with a one-way ticket, then he sure as Christ wouldn't make the trip oozing despair for the clods around him.

Better to ride alone, cover his own tracks, and to hell with the fainthearts.

The trouble had started earlier that night, shortly after they rode into Kosse. Barrickman got himself involved with a saloon girl, and in the heat of the moment, went a little too far. The girl's lover, a gambling man Wes knew from his Brazos days, took exception to Barrickman's pawing and rough talk. Within moments Barrickman was backed into a corner, clearly outclassed and only a step away from the grave. Had it been someone else, Wes would have washed his hands of the whole mess. But this was his cousin, blood kin. After soothing words and a couple of warnings failed, there was only one way out. He killed the gambler.

Though he had been recognized, and the State Police were sure to pick up his trail, that bothered him scarcely at all. The thing that had him boiling was the senselessness of the whole affair. Never before had he killed a man in cold blood, a man who had done him no wrong, knowing even as he forced the fight that the gambler was a walking dead man.

Somehow it grated on him that the gambler hadn't yet cleared leather when the first slug knocked him head over heels. All the more so since it was Barrickman's fight. A killing that served no purpose, could have been avoided except for the goatlike lust of a green plowboy.

Afterward, Wes made no bones about it. Barrickman was to return to the farm, and that was final. More than a liability, he had become a luxury Wes couldn't afford. Killing men who deserved it was one thing. The dead littered along his trail, each and every one, had asked to be buried. But pulling someone else's fat out of the fire, killing when there was no need, was a whole different ball of wax. It made him want to puke.

Barrickman had taken it hard, pleading to be given another chance. The words fell on deaf ears, though. Wes bowed his neck and that was the way it ended. Under a cloud of gloom, tail between his legs, Barrickman headed back to the family farm. The fast life he longed for had, after all, been a little faster than he could handle.

Wes watched him ride away and felt a moment of regret. But in the same instant a flood of relief swept over him. Somehow, by whatever force of nature, he was meant to be a loner, obligated only to himself and the dictates of what was best for Wes Hardin. It was a lesson he wouldn't soon forget.

With that, he pulled the grullo around and struck out for

Mount Calm. A dead gambler, needlessly killed, would soon put the law on his tail. Before it was too late, he had a need to see his folks again. Why or to what purpose was a question that had no answer. But it had to be now. Some inner voice told him that the next time would be a long haul down the trail.

Dusk had fallen as Wes crossed the creek. Avoiding Mount Calm, he'd spent last night and most of the day making a wide swing to the north. It seemed unlikely that the law would have a watch on the farm, but it was a risk to be considered all the same. Better to approach from the blind side, through the fields, just in case. Caution wasn't his strong suit, yet there were times when it paid to step light. Like tonight. Shooting his way out of the Hardin household would be about the last straw.

The one that broke James Hardin's back.

The old man already had a mighty cross to bear, what with his son an outlaw and the congregation clicking their tongues with shock. If the law ever cornered him at the farm, and he had to fight his way out, that would finish it. Preacher Hardin would pass on to his reward out of sheer mortification.

After unsaddling, Wes hobbled the gelding and left him to graze near the creek. A short walk through the woods brought him to a field, and from there he was within a stone's throw of the house. Gaining the barn, he hunkered down in the shadows and spent a quarter hour watching and listening. Satisfied that everything was as it should be, he finally climbed to his feet and made a dash for the back door.

When he entered the parlor, Sarah Hardin uttered a sharp gasp and jumped from her chair as if galvanized. Tears welled up in her eyes and she crossed the room like a distracted ghost, locking him in a fierce hug. Never given to display of emotion, she had changed markedly since his trouble with the law, almost as if the dam had burst and the love hoarded in his childhood must be lavished on him while there was yet time.

Somehow it made him uncomfortable and he pulled back

after giving her a peck on the cheek. "How are you, Ma?"

"Fine, Son. Just fine." She dabbed at the tears and took hold of herself. "Just seeing you does wonders for me."

"Then I'm glad I came."

James Hardin hadn't moved from his rocker, and the youngster sensed that this time was to be no different from his other visits. They were of the same flesh and blood, but in spirit nothing kindred bound them together.

"Hello, Pa."

"Wes, this is your home and you're welcome here night or day. But I don't hold with firearms." He shook a finger at the holstered Colt. "I'd take it kindly if you'll leave that on the back porch."

"Sorry, but I guess I can't do that, Pa. Things the way they are, I rest easier with a gun in reach."

"Tools of Satan! Haven't you learned that yet?"

"Please, James. Please don't spoil it." Sarah Hardin stepped between them, beseeching the old man with her eyes. "We see him so little. Couldn't it be nice for a change? Just once?"

Something passed between them, and after a moment, he nodded. "Sit down, Wes. The way your mother worries about you, I suppose some things just have to be overlooked."

"I don't mean to worry you." Wes lowered himself onto the settee and his mother came to sit beside him. "I'd change it if I could. But that bunch down in Austin don't seem to see it the same way."

"You're trying to reform, then?" His father fixed him with a baleful look. "Is that what you're telling me?"

"Well, in a manner of speakin', I guess you could say that."

"How? What path has this reformation taken?"

Wes shifted uncomfortably. "I'm not sure I follow you, Pa."

"Very well, let's take an example. Have you stopped gambling?"

"No. Not just exactly. But it's an honest livin'. I don't cheat nobody."

"Have you stopped consorting with Jezebels?"

The youngster darted a glance at his mother and saw her redden. "Well, Pa, that's sort of a loaded question. Any way I answer, I'm gonna come up on the short end."

"Have you stopped killing your fellow man?"

"Pa, you're makin' it awful hard for me to hold my tongue. You know well and good I've never killed anyone that wasn't tryin' to kill me."

"According to the State Police, who were here this afternoon, you killed a man not twenty miles from this very room just last night. They say you bulled your way into a private argument and forced him to fight you. I suppose that was self-defense, also?"

"Now, hold on a minute. I can explain—"

"They say that John Wesley Hardin has now killed nine men. Nine human beings."

Wes wasn't about to correct him. The count was ten, but apparently the law hadn't connected him with the circus roustabout. "You want to hear my explanation or are you just gonna sit there and rake me over the coals?"

"What I want to hear," James Hardin countered, "is how my son has set about reforming himself."

"I guess I haven't. Not the way you look at things. I'm just tryin' to mind my own business and stay a step ahead of the Yankees. Maybe someday they'll figure out I'm the wrong fellow to monkey with and then they'll leave me alone."

" 'Whosoever shall exalt himself shall be abased. And he that shall humble himself shall be exalted.' St. Matthew. Chapter Twenty-three. Verse twelve."

"Yeah? Well try this one on. 'Where there is no law, there is no transgression.' Romans. Chapter Four. Verse fifteen."

"Meaning?"

"Meanin', as long as the carpetbaggers are runnin' Texas there's no way somebody like me can come clear. They got my name down on the wanted list and nothin' is gonna change that. Not you or your Scripture or all the hallelujahs this side of kingdom come.''

The old man set his rocker in motion and gazed off into space. "For once, I believe we are in agreement.''

Wes blinked with surprise. "We are?''

"Since this afternoon I have given it a great deal of thought. Until Texas is readmitted to the Union there is no salvation for you here. Afterward, when Texas is again governed by Texans, perhaps some form of amnesty can be worked out. Despite our prayers, that is still a long way off, however.''

James Hardin brought his rocker to a halt and riveted the youngster with an owlish stare. "I believe you should go to Mexico. And stay there until the ashes of war have been scattered. It will be better for you and for all concerned.''

"All concerned, meanin' you and Ma.''

"And your brother. The entire family suffers from the shame you've brought to the Hardin name.''

Curiously, Wes felt nothing. Only a stinging numbness, as if he'd passed his fingers over an open flame. "Maybe you've got somethin', at that, Pa. Mexico might just fit the ticket.''

"I'm glad you agree. It's wisest all around.''

Sarah Hardin stood and looked down at her son. "Could you eat if I put something on the table?''

"Ma, it's the funniest thing.'' Wes jumped to his feet and briskly rubbed his hands together. "All of a sudden, I'm so hungry I could eat a bear.''

As they walked toward the kitchen, the old man's chair creaked and he began rocking slowly back and forth. It was a sad thing he had done. But necessary. However much it sorrowed him personally, it was for the good of the family. Then he heard the youngster laugh out in the kitchen and he nodded, grunting to himself.

That was good. The boy had taken it well.

4

There was no doubt whatever in Jane's mind. When the doorbell rang she knew it was Wes. All along she had held to an unshakable conviction that he would return. It had never been a matter of if he would come back, but only when.

She flew across the parlor, heedless of her father's scathing look. Dutiful, raised to respect her elders and obey unquestioningly, she had at last rebelled on the subject of Wes Hardin. So long as he was an outlaw, she wouldn't marry him. That much she had promised. But she meant to see him whenever and wherever possible. After several stormy sessions, her father resigned himself to this stalemate of sorts. Wisely, he hadn't pressed the issue further. To do so would have driven her into the young hellion's arms all the faster, and perhaps out of the Bowen household forever.

Jane threw open the door and slammed it behind her. Startled, Wes backed up a step as she flung herself on him, peppering his face with warm, sticky kisses. She had saved his letters, knew practically all of them by heart. Stiff and formal and clumsy as they were, she had every certainty that he loved her. Alone in her room at night, she lay wakeful, her mind flooded with wicked thoughts of their moments together. Face flushed, loins and breasts aching, she could close her eyes and feel their bodies engaged. Know again the touch of his corded muscles and his weight upon her, thrusting, filling her emptiness. She needed him and her need knew no shame. However silly or sinful or unwise, she was consumed with want for this boy who wrote clumsy, unforgettable letters.

Wes was no slouch himself when it came to kissing, and he planted one on her that made up for all the months of being apart. At last, when they broke for air, he grinned and gave her a sly look.

"Seems like somethin's changed since the last time I was here."

"Nothing of the kind." Her lips curved in a teasing smile. "I've just decided I love you, that's all."

"That's all!" he blinked, somewhat taken aback. "Holy Moses."

"And I've also decided you love me."

"Well, I'll be double-dipped. You're just a sackful of surprises, aren't you?"

"But that doesn't mean I'll marry you. Not just yet, anyway."

"Here we go again. Same song, second verse."

"Wes Hardin, you're impossible." She kicked him in the shin and stalked off indignantly. "A girl tells you she loves you and is willing to wait for you and give you time to get yourself straightened out, and all you can do is poke fun at her. You're just a big, overgrown ingrate!" She stamped her foot in exasperation.

"Now hold off a minute." The girl's sudden flare of temper left him a little nonplussed and he hobbled across the porch, surprised she could kick so hard. "Hell's fire, you didn't say nothin' about all them things. Waitin' for me, I mean. And givin' me a chance to get clear with the law."

"Land's sakes, I said I loved you, didn't I?" She put on her best pout, casting him a hurt look. "And don't curse. It's not gentlemanly."

Still somewhat baffled, he moved up behind her and gently took hold of her shoulders. "You really meant it? You'll wait?"

"Of course I meant it, you big ninny. Why do you think I waited all this time for you to come back?"

"Danged if I know. I sort of halfway figured you'd be hitched up to some stiff-necked church deacon by now."

"Oh, men! You're all blind as bats." She spun around and thrust herself into his arms. "Mercy sakes alive, leave a girl a little pride. Don't make me spell it out for you."

Wes just stood there, tongue-tied, struck by a sudden fit of speechlessness. There was something different about her.

Older and wiser. More woman than girl. In the face of her unabashed candor, it took him a moment to collect his wits. Presently, he cleared his throat, sensing that she meant to wait him out. Then he smiled.

"Come to think of it, I got a couple of surprises myself. That's why I'm here. To tell you I'm headed for Mexico."

"Mexico!" Jane blurted the word in an incredulous whisper. "You mean across—over the border?"

"Yep, I'm gonna lay low down there till the Yankees call it quits and go home. Way I got it figured, that's about the only way I'll ever come clean with the law."

"But that could take years. Forever."

"Mebbe not. Most all the Confederate states are back in the Union already. My pa says it won't be long before Texas sees the light and gets itself readmitted. Then we'll have Texans runnin' things again and I can work out some kind of amnesty deal."

Jane cocked her head, scrutinizing him closely. "Wes, be honest with me. Whose idea was this—about you going to Mexico?"

Her steady gaze bored into him, insistent, demanding frankness. "It was my pa's idea. He sprung it on me last night. Said it'd be best if I just vamoosed for a while and let the dust settle."

Something in his tone, and the hangdog look on his face, told the tale. Jane scarcely needed an explanation. The elder Hardin had banished his son, and much as Wes tried to hide it, he was grievously hurt. Outlaw and outcast weren't the same. A man could live with one but he could only sorrow with the other. Still, there was something else at work here. A thought that occurred to her only on the moment. In Mexico, Wes at least had a chance. There was nothing for him in Texas but Yankee justice. And the gallows.

She brightened and playfully tugged at his mustache. "Lordy mercy, you got me talking so much I near forgot about this sticker patch. When did you grow that?"

"Few months back." He swiveled around to give her a look from another angle. "Like it?"

Lifting an eyebrow, she studied him with mock seriousness. "Well, it does make you look older." Then she giggled. "They say everybody in Mexico wears mustaches. Maybe if you get one of those sombreros like you used to wear you'll fit right in."

"You might have somethin' at that." Her mood was contagious and his glum look disappeared with mercurial swiftness. "Them señoritas are real pepperpots." Knuckling the ends of his mustache, he grinned. "Wouldn't surprise me none if they swooned dead away when they get a gander at this."

"Now, if that isn't just like a man." She stuck out her lip in a little-girl sulk. "Scarcely betrothed and he's already thinking about other women."

"Betrothed!"

"Well, of course, silly. What did you think I was talking about a minute ago?"

"I dunno." Things were happening a little too fast and he just stared at her, thoroughly dumbfounded. "All I heard you say was that you were gonna wait for me."

"Gracious sakes alive, Wes Hardin! You don't think I would wait on a man I wasn't betrothed to. What kind of a girl do you take me for?"

"Why, sure. I mean, yeah, I understand why—" Flustered now, he stopped and drew a deep breath. "What I'm tryin' to say is that I wouldn't have it any other way. But what changed your mind so sudden?"

"Nothing changed it. I always meant to marry you." She batted her eyelashes and smiled. "I just decided to tell you about it, that's all."

"I'll be damned." His bafflement was profound but it abruptly gave way to concern. "Say, what about your old man?"

"Oh, don't worry about Daddy. When the time comes I'll just twist him around my little finger. I've done it before."

Wes had no doubt of that. He was struck by the thought that inside this innocent-looking creature lurked a real spitfire. Tonight he'd seen a wholly unsuspected side of her character, and like as not, there was more where that came from. He had a sneaking hunch he'd taken on more than he'd bargained for.

Ducking his head back at the house, he grinned suggestively. "If you've got your daddy's number then I don't reckon he'd mind if we took a walk."

Jane laughed. A low, throaty laugh that sounded wicked as sin itself. "You're a naughty man, Wes Hardin. I declare, you just make a girl break out in goose bumps all over."

"What d'you wanna bet I can't cure 'em?"

She giggled and he broke out in a chortled belly laugh. Arm in arm, stifling the temptation to share their high spirits with the world, they stepped off the porch and walked toward the corner of the house.

Within moments, the darkness swallowed them from sight.

An hour later Wes kissed the girl one last time and left her at the front door. As he headed in the direction of the live oak grove, his mind was a grab bag of conflicting emotions. Never in his life had he been so happy. Or so sad. She was his woman. By her own word. Willing to wait however long it took. Yet ahead of him loomed Mexico, and before he saw her again, he had an idea things would get mighty bleak. South of the Rio Grande began to sound worse all the time. A small slice of hell.

Moving through the trees, he was absorbed with the thought, aware of nothing around him. As he halted beside the grullo, hand stretched out to untie the reins, somebody jammed a gun in his back.

"Stand real easy." The man behind the voice nudged him with the pistol. "Just flinch and you're cold meat."

Wes froze stock-still. Whoever the voice belonged to, he was all business. A hand snaked around and relieved the youngster of his Navy, and Mexico suddenly seemed a long way off. An eternity instead of mere miles.

They stopped the next evening beside a small creek. By now Wes saw himself as the greatest jackass of all time. He'd walked into the trap like a dimdot with a head full of sawdust. Suspecting nothing. His captors were divided on the subject. Captain Dan Stokes of the Texas State Police was interested only in the reward and the fame of dragging John Wesley Hardin alive and kicking into the Austin jail. The other one, a black private named Jim Smolly, thought it was funny as hell. The big tough hombre collared with no more fuss than a freshly weaned pup. It was a fine joke.

After ordering the manacled young outlaw to lend a hand with camp chores, Stokes cautioned the black man to remain alert and take no chances. Then he rode off toward a nearby farm to obtain grain for the horses. Smolly flashed a broad, pearly grin, chuckling to himself. The thought of this half-witted kid giving him any trouble was so farfetched he couldn't help but laugh.

"Off yo' hoss, killer." Dismounting, thoroughly amused with himself, he walked to a stump and took a seat. "Start collectin' us some wood fo' the fire. Gonna be a long night."

Watching Stokes disappear in the distance, Wes had an idea it would be the longest night of the black man's life. Stepping down from the saddle, he kept the grullo between himself and Smolly. His wrist flicked, just the way John Collins had taught him, and a derringer appeared in his hand. Unhurried, calm as an undertaker, he moved clear of the horse and shot the black man twice at point-blank range.

Smolly hurtled backward over the stump and fell spread-eagled on the grass. Working faster now, the youngster searched him, found the keys, and unlocked the manacles. Then he retrieved his Navy from the black man's saddlebags, climbed aboard the gelding, and spurred south at a fast lope. The look on Smolly's face at that last instant stuck in his mind and he burst out laughing.

Yassuh, burrhead. It's gonna be a long night.

5

The sun hung suspended in a cloudless sky as Wes rode out of Belton. Nightfall was some three hours off and he meant to be far down the road before darkness. Outside the town he put the gelding into a fast trot and the edgy feeling slowly began to fade. It made him uneasy to travel during daylight, and the risk of entering a town bothered him even more. Still, a man had to eat and vittles didn't grow on trees. The general store in Belton had seemed the safest bet, and despite his misgivings, things had gone pretty smoothly. Near as he could tell, nobody had given him a second glance. All the same, he was glad to be on the road again. Out in the open, with room to maneuver, where he couldn't be taken by surprise.

Here lately, he'd had a gut full of surprises. And then some.

Though he had escaped handily enough, he wasn't interested in another scrape like the one last night. Sticking to back roads and wagon trails, he had skirted Waco and Temple, bearing generally south and west. Early that morning, after riding through the night, he had holed up to let the grullo graze awhile. But a couple of hours was all he allowed himself, then it was back in the saddle. He had in mind to make dust, and lots of it, before word reached Austin. If he didn't make it around the capital sometime tonight, or sunrise at the latest, there was a damn strong likelihood he'd never make it.

Yet, even as he dodged around through the backcountry, skirting the larger towns, Wes was gripped by a sense of self-loathing. He was on the run again. Something he'd sworn wouldn't happen. It was as if he'd taken an oath and broken it. Not to someone else but to himself. Which made it all the harder to swallow.

Thinking back on it, he felt like a willow in a strong wind. Whichever way the breeze blew, that was the way he leaned. One day he would make up his mind to something, determined that it would be just that way, and quicker than scat it got changed. Events or circumstances or some damned thing seemed to be rolling dice with his life. Not to mention people. A whole batch of them, with nothing better to do than nose around in his affairs.

The hell of it was, he let them get away with it. Like this little sashay down to Mexico. He'd let his father browbeat him like some harelipped pisswillie without a mind of his own. Shame him into running. Instead of standing up to the old man, telling him to jam all that sanctimonious crap about God and family, he'd caved in without a fight. Just laughed it off—as if it didn't mean a hill of beans. That was it in a nutshell. A willow bending with the wind. Taking the easiest way out.

Sometimes, looking back, it seemed he had no more spine than a toad. Otherwise, he wouldn't let himself get waltzed around that way. Like a puppet on a string, dancing to whatever tune somebody thought best. Even this thing with the State Police wasn't all that different. Lots of men would have stood their ground and fought it out come hell or high water. The way Simp Dixon had done. Instead of skittering off after every killing like a mouse in a nest full of snakes.

Of course, Simp Dixon was dead. And so was everybody else who had stood and fought. That was no small thing. A dead man, for all the grit he showed, was still dead. Done. Finished. Nothing more than a hunk of meat for the worms to commence pulverizing.

It was damned confusing. This thing of being pushed and pulled in opposite directions. Somewhere along the line, it seemed as though a man ought to make up his mind and stick with it. Quit swapping ends every time the wind shifted. But where to draw the line was a question that defied answer. The more he grappled with it, the less certain he became. Which was goddamned perplexing for a fellow who thought he had life by the short hairs.

Then again, maybe it was like what he'd read in books. Wisdom came not with age but with doubt. A man who knew all the answers actually knew nothing. Only a skeptic discovered the truth. That being the case, though, growing up was a damn sight more trouble than he'd suspected.

Separating the men from the boys was a first-class pain in the ass.

Along about sundown, still pondering the riddle, Wes

forded the Lampasas at the Belton Road Crossing. As he kneed his horse up the far bank, where the road cut through a stand of pecan trees, he decided that maybe there wasn't any answer. That a fellow did the best he could, juggling circumstances whichever way seemed right, and when he got all through, he was a man. What kind of man he turned out to be was perhaps not so much a matter of shifting winds and the tides of fate, but rather how good a juggler he'd become along the way. If he couldn't keep the balls gyrating in the air, sort of harness the vagaries of life to suit himself, then he deserved whatever he got. Boiled down that way, it came out pretty simple. Whatever got shoved up a man's ass was done not just with his consent, but with him lending a helping hand.

The youngster grunted, beaming inwardly, satisfied that at least part of the riddle had come clear. Maybe with time, and poking around in his head a little more, he would solve the whole damn mess. If not, he stood about as much chance as a one-armed juggler in a high wind. The kind that life gobbled up in its own special meat grinder. Only most times the man was spit out, looking much as he always had, and it was his balls that got pulverized.

Which made him no man a'tall.

Jarred loose from his reverie, Wes suddenly hauled back on the reins. He couldn't move, as if somebody had sewed his puckerhole shut and nailed him to the saddle. None of it seemed real, yet queerly enough, it was big as life and a yard wide.

Standing before him in the road was Captain Dan Stokes.

Wes just sat there in a witless stupor for perhaps a half-dozen heartbeats. Before he could collect himself, somebody off to his left thumbed back the hammer on a shotgun. Then, from the other side, came the metallic snick of a Colt being eared back to full cock. They had him stoppered and corked like a jug of molasses.

Stokes shifted to the right a couple of steps, pistol held at his side, and again, the voice was all business. "Hardin, you make any sudden moves and you're a goner. Now step down

out of that saddle real easy like, and don't make me guess
what you're doin' with your hands.''

The young outlaw sighed, weighing the alternative, and
decided it was no choice at all. They had him snookered,
and this time they'd plugged all the holes. Very carefully, he
placed both hands over the saddle horn and stepped down
off the gelding. Footsteps broke out all over the place—front,
and sideways—but he didn't bother looking around. It was
such a pitiful goddamn mess he couldn't bring himself to
look them in the eye. All of a sudden, he felt green as a
gourd and not a hell of a lot smarter.

Ten minutes later they had him trussed up like a Christmas
pig. Hands manacled, feet bound together, and propped back
against a tree with a rope around his throat. Captain Stokes
overlooked none of the salient details this time out. He relieved Wes of the Navy, slipped the derringer out of its
spring-loaded wrist rig, and even collected his jackknife. The
three of them, Stokes and a couple of underlings, stood
around watching him a minute and one of the men made a
crack about a snake with his fangs pulled. Stokes lambasted
him hotly, recalling Jim Smolly's abrupt demise the night
before, and warned both men to be on their toes at all times.

"What we got here ain't a snot-nosed kid," he observed
dryly. "It's a natural disaster. Like a tornado or a prairie fire.
Them that didn't believe it found out the hard way.''

Afterward, with dusk settling over the wooded stream
bank, they made camp for the night. While one of the men
hobbled their horses, the other built a fire for coffee and
broke out jerky and hardtack. When the coffee boiled, Stokes
dug a bottle from his saddlebags and laced everybody's cup
with a short dose. Squatted around the fire, swigging their
brew and munching a cold supper, they congratulated themselves on a good day's work. A short ride come first light
would put them in Austin, and the jingle of gold was so real
it was already burning a hole in their pockets.

Hardly to his surprise, nobody offered to feed Wes. They
had him pegged for the gallows, and as one of the men com-

mented, there was no sense pouring oats down a dead mule. Watching them, a couple of things became apparent to the youngster. They had ridden hard and fast to cut him off, and they weren't about to be done out of the reward money. Over and above that, this bunch was far more dangerous than the mushhead he'd killed last night.

Stokes was a seasoned man hunter. That was plain from his manner and the slick way he had of outguessing those he hunted. Though it went against the grain, Wes couldn't help admiring him the least bit. The man was good at what he did, and that commanded a certain amount of respect. But the other two were a different story entirely. Shiftless and grungy, willing to cut a man's throat for a hot meal or a shot of red-eye. Northern white trash who had been given a badge and a license to kill. If anything, they were more dangerous than Stokes. Given a choice, they would have just shot him in the back and to hell with the manacles.

The thought sparked another, whetting the young outlaw's curiosity. Glancing across the fire, he studied Stokes awhile and finally decided there was no harm in asking.

"Cap'n, you've got me puzzled about somethin'. Mind answerin' a question?"

Stokes's flinty gaze came level and he shrugged. "Seein' as you're the guest of honor, I guess it'd be awright."

"You've had two chances to gun me down. I was just wonderin' why you didn't."

"Best reason on earth. We been huntin' you two years and folks has got to thinkin' you're some kind of cross between the Holy Ghost and a wild tiger. When they stretch your neck down at Austin lots of people is gonna get educated real quick."

"So you held off drillin' me for the good of Texas?"

The lawman allowed himself a tight smile. "Nope. It'd give me considerable satisfaction shootin' you, but I got an idea it's gonna be lots more fun watchin' you swing."

Wes accepted the statement for what it was, a blunt truth. He felt no rancor but he was still curious. "Just one more and I'll shut up. How'd you figure I'd be comin' through at this crossin'? I didn't know myself till I woke up this mornin'."

"Weren't hard. You was headed south and I knew you'd stay clear of big towns. I killed a horse gettin' to Waco and picked up these boys." He ducked his chin at the policemen and they grinned in unison. "Then we rode like hell to beat you here. Less you turned off west somewheres, it figured you'd come through Belton. 'Pears I was right."

The two grinners busted out laughing and Wes lapsed into silence. Stokes just smiled and let it drop there. He wasn't much of a talker anyway and made it a rule never to waste the few words he spoke on the likes of outlaws. The threesome went back to their celebration, passing the bottle back and forth around the fire. The policemen, Anderson and Roberts, did most of the gabbing and Stokes just kept his thoughts to himself. But they all did their share of drinking, and by full dark, the bottle was empty. When Stokes declared it was time for sleep none of them were feeling any pain. Anderson was ordered to stand for the first watch and warned again to stay alert. Just before he rolled into his blanket, Stokes glanced across at the youngster.

"Don't try nothin' funny. Be a shame to havta kill you now."

Wes took him at his word. For the better part of an hour. Then Anderson started nodding, warmed by the fire and the whiskey, and within moments he was fast asleep. Working quietly, Wes slipped the rope off his throat and into his mouth. Gnawing furiously, he cut through the hemp in a matter of minutes. Without a sound, he untied his feet and stood. Briefly he debated making a run for it and just as quickly discarded the idea. It was too risky. Besides, Stokes wasn't a quitter, and the next time out he might just finish the job.

It had to end here.

An inch at a time, silent as a night hunting owl, he moved around the fire. Anderson didn't awaken as he eased the shotgun from the man's slackened grip. But when he earred both hammers back the whole camp came alive. Roberts raised up, directly beside Anderson, and the first blast shredded both men with buckshot. Farther off, back away from the fire, Stokes made a grab for his pistol. Then he stopped, staring into the big black hole centered on his belly. After a moment his gaze came level and their eyes locked.

"Sorry, Cap'n. I'd sort of got to like you."

Stokes shrugged, wooden-faced. "Luck of the draw."

Wes pulled the trigger, gutting him just above the belt buckle. But Stokes's last words hung in his ears over the roar of the shotgun. Slick as he was, the man hunter had lived a lifetime without learning the most important lesson of all.

The luck of the draw depended entirely on who was dealing.

CHAPTER 4

1

Abilene was situated on the edge of a vast prairie which sloped imperceptibly toward the timbered bottomland of the Smoky Hill River. As a town it wasn't much to look at. Just a crude collection of rough-sawn, false-fronted buildings clutched together across from the limestone bluffs on the south side of the shallow stream. Yet, in that sweltering summer of '71, it was one of a kind. A diamond in the rough. The premier cow town on the great western plains.

In Abilene, men who had met under less favorable circumstances, at Shiloh and the Wilderness and Gettysburg, once more came together. They gathered not out of friendship or with the uneasy camaraderie that sometimes exists between former enemies. Nor was there any spirit of reconciliation among them. They met again for a more practical purpose—mutual profit—to exchange Yankee gold for Texas cattle. It was a motive reasonable men understood, and while neither side thought of the other as reasonable, they bartered each summer on the banks of the Smoky Hill in a state of armed truce.

The town itself was a gaudy, ramshackle affair devoted exclusively to avarice and lust. There were some thirty buildings along the main street, dedicated for the most part to separating the Texans from their money. Saloons, dance halls, gambling dives, and whorehouses predominated. With the exception of two hotels, a mercantile emporium, one bank, and a couple of greasy spoon cafes, the entire business community of Abilene was crooked as a dog's hind leg.

When Wes rode into town in early June, he was short on illusions but chock full of great expectations. Bright-eyed and bushy-tailed, if somewhat cynical. Among Texicano trailhands legends had already sprung up about the lusty antics of this Babylon of the plains. While there was every certainty that they would be cheated, flimflammed, and hornswoggled—milked dry of three months' pay in a single week—they came eagerly, with boundless spirits, to this mecca of shady ladies and slick-fingered gamblers. They begrudged the Yankee bloodsuckers every hard-earned nickel, departed town with swollen heads and empty pockets, but they returned each summer with the youthful vigor of bulls in rut. There was nothing like it on the face of the earth, and crooked or not, it was worth the price of admission.

Unlike most cowhands, Wes came to Abilene less out of design than sheer chance. Last summer, after killing four State Police in twenty-four hours, he had struck out for Mexico in a blaze of dust. Newspapers bannered the story in all its gory details, and the name of John Wesley Hardin crackled across Texas like chain lightning. His name became a household word, and the exploits of a lone youth, boldly defying the rascals in Austin, acted as an elixir on the soured spirits of his fellow Texans. The backcountry people, oppressed by Yankee invaders for five long years, took him into their hearts. Among them spread tales of his fearlessness and ferocity, and before long they spoke of him as the daring lad who championed the cause of all men against injustice and tyranny. He was a hero, homegrown and bigger than life. A will-o'-the wisp, with godlike luck and a smoking six-gun, who had made Governor Davis and his ruthless hooligans the laughingstock of Texas.

Still, fame had its price, and the carpetbagger regime quickly upped the ante. Hardly before he crossed the Rio Blanco south of Austin, the young outlaw had a reward of three thousand dollars on his head. Dead or alive. Governor Davis and Attorney General Horace Davidson made no secret of their heartfelt wish that he be brought in stiff as a board. They wanted the man not so much as they wanted his cadaver.

But the youngster was, after all, no less mortal than other men, and scarcely immune to his growing fame. The tales he heard, concocted in equal parts of wishful fancy and pure horsedung, bore only scant resemblance to Preacher Hardin's wayward son. Unfazed, he took a closer look at himself and decided the people had hit the nail on the head. Instead of a desperado and murderer, he was a defender of the faith. Marching in the vanguard of those sworn to oust the Yankee conqueror. Somehow, it had a better ring to it, and with only the slightest effort, he found it wholly believable.

Struck by a random impulse, along with this new vision of himself, he chucked all thoughts of Mexico. Texas was where he belonged, among his own kind, and with spirits restored, he rode east into Gonzales County. There he received a lordly welcome from the Clements tribe, twice-removed cousins of uncertain lineage. Although the family brewed moonshine with a deadly kick, and kept half the country in a suspended state of ossification, its chief claim to fame was four strapping brothers. Hellraisers of the first order—Manning, Gip, Jim, and Joe—they lionized Wes in the manner of the one who had brought glory to the family name. In turn, Wes found himself among kindred souls, and their pride in his quickness with a gun made him cockier than ever.

They were well matched, these four brothers and the young outlaw. The Clements boys were tough as mules, rawboned and coarse, with skin weathered the color of whang leather. There was a noisy vitality about them, and whatever job they tackled, they worked harder than a gang of coons climbing a greased pole. Every spring, ranchers in the county competed to sign them on as trailhands, and after wintering with the tribe, Wes was just naturally considered part of the bargain.

Early in February they hired out as a group to Columbus Carol, a vinegary old cattleman with the disposition of a constipated Gila monster. The spring gather was finished just short of a month later and they headed a herd of fifteen hundred longhorns north toward the Red River, where Texas ended and the Chisholm Trail began. The three-month drive proved uneventful; discounting a couple of stampedes and Wes's killing a *vaquero* in a brief, but memorable, gunfight. The greaser was given an unceremonious burial, and the young outlaw's reputation went up another notch as the Clementses brayed about his speed with childlike gusto. Columbus Carol left the entire crew slack-jawed with astonishment when he went so far as publicly to congratulate the boy and offer him a job as *segundo*. While Carol's demonstrated passion for busthead whiskey and saloon brawls made the job something more akin to bodyguard, Wes found the notion to his liking and readily accepted.

Upon fording the Smoky Hill in early June, Carol's herd was driven to a holding ground at Cottonwood Springs north of town. There the hoary old cattleman intended to wait for a rise in the market and force some Yankee swindler to pay him top dollar. Most of the crew was let go, but Wes and the Clements brothers were kept on the payroll to nursemaid the longhorns through their wait. It promised to be an ordeal, for Kansas summers sizzled one day and scorched the next. All the same, the inducements to stay on were strong. The pay was steady and down the road a piece was that tabernacle dedicated to man's raunchier instincts. The place called Abilene.

Carol selected Manning and Wes to accompany him into town for the first night's winging. Gip, Jim, and Joe grumped around camp a lot, kicking at stones and bellyaching in general, but it was a waste of breath. The old man listened for all of sixty seconds and then blistered them good. Somebody had to watch over the herd, and what with it being a democratic outfit, he'd taken a one-man vote and elected them to office. Their chance to turn the wolf loose would come the next night, and that was that. An hour later, hair slicked back and reeking of bay rum, Carol and the two youngsters rode out of camp.

Along the way, the cattleman mellowed and grew expansive, reminiscing over similar excursions in the past. He'd been up the trail every summer since '69, when Joe McCoy and the Kansas Pacific slapped Abilene together. To hear him tell it, they were headed toward the world's foremost den of iniquity. Wicked, depraved, and dangerous as a teased rattler. All of which seemed to please him mightily. They were off to see the elephant, he declared, and it was a sight to make a sporting man's blood run hot.

Just last summer he'd seen Bear River Tom Smith tame an entire town with nothing but his fists. Whipped the living bejesus out of a half-dozen hardcases, pausing only long enough to dust off his tin star, and spent the rest of the season trading smiles with the politest bunch of trailhands ever hatched. But that didn't last long. Some sodbuster perforated Bear River Tom while he wasn't looking and put an end to his bare-knuckle style of law enforcement. Of course, sodbusters were sneaky, and known backshooters, so it was hardly more than could be expected.

Now, according to word along the trail, Abilene had hired itself a real pisscutter. Fellow name of Hickok, better known as Wild Bill. If the newspapers could be believed, he had killed close to fifty men. But then, newspaper editors were the biggest liars on earth, so most of it was likely horsefeathers and hogwash. Just the same, this Hickok had killed three or four toughnuts over in Hays City, and there was a story around that he'd stood up to a tinhorn in Springfield and drilled him dead center at seventy-five yards. What with one thing and another, it seemed like Hickok might be the real article after all, even if he hadn't killed the full fifty. Folks that had seen him said he was a fish-eyed bastard, cold as a witch's tit and mighty intolerant. Took a dim view of Texans trying to hurrah his town.

Columbus Carol was a man quick to give advice, but he seldom took it. His own or anyone else's. After lecturing the boys all the way into town, cautioning them to steer clear of the law in general and Wild Bill Hickok most particularly, he proceeded to cut the wolf loose with a vengeance. They hit four saloons and a whorehouse in rapid succession, leaving in their wake two crippled bouncers and an apoplectic madam. When they slammed through the doors of the Alamo Saloon Carol was pickled to the eyeballs and had himself primed for a real knock-down-drag-out.

Bulling his way through the crowd, Carol elbowed room for the three of them at the bar and stood there staring at a huge ornate mirror flanked on either side by fake Renaissance nudes. After a couple of minutes he swelled up like a dead toad in a hot sun and commenced pounding the counter with a meaty fist.

"I can lick any lily-livered sonovabitch in this joint!" Listing to port, he slowly came around and faced the crowd. "First come, first served. Who wants to get knocked on his ass?"

Dimly, he became aware that somebody had already taken him up on the offer. Only it was all out of kilter, wrong somehow. The man standing before him was wearing a star and he had a gun rammed into Carol's belly.

"Mister, you're headed for the lockup. 'Bout the only choice you got is how you go. Which way's it gonna be?"

Manning Clements was blind drunk and could hardly keep his feet. But Wes had been sipping all night and was stone cold sober. Shifting away from the bar, he assessed the lawman with a quick once-over.

"You Wild Bill Hickok?"

"Not that it makes a whole hell of a lot of difference, but I'm Carson, chief deputy. Any objections?"

The youngster's arm moved and the Navy appeared in his hand, cocked and centered on the deputy's shiny badge. "Only objection I've got is that you're standin' in my friend's road. Suppose you put that popgun back in the scabbard and haul ass out of here."

Carson regarded him with a quizzical scowl. "Sonny, you're gonna meet Mr. Hickok sooner'n you expected. And you won't like what he's got to say."

"Last man that called me sonny ended up worm meat. Now, you gonna pull freight or do I have to shoot your ears off?"

The lawman spun on his heel, holstering his pistol, and stalked off through the crowd. As he slammed the batwing doors open, Wes gave him a parting volley.

"Tell Mr. Hickok the name's Hardin. Wes Hardin."

2

The name John Wesley Hardin was not unknown in Abilene. Reward dodgers had been circulated from Texas to neighboring states, and the young outlaw was the subject of idle speculation among peace officers throughout the Southwest. A kid of eighteen who had killed ten men was a curiosity in itself, and hardly to be taken lightly. While Texans were known to exaggerate on occasion, the circulars were taken at face value. Anybody who had walked away from that many gunfights, whatever his age, was no joke. Quite clearly he played for keeps, and wasn't overly concerned with the rules.

The marshal of Abilene had given the matter weighty consideration. Though his name implied differently, Wild Bill Hickok was a man of craft and cunning, wily in a deceptive sort of a way. It was this unobtrusive canniness, rather than his speed with a gun, which had kept him alive through a long and checkered career as a lawman. Last evening, when Tom Carson returned to the office in a rage, Hickok had done nothing. Sifting his options, he chose to ignore the brash young gunman. The alternative was to take his four deputies and invade the Alamo, which was bursting at the seams with drunk Texans. Likely that would have resulted in a pitched battle and left the saloon littered with dead men. Among them, perhaps, Mr. James Butler Hickok. It was an idea he found both repugnant and rash. Better simply to wait and let it fizzle out in its own time.

By morning, Hickok was convinced he had acted wisely.

He ran a wide-open town, allowing the Texans considerable leeway in their rowdy, end-of-the-trail celebrations. Never once had he tried to enforce the gun ordinance, knowing that any attempt to disarm the quarrelsome Southerners would provoke an all-out war. This same policy extended to wanted men. Outlaws from many states had drifted through Abilene; he watched them come and go without a word. The crimes they committed elsewhere were not his lookout; his sole concern was keeping the peace in Abilene. Gunfights and shooting up the town weren't to be tolerated. But so long as men behaved themselves in general, he tended to take the broad view.

Still, there was nothing benevolent, or even remotely charitable, in his attitude. Hickok was callous and dispassionate by nature, a man who had killed in cold blood more times than anyone suspected. Just last year he had been fired as marshal of Hays City for gunning down a harmless drunk. The same thing could happen in Abilene if he allowed a bloodbath to evolve from some minor irritant. Like Carson being jackassed around by a hard-nosed kid. He meant to keep the peace, as well as his job, and despite the city council's professed support, that was easier said than done. Reflecting on it over his morning coffee, Hickok silently patted himself on the back for his clever handling of last night's fracas.

John Wesley Hardin was but a single gnat in a swarm of insects. One he couldn't afford to swat. Not just yet, at any rate. Time was on his side, and if a man studied on it hard enough, there was generally a way to exterminate a troublemaker without upsetting his own applecart. Several ways, in fact. Most of which, somewhere along the line, he had employed with considerable guile.

Down the street at that very moment, another man was considering the same problem, although from a slightly different vantage point. In the back room of the Bull's Head Saloon, Ben Thompson had embarked on a scheme that for cold and ruthless calculation was the equal of Hickok's spidery patience. Thompson, in partnership with Phil Coe, was the owner of Abilene's most profitable gaming dive. Squat and pugnacious in appearance, with piercing eyes and a dark bristly mustache, he was a Texan by birth and a gambler by trade. Strictly as a sideline, sort of a sporting diversion, he was also a deadly gunfighter. But like Hickok, he was a man who played the odds, weighing each move with the precise care of one versed in the art of survival.

Seated across from him was Abilene's latest celebrity. The young man who only last night had tied a can to Deputy Carson's tail. While the gambler's purpose had not yet been made clear, he had invited Wes over to discuss the matter of mutual interest. The fact that it served Thompson's interest more than the boy's was only incidental. Long ago, Thompson had made what he considered a vital discovery about life and death. Sometimes it was easier to kill a man, and personally less dangerous, simply by planting a seed and watching it grow.

Thompson had talked around in circles for the better part of twenty minutes, playing on the youngster's cock-of-the-walk manner. Everyone in Texas had heard of Ben Thompson and his skill with a gun, and the boy positively glowed with each word of praise. Presently, the gambler decided it was time to sink the gaff. Leaning back in his chair, hands locked behind his head, he chuckled warmly.

"Yeah, they'll be tellin' that story for a long time to come. Tom Carson euchred like some greenhorn fresh off the train. You know, he claims he's kin to ol' Kit Carson. Always braggin' about his famous relative. I got an idea there's gonna be a lot of salt rubbed in that wound."

"I hadn't heard that." Wes shook his head in mild disbelief. "If it's a fact then the blood must've got thin as beet juice by the time it sifted down to Tiger Tom."

"Tiger Tom!" Thompson erupted in a whooping belly laugh. "Christ A'mighty, I'll have to remember that one. The boys won't never let him live it down."

They sat there for several moments, Wes beaming and the gambler chortling appreciatively. After a while, though,

Thompson seemed to sober, as if struck by a sudden thought, and his eyes took on a somber cast.

"There's another side to that coin, of course. Carson's strictly penny-ante. Nothin' you couldn't handle. But Hickok's a bad man to tangle with. You're gonna have to watch out he don't get the drop on you."

"Get the drop on me?" The youngster gave him a quizzical frown. "You mean he don't come at a fellow straight out?"

"That's exactly what I mean. Most of them he's killed got took from the blind side. Never had a chance. Case you haven't heard, he's got no love for Texans, neither. What with him havin' fought for the bluebellies, he figures Southerners are lower'n snake turds."

"Well you damn bet'cha I'll be on the lookout. Course, I'm not tootin' my own horn, you understand, but I'll tell you one thing. He starts any monkeyshines with me and I'll put some leaks in him they'll never get plugged up. That Wild Bill stuff don't faze me none. He bleeds just like everybody else."

Thompson rubbed his jaw, mulling something over, and finally looked up. "You know, it just come to me. You might be the one."

Wes blinked. "The one what?"

"Why, the one all the trailhands have been waitin' on. Hickok gives 'em a hard way to go, bustin' heads and throwin' people in the lockup if they look at him cross-eyed. So far, though, nobody's had the gumption to try punchin' his ticket. I got an idea you're the one that could cut him down to size."

"You're talkin' about killin' him."

The gambler's mouth creased in a tight smile. "You just got through sayin' a minute ago that he bleeds like everyone else."

Something in Thompson's eyes touched a nerve, and the youngster instantly came alert. "If he needs killin' so bad, why don't you do it yourself? What I heard, you're no slouch with a gun."

"Well, you know how it is. A man operatin' a business can't get involved in these things. In a manner of speakin', I'm kind of like the cowhands. Just have to wait till someone comes along that can give Hickok a dose of what he deserves. Way you talked, I thought it might be you."

Wes wasn't quite sure of the game, but one thing was plain to see. Whatever his reason, the gambler wanted Bill Hickok dead and buried. However slyly, a baited hook had just been dangled in front of his mouth.

"Ben, I'll tell you how it is with me. I don't do nobody's fightin' but my own." Uncoiling from the chair, he came to his feet. "Much obliged for the invite and the conversation."

They stared at one another a moment, understanding of sorts passing between them, then Hardin turned and walked through the door. Thompson muttered an oath, scowling, and slammed his chair to the floor. Somehow, he felt as though he had egg on his face.

Late that afternoon Wes wandered into the Alamo Saloon. Columbus Carol had given him the day off, a reward of sorts for saving the cattleman from a night in Abilene's jail. The youngster found it an excellent idea, but for reasons all his own. After making his brag last night, all but daring Hickok to come after him, it wouldn't do to hide out in a cow camp. That would mark him as gutless or scatterbrained, or both. Make him a laughingstock, and through him, put all Texans to shame. What with the Clements boys beating the drum about his bulldog grit, and everybody glad-handing him all over the place, he felt a certain obligation not to let them down. Things being the way they were, he had a reputation to maintain. Not so much for himself as for Texas and Texans.

Or so he told himself, at any rate.

Throughout the day he had leisurely prowled the town, inspecting the stores and the stockyards, taking dinner in one of the cafes and pausing for drinks in a couple of the saloons. Abilene in daylight was pretty tame, and sort of hard on the eyes. The buildings were constructed of bare, ripsawed lumber and looked as if they had been thrown together with spit and poster glue. But the town itself interested him little, if at all. He merely wanted to be seen, to let folks know that he was out and about and available. Just in case Abilene's fire-eating marshal had any notions about settling last night's score.

Apparently that wasn't the case. Hickok failed to put in an appearance and the only man Wes spoke with at any length was Ben Thompson. Nursing a drink, seated at a table in the back of the Alamo, the youngster was still hashing that one around. A word here and a word there, mainly from bartenders, had erased part of the mystery. Earlier in the season, Hickok and Thompson had evidently had a falling out. Something about a bawdy sign Thompson had hung outside the Bull's Head. Harsh words had been exchanged, and it was even money that the two men would butt heads before the trailing season ended. Plain to see, Thompson figured he'd save himself some trouble by egging a slick-eared squirt into starting a shoot-out with the marshal.

Only it hadn't worked. Wes had made himself available, but as he'd told Thompson, it was strictly his own fight. Other people, the gambler included, would have to do their own dirty work. Except that there hadn't been any fight. Nor the least sign of Hickok. That was a new riddle to ponder, but for the moment the young outlaw set it aside. The Clements boys were due in town any minute now and his mind turned to the night ahead. Swigging his drink, he commenced planning how he'd show them the elephant. A guided tour of Abilene's spiffy cathouses and the better watering holes.

Along about the third sip, though, he started thinking on a different kind of game altogether. Bill Hickok marched through the door, walked straight to the bar, and proceeded to knock back a couple of quick ones. Wes had heard about him, but in person the lawman was a real eye-duster. Black frock coat, hair that hung down over his shoulders, and a droopy mustache that cleared his jawbone. The face was sullen, like an old bull on the prod, and his eyes put the boy in mind of smoky agates, opaque and lusterless, lacking expression.

Still, appraising him closer, Wes decided he wasn't half as fearsome as folks made out. Likely he got into his pants one leg at a time, just like everybody else, and he damn sure wasn't immune to lead poisoning. Anybody that'd march around in a getup like that, odds were he'd assay out to about twelve ounces of bullshit to the pound. Slick and cagey, dangerous in an underhanded sort of way, the same as Thompson had warned him.

Hickok wheeled away from the bar and headed toward the back of the saloon. His manner was casual, unhurried, and as he stopped in front of the table, he nodded agreeably.

"I reckon you must be Wes Hardin."

The youngster smiled, looking him over. "And I could make a wad of money bettin' you're Wild Bill Hickok."

"Mind if I take a chair?"

"Help yourself."

The lawman seated himself and slouched back, folding his hands across his stomach. "Figured we might have ourselves a little talk."

"Folks always said I was a good listener. What you got on your mind?"

The cocky tone grated on Hickok's nerves, but he restrained himself, playing it loose and easy. "Well, for openers, let's just forget about last night. Carson made a horse's ass out of himself and we'll let it drop there."

"Sounds fair." Wes couldn't figure it, but he was curious to see how the next card fell. "Where's that leave us?"

Hickok's gaze clouded over, and it was a moment before he spoke. "I understand you had a powwow with Ben Thompson this mornin'."

"Word gets around, don't it?"

"Soon enough. Which brings up the question I come here to ask. Are you plannin' on takin' a hand in Thompson's fight?"

Wes smiled, glad to have it out in the open. "Marshal, I

make it a habit to stick to my own business. The only fight I've got is what the other fellow starts. Course, I also make it a habit never to back off if a man steps on my toes.''

Hickok bristled, unaccustomed to threats, veiled or otherwise. ''I guess you know I got a dodger on you. Pretty fat reward, too.''

The young outlaw regarded him evenly, still smiling. ''Lots of men have tried collectin' it. Turned out a little different'n they expected, though.''

They stared at each other in silence for a long while. Then, cocking one eye, Hickok smiled. It was an odd look, somehow out of character, as if his face might crack from the smile and shatter into small pieces.

''You're a game lad, Hardin. I like that. You stay away from Thompson, and behave yourself, and we'll get along just fine.''

''Why, sure we will, Marshal. Live and let live. That way nobody steps on the other fellow's toes. Pleases me a whole lot, you feelin' the same way about it.''

Hickok had the distinct feeling this smart-aleck kid was laughing at him. But he didn't press it further. Standing, he scraped back his chair and nodded, then headed for the door. As he walked off, Wes grinned, holding back hard on a chuckle.

The game was getting better all the time. Fast and foxy, and more fun than a barrel of monkeys. A real gutbuster.

3

The truce lasted four days.

On the evening of the fourth day, while taking supper in Abilene's leading greasy spoon, Wes became involved in a slight misunderstanding with a Yankee mule skinner. They exchanged a few heated words, and in the salty parlance of his trade, the teamster thoughtlessly remarked on the ancestry of Texans. Something about bitches in heat whelping flannel-mouthed kids. At that point, things got serious. They quit

trading insults and started swapping lead, and the mule skinner wound up on the cafe floor. Stone cold and stiffening
fast.

Wes had a fair idea as to what came next. The marshal
and his four deputies would swarm over the place like a herd
of bee-stung bears. What with the reward on his head, and
his sassy attitude toward Hickok & Company, it would be
shoot first and ask questions later. The odds told him to fold
his cards and await a new deal. Which was precisely what
he did.

Hardly before the gunsmoke settled, he charged out of the
cafe and scampered aboard the grullo. Then, as if the gelding's tail was on fire, he beat a hasty retreat to Cottonwood
Springs. It wasn't exactly the proudest moment of his life.
Nor was it an act designed to boost his stock among Texans.
But under the circumstances, it was judicious as hell. While
nobody liked a quitter, especially if they were merely spectators to the blood and gore, he had lived to fight another
day.

Overnight, tossing and turning in his blankets, he wrestled
with that stickery bit of wisdom. It was but a minor skirmish,
he told himself. Insignificant and without lasting effect. Certainly one battle didn't make a war. And a single step backward didn't offset what had gone before.

All the same, his pride had taken quite a drubbing. Everybody in Abilene, particularly the Texans, thought he was the
Curly Wolf from Bitter Creek. The way he'd strutted his stuff
around town, and lipped off to Hickok face to face, was by
now a tale of stupendous proportions. A whopper that gathered momentum, and considerable embellishment, with each
telling around cow camp fires. Yet, despite the wisdom and
foresight and common ordinary horse sense of last night's
decision, one fact stood out like a diamond in a goat's ass.

He had tucked tail in a cloud of dust.

The thought left his mouth bitter with the taste of ashes.
When he crawled out of his blankets with first light, he could
scarcely face himself, much less the Clements brothers and

old man Carol. That they thought none the less of him, voicing agreement that he had played it cagey, did little to salve his gloomy spirits. In other camps, around other cook fires, men wouldn't be so charitable. Instead of Curly Wolf, he'd likely get dubbed with a new nickname. Something like Lickety-Split. Ol' Cut' 'n Run. Or Balls o' Fire.

Worse yet, Columbus Carol wanted him to keep right on running. After a pot of coffee, and a couple of thunderous farts, the old vinegarroon lit into him with spurs flying.

"Use your gawddamn brain. The same as you done last night. That was smart thinkin', scootin' out of town the way you did. And you'd better go right on thinkin' the same way. Hickok and his pack of lawdogs are gonna come lookin' for you sure as shit stinks. Hang around and they'll nail your hide to the wall."

"I'll be go to hell if that's so!" Manning Clements glanced around at his brothers and they nodded vigorously. "Long as we're backin' his play, they'll get more'n they bargained for."

"Close that flytrap and keep it shut," Carol growled. "Between the four of you there ain't enough sense to fill a thimble. You try backin' his play and the whole lot of you will get yourselves killed."

"Boys, I hate to admit it, but he's right." Wes gave his cousins a glum look. "This is my fight, and you'd just be buyin' yourselves a peck of trouble."

Carol squinted hard. "Mebbe you ain't any brighter'n they are. This ain't Texas, y'know. You kill any lawmen up here and ever' sonovabitch and his dog'll be out takin' potshots at you."

"Guess I can't argue with you there." The youngster studied on it a moment, torn between an acute case of pride and the old man's unassailable logic. "Tell you how it is, though. That teamster pulled first, and I killed him fair and square. If Hickok wants to make somethin' of that, then I reckon I'll just stick around and oblige him."

There was a long silence as they waited for Carol to explode. But he was curiously quiet, staring off into the distance with a tight scowl. At last, he grunted and jerked his chin in the direction of town.

"Well it appears like you're gonna get your chance. Unless I'm wide of the mark, that's the law, and they ain't out huntin' jackrabbits."

Everybody swiveled around with a start and caught sight of a tiny dust cloud far across the prairie. As they watched, it steadily grew larger, moving ever closer. Whoever it was, they were on a beeline leading straight to the camp.

"Whole bunch of 'em," Gip Clements muttered grimly.

"I make out three." Carol shaded his eyes against the early morning sun. "Four at the outside."

Wes popped to his feet, suddenly galvanized into action. "Manning, you and the boys saddle up and get on out with the herd. Whatever happens, just stay clear of it. I'm not funnin', neither. Stick to your business and let me handle this my own way."

Unhurried, moving with icy calm, he walked to the wagon and pulled a double-barreled shotgun from beneath the seat. Times before, when he had been outnumbered, he'd learned a fundamental truth. There was nothing like a double dose of buckshot to even out the odds. By the time he'd checked the loads and turned back, the Clementses were at the picket line, hastily slapping saddles on their ponies. Carol hadn't moved, still squatted before the fire, watching the dust cloud. Wes walked directly to a shallow gully, some half-dozen paces behind the old man. As the Clements brothers mounted and rode off, the youngster hunkered down in the draw and eared back both hammers on the shotgun.

Some minutes later, Tom Carson rode into camp, flanked by a couple of hard-eyed deputies. They reined to a halt, alert and tense, eyes flickering around the clearing. Carol held his spot before the fire, watching them, and at last Carson's gaze swung around.

"We're lookin' for Wes Hardin."

"You're a mite late, Deputy. He headed south last night." The cattleman gestured with his cup. "Welcome to coffee, though. Even got some beans left over if you're hungry."

Carson dismounted and the other men stepped down beside him. Advancing on a line, still somewhat skittish, they stopped on the far side of the fire. Heaving a sigh of disgust, Carson screwed up his face in a baleful frown.

"Old man, you give us some straight talk or I'm gonna peel your head. Get the idea?"

"Boys, the only thing I can give you is some coffee." Carol stood and walked to the end of the fire, where a coffeepot hung suspended over a bed of coals. The lawmen watched suspiciously as he slung grounds out of a cup and filled it from the pot. "Ain't the best coffee you ever drunk, but it's hot and black."

"Freeze!"

Startled, Carson and his deputies looked around and found themselves staring into the beady black eyes of a ten-gauge greener. Behind it, looming up out of the gully, stood the young outlaw. At that range, centered about chest-high, the scattergun looked like a double-barreled cannon.

They froze stiff as marble statues.

Wes had a finger curled around both triggers, and with Carol out of the line of fire, he held all the aces. If he touched off a double blast the lawmen were dead in their tracks. They knew it and he knew it. After a moment, fairly certain they wouldn't try their luck, he smiled.

"Shuck them guns. Slow and easy."

The lawmen obeyed, carefully exaggerating each move. When their pistols hit the dirt, Wes relaxed a little and his mouth split in a wide grin.

"Now shuck your duds. And don't nobody get sudden."

Carson stared at him dumbly for a second, then blanched with rage. "Goddamnit, Hardin, there's no call for that. It's enough you got the drop on us. Just call it quits and let us ride off."

"C'mon, Tiger Tom." Wes waggled the end of the shotgun. "Skin down."

The deputy glared and gritted his teeth, making knots in his jaws. But he skinned down. So did the other two, all the while eyeing the scattergun nervously. Within moments they stood barefooted and stripped, Carson in underdrawers and the pair of hardcases in filthy long johns.

Wes looked them over and then grunted, satisfied, "If I was you boys, I'd make it back to town before the sun gets too high. And give the marshal a message. Tell him the next time somebody steps on my toes they won't get off so light."

The lawmen hobbled back to their horses and gingerly mounted. Without a word they reined about and struck off toward Abilene. Wes scrambled out of the gully and walked forward to stand beside the old man. They watched in silence as the horses and their lily-skinned riders disappeared across the prairie. After a while Carol snorted and shook his head.

"Bub, I'll say one thing. You sure know how to rub a man's nose in it."

4

Wes hadn't left camp for nearly a week. Most of the time he sat beside the creek, beneath a towering cottonwood, brooding on his troubles. One day blended into the next, and with each passing sunrise he grew increasingly surly and cross-tempered. Try as they might, the Clementses and Columbus Carol couldn't get him to talk. It seemed he had shut them out, withdrawn into himself, and they were completely baffled. The John Wesley Hardin they knew was alive, full of piss and vinegar, scrappy as a bobcat. This man was a stranger, someone who might have wandered in off the trail. He ate and slept and worked. But mostly he just brooded, and kept to himself.

It all started the morning he'd jackassed the lawmen.

The Clements brothers hadn't quit laughing for hours afterward, doubling up convulsively every time somebody retold the story. Old man Carol, who tended to take the dim view, even cackled about it in a dour sort of way. Yet, for all their joshing and high spirits, the most they got out of

Wes was a bemused smile. That afternoon he turned moody and went off to sulk beneath the cottonwood.

What the others didn't understand was that the youngster himself was thoroughly bumfoozled. He'd turned the tables on Abilene's lawdogs, restoring his standing among Texicanos, but he still couldn't set foot in town. According to the grapevine, Hickok had threatened to kill him on sight, and to compound matters, the marshal kept himself surrounded by a gang of deputies at all times. It took Wes a couple of days to sift it all out in his head, and even then, the question was thorny as a briar patch. How to regain the limelight in Abilene without getting himself, and a whole bunch of well-meaning friends, shot to pieces in the process?

The only solution he saw was to kill Hickok.

But that was a damn sight easier said than done. Especially when the sorry devil never stepped outdoors without a couple of gunhands flanking him on either side. The real stickler, though, was why it even mattered. What difference would it make if John Wesley Hardin never again set foot in Abilene? Why didn't he just climb on his horse and get the hell on back to Texas? Puzzling on it, the young outlaw went round and round in circles, arriving every time at what seemed the dumbest answer of all. He was just too muleheaded—too infernal proud—to quit the fight. Which left him exactly where he'd started.

Stalemated. An impasse which seemingly defied answer.

Wes was still scratching his head when the big dogs rode into camp. Shanghai Pierce, Print Olive, and Bob McCulloch. Three of the largest cattlemen in the Lone Star State. Their outfits trailed close to fifty thousand steers to railhead every year, and when they talked, men stopped to listen. That they had come to the camp of Columbus Carol was no small event. The old man and his hands couldn't have been more surprised if the three wise men had galloped in aboard wild-eyed camels.

The queer part was that they had come to see Wes. After everyone squatted down around the fire, and coffee had been poured, the cattlemen wasted little time. Shanghai Pierce started it off.

"Hardin, we've come to ask a favor. You ever hear of a fella named Billy Coran?"

"Why, sure," Wes acknowledged. "He's foreman of the XL. Their camp's about five miles east of here."

"He *was* foreman of the XL," Pierce corrected him. "This mornin' one of his hands shot him in the back. A greaser that calls himself Juan Bideno."

Carol muttered a curse under his breath and the Clementses glanced at one another with shock. Billy Coran was widely respected among cattlemen and that he'd been murdered made his death doubly distressing. Wes hadn't known the man personally, but he could understand the anger of the three ranchers squatted across the fire.

"I'm sorry to hear that. From what I've heard about Coran, he deserved better."

"Goddamn right, he did!" Print Olive rasped. "Never even had a chance. Bideno gunned him down with no warnin' a'tall. Nothin'!"

"That's why we're here," Pierce added. "The greaser took off like a scalded goose. We sorta hoped you wouldn't have no objections to runnin' him down."

"Me?" Wes was genuinely surprised.

"There'd be a reward in it. A thousand, anyway. Mebbe more after we pass the hat."

"You're barkin' up the wrong tree. I never killed anybody yet for blood money."

"Well, it ain't the money, just exactly, that brought us here. We're askin' as one Texan to another."

"Yeah, but why me? Why don't you sic the law on him?"

Olive broke in, his voice husky and short. "Hardin, I'm gonna level with you. We don't want that greaseball brought in. We want him dead and buried. Everybody says you're chain lightnin' with a gun and we figure you're the man for the job. It's just that simple."

"Besides which," Bob McCulloch observed, "the nearest

U.S. marshal is in Topeka. By the time he got on the trail Bideno would be in the Nations. That happens, we might as well kiss him goodbye.''

"There's another thing, too." Pierce studied the ground a moment, then looked up. "You been on the dodge longer'n most and you ain't never been caught. That gives you an edge nobody else has got."

Wes smiled in spite of himself. "Meanin' it takes one to catch one."

"Naw, hell, that ain't what I meant a'tall." Pierce bit the words off, gruff and hard. "I just meant there's less chance of him foolin' you than anybody we can think of." Then he stopped, struck by what he'd just said, and a slow grin spread across his face. "Come to think of it, I guess that's the same thing, ain't it?"

The youngster couldn't help but like these men. They'd told him straight out, making no bones about it. What with him on the owlhoot so long, they figured he could outguess a common backshooter. It was a form of honesty, raw and simple, that he could appreciate. Besides, as they'd said, Coran was a Texan. So it was only right that a Texan be the one to down his killer.

"Lemme ask you a couple of questions. Has this Bideno ever been on the dodge before? For killin' or anything else?"

Olive took the lead on that. "Nope. I asked the same question myself. Up till this mornin' he was straight as a string. Last night him and Billy had words, and evidently he got juiced up and went off his rocker. That don't excuse it none, though. He's still got to pay the price."

"After he killed Coran which way did he head?"

"Due south," McCulloch said. "Like as not he'll make a run for the Nations."

Wes nodded, as if the answer merely confirmed his own suspicions. "Gents, I'll run him down on two conditions."

The cattlemen stared back at him, waiting.

"First, I want a warrant chargin' him with murder."

"You'll have it," Pierce agreed.

"Second, I want a lawful commission as deputy sheriff."

"Holy jumpin' Christ!" Olive barked. "You don't want much, d'you?"

"I've already got my own troubles with the Kansas law. If I kill another man, I want it legal and aboveboard."

"You got yourself a deal." Pierce came to his feet. "I don't know how the hell we're gonna do it, but we'll get you a badge. Now, when can you be ready to ride?"

"The minute I see that tin star."

"Fair enough."

The three men walked briskly to their horses and mounted. But at the last minute Shanghai Pierce turned in the saddle and looked back.

"Say, we heard how you snookered Hickok's boys. Pretty slick. Everybody sorta figures you chalked one up for our side."

Then they were gone, pounding back toward Abilene. Carol and the boys stood there watching for a while and the old man finally glanced over at Wes.

"If I was a bettin' man, I'd say you had something up your sleeve."

The young outlaw grinned. "You'd be bettin' a surefire cinch. Them fellas don't know it, but they just put Mr. Wild Bill Hickok between a rock and a hard place."

Shortly before noon two days later, Wes Hardin and Jim Rodgers rode into the town of Bluff Creek. A mile or so outside the town limits was the state line, and across it, Indian Territory. The Nations. Here was where the chase ended. If their quarry had eluded them, taking refuge somewhere on tribal lands, then the hunt was finished. A washout. Yet, it was just possible the Mexican thought he was safe this far south. Whichever way the coin fell, there was only one way to find out.

The men separated and started checking opposite sides of the street.

Rodgers was an XL hand and could recognize Bideno on sight. Shanghai Pierce and the others had sent him along so identification would be certain if the *vaquero* was caught.

Hardin was to call the shots otherwise, and that's how it had worked out.

The young outlaw set a killing pace right from the start. They had been out of the saddle only three times in the last thirty-six hours, just long enough to swap horses with trail crews outside Newton, Wichita, and Cow House Creek. Along the way cowhands told them of a Mexican headed south at a fast clip, and what Wes suspected from the outset became more evident by the hour. Bideno was an amateur bad man, and like most beginners, he had reacted out of blind panic. Instead of twisting and doubling back, trying to hide his tracks, he had stuck to the Chisholm Trail as if glued on course. By the end of the first day it was no longer a matter of outguessing him. It came down to the knotty imponderable of whether or not they could overtake him.

And now they were about to find out.

Before Wes had gone halfway down the street a cow pony erased the question mark. It was standing hipshot, lathered with sweat, at a hitchrack in front of a saloon and hash house. And burned on its rump was the XL brand.

Taking it slow and easy, just another cowhand looking for a drink, he pushed through the doors. The place was empty, quiet as a tomb. A bartender was polishing glasses and looked up without interest as he approached.

"Saw your sign out front. Where d'you serve the eats?"

The barkeep jerked his thumb toward the rear. "Back room."

"Lookin' for a friend of mine. Mexican. He back there?"

"Could be. One came in about ten minutes ago."

"Guess I'm done lookin'. Much obliged."

Wes walked to the rear of the saloon, pulled his gun, and stepped through the door with the pistol at his side. Bideno was alone in the room, seated with his back to the wall. He looked up, fork caught in midair as the youngster entered.

"Bideno, you're under arrest for murder."

The Mexican just stared at him for a couple of heartbeats, completely befuddled. Then he dropped the fork, shoving away from the table, and made a grab for his gun. Wes shot him once, squarely in the forehead, splattering brains and bone matter across the far wall. Bideno pitched forward, up-ending the table, and crashed to the floor in a storm of broken glass and dinnerware.

Standing over him, it occurred to Wes that the man really was an amateur. The rankest kind. Fool enough to make his play when somebody had the drop on him. Then again, maybe he'd had the right idea after all. This was quick, over and done with, even painless. Brought back alive, the Texans would have strung him up slowly and let him swing a while. Most likely by the balls.

The young outlaw grunted, smiling to himself, and tipped his hat to the corpse.

Goodbye, Bideno. Hello, Mr. Hickok.

5

The celebration was long and noisy, punctuated time and again by a chorus of eerie, high-pitched Rebel yells. The gang of Texans floated from one dive to the next on a sea of busthead whiskey, and wherever they went, the drinks were on the house. Abilene welcomed John Wesley Hardin back with open arms. Already the story had circulated about his daring ride south and the gunfight that brought speedy justice to a godless assassin. Cowhands and townspeople stood in line to shake his hand, pat him on the back, and tell him what a grand fellow he was. While the Fourth of July was still a week off, the youngster's return seemed a tailor-made excuse to commence the festivities a little early. The town had itself a genuine, dyed-in-the-wool hero. And its citizens pulled out all the stops, toasting him in a raucous, earsplitting orgy of good cheer.

Just as Shanghai Pierce had promised, the hat was passed and the young outlaw came up with a purse of better than a thousand dollars. Pierce, along with Olive and McCulloch and Carol and the Clementses and the XL hands, appointed themselves his official escort. Wherever he went they formed a beefy wedge around him, clearing a path through the wild and unruly crowd. They toured cathouses, dance halls, gambling dens, and saloons in the whirlwind of shouted toasts and riotous laughter. Shanghai Pierce and the Clements brothers were especially vocal in their praise, bragging long and loud to each new audience. But they held the limelight only briefly.

It was the youngster that people had come to see. He was the star attraction of this impromptu road show and they demanded to hear him speak. The first couple of times, Wes was flustered, unaccustomed to addressing large throngs of gaping onlookers. Slowly, though, he warmed to the subject, aided in no small part by the liberal doses of popskull forced on him at each stop. With every retelling of the story his memory was jogged, and little details began drifting back to mind. The look on Bideno's face. The sheriff of Bluff Creek turning apoplectic at the thought of a corpse on his hands. The spontaneous roar of approval from spectators when Wes offered to stand the cost of burial. Adding a piece here and a piece there, he embroidered a story as he went along, lending it embellishments that made the telling more colorful, if not exactly accurate.

The crowds ate it up, stomping and shouting and straining to touch him. And at the very last, when he pulled Jim Rodgers forward to share the credit, they went jubilantly mad. It was a fine touch, the mark of a generous man, and he played it all with the aplomb of a medicine-show quack pitching the rubes.

Curiously enough, though, Abilene's leading citizen had failed to put in an appearance. Wild Bill Hickok was conspicuous by his absence, and the fact scarcely went unnoticed. The marshal had sworn to kill this young Texan on sight, and among the town's gamblers, there were many laying odds that he might yet give it a try.

If the thought had crossed Wes's mind, it apparently bothered him not at all. He was having the time of his life, the center of attention in a swirling maelstrom of rabid admirers, and living it to the hilt. Whatever happened would happen, and when it did, he had every confidence he could handle it slick as spit. This was his night to howl. The highwater mark in a not uneventful month along the Smoky Hill. And he meant to make the most of it.

Standing at the bar in the Alamo, surrounded by friends and well-wishers, he found the life of a celebrity much to his liking. It was the first time anyone had ever patted him on the back for killing a man, much less lined his pockets with gold. Aside from the firewater he'd downed, the experience itself was a heady sensation. Yet, back in some hidden cranny of his mind, the irony was all but inescapable. Bideno had made it an even dozen, and for this last killing he was lionized and swamped with accolades. But of the twelve men who had fallen before his gun, the Mexican deserved death neither more nor less than the others. In every case, they had gone up the flume with reason.

It was a special blend of irony. Bittersweet and somehow confounding.

Shanghai Pierce was holding forth in the voice he generally reserved for special occasions, such as weddings, funerals and saloon-room ,oratory. It had been likened to the trumpeting of a bull elephant in mating season. Only louder.

"Boys, I'm here to tell you, I've seen 'em all." He paused, flashing a mouthful of teeth, and threw an arm over the youngster's shoulders. "Saw Thompson down in Austin. And King Fisher in Tascosa. Even saw Clay Allison in a shoot-out once. But there ain't nobody—*nobody on God's green earth*—that can hold a candle to this boy. He's greased lightnin'. Half wolf and half alligator. A natural-born buzz saw. So fast he leaves ordinary men blinded and suckin' wind."

"Hey, Wes," somebody shouted, "show us yer draw!"

"Yeh, Wes, c'mon! Whip out that ol' thumb-buster."

The crowd took up the chant, demanding a demonstration. Shanghai Pierce beamed proudly, and the Clements brothers danced and shouted louder than anybody else. They weren't to be denied, and presently, when the din became thunderous, Wes shrugged modestly. He stepped away from the bar, flexing his wrists, and a deadened silence swept back over the room. Every eye in the saloon was wide and unblinking, riveted on the nervy young gunfighter.

Wes dropped into a crouch, hand poised over his holster. He froze there for the merest fraction of an instant, then relaxed and stood erect. The room was quiet as a graveyard, and the men waited breathlessly, expecting him to make his move at any moment.

He grinned, glancing around at the rapt faces. "Wanna see it again?"

There was an interval of leaden silence as the crowd stared at him in oxlike amazement. Then someone caught on. It was a joke. He hadn't moved at all. The entire room exploded in paroxysms of laughter. Men doubled over, clutching their bellies, and others reeled drunkenly as tears sluiced down over their cheeks. Shanghai Pierce was right, they bellowed at one another, choking on fresh bursts of laughter.

The kid was so goddamned fast you couldn't even see it!

Smiling, pointing his finger at the thunderstruck Clementses, Wes joined in the merriment. After a while, when the laughter subsided a bit, Shanghai Pierce swelled up like a rooster and waved his arms for quiet.

"What d'ya think now? Ain't that the suddenest thing you *never* seen?"

This brought on a fresh burst of knee-slapping but back in the crowd someone shouted over the uproar, "That's quick awright, Shanghai. But there's one gunhand you ain't yet mentioned."

Pierce glared back at the doubter with an owlish frown. "Yeah, who's that?"

"Ol' sour-mouth himself. Wild Bill Hickok!"

"Jesus Pesus Christ," Pierce groaned. "You haven't got sense enough to come in out of the rain. Why, it wouldn't be no contest a'tall. This boy has got him shaded seven ways to Sunday. You stand them up against one another and it'd be like askin' Wes Hardin to commit murder." The cattleman grinned and looked around at the youngster. "Ain't that right, Wes?"

Abilene's star attraction didn't say a word. His eyes were fastened on the door and it was several moments before it registered on the crowd that he wasn't just stargazing. They turned as a man, and there was a sudden intake of breath, as if everybody in the room had been goosed with a hot poker.

Standing in the door was Bill Hickok.

The marshal strolled forward and a path opened before him through the crowd. He halted a couple of paces off and nodded to Wes. Then his head swiveled around and he nailed Shanghai Pierce with a sullen scowl.

"Mister, you got a big mouth."

Pierce swallowed hard. "If a man don't wanna hear then he shouldn't listen."

"In my town there's not much I don't hear. Scissorbills like you, I got a special place for 'em down at the jail. Maybe you'd like to see it?"

"Guess not."

"Then keep your lip buttoned." Hickok's gaze came back to the young outlaw. "Hardin, it appears you're keepin' bad company. Thing like that could get a fellow behind the eight ball real easy."

Wes smiled but a pale glint surfaced in his eyes. "I'm generally pretty picky about my friends. That way I don't have to think about it if it comes down to backin' their play."

The challenge was unmistakable and Hickok went stiff as a ramrod. Everyone in the saloon held their breath, waiting for him to make his move, but he just stood there knotting his jaws. At last, the tension seemed to drain out of him and he shook his head in mild wonderment.

"You got your share of grit. I'll give you that."

"Why, Marshal, down where we come from"—Wes gestured at the men lining the bar—"that's common as milkweed. Thought everybody knew that. Texans have just naturally got more sand in their craw than any creature there is."

Hickok grunted. "Well, I suppose that's another can of worms altogether, and I didn't come here to spoil your party.

Just wanted to congratulate you on catchin' your man. That was a right smart piece of work."

"Thank you, Marshal. I'm obliged for the kind words."

"Look me up when you've got some time. We'll have a drink on it."

With that, Bill Hickok turned and walked from the Alamo. Not a man in the room could credit his own ears. Abilene's fire-eating lawman had refused the goad and pulled in his horns. It surpassed belief. But more than that, it boggled the mind. Left a man's throat scratchy and raw with thirst.

And dumbstruck. Unable to fathom what he'd just seen.

Late that night, Wes lay restless and wakeful in his room at the American Hotel. Sleep eluded him, but it had nothing to do with the carousing or the excitement of his jubilant welcome back to Abilene. His thoughts dwelt solely on one man, an enigma that made little sense and even less reason. Oddly, he was reminded of one of his father's favorite homilies. The dog that barks least bites the worst.

Suddenly there was a click as the door latch sprang loose and he came erect in bed. Snatching the Navy from under his pillow, he thumbed the hammer back and waited. Slowly, an inch at a time, the door swung open. Silhouetted in the entranceway was the shadowy form of a man. Tall and heavyset. Something glinted in his hand, reflecting light from the dimmed hall lamp. Then he moved. The spill of light became brighter. And the thing in his hand was a knife.

Wes shot him and he lurched back through the doorway, disappearing from view. The youngster bounded out of bed, and crouching low, ducked into the hall. Down the passageway, he saw the man staggering toward the stairs, supporting himself with one hand against the wall. Wes thumbed off three shots, dusting him squarely between the shoulder blades. Like a great tree uprooted from the earth, the man swayed, stumbled forward another step, and then pitched headlong down the stairs.

Baffled, Wes started after him and abruptly slammed to a halt. Through the open window in his room, he heard the sound of running footsteps on the boardwalk outside. Darting back through the door, he moved to the window and looked out onto the street. Pounding toward the hotel at a steady lope was the town's entire police force. Hickok and Carson and three deputies.

The coincidence of it confounded him. Hickok and his whole pack of lawdogs so close to the very hotel where John Wesley Hardin was involved in a shooting. Then, in a great flash of illumination, it came to him.

This was no coincidence. Not by a damn sight.

The young outlaw stopped thinking and simply reacted. Jamming his hat on his head, he grabbed his boots and gun belt in one hand, scooped up his shirt and pants in the other, and stepped through the window onto the roof of the porch. When the lawmen burst into the hotel lobby, he leaped to the street and took off running in a spurt of dust. Somehow, though, he couldn't help but chuckle as he ran. Things seemed to have come full circle. Irony heaped on irony.

The bastards had sent him packing in his underdrawers.

BOOK TWO
1872–1874

CHAPTER 5

1

"Bump it a hundred."

"Friend, I got an idea you're tryin' to run a sandy on this ol' country boy. There's your hundred and I'll just kick 'er another two hundred."

"That's a lot of simoleons."

Wes flicked a sulphurhead and took his time lighting a cheroot. He puffed on it abstractedly, regarding the man across from him through a bluish haze of smoke. His appraisal was swift and penetrating. Invariably, when this man bluffed he made some flippant remark. Otherwise, if he held a strong hand, he kept quiet and tried to sucker his opponent into raising. It was a dead giveaway, an unconscious mental tic that sprang to life defensively, without thought or awareness. Thinking back over the night, better than twelve straight hours of steady poker, Wes couldn't recall a single time the man had deviated from this pattern. Now, with just the two of them left in the game, it was time to end it. Sink the gaff and put the poor bastard out of his misery.

"Tell you what, sport. I think I'm gonna have to stick with you. You caught me with my dauber down a couple of times tonight, but I figure I got your number this trip."

The youngster fumbled a fistful of coins from the pile in front of him, letting the tremor in his hand belie the braggadocio in his voice. Licking his lips with a quick, nervous swipe, he scattered several coins over the table.

"Your two hundred and I'll raise it another fifty."

"Fifty?" The man snorted and his mouth twisted in a derisive smirk. "Bucko, you're tryin' to buy yourself a pot. Trouble is, you're a little too cheap for your own good. I reckon I'm just gonna have to send you back to the well." He flung a handful of coins onto the table, then shot the boy a mocking smile and dumped a second handful into the pot. "Call your fifty and goose it three hundred."

The clink of gold was melodic, sweeter than song itself, a tune that convinced Wes he'd pegged his man right. With an idle air of disinterest, he pulled the cheroot from his mouth and gestured at the dwindling stack of coins in front of his opponent.

"How much you got there?"

The man blinked and his Adam's apple bobbed in a jerky gulp. Hastily, he counted his pile and glanced up. "Two hundred twenty."

Wes clamped the cheroot between his teeth and smiled. "I tap you."

Dazed, the man stared at him blank-eyed for a couple of seconds. Then he barked a shaky, gargled laugh and flipped his cards face up on the table. "I'm callin' your bluff, cousin. Read 'em and weep."

Wes studied the pair of aces a moment, saddened somehow that it had been so easy. Sighing, he spread his hand. "Three ladies."

Across from him, the man flinched, batting his eyes furiously. Abruptly, he shoved back in his chair and stood. "Think you're pretty slick, don't you? Well, lemme tell you something, bud. There'll be a next time. You just wait and see."

"I won't be hard to find. Johnny-on-the-spot, that's me."

The man muttered something unintelligible and stalked off. When he went through the saloon door he slammed it so hard the front windows rattled. The bartender glanced over at the boy with a look of profound relief and went back to polishing glasses.

Wearily, Wes slumped back in his chair, the money untouched. His eyes felt pebbled and gritty, and his mouth tasted like the inside of a bat cave. Sort of rancid and foul. There was a steady, throbbing beat at his temples, and his bones ached as if he'd just been poured through a rock-crusher. Daylight streamed through the front windows, searing his eyeballs, and it occurred to him that one more drag on the cheroot would just about polish him off.

Yessir. It was a great life. A laugh a minute.

Bad as he felt, the thought sparked a sardonic chuckle. The trouble with being a gamblin' man was the suckers. Like this peckerhead he'd just skinned. They were dull and witless, and most of them shouldn't be allowed loose without a keeper. Trimming them was childishly simple, downright boring. So easy a man had no need for the tricks of the trade. He had only to play the cards he was dealt, watch closely, and the damn fools would pinpoint their own weaknesses every time.

The real high rollers were few and far between. Mostly in the mining camps farther west, out in the mountains. Once in a blue moon would he run across a game that put him to the test, challenged his skill. The rest of the time was like tonight. Long and tedious and boring. Deadly boring. When it was over, he had the money but damned little satisfaction. And in the end, that's what it was all about. He was bored stiff. Winning wasn't fun anymore. Wasn't enough.

And hadn't been for a long time now.

Last summer, after departing Abilene one jump ahead of Hickok and his assassins, Wes had returned to Texas. The Clements boys had tagged along and they'd ended up right back where they started, in Gonzales. But things had changed while they were in Kansas. The State Police had perfected an enviable spy system, and within days, word of his whereabouts spread to Austin. Reckless and headstrong as ever, Wes hung around in town as if he owned the place, seemingly oblivious to the gathering storm generated by his return.

Texas' most wanted desperado had become a source of acute embarrassment to Governor E. J. Davis. Over the past three years the young outlaw had killed seven law-enforcement officers, and to pile insult on injury, the State Police had twice had him within their grasp. Unless he could be run to earth, hung or killed outright, the system of intimidation employed by Davis and his mercenaries was apt to collapse throughout the entire state.

In September two black officers surprised Wes in a Gonzales grocery store. He killed both of them in a gun battle lasting all of ten seconds. Later that month five State Police rode into Gonzales County. But Wes had a spy system of his own, comprised of friends and a whole gaggle of relatives. He ambushed the man hunters on a backcountry road, dosing them with a double load of buckshot, and two of the five made it back to Austin.

About then, Wes got the idea that Gonzales wasn't exactly a health resort. He bid the Clements brothers goodbye and rode west, headed back to the gambling circuit. It was an easy life, with poker games and horse races to occupy his time, and he drifted from town to town as the mood struck him. Understandably, he found fame, not to mention a certain notoriety, to be an asset among the sporting crowd. Men spoke softly in his presence, the shady ladies thought him an adorable young scamp, and he thoroughly enjoyed the loose camaraderie of professional gamblers. But only for a while.

Slowly, the life began to pale on him. He drank more and slept less, and became bored to distraction with the unending grind. Towns ceased to have names, and the suckers all started to look alike. Beneath his cold eyes and slick manner, he was bedeviled by the need for something more. What, just exactly, he wasn't certain. But one thing was for sure. Fun and games aside, he wasn't cut out for the life of a wastrel. Somewhere along the line, the scales had tipped, and he found himself growing envious of men who lived straight and slept without a gun under their pillow.

At least once a month, when he couldn't stand it any longer, the youngster would sneak into Pisga to see Jane. This went on throughout the winter, and every time they were together he tried to work out some sort of compromise.

All of which came to nothing. However much he wheedled and coaxed, Jane wouldn't budge. She still loved him—and proved it with the abandon of a female wildcat—but she refused to marry him. Unless he quit the sporting life altogether, and somehow got himself straightened out, she was determined to stand her ground.

As winter passed, and the rolling grasslands again turned green, his thoughts came to dwell more frequently on Jane and the kind of life they could have together. Yet the where and the how continued to elude him. His alternatives were what they had always been, bad and worse. Surrender to the State Police was out of the question, something he never even considered. The next choice, skipping off to California or Oregon or New Mexico Territory, left him equally cold. Perhaps he was muleheaded, too stubborn for his own good, but he refused to be driven from his homeland. That narrowed it down to a single option. Head west and lose himself in the vast stretch of wilderness along the Brazos.

The thought alone appalled him. No towns. No people. No more poker games or horse races or fast times. Just the wind and the empty sky and the limitless plains stretching endlessly to nowhere. All it had to offer was Jane, and at first, she wasn't counterweight enough to offset what seemed a monumental sacrifice. The sporting life.

But as he considered it now, staring bleary-eyed at the pile of double-eagles in front of him, the sporting life had somehow lost its zing. Today, tomorrow, and yesterday all seemed to run together. Another town, another poker game, another night in some dingy whorehouse. There was a sameness about it—a grinding, monotonous, never-changing void—that suddenly overwhelmed him. Kicking his chair aside, he began stuffing coins in his pockets, determined at last how it would be.

Then he walked from the saloon and turned uptown toward the livery stable.

Three nights later, his mother beside him on the settee, he sat facing James Hardin again. They hadn't seen each other in close to a year, and at first, the old man had raised cain about the aborted trip to Mexico. Then, gaining his second wind, he had thundered hellfire and damnation about Gonzales County, and the killing of three more peace officers. A year older, more experienced, Wes simply let him sputter and fume and finally run down. At last, when the tirade ended, Wes told them what he'd ridden a hundred miles to say.

"I'm leavin' this part of the country, headin' out west. Don't know exactly where I'm going, or when I'll be back, so I felt obliged to tell you all goodbye. You done your best to raise me proper and I figure it's time I tried puttin' it to use."

There was a stunned silence as the elder Hardin and his wife exchanged glances. Several moments passed before the old man could collect his thoughts, and when he spoke, there was a slight quavering in his voice. "Son, that's all I ever wanted. I know you scoff at my ways, but what you've just said simply strengthens my faith. The Lord has answered my every prayer."

Sarah Hardin touched the boy's arm, willing herself not to cry. "Where out west, Son? It would set my heart at rest if I knew where you were and what you're doing."

"Ma, I can't tell you 'cause I don't know myself. I'm just gonna head west along the Brazos and keep ridin' till I come across the right spot. I'll know it when I find it. That's one thing I've got no doubts about a'tall."

James Hardin lowered his head. "This my son was dead, and is alive again. He was lost, and is found."

2

The sun dipped lower, where river and earth linked as one, splashing great ripples of orange and gold across the water. Overhead a hawk floated past on smothered wings, veered slowly into the wind, and settled high on a cottonwood beside the stream. The bird sat perfectly still, a feathered sculpture, flecked through with burnt amber and bronzed ebony in the deepening sunlight. Then, with the lordly hauteur of taloned killers, it cocked its head in a fierce glare and looked down upon the intruders.

There were five men. A black and four whites scorched the weathered mahogany of ancient saddle leather. Their faces glistened with sweat as they wrestled a stout log onto their shoulders, lifted it high, and jammed the butt end into a freshly dug hole. Small rocks and dirt were then tamped down solidly around the log until it stood anchored to the earth as if set in stone. This was the last in a rough circle of wooden pillars embedded in the flinty soil. The men stood back a moment, breathing hard, and inspected their handiwork with a critical eye.

The black pulled out a filthy bandanna and mopped his face. "Jes' might hold 'em. If we's lucky."

A man next to him, shorter and sandy-haired, squirted the nearest post with tobacco juice. "Shit! Who you funnin', Lon? A goddamn grizzle bear with dynamite up his ass couldn't move one of them logs."

The black man just smiled. "You evah seen a bunch of mustangs when they was spooked?"

"What the sam hill's that got to do with anything? They're just critters, ain't they? Only got four legs, same as a cow."

"Lawdy me. Ain't you in for a s'prise, though. A mustang ain't no critter, Chub. It's a freak o' nature. Cross betwixt a ball o' fire and one o' them steam locomotives."

"What a crock! A critter is a critter. Hoss or cow don't make no nevermind."

"Boys, we got about an hour of daylight left. Little less jabber and come dark we might just have ourselves a corral."

The men turned to look at the rawboned youngster who paid their wages. While they were older, and perhaps more experienced, everyone understood who was boss. There was a quiet undercurrent of authority to his words, and when his pale eyes settled on a man, they seemed to bore right through. It was uncanny, this feeling, spooky in a weird sort of way. As if he could read the other fellow's mind, leave him stripped and vulnerable, his secrets a secret no longer.

They knew little or nothing of this youngster with the brushy mustache and the cold eyes. He was called Earl Roebuck. So far as they could determine he had neither family nor past. He volunteered nothing, and having looked him over, the men felt no great urge to ask questions. From his speech and manner of dress, they pegged him as a Texan; anything else was pure speculation, and best left that way. Yet there were many things they did know about him, bits and pieces gleaned from observation. A thinly sketched mosaic which told them not all, but perhaps as much as they wanted to know.

Earl Roebuck had a seemingly inexhaustible supply of bright golden coins. After hiring them in Fort Worth, he had outfitted them with extra horses; bought a wagonload of tools and gear; and laid in enough grub to feed a pack of wolves through the winter. He had asked few questions, satisfying himself that they were unmarried, in good health, and acquainted with the quarrelsome nature of cow ponies. In return, he told them he was outfitting a crew to hunt mustangs. The pay was forty a month and found, which was generous, although not unusual, considering the hazards of the job.

But the oddest thing about Earl Roebuck, and perhaps the most revealing, was that he evidenced not the slightest fear of being robbed. Not by them—though he had hired them out of saloons and knew nothing of their character—or by anyone else. Privately, and among themselves when Roebuck wasn't around, the men estimated that his saddlebags contained upward of three thousand dollars. A handsome sum by any yardstick, more than most men earned in a decade of back-breaking toil. Yet his attitude was cool and collected, utterly devoid of concern, as if he couldn't imagine anyone foolish enough to try robbing him. That alone told them much about their boss. The cocksure manner, the pale gray eyes, and the care he lavished on his Navy Colt simply rounded out the tale.

Earl Roebuck was a man who played for keeps.

All of the men had seen their share of hardcases. In Texas there was no scarcity of the breed. The young man who led them now was cast from a similar mold, and yet, there was something different about him. If anything, more deadly. He never raised his voice, nor did he attempt to bully or browbeat, tactics commonly employed by self-styled bad men. Instead, there was an inner calm about him, the quiet, cocksure certainty more menacing than a bald-faced threat. It was a warning sign, a simple statement of fact. He was one of those oddities of God's handiwork, a man who had purged himself of fear. Looking into his eyes, they knew that if his bloodlust were aroused, he would kill with the icy detachment of a slaughterhouse executioner.

Still, as Earl Roebuck led them west along the Brazos, they came to like and respect him. Though he was a hard taskmaster, he demanded less of the men than he did of himself. Moreover, he was damned fine company, standoffish at first, but slowly warming as he got to know them. By the time their little column skirted Fort Griffin, which Roebuck insisted be done at the crack of dawn, they discovered that he had a dry incisive wit and a natural flair for leadership. His orders were generally in the form of a request, stated in a tone that was at once pleasant and persistently firm. He chose good campsites, was constantly on the scout for Indians, and rotated the men on night watch without a hint of favoritism. Their respect increased manyfold when it became apparent that he had permanently assigned himself to the dawn watch. Hostiles were partial to the early morning hours for surprise attack, and every man in the crew knew it to be the most dangerous time. It was but another clue to Roebuck's character, and while the men's trust and regard steadily multiplied, they never lost sight of the fact that he was different.

In a way, it was like keeping company with an amiable bear. So long as he wasn't crossed, he was the salt of the earth. Aroused, he might just bite your head off.

West of Fort Griffin, where the Brazos split, Roebuck led them along the Double Mountain Fork. This was virgin country, unknown to white men except for the military and buffalo hunters. These rolling plains were the ancient hunting

grounds of the Comanche and Kiowa, abounding with wild-
life. A vast, limitless land that swept westward in an emerald
sea of grass. The party moved at a snail's pace, for the wagon
slowed them considerably, and in a fortnight of travel they
sighted not a single human being. In an eerie sort of way, it
was as if they had entered another world, where man was
the outsider, marching backward in time and space into a
land where an older law prevailed, an atavistic law founded
on that most simple and most ancient expedient of all, survival.

Toward the end of May, near the headwaters of the Double
Mountain Fork and some hundred miles west of Fort Griffin,
Earl Roebuck found what he was looking for. A wide expanse of woodland, with cottonwoods along the river and a
grove of live oaks stretching southward for a quarter mile.
Bordering the shoreline there was a natural clearing, with a
rocky ford and stunted hills to the north, which would protect
it from the chill winter blast of a plains blizzard. He called
a halt and announced to the crew that their journey had
ended.

Standing there, gazing around the clearing, he felt a warm
glow down in the pit of his belly. The spot was made to
order, and somehow he sensed the rightness of it. Perhaps
of greater significance, though he was scarcely the superstitious type, he felt that time and place had joined hands to
give him a sign. That morning Earl Roebuck had turned nineteen.

The ensuing month had passed quickly, a time of sweat,
excruciating labor, and immense progress. Roebuck drove
himself and the men at a furious pace, working from dawn
to dusk, seven days a week. At the head of the list was a
project that left the crew more puzzled than ever about this
strange young man who had led them into the wilderness.
He informed them that two buildings must be erected, a main
house and a bunkhouse. Again, the men asked no questions.
They felled trees, snaked logs to the clearing, and worked
like demons under his relentless urging. Both buildings were
completed, including roughhewn floors and stone fireplaces,

within three weeks, although there still remained the moot question of who, besides Roebuck, was to occupy the main house.

Afterward, erecting the corral was child's play. Roebuck inscribed a circle on the ground, large enough to hold a hundred horses, and the men set about digging post holes. Once more, he drove them like a man possessed, never sharp or ill-tempered, but merely determined to see his vision a reality at last. For every drop of sweat they shed he shed double, and somewhere along the line a strange thing happened. He was still boss, and what he wanted was what he got, but curiously enough, the men came to feel that they were working not so much for him as with him. They had become a team.

Now, as dusk settled over the clearing, they stood back, weary and exhausted, and marveled on the fruit of their labors. Set off away from the river, shaded by tall cottonwoods, was a sturdy, shake-roofed log cabin. It had three rooms with windows overlooking the stream and an oak door four inches thick. Thinking back to the day they had hung that massive slab in the entranceway, the men still weren't sure if Roebuck meant to keep somebody on the outside from getting in or somebody on the inside from getting out. With time, they had come to accept these little mysteries as part of Roebuck's character. Simply another riddle to be dusted off occasionally and inspected as a child would scrutinize an old and treasured toy.

Across the clearing from the cabin, set flush with the tree line, was the bunkhouse. It was large but compactly built, with bunks on one side and the fireplace and a dining area on the other. Behind it, off in the woods, sat the men's pride and joy. A spiffy two-holer. So far as they knew, it was the first outhouse ever erected on the Double Mountain Fork of the Brazos, their elegant, if somewhat breezy, contribution to the advancement of civilization.

The corral sat squarely in the middle of the clearing, a short distance from the river. The cross posts were springy young logs, designed to absorb punishment from milling horses without breaking. They had been lashed to the ground posts with wet rawhide, and as the leather dried and shrank, the corral was fused solid, as though girded with steel bands. Looking at it now, the men agreed that Chub Poole might have been right after all. Nothing short of a cyclone on wheels would bust out of there. Common ordinary horseflesh wouldn't stand a chance.

Bunched in a loose knot, the five men stood there for a long while, recalling a grueling month comprised of aches and sprains and sweat-drenched days. They didn't say much, just nodding and looking, for none of them especially felt the need for words. Their creation spoke eloquently for itself. It wasn't fancy, or just exactly what a man would call hand-some, but it was built to last.

Lon Hill, the black man, finally grunted and flashed a mouthful of ivory. "I got a notion Gawd never worked no harder buildin' the world. My bones feels like somebody been beatin' me with a iron switch."

"Cripes a'mighty, that ain't nothin'." Hank Musgrave, eldest of the bunch, sighed heavily. "My frazzle's fizzled so bad I couldn't pull my pecker out of a bucket of lard."

That got a chuckle, and heads bobbed in agreement. Not a man among them had energy left to work up a good spit. There was a moment of silence, as if everybody was waiting, and at last Earl Roebuck cleared his throat.

"Gents, you done yourselves proud. I'm beholden."

Looking from one to another, he held each man's gaze for a second and smiled. Then he turned and walked toward the main house. They stared after him, thick lumps clogging their throats, sort of tingly all over, and when he went through the door they still didn't move. None of them quite understood why, but his words had touched a nerve.

It was the finest compliment they'd ever been paid.

3

They came to the escarpment that guarded *Llano Estacado* in early July. Lon Hill was in the lead, for of the five men, he alone had seen the barren land that lay above. It was for this reason Earl Roebuck had hired him back in Fort Worth. The black man was many things—wrangler, bronc buster, mustanger—yet it was something more which set him apart from the others. He had trapped wild horses on the Staked Plains twice before, and returned to tell the tale. Locked in his brain was a map of this uncharted wilderness, their key into and out of a deadly hostile land. Without Lon Hill, or someone like him, venturing onto the high plains was a hazard few men cared to risk.

Late that afternoon they emerged from the steep, winding trail onto the plateau above. They halted to give the horses a breather and the men had their first look at *Llano Estacado*. Lon Hill had talked of little else since departing the Brazos, but nothing he'd said could have prepared them for the real article itself.

The plains stretched endlessly to the horizon, flat and featureless, evoking a sense of something lost forever. A thick mat of mesquite grass covered the earth, but hardly a tree or a bush was to be seen in the vast emptiness sweeping westward. It was a land of sun and solitude, a lonesome land. As if nature had flung together earth and sky, mixed it with deafening silence, and then forgotten about the whole mess. Nothing moved as far as the eye could see, almost as though, in some ancient age, the plains had frozen motionless for all time. A gentle breeze rippled over the curly mesquite, disturbing nothing, as if the wispy breath of a ghost had quietly drifted past. Perhaps more than anything else, it was this silence, without movement or life, which left a man feeling puny and insignificant, a mere speck on the sands of the universe. The Staked Plains did that to men, for in an eerie sense, it was like the solitude of God.

Distant, somehow unreal, yet faintly ominous.

Farther west the high plateau was broken by a latticework of wooded canyons, and it was in this direction that Lon Hill led Roebuck and his crew. These rocky gorges were all but invisible from a distance, and a man sometimes found himself standing on the edge of a sheer precipice where moments before there had been nothing but solitary space. Within these canyons was the breath of life, water, the only known streams in *Llano Estacado*. The men rode west not for the water itself, but instead because it served as a lure. A bait of sorts. It was near these streams that the wild horses roamed.

As they moved deeper into the trackless plains, Earl Roebuck had reason to feel pleased with himself. Back in Fort Worth, rather than hiring men at random, he had taken his time and selected with care. Every man in the crew had been chosen for a purpose, and while his judgment was hardly flawless, there was no deadwood among them. The past six weeks had proved a stern test, one that would have scattered lesser men by the wayside. Yet each of them had stuck, pulling his own weight, and by the sheer dint of hardships endured, they had dispelled any lingering doubt. These were tough men, determined and able, seared by wind and sun and time. They would stick to the last.

Lon Hill was perhaps the choice find of the lot. Freed at the end of the war, he had drifted into ranch work and quite soon shown a remarkable gift for the ways of horses. Though lean, he appeared built of gristle and spring steel, and it was a rare bronc that could unseat him. Better still, he had a head on his shoulders and knew how to use it. He was smarter than he let on, and while he played the feckless darky in front of white men, Roebuck observed that he generally got things his own way. That he outfoxed the others without them knowing it made him a prize catch indeed. Horse sense and brains seldom came in the same package.

Dolph Briscoe and Hank Musgrave were two of a kind. Not too bright but long on savvy. They understood hooved creatures better than they did men, and most of their lives had been spent aboard a horse. Their legs looked warped;

they were so bowlegged they tended to wobble when they walked. But when they stepped into a saddle some change came over them. They sat tall and easy, taking on the grace of men who had found their niche astride a spirited cow pony. Moreover, they were magicians with a rope, and it was for this reason that Roebuck had hired them. They could flatten a steer with loops that confounded the eye, and in another flick of the wrist have him hog-tied and begging for mercy. Savvy like theirs wasn't a gift so much as an art. It came only with time and unending practice.

The fourth member of the crew, Chub Poole, was also a specialist of sorts. Short and chunky, built low to the ground, but he had catlike reflexes and the strength of a young bull. There were few men his equal at wrestling steers or earring down a spooky horse. Unlike Briscoe and Musgrave, he also had something between his ears besides wax. His mind was as agile as his feet, and in a tight situation he was a handy man to have around. Aside from these more apparent traits, Poole had been selected for yet another reason. Earl Roebuck had a sixth sense for spotting men who could handle a gun. He suspected Poole's quickness and sharp reflexes weren't limited to manhandling livestock, and off in the wilderness as they were, having another fast gun along was something akin to an ace in the hole.

All in all, Roebuck felt like a man who had drawn to an inside straight and caught the right card. Watching them, as the little party moved across the high plains, a surge of confidence came over him. He had four good men, each leading an extra mount loaded with supplies, and they were headed into a country where mustangs were thick as blueberries. Suddenly he wanted to laugh. Jump up in the air and click his heels. For a man with a price on his head, he had the world by the balls.

A fortnight later, the trap was ready. Roebuck and his crew waited in a broad canyon, hidden against the sheer walls along both sides. Lon Hill was closest to the mouth of the canyon, the crucial position. The others were split into pairs

and spaced at half-mile intervals across from one another
farther down. All of the men had taken great care in con-
cealing themselves behind rocks and in scrub-choked gullies,
and now they stood fretful and anxious beside their fastest
horses. This was the day, and if they had calculated right,
all hell was about to break loose.

Their first herd of mustangs was due any minute now.

This was the hardest part. The waiting. Finding the canyon
had been fairly simple, for the grassy floor and the tree-
studded creek were alive with hoofprints. After that it was a
matter of Lon Hill bird-dogging the herd and determining
from their movements the best place to construct a trap.

The black man had needed less than a week to sniff out
the mustangs' grazing habits. Tagging along behind them, he
found that this herd was much like all bands of wild horses.
They browsed over a wide expanse of the high plains, always
drifting into the wind, and covered about twenty miles in
four days. What made it interesting was that it was always
the same twenty miles. The herd moved in a set pattern,
roughly an elongated circle, which ultimately brought them
back to their starting point. They stopped once a day to water, mostly at remote, pan-shaped basins on the plateau. But
every fourth day, a couple of hours before sundown, they
watered in the canyon. Warily, they then returned to the
plains along about dusk and spent the night in the safety of
open spaces.

Hill trailed them for six nights and five days before he was
certain of the pattern. Then he rode back to camp with the
news. Their grazing habits were regular as clockwork. And
just as predictable. With any luck at all, they could be
trapped in the canyon like a herd of sheep.

Roebuck listened, asked an endless stream of questions,
and followed the black man's advice to the letter. The men
worked three days out of four, avoiding the canyon completely on the day the herd came there to water. This was
part of the plan laid out by Hill, and it was based in no small
part on the cunning of the dun stallion that ruled the herd.

Sleek and barrel-chested, the stallion was heavily scarred

from a lifetime of fighting wolves and doing battle with young studs who tried to steal his harem. It was a full-time job, for the herd contained close to thirty mares, half again as many colts, and several yearlings. But the stallion was equal to the task. His strength and ferocity in a fight were balanced by the wisdom of age and an ever constant vigilance. He suspicioned anything that moved, and at the first sign of danger sent the herd flying with iron-jawed nips and whistling squeals of outrage. If the herd was to be captured, it was the stallion who must be outwitted. Under Lon Hill's directions, Roebuck and his crew set about accomplishing that very thing.

The trap itself was a simple affair, constructed along the lines of a funnel, but it was hellishly difficult to disguise. Since this was not a box canyon—the stallion would never water in a place that lacked an alternate means of escape— it was necessary to build two corrals where the sheer walls squeezed down to a narrow gorge. Built back to back, with a gate in between, the first was a catch corral, and the second was a larger holding pen to contain those already caught. The next step was by far the hardest. After cutting posts, the men constructed a half-mile-long fence on either side of the canyon. The fence fanned out from the corral entrance in a V shape, with the broad mouth facing the upper end of the canyon floor. If it worked, the herd would be tricked into the open throat of the funnel, then hazed down the narrowing fence and driven into the corral. With everything completed, the men came to the canyon before dawn on the eighth day and worked like demons cutting green junipers. These were used to hide the fences and corral, giving the trap a natural appearance. Once it was done, the men brushed their tracks from the canyon floor, erasing all human signs, and concealed themselves in the positions designated earlier by Lon Hill.

And now they waited. Deep shadows had already fallen over the canyon's westerly wall and sundown was but an hour away. The men began to sweat, despite a cool breeze, and their apprehension mounted as the fleeting sun dropped lower in the sky. Never before had the mustangs been this late. Unless they came to water soon it meant they weren't coming at all. Not tonight. Perhaps never again.

Then, quite suddenly, the herd appeared. One moment the mouth of the canyon stood empty and in the next, like some ghostly apparition, the mustangs simply materialized. A barren old mare, the herd sentinel, was in the lead. She came on at a stiff-legged walk, ears cocked warily, eyeing the canyon for anything out of the ordinary. At last, satisfied, she broke into a trot and led the herd toward the creek.

These wild horses were a sturdy breed, high in the withers and long in the shoulders, with a wide forehead, small ears, and a tapered muzzle. They had the spirit of their noble ancestors, the Barbs, and from generations of battling both the elements and predators, possessed an almost supernatural endurance. Honed by adversity to a single purpose—survival—they were the freest of all the earth's creatures. In motion, swallowing the wind, they could gallop to the edge of eternity and back again.

Behind the herd, the dun stallion came on at a prancing walk. Larger than the others, heavily muscled, he moved with the pride of power and lordship. Yet he was skittish as ever, nervously testing the wind, scanning the canyon floor with a fierce eye that missed not a rock or a blade of grass. He would water only at the very last, when the herd had taken its fill. Until then, protector as much as ruler, he would remain watchful and on guard, alert to any sign of danger.

Halfway between the canyon entrance and the creek, the stallion suddenly stiffened and whirled back. A vagrant breeze had shifted and with it came the most dreaded scent of all. The man scent. Pawing at the earth, nostrils flared wide, he arched his neck to sound the whistling snort of alarm.

Lon Hill shot him at that exact instant.

As the stallion went down, fighting death as he had fought life, the black man charged the herd. Instinctively, they wheeled away from the creek, prepared for flight. But their leader was down, legs jerking in death, and this strange new creature barreled toward them. It uttered the bloodcurdling scream of a cougar, and in its hand was an object that flashed fire and roared like thunder. Without their leader to command them, crazed with fright, the herd broke before Hill's charge and bolted down the canyon in a clattering lope.

The mustangs had gone only a short distance when other strange creatures came at them from either flank, screaming and firing guns. Their pace quickened, and tails streaming in the wind, the herd took off in headlong flight. Then, out of nowhere, two more riders appeared, forcing the herd straight down the middle of the canyon. Terrified, racing blindly in a thunderous wedge, the mustangs entered the juniper-lined funnel without breaking stride. The men on horseback stuck tightly to their flanks, hazing them onward with shouts and gunshots. Suddenly the funnel squeezed down to nothing, the only escape a narrow opening dead ahead.

Never faltering, the herd blasted through the corral entrance at a full gallop. The barren old mare and a yearling hit the far wall with a shuddering impact and toppled over backward, their necks broken. The rest of the herd slid to a dust-smothered halt, confused, then turned and started to retreat the way they had come. But the men were there, sliding long poles across the opening, and suddenly there was no escape. The mustangs milled about, wild-eyed and squealing, slamming against the corral at several spots. They tested the fence cautionsly, though, with respect. For they had seen what happened to the old mare and it was lesson enough. Slowly their panic faded and they huddled together in the center of the corral, trembling and frightened, staring watchfully at the creatures who had captured them.

The men were shouting and laughing and slapping one another across the back. Briscoe and Poole even linked arms and danced a mad jig. But like the mustangs, their excitement slowly drained away. Instead, the hoots and laughter became a stilled amazement. Gathered before the corral gate, they just stood there, staring back at the horses. Somehow it wasn't yet believable, but what they saw was no mirage. They had actually done it. Trapped themselves a herd of woolly-booger mustangs.

Lon Hill was flashing ivory all over the place, proud as a peacock, and he finally got around to shaking hands with the boss. "Lawdy me, Mistuh Earl, ain't they a prize? Nothin' Gawd evah made that's prettier'n a wild horse."

"I guess not." Roebuck grinned, but his eyes were thoughtful, somehow distant. "Sorry you had to kill that stallion. I was hopin' to get a good stud horse for breedin'."

"Weren't no other way, Mistuh Earl." The black man met his gaze and held it. "The devil caught my scent, and he was fixin' to take 'em outta here lickety-split."

"You did what you had to. I know that, Lon. Guess I was just wishin' out loud."

"Well, bossman, you done got your wish." Hill dazzled him with a mouthful of teeth and gestured toward the corral. "Case you ain't had a gander, there's a couple of studs in there pushin' two years. And if I'm any jedge, they got their daddy's blood in 'em."

Roebuck studied the milling herd for a long while, sorting them in his mind. The studs were there right enough, a matched pair. In another year a man would be hard put to tell them from their sire. Of more immediate consequence, there were better than twenty head that could be sold off this year. His inspection finished, Roebuck turned back to the black man, and the corners of his mustache lifted in a wry smile.

"Lon, how long you reckon it'll take us to catch the next herd?"

4

A tangle of arms and legs, breathing hard, they slowly came apart. Jane sat up, straightening her skirts, and patted a stray lock back in place. Then she came into his arms again, suddenly reluctant to have it end so quickly. They didn't say anything for a while, just sat there underneath the oak hugging and kissing, listening to the katydids serenade the night. But the stillness gradually fanned her curiosity, and when she could bear it no longer, she pushed him away.

"Now that's enough! You promised to tell me and so far you haven't done anything but muss me up something awful."

"I don't recollect you puttin' up much of a fight."

"Wes Hardin, you—you're incorrigible! That's what you are. A wicked, naughty boy. Now, are you going to tell me or not?"

He smiled. "Well, first off, you've got the right fella but the wrong name. Figured if I was gonna have a new life I might as well have a new handle. Picked one out of a hat and came up with Earl Roebuck."

"Earl Roebuck?" Jane blurted the name, astonished and not a little mystified. Then she paused, repeating it several times to herself. At last, her cheeks dimpled in a smile and she gave his hand a big squeeze. "Oh, I like it! It's so dignified and—well, I don't know, almost like a banker's name."

"That's where I got it!" He let go a burst of laughter. "Off a bank window in Fort Worth."

"You didn't rob the bank."

"Course not. I just borrowed the name."

"But I don't understand, Wes. Why did—"

"Just for openers, you better get used to callin' me Earl."

"Oh, fiddlesticks. Stop playing silly games and tell me where you've been for the last three months."

"I'm not playin' silly games. That's my name now. And where I've been is out catchin' a bunch of wild horses."

She stared at him, thunderstruck, and repeated it in a tiny voice. "Wild horses. You mean real honest-to-goodness wild horses?"

"Yep, hired myself a crew of men and went pretty near to the headwaters of the Brazos before I found the spot I was lookin' for." He hesitated and gave her an earnest look. "Built a humdinger of a cabin. Got a parlor with a fireplace, and a bedroom, and a kitchen. Real fancy.'' Then, before she had time to interrupt, he went on. ''Anyway, me and the boys took a little sashay out to the Staked Plains and when we come back we had ourselves close to two hundred head of mustangs. You're lookin' at a man of means, case you didn't know it. All honest and aboveboard, too.''

''But I still don't understand.'' Her face crinkled in an exasperated little frown. ''What earthly good are wild horses?''

''Money, woman. Money!'' He cupped her face between his hands. ''We're gonna break them horses and teach 'em some manners, and come fall, I figure to make myself about four thousand dollars.''

Jane was visibly startled. That was almost as much as her father made in a year. And his was the most successful store in Pisga.

''That's wonderful, Wes. But how long can you go on catching wild horses? I mean, it's dangerous work, and surely it couldn't be too steady.''

''The name's Earl. And don't you worry your head about wild horses. I don't plan on being a mustanger much longer. Just till we can get a herd of brood mares built up and start ourselves a real ranch.''

''You mean it? You're going to be a rancher?''

''God A'mighty, haven't you been listenin' to a word I said? Why do you think I went to the trouble of buildin' a cabin and a bunkhouse and a corral? And near busted my back catchin' all them horses?''

Suddenly Jane was listening, very intently, and she understood at last. She fluttered her eyelashes and prompted him with a coy smile. ''Tell me—Mr. Roebuck—why did you do all those things?''

'' 'Cause I figured it was time I made an honest woman of you.'' He cocked one eyebrow in a mock scowl. ''Unless you couldn't abide folks callin' you Mrs. Roebuck.''

She laughed and clapped her hands like an exuberant child. ''Oh, I could! Honestly, I could. I just don't care anymore, Wes. Just so long as we're together.''

"Earl, damnit. Honey, you gotta get used to that. The name's Earl."

"I'll remember, I promise." She threw her arms around his neck and embraced him fiercely. "I wouldn't care if your name was Judas Iscariot. Just so we can get married."

Neal Bowen hardly shared his daughter's sentiments. In fact, he was livid with rage. He had hoped, with time, that she would outgrow her infatuation. Failing that, he had every confidence Hardin would get himself killed before too long. Either way the Bowen family would be shed of their own personal albatross and his daughter would again return to her senses.

When the youngster swept into the parlor with the news that they were to be married that very night, he was at first speechless. Then he went red as ox blood and began shouting. They stood there smiling at one another, arm in arm, as if he were some spoiled brat throwing a temper tantrum. Only by imposing an iron will was he able to calm himself. If anger wouldn't work, perhaps reason would. Facing them now, he took a firm grip on his rage and reversed tactics.

"Think for a minute, both of you. What kind of a life could you have together? Always running and hiding, never knowing when the law will kick down your door in the dead of night. That's not what you want for Jane, now is it, Wes?"

Jane countered with a fetching smile. "Mercy sakes alive, Daddy! You're just working yourself up for nothing. It's already settled. We have a ranch and a herd of horses and there won't be any more trouble with the law."

"But you can't know that for sure." The storekeeper was sweating freely now. "Why couldn't you wait a while? A year, even six months. Give yourselves a little time. If you really love each other a few more months won't make any difference. Now will it?"

That was his best shot, the irrefutable logic used by fathers since biblical times. But when he saw the look on their faces Neal Bowen knew he was licked. His last-ditch effort had just shattered to smithereens against a stone wall.

"Daddy," Jane said sweetly, "will you call the preacher over, or do you want us to run off and live in sin?"

Reverend Ira Suggs opened the good book and blinked sleep from his eyes. This whole affair seemed a trifle unorthodox and he had a strong hunch the Bowen girl was in a family way. If not, then he was going to be strongly indignant with Neal Bowen for rousing him at this ungodly hour. Barring a shotgun wedding or sudden illness, there was very little that couldn't await the light of day. The Lord hadn't said it just exactly that way, but Ira Suggs felt sure He would agree.

Still, the youngsters did make a handsome couple. And from the looks of her folks, it was entirely possible the girl was in a family way. Neal Bowen looked mad enough to chew nails, and his wife had reduced her handkerchief to a sodden ball of snot. The preacher sighed wearily and in a resigned monotone began the service.

"Dearly beloved, we are gathered together to join this man and this woman in holy wedlock—"

There was a short pause while Ira Suggs stifled a yawn. Then he graced the youngsters with a benign smile and went ahead. The bride and groom scarcely seemed to notice. Holding hands, eyes fastened on one another, the only sound they heard was silent.

Warm and throbbing, it passed softly between them.

5

Briscoe and Musgrave roped the horses selected by Lon Hill and dragged them fighting and kicking out of the corral. These were the mustangs the black man had picked to work on that particular day. Half of them were raw and untried, yet to feel a saddle or the weight of a man on their backs. The others were about half-broke, having been ridden and accustomed to a bridle, but they were still in school. As Hill had commented, they had a ways to go before earning a diploma from his bronc-bustin' academy.

The day's pupils were hauled down near the river and tethered to trees. Then the rest of the herd was driven from the corral and hazed through the ford to a lush grassland on the north side of the stream. There they could graze and water throughout the day, and toward sundown they would be driven back to the corral. Hank Musgrave was left to keep an eye on them, just in case some hammerhead took a notion to quit the bunch and head back to the wide-open spaces.

There was only a slim chance of this happening, though. The mustangs had learned that a bunch quitter quickly came upon hard times. Shortly after being captured on the Staked Plains, each of the horses had been roped and thrown to the ground. When released, the horse discovered that one of its front feet had been tied to its tail with a piece of rope. It was a practical device that kept the mustangs from running, and after they had dumped themselves a couple of times, they simply gave up trying. The men drove them out of the canyon and trailed them for two days in this manner. Afterward, with the ropes removed, the mustangs behaved themselves. They could be herded any way the men wanted them to move, and few of them needed a second dose. Another day roped foot to tail convinced even the most stubborn of the lot that it was better to stick with the bunch.

With the herd grazing peacefully now, the workday began. Dolph Briscoe brought one of the tethered horses back from the river and released it in the corral. This was a raw bronc, a big rangy buckskin, and it looked to be a lively session. Briscoe hitched his own horse outside the corral and stepped down with a lariat in his hand. Roebuck, along with Hill and Poole, awaited him at the gate, and they all four entered the corral at once. This was a job they had been at steadily for the past three weeks and there was little lost motion in their actions. Like a freshly oiled machine, with all the parts functioning properly, they worked well together.

The buckskin started racing around the far side of the corral as they fanned out and walked forward. Suddenly Briscoe's arm moved and the lariat snaked out, catching the mustang's front legs in a loop just as its hooves left the ground. Briscoe hauled back, setting his weight into the rope, and the horse went down with a jarring thud. Working smoothly, every man to his own job, the other three swarmed over the buckskin in a cloud of dust and flailing arms.

Poole wrapped himself around the horse's neck, grabbing an ear in each hand, and jerked it back to earth just as it started to rise. Almost at the same instant, Roebuck darted in with a length of braided rawhide and lashed the animal's back legs tight. While Poole kept the horse earred down, Hill slipped a hackamore over its head and Roebuck clamped hobbles around its front legs. Pushing and tugging, sometimes rolling the horse up on its withers, Hill and Roebuck then managed to cinch a center-fire saddle in place. As Hill jerked the latigo taut, Roebuck eased forward and tied a blindfold around the mustang's eyes.

The entire operation had taken less than a minute.

Quickly, the ropes were removed from the buckskin's legs and it was allowed to regain its feet. Blinded and dazed, still winded from the fall, the horse stood absolutely motionless. The hobbles around its front legs kept it from rearing or jumping away, and the blindfold calmed it into a numbed stupor. However unwilling, the bronc was ready for its first lesson.

Briscoe and Roebuck backed off and scrambled over the fence just as Jane walked down from the house. She couldn't bear to watch as the mustangs were thrown and tied—although she readily admitted that it was the most practical means of strapping a saddle on a wild horse—but she loved to watch the bucking. Briscoe touched his hat, grinning like a possum, and Jane gave him a winsome smile.

The sight of her was a constant source of agony to the men, for until Roebuck showed up with his new bride, they hadn't seen a woman in close to four months. The dresses she wore were simple gingham affairs, not meant to be suggestive, but they fit snugly across her tightly rounded buttocks and her fruity breasts. There was considerable moaning in the bunkhouse late at night, but the men treated her like a fairy princess come to life. Though unspoken, there was general accord that it was better to look and not touch than to have nothing at all to look at. They suffered in quiet agony.

Standing between her husband and Briscoe, Jane felt her pulse quicken. Poole had just handed the reins to Lon Hill and retreated back to the fence. The black man tugged his hat down tight and scrambled aboard the mustang. Whenever he mounted, no matter how many times Jane watched, she was always reminded of a monkey leaping nimbly to the back of a circus pony. One moment Hill was just standing there, and in the blink of an eye, as if springs had uncoiled in his legs, he was seated firmly in the saddle.

Leaning forward, Hill jerked the blindfold loose and let it fall to the ground. For perhaps ten seconds the buckskin remained perfectly still. The black man sat loose and easy, just waiting, his lips skinned back in a faint smile. Then he moved his foot, and in the breathless quiet of the corral, the jingle-bobs on his spurs gave off the thunderous chime of cathedral bells.

The buckskin exploded at both ends, like a firecracker bursting within itself. All four feet left the ground as the horse bowed its back and in the next instant came unglued in a bone-jarring snap. Then it swapped ends in midair and sunfished across the corral in a series of bounding, catlike leaps. Hill was all over the horse, bouncing from one side to the other, never twice in the same spot. Veering away from the fence, the bronc whirled and kicked, slamming the black man front to rear in the saddle, and sent his hat spinning skyward in a lazy arc.

Hill gave a whooping shout, and in the middle of a jump, decided it was time they got down to serious business. Lifting his boots high, he raked hard across the shoulders with his spurs, and the spiked rowels whirred like a buzz saw. The buckskin roared a great squeal of outrage, and this time went off like a ton of dynamite with a short fuse.

Leaping straight up in the air, the bronc swallowed its head and humped its back, popping the black man's neck with the searing crack of a bullwhip. A moment later it hit on all four feet with a jolt that shook the earth. Then the horse went berserk. As if willing to commit suicide in order to kill the man, it erupted in a pounding beeline toward the corral fence. Hill saw it coming and effortlessly swung out of the saddle at the exact instant the mustang collided with the springy cross timbers. Staggered, the horse buckled at the knees and fell back on its rump. Like a drunk man, it just sat there for several moments, shaking its head and making pitiful little grunts.

Hill casually stepped back into the saddle as the mustang regained its feet, then he rammed his spurs clean up to the haft. This time there was less rage and less fight, ending in a series of stiff-legged crowhops that lacked punch. The black man hauled back on the hackamore for the first time, shutting off the horse's wind, and reined it around the corral in a simple turning maneuver. At last, he eased to a halt and climbed down out of the saddle. The buckskin stood where he left it, head bowed and sides heaving as it gasped for air.

Hill retrieved his hat and dusted it off. Jamming it on his head, he walked toward the grinning foursome gathered outside the corral.

"That's gonna be a good hoss." He smiled and jerked his thumb back at the spent mustang. "Got plenty of starch."

"He don't look so starchy now," Chub Poole cackled. "Looks like somebody twisted all the kinks out of his tail."

"Aw, he's jest restin'. Figgerin' what he's gonna do next time. Course, I'd bet a heap he don't run into that fence no more."

Earl Roebuck laughed and squeezed Jane around the waist. She had never seen him in such good spirits. Nor had the men. They talked of it often in the bunkhouse. Since the lady had come to stay, and Lon Hill started busting broncs, the grim-eyed youngster was a changed man. Like night and day.

That evening the young couple came to sit on the front step of their cabin. The sweet coolness of night had fallen over the land and they could hear the crickets warming up along the riverbank. There was a serenity about this place, something they both felt, almost as if there had never been another life except the one they shared here on the Brazos. Thinking about it now, Jane felt warm and giddy inside. These were the happiest days she had ever known. And she need look no farther for the reason than the man seated beside her.

"Penny for your thoughts."

His words jarred her reverie. She snuggled closer, burrowing deep into the hollow of his arm, and smiled. "I'm not sure I should tell you."

"Keepin' secrets on me?"

"No, but your head might swell up and bust."

He chuckled and gave her a bearish squeeze. "Try me. Can't hardly be worse'n it already is."

"I was just thinking how proud you make me. That it was you who built all this. The cabin and the horse herd and everything. Sometimes I have to pinch myself to make sure it's all real."

"Well, I had some help, y'know. It wasn't like I walked in here with an ax and a mouthful of nails and slapped it together all by myself."

"You're a paragon of modesty, Mr. Roebuck." Her voice had a teasing lilt. "I wouldn't be surprised but what you're blushing."

"Nope, I clean forgot how. Been too busy buildin' empires."

"See, I told you. It went right straight to your head."

"Judas Priest, can't a fella speak the truth in his own house?"

"Oh, you really are vain, Wes Har—" She clamped a hand over her mouth and giggled softly. "I mean, Mr. Roebuck. But it's still true. You're the vainest man I ever met."

"Caught you, didn't I? Any man that did that has got reason to be proud."

She laughed a deep, throaty laugh. "Maybe you don't catch me enough."

He considered it a moment and she could tell he was smiling. Then he chuckled, "I think you got somethin' there. What d'you say we hit the hay early tonight?"

"Mr. Roebuck, I thought you'd never ask."

Since they were of a mind, there seemed no reason for further talk. They stood and he lifted her over the step and set her on the floor inside the cabin. As he swung the massive oak door closed and barred it, she crossed the parlor and blew out the lamp. Then she laughed that laugh again, and he heard the rustle of her skirts as she headed toward the bedroom.

Curiously, he had no trouble finding her in the dark.

CHAPTER 6

1

Roebuck left the crew camped along the river outside town. There were several hours of daylight remaining but nobody questioned his decision to halt in midafternoon. The men were still hungover pretty bad, and just then, their only interest was in ridding themselves of the miseries. Trinity was scarcely more than a wide spot in the road, but it had a couple of saloons, and that was what counted most. A man wasn't picky about watering holes when his throat was on fire and his head felt like a melon about to burst. So far as the crew was concerned, Trinity would do nicely.

When he rode off headed south along the river road, the men gave him little more than a second glance. Trinity was in the opposite direction, but in the past year they had learned a vital lesson about Earl Roebuck. Like God, he moved in mysterious ways, and he didn't take kindly to questions. If he wanted them to know something, he told them. Otherwise, it was best to lie back and wait. While he was a damn good man to work for, and never put on any highfalutin airs, he still held his own counsel. That was his way, and however close the men felt to him, they knew better than to step over the line.

After he was out of sight, where the river took a sharp bend, Roebuck swung east and put the grullo into a steady lope. It pleased him that they hadn't asked questions. The fact that he had kin nearby was none of their business, and under the circumstances, hardly explainable. The three-day spree in Galveston had dampened their curiosity at any rate. Busthead whiskey and fancy cathouses had a way of sapping the juices, and right now they were more interested in regaining their wind than they were in his little jaunt downriver. Satisfied with the way everything had worked out, he put it from his mind and rode toward Barnett Hardin's farm.

Somehow, as his thoughts drifted back, there was a sense of the unreal about this visit. It had all started here—not quite four years ago—the day he'd killed the black freedman. Yet it seemed he had lived a couple of lifetimes since that day. Instead of twenty, he felt forty going on a hundred. A man with few illusions left intact. Someone who saw life and people not as he would have wished them to be, but simply as they were. And the dozen dead men littered along his back trail made the feeling no less intense. Coming here again, where it had started, was strangely out of focus. As if it had happened to someone else, in another lifetime, and he was merely an observer peering through a frosted windowpane.

Still, for all the close shaves he'd gone through, things had worked out pretty well in the end. This past year had been as good as any man could ask for, and he had no complaints about the time before. That was water under the bridge, and with what he had now, there was nothing to be gained in dwelling on the bad times.

It had been an eventful year on the Brazos. Last fall they had sold close to a hundred head of saddle stock. Not mustangs but mannered horses, instilled with a healthy respect for all mankind at the sure hands of Lon Hill. Trapping on the Staked Plains had also been good, providing the Roebuck spread with a fine herd of brood mares and another batch of stock to be broken and sold. After a long winter, and a hectic six weeks in the breaking corral, this new bunch had been trailed to Galveston and sold to a dealer. From there they would be shipped to various markets in the South where men prized fiery-spirited horses. All in all, it paid handsomely. Roebuck had cleared almost four thousand dollars for the year and his brood mares would begin foaling next spring.

His vision of a horse ranch was only one step removed from becoming a reality.

Yet, the highlight of the year had nothing to do with horses. In May, a few days before Roebuck's own birthday, Jane had given birth to a squalling, lusty-lunged baby. It was a girl, which disappointed Roebuck only slightly, and they had named her Molly. Like her mother, she had a way with men, and inside of a couple of days everybody on the place had been bewitched by the tiny newcomer. Where the crew had simply been awkward and shy around Jane, they were completely spellbound by the baby. Somehow, in a way that seemed very personal, each of the men thought of himself as Molly's uncle. They never discussed it, and would have been mortified had anyone suspected their inner thoughts, but they felt it nonetheless strongly.

Jane herself had bloomed like a wild flower. Though reared to expect certain luxuries, she had taken to the frontier life with astounding gusto. There was nothing that fazed her, from cooking over an open fireplace to having her own husband as midwife, and she positively thrived where most women would have swooned dead away. The men thought her a great lady, and among themselves agreed that the boss was the luckiest sonovabitch on the face of the earth.

Earl Roebuck felt the same way. He had a fine ranch, a well-seasoned crew, and some nifty prospects for the future. But more importantly, he had Jane. And Molly. And a life that left him answerable to no man. So far as he could see, he had it all.

That thought was uppermost in his mind as he crossed a creek and heeled the grullo onto a rutted wagon road. The boy who had once killed a burrhead on this same road no longer existed. In his place rode a man who had won all the marbles. And on his own terms.

Barnett Hardin and the youngster came outside after supper to sit on the porch. They were stuffed full and feeling a bit sluggish from the heavy meal. But this hardly put a damper on their high spirits. There was an affinity between them that hadn't been dispelled by time or circumstance. More than blood, it was the kinship of strong men who each saw something of himself mirrored in the other. Hardin took a seat in a creaky rocker, motioning his nephew to another chair, and began loading his pipe. Then he struck a sulphurhead on his thumbnail and noisily sucked the pipe to life. Glancing up, he exhaled a thick cloud of smoke and smiled.

"Y'know, I hate to admit it, but I'm just the least mite envious. This place you got on the Brazos makes me wish I was twenty years younger. In a queer sort of way, a man's first scrap with the wilderness is the best time of his life. I don't understand just exactly why it's that way, but it's a fact all the same."

The younger man nodded, digesting the thought, and a slow grin spread over his face. "I never thought of it like that but I've got an idea you're right. Least ways this last year's been real good to me. Lots better'n I ever expected, that's for damn sure."

"Well, Christ A'mighty, boy! You had rough sleddin' there for a while." Hardin's words came out in little spurts of smoke. "What with one thing and another, it's a wonder you didn't get yourself skinned and hung out to dry."

"Yeh, I s'pose it is. Course, things have calmed down some since then."

"Not just exactly, it ain't. Mebbe Texas is back in the Union, but we still got Davis for governor. Long as he's got them nigger police backin' his play you're gonna stay on the wanted list. No two ways about it."

"I guess you're right." A sardonic smile flickered and in the next instant was gone. "Likely they figure I owe 'em some on account."

"Ain't no likely about it. Many of 'em as you killed they won't never forget your name. That's why I was so tickled when you told me you got a new handle. Best thing you could've done."

"Things the way they were, I didn't have much choice. Still goes against the grain, though, havin' to hide behind somebody else's name."

"Sure it does. But you got a wife and baby and a ranch to think about now. Like I said, it's the smartest thing you ever done."

The youngster got a far-off look in his eye, saying nothing, and after a moment Barnett Hardin snorted. "Hell's bells and little fishes! It ain't like it'll last forever. Lemme tell you somethin', Wes. Elections are comin' up next year, and there's a damn good chance Davis is gonna get his nose rubbed in it. If we can get a Democrat as governor, I got a notion the law might just forgive and forget."

"I'm not bankin' on it, but it'd sure be nice to quit this play-actin'. Sort of chafes a fellow's nerves after a while."

"I s'pect it does. All the same, you ain't killed nobody in over a year and the State Police ain't campin' on your tail. It's that new name that turned the trick. 'Cept for that there wouldn't be no Jane and there wouldn't be no baby girl. You can chew on that and you'll see I'm right."

"Course you are. I didn't mean I was thinkin' of pullin' anything stupid. Hell, I'm happy as a pig in mud the way things are. My name's Earl Roebuck and it's gonna stay that way."

"That's the ticket. You're young and you got plenty of time. Just keep the hell out on the Brazos till we get these carpetbaggers run off."

"Don't worry none on that score. Only time I come east of Fort Griffin is to sell horses. Got everything I need right where I am."

"By God, I'm glad to hear you say it. Only next time I want you to bring Jane and the baby. Don't rightly seem fair that you got a young'un and I ain't never seen her."

"Well, I would've brought 'em, but what with Jane just gettin' back on her feet I figured it was best to leave 'em at her folks. Just comin' in from the Brazos sort of took the starch out of her. Not that she's sickly or anything, but the rest will do her good. Next spring I'll bring 'em by for sure, though. You can count on it."

"Good. Your aunt would purely love to see that baby." Hardin puffed on his pipe a minute and gave the youngster a speculative look. "What about your folks? You plannin' on seein' them this trip?"

"Matter of fact, I am. Thought I'd sneak in for a quick visit on the way back to get Jane and Molly."

The older man smiled. "I'm real proud you patched things up with your pa. Every time we get a letter he don't hardly talk about nothin' but you. And, o' course, your ma misses you something fierce. They'll be tickled pink to see you're makin' out so well."

Bessie Hardin came through the door, drying her hands on a dish towel. The youngster stood and she motioned him back to the chair. "Now keep your seat and go right on visiting. I just thought you might want coffee, or maybe some more cobbler."

"Couldn't if I wanted to. I'm full as a tick. Besides, I told the boys I'd meet 'em in Trinity along about dark. Guess I oughta pull out pretty quick now."

"Think that's wise?" Hardin's gaze narrowed. "You go hangin' around towns and there's always the chance somebody'll spot you."

"Well, we didn't have any trouble in Galveston. And Trinity's sort of off the beaten path. I'd be surprised if anybody got curious."

"Just watch yourself. It only takes one miscue, y'know."

"Yeah, I learned that the hard way. Course, the way it worked out, the joke was always on the other fellow."

Barnett Hardin and his wife exchanged a quick glance. Then the older man grinned and a deep belly laugh rumbled up from his gut. He stood and clapped a thorny paw over the youngster's shoulder.

"I reckon it never was you that needed advice. It was them other fellers."

"Yessir, I guess it was. And hallelujah to that."

2

The game was less than an hour old and already Roebuck was far and away the big winner. While the stakes were small potatoes to him, it was plain that the other men were playing desperation poker. The money on the table was either all they had or more than they could afford to lose; they were taking reckless chances, defying both the odds and common sense, in an effort to recoup their losses. Some stayed, blindly counting on the draw, when they should have got out; others sweated inside straights or stupidly called raises when it was clear they were beat on the board. Fickle as ever, the lady allowed some of them to drag down an occasional pot. Since they wanted to believe, this was enough to convince them all that the worm would shortly turn. That luck would again come sit beside them. Lead them to that elusive pot of gold.

Roebuck was tempted several times to fold a winning hand, simply to lessen the mounting tension. But this went against his every instinct as a gambler. These men were both thick-headed and stubborn, and whatever drubbing they took was not so much a result of his skill as it was their own foolishness. They had ignored the cardinal rule of gambling—a man who bets money he can't afford to lose is beat before he starts. Roebuck wasn't a Good Samaritan where poker was concerned. Nor did he believe in charity to fools. He played the cards dealt him and he played to win.

Given different circumstances, perhaps Roebuck wouldn't have joined the game at all. Upon leaving Jane he had half-way promised he wouldn't backslide and let himself be lured to the gambling tables. Until tonight, it was a promise he had kept. But when he rode into Trinity, and found the crew at Gate's Saloon, he was quickly persuaded to change his mind. The men were already pretty well ossified, having hit the saloon some hours earlier, and he suddenly found their antics a little boring. The spree in Galveston had been enough to hold him for the year, but the men apparently meant to make the most of their brief respite from the Brazos. Briscoe and Musgrave were the worst, loudly proclaiming themselves the greatest mustangers ever to come down the pike. Poole wasn't far behind, and gaining ground with every shot of red-eye. Of the group, only Lon Hill still had his wits about him. The black man was the watchful type, particularly in a white saloon, and where the others swilled, he merely sipped.

Their tomfoolery was about what Roebuck had expected, though, and he didn't begrudge them another fling. They had worked long and hard over the past year, and he figured they'd earned the right to celebrate. But that didn't mean he had to get down and wallow with them. All the more so since whiskey generally left the taste of sheep dip in his mouth. After a couple of sociable belts, he left them to their own devices and wandered back to join the poker game.

Now, with most of the money on the table piled in front of him, Roebuck took up the cards to deal. The other men were about what he would have expected to find in a back-country poker game. Two hardscrabble farmers, a store-keeper, and the town loudmouth, who worked at the local livery stable. All of them had lost heavily and they were showing the strain, but the loudmouth was the only one who had so far voiced any grievance. Roebuck knew the type. A dimdot who gulped his whiskey and considered himself the world's shrewdest card player. The kind who was all wind and no whistle. A born loser.

Still, Roebuck had no qualms about trimming them. Anybody old enough to play was old enough to know when to quit. That most men didn't, and just sat there flinging good money after bad, wasn't his lookout. Nor did he have any misgivings that they might believe he was cheating. The deal passed from player to player, and regardless of who dealt, he was winning consistently. That spoke for itself.

After shuffling, and allowing the farmer seated on his right to cut, he dealt a hand of five-card draw. The man on his left, the storekeeper, opened for five dollars. The other farmer called, and with a gleeful cackle, the loudmouth raised ten.

The last man, the farmer who had cut, hesitated a long time, as if trying to change the spots on his cards. Finally he called. Roebuck had all he could do to keep a wooden face as he spread his own hand. Staring back at him were two pairs. Aces and treys.

"See the fifteen and bump it ten."

The storekeeper and the farmer swore in unison and pitched their cards to the center of the table. The loudmouth grumbled to himself a little bit, sneaking dark looks at Roebuck, and at last snorted derisively. He grabbed up a bunch of coins and flung them into the pot.

"Gonna make you stretch, Laddy. Your ten and ten more."

The farmer cursed under his breath and folded.

Roebuck merely smiled and started counting from the stack in front of him. "Like the fella said, when you got 'em, bet 'em. Call the ten and raise it"—he glanced up, still smiling—"how's fifty sound?"

The stablehand grunted as if he'd been kicked in the belly. But the whiskey had taken hold and he was too stubborn to back off now. "Call, by God! You ain't the only man that knows tit from tether."

Ignoring the jibe, Roebuck picked up the deck. "Cards to the players."

"Gimme two. And make 'em good uns."

Apparently the loudmouth had three of a kind. Or maybe a pair with an ace kicker. Either way it didn't matter. Roebuck dealt him two cards and carefully laid the deck on the table. Then he placed a double-eagle on top of his own hand.

"Dealer stands pat." He gave the other man a sardonic smile. "Your bet."

The stablehand blinked a couple of times and sweated out his draw. Evidently the cards failed to improve his hand, for when he glanced up his face was ocherous. "Check."

"Bet two hundred."

"Goddamnit, you know I ain't got that much."

"I'll tap you then. Call for what's in front of you."

Roebuck knew he wouldn't call. The hangdog expression

on his face told the tale. The bluff had worked. A moment elapsed, then the loudmouth slammed his cards to the table and knocked back a glass of whiskey in a single gulp. Smiling, Roebuck threw his hand on the deadwood and started to drag in the pot.

Suddenly the man snatched at the deadwood, trying to grab Roebuck's discarded hand. Roebuck leaned across the table and backhanded him in the mouth. The man's lip split, spurting blood, and he lurched erect.

"You sonovabitch! Nobody does that to me."

"Friend, I'll do worse than that if you don't keep your mitts out of the deadwood."

The stablehand was unarmed, so that meant rough-and-tumble if it came to a showdown. But forty years of beans and sowbelly were beginning to show at his waistline, and Roebuck had little doubt of the outcome. The youngster kicked his chair back and stood just as the saloonkeeper materialized at his elbow.

"Mister, don't pay no attention to Sam. He didn't mean nothin', honest. It's just whiskey talk. Look for yourself. He's so drunk he couldn't ride a hobbyhorse."

Roebuck's flinty gaze bored into the stablehand for a moment, then he shrugged. His voice was low-keyed, restrained somehow, but there was an undercurrent of deadliness in the words. "Get the peckerhead out of here. He's got no business playin' poker with grown men."

The barkeep circled the table and grabbed Sam by the shirt collar and the seat of his pants. Then he waltzed him across the room at a lively clip. But as they went through the door the stablehand twisted around and hollered back over his shoulder.

"You ain't through with me yet, you sorry bastard. Just hide and watch. You'll see!"

Drunk as they were, Roebuck's crew had wheeled away from the bar at the first sign of trouble. Now he smiled and waved them back, his brief flare of temper once again under control. Righting his chair he took a seat and glanced around at the dumbstruck players.

"Pardon the intrusion, gents. Who's dealin'?"

The storekeeper fumbled the cards together and commenced shuffling. Like a couple of mesmerized sheep, the farmers just sat there, staring vacantly at his shaking hands.

Late that night Roebuck emerged from the saloon trailed by three drunks and someone who looked like a glassy-eyed owl that had been dipped in tar. The notable difference was that Lon Hill could still walk, whereas the others sort of listed and swayed, taking two steps backward for every one step forward. Roebuck was somewhat ahead of the others and had just stepped off the boardwalk when a brilliant orange flash erupted across the street.

A sliver of fire seared his side and in the same instant he heard the deep roar of a shotgun. He knew he'd been hit, but somehow that seemed incidental, a mere trifle. Without thought, acting out of sheer reflex, he jerked the Navy and placed five shots in the precise spot he had seen the muzzle flash. There was a momentary lull while everyone stood rooted in their tracks, then the stablehand lurched out of a dark passageway between two buildings. The shotgun fell from his hand, clattering on the boardwalk, and he teetered there like a tree rocking in the wind. His legs gave way all of a sudden, as if chopped from beneath him, and he pitched face down in the street.

Roebuck felt something warm and sticky soaking his shirt front, and bright swirling dots appeared before his eyes. Quite without realizing it, his knees buckled and he found himself sitting in the road. Lon Hill loomed over him, and from a great distance he heard the raspy croak of his own voice.

"Can you beat that? The sonovabitch killed me."

As it turned out, the youngster was only half right. According to Dr. Jonas Stroud he should have been dead, but by some inexplicable quirk of fate, he wasn't. Less than an hour after the shooting, the physician operated and removed two buckshot that had passed through the kidney and lodged between the backbone and ribs. In the process he recognized Barnett Hardin's nephew for who he was, and inadvertently let slip to the crew that they were riding in fast company. All of which seemed a moot point since Stroud gave the young outlaw a fifty-fifty chance at best of pulling through. Unless he was confined to bed and kept completely inactive there were no odds. He would simply die.

Fearful of using opiates, due to the youngster's weakened condition, Stroud had operated without a pain-killer. Wes had stoically endured the scapel, and gritted his teeth all the harder when he heard the physician expose his identity. Now, stitched back together and bandaged tightly, he asked Stroud to summon his crew. They trooped in and ganged around the operating table, stone-cold sober and looking just the least bit sheepish. The youngster was ashen, but in full control of himself, and he smiled weakly.

"Boys, I guess the jig's up. I'm sorry I had to fool you like that, but it was better you didn't know who I was. Now that you do, I want you to make tracks and forget you ever heard of me."

Poole puffed up like a banty rooster. "Now just hold on a goldarned minute, Earl."

The young outlaw stopped him with a slight motion of his hand. "Chub, it's a little late to start arguin' with me. The doc will pay you fellows off out of my money belt and then I want you to vamoose. The State Police are gonna get wind of this, and if they catch us together you boys will swing right alongside me. You think about it and you'll see I'm right." Drained of strength, he managed one last smile. "Now scat, the whole bunch of you."

The men stood there several moments, wavering between loyalty to the man they knew as Earl Roebuck and the uncertain fate of riding with Wes Hardin. Bitter as it was, they had to admit he was right. Hank Musgrave started it off, and then, one at a time, they filed by and gave his hand a soft squeeze. None of them said anything and somehow that didn't seem in the least strange. It had all been said back on the Brazos.

When the door closed Wes lay there for a long while, trying to collect his thoughts and plan what to do next. Then, quite suddenly, he sensed that he wasn't alone. Turning his head, he saw Lon Hill standing just inside the doorway. The black man flashed a mouthful of ivory and met his stare straight on.

"Boss, you'd jest be wastin' your breath. Like it or not, you done stuck with me."

Hill cocked his hat back, grinned, and took a chair beside the door.

3

The room was still dark when Wes awoke. Through the window he saw a grayish tinge in the sky and estimated dawn was yet an hour away. Some inner mechanism had awakened him, a warning of sorts, and he lay there trying to unravel what it meant. Nothing stirred, and so far as he could tell there was no reason to take alarm. The house was quiet and there were no unusual noises from the farmyard. All of which didn't mean a hill of beans. Not after the last two months. The quiet times, especially when a man was sleeping, were the most dangerous of all.

Slowly, he ran his hand under the pillow and took hold of the Navy. Then he rolled sideways and eased his feet onto the floor. The wound in his side had healed nicely, but he favored it nonetheless. Sudden movements still brought a sharp pain, and while it curried him the wrong way, he had conditioned himself to taking things easy. Standing, he hobbled around the room, barefooted and silent. There were two windows, one at the side of the house and the other at the back. Some minutes passed as he scanned the yard, which was off a ways to the rear. He detected nothing out of the ordinary, but that did little to ease his jumpy feeling.

It was no false alarm. Not when it tugged him awake like this.

The past couple of months had given him a strong conviction about these hunches. Whether it was sixth sense or a deeper instinct of some sort seemed unimportant. He knew that he possessed it, whatever it was, and more significantly, he knew that it was almost unerring. Not infallible, but close. Damned close. The feeling was triggered by something inside him, always unexpected, and never once concerning itself with trifles. When it came, it came with dazzling clarity. And there was no muck of uncertainty. It struck hard and fast, and most of the time, dead center. On center often enough that only a fool would have ignored it. The proof was not so much in his head as in the simple function of his lungs.

This thing, whatever its name, had kept him alive.

Alert and edgy, he returned to bed and again lay down, with the Navy resting across his chest. Despite the early morning calm—what his eyes and ears took to be a good sign—he couldn't relax. Too much had happened since that night in Trinity. And none of it good. Looking back, he felt a profound sense of wonder. Not that he had survived that night, or recovered from the shotgun blast. But instead, that by hunch and a long streak of luck he had lived to greet the gloomy dawn of a September day.

Lon Hill had been as good as his word. The black man stuck with him, and foxy as ever, had cleverly engineered his escape. That same night Hill had cut the telegraph lines out of Trinity, sealing it off and delaying word of the shootout from reaching Austin. Then, shortly before dawn, he spirited Wes out of town in the back of a buckboard. It was rough going at first, for they were forced to hide in the heavy thickets along the river. After a week, though, Hill managed to sneak a quick powwow with Barnett Hardin and they were able to quit living like animals.

But instead of getting better, things got worse. Though Barnett Hardin's place was under constant surveillance, making it unsafe for them to stay there, he arranged for them to hole up with friends in Walker County. Texans were a prideful and independent lot, but they were united in one thing, their hatred of the carpetbagger regime. The name Wes Hardin had a certain magic about it, a symbol of sorts. One man fighting a lone fight against the brutality and injustice of Yankee tyranny. The youngster and his dusky watchdog were welcomed like victorious soldiers home from the war.

The jubilation proved somewhat premature, though. The State Police sniffed out their trail early in July, and within a span of six weeks they were forced to run on seven separate occasions. Wes was weak as a kitten throughout the entire ordeal, unable to sit a horse, much less turn and give fight as he had in the past. Lon Hill carted him from farm to farm in the buckboard, and each time, they escaped capture by what seemed a sheer stroke of luck.

It was during this deadly game of hide-and-seek that Wes first became aware of his hunches. Something akin to an itchy feeling would come over him, and an inner voice warned him of impending danger. Lon Hill believed in many things—among them voodoo witchcraft and the Lord God Jehovah—but his strongest faith was in the wolflike instincts possessed by certain men. Men like Wes Hardin. Whenever the young outlaw showed signs of that itchy feeling, Hill hurriedly packed the buckboard and they took off in a blaze of dust. That the hunches were virtually foolproof was borne out by the fact that they had misfired only twice. Of the seven times they ran, State Police stormed five hideouts shortly after they departed.

As if his wound and the relentless hounding weren't enough, Wes was further made miserable by concern for his family. Jane and the baby were still in Pisga, and through friends, he was able to send an occasional letter. But there was no way Jane could reply, and it was this loss of contact which he found unbearable. So long as they remained with the Bowens, she and the baby were safe, and for that he was thankful. Still, it did little to salve his need for them. Though the admission came hard, he couldn't elude a stark sense of emptiness. He was lonely, and for the first time in his life, he needed someone besides himself. It was a troublesome feeling, one he had difficulty in handling, particularly at night without Jane's soft warmth snuggled close to him.

Beneath it all, compounding his more immediate worries, was a hurt of a different sort. He had lost the ranch, and while the thought was bitter as wormwood, he never once tried kidding himself on that score. A year on the Brazos, filled with sweat and hope and great accomplishment, had simply gone down the drain. Poole and Musgrave and Briscoe were good men, loyal in a way he wouldn't have expected from hired hands. But they were heavy drinkers as well, and liquor tended to loosen a man's tongue. Despite their best intentions, sooner or later one of them would get crocked and spill the beans. Nothing was more natural when a man kept steady company with John Barleycorn, and before long they would all be bragging. Telling the world how they'd trapped mustangs with a fellow whose real name happened to be John Wesley Hardin. Much as it galled him, the young outlaw couldn't avoid facts.

Earl Roebuck was dead. And his dream on the Brazos had vanished in a puff of smoke.

None of this concerned him now, though. Instead, he lay in bed, wide awake and fretful, wondering if he was jumping at shadows. His nerves had been on edge for close to two months, and he was strung so tight he had begun to suspect his own hunches. Perhaps of greater consequence, he was just plain fed up with running. A week ago, with a premonition this strong, he would have rousted Hill from bed and made tracks. Now, irked by the constant harassment and feeling more his old self, he simply waited. The State Police weren't about to call it quits, and all of a sudden he just didn't give a damn. It was time to shove back.

A light rap on the door brought him out of bed in a single motion. He thumbed the hammer back on the Navy and waited. Then the doorknob turned, and in the deadened silence of the room, the creaky hinges sounded like the clatterwheels of hell. Lon Hill stuck his head inside.

"It's jest me, boss."

"Hell, c'mon in, Lon." Wes glanced sheepishly at the cocked pistol and slowly lowered the hammer. "Guess I'm a little spooky these days."

The black man swung the door open but held his position in the hall. "I s'pect you got reason." He jerked his thumb toward the front of the house. "Couple of fellas left their horses in the trees over by the creek. They's pussyfootin' this way and they got rifles."

Wes smiled grimly. "Looks like my itch was real after all." Snatching up his pants, he pulled them on, hurriedly hooked the top button, and jammed the Navy in his waistband. "Where are Dave and his wife?"

"Still sleepin'."

The young outlaw heaved a sigh of relief. Dave Harrel was an old friend of Barnett Hardin's, and it would be easier if he had no part in whatever happened. With that off his mind, he grabbed a shotgun leaning against the wall by the bed and turned back to the black man.

"You say there's only two of 'em?"

"That's all I seen."

"Good. Two're just about right. Say, how come you to spot 'em, anyway?"

Hill grinned. "Reckon I done caught your itch."

"Well, that's all you've caught. Get on back to your room and stay"—the black man's jaw clicked open but Wes's harsh scowl stopped him cold—"I haven't got time to argue. Just do like I say. And if they get me, you play dumb and act like you're Dave's hired help."

He brushed past Hill and hobbled off down the hallway. Entering the parlor, he moved quietly to a front window and peeked through the curtains. Two men were crossing the yard, rifles thrust out in front of them, peering suspiciously at the house. They both wore badges and had the unmistakable stamp of Yankee written all over them. Quickly, he moved across the room, earring back the hammers on the shotgun, and halted beside the door. Grasping the greener in his right hand, he threw the door open and dropped to one knee in the entranceway.

"Hands up!"

The policemen froze at his barked command. They gawked at him for an instant, goggle-eyed with disbelief, then the one on the right moved his rifle barrel. Wes pulled both triggers and the scattergun vomited a double load of buckshot. The officers hurtled backward, lifted from their feet by the impact, and slammed to earth with a dusty thud. One man's head was half gone and the other one had a hole the size of a saucer where his badge had been. The ground around them puddled with blood and muddy gore; there was scarcely any question about the outcome. They were dead and ripening fast.

Wes climbed to his feet and turned back into the house. Lon Hill was standing just behind him, clutching a battered Spencer carbine. The black man grinned.

"Looks like the magpies is gonna have eyeballs for breakfast."

"I thought I told you to stay put."

"Boss, you gonna have to speak louder. This ol' niggah's hard of hearin'."

"Yeah, sure you are. Like a fox." Wes smiled and shook his head. "Well, long as you're here, see if you can round up a shovel and we'll get those bastards planted."

"Yassuh, Mistuh Wes. You want one hole or two?"

The young outlaw flicked a glance back at the sprawled bodies. "One'll do fine. They can keep each other company."

Then he walked off down the hall. He could hear Maude Harrel screeching at her husband in their bedroom, and it grated on him that he had brought trouble to their doorstep. Suddenly he felt very tired and his side ached something fierce. A year on the Brazos had changed things not at all. It was like a lost man wandering in circles.

He was right back where he'd started.

4

The air was damp and chill along the river. Wes huddled deeper inside his blanket and tried to draw some warmth to his body. Though it was pitch dark, and the heavy thickets screened the campsite, he dared not light a fire. Instead, he sat with his back against a wagon wheel and shivered, forcing himself to ignore the pain in his side. Despite the cold, he felt flushed, just the least bit woozy, and sensed that he was running a fever. But this he also put from his mind. Until Hill returned there was nothing to be done. He closed his eyes, resigned to the wait, and blocked out all thought of pain and cold and chattering teeth.

They had been on the run for almost a week. Harried like animals with hounds set loose on their trail. There seemed no sanctuary, not after the gunfight at Dave Harrel's place; no matter how hard they pushed themselves, or how often they changed hideouts, the State Police were only a step behind. Finally, out of desperation, they had once again taken to the thickets. Here, at least, they could lose themselves for a while, and gain time to think.

Burying the dead officers at Harrel's had been futile, wasted effort. State Police were fanned out across Walker County in a massive search, and other officers had appeared that very afternoon asking questions. That they would return, nosing out the trail of the dead men, Wes had no doubt whatever. Yet he was in worse shape than ever, and hardly fit to run. The recoil from the shotgun, where he'd held it jammed against his side, had ruptured his wound. Maude Harrel fixed him a poultice of spider webs and chimney soot, but it merely slowed the bleeding to a steady leak. Late that night, though, he and Lon Hill took off in the buckboard anyway. As long as they remained at the farm, the Harrels were in danger of being killed, for it was only a matter of time until the law trapped them there. With them gone, Dave Harrel could claim he had harbored them at gunpoint, and there was no way of proving otherwise. It was no choice at all.

They ran and kept on running, driven, at last, into the thickets.

Now Wes gritted his teeth, closing his mind to the pain and the sweaty chills that swept over him. He focused instead on what seemed a more unsettling problem. Lon Hill was long past overdue, and it was unlike the black man to be late. Hill had ridden out around sunset, expecting to reach Barnett Hardin's place shortly after dark. Wes disliked drawing the old man deeper into his troubles, but he desperately needed a safe hideout. Someplace he could lay up until his wound healed fully and he was again fit to ride a horse. However distasteful the idea, he had nowhere else to turn for help. Barnett Hardin was his last hope. Yet, even as he mulled this over, it merely increased his concern for Lon Hill.

The black man might easily have been trapped at Hardin's farm. Or perhaps he was just fed up with the whole sorry mess and had kept on riding for parts unknown. The thought no sooner entered Wes's head than he discarded it. Lon Hill wasn't a quitter. Once he started something, he finished it, and he wasn't the kind to turn his back on a friend. The more likely possibility was that he had fallen into the hands of the State Police. And if so, God have mercy on his soul. They would brand him a renegade black, traitor to the very cause that had freed him. Justice would be swift and harsh. A shot in the back or a rope strung over the nearest tree. Wes saw it happening, etched clearly in his mind's eye, and the sight of it made his stomach churn.

Lon Hill deserved better than that.

The young outlaw was suddenly jarred out of his funk by a sound. A horse moving through the thickets along his side of the river. But there was something out of kilter, not as it should be. He listened closer, straining to catch the rustling sounds. Then he stiffened and threw the blanket aside. There were two horses. And Lon Hill hadn't left with an extra mount.

Scrambling to his feet, he grabbed the shotgun and ducked around behind the buckboard. Quietly, one notch at a time, he earred back both hammers and rested the barrels across the rear wheel. The horses came nearer, and while he could see nothing in the inky darkness, the noise pinpointed his target. That was the edge a scattergun gave a man, and why he always had one close at hand these days. Even in the dark it was deadly accurate, chunking a murderous storm of buckshot some thirty yards or farther. Shifting slightly, he trained the small cannon directly on the approaching sounds.

"Hold your fire, boss! We're comin' in."

Wes felt such a surge of relief that his knees went weak. Then his temper flared and he jerked erect. "Goddamnit, Lon, why didn't you call out sooner? And what the hell business you got bringin' back a spare horse?"

"Quit your cussin', boy. Both these saddles is filled."

Dumbfounded, Wes stared into the darkness with his mouth open. The voice was unmistakable, but it took him a moment to collect his wits. "Uncle Barnett?"

"Who'd you expect—Abe Lincoln?"

He heard the creak of saddle leather, and saw shadowy forms dismounting from horses. Lowering the hammers on the shotgun, he laid it in the buckboard and walked forward. The shadows became indistinct blobs, and the sheer bulk of one made mistake all but impossible.

"Guess you kind of threw me." Wes fumbled for words, still a little taken aback. "I never figured Lon'd bring you back out here."

Barnett Hardin laughed and clapped a bristly paw over his shoulder. "Lon didn't bring nobody. I brung myself."

"That's sure 'nough right, boss." The black man's ivories flashed in the dark. "Mistuh Barnett wouldn't have it no other way. Jest pointed me toward the river and said—*GIT!*"

"Well, to tell you the truth, Uncle Barnett, I wish you hadn't come. Don't misunderstand. I'm glad to see you and all that. But if the Yankees catch you with me that'll be all she wrote."

"Don't fret yourself about me. Case you forgot, I was killin' bluebellies before you learned to quit pickin' your nose." The old man's head swiveled around and even in the dark he seemed to be frowning. "What the hell you mean sittin' around here without a fire? Gawd A'mighty, boy, don't you know you can catch your death that way?"

''Things like they are,'' Wes said, ''fires have a way of drawin' crowds. Lately most of 'em been wearin' a badge, too.''

''Horseapples! Them police got more sense than to be stumblin' around in the thickets on a night like this.'' Hardin turned to the black man. ''Lon, how 'bout rustlin' up a fire? Let's get this boy toasted a little on both sides and then we'll pour some of his aunt's special potion down him.''

''Yassuh! Have 'er ready in a jiffy.'' Hill went into his darky routine and shuffled off to gather wood. ''Lawdy me, I's glad you is here, Mistuh Barnett. He's been needin' the double whammy longer'n I can remember.''

Wes narrowed his eyes suspiciously. ''Just exactly what'd Aunt Bess send out here?''

''Why, I told you. It's her special potion.'' Hardin chuckled. ''Sort of a broth—yellowroot, fresh kidney, oak bark—cures whatever ails you. Builds up your blood and flushes you out all at the same time.''

The young outlaw groaned and sank down beside the buckboard. ''Meanin', if it don't kill you then you're pretty sure of survivin' whatever it was that ailed you to start with.''

The broth wasn't half bad, though. Presently, Lon Hill had a fire blazing, and after downing his aunt's magic remedy, Wes perked up considerably. Whether it was the curious-tasting broth, or simply having his chilled bones warm again, Wes didn't know and didn't really care. He was toasted to a crisp, pleasantly light-headed, and feeling no pain whatever. His only regret was that Bessie Hardin hadn't sent along a barrelful of the stuff. Even if it killed a man, at least he'd die happy.

After he'd finished, Wes glanced around the fire and gave the other men a dopey smile. ''Whatever it was, that was mighty fine. We ought to bottle it and make ourselves a fortune.''

Barnett Hardin just nodded, sucking on his pipe. Lon Hill hauled out the makings and started building himself a smoke. They exchanged glances and something unspoken passed between them. Several moments elapsed before the old man knocked the dottle from his pipe and looked up.

"Wes, I was talkin' things over with Lon, and the way we got it figured, you're about at the end of your string."

"The hell you say!" Wes slapped his knee and let go a goofy laugh. "I got lots of string left."

"Mebbe so. But if you don't get that hole plugged up decent, and stop flittin' around like a June bug, you're gonna have to unravel it six feet under."

"What're you talkin' about? I'm healthy as a horse."

"Sure you are. Any luck a'tall, you might last out the week."

"Your uncle's tellin' you right, boss." Hill lit his cigarette with a flaming stick, then let his gaze come level. "You got a leak that's gonna bleed you dry. And if that don't get you, the lung fever will." He gestured at the damp ground fog and the thickets surrounding them. "Man in your shape can't take it in a place like this."

"So what am I s'posed to do? Get the law to look the other way while I find myself a warm bed?"

"That's sort of what we had in mind." Hardin's lips were set in a grim line. "Leastways if we can get you to act sensible."

"Why hell, all us Hardins is sensible people." He gave them a glazed smile. "I thought everybody knowed that."

Barnett Hardin studied something in the fire for a moment. "Y'know, I got a good friend that's sheriff of Cherokee County. Fella name of Dick Reagan. He's a square shooter, and honest as sin."

"That a fact?"

"Yep. I was tellin' Lon about him. Said if we was to work it just right, Reagan would probably let you rest up in his jail."

Wes blinked and cocked one eye in a bemused scowl. "How's that again?"

"Well, it come to me, don't y'see, that Reagan's jail is a couple of counties away from here. Now, if we was to get him to hold you on some trumped-up charge and—"

"Whoa back!" Wes recoiled so hard he almost fell over. "That idea don't exactly touch my funny bone."

"Goddamn, lemme finish before you get your nose out of joint. Now, unless I heard wrong, you're wanted for a bunch of killin's down in Gonzales."

"What's that got to do with anything?"

"Suppose we was to have Reagan arrest you on some charge or other, and tell folks he was holdin' you for the Gonzales authorities." Hardin threw up his hand as the youngster started to interrupt. "Just hold your horses. That'd make it a county matter, wouldn't it? And the State Police couldn't touch you—ain't that right?"

"Hell, I guess so. I'm not no lawyer."

"Take my word for it. Now the other part is that Gonzales is a long ways off. And it could take them Gonzales lawmen a long time to hear that Dick Reagan is holdin' you for 'em. Maybe even a couple of weeks. Long enough, anyhow, for you to get yourself mended back together."

Hardin paused, and shot him a crafty look. "You startin' to get my drift?"

Wes digested it slowly, letting the words seep through his pleasant stupor. At last, he shook his head and grinned. "Maybe I'm crazy as a loon, but that's about the best sonovabitchin' idea I ever heard in my life."

The old man beamed and traded smiles with Lon Hill. "I thought you might like it."

"I only got one question."

"Ask me anything. Solomon couldn't hold a candle to me tonight."

"How much liquor did you put in that soup?"

"Hell, that weren't liquor, boy. It was white lightnin'. Double distilled and spiked with tarantula juice."

They all burst out laughing, and Barnett Hardin's belly shook like a great mound of jelly. While everyone was in a good mood he fed Wes some more broth, and before long the youngster's eyes took on the luster of polished stones. After a while he just sort of keeled over and commenced snoring loud enough to raise the dead. The old man and Lon

Hill swapped looks again, and a rare feeling of kinship settled over them.

It had been a good night's work.

5

The soft metallic whine of a hacksaw on iron was lost in
the mournful chorus of hounds baying at the sky. Obscured
by low-scudding clouds, the moon cast a dim glow over the
earth, and the town of Rusk slumbered peacefully in the brisk
autumn stillness. It was past midnight, time for all respectable people to be in bed, and the citizens of Rusk were nothing if not respectable. They slept on untroubled and
undisturbed, secure in the blissful serenity of those committed to the straight and narrow.

Like the town and its people, the jail lay becalmed beneath
a shadowed moon. The only sound was that of steel teeth
steadily devouring iron bars. Yet it was a small sound, not
unpleasant in its hungry drone. Through the thick oak door
of the cellblock the sound was muffled further still, and the
night deputy, dozing quietly in the front office, heard nothing.

The jail's single occupant, Cherokee County's most illustrious boarder, took care that the steely blade hummed
smoothly, without distraction or undue noise. There was
every reason that the jailbreak should appear convincing, the
work of a lone prisoner aided by unknown confederates.
While hardly respectable by local standards—the townspeople thought of him as a misguided rogue—Wes Hardin was
nonetheless an honorable man. He had been well fed and
fairly treated during his brief confinement, and he meant to
leave the lawmen of Cherokee County with their reputations
intact. In all fairness, he could do no less. They were genial
hosts, ever willing to accommodate an old friend, and embarrassing them would have made it awkward as well for
Barnett Hardin.

Through an arrangement between his uncle and Sheriff

Dick Reagan, the young outlaw had surrendered himself on the courthouse steps some two weeks back. Word of his capture spread rapidly throughout Rusk, and in that time he had been the object of considerable speculation among the townspeople. At first, curious citizens flocked to the jail in droves, hoping to catch a glimpse of Texas' most famous desperado. But as quickly as they crowded through the door they were turned away, left to gather on the street and stare expectantly at the cellblock window. Sheriff Reagan made it plain that his prisoner was not to be put on public display. Instead, he would be held quietly and safely until Gonzales authorities came to collect him on several outstanding murder warrants.

Still, despite Reagan's discreet and somewhat stingy announcements, news of the capture spread within the week to other counties. As expected, State Police descended on the jail like sharks scenting warm blood, demanding custody of the prisoner. Reagan politely, but firmly, refused. They were told of the Gonzales warrants and informed that only a higher court order could supersede outstanding murder charges. Promising to return, they stormed from the jail and rode off toward Austin. The sheriff merely smiled and went on about his business. Nor was his prisoner overly concerned. The wheels of justice ground finely, and with elections approaching, Austin would consider at length before interfering in county politics.

Thereafter, young Hardin virtually had the jail to himself. A local sawbones, the only outsider allowed to see him, came by every day, and while patching him back together pumped him for juicy tidbits to pass along to the townspeople. His cell was warm and clean, the grub he ate came from the best cafe in town, and the Ladies Temperance Society kept him supplied with plenty of interesting reading material. Sheriff Reagan allowed him to exercise in the cellblock corridor, and once, late at night, even sneaked Barnett Hardin in for a quick visit. All in all, Wes took to it like a starved dog trailing a gut wagon. In close to two months of running, it was the first time he'd really stopped to draw a deep breath.

Perhaps as much as a good rest, it also gave him time to

think. Stretched out in his bunk, hands locked behind his head, he stared at the ceiling and slowly dissected his life. Taken as a whole, it wasn't much to talk about. Except for Jane and the baby he had little or nothing to show for his efforts. The ranch was gone, and with it his dreams of leading a straight life. In less than two months he had killed three more men, bringing the total to something over twenty. The state and several counties were keenly interested in stretching his neck. There was no sanctuary in any of his old haunts. Not on the Brazos or with the Clementses, and certainly not with his folks. And unless things changed drastically, he might as well forget about any kind of life with his own wife and child.

What with one thing and another, it was about as sorry as sorry could get.

But he'd never been one to dwell on past miseries. After hashing it over, and mentally kicking himself in the rump a couple of times, he began casting around for a solution. Something safe, so he could have his family with him, and yet nothing sneaky or fainthearted, for he still had to live with himself. That was a tall order, a compromise of sorts, and for a while it put him in a royal quandary. Then, out of a clear blue, he happened to remember Dewitt County and the Taylors.

The moment he thought of it he cursed himself for having overlooked it before. The Taylors weren't Hardin stock, and they were none too civilized, but they were still kin. As near as he could recall, old Pitkin Taylor was his mother's first cousin, and in Texas that made for close blood ties. Somewhat like a tribe, the Taylors stuck close to one another, and after whelping several generations of offspring, their numbers comprised a small army. He recollected his father commenting on occasion that the Taylor clan pretty well ran things to suit themselves in Dewitt County. While that had meant nothing at the time, it might now mean the difference between living free or resuming his one-sided race with the State Police. A county where his own kin called the shots seemed made to order. Not unlike a blind hog stumbling over an acorn, he had found a nifty compromise to all his problems.

That very night he made arrangements for his escape.

And now, as the shrouded moon played hide-and-seek in the clouds, and the town dogs closed down their nightly serenade, he sawed through the last bar. Gently, he lifted it from the window and laid it on the bunk, alongside its three mates. The hacksaw was placed squarely on the pillow, where it would be found and later marveled over as the townspeople recounted assorted versions of the daring escape.

Dusting iron filings from his hands, he turned and gave the cell a last inspection. Then, satisfied that everything was in order, he scrambled up the wall and disappeared through the window.

Outside, he kept low, sticking to the shadows, and sprinted toward the back of the jail. When he rounded the corner it was just as he had expected. A reunion of sorts. Lon Hill sat astride a flashy roan and beside him was the grullo gelding. Without a word, Wes swung into the saddle and they calmly walked their horses to the edge of town. There, no longer concerned with attracting attention, they spurred hard and took off in a pounding lope. Behind, they left a rooster tail of dust and the blissful, if somewhat unsuspecting, citizens of Cherokee County.

An hour later they reined to a halt along the banks of the Neches River. Wes unstrapped the holstered Navy from the saddle horn and buckled it around his waist. Then he laughed, suddenly galvanized by the sweet smell of freedom, and slapped the black man across the shoulder.

"Lon, you're a ring-tailed stemwinder. Damned if you're not! I don't know but a couple of men I would've trusted to pull that off tonight, and by Jesus, your name heads the list."

In all the months they'd been together it was the first time this mercurial youngster had spoken to him with such openness. Confused, his heart hammering with pride, Hill retreated behind his darky patter. "Weren't nothin', boss. Jest done what you tol' me, that's all. Hardest part was waitin'.

Not knowin' how you and that saw was gettin' along.''

"Hell, that's what I'm talkin' about. Any peckerhead can let fling when things bust loose. It takes guts to wait and play your cards right. Most men haven't got the sand for it. Just eats 'em up alive.''

The black man ducked his head, faltering for words. A moment passed and then Wes again started to speak. But something in his voice had changed. It was sober, the lightness gone, somehow reluctant.

"Lon, I sort of stretched it a minute ago. There's not another man on earth I'd sooner have side me than you. For my money, you're the pick of the litter. But I guess we don't always get things the way we'd like 'em. What I'm buildin' up steam to get said is that this here's where we part trails.''

Hill's chin snapped up and his muddy eyes glinted in the moonlight. "That a fancy way of tellin' me to haul ass?''

"Nope, it's a fancy way of sayin' I like you better'n any man I ever rode with. White or black. You stick with me and you'll get yourself killed. I know you'd do it anyway, regardless, so it's me that has to cut the knot. I hate it worse'n anything I ever done, but that's the way she's got to be.''

The black man studied him a long while, then quickly looked away. "Funny thing. What you said about likin' me. Guess I always felt the same way and jest didn't know how to say it.''

"Wasn't any need to say it, Lon. You showed it. Hadn't been for you I'd be worm meat right now.''

"Lawdy me, lissen to that man carry on. Feel like I been dipped in goosebutter.''

"Yeah, but it's a fact, all the same. I owe you, and the way I got it figured, there's only one thing that'll square accounts.'' Wes paused and gestured on an angle away from the river. "You head due west till you hit the Brazos and then you just keep right on ridin'. When you come to the ranch, step down and hang your hat. It's yours. I don't know anyone this side of hell I'd rather see have it than you.''

Hill swallowed hard and had to clear his throat. "Mistuh Wes, I know how much that place means to you. If you ever gets a notion—"

"Don't sit around lookin' for me. I'm headed in another direction. You just go on back to catchin' horses. And somethin' else. Anybody gives you trouble about ownin' that place, you tell 'em to button their lip or Wes Hardin'll come out there and shoot their balls off."

"I'll tell 'em that very thing. Be like showin' a spook the holy cross."

The young outlaw stuck out his hand. "Walk soft."

Lon Hill gave him one last flash of ivory. "You sleep light."

Their parting was as simple as that. With a final squeeze their hands came unstuck and they wheeled their horses in opposite directions. The pale moonlight filtered down over the plains, and they were in sight for a long while. But neither man looked back. There was no need.

CHAPTER 7

1

Spring came early to Dewitt County that year. It brought new life to the prairie and death to the Taylor clan. Along the Guadalupe, as the earth sprouted tall grasses and wild flowers bloomed, time was measured not by date or calendar, but by the day certain men were killed.

Pitkin Taylor, patriarch of the clan, had been murdered in his own front yard. His sons-in-law, Bill and Henry Kelly, were callously gunned down after being captured and disarmed. In retaliation, Bill Taylor, the old man's son, blasted William Sutton in the poolroom shoot-out, but unaccountably failed to kill him. There the matter stood on April Fools' Day.

A grim joke inscribed in blood.

Yet there was no laughter in Dewitt County, and few men took solace in graveside humor. Least of all John Wesley Hardin. In a very real sense, he had bought chips in a game where everyone lost. The stakes were ashes to ashes and dust to dust; aside from a glowing eulogy and plenty of company, the players could expect little on their journey to the Promised Land.

The young outlaw and his family had arrived on the Guadalupe in early January. Their Christmas had been sparse, spent dodging around backcountry roads, and they entered Dewitt County only one step ahead of the law. But all pursuit stopped there, and for a brief time they rejoiced quietly. The

Taylors gave them haven, and not even the dread State Police dared challenge their kinsmen. It seemed, at last, that they were safe, in a world apart, where carpetbagger justice was a thing of the past, and men could again get on with the business of living.

Quite soon, though, the bubble burst. Their refuge proved an illusion, and in the light of day, reality was stark and cold and never more blunt. They had merely traded one enemy for another. And while at first it had seemed the lesser of two evils, in some ways the State Police were a catwalk compared to the dangers they now faced.

Not unlike many sections of Texas, where cattle was king, Dewitt County was in the midst of a power struggle. Since before the Civil War the Taylor clan had controlled the county, and run it much to suit themselves. But with the advent of carpetbagger rule times began to change. Certain elements in Dewitt County, led by William Sutton, aligned themselves with the Davis regime in Austin. Slowly, over a period of years, the Sutton faction had gained influence. At first their efforts to undermine the Taylors had been insidious, chipping away at the edges, just as a river at floodtide erodes and weakens the shoreline. Within the last year, though, their efforts had become bolder. And somewhat murderous, in a pragmatic, backwoods sort of way.

Still, those who knew William Sutton found nothing strange in that. For he was a pragmatic man, a firm believer in the old adage that the end justified the means. At stake was the land itself, the very foundation of power and wealth. Dewitt County, situated some seventy miles southeast of San Antonio, was split down the middle by the Guadalupe River. The Taylor clan's domain lay south of the river, and as the power struggle intensified, the Sutton forces came to control the lands north of the Guadalupe. Yet whoever had a hammerlock on county politics might well end up with control of both the river and the land. It was the classic battle of the haves against the have-nots. Cattle was king, but the cornerstones of that kingdom were water and graze. The stakes were monumental, and unlike man's lesser games, there were no rules.

Just last year, with an organized and well-financed campaign, the Sutton faction had gained control of several county offices. Perhaps their most critical victory was the election of Jack Helms to the post of sheriff. For Helms was a practical man, with all the moral conscience of a scorpion. He devoted himself not to causes but to the highest bidder. In this instance that happened to be the Sutton forces. And with the law behind him, William Sutton set in motion the oldest and most expedient of all power plays. He began murdering his opponents.

Several lesser members of the Taylor clan were killed first. Charged with rustling, they were taken captive by Helms' Vigilance Committee, and according to reports, gunned down while attempting to escape. Retribution was swift and decisive. Several Sutton men were bushwhacked with brutal efficiency. Obviously, stronger measures were needed, something closer to home. The Kelly brothers, married to Pitkin Taylor's eldest daughters, were run to earth and shot. The coroner's verdict was but another verse of an old song— killed while attempting to escape.

Yet the desired effect was not forthcoming. Instead of quaking submission, the Taylor clan bowed its neck and prepared to fight. Apparently still stronger medicine was needed, an object lesson that would destroy all will to resist. The patriarch himself, Pitkin Taylor, was lured from his house on a dark, moonless night and blown to kingdom come by several quarts of buckshot.

Again, the Sutton forces had misjudged their adversary. Bill Taylor, the old man's son, hadn't been shorted on grit. He marched into a billiard parlor the next night and accused William Sutton of murder. When the smoke cleared Sutton was badly wounded and Billy Taylor assumed leadership of the clan. But even as Taylor walked from the pool hall the name of the game changed.

The fight had become a feud.

As a spectator to the gathering storm, Wes Hardin felt a queer sense of being sucked along by forces beyond his control. Yet, for the first time in his life, he allowed himself to be drawn into somebody else's troubles. The Taylors had given him sanctuary—made a place for him and his family on their lands—and it wasn't an obligation to be shunted aside lightly. While it gave him an occasional fitless night, this idea of fighting another man's fight, he threw his support behind the Taylors all the same. And in Texas the support of John Wesley Hardin was a matter of no small consequence. His name was a household word, and unlike most outlaws, it was common knowledge that he had never resorted to murder or backshooting. This, coupled with the fact that he had killed more than twenty men, made him a formidable enemy.

The Sutton forces treated him with kid gloves, and since the day he rode into Dewitt County, they had never once attempted to brace him. Quite the contrary, Sheriff Helms had made several overtures of peace, suggesting that he remain neutral in the days ahead. Wes turned him down out of hand, and calmly went on about his business. He rode where he pleased, when he pleased, and it was plain he feared neither Sutton nor the Vigilance Committee.

Shortly after joining the Taylors, Wes had entered the cattle business. He had a family to support, and with the cow market at its peak, he saw a chance for quick gain. But he quickly discarded the idea of buying land and making another stab at ranching. The year on the Brazos had taught him much about the vagaries of life; he meant to wait and watch for a while before sinking roots. Instead of a rancher, he became a cattle buyer. After hiring a crew, he traveled around the county contracting ahead of season with various outfits. He offered the ranchers a fair price, thereby assuming the risk that the market would hold and he could later turn a profit. The cattlemen took to the idea readily, for it gave them a fair price on part of their herd and acted as a hedge against fluctuations in the summer market.

With spring, Wes and his crew began trailing small

bunches to holding pens at Cuero, the nearest railhead. From there the cows were freighted to Indianola, the closest port on the Gulf Coast, and then shipped to a contractor in New Orleans. As he'd suspected from the start, the venture turned a neat profit. The cattle market held strong throughout early April and it appeared he had drummed together a thriving little business. Though he was a speculator of sorts, the hazards entailed never bothered him. Life itself was a gamble, with shorter odds than poker or faro or chuck-a-luck, and cattle speculation seemed tame by comparison.

Some ten days after Bill Taylor shot William Sutton, Wes and his crew drove a small herd into Cuero. This was the last batch needed to round out a trainload; by late afternoon the holding pens were empty and the cattle cars packed with bawling cows. It was hot, dusty work—longhorns were contrary beasts and had an inborn fear of being hazed up loading chutes—the men were soaked with sweat and grime when the last door clanged shut. Wes felt parched, and he could almost taste the foam on a cool beer, but he still had affairs to conduct at the bank. After debating pleasure before business for a moment, he sent the crew on to a saloon and headed uptown toward the square.

Cuero was the county seat, and as with most country towns, the courthouse had been built in the center of the square. Wes cut across the courthouse lawn to the bank, and withdrew enough money to pay his crew and meet current expenses. Stuffing the money in his pocket, he retraced his steps and entered a saloon on the southwest corner of the square. While he gave it little thought at the moment, he was aware that Sheriff Jack Helms had watched him the entire time from a downstairs window in the courthouse. He considered Helms a four-flusher, all brag and no show, and promptly put the incident from his mind.

He found the crew bellied up to the bar and spent a few minutes settling accounts. Then he ordered a large schooner of beer and downed half of it in a long, thirsty gulp. He was still wiping foam off his mustache when the door swung open and Jed Morgan, a deputy sheriff, stepped inside. Normally he wouldn't have given the man a second glance. But coming on the heels of the Sutton shooting and the sheriff's undisguised interest in his movements, he was the least bit leery. Something about the man's bearing alerted him as well, a furtive look, as if a quick appraisal had just been made. He straightened and shifted the schooner to his left hand, watching Morgan from the corner of his eye.

The lawman walked to the bar, ordered a drink, and knocked it back in a single motion. Then he stood there a few moments, as if deliberating something, and beads of sweat popped out on his forehead. Finally he drew a deep breath and glanced over at the bartender.

"Guess you heard we're gonna clean them Taylors out."

Everybody in the saloon stopped talking at once. The barkeep went rigid, slewing a sideways look at Wes, but the young outlaw merely studied his beer with wooden detachment. Swallowing hard, as though he had something lodged in his throat, the deputy tried again.

"Them Taylors are a bunch of backshootin' sneaks anyway. We're just gonna give 'em what they deserve."

Wes smiled and carefully set his glass on the bar. "Morgan, you're so full of crap your breath stinks."

Silence in the room deepened to a turgid stillness, and the lawman flushed cherry red. Then he flicked a glance toward the back of the saloon and his backbone seemed to stiffen. He stepped away from the bar, hand on his gun, and turned.

"Hardin, you're under arrest."

Wes waited for the deputy's gun hand to move, then threw himself away from the bar, drawing and firing as he dropped to the floor. The slug caught Morgan just over the shirt pocket, above his badge, and he cartwheeled backward in a nerveless dance. Wes had hesitated only long enough to snap off the shot and then rolled sideways across the floor. Now he reversed himself, rolling backward a full turn, and came up on one elbow facing the rear of the saloon. A rifle barrel was suddenly withdrawn from outside and the back door slammed shut. He drilled two shots through the door, knowing it was wasted lead. The bushwhacker was off and running by now, but he wouldn't forget the splintering whine behind him an instant after he turned away. Next time he would be even shakier when he tried to backshoot somebody.

Uncoiling, Wes climbed to his feet and holstered the Navy. He slapped dust from his shirt and let his gaze drift around the room. Everybody but his own men suddenly got busy with their drinks, apparently unwilling to meet his stare. After a while his pale eyes settled on the bartender and he smiled.

"I got an idea the sheriff won't show up till I'm gone, so give him a message. Tell him I said it didn't work." The barkeep bobbed his head and Wes turned away. But as he neared the door, he stopped and looked back. "One more thing. Tell him if he comes lookin' for the Taylors I'll personally send him home in a box."

The young outlaw jerked his chin at the crew and strode from the saloon. The men trooped along behind him and outside they found a crowd gathered in the street, drawn by the sound of gunshots. Wes ignored them and walked toward the hitchrail. Their morbid curiosity irked him somehow, but as he stepped aboard the grullo, it came to him that they would soon have plenty to talk about.

Plainly the Vigilance Committee was set to raid the Taylors. Otherwise Morgan wouldn't have spouted off so strongly. But Helms had made a big mistake. In trying to weed out one fast gun, he hadn't just tipped his hand. He had pushed an outsider off the fence and made himself another enemy. For there was no longer any lingering doubt. Not so much as an iota.

All of a sudden it had become a very personal fight.

2

"Boys, I reckon it's time we faced facts."

Billy Taylor was tall and lean, with a ruddy face, eyes deeply socketed between high cheekbones and a big hawk-like nose. As he spoke a fiery glint appeared in his eyes, and

his head swung from side to side, studying faces around the
room. Upon hearing of Deputy Morgan's death he had acted
at once, calling the clan to a council of war in his parlor
shortly after supper. Men were jammed up back to the door,
filling every chair and lining the walls in a crush of hard,
sweaty bodies.

Down front were Taylor's three younger brothers, Jim,
John, and Scrap. Seated next to them was Wes, and beside
him, Jeff Hardin, a distant cousin who had drifted into Dewitt
County some months back. Off to one side were the Dixon
brothers, Bud and Tom, and with them, Bill Cunningham.
Standing behind the settee were the Andersons, James and
Ham, and their brother-in-law, Jim Milligan. All told some
twenty men had squeezed into the crackerbox room, and
while a few were missing, they comprised the Taylor clan.
Whether by blood or marriage, they were related in some
way, and south of the Guadalupe their word was law. Or had
been, at least, in years past.

Now, crowded together in a stifling parlor, their numbers
seemed pitifully inadequate for the task that lay ahead. Already they had lost nearly ten men, and not one among them
doubted that the toll would mount higher before the fight
was done. Yet, they came and they would fight, knowing in
advance that some were marked for death. They had no
choice, really. It had come down to sink or swim. And
whichever way it fell, they would go together. Old Pitkin
Taylor had drilled that into their heads relentlessly over the
years, and they had come to accept it as gospel truth. Divided, they were nothing. But if they stood together, strong
in their solidarity, the family could have anything it wanted.
Dewitt County, most especially.

At last, Billy Taylor finished his inspection. Since assuming the reins, this was the first time he had called them to
council, and they waited patiently to hear him speak. He was
the patriarch's eldest, the rightful leader of the Taylor clan,
but they would follow him only so long as he won. Though
unspoken, every man in the room knew it, and perhaps no
one sensed it so strongly as Billy Taylor himself. He drew a

deep breath and let it out between his teeth. Then, choosing his words carefully, he began to talk.

"Seems to me Wes Hardin is right. The fat's in the fire. Now, I don't know whether Sutton is pullin' the strings from his sickbed or whether Jack Helms just decided to go whole hog. But one thing is plumb certain. They mean to burn us down and run us out of the county. And they're not gonna be long in makin' their play."

Ham Anderson screwed up his face in a tight frown. "Billy, I'm not throwin' rocks, but it seems like somebody ought to say it before this goes too far. If Wes hadn't killed Jed Morgan we might've just sat tight and weathered this out. Fact is, there's some of us here that still thinks that way. If you was to go have a talk with Helms and—"

The young outlaw started out of his chair but Taylor motioned him down. This was the first challenge to his leadership, and if it was to be the last, Taylor had to handle it in his own way. "Ham, I'll slap the puddin' out of the next man that says anything against Wes. This fight's been buildin' for a long time, and him killin' Morgan don't mean a hill of beans. Helms was already set to raid us and the only choice we got is how we're gonna put a knot in his tail."

"Well, I'll tell you one thing," Jim Milligan snorted, "you shore sound like your daddy. If ol' Pitkin had been willin' to bend a little a few years back we wouldn't be in this fix now. The Sutton bunch is rared up and ready to fight 'cause that's the only way they can get us to budge a notch."

"Now, Jim, you and the Andersons listen to me real close." Taylor barked the words out, squinting hard at the three men. "My daddy fought to get this county and he kept it for better'n twenty years 'cause he was willin' to bust heads anytime somebody looked at him cross-eyed. And that's the only way we're gonna keep what we got left. Fight for it. Talkin' to the likes of Sutton and Helms won't get you nothin' but a quick buryin'. That's the way I see it and that's the way I'm gonna run things. Only one man can call the shots, and unless you fellas vote me out, I'm him. Savvy?"

Milligan and the Anderson brothers shifted uncomfortably, darting sheepish glances at one another. The other men remained silent for the most part, but a few nodded their heads in agreement, and everybody seemed satisfied with the way Taylor had handled the situation. After allowing several moments to pass, just to drive the point home, Taylor took up where he'd left off.

"Like I said, it's not a matter of whether we fight. The only question is how we go about it. I got some ideas of my own but I'd like to hear what you boys've got to say. Floor's open to anybody that wants to talk."

Ham Anderson stood up. Taylor stared at him a moment then nodded. Anderson glanced around at the group and it was clear from their expressions that they expected more talk of peace.

"If we've got to fight, then I say let's go about it the right way. I served under some good officers in the war, and they all stuck pretty close to the same rule of thumb. Protect what you got before you go after more. Where we're concerned, that means we got women and kids and horses and cattle to think about. Some way or other, we got to come up with a plan to protect that before we get itchy and go lookin' for a fight."

Bud Dixon grunted. "What the sam hill you talkin' about, Ham? Fortin' up or some such thing?"

"Be sort of hard to fort up all them cows," Anderson replied quietly. "No, what I'm talkin' about is sentries, or scouts. Whatever you want to call 'em. Patrols of some kind to give us warnin' whenever Helms and his bunch head our way."

"Great Gawd Jesus!" Tom Dixon crowed. "You got any idea what that'd mean? Hell, there's better'n thirty miles of river where they can cross anywhere it suits their fancy."

"Hold off a minute." Taylor threw up his hands as several men began talking at once. "Seems to me Ham's got a point. I grant you they could come through lots of places, but there's only three or four good fords. And that's where they'll most likely come through. If we had scouts watchin'

those spots, we'd get warnin' enough to spring a little surprise on Helms.''

The men wrestled with that for a while and it was finally
decided to place Ham Anderson in charge of the scouts. If
and when the alert was sounded everybody was to gather at
the Taylor house. Some talk developed as the best way to
meet such an attack and everyone in the room suddenly
turned into a general. At last, Wes Hardin climbed to his feet
and stood watching them until an uneasy-quiet settled over
the room. Then he turned and looked straight at Taylor.

''I've never fought in a war but I have come clear of a
few scrapes. Just listenin' to you fellows talk, it seems to me
we're barkin' up the wrong tree. Near as I recollect, fights
are generally won by the man that gets in the first lick and
keeps stompin' till it's all done with.''

''By golly, he's right!'' Jim Taylor jumped to his feet with
a shout. The four brothers were almost indistinguishable,
alike as peas in a pod, but Jim was the youngest, and by far
the loudest. ''Don't wait for 'em. Go get 'em!''

''My sentiments persactly,'' Bud Dixon chimed in from
over against the wall. ''I'd a heap sooner carry a fight to a
man than have him bring it to me.''

''Hogwash,'' Jim Milligan growled. ''At best we got
maybe thirty men. We'll be facin' twice that many, easy.''

''All the more reason to hit 'em first,'' Wes observed.
''Fast and hard. Clobber 'em good and get the hell out. Couple of shots like that and they'll call it quits.''

James Anderson cut the others off short. ''Wes, I gotta
say I think you're wrong. I served in the war, too, and believe
me, it was just plain suicide to try attackin' when you was
outnumbered two to one. Take my word for it, we'd get
chopped up in little pieces.''

''Yeah, but we're not fightin' a war,'' Wes countered.
''We've got our backs to the wall, and like as not, there'll
only be one battle. If we wait and let 'em come after us,
they'll gobble us up a piece at a time.''

Taylor broke in. ''Boys, you could hash that around all
night. Trouble is, you're overlookin' the big problem.

There's no way we can just haul off and attack the law. Not without stirrin' up a hornet's nest in Austin. We've got to let them start it and then figure out some way to finish it.'' He paused and looked around the room. ''Suppose we leave it at this. Until somethin' changes, we'll just sit tight and let them make the first move. After that it'll be dog eat dog and nobody'll be able to say we took the law in our own hands.''

Not everyone in the parlor was satisfied, but they were forced to admit that he had a point. None of them wanted the county overrun with State Police, and it could happen if they struck the first blow. A short while later the meeting was adjourned. Taylor had assigned men to Ham Anderson's scouts, and ticked off others to sound the alarm in case of attack. From there on out, he concluded, they would just have to play it by ear. Wes wasn't overly impressed with the tactics; he remained convinced that they were borrowing trouble by sitting back and waiting. But as he filed out the door it suddenly came to him that he should have kept his lip buttoned.

It was their fight. And they had a right to lose it any way that suited them.

3

Pitkin Taylor had built the main house to last. It was a rambling affair of log and stone, constructed to withstand the ravages of time and the elements. For a site he had selected a majestic grove of live oaks on a slight knoll, commanding a view of the shimmering prairie in all directions. The house had weathered well, surviving Indian raids, blue howlers hurtling down out of the wintry north, and coastal squalls that sometimes swept far inland. As the years passed, and his sons married, the old man built other houses nearby. Wedding presents, he called the smaller houses, though everyone was painfully aware that he wanted only to keep his sons close at hand. Or under thumb, according to men like the Andersons and Jim Milligan, who sometimes thought for themselves.

Still, if Pitkin Taylor had been a tyrant of sorts, there was never any question of his generosity. Three sons married—Billy, John, and Scrap—and three houses complete with furnishings. Only Jim, spoiled and unruly, remained in the big house. But the grove of stately oaks was not merely for living. It was also a place of work. As outbuildings sprouted around the base of the knoll, it became a complex of rough-hewn structures resembling a small town. There were corrals and barns, several bunkhouses, and a scattering of pens and sheds thrown up as the need arose. From a distance it looked like a handful of dice sprinkled haphazardly across the earth, but up close there was something foreboding about it, as if it had need of nothing save itself, and those who rode in unasked did so at their own risk. And in truth, except for Indians, the Taylor compound had never been threatened by an outside force. Until that night the bushwhackers left Pitkin Taylor riddled with buckshot.

Now, the Taylor ranch was inviolate no longer. Men of greed and ambition were even then mounting an attack. What Pitkin Taylor had built over a lifetime, a legacy to his sons and their sons after them, was in danger of being destroyed in a single night. There was a somber air to the compound. Lamps had been turned low and the laughter of children was curiously missing. Men stuck close to home, near their families, and the bunkhouses were unusually quiet. Oddly, not a single dog had barked since sundown, as if in some brutish way they had been spooked by fears beyond their ken. For fear was thick, like a noxious mist, and those men who slept at all slept lightly, with their guns never far out of reach.

Like the others, Wes felt the growing tension and he was in a skittish mood. Waiting curried him the wrong way, and given a choice, he would have ridden on the Sutton forces that very night. Still, the decision had been made and he was willing to follow Taylor's lead. For the moment anyway. If a hitch developed then he'd shuffle and see about dealing new cards all around.

Seated on a porch step, gazing out over the compound, it occurred to him that he owed Taylor the chance to make his own mistakes. The house he and Jane were living in had been Taylor's, and they had it to themselves because of his openhanded nature. After the old man's murder Taylor had moved into the big house, and despite grumbling from certain quarters, he had given the Hardins his own home. Which suited Wes just fine. There was too much commotion in the big house, people coming and going at all hours, and he much preferred to be off by himself. Besides, what with Jane expecting again, it had worked out better all the way around. She got a little snippy when she was in a family way, and had never felt at ease with the gang of women constantly swarming through the big house.

Overhead a shooting star flashed through the sky and he watched it fizzle out in a silvery streamer. Out of nowhere came the thought that people played out their lives in much the same manner. A brief spurt, snatching at the goodies and hollering to beat the band, and then it was all over. They hadn't accomplished much—except to whelp a bunch of kids and make fools of themselves—and when it was done with there wasn't much left to show. Just a few teary-eyed mourners and a headstone with some nitwit inscription a man wouldn't rightly have picked out for himself. The hell of it was, most folks didn't know any better. They went out thinking they'd really left their mark on things. In spades.

Suddenly it struck him that he was being mighty goddamn pompous. Anybody with a half brain would see that he hadn't made any great shakes of his own life. He had a wife and a family, which took care of the whelping department. Then he had a good horse and a few thousand dollars in gold. Other than that, he didn't have much more than the clothes on his back. Not a square foot of land or a house or the first stick of furniture. Matter of fact, the roof over his head had been built by someone else and he was sleeping in another man's bed. Which sort of put him to rowing the same boat as the nincompoops he'd just been sneering at.

He grunted sardonically and a mocking chuckle rumbled

up out of his gut. Yessir. He had a lot of room to talk.

"Must be awfully funny."

Wes craned around and saw Jane standing in the doorway. The lamp inside silhouetted her figure, outlining the barest hint of what he hoped would be a son. She was some months away from being ungainly, but the thought of what was to come had put her out of sorts lately. Not unlike most attractive women, she disliked losing her looks, and absolutely despised waddling around like a clumsy she-bear. Still, she'd wanted lots of babies, and she damn sure couldn't blame him for being accommodating. Besides which, he kind of liked it when her belly was big and round and her face filled out. Gave her a nice rosy glow, all flushed and apple-ripe, that she didn't have other times.

"Lady, don't you know it's not polite to eavesdrop?"

"Not on your husband, it's not." She came out of the house and sat beside him on the step. "I even listen when you talk in your sleep."

"Judas Priest! Just ain't no privacy anywhere, is there?"

"Well, how else is a woman to learn? You big hairy men walk around like you had lockjaw all the time. Besides, I find out some very interesting things that way."

"Yeah. Like what for instance?"

She smiled and flashed a mischievous look. "I'll never tell. But you don't have as many secrets as you thought you did. That's for sure."

Her light mood both surprised and pleased him. The last couple of weeks she had been cross and mighty hard to live with. He put an arm around her shoulders and drew her closer. "Woman, why don't you quit walkin' around in a man's mind? Like I said, it's not polite."

"You still haven't told me."

"Told you what?"

"What tickled your funny bone a minute ago."

"That? Wasn't nothin' at all. Just ruminatin'."

"Wes Hardin, don't you dare pull that lockjaw stunt again. Ruminating about what?"

His tailbone suddenly felt as though it was spiked to the

porch, and he found himself faltering for words. "Awww, hell, honey, it wasn't nothin'. Honest. I was just thinkin' about people and how most of 'em sort of piddle around trying to make something of their lives."

"And?"

"What do you mean *and?*" he demanded. "That's what I was thinkin'."

"There you go again. Shutting me out." She arched her head back like a schoolmarm and gave him a quizzical little frown. "There was more to it than that. Now, be truthful. Wasn't there?"

Sometimes he thought he never would understand women. Especially when they were in a family way. Seemed as if their brains took curiosity, then multiplied it by nosiness, and somehow came up with a wife's right to know. It left a man damn little privacy, and even less peace of mind.

"Well, if it's that al'fired important, I was thinkin' that most folks go to their graves never havin' done half of what they set out to do. Then I chewed that over a little more, and much as I hate to admit it, I guess I couldn't say much better of myself."

"What a horrible thing to say!" She was positively indignant. "You've done lots of worthwhile things."

"Yeah? Name me a couple."

"Why, you've built a ranch—"

"And lost it."

"—and made a pile of money."

"And spent it."

"Oh, Wes, stop mocking me. Good Lord, you're barely twenty. You've already accomplished more than some men twice your age."

"Sure have. Livin' off my kin. Can't even give my family a house of their own. Just a regular ball of fire."

Jane caught her breath, then snuggled closer and buried her head against his chest. "Sugar, it scares me when you talk like that. It's not like you. And I'm scared enough already without having a stranger in my bed."

His hand came up, stroking her hair, and he gave her a

gentle squeeze. "What kind of foolishness is that? There's nothin' for you to be scared about."

"It isn't either foolishness. And you know it very well."

"You're talkin' riddles. What d'you mean?"

"I mean the man you killed today. And all those other men. There's just no end to it."

"Janey, lemme tell you somethin'." His words were soft, almost inaudible, so quiet she had to strain to hear. "I never in my life killed a man that wasn't tryin' to kill me. Don't you know that?"

She sniffed and poked him in the ribs. "Wes Hardin, you're thick as a rock sometimes. That's what I'm talking about. All these men trying to kill you. The State Police and now you've taken sides in the Taylors' fight. Where does it stop?"

"Gawd A'mighty!" He'd finally caught the clue. "You're not worryin' yourself silly thinkin' somebody's gonna put me under?"

"Of course I am, you big ninny!" She jerked away from him. "I have a baby in my arms and another one on the way and half the men in Texas want to kill my husband. And you have the gall to sit there and tell me I shouldn't worry. You're—oh, damn! I don't know what you are."

"Quit sputterin' and listen a minute." He pulled her back into his arms and hugged her tight. "There's nothin' gonna happen to me. That's a natural-born fact, and you can bank on it."

She turned her head up, entreating him with her eyes. "Promise?"

"Take my word on it." His voice went husky and something odd happened to his face. "The man ain't been born that can punch my ticket."

"God, I pray not, Wes. Every night I pray that."

"Then you can quit worryin'. Looks like somebody's listenin'."

High overhead a star fell from the heavens and rocketed earthward. Then the sky settled once more into velvety darkness and the winking stars were like a zillion eyes staring down at them. Drawing her close, Wes closed his mind to all but the inky sky and the woman and the little cameo doll that slept inside.

It was enough. Let tomorrow worry about itself.

4

A scout rode in on a lathered horse early the next evening. The Sutton forces, some fifty men strong and led by Sheriff Helms, were headed toward the Guadalupe. Under stiff questioning by Taylor, it came out that Ham Anderson had sent men snooping around Cuero. Toward sundown the vigilantes began gathering in front of the courthouse and there was little doubt as to their purpose. The scouts raced back to the river, informing Anderson, and he in turn sent riders fanning out across the southern half of the county to sound the alarm. However much he resented Anderson's casual disregard of orders, Billy Taylor could hardly fault the man. It was a shrewd move, and because of it, the Taylor faction had gained a couple of precious hours.

Shortly after nightfall the clan began pouring into the compound, and by full dark close to thirty men were formed in a loose knot before the steps of the big house. They were armed to the teeth, many of them carrying the new repeating Winchesters, and spoiling for a fight. Young Hardin still favored the shotgun for hunting men, but he was packing a .45 Colt Peacemaker. Just on a whim he'd bought the pistol earlier in the year in Indianola. It was the latest model, firing cartridges instead of cap and ball. Yet, for all its advantages, he had never used it. The battered old Navy rested squarely on his right hip, and the Peacemaker was stuck in the waistband of his trousers. He'd brought it along as something in reserve, and from all reports, he had picked the right night. It promised to be a fight where a backup gun would come in mighty handy indeed.

The men were talking in low tones, speculating on what they faced, when Billy Taylor walked out of the house. He stopped at the edge of the porch, grim-faced and watchful, waiting for the murmured conversation to slack off. After the men fell silent, he waited a moment longer, then cleared his throat.

"Boys, I guess you've all heard what's headed our way. Last time we met I told you I had some ideas of my own about how to handle this. I've give it lots of thought since then and I'm still convinced it'll work."

He paused and gestured out over the compound. "It stands to reason they'll hit this place first. If they burn us out here then the waltz is pretty well done with. But there's one thing they didn't count on. This whole hill is ringed with buildings of one sort or another. That makes it real easy to defend. I figure if we put men in ever' building, and give 'em a hot welcome, they'll play holy hell bustin' through. After a couple of blasts right up their nose, I got an idea they'll take off like scalded dogs."

There was a moment of silence while the men digested that. The porch lantern cast a dim glow out over their ranks, and it was apparent that many of them were having a hard time swallowing Taylor's plan. Considerable grumbling broke out, and several men muttered outright disagreement. Finally, James Anderson stepped forward.

"Bill, I hate to be the one to say it, but I don't think your idea'll work. First off, we got too few men as it is. You stick 'em off in them buildin's and we're gonna be spread mighty thin. If Helms was to keep his bunch all together, and charge one spot, they'd bust through this defense of yours like a hot knife cuttin' through butter. Then they would be behind us and we'd find ourselves in some fix."

A hoarse murmur swept back over the men, but Anderson motioned for quiet. "Now, lemme finish, then anybody that wants can have his say. There's another thing Helms could do and that worries me even more. Bill, just suppose we greet 'em with lead like you was talkin' about and they back off. You think they're gonna call it quits and ride on back to town? Not by a damn sight they won't. They'll just ride off and put the torch to ever' house south of here. And we'll be

sittin' on our butts back here watchin' 'em do it. Now I grant
you, that'd save this place. But it'd sure play hob with the
rest of us. We'd get home and not find nothin' but a pile of
ashes.''

Before anyone could get his jaws unlocked, Wes Hardin
stepped out of the crowd. He walked to the bottom step and
looked up at Taylor. "I owe you a lot, Billy, and I don't like
causin' you grief. But I agree with Anderson. Only for a
different reason. It just don't make sense to fight that bunch
where we got women and kids to worry about. If they ever
busted through and got up here our families wouldn't stand
a chance. I'm still of the notion that we ought to ride out
and meet 'em somewhere. Ambush 'em maybe. Like I said
before, take the fight to them and hurt 'em bad.''

A moment elapsed while the two men stared at one another, and then the young outlaw's gaze went hard as flint.
"You know I'm not a quitter, and I'm willin' to oblige any
man here that thinks different. But I won't take a chance on
my wife and baby gettin' caught slambang in the middle of
a shoot-out. If you can't see your way clear to fightin' Helms
somewhere else, then I don't have no choice but to pull out.
I'd sooner back your play and have this thing done with, but
that's up to you.''

Bud Dixon and Jim Taylor stepped forward flanking Wes.
Dixon pulled himself up straight and squared his shoulders.
"Billy, none of us wants to go against you, but it 'pears to
me Wes is talkin' sense.''

Young Taylor bobbed his chin. "And Jim Anderson, too.
You're my brother, and I wouldn't cross you for the world,
but it ain't fair to ask these fellas to protect our place while
their own gets burned to the ground.''

Billy Taylor's ruddy face paled and little knots bunched
tight at the back of his jaws. He stood there for a long time,
staring at the four men who had stepped forward, and the
still night seemed charged with tension. At last, he let go a
deep breath and looked out across the waiting crowd.

"What do the rest of you boys say? You of the same
mind?''

Aside from the other Taylor brothers, none of the men could meet his gaze. They ducked their heads, hawked and spat, and looked everywhere except at the tall man on the porch. Quite plainly, they had swung over to Anderson and Hardin. But they couldn't bring themselves to tell Pitkin Taylor's eldest son that he'd already been outvoted.

After a while Taylor shrugged and made a chopping motion with his hand. "That's answer enough, I guess. Put it to a vote and pick yourselves a new ramrod. But don't fiddle around. We stand here runnin' our gums much longer and Helms will be lookin' down our throats."

The men all started yammering at once, but Wes suddenly jumped up on the steps and faced them. "Hold your horses! Just slow down a minute and listen." Taken by surprise, they fell silent and stared back at him in mild puzzlement. "Now I'm sort of a Johnny-come-lately around here. And I reckon most of you figure it's not up to me to commence preachin', but I'm gonna speak my piece just the same, and I'll make it sweet and short. Any man that can admit he's wrong has got lots of sand. Leastways he does in my book. Seems to me Billy is the best man to lead this outfit, and to my way of thinkin', he deserves the chance. Hell's bells, how's a man gonna get to be a general if he don't get his feet wet? And besides, now that I take a closer look, I don't see no Stonewall Jacksons among you, anyhow."

The lantern sputtered and the men stood there gawking at him for a couple of seconds, baffled that he had switched horses in midstream. Wes was a little confused himself, but his feeling was genuine. He somehow sensed that Taylor had the stuff to make a good leader if given the chance to prove himself. All of a sudden someone at the back of the crowd let go with a snorty chuckle.

"Looks to me like there ain't no Robert E. Lees here, neither."

Everyone broke up laughing and the tension drained away, restoring their spirit of solidarity. Soon they got down to the real problem—where to jump the vigilantes—and began batting various schemes back and forth. All of them knew the countryside in the way of men born to the land, and a lively discussion evolved as the best place for an ambush. Then, quite unexpectedly, Ham Anderson rode in and stepped down from a jaded horse. His message needed no elaboration. Helms and the vigilantes were headed south along the Yorkstown Road.

And that put an end to the debate. Every man in the group was thinking of the same spot. The perfect place to throw a surprise party.

Tomlinson Creek.

Less than an hour later Billy Taylor had his men spread out along the south bank of the creek. The night was dark, with ghostly patches where starlight filtered down through the trees. Taylor had chosen well, selecting a site that afforded both cover and a clear field of fire. The men were hidden behind massive cottonwoods, far back in the shadows; he had positioned them on angles, two men to a tree, so that on signal their fire could be directed to the exact center of the creek. Across the stream there was a small clearing in the woods, where the road sloped down to the ford. Both the stream and the clearing shimmered faintly in a soft haze of starglow. Any movement toward the crossing, could be seen. And a man on horseback—or a whole gaggle of horsemen— would stick out like a parade of elephants.

Wes had been assigned a choice spot. Beside the road, not ten yards from the ford, where his shotgun would do the most damage. He stood with his back to a tree, loose and easy, with just the slightest tingle dancing over his nerve ends. It was a feeling he knew well, an old companion. A sign that he was alert and ready and keyed to just the right pitch. On the other side of the tree, Jim Taylor was squatted down on one knee, rifle butt resting against his hip. Directly across the road, screened by a cottonwood, Billy Taylor had his eyes glued on the dimly lighted clearing.

Nothing moved and the sounds of the night went undisturbed.

Their wait was prolonged only a short while. Hoofbeats drifted in on a faint breeze and then the earth quivered under the thudding rhythmic pace of animals moving at a steady gait. One moment the clearing stood empty, a silvery blur, and in the next a solid wedge of horsemen materialized out of the night. They came on at a fast walk, unsuspecting and careless, bunching up where the road sloped off to meet the creek. When they hit the center of the ford, water splashing up around their stirrups, Billy Taylor edged out from behind the tree.

"Surrender or get your heads blowed off!"

The lead rider reached for his gun and Wes blasted him out of the saddle. Others screamed and clutched at wounds as the double load of buckshot whistled through their ranks like snarling hornets. Their horses went berserk, wheeling and bucking, as the night came alive with the orangy splat of rifle fire. Wes flung the shotgun aside and jerked his Navy, amazed that some of the vigilantes were actually firing back. He thumbed off three shots in a blinding roar, and then froze as the Navy snapped on a dead cap. Just for a moment he couldn't believe it—the Navy had misfied—but his stupor lasted only an instant. He dropped the gun, cursing savagely, and pulled the Peacemaker from his waistband. As he earred the hammer back, he saw another rider topple over and splash headlong into the creek. Then, maddened with fear, the vigilantes somehow got themselves unscrambled and spurred back the way they had come.

Stepping clear of the tree, Wes emptied the Peacemaker in a spitting, staccato bark. Around him, the drum of rifle fire increased at a steady beat, but so far as he could tell none of the riders were hit. Suddenly, like specters on horseback, the vigilantes simply vanished into the woods and were gone. An eerie silence settled over the clearing, and along the tree line a dense cloud of gunsmoke hung still for a moment, then scudded away on the breeze. Men appeared all up and down the creek bank, staring quietly across the stream. It had happened so fast—the rout was so complete—

that they could scarcely believe it. Words seemed inadequate, somehow wanting, and so they said nothing. They just stared, dazed and vastly relieved.

But Wes Hardin shared none of their wonder. Nor did he feel any sense of relief. In fact, he was angry, and just the least bit unnerved. An old friend had betrayed him. And under less favorable circumstances might easily have gotten him killed. Still cursing, he gave the Navy a sharp kick and watched as it hit the creek and sank to the bottom.

Then he hefted the Peacemaker, smiling, and calmly reloaded it.

5

The fight at Tomlinson Creek was hardly decisive. Helms's vigilantes left behind two dead, and according to word from town, several had been wounded. Curiously enough, most of the casualties were suffering from buckshot wounds, but the *Cuero Eagle* reported that none of them were expected to die. Yet, in some small way, it was a victory for the Taylor clan. They had driven the Sutton forces from their land, and not one of their own had received so much as a scratch.

There was considerable rejoicing among the womenfolk, and some talk that the victory might at last put an end to the feud. However much they wished it were true, wiser heads knew different. William Sutton, though still confined to bed, was not a man so easily dissuaded. Ham Anderson observed that the vigilantes were like a rattler. It remained dangerous until somebody cut off its head. And the feud would end when Sutton was dead. Not before.

But if their victory had a hollow ring, the Taylors at least had themselves a ring-tailed bravo to admire. Wes Hardin not only had real grit, he also had something between his ears besides mush. From the beginning, he alone had counseled the wisdom of an ambush, and while it hadn't been a spectacular success, it had damn well put the vigilantes to rout. Over and above that, tales began circulating about his deadliness in a fight. Even in the heat of battle men had seen him step from behind the tree, opening the fight with a double load of buckshot and then coolly emptying his revolvers into the massed riders. And all the time slugs whistling about his head and thunking into the tree at his shoulder. There were no longer any skeptics among them. Everything they had heard about young Hardin—the twenty-odd men he'd killed and his ice-cold nerves—was the straight goods. He was a slick article, sharp as a tack and deadly to boot, and they took immense pride in knowing he was on their side.

For his part, West hardly seemed to notice the change in attitude, the way everybody had commenced buttering up to him. Though he accepted their version of the fight, he had no recollection whatever of slugs chunking around him. He remembered firing and cursing the Navy and the heavy rattle of rifle fire. And in looking back, he remembered that those rifles, some thirty strong, had killed only one man. It was a chilling thought, and one he wouldn't soon forget. If a man wanted to go on breathing, particularly in a shoot-out at night, he was well advised to keep a shotgun close to hand.

All in all, it came as no surprise when Wes announced two days after the fight that he was going into town. Nor was anyone overly shocked that he meant to go alone. It merely confirmed what they had seen on the banks of Tomlinson Creek. The youngster had more guts than a three-legged bulldog.

Billy Taylor tried to argue him out of it and Jane pitched a fit that could be heard clear across the compound. But his mind was set and he wouldn't budge. He had business to conduct and the likes of Jack Helms was no reason to avoid Cuero. Matter of fact, he observed dryly, it was all the more reason to ride into town bold as brass. If backshooters ever thought they'd run a sandy on a man, there'd be no end to it. Better to let them know right from the start. Anybody who tried any monkey business was fair game. And deserved whatever he got.

Down the road a piece, Wes heard hoofbeats coming on

fast and reined up. Jim Taylor appeared a couple of moments later, fogging it at a dead gallop, and slid his horse to a halt. He had a big, toothy grin plastered across his face and looked as though he had just swallowed a canary.

"Thought I'd ride along with you." His eyes glittered with excitement. "Few things I need from town."

"Yeah?" Wes gave him a slow up-and-down scrutiny. "What's that?"

The question flustered him, but Taylor dismissed it with an idle gesture. "Oh, y'know. Tobacco and rollin' papers and stuff like that. Just little things."

"Stuff that just wouldn't wait, huh?" Wes studied him a moment longer, then smiled. "Billy know you tagged along after me?"

"Aw, hell's fire, Wes, I'm full-growed. Billy don't have to wipe my nose."

Which was true, after a fashion. Though three years younger than his cousin, Jim Taylor pulled his own weight and did a man's work. Thinking back to earlier days, Wes had to admit that the boy had a point. Every man was entitled to get his nose bloodied whichever way it suited him. And if he needed permission, then he wasn't big enough to try.

Wes reined the grullo north, toward town. "Glad to have the company."

Taylor brightened and pulled alongside. "Think there'll be any trouble in town?"

"Not unless somebody else starts it. Why, you lookin' for trouble?"

"Not me! Just askin', that's all." The boy's reply was overdrawn, a little too guileless. They rode in silence for a while, though it was obvious Taylor had something on his mind. Finally, clearing his throat, he worked up the nerve to spit it out. "Y'know, I got a confession to make. The fight at the creek the other night? That was the first time in my whole life I fired a gun at another man."

Wes gave him a sidewise glance, holding back hard on a smile. "That a fact? Well, you could've fooled me. I thought you did real good."

"You did—honest?" Taylor perked up and his chest swelled a couple of notches. "Cripes, I didn't even know you was watchin'. Tell you the truth, I was so scared I don't hardly recollect much of anything."

"Nothin' wrong with that. Plumb natural."

"Aw, c'mon. You wasn't scared. Not the way you was slingin' lead."

Wes smiled cryptically. "You think Ham Anderson's right? That this thing won't end till Sutton's been planted?"

Taylor was young but he was no fool. He took the hint, and set aside the string of questions he wanted to ask about gunfighting. "Can't see how it'd end any other way. Leastways, according' to Billy, Helms don't hardly take a leak less he checks with Sutton first."

"Yeah, that was sort of the impression I got. Too bad Billy didn't finish him off when he had the chance."

"Cripes, Wes, Sutton was down and bleedin' like a stuck pig. Billy couldn't hardly shoot him again. I mean—well, hell—it'd almost be like murder."

"Hadn't Sutton tried to shoot him?"

"Sure he did. Billy cussed him out so bad he had to draw."

Wes stared straight ahead, revealing nothing. "All the more reason Billy should have finished him. If there's cause to shoot a man, then there's cause to kill him. However it's gotta be done. Leave him alive and you wind up lookin' over your shoulder the rest of your life."

Jim Taylor started to say something but it clogged down in his wind pipe. What he'd just heard sent a chill rippling up his spine. But it made a hell of a lot of sense. So much so that only a lame brain would argue otherwise.

It was the real article. Straight from the horse's mouth.

They rode into Cuero shortly after the noon hour. The grullo needed to be shod, which was one reason for the trip to town, and their first stop was at the blacksmith's shop. Taylor wanted some odds and ends from the mercantile, so they separated at the northeast corner of the square. Crossing the street, with one eye glued on the courthouse, Wes strolled off toward the bank. Unlike the last time he was here, the sheriff wasn't gawking at him from the office window. But he had the feeling of being watched all the same. Some enterprising citizen would spot him and scurry off to inform the sheriff. Of that, he had no doubt whatever. Still, it didn't trouble him one way or the other. He had legitimate business here, and them that didn't like it could damn well lump it. Or try something stupid, if they were feeling lucky and right with God.

Whistling a cheery refrain from "The Old Rugged Cross," he entered the bank feeling cocky and light on his feet. Twenty minutes later, with the institution's flabbergasted president trailing him to the door, he walked out about thirty pounds heavier. In the money belt around his waist was five hundred dollars in gold and three letters of credit totaling nearly four thousand.

Headed back the way he'd come, his conviction remained strong that it was a wise move. And none too soon, either. The feud with Sutton had only just begun, and as any fool knew, it was always darkest before the storm. The way things were shaping up it was going to get a hell of a lot worse. And there looked to be a long dry spell before it got better. Which seemed ample reason to have his money out of the People's Bank of Cuero. Chances were better than even that he wouldn't have another opportunity anytime soon. If ever.

Feeling pretty smug, and just the least bit foxy, he set a brisk pace along the block east of the square. But as he came around the corner his cockiness went numb as an icicle and he slammed to a halt. The blacksmith shop was on the other side of the street, in the middle of the block, and in front of it stood Jack Helms. There was a gun in his hand and he had it pointed at something inside the smithy. Wes had a moment of gut-wrenching fear, a dead certainty that the lawman was only an instant away from killing Jim Taylor.

"Helms!"

The sheriff's head jerked around at the sharp cry, and he blanched, staring wide-eyed with terror at the young outlaw.

Then he spun, clumsily setting himself in a crouch, and brought the gun to bear. But his hand shook so violently that he couldn't align the sights, and he quickly brought his other hand up to steady the pistol.

Under different circumstances Wes would have laughed. It was a bumbling performance. All the same, Helms's intent was real enough, and in that he found nothing amusing. The Peacemaker was already out and cocked, and as he squeezed the trigger a gusher of red blossomed just above the sheriff's belt buckle. Aiming higher, he stitched a row of bright little dots straight up Helms's shirtfront. The big slugs jolted the lawman back a step at a time, like a puppet with his strings gone haywire. The last one caught him in the brisket, splattering bone and gore with the impact of a thunderbolt, and he went down in a jarring, head-over-heels somersault.

Jim Taylor ran from the smithy, his face wild and crazed. He halted, towering over Helms, and the body suddenly twitched in a final spasm of death. Unnerved, past caring that the man was dead, Taylor's reaction was one of sheer reflex. The gun in his hand came up and he methodically emptied it into Jack Helms's head.

Hurrying forward, Wes tried to call out, but the words wouldn't come. The act was so fundamental that its savagery spoke eloquently enough. When a man goes down make sure he stays there for keeps. And green as he was, the kid had taken the message to heart.

Jack Helms would rise no more.

CHAPTER 8

1

Peace of sorts had come to Dewitt County. Though the Sutton-Taylor feud flared sporadically the balance of '73, neither party seemed anxious for another full-scale battle. Instead they went back to bushwhacking one another, engaging in a prolonged if indecisive campaign of attrition.

With Jack Helms dead and William Sutton once again on his feet, the feud settled into a slow and deadly chess game, one in which the players painstakingly stalked each other, patiently awaiting the day that time and circumstance might sandbag the odds. Both sides hoped to whittle the other down, seemingly satisfied to destroy their enemies piecemeal rather than in a body. While there were long stretches of calm, there were also isolated spurts of violence, and those who sacrificed their lives rarely had any warning. They were simply murdered. Quickly, efficiently, and in ways that could never be traced.

A Taylor man was shot to death outside the Yorkstown general store. Another was picked off while hunting strays in a remote section of brush. One of Sutton's men was gunned down on a dark night as he made a final trip to the privy. And Sutton himself was ambushed twice. Both times his horse was shot from beneath him, and by whatever quirks that guide men's lives, he escaped injury. Curiously, there were no witnesses to the shootings. Like the three wise monkeys, the citizens of Dewitt County neither saw nor heard nor spoke. They merely watched and waited, content with the role of spectators. On the strength of this silence they bought the privilege to go on breathing. And if they kept quiet long enough, it seemed not unlikely that they would outlive the men who savaged one another in the struggle for power.

Shortly after New Year's, though, some of the more influential citizens came down off the fence. However misguided, they felt there was a genuine chance for peace. Secret meetings were arranged between William Sutton and Billy Taylor, and articles of truce were actually signed in the county courthouse. But the armistice was short-lived, if not stillborn. A spate of killings erupted and things went back to normal. Once again it became dog eat dog, and devil take the hindmost.

Throughout the winter Wes rode the countryside unmolested. Apparently the Sutton forces wanted no part of the brash young outlaw; he came and went as he pleased. Working both sides of the Guadalupe, he called on ranchers scattered across the county, again dickering ahead of time and allowing them to hedge against market fluctuations. Since spring roundup began early in southern Texas, he contracted for cattle to be delivered commencing in March and extending throughout the summer. But he rarely rode into Cuero except on urgent business, and even then, he never went alone.

Murder warrants were outstanding on Wes for killings of both Sheriff Jack Helms and Deputy Jed Morgan. Successors to the dead lawmen, appointed to fill their abruptly vacated terms, were deliberate rather than rash. They studiously avoided Wes, generally sticking close to the courthouse whenever he was in town. But as the months passed, and the old year gave way to the new, it became clear that local peace officers were the least of his worries. Nor were the State Police any longer a concern. The tides of change had swept over Austin, and in their wake was born a new and more formidable threat.

Edmund Davis, long the carpetbagger governor of Texas,

had at last been defeated at the polls. Elections were held
shortly before Christmas of '73 and Davis had been soundly
trounced by a former Confederate, Richard Coke. Upon taking office, one of Coke's first acts was to abolish the dread
State Police. But if Texans thought the slate had been wiped
clean they were sadly mistaken.

Governor Coke resurrected the famed Ranger Battalions,
disbanded in '65 by the Army of Occupation, and ordered
them to rid the state of outlaws. They were given a free hand,
what amounted to a license to kill, and told not to bother
themselves overly much with prisoners. The attorney general's office drew up a wanted list, one considerably longer
than that of the former State Police, and the Rangers were
turned loose.

Unequaled as man hunters, the Ranger Battalions went
through several counties like croton oil, flushing wanted men
with remorseless efficiency. Some outlaws were captured and
jailed, others fled west, but most were either shot dead or
hung to the nearest tree limb. Unlike the State Police, the
Rangers made little pretense of upholding the judiciary process. Their orders were to clean out Texas and they set about
it with the most expedient means at hand. Justice was arbi-
trary and swift, a kangaroo court where the Rangers sat as
judge, jury, and executioner.

One of the names heading the wanted list was that of John
Wesley Hardin, and the young outlaw watched with more
than passing interest as the Rangers worked their way toward
Dewitt County. While he had hoped for a general amnesty
with Coke's election, he was neither shocked nor disturbed
by the turn of events. It was simply another roll of the dice,
a matter over which he had no control whatever, and he took
it in stride. That his pursuers were Texans, rather than Yankee troops or carpetbagger police, seemed somehow strange
and just the least bit unfair. But he lost little sleep pondering
the inequities of life. After being hounded for five years,
killing peace officers had become something of a pastime, if
not habit. It hardly seemed important what badge they wore,
or under whose authority they rode. Stripped of political jar-

gon, it was simply him against them. Root hog or die. The man hunters sought to kill him and he in turn tried to stay alive.

That he was better at it than the lawmen was plainly their lookout. If they left him alone then he'd leave them alone. Otherwise they took their licks just like everybody else.

All the same, despite his jaundiced view, Wes had grown more cautious with time. It had nothing to do with fear, and only in a small way did his own safety bear in the issue. Instead, it had to do with his family. And an admission he had come to after much inner searching.

To live or die was no longer his choice alone.

In January Jane had given birth to a son. He was chubby and strong and the spitting image of his father. And they had named him John Junior, for it was the proudest moment of Wes's life. But with a new baby in her arms, Jane became oppressed with fear. She brooded constantly, afraid that Wes would ride off one day and be returned home in a box. Or worse, killed by the Suttons or lawmen and left for the carrion eaters on some remote stretch of prairie. Her fear was pervasive, touching their lives like an insidious growth, and she never let him forget.

Half the men in Texas want to kill my husband.

At first Wes joshed her for being a worrywart. But with the birth of their son his attitude underwent a curious change. Slowly, he came to grips with the fact that he was no longer a loner, answerable only to himself. Those days were past, and however reluctantly, he was forced to look at things in a new light. He had responsibilities that refused to be shunted aside—a wife and two children—and for them, if not for himself, he must somehow persevere. It was not enough that his daughter and son have as their legacy the hand-me-down tales of their daddy's fearlessness and daring. They must have a father, alive and kicking, to show them the way. On a chill wintry night, bundled close in their bed, it was a promise he had made to Jane. And he was as good as his word.

Unlike the old days, he had become an exceedingly cautious man.

But it was a curious brand of prudence, somewhat unorthodox and characteristic of the man himself. A stout right arm being the best defense, he sought to avoid his enemies not so much as he dwelled on ways to eliminate them.

Early in March, returning from the railhead at Cuero, he called a meeting with the Taylors. After supper he strolled across the compound and entered the main house. There he found the four brothers seated before the fireplace in the parlor. They had come to accept him as family, more brother than cousin, one of their own. The feeling stemmed in no small part from the fact that he had saved Jim Taylor's life. But aside from that, they admired him for his cool judgment and nervy quickness in a tight situation, qualities that had served the Taylor clan well, and repaid them manyfold for offering a kinsman shelter.

And now they waited expectantly to hear what he had to say. Plainly it was a matter of some consequence or he wouldn't have called them together. They had left him the place of honor, Pitkin Taylor's old rocker, and after seating himself, he wasted no time on formalities.

"Boys, I picked up an interesting piece of news in town today. Word's out that Sutton is gonna cut and run."

The brothers came up on their chairs, gaping at him in disbelief. Just for a moment they were shocked into speechlessness. Then Billy Taylor collected his wits and blurted out what they were all thinking.

"You mean he's quit the fight—give in?"

"Nope. Not just exactly, leastways. Seems like gettin' that last horse shot out from under him sort of soured his milk. He's gonna hole up in New Orleans awhile and let things blow over. Then, when he gets to feelin' lucky again, he'll come back and have another go. Course, that's all second-hand, y'understand, but it's the straight goods."

Scrap Taylor cocked one eye skeptically. "What makes you so sure?"

Wes gave them a wolfish grin. "He's got tickets on a boat out of Indianola a week from Saturday."

"Just him?" Jim Taylor demanded.

"Him and Gabe Slaughter." Wes paused and his grin widened. "And their wives."

"By Jesus Christ!" Billy Taylor slammed a meaty fist into his palm. "You're right. They're runnin'."

"And somebody really tricky," John Taylor crowed, "might catch 'em with their pants down."

"While they haven't got an army surrounding 'em!" Jim Taylor whooped. "Just the two of 'em by their lonesome."

Wes chuckled and set the rocker in motion. "I thought you boys might see it that way."

Billy Taylor shot him a quick look. "Was you figgerin' to deal yourself a hand in this?"

"Not unless I'm asked. Seemed to me it's a private game."

"I'm obliged, Wes. It's sorta personal. Just between us."

"Yeah. If somebody killed my daddy I guess I'd take it personal, too."

The four brothers nodded, glancing at one another and back at him. It was a gesture they wouldn't forget. And could never repay. After a moment he climbed to his feet, shook hands all around, and headed toward the door. As he hit the porch, they started talking at once, and he laughed softly.

Pitkin Taylor would have been proud of his sons.

2

Cuero was alive with rumors.

On every corner of the square men gathered in little knots to swap the latest gossip. Depending on which corner a man stood, and who was doing the talking, the speculation soared wildly. Local peace officers meant to brace Wes Hardin before the day was out. Lawmen from a neighboring county were in town, determined to collect the bounty on the young outlaw's head. The Texas Rangers were riding on Cuero, prepared at last to clean out the Taylors and their deadly kinsman. The rumors grew farfetched, even zany, as the day wore on, and the mood quickened as more and more people thronged to the square. Whatever took place, it promised to be spectacular. Nothing this exciting had happened since the circus came to town. And the townspeople meant to be on hand when the final curtain rang down.

It was the stuff of legend. A story to outlive them all. Or so they told one another as they stood gawking at the batwing doors of Wright's Saloon.

On the other side of those doors, Wes Hardin was bellied up to the bar, flanked by Jim Taylor and Bud Dixon. But the rumors, and the frenzied air of the town, seemed to concern him not at all. It was his birthday, and he had no time for fainthearts and their flimsy speculations. Today he was twenty-one years old, and celebrating it in a manner suitable to the occasion. Free, white, and twenty-one. A rare event in a man's life. All the more so since the law had done its damnedest to put him under before he reached voting age. And at the very least would have robbed him of his freedom. Tossed him in some stinking dungeon and thrown away the key.

He had earned a celebration. The hard way.

Not that he wasn't aware of an impending showdown. The state of things in Dewitt County had altered drastically, and again, he sensed a brewing storm. Only this time it wouldn't be so easily handled. Or so quickly ended.

Back in March, some two months past, the Taylor brothers had ridden down to Indianola. Docked at the wharf, they found the steamboat *Clinton*. And aboard the boat they found William Sutton. While John and Scrap guarded the dock, with four fresh horses hitched nearby, Billy and Jim mounted the gangplank. On the upper deck they cornered Sutton and his partner, Gabe Slaughter. The gunfight was fast and bloody, if somewhat one-sided. Sutton and Slaughter both went down, one dead and the other mortally wounded. But neither of the Taylor brothers received so much as a scratch.

It was a testament to their accuracy that every bullet fired found the mark. The dead men's wives stood shrieking hysterically throughout the whole affair, but the only wounds they suffered were those of anguish and sorrow. Clambering back down the gangplank, Billy and Jim swung aboard their waiting horses and the four Taylors made a beeline for Dewitt County.

With the death of William Sutton, a calm settled over the Guadalupe. The faction he had organized and commanded for so long fell to fighting among themselves. The King was dead and a royal squabble broke out as to who would take his place. Like their former leader, the men of the Vigilance Committee still coveted the lands south of the Guadalupe. And within their ranks were those who believed they could succeed where William Sutton had failed.

This struggle for leadership gave the Taylor clan a momentary respite, and left them to fret over a new and more resourceful adversary. The Texas Rangers.

Word seeped down from Austin that the killing of William Sutton had been the last straw. The Rangers just then had their hands full scourging Gonzales County, where the Clements family had ridden roughshod over their neighbors since the end of the war. But once done in Gonzales, the lawmen had explicit orders from Governor Coke. Their next task was to clean out Dewitt County, and the natural place to start, according to the big augurs in Austin, was with the Taylor clan.

And a gold watch to the man who got John Wesley Hardin.

Hardly a bystander, Wes gave as much, if not more, thought to the Rangers than did his kinfolk. In Dewitt County alone he was wanted for the killing of two lawmen. Not to mention a clutch of old warrants charging him with a dozen or so murders. The fact that most of those he had killed were either Yankees or carpetbaggers seemed to matter little. Not to Austin or the Rangers. And certainly not to him, if he was caught. They would stretch his neck from the nearest tree, and the question of whom he had killed would soon be forgotten. Hung was hung, and it was just as final for drilling a Yankee as it was for drilling a corrupt sheriff. Such hairline distinctions clearly left the Rangers unimpressed, and for a man facing the rope, they simply ceased to exist.

Still, even with time growing short, Wes hadn't broken out in a nervous sweat. The Rangers had bitten off a mouthful in Gonzales. Unless they were something out of the ordinary—which he doubted, despite all reports—it would be a while before they got around to tackling Dewitt County. And when that time came he'd give them a dose of something they hadn't run across elsewhere. After all, they were just lawmen, mortal men at that, and they weren't any more bulletproof than the other toughnuts he'd laid to rest.

All in all, the situation left him unperturbed. He was pleased with himself for arranging William Sutton's abrupt demise, and thoroughly confident he could settle the Rangers' hash when it became necessary. Until then, he wasn't about to give himself a case of blue swivets with needless worry.

Instead, feeling his oats, he had come into town to celebrate his birthday. Accompanied by young Taylor and Dixon, he started the festivities with an afternoon at the horse races. This was a regular event, held every Saturday, and drew people from all over the county. Betting was generally heavy, and with an eye for good horseflesh, Wes won handily, which was all the more reason to celebrate.

After the races, their spirits soaring, the threesome retired to Wright's Saloon. There Wes bought several rounds for the house and began promoting a poker game. Though it was hardly sundown, he hoped to lure some of the town's sporting men into a little session of cutthroat stud. His luck was running strong, the ponies had proved that, and he had a hunch it was his night to howl.

Free, white, and twenty-one! Frisky and furry and full of fleas! Never been curried above the knees! A ring-tailed lalapalooza from Bitter Creek!

Everybody laughed and drank heartily, since he was paying, but they couldn't be suckered into playing poker with him. An hour later he was still trying to cajole someone into a game when the doors swung open and Cuero's new deputy sheriff walked through. He was a long drink of water named Dave Karnes, and until tonight he'd given the young outlaw plenty of elbow room. The saloon went still as a graveyard while he crossed the room and came to a halt in front of the threesome. Wes eyed him narrowly, not at all pleased to have a damper put on his celebration. The deputy darted a sheepish glance at the crowd and finally cleared his throat.

"Mr. Hardin, I wonder if we could have a few words?"

"Why sure, Deputy. What you got on your mind?"

"Well, it's sorta private." Karnes licked his lips nervously. "Reckon we could step outside?"

Wes gave him an inscrutable look, wondering if the sheriff had some notion of springing a trap right on the public square. If so, he'd gone about it in a mighty clumsy fashion. In fact, the idea was so absurd it was downright ridiculous. At last, the youngster shrugged and smiled at Karnes.

"Why not? Guess you wouldn't mind if my friends went along." It was more statement than request, and when the deputy bobbed his head, Wes gestured toward the door. "After you."

Karnes led off, with Wes trailing him. Taylor and Dixon brought up the rear, still a little confused by the swift turn of events. Outside they all came to a halt and Wes stiffened as he spotted the crowd. The square was jammed, and he was struck by the curious thought that it was him they had come to see. Suddenly alert, he turned a flinty gaze on Karnes.

"Deputy, I've got a hunch you know somethin' we don't."

"That's what I come to see you about, Mr. Hardin." Karnes broke out in a cold sweat and his words tumbled over one another. "The sheriff sent me over here to warn you. See, he's got an idea the Taylors could wind up runnin' the county and he wants 'em to remember that he did you a good turn."

"Warn me about what?"

"See that bunch up on the corner?"

Wes glanced up the street and saw a group of men standing off by themselves. They were strangers, and from the looks of them, a hardcase lot. Even as he watched, a man separated from the others and walked toward the saloon.

"Holy moses!" Karnes rasped. "The fat's in the fire now."

"Mister, you better do some fast talkin'." Wes scowled ominously. "Who's the jasper headed this way?"

"That's what I was tryin' to tell you, Mr. Hardin. Y'see, this fellar name of Charlie Webb, he's head deputy over in Brown County, and he got a posse together and they come over here—"

"To get me."

Karnes swallowed hard. " 'Cause of the reward money."

Webb pulled up in front of them and Karnes's shoulders sagged like a wilted sunflower. The Brown County lawman and the outlaw stared at one another for a moment, saying nothing. Finally, Karnes got himself untracked, and in a froggy croak, made the introductions.

"Charlie Webb, this here's Wes Hardin."

"John Wesley Hardin." Webb beamed and stuck out his hand. "Been waitin' a long time to meet you."

Wes took the lawman's hand and nodded. "Pleased to make—"

Too late, he realized that Webb was packing a brace of Colts. Before he could move the lawman locked his hand tight, jerked the offside pistol, and shot him. Wes lurched backward, a dark blotch staining his shirtfront. But as he fell, he pulled the Peacemaker and thumbed off a single shot. The slug caught Webb in the face, tearing away his jawbone, and he slammed up against the wall. He hung there a moment, drilling another round into the boardwalk, then toppled forward. As he went down, Taylor and Dixon shot him four times in the back.

Suddenly Webb's posse opened fire from the corner and lead whistled all around them. Taylor and Dixon hammered off several shots, dropping one of the men, and the rest scurried around the corner. Working quickly, they grabbed Wes under the arms and got him aboard his horse. Then they mounted, leading the youngster's horse, and took off down the street at a dead lope. A moment later they turned the corner and disappeared from sight.

Dave Karnes suddenly doubled up and puked all over his boots.

3

The Texas Rangers rode into Cuero three days later. Though their bloody work was not yet done in Gonzales, one company had been detached from the Special Forces Battalion. Twenty men strong, their mission was to restore the law in Dewitt County. Other than that, they had blanket license to take whatever action deemed necessary. Austin was interested in results, not methods, and the Rangers' orders were both chilling and terse.

Convert the lawless. Make believers of them all.

This left the Ranger commander, Captain Sam Waller, considerable latitude in judgment. An avowed pragmatist, he chose not the best way, but the quickest. The big augurs in Austin had little patience with commanders who pussyfooted around, and Captain Waller was of the lean and hungry school. While not overly bright, he was exceedingly ambitious, and he knew that nothing impressed politicians quite so much as blood and thunder. A quick and violent campaign, with citations for bravery under fire, would be better for all concerned. Particularly Sam Waller.

With the problem reduced to fundamentals, Waller spent a day mapping his strategy. Basically, it was rather simple. There were two factions—the Taylors and the Vigilance Committee. And while the Taylors were acknowledged desperadoes, the Vigilantes at least had some tenuous alliance with the law. If he could eliminate the Taylors a semblance of order would be restored. Fast and efficiently. Then, if it was still necessary, he could turn and destroy the Vigilantes.

Yet he doubted that the second step would be required. A single campaign, conducted brutally and without quarter, was generally object lesson enough.

The strategy was neither remarkable nor inventive. It was merely the shifty reasoning of a pragmatic man, employing the expedients of ruthlessness and fear. And for Sam Waller, zealot without mercy, it was nothing less than a holy quest.

He would convert the Taylors with a baptismal of fire.

The Rangers' sudden appearance in Cuero was unexpected, but hardly a secret. Word travels fast in a small town, and by noon the grapevine was working overtime. Before nightfall the news had spread throughout the county, and the most avid listeners were known partisans of the Taylor cause. None more so than John Wesley Hardin.

Though he was not a deliberate man, tending to react as the situation demanded, Wes had already sorted through his alternatives. The three days' grace, laid up in bed with Jane playing nurse, had given him time to think. His wound was superficial, if painful, a neat hole drilled front and back through the side. So there was nothing to stop him from simply riding out and making himself scarce. Except loyalty to the Taylors.

Yet that bothered him only briefly. The clan itself was divided on the wisest course of action. Some intended to run. Others meant to hold their ground. What it came down to was how much trust a man placed in the law. That the Rangers were partial to bloodbaths, having demonstrated it in several counties, was apparent to many Taylor supporters. But most were determined to stand pat and take their chances. They felt they were in the right, that once the facts were known the law would declare them the aggrieved party. With some slight reservations, they welcomed the Rangers to Dewitt County. Now their families could rest easy, and a man might go about his work without fear of being bushwhacked.

Wes found it difficult to share that conviction. Years of dealing with lawmen had left him with an unshakable cynicism for the breed. They weren't to be trusted, however much they spouted slogans of equal justice for all the people.

Somehow it generally worked out that certain people were more equal than others. And based on past experience, not to mention the governor's wanted list, he figured his name had already been entered on the wrong side of the ledger.

The swing vote, though, was cast by the Taylor brothers themselves. They were split down the middle, and this fracture dispelled any lingering sense of loyalty the young outlaw might have had. John Taylor took off like a turpentined bear for parts unknown. Billy and Scrap forted up in the big house and declared themselves ready to fight till the last. Young Jim simply crossed the compound and threw in his lot with Wes. Guileless to the end, he made no bones about his decision. The chances of coming out alive were vastly improved by sticking with someone who had managed to survive similar predicaments. It was just that elemental.

Wes couldn't have agreed more. Only a fool fought the law on its own terms. The way to beat the Rangers was to play cat and mouse. Hit and run. Keep them guessing. Never give them a chance to get set. It had worked with the Yankees and the State Police, and it would work with the Rangers. After a couple of weeks of being led in circles, they'd call it quits and head on back to Austin. Lawdogs were a sorry bunch, as everyone knew, and had never been known for their gumption.

That night, after a teary farewell with Jane, Wes and young Taylor went on the dodge. They traveled light, carrying bedrolls and grub, and by dawn they were some miles south on the Guadalupe. There, they holed up for the day in a grove of pecan trees along the riverbank. Wes planned to shift their hideout each day, traveling only at night. While he entertained little hope of eluding the Rangers altogether, he knew the odds improved if they kept moving.

Downstream from camp, they hobbled the horses and turned them loose to graze on a grassy patch of bottomland. Afterward, they washed down cold biscuits and beef with river water. That part of being on the run was what Wes resented most. He missed his coffee. Thick and black and heavily larded with sugar. Being chased was an inconven-

ience. And people taking potshots at him was a bother of
sorts. But to be denied his coffee seemed the ultimate sacrifice. Damn near intolerable. Still, a fire was a luxury they
could hardly afford. Smoke on a clear day was a dead giveaway. Better to hire a brass band and parade into Cuero in
style.

The thought made him smile inwardly. A sardonic smile,
mocking himself. He was getting too old for this nonsense.
Like some crotchety vinegarroon, he sat there bemoaning his
coffee when he was lucky as hell somebody hadn't already
planted daisies over him. It just went to prove that God
should've given a man an extra bunghole and shorted him
on brains. Thinking could get a fellow in real trouble.

Watching him, Jim Taylor swallowed a mouthful of dusty
biscuit and arched one eyebrow. "You look like somebody
just gigged your funny bone."

Wes grinned and shook his head. "Not lately. Fact is, I
was thinkin' this outlaw business is gettin' to be a pain in
the rump."

"Sounds sorta queer comin' from you. I mean, hell, you
been on the dodge so long. I always figgered it was the kind
o' life you just naturally cottoned to."

"You mean like I picked it out special? The way some
people set their cap to be a doctor or a lawyer?"

"Well, no, not just exactly." Taylor frowned, searching
for the right words. "I know you sorta backed into it. But I
always thought"—his voice trailed off lamely—"well, you
know."

"That I got a charge out of killin' people?"

"Now, Wes, I didn't say that neither. It's just that"—
flustered, his face turned red as cherry pits—"I just s'posed
you liked the excitement. The way some folks get weaned
into likker. Guess I was wrong."

Wes grunted, fixing him with a rueful stare. "Lemme tell
you somethin', Jim. This stuff of being a badman ain't all
it's cracked up to be. It's a mighty lonesome occupation."

"Lonesome? Cripes, you got more friends'n any man I
know."

"And more enemies. Ever think of it like that?"

"Sure, I reckon that's part of it. But your name stands for somethin'. Hell, people all over Texas look up to you. You ain't some saddle tramp with a boil on his ass. You're special."

"Think so, huh? Well, you try cuddlin' up to that some night when all you got between your butt and the ground is a sweaty blanket. I guaran-dam-tee you there's nothin' *special* about it. After a while you get to wishin' you'd signed on as a ribbon clerk, so you could go home to a hot meal and a little nuzzlin'. 'Cause, Jimbo, when you get right down to the nubbin, that's what special really is."

"You ain't talkin' about a wife and kids and all that stuff?"

"That's exactly what I'm talkin' about. I had it for a year one time out on the Brazos. And there hasn't been a day since that I wouldn't 've traded my left nut to still be there. It was a good life. Lots better'n a man knows till he loses it."

"Christ A'mighty, Wes, that don't hardly make sense. Not the way you was livin' it up in town the other night. And the look on your face when you get in a fight. Hell, I've been there. I seen it for myself. You got a natural-born taste for them things. Sticks out like a sore thumb."

"Yeah, I guess it does. What I'm tryin' to tell you, though, is that there's things I like better. Y'know, sometimes a fellow has to play the cards he's been dealt and just do the best he can. But you stick with it long enough and that sportin' life, and all the time windin' up in a gunfight, gets old real quick. Take my word for it."

Taylor fell silent for a long while, staring distractedly at his biscuit. At last, he sighed and looked up with a bemused frown. "Well, that's shore a revelation. I don't mind tellin' you, it purely is. All this time I had it figgered that you was hard as nails and sudden death 'cause that's the way you liked it. Now you up an tell me you'd sooner been a ribbon clerk. Damned if that don't take the cake."

Wes knuckled his mustache back and drew a deep breath.

"Jim, lemme give you some free advice. When we come clear of this thing with the Rangers, you forget about the fast life and settle down. The only thing special about being a big, tough hombre is that you generally wind up lookin' like a sieve. And sooner or later somebody's gonna put a leak in you that a sawbones won't be able to get corked up. It's not a hell of a lot to look forward to."

The young outlaw's words proved prophetic. Shortly after dusk the next evening they stopped at Bill Cunningham's place to grain their horses. Cunningham met them at the door with a shotgun, his house darkened, and the tale he related left them dumb with shock.

While the Rangers were busy chasing Wes Hardin, the Vigilantes swept across Dewitt County exacting deadly retribution. In a single night they had lynched Jeff Hardin and the Dixon brothers, Bud and Tom. Then, their bloodlust aroused, they attacked the Anderson place. Ham and James had finally surrendered, fearing the women and children would be harmed, and the Vigilantes riddled them with buckshot right in their own front yard. Oddly enough, the Rangers didn't bat an eye. It was as if the law had joined forces with a pack of mad-dog killers. All in the name of justice. And however murky the alliance, their purpose was clear. The Taylor clan was to be hunted down and exterminated.

Wiped clean from the face of Dewitt County.

4

The hunt was well organized and relentless as death itself. Working separately, the Rangers and the Vigilantes methodically scoured the backcountry south of the Guadalupe. After their mindless night of savagery, which had cost the lives of five men, the Vigilantes' thirst for revenge appeared slaked somewhat. Their bloodlust had been curbed in no small part by Joe Tomlin, the man who now led them. Tomlin was crafty and unburdened by scruples, but he was an astute judge of character. All of which had helped him outwit his rivals in the struggle for leadership of the Vigilance Committee. Upon taking command, he focused that same shrewdness on the problem at hand, and quickly put an end to needless violence.

With Ham Anderson and Bud Dixon dead, the Taylor clan's lieutenants had been effectively eliminated. Those who remained were either unwilling or incapable of leading the ranchers below the Guadalupe. That left only the Taylor brothers themselves. And their upstart kinsman, Wes Hardin. Once they were dealt with, Dewitt County would become a fat, juicy plum, ripe for the picking.

Word had leaked out that two of the Taylor brothers, John and Jim, had taken to their heels. It was also known that the other brothers, Bill and Scrap, had barricaded themselves in the main house. Tomlin had seen that house, remembered old Pitkin Taylor bragging that it had been built along the lines of a fort, and he wanted no part of it. Wisely, he left it to the Rangers to flush Billy and Scrap. At the head of the Vigilantes, he rode off in search of John and young Jim. That seemed the more prudent course, chasing the pair who had taken flight, and if nothing else, Joe Tomlin was a prudent man. He meant to live a long time, and enjoy his newly won position as the he-wolf of Dewitt County.

But the best-laid plans, even those of prudent men, all too often run afoul of the unknown. Tomlin had made a single miscalculation—he assumed Jim Taylor had tagged along with John, the second-eldest brother. It was a serious error in judgment, one that became evident only when it was too late.

Toward sundown on the second day of their hunt, the Vigilantes found a spot on Salt Creek where two men had made a cold camp. Horse droppings and other signs indicated that the men had spent the day hidden in a small stand of trees. And most revealing was the fact that they hadn't built a fire. Translated, it meant the men had reason not to be seen.

The tracks were still fresh, less than an hour old, headed due southwest out of the woods. Like coonhounds on warm scent, the Vigilantes set off at a fast pace in the failing light.

They trailed the two horsemen straight as a string to the farm of Everett Nix, scarcely three miles from the cold camp on Salt Creek. A known Taylor supporter, Nix was a hard-scrabble sodbuster who had little stomach for gunplay. The hunters had every confidence that the Taylor boys would surrender rather than endanger Nix and his family. Boldly, just as dusk settled over the land, they rode into the front yard, fanned out in a rough crescent. This was Tomlin's idea. He wanted the Taylors to see them, to understand that there was no escape. It was his second mistake, but not his last. That came when he stood tall in his stirrups and shouted toward the house.

"You Taylors got ten seconds to give up! Then we open fire."

Tomlin's jaw popped open as Wes Hardin appeared at the parlor window and laid a double-barreled greener over the sill. For an instant in time, frozen in space and motion, the Vigilantes stared bug-eyed at the young outlaw. Then the scattergun exploded in their faces. The first charge snatched Tomlin from the saddle and sent him tumbling over the back of his horse. A moment later another quart of buckshot sizzled through the air, wounding several men and stampeding their horses. From the kitchen window a Winchester opened fire, and the ugly snout of a Peacemaker replaced the shotgun in the parlor window. Caught flat-footed, the Vigilantes panicked and took off in a wild melee of squealing horses and cursing men. The Winchester and the Colt peppered their backsides, wounding two more men, and within seconds they disappeared into the dusky night.

Joe Tomlin stayed behind. Dead as a doornail.

The Vigilantes were hardly out of sight when the back door flew open. Wes and Jim Taylor rushed out and ran toward the barn. Several moments later, saddles hastily cinched and spurs whirling, they quit Everett Nix's farm in a thundering gallop. Circling west for a mile or so, they turned and doubled back, then struck off toward the Guadalupe. Neither of them said a word the whole time. And in truth, there was no need. They were both thinking the same thing. Their escape had nothing to do with foresight or brains. Nor was it a favorable commentary on their cunning.

It was a fluke. Sheer outhouse luck. One in a zillion.

Late the next night, the young fugitives warily rode into Slim Joiner's place. They had spent the day hidden in a marsh bordering Slough Creek; their clothes were crusted with swamp mud, they were hungry and frazzled, and their horses shuffled along like crippled elephants. They needed hot food, grain for their mounts, and a good scrubbing with lye soap. Taylor had suggested Joiner's place since it was off the beaten track and less likely to attract the law. Just at the moment, however tempting a soapy tub and a decent meal, that was their main lookout. Avoiding the law.

Slim Joiner could offer them little cheer, though. Aside from corn bread and a pot of warmed-over stew, his news was all bad. The worst yet.

Upon returning to town the night before, the Vigilantes discovered that a small battle of sorts had been waged at the Taylor compound. Early that morning the Rangers had attacked, surrounding the main house. But after a long, and mostly wasted, exchange of gunfire, it became apparent that they would never dislodge the Taylors from their fort. Captain Sam Waller ordered hay wagons set afire and sent them barreling into the house from front and rear. Within an hour the house was shrouded in flames and roiling clouds of smoke. Shortly afterward, with a choice of being roasted alive or surrendering, the survivors called it quits. Three of the defenders had been killed in the gunfight, but the Rangers took into custody Scrap Taylor, Joe Tuggle, and Dan White. Incredibly, Billy Taylor somehow managed to escape in the smoke and confusion.

The captured men were manacled and whisked off to jail in Cuero. That night, smarting over the death of Joe Tomlin and fueled with Dutch courage, the Vigilantes stormed the jail. They demanded the prisoners, threatening to take them by force if necessary. Captain Sam Waller, ever the pragmatist, formed his Rangers and beat a hasty retreat to the hotel. Still in chains, Scrap Taylor and the two unfortunates with him were promptly marched to the courthouse steps. There, without any great ceremony, the Vigilantes hung them from an overhead railing. The entire town turned out to watch and it was generally agreed that justice had been served.

Then, next morning, irony had the last laugh. Billy Taylor was captured attempting to board a boat in Indianola. It was the *Clinton*, the same boat on which he had killed William Sutton. Word came over the telegraph that he was being held without bail, awaiting arrival of the Rangers. Beaming, Sam Waller sent a squad to collect the prisoner, and then strutted around town as though he'd rolled in catnip. And as any fool could see, he had reason to be proud. The Sutton-Taylor feud was history. However questionable their tactics, the Rangers had ended a decade of bloodshed in a single week, and their captain had every confidence that he was about to become Austin's fair-haired boy.

When Slim Joiner finished his grisly tale, young Taylor was woozy with shock and Wes had his jaws clenched in a tight knot. But the outlaw's thoughts dwelled only momentarily on the dead. His mind turned instead to the living. Joiner had related all there was to tell, but in deference to his guests, he had left out one salient detail. There were two fugitives still to be caught. And come morning both the Vigilantes and the Rangers would be combing the countryside. For however much the lawmen gloated and swaggered about town, there were a couple of loose ends yet to be trimmed. One named Taylor and the other named Hardin.

And not until then would the matter be officially closed.

Joiner thoughtfully passed around a jug of his own white lightning, and the jolt of hard liquor seemed to snap Taylor out of his funk. Afterward, Wes took him outside and gave him some hard talk. It was straight from the shoulder, and the youngster winced a couple of times, but it had to be said.

Grim as it was, he had to face the fact that one of his brothers was dead, another would face the hangman very shortly, and the third was probably halfway to China by now. That meant he was the last of the clan. The last of Pitkin Taylor's sons still in Texas. If he had any hope of living— of returning someday to claim the family birthright—then he must run fast and run far. Otherwise there would be another Taylor sent to the boneyard before the week was out. Better to run, and find a hole, and live to fight another day.

Jim Taylor bowed his neck at first, but Wes persisted, and the boy finally caved in. They talked, weighing various hiding places, and Wes eventually remembered Barnett Hardin. Polk County was better than a hundred miles north and the Hardin farm was back off in the sticks. A perfect hideout. The kind of spot where a fellow could change his name, walk the straight and narrow, and get himself fixed for a comeback in Dewitt County.

An hour later, they shook hands and the youngster stepped aboard his horse. When he rode out of Slim Joiner's yard there were tears in his eyes. Green as he was, he knew it was a pipe dream. He would never come this way again. But he also understood why Wes had saved his life, and somehow he felt as though he'd lost the only friend he ever had.

Shortly before sundown next day Wes ambushed the Rangers. He figured they had earned some licks and he'd gone looking for them early that morning. They weren't hard to find. Just as he expected, they were out looking for him, and he cut their trail in late afternoon. After tagging along for a while it became clear that they were headed for the Thomaston Crossing on the Guadalupe. Thinking it over, he decided it was as good a spot as any for a surprise party. It was a deep ford, heavily screened by brush on both sides, and damned hard to back out of once a horse was in the water. Satisfied, he'd circled north ahead of the lawmen and took a position on the far side of the stream.

Not unlike times past, when he'd ambushed Yankee soldiers and State Police, he felt no remorse whatever. They were worse than the men they hunted, using the law as a license to kill, and they deserved everything the got. His only regret was that he had but one shotgun. A dozen would have been better. And a cannon better still.

Nerveless, holding off till the last second, he waited until they were in the deepest part of the ford. Then he blasted Captain Sam Waller straight into kingdom come. The second load he emptied into the men behind, chuckling to himself as their horses reared and another man splashed dead in the water. As they sawed at the reins, hauling their horses around, he jerked the Colt and thumbed off five shots in a blinding roar. A third man pitched from his saddle on the far bank and an instant later the Rangers were gone, pounding back the way they had come.

Without moving, Wes calmly reloaded, satisfied that in his own way he had helped even the score. Hefting the shotgun, he walked back to where the grullo was tied. Then he mounted and rode toward the Taylor compound.

5

The night was still and black under an overcast sky. There was a smell of rain in the air; the katydids were silent; nothing moved in the compound. Light blazed in the smaller buildings, but what had once been the big house lay ominously dark and quiet, a pile of charred rubble. A soft breeze carried the scent of burnt timbers, and unless a man put it from his mind, there was even a faint trace of scorched flesh.

Try as he might, it was a smell Wes couldn't set aside. It clung in his nostrils, thick and cloyed, sickly sweet yet putrid in the way of something tainted and gone to rot. He knew his mind was playing tricks, a ghoulish joke of some sort, for by now the dead men had been removed from the ashes and buried deep. But the odor stuck with him all the same.

He was hunkered down behind a tree, at the base of the knoll, and for the past hour he had been watching the compound. It was unlikely that either Vigilantes or the Rangers would return to this place on this night. Yet the risk was always there, and this late in the game it was better to hedge his bet. Another hour, waiting and watching, would cost him nothing. Yet it might easily spell the difference between a new life and a hangman's knot. For John Wesley Hardin had decided to take his own advice.

He was leaving Texas.

After convincing Jim Taylor to quit the fight, Wes had given it considerable thought. The advice was sound, wholly realistic, yet coming from him it was laughably absurd. Worse than that, it made him the world's greatest hypocrite. For in all truth, Jim Taylor was small potatoes, a piker where the law was concerned. If ever a man had reason to run fast and run far, it was Preacher Hardin's wayward son. The stiff lecture he'd given the boy went double for himself. But only after mouthing the words to someone else, listening to his own pearly wisdom, did it jar his brain loose, force him to separate illusion from reality, and to take a long, hard look at the folly of muleheaded pride. From the Rio Grande to the Red, there had never been a man with more reason to call it quits in Texas.

Nor was there any reason to stay. The opposite side of the coin made that painfully clear. Bitter as it was to swallow, loathsome even, an era had ended. He was no longer a knight in shining armor, the people's champion against tyranny and injustice. He was merely a common outlaw.

The people themselves, across the breadth of Texas, had proved that. There had been no outcry of public indignation over the Rangers' murderous campaign against lawbreakers. The Clementses and the Taylors and the Hardins, once a breed apart, had outlived their time. Union troops no longer ruled Texas. The carpetbaggers had moved on to new swindles. And the dread State Police were now a nightmare of the past. Texas was once again governed by Texans, and its citizens no longer sanctioned the wanton slaughter of lawmen. The people wanted peace and an end to the terrors of Reconstruction. In short, the Rangers were Texans, not Yankees, and that made the difference. However savage their bloodletting, the people backed them solidly.

And at the jaded age of twenty-one Wes Hardin found himself an anachronism. A legend who had outlived his era and suddenly had no place in the new scheme of things.

This realization was all the more painful because Wes had come to it so late. Almost too late. Years ago his father had advised him to run, to leave Texas. Mustanging on the Brazos had been a compromise of sorts, but stubborn pride wouldn't allow him to run farther. Had he done so things might have been different. And not just for him alone.

That was a thought much on his mind as he watched the Taylor compound. Had Billy Taylor been right after all? Would the politicians in Austin have supported the Taylor cause if that first ambush had never taken place? The ambush Wes had argued so strongly to bring about. And what of the lawmen he himself had killed in Cuero—Jed Morgan, Jack Helms, and Charlie Webb? Would the Rangers have ridden against the Vigilantes instead of the Taylors if an outlaw named Hardin hadn't stripped Dewitt County of peace officers? These questions vexed him, and yet they were moot, unanswerable. Whatever he'd contributed to the Taylors' downfall had been done with their blessing, and while he felt sadness, he felt no guilt. The dead were dead and flailing himself wouldn't bring them back.

But what of the living?

His eyes wandered to the compound, settled on the house where even at that moment Jane sat in mourning with the Taylor widows, doubtless waiting for word of his own death. What of her and Molly and the baby? That was a question which could be answered. A question, in fact, that had already been resolved. They deserved happiness and protection and freedom from fear. And above all else, it was for them that he had set aside his pride. Taken his own advice. Yielded to common sense and determined to put Texas behind him for good.

Yet there were things he mustn't tell her. Not until later. Like this latest stunt. One man ambushing an entire company of Rangers. There had been enough death and bloodshed to last her a lifetime, and to tell her now would merely add to the burden. It could wait until they were clear of Texas, the killing behind them.

Still, mulling it over, he wasn't sorry about the ambush. It had worked out well. All things considered, a pretty tricky maneuver. A little risky, perhaps, something he'd done in the heat of anger. But it had bought him a couple of days' grace, and at a moment when he desperately needed time. With Waller dead it would take the Rangers a few days to get organized. After the licking they'd taken, it wasn't likely they would go looking for a fight until Austin sent in a new commander. As for the Vigilantes, they already had what they wanted. The Taylors were dead or scattered to the winds. Which meant there was little chance of anyone organizing a fresh manhunt. Not anytime soon.

The thought sounded good, just logical as hell, but it made him laugh. However much it justified the risk, time wasn't the reason he'd ambushed the Rangers. He'd done it for the Taylors and the Dixons and the Andersons. And for himself. It was a damned fine way to leave Texas.

When the compound finally went dark, with the last lamp snuffed out for the night, Wes figured it was safe to move. Shotgun in hand, he left the grullo tied in the trees and cautiously worked his way up the knoll. Skirting open spots, he stuck to the shadows and within ten minutes he was standing alongside the house. He waited a while longer, letting his eyes roam from building to building, until he'd satisfied himself there was nothing out of kilter. Then he edged around the front of the house and eased quietly through the door.

Silently, he moved to the bedroom and found Jane snuggled up with both children. It was about what he'd expected. With the big house in ashes it made sense that Billy Taylor's wife and the old woman would take over the spare bedroom. He leaned the shotgun against a wall and very gently placed his hand over Jane's mouth. She came awake with a start, eyes wide with fear, a muffled scream choked back in her throat.

"Sshhh," he whispered, "it's me."

She whimpered, then big tears puddled up in her eyes and

she threw her arms around his neck. They clung to one another, rocking back and forth, and she smeared his face with salty kisses. Suddenly she began to shake, heaving great sobs, and she buried her face against his shoulder to hide the sound. He stroked her hair, gentle and soothing, and after a while she seemed to get hold of herself. With one eye on the children, he eased her back onto the pillow. Then, tapping his lips with one forefinger, he cautioned her to whisper.

"Stay quiet. I don't wanna draw a crowd."

"Oh, God, Wes." Tears brimmed over and spilled down her cheeks. But she sniffed softly and kept her voice low. "I thought you were dead. We heard about the fight at Nix's place and then somebody brought word that the Rangers were after you. I prayed and prayed, but I just knew they would find you. And then—"

He stilled her with a soft touch on her lips. "Take it easy. I'm fit as a fiddle. Matter of fact, you can quit worryin' altogether. I'm finished."

"Finished? I don't understand. What's finished?"

"The fightin' and killin' and everything else." He drew her close and breathed the words in her ear. "We're leaving Texas."

She gave a little yip of joy and threw herself into his arms. "Do you mean it? Sugar, do you really mean it? Oh, thank God. Thank the Lord and all the stars. It's a miracle. I can't believe it. Are you sure? We're actually leaving?"

"I mean it. Cross my heart. Now quit raisin' such a ruckus. I'd just as soon not wake the Taylor women."

"You couldn't. They have cried themselves sick with grief. But I don't understand, Wes. Why can't we let them know? They'd never tell. Never."

"Never's a long time. And people have a way of gabbin' when they shouldn't. This here's our little secret. Just between us Hardins. Now get your clothes on and let's see if we can get the kids dressed without any big commotion."

She sat bolt upright. "You mean we're leaving now? Tonight!"

"I mean we're pullin' out quicker'n scat. Now quit talkin'

and get busy packin'. I'll tell you all about it when we're down the road a ways.''

Jane Hardin wasted little time. While Wes hitched a team to a buckboard, she packed their meager belongings, and when he returned she was ready to go. The children were bundled warmly in blankets, still fast asleep, and Wes carried them out in his arms. Jane trailed along with a carpetbag in one hand and a tow sack stuffed full with food in the other. Within the hour they were off the knoll, the grullo tied behind the buckboard, and headed eastward into a gloaming dawn. By dead reckoning, Wes calculated it was two hundred miles to the Louisiana border.

And beyond that a new life in a new land. A land of fruit and honey, where people didn't know John Wesley Hardin from Adam's off ox.

What the good book called the Promised Land.

BOOK THREE
1875–1877

CHAPTER 9

1

The train rattled northward like a scorched centipede trying to escape the fireball lodged high in a cloudless sky. Smoke belched from the engine in thick black spurts, wheels meshing with steel rails in what seemed a slow and tortuous race with time. The noonday heat was oppressive, a brutal mace hammering down against the coach roofs, and inside, the passengers sweltered as if trapped in a crackerbox rocketing through the fires of hell.

Seated beside a window, Wes Hardin stared wearily at the monotonous landscape rushing past. His eyeballs were gritty and raw, smarting with flecks of engine soot, and his clothes were covered with a fine layer of powdered grime. The damp tropical heat left him sitting in a puddle of sweat, and his mind felt numbed, somehow sated, with the sight of palmettos and Spanish moss. Swaying with the motion of the coach, caught up in the mesmerizing *clickety-clack* of the wheels and the stifling heat, he fought against the drowsy lassitude that threatened to suck him under.

While he sat at the rear of the coach, his back against the compartment wall, he still felt jumpy and on edge. And that bothered him. There were no Pinkertons aboard this train, on that score he was certain, and the knowledge should have relaxed him, allowed him to settle back and catnap through the noonday inferno. But it hadn't and probably wouldn't until he was across the state line. Although what difference it made, skipping from Florida into Georgia, he wasn't all that sure. State borders meant nothing to the Pinks, as he'd learned the hard way, and even now they were probably sniffing out his trail.

Which was what he wanted. To lure them away from Jane and the kids. And perhaps that's what had him nettled. Some inner foreboding that the dodge hadn't worked. The Pinkertons were a dogged bunch, and nobody's dumbbells. Slippery as his maneuver had been, they might well have tumbled to the game.

Thinking about it, as the train chuffed northward toward Georgia, he had to admit it was a little childish. If anything, he had spooked himself. His unease was founded on nothing more than superstitious nonsense. The mind playing tricks on itself. A damnfool notion that Florida was a hex. That the Pinks had gotten the Indian sign on him, and that he wouldn't be rid of it until he was safely out of the land of sand and sun.

The hell of it was, everything had started out so well. And he had been so careful. Playing it cagey right from the outset. Looking back, though, hindsight was an illuminating if somewhat mortifying eye-opener. Clearly, he hadn't been cagey enough. Or else the Pinkertons had just been slicker. Or luckier. Or maybe both. But however the chips had fallen, he could see now that his first mistake was that paddle-wheeler.

A mistake he had compounded every step of the way.

Upon reaching New Orleans last summer, Wes had felt safe for the first time in years. The buckboard ride from Texas hadn't been any picnic, but Jane and the kids had held up well. All the same, they had needed a breather, rest and soft beds and some decent food. He'd picked a new name for himself—Harry Swain—and taken rooms in a swanky hotel. They spent the next week roaming the French Quarter, stuffing themselves with fancy meals, and generally lazing around. Then, with everyone back on their mettle, Wes decided it was time to lose himself for good. And the farther from Texas the better.

While Florida wasn't exactly the end of the earth, the young outlaw figured it was far enough. He booked passage on a steamboat to Cedar Key, a small port on the Gulf. Although he stayed seasick most of the voyage, the family enjoyed it immensely, and from Cedar Key they took a train to Gainesville. Wes had chosen the town because it was off the beaten path, about halfway across the state, and yet still large enough for a newcomer to pass relatively unnoticed. A couple of days spent looking the place over seemed to confirm his judgment.

It was sleepy and slow-paced, like most southern towns, and other than church socials, rarely had any excitement. All in all, it appeared perfect. A most unlikely place to stumble across the Texas Rangers.

Harry Swain rented a house, got his family settled, and then began scouting the business opportunities. Within a week he bought a saloon and quietly set about fading into obscurity. Over the next several months he refrained from gambling and operated an orderly, well-run drinking establishment. The townspeople came to know him as a friendly, if somewhat laconic, saloonkeeper, and the Swains were slowly accepted into the community. At Jane's insistence, the family joined the Methodist church, and everyone was pleasantly surprised by Saloonkeeper Swain's rather remarkable grasp of the good book. Quite shortly he was invited to join the fraternal order of the Masons, and being a devout Christian as well as a devoted family man, he readily accepted. With some reluctance on his part, Harry Swain had become the talk of Gainesville, and the townspeople counted themselves fortunate to have a real up-and-comer in their midst.

Not long after the New Year, however, Harry Swain's house of cards began to fall apart. The sheriff, who coincidentally happened to be a Mason, came to him with a disturbing story. There was a stranger in town asking questions, and despite a clever smoke screen, he quite obviously was a Pinkerton agent. More to the point, the questions he asked had to do with a man whose description bore an uncanny resemblance to the young saloonkeeper. Like most Southerners, the sheriff had little use for the Pinkertons, who had served the Union cause throughout the late war. While he had told the detective nothing, and refrained from asking questions of his own, the sheriff advised Swain to watch his step. It wouldn't do for a good Christian and a brother Mason to wind up in the pokey.

Harry Swain couldn't have agreed more. That afternoon he gave his lawyer power of attorney to sell the saloon and closed out his rather sizable account at the local bank. Shortly after sundown, the Swain family appeared at the depot and caught the evening train for Jacksonville. Somewhat stunned, the people of Gainesville awakened next morning to find that the personable young saloonkeeper had departed town bag and baggage. Without so much as a fare-thee-well.

But certain men not only knew of Swain's whereabouts, they gave him a brotherly boost as well. In Jacksonville he was put in touch with George Haddock, owner of a slaughterhouse and by no mere coincidence, a fellow Mason. They exchanged the secret handshake and Swain became a contract cattle buyer for Haddock & Company.

Once again the Swain family rented a house, joined the church, and became active in community affairs. Jacksonville was a sprawling city, bustling with growth, and Swain felt confident he could lose himself for good this time. As the months passed, his business grew and prospered, and his family settled down at long last to a peaceful, untroubled life. Yet, blissful as things seemed, he had reckoned without the bulldog determination of the Pinkertons.

Toward the end of June he returned from a cattle-buying trip and was informed by George Haddock that a stranger had appeared just that morning asking questions. Haddock told the man that Swain had moved to Tallahassee and let the matter drop there. But from his description of the stranger, Swain had little doubt that it was the same Pinkerton who had traced him to Gainesville. Why the Pinkertons were after him was a question that had perplexed Swain for the past six months. And despite many sleepless nights, he still hadn't resolved who might have sicced the detectives on him. Yet there was one part to the puzzle about which he no longer had even a smidgen of doubt. The Pinks were some-how tracing him through the transportation he used. First the steamboat from New Orleans. Then the train out of Cedar Key. And now the train from Gainesville to Jacksonville. It was the only answer that made sense.

With any luck at all, though, it might be made to work against the Pinkertons. Sucker them into a real Texas-type wild-goose chase.

Rushing home, he broke the bad news to Jane. She became despondent for a time, shattered that they were again forced to flee their home. All her apprehensions of the past boiled over and she burst into tears, fearful that they would be hounded the rest of their lives. But as he outlined his plan she slowly got hold of herself. And by the time he finished she was positively glowing.

Jane and the children were to hire a buckboard and drive to Baldwin, farther west along the railroad. From there they were to catch a train and make their way to Alabama, where Jane had relatives in a small farm town. Wes, meantime, would be acting as a decoy to lure the Pinkertons in the opposite direction. If they could pull it off, they might just lose the law forever.

And it had worked perfectly. Leaving everything behind, as if they were merely off for an afternoon in the country, Jane and the children headed west in a rented buggy. Wes appeared at the depot shortly afterward and bought a ticket on the noon train to Savannah. Quite innocently, he sparked a conversation with the ticket agent and managed to let slip that he was Harry Swain with Haddock & Company. When he boarded the train he was feeling pretty smug with himself. The hook had been baited and he had every confidence the Pinkertons would swallow it whole. They would follow him to Savannah and then on to Atlanta, and there the trail would vanish. For once in Atlanta Wes was finished with trains.

Aboard a horse, he would simply melt into the countryside, invisible among the crowds of horsemen entering and leaving Atlanta every day of the week.

Late that night, when the train arrived in Savannah, Wes found a nearby cafe and ate supper. Then he returned to the depot. This, too, was part of the plan. He purchased a ticket for Atlanta, spent a few minutes chatting with the agent, and finally stretched out on a bench to catch a nap. The train for Atlanta departed early in the morning, and when it left he meant for the ticket agent to remember him quite clearly. Naturally, being crackerjack detectives, the Pinkertons would have no trouble at all in following his trail.

The thought amused him, but he suppressed a mild chuckle. Hitching himself around on the hard bench, he was asleep an instant after closing his eyes.

Some hours later he came awake with a start. It took a moment for it to register, then it dawned on him that a train was slowly screeching to a halt outside. And it had come in from the south.

He bolted to his feet as the ticket agent came around the counter. "What train is that?"

Rubbing sleep from his eyes, the agent gave him a puzzled look. "Beats me, mister. Nothin' due in here from Jacksonville till tomorrow. Somebody must've run a special."

Wes had a sinking feeling who that somebody was. Striding past the agent, he slammed out the door just as the train groaned to a halt. Hardly to his surprise, the train consisted of an engine and a single coach. Apparently the Pinks had made up in speed what they had lost in time. Out of the corner of his eye he saw three men step off the coach and he began walking faster. Suddenly a voice behind him racketed over the hiss of steam.

"You, there! Stop right where you are."

Wes leaped from the platform and took off running across the train yard. Back at the depot, he heard shouts and the thud of heavy brogans pounding along the platform. Then something hot and angry fried the air beside his head, followed an instant later by the report of a gun. Disgusted, cursing inwardly, he skidded to a halt.

The bastards could never let well enough alone. Chasing him was one thing. Like gnats, it was an irritant he could overlook. But when they started shooting, that was just too damn much. Whirling about, he jerked the Colt and dropped to one knee. The Pinkertons were standing at the edge of the platform, blasting away as if they were lined up in a shooting gallery. Lead whistled all around Wes, kicking up cinders and zinging off rails, but he closed his mind to everything except the men on the platform. They were standing almost shoulder to shoulder, silhouetted perfectly against the depot lantern, and the muzzle flash from their guns winked orangy-gold in the night. He raised the Peace-maker, supporting his gun hand in the palm of his left hand, and aimed deliberately.

Suddenly the tables were reversed, and quite literally, the Pinkertons became sitting ducks. The first slug sent the man on the left reeling backward in a windmill of arms and legs. Shifting aim slightly, Wes thumbed off another shot and saw the next man buckle at the knees, then pitch headlong off the platform. The third man caught on that it was his turn next and he abruptly quit the fight. Spinning away, he ducked low and ran toward the station house. Turning back saved his life, but he hardly escaped unscathed. Wes snapped off a hurried shot that was just wide of the mark. It drilled into the doorframe beside the detective's head and a jagged splinter laid his cheek open to the bone. An instant later, leaving his feet in a headlong dive, he disappeared through the door into the depot.

Wes came to his feet and moved off through the train yard. As he walked, he reloaded, still cursing the Pinkertons. Rather neatly, they had upset his little red wagon, and the plan would have to be changed. Damned fast. Then he grunted, smiling to himself. Somewhere in Savannah there was a man who was about to sell him a horse.

Even if the transaction took place at the point of a gun.

2

Ed Duncan was a not a man easily intimidated. He had served with honor during the late war, sending a small legion of Johnny Rebs to their reward. And more recently he had exchanged lead with the James Boys and the Youngers, receiving both a raise and a citation from the agency for his coolness under fire. Few men sported such impressive credentials, and among his professional colleagues, it was said that the pale-eyed Scotsman had the brass of a billy goat. In short, he was tough, resourceful, and hard as nails.

But as Duncan walked along the hotel corridor he felt just the least bit shaky, and there was a brackish taste in his mouth. Waiting in a room down the hall was the Old Man himself, Allan Pinkerton. And for all his daring under fire, Duncan's qualms about this meeting were not without reason. Agents who muffed an assignment go the pucker reamed out of their puckerhole, and the Old Man seldom minced words in the process. He was hell on wheels, with the sting of a yellowjacket and all the warmth of an aroused cobra.

On the long train ride to Atlanta Duncan had thought of little besides the upcoming confrontation. What he might say in his own defense still eluded him. Or more precisely, it posed yet a more vexing question. What was there to say in defense of an agent who not only had queered a manhunt but at the same time managed to get two of his fellow agents killed? So far as he could see, the answer was plain and simple—not much. Certainly nothing that would get him off the hook.

In retrospect, Duncan found himself wishing he had never heard of John Wesley Hardin. Jesse James and his gang of cutthroats were cream puffs by comparison. The young Texan seemed to have more lives than a cat, and the luck of the Irish as well. Which in itself was a dirty word to the square-jawed Scotsman.

Yet, from the very outset, he had felt a grudging respect

for Hardin. Admittedly, the youngster was cold-blooded as a shark, and as a man-killer he had few equals. But he wasn't the garden-variety desperado. Nor was he an outlaw in the accepted sense of the word. Despite their best efforts, the Texas Rangers had failed to produce one shred of evidence linking Hardin to cattle rustling or bank robbery, or any other form of skulduggery for profit. It seemed that the most infamous gunman in Texas killed for only one reason—a desire to remain free. Duncan found nothing unnatural about that, and given the circumstances, he couldn't wholly condemn it. Particularly when it was common knowledge that Hardin supported himself and his family through honest labor, and rarely went out of his way to provoke trouble. The problem in a nutshell was that he had a disturbing way of ending arguments. And fully a baker's dozen of those he had killed were peace officers.

Scarcely a year ago, in the capitol building at Austin, Duncan had listened to vitriolic tirades from the governor and the attorney general on this very subject. The Scotsman had thought then that Hardin was perhaps one of a kind—an honest outlaw. But this distinction, however singular, was lost on the governor. Wes Hardin had made the Rangers look like bumbling asses, killing three of them in what could only be described as a turkey shoot. Then he simply vanished, leaving not only the Rangers but the governor himself the laughing stock of Texas. It appeared certain that Hardin had departed Texas and the governor wanted him run to earth. With one proviso. The Pinkertons were to take him alive and return him to Texas for trial. Only then would the good name and reputation of the Coke administration be restored.

Though unimaginative, Duncan was a student of logic, and he spent several months investigating the most obvious escape routes from Texas. Doggedly persistent, he questioned ticket agents at train depots and ship lines all along the Gulf Coast, slowly working his way into Louisiana. Finally, in a steamboat office in New Orleans, he struck pay dirt. From there the trail led to Cedar Key and then on to Gainesville. After talking with the sheriff, who was a poor liar, Duncan knew he was very close. The tradesmen he questioned around town—who were by turn reserved and startled and hostile—merely confirmed his judgment. Still, more than a week elapsed before he discovered that Hardin, posing as Harry Swain, had once again slipped through the net.

Simple deduction, and a small bribe to the depot agent, led him next to Jacksonville. There he called for support, and Allan Pinkerton assigned two agents to work under his supervision. They combed the city, slowly eliminating all possibility that Hardin had bought a saloon or returned to gambling. Then, Duncan had a brainstorm. He recalled Hardin's dealings in cattle and began investigating the city's slaughterhouses. Again he struck pay dirt in the form of a poor liar—George Haddock. And again Hardin slipped through his grasp. Only this time it was by a mere whisker. Duncan and his men traced Hardin to the depot less than two hours after the train had departed for Savannah.

The Scotsman wired Pinkerton in Chicago and within the hour he had a special train at his disposal. Later that night they roared into Savannah and through sheer happenstance almost stumbled over Hardin. Except that Duncan's orders were to take the outlaw alive, and he in turn shouted orders for his men to aim low. Try for a crippling shot.

It had been a harsh and costly introduction to John Wesley Hardin. Duncan's agents had been killed where they stood, and the Scotsman would carry a livid scar to his grave. He still remembered the leaden thunk as a slug slammed into the doorjamb beside his head, and at times he could even feel the splinter knifing through to his cheekbone. But what he recalled most was that the youngster had fired only three shots, which was not so much a testimonial to Sam Colt's equalizer as to Wes Hardin's accuracy. And it had stimulated a healthy respect in Ed Duncan for this one-of-a-kind outlaw.

He now knew what it was to have a shark turn and fight.

But while all of this mitigated his failure, none of it stacked up well as a defense. The unvarnished facts, galling as they were, told the tale. He'd had three chances to trap his man, and at every juncture Hardin had made a monkey of both him and the Pinkertons. It was the cardinal sin, besmirching the reputation of the agency, and on that score he must answer to the Old Man himself. Pinkerton rarely stirred from his headquarters in Chicago, and his presence in Atlanta could mean only one thing. Heads were about to roll.

Duncan halted before the door, removing his hat, and knocked. A gruff voice ordered him to enter, and as he stepped inside the room, any lingering hope went by the boards. The agency chief was standing in front of the fireplace, scowling one of his famous scowls. Quite pointedly, he declined to shake hands. Instead, he motioned to a chair and cut straight to the heart of the matter.

"I would like to know the present whereabouts of John Wesley Hardin."

"So would I, Mr. Pinkerton." Duncan lowered himself into the chair and squirmed about uncomfortably. "However, I'm forced to report that we've come up empty. He simply vanished into thin air."

Defeat in any form was unacceptable to Allan Pinkerton. Short in stature, pushing sixty, with a graying beard and muddy brown eyes, he seemed an unlikely hunter of men. Yet his looks were deceptive, cloaking an iron will and a fierce determination to win. In 1860 he had saved Abraham Lincoln from assassination, and afterward established the Secret Service. During the war he commanded all espionage and intelligence-gathering activities for the Union, and came away with a record unblemished by failure. He was shrewd, chillingly perceptive, and at heart, tougher than any outlaw he'd ever chased. Now, something flickered in his eyes, and he nailed Ed Duncan with a corrosive stare.

"Suppose you tell me how a man vanishes?"

Sweat beaded Duncan's forehead, but he returned the look squarely. "I don't know, Mr. Pinkerton. He's a will-o'-the-wisp. Like smoke. You reach out to grab him and all of a sudden he's not there."

"Am I to understand that after three weeks you still have

no clues whatever? That with two of our agents shot dead
and the reputation of this firm at stake, you've turned up
nothing?''

Duncan bristled at the tone and his pale eyes went stony
cold. "That's correct, sir. Nothing. I've turned Savannah upside down and have yet to find a trace of Hardin. But I'm
still looking, and unless you take me off the case, I'll find
him. And that isn't an idle promise, Mr. Pinkerton. It's a
statement of fact.''

Pinkerton glared back at him for several moments, then
the muddy gaze abruptly softened and he smiled. "Ed, that's
what I came all this way to hear. You are as good an oper-
ative as we have in the agency, and I never for a moment
doubted that you would fail me. But I wanted you to hear
yourself say it. Most of the time, it's what a man believes
of himself that makes the difference.''

The Scotsman's mouth quirked in a dour smile. "I'll get
him. It's just a question of when and where and''—he
paused, no longer smiling—"whether or not you still want
him alive.''

There was a long silence, and at last the older man nodded.
"Take him alive. We'll make an example of young Mr. Hardin.''

Allan Pinkerton took a chair and thoughtfully steepled his
fingers. After a moment's contemplation a foxy look settled
over his face, and he peered across at Duncan with an intensity that fairly crackled.

"Now let's discuss tactics. I have a few ideas I believe
might interest you.''

3

Polland in many ways reminded Wes of Mount Calm. It
was a quiet little town, somewhat backwoodsy, and people
tended to follow the rule of live and let live. Not unlike most
small communities in Alabama, it was neither prosperous nor
destitute. There were a couple of wealthy men who pretty

well controlled things, notably the local banker and a former plantation owner who had managed to fend off the carpetbaggers and scalawags. But for the most part people made do with what the Good Lord provided and counted it a blessing after the horrors of Reconstruction.

Not that ambition in Polland was dormant. Nor was it suffering some acute form of stagnation. There were several small businesses, owned by men whose moderate means adequately satisfied their moderate needs. Yet everybody else, when they worked, generally found themselves in the employ of the banker and his major depositor, or if things got desperate, they trudged five miles to the sawmill at Wawbeek and hired out for the day. Things seldom got that desperate, though. For the people of Polland were content with chicken on Sunday, grits the rest of the week, and old-time religion around the clock.

Except that their pace was a little slower and their drawl a little heavier, Wes found them not all that different from the people back in Mount Calm. In many ways, it was as if he had come home again. Particularly when he discovered himself living among a regular beehive of Bowens.

Somewhat like the Taylors and the Clementses back in Texas, the Bowens were a loving, close-knit clan. An offshoot of Jane's family, blood kin to her father, they were easygoing and rarely bothered themselves with things outside their own small world. They knew, of course, that Jane's husband was a wanted man, and it rather tickled their fancy to have a famous outlaw as part of the family. The scars of Reconstruction were hardly healed, even in tiny Polland, and a man who had killed so many Yankees was a prize catch indeed. The Bowens welcomed him into the clan with open arms, but his identity remained their own-guarded secret, a private joke of sorts on the community, and so far as anyone knew, he was simply Harry Swain, young, obviously well-to-do, and come to Polland to settle among his wife's family.

All of which suited Harry Swain very much indeed. He was tired of running, wearied even with the killing, and he wanted to sink roots. The time had come to commence building something for his family, to give their lives a measure of peace and stability. While that could never become a reality in Texas—he had discarded all hope of ever returning west—it might well come to pass in Alabama. Polland was isolated to a great extent, the nearest city some fifty miles across the Florida line, and if he kept his nose clean it was doubtful the world would ever again hear of John Wesley Hardin.

Yet his rosy outlook for the future was mixed with just a tinge of watchfulness. Never again would he underestimate the Pinkertons. After his near disaster in the Savannah depot they had won his grudging admiration, if not for their marksmanship then at least for their genius as bloodhounds. Perhaps more precisely, he had developed a keen appreciation for the skills of a stumpy little Scotsman with pale frosty eyes and a square jaw.

Newspapers across the South had ballyhooed the Savannah shoot-out in front-page headlines. Liberal quotes were also included from one Edward S. Duncan, Special Agent in charge of the manhunt for John Wesley Hardin. Duncan freely admitted that he had lost the trail in Savannah, but went on to observe that this presented nothing more than a temporary setback. He had tracked Hardin from Texas to Louisiana to Florida to Georgia, and he planned to go right on tracking. Furthermore, he had every confidence that the wanted man would be taken into custody within a very short while. The newspapers ate it up. Having a woolly-booger western desperado loose in the southland made hot copy. Editorials teetered between outraged indignation and droll amusement, and the public couldn't get enough. For weeks every new development was trumpeted in Gothic bold, and reporters employed prose so livid it all but glowed in the dark. Then, quite abruptly, there was nothing. No news stories. No editorials. And no quotes from Edward S. Duncan. The detective had dropped out of sight, and with him, all speculation about the manhunt.

But if the public quickly forgot, the wanted man himself grew all the more reflective. Having devoured the news stories as avidly as everyone else, he now knew something of his pursuer. The man had a name, and a souvenir from their gunfight in Savannah, which tended to make it more personal. He was obviously resourceful, double-wolf on guts, and not in the least discouraged by what he termed a temporary setback. And the fact that he had dropped from sight was not a matter to be taken lightly. Detectives seemed to be most dangerous, judging from past experience, when they suddenly turned unobtrusive and silent. And so it evolved, in the little town of Polland, that while Edward S. Duncan was out of sight he was hardly out of mind.

Harry Swain had much going for him in Polland. After escaping Savannah on a hastily purchased horse, he made his way across Georgia and Alabama, sticking to backcountry roads, and had come at last to the home of Brown Bowen. As the eldest in the family, Bowen had made him welcome, offering both friendship and refuge. Jane and the children had arrived some three weeks previously, and since then, the clan had been waiting expectantly for the daring young outlaw to make an appearance. They threw a celebration in his honor, with hickory-smoked hog and hoedown dancing and a hair-curling blend of white lightning. And when it was over, his eyeballs afloat and his step none too steady, the guest of honor found himself adopted. The Bowens, it seemed wouldn't take no for an answer. He and Jane and the children were to remain in Polland, settle down, and consider themselves full-fledged members of the family.

The lazy summer days slowly drifted into fall, and as the nights became cooler, Harry Swain made his decision. While he'd never refused the Bowens' offer, he felt it best to await events before sinking roots in yet another town. But with the coming of October, and still no sign of the Pinkertons, he concluded it was safe to try his hand at some form of business. After all, his family had to eat, and since money didn't grow on trees, it was high time he set about making some.

But as things worked out, it appeared that money did, in fact, grow on trees. Scouting around town for likely investments, Swain quickly learned that prospects were far from bright. Polland already had a saloon, which served its needs nicely; gambling was looked upon as a sin only slightly less heinous than adultery; and the cattle business, as such, was virtually nonexistent. By process of elimination the trades in which he had a working knowledge seemed to have been chalked off rather neatly.

Then, quite by accident, opportunity came knocking. Having exhausted the more attractive possibilities, Swain marched into the local bank, unstrapped his money belt, and made a sizable deposit. This fact was duly noted by Lionel Culpepper, the bank president, and Swain was shortly ushered into his office for a private chat. Culpepper had his finger on the pulse of things and there was little in Polland that escaped his scrutiny. While he had long since dismissed the Bowens as a vital force in the community, he sensed something altogether different about their young kinsman. Like most bankers, Culpepper believed that money talked loudest, and Swain's deposit slip was a highly persuasive introduction.

Which was no great revelation to Harry Swain. It was what he had expected, and the reason he'd played the money belt as if it were the case ace in high-stakes showdown.

After a bit of small talk, Swain let it drop that he was looking for an investment. Nothing speculative but something solid and reliable. Something a family man could get his teeth into and build with an eye toward the future. Having determined to settle in Polland, he wanted to contribute to the growth of the community and at the same time further his own fortunes in some small way.

This was the kind of talk to warm a banker's heart, and Culpepper took a fancy to the young man right off. It so happened that he did know of an investment. One of the bank's oldest customers, owner of a small logging company, was currently in a financial bind. While the company was basically sound, the owner, Joe Dan Adair, was a good logger but a poor manager of money. Forced to take the conservative view, the bank had recently declined his request for a loan. But a man with a head on his shoulders, who was willing to pitch in and work hard, might well make his fortune in partnership with Adair.

A meeting was arranged between Adair and Swain, and the two men struck it off immediately. Adair was on the sundown side of forty, clearly a hard drinker with an Irishman's mercurial temper. But he needed money and he was bright enough to recognize that a partner with brains could prove a real asset. It took only a brief discussion, especially the part dealing with money, to see that Swain qualified on both counts.

Playing it cozy, the young investor spent a full week inspecting Adair's operation. The logging itself was done along the upper tributaries of the Escambia River, some ten miles west of Polland. After being felled and stripped, the logs were snaked through the woods by mule teams and eventually brought to the river. There they were floated downstream and sold outright to the sawmill at Wawbeek.

And it was at the sawmill that Adair was slowly losing his shirt. The owner of the sawmill had a hammerlock on the loggers, since his was the only mill along the stretch of river that flowed through Alabama. He could set his own price, take it or leave it, and thumb his nose at anybody who yelled about the rules. There were plenty of loggers, but as he was quick to point out, there was only one sawmill.

Swain disappeared from Polland for a few days, giving Adair a mild case of heart flutters, and returned looking as as though he'd just swallowed a canary. They sat down for another talk, and while Swain was oddly cryptic about his trip, he proved that he had brains enough for both of them. The dickering went on far into the night, at times verging on a bare-knuckle donnybrook, but the younger man couldn't be swayed from a telling argument. He had the money and without it Adair would sink like a rock. When they finally shook hands, Swain was a full partner with authority to run the business end of the operation any way he saw fit. All Joe Dan Adair had to do was get the logs to river. From there, Polland's newest entrepreneur would handle the rest.

Harry Swain came away from the meeting walking on air.

He had big plans for the future, and with a gambler's instinct for a winner, he knew he'd backed a sure thing. But he also knew there was risk involved, that he might well be constructing another house of cards. And though he allowed himself a pat on the back, he wasn't quite ready to stop looking over his shoulder.

Not until he knew the whereabouts of one Edward S. Duncan.

4

Polland was agog with wonder.

Joe Dan Adair's young partner had just turned the logging industry topsy-turvy. People around town could talk of nothing else, and wherever they gathered the topic of conversation seldom strayed from Harry Swain's nifty sleight of hand. The Bowens were beside themselves with glee, flushed and jubilant that the family had at last produced a live-wire eager beaver with the magic touch. Lionel Culpepper, though equally impressed, merely sat in his office at the bank and brooded. Somehow he couldn't shake the feeling that this Johnny-come-lately had stolen the march on him. And worse yet, hoodwinked him into helping.

It was a day that shook the order of things.

That afternoon Joe Dan Adair and his crew hit town howling like banshees. They tromped into Polland's one saloon and promptly ordered drinks for the house. Then, though the youngster himself had declined to join them, they proceeded to tell everyone within shouting distance of the tricky, underhanded, positively dazzling cunning of Mr. Harry Swain.

Adair & Company had felled their usual quota of logs that week. But when it came time to make the run downstream, Harry Swain had a little surprise for them. And it revolved around his mysterious trip a few weeks past, those two days he'd disappeared from town.

Horseback, Swain had ridden the shoreline of the Escam-

bia River all the way to Pensacola. There, as any fool could
have told him, he found a sawmill at the mouth of Escambia
Bay. Being neither a fool nor a logging man, which many
people considered one and the same, he sat down to talk
turkey with the mill owner. When he departed, he had a firm
offer for all the logs Adair & Company could deliver—at
twice the price being paid in Wawbeek.

Ignorance is bliss, according to know-it-alls, and if so,
then Swain was riding on a cloud. But it was a thin and
delusive cloud, the stuff of pipe dreams. For no one had
thought to tell him that logs couldn't be floated down seventy
miles of winding, treacherous river. At least it hadn't occurred to anyone to mention it until he announced the scheme
that day along the upper Escambia.

Then Joe Dan Adair told him. Loudly, in no uncertain
terms, and with the profane artistry of a drunken mule skinner. After the sour-tempered Irishman sputtered to a halt,
Swain fixed him with that stony look and asked a single
question.

"How do you know it can't be done?"

"Because, goddamnit," Adair thundered, rolling his eyes
at the innocence of fools, "nobody's ever done it before."

Swain just smiled. "Then it's time someone tried."

There was plenty more cursing after that, and at one point
the two men almost came to blows. But at last Swain gave
his partner the double whammy. First off, he had ridden
every foot of the river, and logger or not, he was of the
opinion it could be done. More to the point, their contract
gave him the authority to call the shots, and like it or not,
he was exercising that power.

Joe Dan Adair fumed and cussed and kicked at rocks. But
he was snookered and he knew it. They set the logs afloat.

Later, recalling it for his goggle-eyed audience in the saloon, Adair admitted that the high point of his life was when
they drifted past the sawmill at Wawbeek. The owner, Pud
Moore, stood on the landing like a hayseed gawking at his
first tent-show freak. That dumbfounded look, Adair cackled,

a mixture of raw disbelief and faunching rage, was worth the price of admission. Even if they'd lost every log in the run, he would have felt amply rewarded.

But as it came about, they lost very few logs. The only hitch they encountered was below Century City, at a sharp bend in the river. There, everything came to a halt in a massive logjam, a bottleneck of sorts that had Adair stumped and the rest of the men scratching their heads. Swain, who hadn't yet got the hang of walking logs, was trailing them along the shoreline. He stepped down off his horse, pulled a stick of dynamite from his saddlebags, and calmly lit the fuse. As the loggers scattered like peppered ducks, he tossed the dynamite into the bottleneck.

Afterward, laughing about it, the men labeled it a stroke of genius. The explosion made kindling of the logjam, sending a plume of debris rocketing skyward, and in the blink of an eye the pileup simply ceased to exist. They again started the logs downriver and from there on out it was smoother than a ride on a brand-new hobbyhorse.

They roared into Escambia Bay cocky as a bunch of bulldog pups. What nobody had ever tried before, they had just done. And if they could do it once, they could do it again. Any damn time they pleased. Yet the frosting on the cake was still to come. They got that when everybody ganged around and watched the mill owner pay Harry Swain double the price their logs would have brought upriver.

The partners called a stockholders' meeting of Adair & Company right on the spot, and voted a week's bonus for every man in the crew. Then they swaggered into Pensacola and got blind, stinking drunk. Somewhere along the line— Adair seemed to recall it was after they'd wrecked the third saloon—Swain pulled another disappearing act. Him being a family man and all, they figured he'd headed on home. Which was the Christian thing to do, and dampened the spirit of their celebration not at all. With a full load under their belts, they invaded Ma Smalley's riding academy, the fanciest sporting house in town. And as the police informed them later, they put the girls out of commission, pretty near demolished the house, and gave Ma herself a case of the nervous twitters.

All in all, it had been a mortally satisfying experience.

Their story finished, Adair and his men announced that they were holding a little contest. And they needed the counsel of the sage minds gathered there at the bar. Somehow it didn't seem proper that young Swain be stuck with such a commonplace given name. After all, with what he'd done *Harry* just didn't fit the ticket anymore. The opening of the Escambia to loggers demanded something more elegant, a moniker with class.

The trouble was, Adair and crew had come up with a couple of dandy names but they couldn't decide between them. Trailblazer Swain had a good ring to it. But the other one, Pathfinder Swain, wasn't anything to sneeze at either. So they were going to leave it up to the town. Whatever folks started calling the youngster, that's how he'd be known.

Personally, Joe Dan Adair observed, he didn't give two hoots and a holler. Whether it was Trailblazer or Pathfinder, it all worked down to the same thing. That Swain kid was a goddamn wizard. Still squiffed to the eyeballs, Adair was soon overcome by the blubbery look common to all melancholy Irishmen with short fuses and tender hearts. So he saved the moment with that honored and most ancient of all Gaelic traditions.

Hammering the bar, he ordered another round for the house.

Jane Bowen Hardin Swain was proud as punch and mad as a wet hen, which was a little hard to manage all at one time. She gave the cake batter a vicious lick and grumped something very unladylike to herself. The more she thought about it the madder she got, and just then, she was thinking about it plenty.

Her husband had again proved himself. Shown that he was something more than a common outlaw and killer of men. He had a keen head for business, not to mention shrewd judgment, and the gift of swaying others with nothing more

than reason and soft words. That was apparent in the way
he'd made this logging venture pay so handsomely. While
stodgy old-timers sat mired in worn-out methods and hide-
bound customs, he looked deeper, sought new insights, and
came up with a better way. Like visualizing the Escambia as
one long water chute. Daring something no one else had ever
tried. And doubling the profits!

It was grand and glorious. To her, almost godlike.

But how did that fool Irishman repay him? Not to mention
the townspeople and her own family. With a childlike contest
and a name pirated straight out of Fenimore Cooper's books.
It was outrageous. Humiliating. More than that, it was crude
as spit.

She heard footsteps and got busy whipping the batter. A
moment later her husband came through the kitchen door,
whistling softly, and gave her a swat on the rump.

"What's for supper, woman? I'm hungry as a bear."

Sniffing, she gave the batter a savage whack. "You seem
awfully chipper."

"Well, I oughta be. Just got Adair and his boys sobered
up and packed off to camp. Which, in case you don't know
it, is one mighty full day's work." She thumped the batter
harder, saying nothing, and studied her a bit closer.
"Somethin' the matter? You look like you just swallowed a
mouthful of hornets."

"Very funny. I must say, you're certainly taking it
calmly."

"Taking what calmly?" Puzzled, he shot a glance back
toward the front of the house. "Is there somethin' wrong
with the kids?"

"No, there is nothing wrong with the children. They're
having a nap. And you know perfectly well what I mean."

"Well, if I do it's news to me. What the sam hill are you
gettin' at, anyway?"

"What I'm getting at is the latest town joke." She
slammed the batter in a cake pan, then spat out the words,
her lips pinched tight. "Trailblazer Swain."

"Great God A'mighty. Is that what's got your goat? They

was just havin' some fun. Nothin' but a bunch of drunks jabberin' whiskey talk.''

"That's exactly what I mean!'' Her eyes blazed and she waved the mixing spoon overhead like a broadsword. "Drunks sit around giving you nicknames and the good people of this town laugh themselves hoarse. It degrades everything you've accomplished in the last month.''

"Now is that a fact?'' He grinned and cocked one eyebrow. "What would you say if I told you that Mr. Lionel Culpepper—the big-dog banker himself—asked me in for a little chat today?''

"He did?'' She blinked and lowered the spoon.

"Yes ma'am, he did. Thought I might be interested in a deal he's been hatchin' up. And I was.''

"You were?''

"Yep. Seems like he's got his hooks on some timberland down below Wawbeek and he thought we might figure some way to divvy up the profit. Turned out to be simple as pie. He wanted half and I let him twist my arm into givin' him a quarter.''

"But why did he—I mean, he owns the timber.''

"Yeah, but I know how to get it to Pensacola. See, that's what had him stumped all these years. There ain't no way to float logs upstream.''

Her cheeks went red as beet juice. "I was silly to worry, wasn't I?''

"Sure you were. Them swells, the good people you was talkin' about, they don't care what handle a man goes by. Not so long as he can make 'em some money. You just wait and see, before long they'll be invitin' us to come have supper at their big fine houses.''

"You really think so?''

"Know so. Fact is, I'm givin' odds.''

Jane grabbed up the cake pan and whirled across the kitchen in lazy circles. "Oh, Wes, I'm happy as a pig in mud.''

"The name's Trailblazer, ma'am. And I'm right proud to see you smilin' again. 'Course, you oughta be, squatted down amongst all these Bowens. It's like havin' a whole tribe for your very own family.''

She shushed him. "You know that's not it. It's being clear of the law and you so successful and having men like Mr. Culpepper seek out your advice. Don't you see, we might really make it this time. Have—well, you know—all those things we talked about and didn't really believe.''

"Speakin' of which.'' A funny little gleam flickered in his eyes. "How long you reckon we've got before the kids wake up?''

She slid the cake pan in the oven and spun like a dizzy butterfly to the door. Then she turned, tossed her apron in the air, and gave him a lewd wink. "Mr. Trailblazer, I figger we got an hour 'fore that cake is done. Now, if you need any help findin' the path, jest stick with me.''

She danced away and he followed her through the door.

5

The preacher lifted his hands to heaven.

"Now, if y'all will stand and please turn to page one-nine-three in your hymnals.''

The congregation rose, an obedient flock, and there was a rustling flutter as they thumbed through their hymnbooks. From the front of the church, hidden by a screened partition, came a muffled *thump-thump-thump* as one of the Butler kids jackhammered air through the pump. Then the organ wheezed to life, and Maybelle Floskins, grinning like a horse eating briars, assaulted the keyboard with her stubby fingers. The faithful drew a collective breath, watching Preacher Cleve Blalock's lead, and raised their voices on high as the organ thundered out of the prelude.

On a hill far away
Stood an old rugged cross
The emblem of suffering and shame

Singing loudly, if slightly off key, Harry Swain stood in the second pew from the front, on the left side of the aisle.

Beside him were his wife and children, and together they comprised a living model of what every Methodist family aspired to be. Little Molly, going on four, was starched and fluffed, a flaxen-haired cameo of her mother. The youngest Swain, two-year-old Johnny, was decked out in a little man's suit and already displayed the roughly chiseled features of his sire. Jane, whose clear alto compensated somewhat for her husband's jarring baritone, was never more radiant.

And never more proud. Deacon Ura Suggs, not ten minutes past, had ushered them down the aisle and seated them only one pew from the front on the left-hand side, directly behind banker Lionel Culpepper and his family. In the Polland scheme of things, it was an engraved announcement to one and all. The Swains had arrived.

After the hymn, Reverend Blalock led his flock through the Lord's Prayer and motioned for them to resume their seats. Then he drew himself up to his full height, eyes glittering with fire and brimstone, and launched into a fist-pounding sermon on the insidious horrors of demon rum. His topic for the morning was prompted in no small part by a courtesy call from the Ladies Temperance League earlier in the week. The good reverend, not only supported their cause with fervor and straitlaced rectitude, he also knew who wore the pants in most Polland families. His sepulchral wrath set the church rafters to vibrating, and predictably enough, John Barleycorn took a real thrashing from Christ as the sermon built to a crescendo.

Harry Swain listened with only half an ear. Demon rum posed no threat to him personally. He could take it or leave it, and mostly he left it. Moreover, several Sundays each year throughout his boyhood, he had heard John Barleycorn raked over the coals in a manner that made Preacher Blalock's sermon a pale imitation of the real article.

The thought made him smile inwardly. Reverend James Hardin had few equals when it came to Fundamentalist, Bible-thumping old-time religion. The mellifluous, honey-tongued voice—interspersed at key moments with a crisp, barking jolt—kept his congregation wide awake and in fear of their mortal souls. Looking back, it seemed that his delivery was inspired, evangelical more than rehearsed, the stuff that made believers of fornicators and idolaters alike. After one of James Hardin's sermons the people of Mount Calm knew better than to monkey with God.

Here lately the young businessman's thoughts had returned frequently to those days. The time of his boyhood. Warm, golden years filled with discovery and never-ceasing marvels. He felt a void, an aching lonesomeness, something unfulfilled. And however much he resisted the idea, he knew it stemmed from his folks.

The plain and simple truth was that he missed them. Perhaps living among the Bowen tribe, seeing the love and tenderness they lavished on one another, had triggered some wistful memory of his own family. Not that it was enervating, or caused him to brood himself into the dumps. His folks had been strict and unbending, never the kind to display affection. So it wasn't that. They loved him, and had proved it in their own way, and he'd never felt the need for syrupy talk and hugs and kisses. It just boiled down to something he sensed in his gut, something he couldn't put a name to or label or spell out even in his own head. He missed them.

Sitting there in the pew, only dimly aware of Preacher Blalock's fire and fury, it came to him that the Hardins hadn't derived much joy from their youngest son. How long ago was it that they'd set their sights on him becoming a schoolteacher? Only seven years. Yet it somehow seemed like more. Another lifetime. And instead he'd brought a different sort of fame to the Hardin name. Scarcely anything to make his folks burst with pride or beat the drum about their secondborn.

Of course, the last couple of years had been better. While there was no way of returning home, or bringing them to visit Polland, he did write them fairly often. The letters were long, filled with news of the kids, and the logging venture, and the fine life he and Jane had made for themselves. But it disturbed him, even after all this time, that his folks couldn't reply. The only word he had of them was through

Jane's family, for she could write her parents using the Bowens as a cover. His letters were mailed on business trips to Pensacola, just in case the Rangers were still nosy about who was writing the Hardins.

Yet, as he considered it now, the whole thing struck him as a little overcautious. It was close to two years since he'd skipped Texas, and just shy of a year since his shoot-out with the Pinks in Savannah. In all likelihood the law had chalked him off as a lost cause and gone on to fresher game. Perhaps things weren't so risky anymore, and handled just right, he might work out a way for his folks to write back. If he got a post-office box in Pensacola, under still another alias—who would be the wiser? It was something to think about anyway. And it would damn sure beat getting the news secondhand. Which was what it amounted to with the tidbits passed along by Jane's mother.

Just for a moment his mind drifted back to the sermon and he was reminded that it was Cleve Blalock who had baptized his children. That must have hurt the old man mightily. To know that some footwasher in Alabama had done the hocus-pocus on his own grandchildren. Doubtless his folks were proud to see him back in the fold, and to know that he had arranged salvation for the kids, but it must have chafed all the same. James Hardin was made of stern stuff, but he wasn't as hard as he put on. Dunking his own grandkids would have been a mortal delight. All the more so since he'd never seen them. But, as every preacher knew, life was no bowl of cherries. Otherwise there would be no need for religion. Or preachers.

Somehow, although he couldn't quite make the connection between preachers and bankers, his mind suddenly jumped to Lionel Culpepper. The banker was seated directly in front of him, and it passed through his mind that for all of Culpepper's righteous ways, there was no forgiveness in the man. Over the last several months they had become thick as thieves, working out a number of deals that had proved mutually profitable. Along the way, though, he had learned much about the man who cracked the whip in Polland. Harry

Swain was accumulating a tidy little nest egg not because Culpepper liked him, but because the banker occasionally needed a front man who was quick with his head. Culpepper called him astute and gifted, buttering him up with four-bit words, but beneath that oily smile beat the heart of a real man-eater. One miscue, like that fiasco last month in Mobile, and Culpepper would toss him to the wolves. Which meant he would have to watch himself closer in the future. A damn sight closer.

He still couldn't figure how things like that happened. It wasn't just that he was a backslider and couldn't resist temptation. There was more to it than that. Had to be. Like maybe some voodoo cloud trailed him around—his own special hex—read to dump on his head whenever he strayed off the straight and narrow. And the hell of it was, he hadn't strayed all that far.

After delivering on a big timber contract, he and Adair had taken the boys to Mobile for a well-earned spree. While the others had swilled booze and sampled half the brothels in town, he'd played it close to the vest. Kept his nose clean, and more than anything else, hung around to bail them out when they finally landed in jail. But after a couple of nights of such nonsense, he'd gotten bored and let himself get sucked into a poker game. And like any damn fool should have expected, there sat a tinhorn who fancied himself greased lightning with both the cards and a gun. The upshot of it was, he called the man for dealing seconds and had to put a leak in his ticker. Outside the saloon, with Adair and the boys in tow, it went from bad to worse. A trigger-happy constable came running up, already primed for bear by the gunshots, and somehow they ended up swapping lead. That part was still a little hazy, but he finally winged the lawman enough to put him down and they made dust going away. Adair awakened a liveryman, paid top price for a team and wagon, and the whole bunch of them quit Mobile that very night.

It was the kind of tomfoolery he could no longer afford. Not just because of the Pinkertons, either. Had anyone tied him to the shootings it would have reflected badly on Culpepper. Everybody knew the banker had taken him under wing, and a scrape like that would have seriously compromised Culpepper's position in the community. And if it was dangerous to monkey with God, it was sheer lunacy to jeopardize the social standing of Lionel Culpepper. A miscue in that direction, just one little slip, would put Harry Swain and family back on the road again. Without a pot and nowhere to squat.

Which was something to ponder. Long and carefully.

Reverend Cleve Blalock was coming down to the wire, flailing John Barleycorn with some choice Scripture. As the sermon mounted to a pitch, and the preacher worked himself into a proper frenzy, the head of the Swain family silently swore the oath. No more booze. Or cards. Or honky-tonk saloons. From here on out it was nose to the grindstone, right around the clock.

Straight as an arrow and stiff as starch.

CHAPTER 10

1

The muggy coastal heat hung over Pensacola like a sweaty blanket. Not unlike most Gulf ports, the city in August was hot and fetid and thoroughly unpleasant. That it was a major railhead, gateway to Alabama and the Florida Panhandle, simply made matters all the worse. Tracks fanned out from the city in a latticework of steel, narrow-gauge arteries linking it with hundreds of inland towns and countless whistle-stops. Throughout the day, trains chuffed in and out of Pensacola, a snarl of fire-breathing monsters drawn to the switchyards as dragons to a den. But along with the human cargo disgorged, and tons of freight embarking overland from the wharfs, the trains left an unmistakable spoor. Thick smoke and grimy soot drifted across the city; combined with the soppy heat, it left Pensacola sweltering in a filthy steam bath.

Coat slung over his shoulder, Ed Duncan stood on the depot platform, eyes riveted on the bands of steel running west from the city. Beads of sweat streamed down his face, and in the humid noonday heat, his shirt stuck to him like a mustard plaster. He felt soaked, limp as a dishrag, a human puddle caught in a vapid blast furnace. Lips pinched tight, his mouth a small cavern of salt, he silently cursed the heat and inept railroads and the South. Mostly the South. At times such as this his thoughts returned to the Orkney Islands, off the coast of Scotland, where he had grown to manhood. It was a land of cool ocean breezes and emerald fields and untainted air, and he found himself wishing he'd never left it.

A wish he'd dwelled on much this past year.

Never a believer in luck, except that which a man made for himself, Duncan had come to a brooding uncertainty about the caprice of time and circumstance. Seemingly, the gods had conspired with fortune, and so far as he, personally, was concerned, the outcome had been nothing short of catastrophic. He had crisscrossed this miserable, steamy land since late last summer, and in all that time he had turned up not one lead as to the whereabouts of John Wesley Hardin. The only thing he'd accomplished was to prove to his own satisfaction that southern hospitality was a fable. Outsiders, which included both Yankees and bandy-legged Scotsmen, were as welcome as a plague of locusts.

After the Savannah shoot-out, Allan Pinkerton had ordered him to resume the manhunt. The young fugitive was to be brought in, according to Pinkerton's directive, regardless of how long it took. Neither the agency chief nor the governor of Texas thought it would be a snap. The man they sought was a most uncommon outlaw, as he had demonstrated to the embarrassment of everyone involved. But none of them, Duncan most especially, had believed that the hunt would consume another year.

The search was resumed in Savannah, where Hardin had disappeared, and it quickly became apparent that Duncan was looking for the proverbial needle in a haystack. Pinkerton had made the case his sole responsibility. There was only one outlaw, the Old Man declared, and it should require only one detective to find him. Duncan struck off alone, checking steamboat lines, outlying railroad depots, and fully a hundred livery stables in surrounding counties. Finally, having exhausted the more likely prospects, Duncan was forced to admit that Hardin had outfoxed the hounds. However he had escaped, it broke the pattern he'd followed since departing New Orleans in the summer of '75.

Duncan returned to Savannah, and began a house-to-house

canvass of farms along roads leading from the city. Late in November, what was now the winter of '76, the drudgery at last paid off. He stumbled across a farmer on the Claxton Road who had sold a horse the summer before to a man answering the description of Wes Hardin. The date fitted, and as the stranger had appeared afoot early one morning, the timing dovetailed neatly with the Savannah shoot-out. After four months of dogged legwork, Duncan finally knew how his man had eluded capture. And more than that, he knew Hardin had headed west into Georgia.

But what seemed good fortune quickly proved nothing more than a fluke. The trail simply evaporated, as if Hardin went up in a puff of smoke after buying the horse. Duncan's line of search, which roughly paralleled Sherman's March to the Sea, became a study in futility. The natives were aloof, hostile, and at times downright insulting. They gave him little conversation, and even less information. If any of them had seen a rider fitting the fugitive's description, they betrayed it by not so much as a flicker of an eyelash. Whatever else they were, Duncan wrote in his reports, these Georgia crackers were good haters and damned accomplished liars.

Before long he came to feel like a blind man groping from one cul-de-sac to another, and by the New Year, he reluctantly called it quits. Hardin had once more slipped through his grasp.

Then, as if fate meant to toy with him a while longer, a shot in the dark bore fruit. At their meeting in Atlanta last summer, Allan Pinkerton had ordered him to have a surveillance placed on Reverend James Hardin's mail. Duncan wrote Austin, suggesting some sort of arrangement be worked out with the postmaster in Mount Calm, and the attorney general set the wheels in motion. Afterward, the detective forgot about it, never once dreaming that Hardin would be so foolhardy. But in early January, with his spirits at a low ebb, he received an astounding communiqué from the Pinkerton office in Chicago. According to Austin, the elder Hardin had gotten two letters, a month apart, both postmarked Pensacola. Implicit in this new wrinkle was the curious fact that the letters bore no return address. While scarcely hard evidence, it was enough to galvanize the Scotsman. At an impasse in Georgia, with the letters his only fresh clue in months, he immediately boarded a train for Florida.

Pensacola proved to be—if anything—more of a dud than Savannah. Duncan at first spent his days haunting the post office and his nights sifting through outgoing mail. When that drew a blank, another month down the drain, he began combing the city. Hardin's favorite hangouts—saloons and gambling dens, cattle auctions and slaughterhouses—were investigated with painstaking care. But all to no avail. By late spring the detective was forced to a distasteful conclusion. John Wesley Hardin had changed his method of operating, doubtless disguising himself behind an occupation completely unrelated to his past. That, or he was living elsewhere and merely using Pensacola as a mail drop. Or he might have played it very cagey and done both.

Which brought things full circle. Another cul-de-sac.

Duncan went through the motions, but his heart wasn't in it. As in Savannah, he widened the search to outlying towns, expecting little and finding less. His actions were those of a skilled man hunter reduced again to the drudge of procedure and legwork. The red-necks of Florida were even less co-operative than the crackers of Georgia, and as the summer wore on his mood slowly soured in the juices of its own frustration.

All the more so since communiqués from Allan Pinkerton informed him that letters continued to arrive in Mount Calm. And with the exception of a stray bird from Mobile, the postmark never varied—Pensacola. Clearly, the man he had tracked so far and so long had come to earth within close proximity of the port city. But where, and in what guise, were questions that defied answer. The detective simmered and stewed, more from his sagging spirits than the heat, and doggedly plodded about the countryside in a game of blind-man's buff.

Then, in late July, he received a cryptic telegraph message from Allan Pinkerton. He was to meet Lieutenant John

Armstrong of the Texas Rangers in Pensacola. Armstrong's train would arrive on the first day of August, and at that time he would explain the purpose of the meeting. There the message ended, and Pinkerton left him to grapple as best he could with his own impatience. Not to mention a seething indignation at a move which had all the earmarks of impending demotion. Otherwise, he could think of no logical explanation for calling up the Rangers.

And now, dripping sweat and boiling mad, he waited on the depot platform as the train slowly screeched to a halt. Several passengers stepped off the coaches, but he had little trouble identifying the Ranger. John Armstrong was tall and rawboned, weathered lean with time. His mouth was straight as a razor slit, covered somewhat by a bristly mustache, and his jutting chin had a cleft so wide it might have been split with an ax. The high-crowned hat, spurs, and six-gun were merely window dressing, like ornaments on a Christmas tree. Plainly, he was a Texan, and from the way he carried himself and kept his eyes squinted in a hawklike scowl, he was damned proud of it.

The two men spotted one another and came together on the platform. They made an odd contrast—the tall, lantern-jawed Texan and the diminutive, pale-eyed Scotsman—and a moment passed as they stared at each other with mutual distaste. Armstrong didn't like Yankees, even the imported variety, and Duncan had an aversion to swaggering gunmen who passed themselves off as peace officers. Which sort of got them off to an even start. The Pinkerton stuck out his hand and the Ranger gave it a perfunctory shake. Then Armstrong shifted his cud and squirted tobacco juice off the edge of the platform.

"Take it you must be Duncan."

"Which rather obviously makes you Armstrong."

The Texan grunted. "Anybody tell you why I was comin'?"

"I was informed by our Chicago office that you would tender an explanation upon arrival."

"Meanin' I was to give you the lowdown."

Duncan drew a long breath and sighed. "Yes, I believe we can say that was the gist of the message."

Armstrong's hawklike gaze flicked around the depot and he lowered his voice to a near whisper. "Hardin finally slipped up. Week ago Saturday, his daddy mailed him a letter to a post-office box here in Pensacola." He jerked his chin back toward the train. "It's in the express car. Oughta be put in his box sometime tonight."

"I presume we're to maintain a watch on the post office and take him into custody when he appears."

"That's the gen'ral idea. Leastways, if he don't make a fight of it."

"And if he does?"

"Let's hope he don't. The governor wants him alive, and I'm the kinda fella that likes to follow orders."

"Apparently the governor didn't feel the Pinkertons could handle the situation without help."

The lawman smiled and squirted the cinders again. "Well, s'pose we just say he thought the Rangers oughta be in on the showdown. However it works out."

Duncan gave him a short look. "Translated, that means after I've chased him for two years Texas wants to claim some of the glory for itself."

"Yeah, but you just chased him. You ain't never caught him. Makes a whole heap of difference."

The little Scotsman conceded grudgingly. "Your logic underwhelms me."

Armstrong liked four-bit words even if he didn't always understand them. "Shorty, you and me is gonna get along just fine. Now what d'ya say we find ourselves a waterin' hole and lemme sluice some of the dust out of my innards. Goddamn, I'd sooner take a whippin' than ride a train."

Duncan turned without a word and headed uptown. The Ranger tagged along, lugging a war bag, thoroughly pleased with the way things had gone thus far. Back in Austin they'd told him to watch himself, warning him that the Pinks would

attempt to grab the headlines. But plain to see, he didn't have
nothing whatsoever to worry about.

This little fella was the runt of the litter.

2

Adair and the loggers looked like a bunch of overfed
schoolboys out on a lark. Laughing and yelling and playfully
swapping punches, they walked forward to where Harry
Swain awaited them outside the sawmill. Under Adair's supervision, the crew had just brought a run down driver and
they were in a mood to celebrate. Over the past year this had
become something of a tradition with Adair & Company.
Several weeks' backbusting work in the woods, then skating
the logs down the Escambia, and afterward, a volcanic spree
that left Pensacola's red-light district in a shambles.

The laughter faded to smiles and some of the exuberance
melted away as they halted in front of Swain. A remarkable
change had come over the young businessman in the last six
months. He was decked out in a conservative suit and looked
spiffy as an undertaker. These days he seldom worked with
the crew, and since the blowout in Mobile had never taken
part in their celebrations. That part they could understand—
killing a gambler and wounding a policeman was reason
enough to lay back for a while. But they knew him as a
carouser and a man who loved a good scrap, and they
couldn't quite fathom his sudden taste for the straight and
narrow. His time was now spent flitting about the countryside, wheeling and dealing on assorted ventures, and rumor
had it that he was becoming wealthy as sin. The men still
liked him, and admired his style, but the closeness, that old
sense of easy familiarity, was gone. Somehow, in a way none
of them could articulate, he was no longer a part of the crew.
He was the boss, both to them and his partner, which was
clear in the way Joe Dan Adair deferred to his judgment. It
sort of put a damper on things at times such as this, and for

that reason alone, they lost some of their raucous good humor in his presence.

Smiling, Swain waited till they ganged around, then gave his partner a steady look. "Joe Dan, I hate to spoil your fun, but Timmons is waitin' for us in his office."

"Aw hell, Harry, there ain't no sense in me bein' there." The Irishman's face wrinkled in a hangdog expression. "All that horse tradin' and contracts and such is your bailiwick."

"Just the same, I think you ought to sit in. We're gonna be talkin' tall cotton, and I want him to know we're both of a mind."

Adair grumped something to himself and fell silent. After a moment Swain glanced around at the crew. "Boys, I'm afraid your wingding is liable to be a little short this time. If we pull this deal off I wanna catch the three-ten back to Polland and get things movin'." He pulled a fancy pocket watch from his vest and checked the time. "That gives you about four hours to tie one on. And don't get yourselves tossed in the jug, neither. I wanna see everybody at the depot bright-eyed and bushy-tailed."

The men sulled up, groaning their displeasure. But he cut them short by hauling out a roll of greenbacks and peeling off several bills. He stuffed the bills in the shirt pocket of Monk Birkhead, the foreman.

"That ought to cover drinks and a quick trip to Ma Smalley's for everybody. Just be sure you get 'em to the train station on time." He started away, then turned back and fished a small key from his vest pocket. "Monk, I'd be obliged if you'll do a little errand for me. This here's the key to my mailbox. Pick up any letters I've got and bring 'em on to the depot."

Swain grinned, waved the crew on their way, and walked off toward the sawmill office. Adair ambled along beside him, hands thrust deep in his pockets, plainly out of sorts. They skirted the scrap heap, picking their way over slabs of bark and refuse, and finally the Irishman couldn't hold it any longer.

"Harry, I don't like to be throwin' rocks, but you're makin' it awful hard for me to live with them boys. I mean, hell's fire, they bust their butts for us and they got a right to blow off a little steam."

"Horseapples! We've got 'em spoiled rotten and you know it." Swain stopped and fixed him with a tight scowl. "Joe Dan, lemme tell you somethin'. We're about to talk turkey on the biggest contract we ever negotiated. Now, I haven't got time to wipe noses and listen to people bellyache. If this deal goes through we'll all be sittin' on easy street. But we're gonna have to quit playin' kid games and buckle down to work."

He paused, scrutinizing the older man closely. "I'd like to know you're with me on this."

Adair nodded and ducked his chin. "Hell, I'm here, ain't I? But that easy street ain't as easy as it sounds. What makes you think Timmons won't beat you down on price?"

Swain flashed a cocky grin. "Because I'm holdin' a club over his head. Pud Moore is just itchin' to sell me his sawmill, and that sort of puts Timmons between a rock and a hard place. I suspect he'd roll over and do tricks to keep me out of the millin' business."

Laughing, he threw an arm over Adair's shoulders. "C'mon, you old goat. Let's go get ourselves a contract. And stop actin' like you're gonna swell up and cry. God A'mighty, I never saw a man fight so hard to keep from gettin' rich."

Adair chuckled despite himself and playfully rapped his young partner in the stomach. Then, of a mind, they marched through the sawmill door. It promised to be a lively session, and in a way, the Irishman was glad he'd been strong-armed into coming along. All of a sudden he had an idea that being rich wouldn't be half bad. Not at all.

Things generally slacked off at the post office after noontime, and the rest of the day became a grinding bore. Back in the mail room, Duncan and Armstrong tried to stay awake swapping stories, but by now they had pretty well exhausted their supply of tall tales and anecdotes. Three weeks had passed, and every minute of every day their eyes remained glued on a certain box and the single letter it contained. They arrived at the post office when it opened each morning and left when the doors were locked each night. And the waiting had slowly become a test of their endurance.

That they had endured one another was no small feat in itself. The only thing they had in common was the man they pursued. Their views on politics, religion, the law, and most particular, methods of apprehending the lawless were poles apart. Their storytelling began as a means to pass the time, but gradually evolved into a device to rankle the one listening. They bickered constantly, sparking some heated arguments, and three weeks sequestered in the post office had hardly brought them closer together. Yet they were both under orders, and despite their antipathy, forced to make the best of a bad bargain. Until Hardin showed it was like it or lump it, and for Ranger and Pinkerton alike, it was strictly a matter of lump it.

The two men had suffered one another's company so long that they had finally come round to rehashing stale arguments. Just now Armstrong had his mouth stuffed with Climax and was glaring fiercely at the little detective.

"The hell you say! There ain't one iota of proof. You're like a possum hound barkin' up an empty tree."

Duncan's mouth quirked in a patronizing smile. "And your problem, Lieutenant, is that you seem blinded by facts. First, the postmarked date on a letter mailed from Mobile to Hardin's father. Next, on the day after that date, a gambler is killed—remember now, Hardin likes his poker—and a policeman wounded. Last, and perhaps most significant, was the fancy pistol shooting. There aren't many men that handy with a gun. Not even in Texas."

That stung and Armstrong recoiled. "Fat lot you know. I could name you a dozen men that could've done better'n that. And them's just the Rangers. Why, hell, there must be a hunnert fellers that good with a gun. Mebbe more."

"In Mobile?" Duncan countered dryly.

"Judas Priest! Arguin' with you is like talkin' with an

anvil." Armstrong squirted a spittoon and knuckled tobacco juice off his mustache. "What I'm tryin' to get through your head is that—"

The detective stiffened, staring wide-eyed at the mailbox. Armstrong looked up in time to see a hand extract the letter and slam the door. Both men leaped from their chairs, guns drawn, and ran to a door at the far corner of the mail room. But once through the door they skidded to a halt. The man walking away from the box was wrong in every respect. Too short. Several years too old. And ugly enough to stop an eight-day clock.

"Sonovabitch, that peckerhead ain't Hardin." Armstrong seemed genuinely perplexed. "What the hell do we do now?"

Duncan's stumpy legs were moving even as the man disappeared through the street door. "We follow that letter. Wherever it goes!"

Then he was gone and the Ranger hurried after him. They hit the street, spotted their man turning downtown, and tagged along a half block behind. For the first time in three weeks, their common denominator brought them together in a union of purpose and mutual need.

Harry Swain was seated on the aisle and next to him Joe Dan Adair sat gazing out the coach window. Last-minute pasengers were hurrying to board the train, but Adair seemed oblivious to the commotion, humming softly to himself. Though his drinking time had been cut drastically short, he was pretty well squiffed and feeling no pain. An hour ago they had signed the largest contract in the history of Adair & Company, and he was fairly bubbling over with good cheer. Just as his partner had predicted, he was on the verge of joining the well-to-do. And for that he thanked neither God nor his lucky stars, but Harry Swain, the slickest horse trader to come down the pike since Heck was a pup.

Their crew was spread out through the coach, ossified on cheap liquor and a bit sapped from their brief but hectic tussle with Ma Smalley's girls. While they were accustomed to somewhat longer benders, a couple of days at least, they really couldn't complain. The boss had footed the bill, plus forking over their regular bonus, which showed that his heart was in the right spot after all. They settled back in the stiff, uncomfortable seats, their hunger slaked for the moment, and began daydreaming about the next time.

The young businessman was preoccupied himself, but with matters of a loftier nature. Monk Birkhead had brought a letter from his mailbox—the first letter in two years from his folks—and he was rapidly devouring the hometown news. Although his head swirled with contracts and figures and potential profits, he set such things aside as he skimmed through the letter. Everybody in the family was well and overjoyed that he had again found the Lord, and, of course, they were delighted with his business success. Not to mention the children and the steadying influence of his good wife. Mount Calm was peaceful and thriving, and church membership was on the rise. Old friends often inquired about him, and the family offered prayers each night that he find a horn of plenty in the land where he had built a new life.

Reading that, he chuckled to himself. It seemed that nothing had changed in Mount Calm. Or in the Hardin household either. Maybe that was the way of it, though. How it was meant to be. Some places and some people never changed. Smiling, he again focused on the letter.

"Hands up! Anybody moves gets shot."

The letter fluttered to the floor. Just for a moment he sat there in a witless stupor, hardly able to credit his eyes. A man stood at the front of the coach with a pistol leveled on his chest. And from the garb, and the weathered rawhide look, he scarcely needed to be told who the man was. The Texas Rangers, incredible as it seemed, had found him at last.

Uncoiling, he sprang to his feet, clawing at the Colt in the waistband of his trousers. But the gun refused to budge, its hammer snagged on the bottom of his vest, and he tugged frantically to jerk it clear. Beside him, Joe Dan Adair encountered no problem whatever. Through an alcoholic haze, the old man pegged it as a holdup and fumbled a bulldog pistol from his hip pocket. As he brought it to bear, a little man in a rumpled suit at the back of the coach shot him between the shoulder blades. The impact of the slug drove him forward, angling sideways through the open window, and he fell headlong to the tracks outside.

The young outlaw was still struggling with his own gun, distracted for a moment by Adair's death and the unsettling fact that somebody had him covered from the rear. Then, in the next instant, the Ranger somehow materialized in the aisle, directly in front of him, and clubbed him over the head with a long-barreled Peacemaker. His eyes rolled back in his head like glazed stones and he staggered crazily against the seats. Suddenly he went limp, a huge doll with its stuffing torn loose, then he rebounded off the cushion and slumped unconscious to the floor.

Ed Duncan walked forward, waving his pistol at the rest of the crew. "You men just keep your seats and nobody will get hurt."

He stopped beside Armstrong, who was staring down at the young outlaw. They stood there for a while, hardly able to believe that it had gone so smoothly. That they had captured John Wesley Hardin at last. When the detective finally spoke there was something new in his voice. A note of respect.

"That was a nervy thing you did, John. The lad might well have killed you."

"Naw, hell, there's the nervy one." Armstrong jerked his chin at the crumpled form on the floor. "Had the drop on him and the bastard kept right on tryin' to get that gun untangled."

"You could have shot him, though. I suspect most men would."

"Mebbe. But all I could think of was the governor sayin' he wanted Hardin alive. Been sort of embarrassin' if I'd brought him back in a box."

They fell silent for a moment, then Armstrong glanced down at the detective. "Ed, I'm obliged to you for takin' care of that other feller. What with me bird-doggin' Hardin the way I was, I got an idea you saved my bacon.''

Duncan smiled. ''Professional courtesy, John. You would have done the same for me.''

The Ranger's mouth creased in a small grin. ''Yep, reckon I would at that. But I owe you, all the same.''

Armstrong extended his hand and the little Scotsman gave it a hearty shake. Then, while Duncan kept the logging crew covered, the lanky Texan grabbed Hardin by the heels and dragged him off the train. As he backed through the coach door, Ed Duncan was whistling softly under his breath. A sprightly tune, Scottish in origin, and better played on the bagpipes. But it seemed fitting nonetheless, for he was a happy man, at peace once again with himself.

Two years and twenty-one days. And done with at last.

3

The cell was nothing to write home about. It was small, with a bunk and washstand on one side, and a table with a couple of chairs on the opposite wall. Under the bunk was a slop jar, but as the guards emptied it only once a day, the whole place reeked of an outhouse. The view wasn't bad, though. Not if a man liked to look at the capitol building. The jail fronted San Jacinto Street, right in the heart of Austin, and they had given him a cell on the top floor. Standing at the window, he could gaze out over the bustling city, and ironically enough, had a beeline view of the governor's office.

Which was where he spent the most part of every day. There, staring out the window, or else pacing back and forth like a caged animal. The jailers kept a wary eye on him, for he was restless and seldom off his feet. Not until late at night, when he was worn out from pacing, did he flop on the bunk and try to sleep. But even then, it was difficult to rest. He felt trapped, a great lobo caged in steel, the freedom he prized above all else gone forever. Better had they shot him,

put him in the ground, for a wolf deprived of his freedom
was no wolf at all. He was simply a beast, mindlessly pacing
his stinking lair in numbed rage.

He paused at the window, staring out across at the capitol.
Again he was struck by the question that ate on him, nibbling
at his bowels with sharp little teeth. What good is the law in
a land where there is no justice? Like Texas. Where the men
in power twist the law to suit their own ends.

The governor wanted him caught and caged. So the man
hunters had tracked him down. Taken him captive in a state
where their badges meant nothing. Killed an innocent man
in the process. All without warrant or legal right of seizure.
Then, compounding the illegality of their act, they had spirited him back to Texas. And again, on order from the governor. Simply shunted aside the judiciary process. Ignored
the accused's right of habeas corpus and the fundamental
privilege of extradition proceedings. Slapped him in irons
and shoved him aboard a train. Hustled him across half a
continent in defiance of all laws ever written to protect the
rights of an accused man. The trial had been held in absen-
tia—a kangaroo court invoked by the law-makers themselves—and the verdict rendered. Innocent until proved
guilty ceased to exist. The law and the governor and the state
of Texas had decreed that justice was better served if certain
men were shortchanged on their rights, brought to bay and
caged in the most expeditious manner possible.

Which made them worse than the man they jailed. Their
lawlessness was larded with deceit. The act of hypocrites. A
mockery of the very system they were sworn to uphold. Beside them, an outlaw was an honest man. He risked all in
open defiance. They risked nothing, for it was within their
power to pervert the law according to the needs of the moment. To make justice a sham and evil a virtue. All in the
name of honor and decency and the state's inviolate right to
an eye for an eye.

Standing there, his gaze fixed on the windows of the governor's office, Wes Hardin was an embittered man. Not from

hate or a thirst for revenge. Nor as an outgrowth of his long vendetta with those who enforced the law. They were merely hired help, mercenaries earning their daily bread. Instead, his rancor was for the kingfish. The high and mighty. The men who called the shots. He felt like a gambler who had played the game squarely, calling every bet and never questioning the stakes, only to find in the end that the cards had been marked all along.

A game rigged by the anointed. The lawmakers themselves.

Footsteps in the corridor broke his train of thought, and he became aware that someone had stopped outside his cell. He turned from the window, and seeing them there, such an unlikely pair, made him smile. Standing outside the door was his nemesis, Ed Duncan, and the detective's lanky sidekick, John Armstrong. Curiously, he felt no bitterness toward these men. They had taken him alive, when they might as easily have killed him, and on the long journey back to Texas they had treated him fairly and with respect. Against orders, they had even allowed him to pen a hasty letter to Jane, informing her of his capture. Perhaps they were lawdogs, but they weren't bastards. In a queer sort of way, he'd grown to like them. What his educated lawyer called friendly adversaries.

He crossed the cell and stuck his hand through the bars. "Mornin', gents. How's tricks?"

Both men shook his hand and Duncan returned the smile. "Can't complain. How about yourself?"

"Why, I'm livin' in the lap of luxury, Ed." He motioned back toward the cell. "Soft bed, three squares a day, and somebody to empty my johnny-pot. All the comforts of home."

Armstrong, who rarely smiled anyway, wasn't fooled by the light tone. He shifted his quid to the off-cheek and gave the cell a sour look. "Not much, is it? Seems like they could've done better for a fella of your caliber."

"John, I don't suppose it matters much. However it was fixed up, it'd still be a cage." Wes flashed them a sudden grin, dismissing it with an idle gesture. "Listen here now, that's enough of my troubles. What brings you gents callin' so bright and early?"

"Couple of things," Duncan replied.

"Mebbe three," Armstrong amended, slewing a sidewise glance at the detective. "You recollect that leetle debate, don't you?"

"Yes, to be sure. Our bone of contention. But the good news first." Duncan beamed, thumbs hooked in his vest pockets. "Wes, by rights your lawyer should be telling you this, but since we're feeling particularly fond of you today, we wanted to be the bearers of good tidings. The court has approved the motion for change of venue. Your trial will be held right here in Austin."

Wes was genuinely surprised. "Well, I'll be dipped. Never figured that had the chance of a snowball in hell."

Armstrong clucked, bobbing his head like an old tom turkey. "You're mighty lucky, Wes. Mighty lucky. If that bunch down in Dewitt County had ever got their meat hooks on you, that'd been all she wrote."

"You'll get no argument there. Folks on the Guadalupe wouldn't exactly remember me with what you'd call Christian charity."

He hesitated a moment, studying the lawmen with a quizzical frown. "Speakin' of which. How come you fellows are feelin' especially fond of me today? Old man Pinkerton give you a citation or somethin'?"

"Better'n that." Armstrong managed what passed for a smile.

"Much better." Duncan rocked up on his toes, eyes bright. "Wes, the state has authorized payment of the reward for your capture. John and I will share in it equally. Which is only fair, of course."

"Five thousand simoleons." Armstrong spoke the words with a poor man's reverence.

"Well, kiss my dusty butt!" Wes lit up with a big smile and he pumped their arms in a warm handshake. "By God,

I'm proud as punch. You boys earned it. Ever' nickel of it. If I was out of here I'd stand you to a round of drinks.''

The irony of his statement struck them at the same time and they all burst out laughing. Then, after their laughter slacked off, Duncan gave him a sober look.

"Wes, we're pleased you took it this way. John said you would, and I tended to agree, but we're gratified nonetheless."

"Hell's bells, I don't hold you fellows no grudge. You was just earnin' your keep, and that's all there is to it. Besides, I come out smellin' like a rose. Listen here, I damn near keeled over when I found out they was only gonna prosecute me on one count. And for shootin' Charlie Webb, too! Christ, that's the biggest joke I ever heard.''

"Don't let it tickle you too much," Armstrong commented glumly. "They got witnesses on that one, and the word's out—they're figgerin' on stretchin' your neck."

Wes waved it off. "Hide and watch. We got a few tricks up our sleeves. Might turn out a whole lot different than most folks think.''

The lawmen exchanged a look more eloquent than words. Clearly, they didn't share his optimism. A moment passed in silence, and then Duncan snapped his fingers.

"Say, that reminds me. What John said about our debate. Now, if you would rather not talk about it, we'll understand. And naturally, anything you say is off the record. But we've had this argument going, and if you could clear up a few loose ends, we would certainly be in your debt."

Wes nodded, mildly puzzled. "Argument about what?"

"The fact of the matter is"—Duncan faltered, groping for words—"Wes, there isn't any easy way to ask this. You see, our debate has to do with your gunfights."

"Aw, quit pussyfootin' around, Ed." Armstrong shifted his quid and glanced back at the outlaw. "What he's trying to ask you is how many men you've killed."

The Ranger gave him a sly wink and Wes just nodded, solemn as a judge. Then, pursing his lips, he looked over at the little detective. "Well, Ed, lemme ask you—was you talkin' about white men, or did your argument include Injuns and greasers?"

Duncan's eyes went round as saucers. "Why—uh—I don't know, really. I suppose men are men, regardless of their color." He paused, still uncertain, and shrugged. "In all fairness to John, I think it's the overall number we would have to consider."

Wes rubbed his jaw and spent several moments in deep calculation. Finally he grunted. "Course, you understand, I never notched my guns or any such foolishness. So I might be off a couple either way. But near as I can figure, I'd say forty would come pretty damn close."

Duncan blinked, plainly startled, but Armstrong cackled softly and slapped him across the shoulders. "See there, you little runt. Told you, didn't I? Next time you won't be so quick to put your money where your mouth is."

The Scotsman swallowed, and then, quite softly, "Forty?"

"Give or take a few. Gets a little fuzzy that far back."

"Lad, I've done you a grave injustice. A man should never underestimate his adversary. Particularly in our line of work."

Duncan was still shaking his head when they left, not at all himself. But for once Armstrong actually appeared jovial, as if he had pulled off some rare coup that only a Texan could fully comprehend.

A little later Wes heard footsteps and thought they had returned with more questions. Pleased with the joke, and himself, he crossed the cell ready to lay it on thick. Then he froze, everything suddenly gone blurred and somehow distorted, like looking through a windowpane smeared with the splatter of raindrops.

Standing at the cell door, were James and Sarah Hardin. They had never been a family to show affection, but his arms went through the bars now and embraced them in a tight hug. There were tears streaming down his mother's face, and as far back as memory served, it was the first time he remembered his father turning loose. They held him close through the bars, content just to touch, and for a long while nobody spoke. At last, the old man cleared his throat, swallowing hard, and looked up.

"Son, if it's not too late, we've come to help."

4

The trial was an event. A Texas-style Roman circus. The biggest thing to happen in Austin since the carpetbaggers departed back in '74. The newspaper ballyhooed it with reams of purple prose. John Wesley Hardin, Texas' most notorious desperado, was to be tried for murder. By early September the sensationalism had built to a fever pitch, and people converged on Austin from all directions to see the spectacle. Their mood was carnival, laughing and high-spirited, and a holiday atmosphere settled over the city. They had come to gawk at the most deadly gunfighter of them all, the swaggering young bravo who reputedly had killed a man for every year of his life.

But if the trial was a drawing card, the main attraction would come afterward. At the scaffold, where condemned men spent their last moments dancing on air. Feeling ran strong on that score, though. Some people remembered the days of Yankee oppression, and their sentiments were with the youngster. Yet others had shorter memories, and were perhaps more honest. For those who flocked to Austin on that warm September day—whatever their jangled emotions; whatever their heated disclaimers—were there of one mind and one purpose and but a single expectation.

They came to watch Wes Hardin be hung.

An overflow crowd filled the courtroom, with spectators jammed shoulder to shoulder along the walls. Down front, a company of Rangers, armed to the teeth and primed for trouble, stood ready should the onlookers become unruly. Seated at the defense table was the accused and his attorney, Horace Adams of Waco. Directly behind them, on the other side of the rail in the front row, was Jane Hardin and the defendant's

parents. The prosecution table was across the room, nearer
the jury box, and on the bench sat Judge Marcus White.
Earlier that morning the jury had been impaneled, but only
after Horace Adams exhausted all his peremptory challenges.
A noted criminal lawyer, with a flair for drama and a mellifluous voice, Adams had left the impression that his client
was unlikely to receive a fair trial anywhere in the state of
Texas, much less in the capital city itself.

Afterward, Judge White gave everybody a stiff lecture
about their conduct in his courtroom and the trial began. Tate
Belford, special prosecutor appointed by the governor, made
a lengthy opening address in which John Wesley Hardin
came off as a cross between a depraved scoundrel and a mad-
dog killer. He vowed to prove beyond a shadow of a doubt
that the accused had gunned down Deputy Sheriff Charles
Webb in cold blood. Defense counsel held his opening remarks to a minimum, gently ridiculing the state's inflam-
matory assertions. He drew laughs from the crowd, which
Judge White quickly silenced, and tentative smiles from the
jurors. Having harpooned Belford where it hurt, he quit while
he was ahead.

The prosecutor was an old hand, and while rankled by the
gibes, he was never in any danger of losing his composure.
With the stage set, and the spectators hanging on his every
word, he began to unravel the state's case. Throughout the
morning a half-dozen witnesses, freshly imported from Dewitt County, were paraded to the stand. Without exception,
they were former members of the Sutton Vigilance Committee, and with only minor variations, they all told the same
story. The accused and his kinsmen had killed Deputy Webb
without provocation or reason. Foul murder, three against
one, with the peace officer riddled full of holes. Belford even
managed to sneak in some testimony about a conspiracy,
hinting that the death of Charles Webb was, in fact, premed-
itated murder. Adams strenuously objected and Judge White
ruled the testimony inadmissible. But the jury had heard,
nonetheless. After several gory recountings of the killing itself, and heavy stress on three gunmen against a lone peace

officer, the notion of a conspiracy was easily swallowed.

Adams' cross-examination was brutally incisive, leaving the witnesses rattled and bathed in sweat, but he failed to dislodge them from their story. The prosecution had drawn first blood, and the jurors began eyeing Hardin as if he were a molester of little girls.

Then, pausing for effect, Tate Belford offered up the *coup de grâce*. He called to the witness stand Clarence Spivey, sheriff of Dewitt County. They worked well together, and made a hard act to follow. Tate knew the questions and Spivey had all the answers. In ten chilling minutes, Spivey related how he had stood on the courthouse steps and watched Wes Hardin, assisted by Jim Taylor and Bud Dixon, murder Deputy Charles Webb. There was no doubt as to the identity of the killers, and having witnessed it with his own eyes, he could verify that the dead man never had a chance to defend himself. It was outright murder, with all the mercy of three men slaughtering a hog.

Belford resumed his seat, looking immensely pleased with himself, and Adams rose for cross-examination. He approached the witness stand scratching his head, almost hesitant, apparently puzzled by something he'd heard.

"Sheriff, I confess I'm at a bit of a loss. You stated you were on the courthouse steps when the shooting occurred. Is that correct?"

Spivey was a paunchy, whey-faced man with a nose the color of rotten plums. On guard now, he squinted back at the lawyer through rheumy eyes. "It is."

Adams still looked perplexed. "You weren't in your office?"

"No."

"Afraid to show your face?"

"No."

"And isn't it a fact, Sheriff"—Adams turned to face the jury and his voice cracked like a bullwhip—"that on the day in question you were *dead drunk*?"

Belford leaped to his feet. "Objection! Counsel is badgering the witness, your honor."

"Sustained," Judge White intoned. "Watch your step, Mr. Adams."

Adams nodded and turned back to the witness. "If you weren't drunk, Sheriff, perhaps you could tell us where your deputy was during the shooting. I believe his name is Dave Karnes."

Spivey batted his eyes a couple of times. "Why, I seem to recollect he was back in the office."

"Wasn't that rather odd? That he wasn't with you while a shooting was in progress?"

"Not especially. We had no way of knowin' there was gonna be a fight."

"You didn't know that Charles Webb was in town for the express purpose of confronting John Wesley Hardin?"

"I did not."

"And I suppose you'll tell us next that you did not send Deputy Karnes to warn Wes Hardin of Webb's avowed intention to shoot him dead?"

Spivey bridled with indignation. "That's what I'm gonna tell you awright,'cause it never happened."

"By the way, Sheriff, where is Dave Karnes now?"

"I wouldn't know. Turned out he didn't have the stomach for law work and I had to fire him."

"Oh, when was that?"

Spivey's nose purpled and his store-bought teeth clacked together. "Couple o' weeks back."

"Now, isn't that strange? You mean to say that after three years as your deputy you decided he wasn't fit to be a peace officer?"

"That's right."

"Wasn't that a little—sudden?"

"Nope. He had a family and I just hated to do it, that's all."

"Very commendable. A lawman with a soft heart." Adams stalked back to the defense table, then whirled, leveling his finger at the witness. "Sheriff Spivey, I offer you one last chance. Will you here and now recant the lies you have just told this court?"

Belford bounced out of his chair, sputtering with rage. Judge White waved him silent and looked across at the jurors. "The jury will disregard defense counsel's last question." Then he turned back to Adams. "Counselor, you are bordering on contempt of court. Let this be my last warning."

"I understand perfectly, your honor." Adams took his seat. "Defense has no further questions of this witness."

Presently, after the spectators were quieted and order restored, it became apparent that Spivey was the state's final witness. Belford rested his case for the prosecution and Judge White called noon recess. Adams conferred briefly with his client, expressing guarded optimism. They had lost ground, he admitted, but the day was still young. Wes was allowed a few minutes with Jane and his folks, and he could see from their quivery looks that they were worried. As he was himself. The morning hadn't been a spectacular success. Then, all too suddenly, the jailer tapped him on the shoulder and he was returned to his cell for lunch.

Shortly before two that afternoon court was reconvened. Everyone was in place as Judge White took the bench. He rapped his gavel several times, hammering the crowd into silence, then peered over his glasses at Adams.

"Does defense counsel wish to make an opening statement?"

Adams rose. "No, your honor. Our remarks will be reserved for the summation."

"Very well. You may proceed with your case."

"If it please the court, defense will call but two witnesses. The first is former deputy sheriff of Dewitt County, David R. Karnes."

The crowd erupted in a buzz of speculation and Judge White again hammered them into silence. Dave Karnes, who had been secreted into town only that morning, came forward and took the witness stand. After the oath had been administered Horace Adams crossed the room and stood where he could watch the jurors' faces.

"Mr. Karnes, I believe you served as deputy sheriff of Dewitt County for three years. Is that correct?"

Karnes had put on weight, but he was still fidgety and somewhat unsure of himself. "Yessir, that's correct."

"And you were dismissed from that position two weeks past. On August 27, I believe."

"Yessir, I was."

"Correct me if I'm wrong, Mr. Karnes, but wasn't that just four days after the defendant was captured in Pensacola, Florida?"

"Yessir."

"I see. Now if you will, please tell the court the circumstances prompting your dismissal."

Prosecutor Belford jackknifed to his feet. "Objection! Irrelevant and immaterial, your honor. This has no bearing on the murder of Charles Webb."

"On the contrary," Adams countered. "With the court's indulgence I will show the connection."

Judge White steepled his fingers, considering a moment, then peered down from the bench. "Overruled. Make your point quickly, Mr. Adams. You're skating on thin ice."

Adams smiled and focused once more on the witness. "You may answer the question, Mr. Karnes."

Dave Karnes gulped, took a long breath, and let it all out in a rush of words. "Well, at first, when we heard that Hardin had been captured, nothin' much happened. Ever'body took it real calm. Then a few days later—the twenty-seventh, it was—we got word he was gonna be tried for killin' Webb and quick as scat some of the old Sutton bunch showed up at the sheriff's office."

"You're referring to the followers of William Sutton, who opposed Hardin and his relatives in the Sutton-Taylor feud?"

"Yessir, them's the ones."

"Proceed."

"Well, they shooed me out of the office and there was a lot of yellin' and cussin', and then finally they left. Afterward, the sheriff called me in and told me I was fired. I asks why and he says there's certain people that don't want me around to tell what I know about Webb gettin' hisself killed. When I commenced makin' a fuss the sheriff gave it to me straight. Told me he couldn't protect me. Said if I didn't get out of town, and keep my mouth shut, them same people would turn me into worm meat.''

"So you ran. To protect yourself and your family.''

"Yessir, I shore did. That very day.''

"And why have you come forward now, Mr. Karnes?''

"Why, 'cause you subpoenaed me and had me shanghaied up here. I ain't no damn fool.''

The crowd burst out laughing, and Adams noticed several jurors smothering their smiles. Judge White banged his gavel, and when things settled down, Adams picked up the thread of Karnes's testimony.

"You made a statement that interests me, Mr. Karnes. You said, and I quote—certain people didn't want you around to tell what you knew about Webb getting hisself killed. What did you mean by that phrase—Webb getting hisself killed?''

"Just what I said. Webb come over from Brown County with a bunch of hardcases, all likkered up he was, and commenced braggin' around town how he was gonna kill John Wesley Hardin. Said it'd be easy as shootin' fish in a barrel. Well, a little before sundown, right after the races, the sheriff sent me over to the saloon to warn Hardin. Webb didn't mean nothin' to us, him bein' from another county and all, and the sheriff said he figgered he'd keep hisself in good with the Taylors just in case they won the feud.''

Karnes paused for breath, acutely aware of the jurors watching him and the hushed stillness that had fallen over the courtroom. After a moment, he resumed. "Well, anyhow, I called Hardin outside and about that time Webb walks over. I introduced 'em and Hardin offered to shake hands and that's when Webb shot him.''

"Excuse me, Mr. Karnes. You're absolutely sure of that? Webb shot first? While Hardin was offering to shake hands?''

" 'Course I'm sure. Webb shot him and then Hardin shot him back. Hardin only got off one shot, 'cause he was fallin',

y'see. And then Taylor and Dixon opened up and pumped
Webb full of holes. Never saw nothin' like it. And don't
want to again.''

"Now, let me see if I have it straight. Hardin shot only
once and his companions fired a number of times. Is that
correct?''

"That's exactly correct.''

"Very well, Mr. Karnes. Now think carefully. You were
standing there, the only true eyewitness to the shooting. Is it
possible that Charles Webb could have survived the *one shot*
fired by Hardin?''

Karnes shrugged. "Yeah, I suppose so. Leastways Hardin
lived through the one Webb give him.''

"Quite true. Now consider carefully again, Mr. Karnes. Is
it possible that Charles Webb could have survived the mul-
tiple wounds inflicted on him by Taylor and Dixon?''

"No way on earth! They riddled him like a sieve.''

"Then isn't it extremely likely that Charles Webb was
killed not by John Wesley Hardin but rather by Jim Taylor
and Bud Dixon?''

Belford slammed out of his chair. "Objection! Calls for a
conclusion on the part of the witness.''

"I withdraw the question, your honor.'' Adams moved
away from the jury box, then stopped and looked back. "One
final question, Mr. Karnes. Is it your belief that Hardin fired
in self-defense?''

"Why shore. Webb shot first. 'Sides, Webb didn't have
no business in Dewitt County, anyways. He always was
pushin' in where he didn't belong.''

"Thank you, Mr. Karnes.'' Adams strolled to the defense
table, then turned and gave Tate Belford a genial smile.
"Your witness, counselor.''

The prosecutor tried, but with each question his cross-
examination seemed to spill more worms from the can. He
badgered, bullied, and browbeat, and the witness squirmed
like jelly throughout the ordeal. But for all his fidgets and
gulping of air, Dave Karnes couldn't be swayed from his
story. He told what had happened, what he had seen, and

nothing could change that. Not even an enraged special prosecutor. When he finally left the stand, bathed in a cold sweat, the former lawman's testimony was still intact.

A nervous murmur swept back over the spectators as Karnes walked from the courtroom. They knew what was coming next, the opening refrain in a dance of death. The very thing that had brought them to Austin. And Horace Adams didn't disappoint them. He stepped away from the defense table, nodded to Judge White, and in a deceptively quiet voice spoke the words they waited to hear.

"The defense calls John Wesley Hardin."

Staring straight ahead, wooden-faced, Wes marched to the stand and repeated the oath. Then he lowered himself into the witness chair and waited. Counsel for the defense again positioned himself at the far end of the jury box. He wanted nothing to distract the jurors from his client, or what they were about to hear, and his first question claimed their attention like a clap of thunder.

"Wes, did you or did you not shoot Charles Webb on the afternoon of May 26, 1874?"

"Yessir, I did."

"Had you ever seen Webb before that day?"

"No sir. I hadn't. Fact is, I'd never even heard of him."

"To set the record straight, then, will you please tell this court why you shot him?"

The defendant shifted slightly, and his gaze came to rest squarely on the jurors. "Webb walked up to me friendly and smilin' like, and when he was introduced, I offered to shake. He latched onto my hand and jerked a gun with his left hand, and then he shot me. He was yellow clean through to pull a trick like that, and as long as he'd started it, I figured I was within my rights to shoot him back."

"And you fired solely in self-defense, is that correct?"

"Yessir, it is."

"Were you aware at the time that Charles Webb was then a deputy sheriff of Brown County?"

"I was. Dave Karnes had just got through tellin' me. But Webb had no jurisdiction in Dewitt County, and even if he

had, he never said a word about arrestin' me. He just said
somethin' like, 'Pleased to meet you,' and then he shot me.''

"Other than the shooting itself, do you have any particular
reason to remember the occasion?''

"Yessir, I do. It was my birthday.''

"How old were you that day?''

"Twenty-one.''

"And you were out celebrating with friends?''

"Well, I was. Webb sort of busted up the celebration.''

Adams paused, watching the jurors smile and nod, and
waited for a twitter of laughter to subside among the spectators. "Now, Wes, I have but one final question. I want you
to take your time and answer it in your own words. It is
rumored that you have killed a man for every year of your
life. There is no reason for you to confirm or deny that rumor. Still, it is common knowledge that you have killed a
number of men over the years. And for that reason I ask you
now—before this jury and this court—have you ever in your
life killed a man except in self-defense?''

The courtroom went deathly still. Wes looked from the
lawyer to Jane and his parents, then out over the crowd, and
at last brought his gaze back to the jury box. "When I was
fifteen I killed a man who was tryin' to kill me. Happened
he was black and Yankee soldiers came after me, so I had
to kill some of them. After that the law never let me be.
Someone was always tryin' to kill me—soldiers, carpetbagger police, different kinds of lawmen. But none of 'em ever
gave me a chance to surrender peaceable, to tell my side of
the story. They just came after me and they tried to kill me.
I can't say I regret killin' them, because they brought it on
themselves, and I reckon most of 'em got what they deserved. But as God is my judge, I never killed a man who
didn't try to kill me first. I never robbed nobody or broke
the law in other ways, and I never took pay to kill a man. I
just killed to stay free, and I guess if there's anything worth
killin' for, it's a man's right to freedom.''

He stopped, still looking at the jury, then his eyes moved

to Jane and his mouth ticced in an imperceptible smile. She nodded, blinking away tears, and her lips curved in response. The courtroom remained still, absolutely silent, for perhaps a dozen heartbeats. Then Adams wheeled away from the jury box and strode past the prosecution table.

"Your witness, counselor."

Tate Belford knew better than to monkey with a loaded gun. Never in a month of Sundays could he rattle Hardin. The man appeared made of flint and ice. And just then, it seemed highly improbable that he could even discredit the outlaw for killing a score of men. Somehow, the way Hardin told it, the killings sounded curiously noble, almost patriotic. He would let well enough alone.

"The prosecution has no questions of this witness."

The defendant stepped down from the stand, shoulders squared and head erect, and crossed the courtroom. There was a slight stir in the crowd as he took his seat, then the room froze in utter silence. Horace Adams rose, eyes fastened on the bench, and nodded to Judge White.

"Your honor, the defense rests."

5

Texas was electrified by the news.

John Wesley Hardin would not hang. A jury of his peers had convicted him of second-degree murder. Later polled, the jurors admitted that had it been anyone besides the notorious gunman they would have set him free as a bird. Circumstances surrounding the case, however, made it impossible to render an acquittal verdict. Yet, in all conscience, neither could they send him to the gallows. The outlaw's impassioned, almost eloquent plea from the witness stand had swayed their vote. That, along with the evidence, the jurors readily agreed, had saved him from the rope. Nonetheless, from that same witness chair, he had acknowledged killing a small legion of men. Twenty, perhaps more.

And displayed no sign of either remorse or contrition. Nor did he attempt to excuse the killings, which was to his credit. A proud man to the end, he had not begged.

But if the jurors could not hang him, neither could they turn him loose, perhaps to kill again. However noble a man's intentions—and defending his freedom was perhaps the noblest cause of all—the law demanded payment. Justice must be served. The jury found him guilty of murder in the second degree.

And Judge White sentenced him to twenty-five years.

Newspapers across Texas bannered the story. The youthful outlaw, now only twenty-four, had been spared by the grace of God. And the compassion of twelve very mortal men. Yet, as most editorials agreed, twenty-five years at hard labor in Huntsville Prison was hardly a slap on the wrists. Another jury and another judge might have hung him. But in the end, perhaps mercy was the better choice after all. It was right that Texas bind up its wounds. Set aside its grim memories of Yankee injustice and carpetbagger rule. Turn its eyes onward, to a new day and a fresh beginning.

The time for vengeance had passed.

Oddly enough, everyone seemed satisfied with the verdict except the convicted man himself. Wes Hardin had not compromised himself on the witness stand. Nor had he pandered to the jury, hoping to touch their soft spot and exact some form of clemency. He staunchly believed in man's God-given right to defend the most precious of all possessions—his freedom. The testimony he gave was not meant as an appeal. Nor did he seek to mitigate the act of killing itself, or the fact that in seven brief years he himself had killed some twenty-odd men. Instead, he had played for all the marbles, staking everything on his belief that a man who relinquished the right to defend himself was no man at all.

And in that, he had lost.

But any gambler worth his salt knows when to check the bet. However much he believed himself innocent of wrongdoing—especially in the killing of Charlie Webb—the jury had met him only halfway. That they had not voted acquittal, he found it difficult to accept, or comprehend. That they had shown him mercy, instead, both astounded him and unnerved his deep-rooted conviction that man was the least tolerant of all God's creatures. Yet, the fact remained, he had gambled and lost.

Which was a damn good time to fold his cards and call it a day. There were other murder warrants outstanding, more than he cared to recall. And to appear ungrateful—or even worse, angry—might well goad the state into having another try. They had a grab bag of warrants to choose from, and next time they might dust off one that would give him a short, if somewhat unpleasant, acquaintance with the hangman's noose.

Better to hold his peace. Keep his thoughts to himself. Let them send him to prison. Give the governor his bone. And the public its sugar tit—a substitute of sorts—for not seeing him hang. Then, after biding his time for a while, anything might happen. It was a mortal wonder what a man could do when he set his mind to it. And Huntsville was scarcely impregnable. Either from without or from within.

Freedom was illusive but it wasn't yet lost.

Now wasn't the time, though. Nor was the place just exactly right. He was in the visitors' room of the Austin jail, manacled hand and foot, and outside the door stood a company of Rangers waiting to escort him to the penitentiary. The Ranger captain had allowed time for final farewells, and only moments before his folks had left the room. Their parting had gone well, all things considered. His mother wept, which was to be expected, and his brother Joe, who had finally put in an appearance, smiled a lot and told him to keep his dauber up. But the old man had surprised him. James Hardin talked not of God or those who live by the sword, and made no mention whatever of his youngest son's misspent life. Instead, he spoke of the future, and the dawning of a new era in Texas. And how, in time, Wes would come back to them and take his place in a more orderly world. It was farfetched, little more than a fairy tale, but Wes had indulged the old man's fantasy. If it gave his folks hope and some measure of comfort, then it was the least he could do. A token gesture, perhaps, but one which would let them sleep easier in the years they had remaining.

All the same he hadn't mentioned his true feelings, or his own plans for the future. Nor would he reveal these things to Jane. What people didn't know couldn't hurt them—or worry them—and what he had in mind was not a thing to be shared. It was best kept in the dark, out of sight and out of mind, until the time was right. Then, if his luck held, and the cards fell right, they might yet find the land of milk and honey, where all roamed free.

The door swung open and Jane stepped into the room. He found it incredible, a small miracle of sorts, that she hadn't changed a bit since those long-ago days on the Brazos. Her smile was still smoky and warm, soft as an autumn sunset. And her eyes, like violets glistening damp with morning dew, were a sight he would carry to his grave. She was one of a kind, this woman of his. Full of fire and mettle, tenderness and love. The stuff that made a man more than he might have been. A restorative not just for his soul, but an elixir that gave reason and purpose to life itself.

She came into his outstretched arms, sliding underneath the manacles, and for a long while they said nothing. The warmth and softness he had known so well seemed all the more precious in these last moments, and he was content just to hold her close. At last, their time fleeting swiftly, she eased back, tilting her head upward, and gave him a searching look.

"You'll never be out of my heart or my mind. Not for a moment. And the day you come home I'll be right there waiting."

There were no tears in her eyes, and never had he been prouder of her than at that moment. He forced himself to smile. "The kids still at your folks'?"

She nodded. "I thought we would stay with them awhile and then visit your folks. They're both close enough to Huntsville, so I'll be able to see you every month on visiting day."

"How you fixed for money?"

"You may be a scamp, Wes Hardin, but you're a very good provider." She cocked her head in that funny little smile. "We'll get along very nicely on the investments you made. So just put that out of your mind."

There was a heavy rap on the door and they both stiffened. Suddenly her eyes went misty and she struggled to hold herself in check.

"I love you, sugar. I always have and I always will."

"Maybe I never told you, but I should've. You're the only woman I ever loved, Janey. Even before we were married, there wasn't nobody but you."

She came into his arms and gave him a kiss that was meant to last. They clung to one another, unable to speak, and then, very slowly, he lifted his manacled hands over her head and stepped back. She sensed he wanted it this way and she didn't move, standing proud and tall as he shuffled to the door. He looked so fine, just the way she would always remember him, strong and vital, like a young hawk floating free on a high, soft wind. Somehow, at that moment, there were no manacles or leg-irons. There was just the boy she had married and the wild, free spirit she had grown to love.

At the door he turned back, flashing that old grin. "Remember that sayin', be careful what you wish for 'cause it might come true?"

Her bottom lip trembled, but she gave him a bright nod.

"Wish real hard, and when the moon's down some dark night, keep a sharp lookout. Maybe your wish'll come true."

She understood. "I'll be waiting. Every night of my life."

The door opened and closed and he was gone. Several moments passed while she listened to the rattle of his leg-irons as he hobbled down the hall. There were voices, muted noises for a bit, then all went silent.

And the waiting began.

EPILOGUE

Never had a man tried so hard to keep a promise.

When the gates of Huntsville Penitentiary clanged shut behind John Wesley Hardin it signaled a battle of wills between prison authorities and the determined young outlaw. It was a battle in which an irresistible force quite literally hurled himself against an immovable object—in this case a stone wall. And with only brief interludes, it was to last for five agonizing years.

Less than a month after entering prison Wes Hardin engineered an escape attempt unlike anything Huntsville had ever seen. In scope, it was actually more of an armed insurrection than a prison break. Assigned to the wheelwright's shop, he allowed himself a week to inspect the layout. What interested him most was the armory, located some seventy-five yards across the prison compound. There the weapons of off-duty guards, both rifles and pistols, were stored in a small building that looked as impregnable as a fortress. But he had no intention of storming the armory. Instead, after considerable reflection, he decided to tunnel underneath the prison yard and enter from below.

With his plans perfected, Wes enlisted into the conspiracy some thirty lifers and long-term convicts. His reputation had preceded him inside the walls and he had no trouble whatever in organizing the revolt. The men selected readily acknowledged his leadership, and digging began on the first day of November.

Their goal was to tunnel into the armory, seize the guns, and arm upward of a hundred convicts. Then they would demand surrender of the prison, taking it by force if necessary, and liberate the inmate population of Huntsville. Afterward, in the confusion and uproar, with better than five hundred convicts scurrying across Texas, Wes had every confidence he could pull a vanishing act.

The tunnel progressed smoothly, burrowing on a direct line beneath the carpenter's shop and the superintendent's office. Working from the wheelwright's shop, one man dug at all times while the others covered for him and kept watch. Dirt from the tunnel was secreted outside and scattered in the prison yard during exercise period. Wes had the men organized into shifts, with no one man off the floor for more than a half hour, and the wheelwright guard never once tumbled to their scheme. Three weeks after the digging began, late on the afternoon of November 20, the tunnel was completed. All that remained was to wait for guards supervising work parties outside the walls to return their weapons to the armory. Then the conspirators would break through the floor of the arsenal, distribute guns to everyone in the wheelwright's shop, and seize the prison.

But Wes had failed to reckon with life inside the walls. Huntsville crawled with men willing, if not eager, to play the part of Judas. In exchange for information, they curried the favor of prison officials, which brought them privileges denied other inmates. The young outlaw's single miscalculation proved a fatal flaw.

Shortly before the break was to occur, armed guards swarmed over the wheelwright's shop. The plot had been betrayed at the last minute, and twelve men were hustled off to the warden's office for questioning. Several talked, more concerned with their own skin than honor among thieves, and Wes was quickly tagged as the ringleader. Before nightfall he was thrown in a dank dungeonlike cell, with a ball and chain attached to his leg. There he spent the next fifteen days, isolated in total darkness, subsisting on nothing except bread and water.

Upon being released he was assigned to the shoe factory, more determined than ever to escape. His time in solitary had been spent in analyzing the first attempt, and he saw now that it was doomed from the start. Besides being much too elaborate, it depended on far too many men, which made it susceptible to the prison grapevine, and ultimately exposure to the authorities. Having sampled the folly of trusting others, he reverted to a role more in keeping with his character. He became a loner, and began planning his next break.

On the day after Christmas he was again betrayed, this time by his own cellmate. In his possession the guards found a pistol, which had been smuggled into prison, and a homemade master key which unlocked every door and gate between the cellblock and the front wall. Clearly, Huntsville's most illustrious inmate was not a man to be dissuaded by bread and water alone. Harsher measures, it seemed, were necessary to speed his adjustment to life inside the walls.

That night Wes was stripped naked, spread-eagled on a stone floor, and tied face down. Then the underkeeper, a bullet-headed bruiser who gloried in his trade, stepped forward with the Huntsville nutcracker. This was a whip consisting of four straps, each twenty inches long and constructed from thick harness leather. It was designed to crack toughnuts and hardcases who had proved unresponsive to gentler discipline. Under the supervision of the warden, Wes was administered thirty-nine lashes, all the law allowed. Afterward, his back and buttocks reduced to bloody quivering jelly, he was dragged to solitary row and held in isolation for thirty days.

Yet the lash had somewhat the opposite effect intended. Although half crippled by the flogging, and unable to perform hard labor for some months afterward, Wes was hardly broken in spirit. He set about hatching new plots for escape.

Over the next three years he attempted seven breaks. When he wasn't betrayed by fellow convicts, he was discovered by guards, and again hauled off to solitary. With each attempt he was flogged the limit; his back became a latticework of heavy, discolored welts. And his keepers added a new wrinkle—they tried to starve him into submission.

Nothing worked, though. He was incorrigible, bullheaded, and from the punishment he had absorbed, seemingly indestructible. Within Huntsville he became something of a legend—the man who wouldn't break—and the inmates spoke of him in awed tones. Prison officials grew increasingly bewildered, completely stymied by a man who evidenced only contempt for their brutal methods. At last, convinced that the lash and starvation were a waste of time, they simply chained a ball to his leg and assigned guards to watch him around the clock.

Then, early in 1885, a curious thing happened. After seven years' imprisonment, Wes Hardin got religion.

Some of those in Huntsville, most especially the warden, declared it was nothing short of a miracle. Others, perhaps more skeptical, allowed that all else having failed, Hardin had merely made peace with his God and accepted the inevitable. Those who knew him well, a scant handful within the prison walls, traced his conversion to another source. Soon after the New Year his mother and father had passed on within weeks of one another. Hardin had accepted the news stoically, displaying no emotion whatever, but he was never again the same man.

However the transformation came about—and this remained a bone of contention for years afterward—there was no dispute as to subsequent events. Wes Hardin embraced the Lord God Jehovah with the same fervor and vitality that had made him the most feared gun in Texas. Under the prison minister's guidance, he became an avid student of theology, exploring the Bible and the rudiments of Holy Writ with the zeal of a reformed drunk. Before long he was assisting in church services, and within a few months had been appointed superintendent of the weekly Sunday School class.

On a sweltering Sunday night early that summer, he penned a letter to Jane which read in part:

I can tell you that I spent this day in almost perfect happiness, as I generally spend the Sabbaths here, something I once could not enjoy because I did not know the causes or results of that day. I had no idea before how it benefits a man in my condition. Although we are all prisoners here we are on the road to progress.

That, even from a man who detested braggarts, was something of an understatement. Once on the road to salvation, Wes Hardin pulled out all stops. He ransacked the prison library, in short order mastering Stoddard's *Arithmetic* and Davies' *Algebra*. With that under his belt, he next undertook an intense study of history, broadening his perspective of man's place in the scheme of things. And along the way he discovered what was to become his grand obsession—the law.

The years passed swiftly after that, months rippled off the calendar like golden leaves in an autumn wind. Caught up in his hunger for knowledge, Wes devoured Blackstone, Bishop's *Criminal Law*, Walker's *Introduction to American Law*, and fully a hundred additional volumes ranging across the wide spectrum of jurisprudence. He began corresponding with judges and noted attorneys around the state, seeking interpretations and shadings of what he had read. By 1892 his comprehension of the law *per se* was awesome, and in terms of statutes and legal technicalities, he was acknowledged to be better versed than most practicing attorneys.

Later that year, however, he received a severe blow. Jane Bowen Hardin suddenly sickened of ague and died. She had remained faithful to him throughout his long imprisonment— proud to the end—urging him to continue his studies and hope for a brighter day. Now she was gone, his staunchest supporter through good times and bad, and life without her seemed hardly worth the effort. For a time his mood darkened, and he fell into a fit of depression, unable to shake the thought that she had wasted her best years waiting for him to return. Slowly, though, he came to see that wallowing in self-pity demeaned her memory, belittled the love and happiness she had brought him. While Jane was gone, their children still waited, and what he had never given her, he might yet give to them. He returned to his studies with a vengeance.

Then, early in 1894, judged to be fully rehabilitated, the former outlaw was granted an unconditional pardon by Governor J. S. Hogg. After sixteen years behind the walls at Huntsville, John Wesley Hardin walked through the gates a free man. There to greet him were his children, Molly and John.

While saddened that his wife hadn't lived to see him freed and his citizenship restored, Wes bore no grudge against society. He had matured greatly while in prison—graying a bit at the temples as he approached his fortieth birthday—and he had no wish to dwell on the past. Time laid scars on a man, and whatever else he'd learned in Huntsville, he knew now that wisdom came when a man could accept the bitter with the sweet. There were good years remaining, and instead of looking back, he looked forward, to the future.

And as Jane had believed all along, it was a brighter day.

Before spring Molly, who was married to a storekeeper, made him a grandfather, and a month later he served as best man at John Junior's wedding. Then, in May of that year, shortly before his birthday, the fruition of his love affair with Blackstone came to pass. He was admitted to the bar as an attorney-at-law. It was a warm day, cloudless and not unlike most spring days, but a day that many men, John Wesley Hardin among them, would not soon forget.

Texas' deadliest outlaw had hung up his guns at last.

A Distant Land

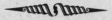

ONE FOR ALL

A brittle silence had now settled over the other poker tables. Toward the rear, Hank stood behind the pool table, listening intently. While he'd never seen the Jarrotts, he was aware of their past efforts at killing Lon. His eyes moved from one brother to the other. He thought Lon would take the younger one, Charley, first.

Hank suddenly stiffened. He saw Morg Brannock rush through the front door and bull a path through the crowd.

"You gonna fight?" Bob Jarrott glowered at Lon. "Or you gonna show your yellow streak?"

A cold tinsel glitter surfaced in Lon's eyes. "You've got me at a disadvantage, Jarrott. Two to one and I'm still in my chair."

"Then get on your gawddamn feet!"

"Lon—!" Morgan called out, hurrying forward.

The Jarrotts were momentarily distracted. In that instant, Lon kicked back his chair and stood erect. The other players hit the floor as his Colt appeared and his arm leveled—at the exact moment that young Charley Jarrott pulled both guns . . .

To Betty
and
all the Moores

ONE

The sky was overcast, threatening rain. A blustery wind whistled across the river and slammed into the ferry landing. The passengers stood huddled at the foot of the gangway.

Clint Brannock waited off to one side. The badge of a deputy U.S. marshal was pinned to his mackinaw and he was leading two horses. With him was a gaunt-faced man whose hands were secured by wrist manacles. The prisoner's name was Abner Hoxletter.

On the opposite shore stood Fort Smith. The river roughly paralleled the boundary separating Arkansas and Indian Territory. There was no bridge spanning the broad stream and ferryboats were the sole means of conveying freight and passengers from one side to the other. Travelers in either direction had no choice but to await the next ferry.

West of the landing was the Nations. Homeland of the Five Civilized Tribes—Cherokee, Chickasaw, Choctaw, Creek, and Seminole—it was so named because they had chosen to follow the white man's path. Bounded by Texas, Kansas, and Arkansas, the Nations was still a long way from civilized. Deputy marshals operating out of Fort Smith were responsible for enforcing the law west of the river.

Three days past, Clint had taken Hoxletter into custody. A horse thief by trade, Hoxletter was one of many white men who sought refuge in the Nations. The chase had lasted the better part of two weeks, ending in the land of the

Cherokees. Wiser than he looked, Hoxletter had prudently offered no resistance. The alternative to arrest and prison was an unmarked grave somewhere in Indian Territory. Dead men were seldom transported back to Fort Smith.

By custom, lawmen and their prisoners were boarded first. After leading their horses up the wide gangway, Clint and Hoxletter moved to the foredeck of the ferry. The other passengers were a mix of tribesmen with business in Fort Smith and white traders returning from the Nations. Once loaded, the gangway was raised and the ferry pulled away from the landing. The crossing was made by a system of towropes working in concert with the swift-running current.

Standing at the bow, Clint watched the approach to Fort Smith. Originally an army post, the town was situated on a sandstone bluff overlooking the juncture of the Arkansas and Poteau rivers. With time, it had become a center of commerce, serving much of Western Arkansas and a good part of Indian Territory. The largest settlement bordering the Nations, it boasted four newspapers, three banks, and thirty saloons. The saloons, in particular, enjoyed a captive trade from transients bound for the great Southwest. By federal law, the sale of firewater was banned throughout the red man's domain.

From the wharf, Clint and Hoxletter followed Garrison Avenue. The street ran through the center of town, which had all the earmarks of a prosperous frontier community. On the far side of the business district, they approached the garrison of the old army post. Abandoned some years before by the military, the compound was now headquarters for the Federal District Court of Western Arkansas. And the indisputable realm of Judge Isaac Charles Parker—the Hanging Judge.

Clint had served under Judge Parker for the past six years. Unlike many federal marshals, he had chosen not to put away his gun with advancing age. He was now in his late forties, but nonetheless an imposing figure of a man. Tall and sledge-shouldered, he was still lean and tough, with the look of vigorous good health. His sandy hair and his mustache were peppered with gray; yet the force of his pale blue gaze was undiminished by time. Nor had age dimmed his zest for the challenge of the chase. He still hunted men.

Not as sudden as he'd once been, Clint was nevertheless widely feared. Time had slowed his gun hand, but he had learned that speed was a marginal factor in a shootout. What counted most was awareness, that blend of instinct and experience that forewarned violence. A man alerted to danger was able to act rather than react, and therefore gained an edge. At that point it became a matter of deliberation, an instant of cool nerve required for an accurate shot.

Over the last twenty-two years Clint had served as a cavalry scout, an army investigator, and a lawman in various guises. In all that time, he'd been wounded twice by men who valued speed over accuracy. Neither wound was serious and neither stopped him from finishing the job. He was reputed to have killed seventeen men by adhering to a simple but deadly credo. His first shot was the last shot of the fight.

The old military garrison was a grim setting for the work carried out by Judge Parker and the marshals. A bleak two-story building housed the courtroom and offices for the federal prosecutors. As many as ten cases a day were tried, and few men were acquitted. The majority were given stiff sentences—all the law would allow—and quickly transported to federal prisons. Convicted murderers were allowed one last visit with immediate family. Then they were hanged.

Another stone building, formerly the post commissary, was situated across the old parade ground. A low, one-story affair, it was headquarters for the U.S. marshal and his complement of deputies. In the center of the compound, within clear view of both buildings, stood the gallows. Constructed of heavy timbers, it had four trapdoors, each three feet wide and twenty feet long. There was adequate space for twelve men to stand side by side and plunge to oblivion on the instant. The structure was roofed and walled, so that executions could be performed even in bad weather.

Crossing the compound, Clint left the horses hitched outside the main building. He marched Hoxletter down a short flight of steps and halted before a stout door. The prison lockup was located in a dungeonous cellar large enough to accommodate almost a hundred inmates. He lifted a heavy door-knocker and gave it three sharp raps.

A judas hole slid open, then slammed shut. Jack Frazer, the prison warden, unlatched the door. He was brutish in appearance and talked like a man with a bad cold. His nose had been broken several times and a gold tooth gleamed from the center of his mouth. He nodded to Clint.

"Who you got there?"

"Abner Hoxletter," Clint said. "Charged with horse stealing."

Frazer grunted coarsely. "Horse thieves always welcome. We got 'em packed eight to a cell."

While Clint unlocked the manacles, Frazer entered the prisoner's name in a ledger. Hoxletter was turned over to a guard and they disappeared down a dim corridor. After closing the ledger, Frazer looked up from his desk. His mouth curled in a wolfish grin.

"You're just in time for the party."

"How so?" Clint asked.

"Hangin' day," Frazer said, chuckling. "We're fixin' to lose some of our steady boarders."

"Anybody I know?"

Frazer ticked off four names. One of them was a man Clint had captured only last month. All were convicted murderers, and their appeals to Judge Parker had been routinely denied. Justice was swift and certain in the Fort Smith court.

"Got the word yesterday," Frazer said. "The judge ordered the four of 'em to take the drop at once. Guess he figures the more the merrier."

Clint shrugged. "Sounds like another one of his object lessons. Ought to make a big splash in the newspapers."

"What the hell!" Frazer crowed. "They don't call him the Hanging Judge for nothin'."

From the prison lockup, Clint walked back across the compound. A crowd was gathering before the gallows and he was reminded that most Westerners approved of Judge Parker's harsh methods. The Eastern press, on the other hand, never missed a chance to slander the jurist. His attitude toward the death sentence was variously termed "barbarous" and "a thing of infamy."

Appointed to the bench in 1875, Isaac Parker had jurisdiction over Western Arkansas and all of the Nations. A wilderness area which encompassed some 74,000 square miles, it was a haven for cutthroats of every description. To enforce his orders, the judge was assigned two hundred U.S. deputy marshals, and the almost impossible task of policing a land virtually devoid of law. Four months after taking office, he had sentenced six convicted murderers to be hanged simultaneously.

The thud of the gallows trap that day called the attention of all America to Judge Parker. Newspapermen poured into Fort Smith, and a crowd of more than five thousand gathered to witness the executions. The press immediately tagged him the Hanging Judge, and decried the brutality of his methods. In the furor, the purpose of his object lesson was completely lost. Yet the reason he'd hanged six men that day—and went on to hang forty-three more in the next twelve years—lay just across the river.

Gangs of white outlaws made forays into Kansas, Missouri, and Texas, and then retreated into Indian Territory. There they found perhaps the oddest sanctuary in the history of crime. Though each tribe had its own courts and Light Horse Police, their authority extended only to Indian citizens. White men were exempt from all prosecution except that of a federal court. Yet there were no extradition laws governing the Nations; federal marshals had to pursue and capture the wanted men. Curiously enough, the problem was compounded by the Indians themselves.

The red man had little use for the white man's laws. All too often the Indians connived with the outlaws, offering them asylum. The marshals were looked upon as intruders in the Nations, and the chore of ferreting out fugitives became a murderous task. It was no job for the faint of heart, as evidenced by the toll in lawmen. Over the past twelve years nearly forty federal marshals had been gunned down in Indian Territory.

Once across the compound, Clint entered the old commissary building. Inside the main office, he found John Carroll, the U.S. marshal, seated at a battered rolltop desk. Carroll was a stocky bulldog of a man, with ruddy features and a brushy ginger mustache. He was a political appointee, rather than a veteran lawman, and reported directly to Judge Parker. His principal job was assignment of cases to the deputy marshals.

"Hello there, Clint," he said, looking up from a stack of papers. "We'd about given you up for lost."

"Took me longer than I expected. Hoxletter was always one jump ahead."

"Any trouble?"

"Nothin' to speak of," Clint said amiably. "Once I caught him, he came along peaceable. I just dropped him off at the lockup."

"Good work," Carroll observed. "All in the nick of time, too."

"How's that?"

"The judge wants to see you."

Clint pulled out the makings. He creased a rolling paper and sprinkled tobacco into the fold. Stores now carried the new tailor-made cigarettes, but he found them too mild for his tastes. He stuck with the roll-your-owns.

Watching him, Carroll marked again that his eyes were never still. The slightest movement or sound attracted Clint's attention. His glance was quick but sharp, and even in the midst of rolling a cigarette, he seemed aware of all about him. Carroll often thought it was why he'd survived six years in the Nations. Nothing took him by surprise.

Clint sealed the rolling paper and popped a sulfurhead on his thumbnail. He looked at Carroll over the flare of the match. "The judge say what he wants?"

"Yes and no," Carroll said with an odd smile. "I suggest you ask him yourself."

"Sounds mysterious."

"Let's just say it's out of the ordinary. Judge Parker prefers to tell you personally."

A commotion from the courtyard interrupted them. Clint turned and moved to the window, followed by Carroll. Outside a growing crowd of spectators was gathered before a roped-off area fronting the gallows. A holiday atmosphere seemed to prevail, and an excited murmur swept through the onlookers as the four condemned murderers were marched across the compound. George Maledon, the official executioner, led them up the gallows steps.

Hushed, the spectators watched as he positioned the prisoners on the center trap. Maledon was a slim, stoop-shouldered man with a full beard and close-set eyes. All business, he went about his work with an air of professional detachment. As the death warrants were read, he moved from man to man, slipping a hangman's noose over their heads. A craftsman of sorts, he prided himself on breaking necks rather than strangling men to death. He was careful to center the knot directly behind the left ear.

A minister began intoning a final prayer. The condemned men stood with their arms strapped to their sides and their ankles tightly bound. Their expressions were strangely resigned and they appeared to be listening intently to the preacher. Maledon once more moved down the line, fitting black hoods over their heads. Then, as the prayer ended, he walked to a wooden lever behind the prisoners. The crowd, morbidly curious, edged closer to the scaffold.

A loud *whump* suddenly echoed across the courtyard. The four men dropped through the trapdoor and hit the end of the ropes with an abrupt jolt. Their necks snapped in unison, and their heads, crooked at a grotesque angle, flopped over their right shoulders. The spectators, staring bug-eyed at the gallows, seemed to hold their breath. An oppressive silence settled over the compound.

Hanging limp, the dead men swayed gently, the scratchy creak of taut rope somehow deafening in the stillness. One eye on his pocket watch, Maledon finally nodded to the prison physician. Working quickly, the doctor moved from body to body, testing for a heartbeat with his stethoscope. A moment later he pronounced the four men officially dead.

The crowd began drifting away. Clint walked back to the desk and snuffed his cigarette in an ashtray. When he turned around, Carroll was still staring out the window. There was a look of ghoulish fascination on the marshal's face.

"Anything else?" Clint asked.

"No," Carroll said quietly. "Nothing else."

"Guess I'll go see what the judge wants."

Carroll merely nodded. Clint stepped into the hallway and moved toward the main door. As he emerged from the building, the bodies were being lowered from the scaffold. Four wooden coffins were positioned beneath the structure and several guards were attending to the dead men. Glancing at them as he went past, he retraced his path across the compound.

Clint marked the date as March 2, 1887. Since signing on as a deputy, it was the third time he'd seen four men hanged at once. In that same six-year period, he had killed seven men by his own hand. Lately he'd come to the conclusion that the threat of death was no deterrent to hardcases and outlaws. Still, there was something to be said for the finality of hanging, and law enforced by the gun. Dead men never again committed murder.

There were times when Clint considered quitting. Elizabeth Brannock, the widow of his eldest brother, still operated the family ranch in New Mexico. In 1881, after his brother had been murdered, he'd taken it upon himself to square the account. Charged with manslaughter, he'd been released on condition that he exile himself for a period of one year. A month later, his reputation untarnished by the incident, he had gone to work for Judge Parker. Had he wished, he could have returned to New Mexico anytime within the past five years.

What kept him from leaving was still another branch of the family. While he was unmarried, Clint nonetheless had a strong sense of duty. His second brother, dead since 1874, had left a widow and two boys. The woman was a full-blood Comanche and continued to live on the reservation in western Indian Territory. Her welfare was of concern to Clint, and he looked upon the boys as his own sons. His work as a marshal allowed him to visit them with some frequency, and the bond had grown closer over the years. For that reason, he had never seriously considered returning to New Mexico.

Earlier today he'd thought to ask for a week off. His last visit to the reservation had been at Christmastime, fully two months past. But now, crossing the compound, his mind turned to other matters. A personal summons from Judge Parker was unusual under any circumstances. All the more so when the reason was shrouded in mystery.

A clerk ushered him into the judge's chambers. Isaac Parker was in his early fifties, a stout six-footer with a well-trimmed mustache and goatee. He was as demanding of himself as he was the officers of the court and the deputy marshals. He observed no holidays except Christmas and Sundays, and he seldom recessed court before early evening. His docket was restricted almost exclusively to criminal cases.

No jurist had ever been invested with such unlimited power. There was no appeal from his pronouncements, and more men had died on the Fort Smith gallows than anywhere else in America. In a newspaper interview, he had once outlined his views on the death sentence. "People have said that I am a cruel and heartless man. But no one has ever pointed to a single case of undue severity. On the bench, I have ever had but a single aim: Permit no innocent man to be punished; let no guilty man escape."

Attired in a black cutaway coat and high starched collar, Parker greeted Clint with genuine warmth. Over the years he'd come to admire Clint's cool judgment and nervy quickness in a tight situation. Of all the deputy marshals, he believed Clint to be the one officer who was more dangerous than the outlaws they hunted. What he had in mind today would require nothing less.

After they were seated, Parker went straight to the point. "I issued orders that no one was to mention it until I'd told you myself. Ernie Wilson was killed last week."

Clint's face took on a sudden hard cast. Ernie Wilson was a fellow marshal and perhaps his closest friend. His voice betrayed nothing of what he felt. "Where'd it happen?"

"Cherokee Nation," Parker said. "Outside the town of Whiteoak."

"Who killed him?"

"Rafe Dixon."

The name required no elaboration. Rafe Dixon was a white man, the leader of a band of outlaws. Within the last few months, the gang had robbed a bank in Arkansas, another bank in Kansas, and a railroad express car in southern Missouri. After each holdup, the robbers scattered to the winds and took sanctuary in the Nations. Ernie Wilson had been assigned the job of bringing Dixon to justice.

"Ernie was no greenhorn," Clint said at length. "Dixon must've taken him unawares."

Parker nodded dourly. "From what I gather, Dixon ambushed him. Wilson was apparently shot in the chest and fell off his horse. Then he was deliberately shot in the head. There were powder burns on his temple."

"Dirty sonovabitch," Clint said in a flat monotone. "He executed Ernie, didn't he?"

"I'm afraid so."

There was a long beat of silence. Clint seemed turned to stone, his eyes cold and remote. "Ernie deserved better," he said finally. "That's no way to die."

Parker's expression darkened. When he spoke, there was an undercurrent of rage in his voice. "I intend to make an example of Rafe Dixon. No man murders one of my marshals with impunity."

"Are you assigning me to the case?"

"Yes," Parker said without inflection. "However long it takes, I want you to find Dixon."

"And after I find him—?"

Parker paused as though weighing his words. He looked

curiously like a philosopher contemplating some complex abstraction. "Given my choice," he said, "I would prefer to hang Dixon. On the other hand, if his death were reported in the Nations, justice would be served equally well. Do you take my meaning, Mr. Brannock?"

"Yessir, I do."

"In that event, I wish you good hunting."

Clint heaved himself to his feet. He nodded once, then turned and walked to the door. With his hand on the knob, he looked back. "Judge, would you like me to wire you the news?"

"I'd like that very much, Mr. Brannock."

"Consider it done."

The door opened and closed. Isaac Parker tilted back in his chair, put his fingertips together. A slight smile played at the corner of his mouth.

He thought Rafe Dixon was as good as dead.

TWO

A wind mourned through the leaves of the cottonwoods. Hazy sunlight rippled across the waters of the Rio Hondo, warming the valley. Umber grasslands, like a wave crashing against a wall of stone, swelled toward the distant mountains.

Elizabeth stood at the parlor window. She was lost in reflection, and her mind wandered down odd little byways of memory. She remembered the day Virgil had brought her to the Hondo, how proud he'd been. Working together, partners as well as man and wife, they had put down their roots here. Those were the golden years, when they'd transformed the valley into a great ranch and called it Spur. And now, strangely, it seemed so long ago. Another life.

A striking woman, Elizabeth was tall and statuesque. Her features were exquisite, and though she was forty-two, she looked ten years younger. Her eyes were hazel, alert and inquisitive, and she wore her hair in the upswept fashion. Yet, for all her beauty, there was something in her manner that commanded attention. Her force of character ensured that people were rarely unaware of her presence. The *mexicanos* had aptly nicknamed her *La Mariposa de Hierro*—the Iron Butterfly.

The name was now known throughout New Mexico Territory. In 1881, following her husband's death, she had assumed the reins of Spur. While she shared the inheritance with her daughter Jennifer and her son Morgan, there was little doubt as to whose will prevailed. Nor was there any question that she'd become a persuasive force in territorial politics. Her coalition of Anglos and *mexicanos* controlled almost half the seats in the legislature. Still, quite apart from her political power, the ranch remained her touchstone. She drew strength from the land, the Rio Hondo and the valley.

Headquarters for all of Spur was a large compound in the center of the valley. Along the north bank of the Rio Hondo, the buildings were formed in an irregular crescent beyond the main house. Situated opposite a central commissary were the bunkhouse and a combination kitchen and dining hall. Nearby were the corrals and various outbuildings for blacksmithing, carpentry, and general storage.

The main house overlooked the river. Shaded by cottonwoods, it was a vast sprawl of adobe, built along the lines of a *hacienda*. The walls were three feet thick, with deep-set windows and hewn rafters protruding from a flat roof. A galleried veranda, with rockers and a porch swing, ran the length of the front wall. Comfortable winter and summer, the house was sheltered by foothills to the south.

Some thirteen years past, the Brannocks had purchased a Spanish land grant totaling 100,000 acres. The holdings were located in the center of the valley and surrounded on all sides by public-domain lands. With the death of John Chisum in 1884, the vast Jinglebob spread on the Pecos had been sold off piecemeal. Spur then became the largest outfit in Lincoln County, breeding both cattle and horses. Fifty cowhands worked the livestock herds that wore the ✳ brand.

Hondo Valley was situated in the foothills of the Capitan Mountains. The river meandered through a lush grazeland roughly twenty miles long and some three miles wide. To the west lay the town of Lincoln, and eastward the Rio Hondo eventually converged with the Pecos River. Surrounded by craggy slopes, the valley was sheltered from the harsh blast of winter and watered by spring melt-off from the mountains. A natural basin, hidden away from the world, it seemed fashioned for raising livestock.

Staring out the window, Elizabeth looked toward the

snowcapped mountains. She was waiting for Morg and his
cousin, Brad Dawson, who was the ranch foreman. A vagrant thought surfaced, prompted by her daydreaming about
family. Her last letter to Clint had gone unanswered and she
wondered why he hadn't replied. That was unlike him and it
left her vaguely troubled.

When time permitted, she and Clint managed to visit one
another. She considered him her dearest and oldest friend, a
brother rather than a brother-in-law. Yet they hadn't seen
each other in nearly a year, and she missed him terribly. All
too often she found herself wishing he would return to New
Mexico, join her in operating Spur. But then, upon reflection, she knew it would never happen. He was wedded to the
law and would likely die wearing a badge. She nonetheless
dreamt of having him near and refused to abandon hope.

Morg and Brad rode up to the house. As they dismounted,
she was reminded that the Brannock blood always showed.
They were both tall and rangy, strapping six-footers, larded
with muscle. Morg was cleanshaven, with wavy blond hair
and his father's blue eyes. While Brad's mother had married
a Dawson, his Brannock heritage was nonetheless apparent.
His eyes were the color of carpenter's chalk and his wheat-
colored hair was matched by a bristly mustache. He was a
second cousin to Morg and Jennifer, and his looks pegged
him as family. He might well have been their brother.

For all the similarity, Morg and Brad were a study in contrasts. At twenty-five, Brad was more mature and somewhat
serious by nature. He was a slow, thoughtful talker, with an
easy smile and a wry, offhand humor. Morg, who had just
turned twenty, exuded the vitality and vigor of youth. Yet his
brash self-assurance and cocky manner was deceptive. He
had inherited his father's head for business, and beneath the
sportive manner there was a shrewd mind at work. Older
men quickly learned to respect his opinion.

Today's meeting was to review the business affairs of
Spur. Late that afternoon, Elizabeth was departing for Santa
Fe, where political matters demanded her attention. She

wanted a report from Brad, who was in the midst of preparing for spring roundup. As for Morg, she had recently entrusted him with additional responsibility. An offshoot of the family holdings was a ranch located in the Cherokee Outlet, at the northern boundary of Indian Territory. Though the foreman was reliable enough, Elizabeth generally made three trips a year to inspect the operation. Tomorrow, for the first time, Morg was scheduled to go in her place.

A room off the central hallway had been converted into an office. There, seated around a large desk, Elizabeth and the boys reviewed their business interests. To a great extent, Brad's report was the reason for the meeting. Not quite seven years ago, he had come west from Missouri, the original home of the Brannock clan. After starting as a cowhand, he had worked his way up to *segundo* and then to trail boss. He displayed a natural savvy of cattle and possessed all the qualities of leadership. Three years past, he had been promoted to foreman of Spur.

Under Brad's guidance, the longhorn herds were gradually phased out. The ranch had switched instead to breeding shorthorn Durhams, relying on blooded stock. A chunky animal, far beefier than the old longhorns, the Durhams had proved to be a profitable venture. Horses were no less a mainstay of the Spur operation. Several breeding pastures were maintained for cowponies, draft horses, and general work animals. Across the West, cattlemen and farmers, as well as livestock traders, provided a steady market. The proceeds from horse sales rivaled those generated by the Durhams.

Elizabeth was an astute businesswoman. Following Brad's report, she paused, weighing all she'd heard. Then she lifted an eyebrow in question. "When can you start roundup?"

"Depends on the weather," Brad explained. "So far, it looks to be an early spring. I'd judge we'll get under way about mid-April."

"And the first trail drive?"

Spur was roughly a hundred miles from the nearest rail-head. Brad scratched his jaw, reflective a moment. "Give or take a week," he said at length, "I'd calculate the middle of May. What with the gather and branding, it'll take nearabout a month."

"How large an increase do you expect?"

A flicker of humor showed in Brad's eyes. "Well, our bulls are mighty dependable critters. I'd say we'll equal last year's calf crop. Maybe even better it."

Elizabeth nodded with an approving smile. She then turned her attention to another matter. Unlike the old days, Spur no longer laid claim to public-domain lands within the Hondo Valley. Times had changed, and she considered it morally reprehensible to hold grazeland by right of force. Nor was she an advocate of stringing barbed wire; the only fences on Spur were those enclosing the breeding pastures. Still, a large ranch always needed more graze, and she'd undertaken a program of acquiring privately held land.

To that end, she had placed Morg in charge of the project. One group of landowners was the homesteaders, who began moving into the valley the summer of 1882. Five years were required to prove their claim and many would shortly receive valid title. The other group was composed of *mexicano* farmers who held title by virtue of ancient Spanish land grants. Morg was a personable negotiator and he spoke fluent Spanish. His days were spent cajoling landowners and haggling over price.

Elizabeth looked at him now. "Have you made any progress with the Horrells?"

"The Horrells," Morg said with a sudden grin, "and the Tuckers. They've both got an itch to pull up stakes."

"Are they agreeable to our offer?"

"It's in the bag." Morg's grin broadened. "Got 'em to sign the papers just this morning. Counting all the relatives, we'll come out with another full section."

Elizabeth appeared pleased at the prospect. "Aren't you the sly one?" she said. "That's almost a thousand acres in the past month."

"Nothin' to it," Morg said bluffly. "All you need's a gift for gab and a wad of greenbacks. Works every time."

Elizabeth smiled. "If that's true, why haven't you convinced the Pérez family? Aren't they susceptible to your charm?"

"Don't worry," Morg assured her. "Nobody holds out forever. I'll get 'em yet."

"Listen to him," Brad joked. "Sounds like a drummer selling corsets. Pure hokum."

"Says you!" Morg countered. "How'd you like to make a small wager?"

"Another time," Elizabeth cut in. "I have to leave in a few minutes. Have we anything more to discuss?"

"Guess not," Morg said. "Unless you want to talk about the Outlet."

"I've already told you what you need to know. Go there and learn the operation for yourself. We'll talk when you return."

The meeting ended on that note. Elizabeth shooed them out of the office and went to pack her bag. Brad declined Morg's invitation for a cup of coffee. He was expected at one of the breeding pastures and already running late. He rode off toward the northern foothills.

Morg wandered back to his bedroom. He found his wife seated in a rocker, staring listlessly out the window. Scarcely six months past, they had been married at the Methodist Church in Lincoln. She'd gotten pregnant on their wedding night, and in his view, she hadn't been the same since.

Formerly Louise Stockton, she was the daughter of a rancher on the Rio Felix. At nineteen, she was a blond tawny cat of a girl with bold eyes and a delicate oval face. Her features, not to mention the swell of her abdomen, had filled out as her term progressed. She was thrilled by the prospect of motherhood, but disconsolate over her condition. She felt ugly and unwanted, and desperately unloved.

Entering the bedroom, Morg tried to divine her mood. These days she was either warmly affectionate or irritable and waspish, with no middle ground. She was particularly bitter about his forthcoming trip to Indian Territory. As though walking on eggshells, he crossed to the rocker and bussed her on the cheek. She sniffed, averting her face.

"Well?" she demanded tartly. "Have you got your marching orders?"

Morg stared at her in mild astonishment. "What are you talking about?"

Her chin tilted. "Wasn't that what your mother was doing just now—issuing final instructions?"

"For Chrissake," Morg said, rolling his eyes. "Just leave her out of it, will you? I'm going because I have to go."

"No, you're not." She sulked. "You're going because you *want* to go. To get away from me."

Louise felt somehow like a castaway. Before she'd become large with child, Morg had been tender and unstintingly passionate. She remembered him as an ardent lover, infinitely wise in the ways of a man and woman. By breathtaking stages, he had never failed to bring her to complete and wondrous satisfaction. She cherished those intimate moments and still ached for him with an imperishable desire. All of which merely underscored her melancholy moods. He hadn't touched her in almost a month.

"Won't you change your mind?" She entreated him with her eyes. "Wait till after the baby's born—please."

"I can't," Morg said with an aimless shrug. "That's three months off, and we've got a business to run. I don't have any choice."

"What about me?" she stormed. "You're leaving and your mother's leaving. And I'll be here all alone!"

A shadow of irritation crossed Morg's features. He saw tears well up in her eyes and he tried to fathom why she was being so unreasonable. Words failed him and he suddenly turned away. She burst out crying as he went through the door.

He wondered why the hell he'd ever gotten married.

A short while later Elizabeth emerged from the house. John Taylor was waiting with a buckboard and team, and he assisted her into the front seat. Her leather carryall was already stowed in back with his warbag.

Taylor was a retired gunman. Years ago, when Elizabeth and her husband were threatened by political assassins, Taylor had been hired as her bodyguard. After her husband was killed, the political climate in New Mexico had calmed somewhat. But Taylor had elected to stay on at Spur and Elizabeth welcomed the decision. By then, she'd come to think of him as a companion and a loyal friend.

Elizabeth seldom entertained the notion of marrying again. Her time was devoted instead to the ranch and a whirlwind of political activities. Yet she was not unaware of the gossip surrounding herself and John Taylor. He was a man of saturnine good looks, on the sundown side of forty, with a tough, rather sinister visage. Wherever she went, he accompanied her, for a woman could hardly travel the backcountry alone. Still, in all their travels, she'd never once considered him anything more than a friend. She was comfortable with his company.

For his part, Taylor treated her with understated reverence. He was beguiled by her elegance and thought her the most desirable woman he'd ever known. But he had long since parted with the idea that the feeling was mutual. Nor was he blind to the chasm separating them on a social level. She was a lady of prominence and wealth, and a political activist of enormous prestige. At best, he was a retired "shootist" who had killed more men than he cared to remember. He contented himself with being her companion and her trusted confidant. So far as he knew, there were no secrets between them.

Glancing at her now, he kept his tone light. "How long we stayin' in Santa Fe?"

"Only a day or so," Elizabeth said. "I've arranged a meeting with Salazar and Martínez."

"In the same room?" Taylor smiled lazily. "That oughta be a regular cat-and-dog fight."

Lorenzo Salazar was an influential *rico,* one of the oldline political aristocracy. His rival, Antonio Martínez, was a young *jefe político,* idealistic and ambitious. One sought to maintain the time-honored hierarchy and the other sought widespread political reform. Their antagonism threatened to split Elizabeth's coalition along factional lines. She had arranged the meeting in the hope of negotiating a compromise.

"I'm afraid you're right," Elizabeth said, almost to herself. "Neither of them has any respect for the other. It's a touchy situation."

Taylor chuckled softly. "Just lemme know if you need a referee. I'm a old hand at settlin' disputes."

"Let's hope it doesn't come to that."

Elizabeth fell silent. She remained thoughtful and somewhat distracted during the drive to town. They arrived late that afternoon, with the sun dropping lower toward the mountains. From Lincoln they would take the overnight stage to Socorro, the nearest railhead with passenger service. Tomorrow, by train, they would travel on to Santa Fe.

Lincoln was the county seat, a center of trade for outlying farms and ranches. Taylor dropped her off at a house on the north side of the town's main street. He then drove on to the livery stable, where the horses would be stalled until their return. Elizabeth proceeded up the walkway to a small frame house painted white with green shutters. A simple hand-lettered sign was mounted beside the door.

JENNIFER BRANNOCK, M.D.
Clinic Hours Tuesday & Friday

Twelve years ago Elizabeth had organized a free clinic for poor *mexicanos*. The local physician, Dr. Chester Wood, had been her strongest supporter. Jennifer, who was only a girl at the time, had become fascinated with the world of medicine. Dr. Wood encouraged her interest, and was largely responsible for her decision to enter medical school. At age twenty, she had graduated from Tufts University, located in Boston. She was the first woman doctor to establish practice in New Mexico.

A year had passed since her return to Lincoln. In that period, with Chester Wood's public support, Jennifer had overcome the pervasive distrust of lady doctors. Four months ago, when Wood died of a stroke, she'd bought the house and continued to operate the clinic. She practiced general medicine, and though barely twenty-one, she had already developed a reputation as a skilled surgeon. She was now the only physician within a forty-mile radius of Lincoln.

The last patient was leaving as Elizabeth entered the clinic. Jennifer greeted her with a warm hug and a look of pleasant surprise. Apart from the normal affection of a mother and daughter, there was a sense of mutual respect between them. In their own way, each of them had made her mark in what was essentially a man's world. Elizabeth was particularly proud that her daughter had stormed the barriers excluding women from the medical profession.

"I've only a minute," she said quickly. "John and I are catching the evening stage."

"Oh?" Jennifer said, smiling. "What's the burning issue this time?"

"Nothing too exciting," Elizabeth confessed. "Another squabble between the old guard and one of the young *jefes*. Sometimes I wonder why I bother."

"You wouldn't have it any other way. I think you enjoy all the backbiting and intrigue."

Jennifer looked amused. She wore a pleated skirt and a ruffled blouse with a high collar. Tall and willowy, she had a stemlike waist and long, lissome legs. Her eyes were hazel and her auburn hair was drawn back and pinned, accentuating her expressive features. She was compellingly attractive, a mirror image of her mother.

"Well, anyway," Elizabeth said, changing the subject. "How are things with you? Any news yet?"

"News—?"

"Don't be coy, Jen. You know very well I'm talking about Blake. Has he asked you or not?"

"Honestly, Mother," Jennifer groaned. "You really are incorrigible. Anyone would think you're in a rush to marry me off."

"I am," Elizabeth said with mock seriousness. "I won't have a daughter of mine end up a spinster."

Jennifer had been keeping company with Blake Hazlett, a local attorney. Elizabeth approved of the match and never failed to voice her opinion. Their bantering was by now something of a ritual.

"Spinster indeed!" Jennifer said indignantly. "I'll marry when I'm ready to marry, thank you very much."

Elizabeth laughed happily. "I suggest you not wait too long. Good men are hard to find."

"Oh, what a terrible thing to say! And you one of the original suffragists."

"Women's rights have nothing to do with a warm bed. Your father and I reconciled that point very nicely."

The west-bound stage clattered past. Through the window, Elizabeth saw it roll to a halt in front of the express office. She kissed Jennifer on the cheek, waving gaily, and hurried out the door. On the street, she set off at a brisk pace uptown.

Jennifer watched from the doorway. She thought how proud her mother looked, almost stately. There was a strength about the matriarch of the Brannock family that touched something in others. People were instinctively drawn to her, infused with her energy and determination. She was, in a word, indomitable.

A small irony flashed through Jennifer's mind. Her mother was forever coaxing her toward the wedding altar. Yet, though she was still a stunning woman, Elizabeth ignored the overtures of her many male admirers. In that respect, she seemed perfectly content with memories, a time of unexpired emotions. A bright remembrance of days past.

The memory of her father was no less real to Jennifer. And the thought occurred that her mother had used a shopworn phrase to express a deeper truth. Perhaps, after all, good men were hard to find.

THREE

Younger's Bend was located in the Cherokee Nation. There one of the frontier's most notorious bandits maintained a stronghold. Her name was Belle Starr.

Clint was looking for a lead. Like many lawmen, he relied heavily on informants when tracking a fugitive. Belle Starr was a convicted horse thief and reportedly involved in a string of penny-ante holdups. She also swapped information when it was to her advantage. Clint planned to ask her about Rafe Dixon.

Three days had passed since his meeting with Judge Parker. Clint was mounted on a sorrel gelding and traveling light. Late yesterday he'd camped at the juncture of the Arkansas and Canadian rivers. From there, he had followed the Canadian in a southwesterly direction. He was now some forty miles upstream.

Farther west lay the Creek Nation and a short distance south lay the Choctaw Nation. Younger's Bend, which was on the fringe of the Cherokee Nation, was ideally situated to the boundary lines of all three tribes. Belle Starr's place was hacked out of the wilderness, well off the beaten path. She lived there with a Creek half-breed who called himself Jim July.

Clint considered the Nations as hostile territory. Law enforcement among the tribes was conducted under the strangest circumstances ever faced by men who wore a badge. With the advance of civilization, a new pattern of

lawlessness began to emerge on the western plains. The era
of the lone bandit gradually faded into obscurity, evolving
into something far worse. Outlaws began to run in packs.

Local peace officers found themselves unable to cope
with the vast distances involved. Gangs made lightning
strikes into surrounding border states, and then retreated into
Indian Territory. In time, due to the limits of state jurisdiction, the war became a grisly contest between the gangs and
the federal marshals. Yet it was hide-and-seek with a unique
advantage falling to the outlaws.

A wanted man could easily lose himself in the mountains
or along wooded river bottoms. The favorable terrain and
general atmosphere of sanctuary were improved by too few
lawmen chasing too many desperadoes. The Nations
swarmed with killers and robbers and dozens of small gangs
like the one led by Rafe Dixon. Outnumbered and out-
gunned, the marshals were seldom afforded the luxury of
conducting a manhunt in force. They generally rode alone
into Indian Territory.

Adding to their burden was the trade in whiskey. By federal law spirits in any form were illegal in Indian Territory.
For selling or bartering, there was a five-hundred-dollar fine.
Smuggling or attempting to transport alcohol into the Nations brought a three-hundred-dollar fine. Operating a still
for the manufacture of spirits carried a fine of one thousand
dollars. Popskull and rotgut were nonetheless staple com-
modities of trade throughout the tribes. From the marshals'
standpoint, the problem was compounded by the attitude toward lawmen. Whiskey traders, whether white or red, were
willing to kill to avoid arrest.

To survive, a marshal had no choice but to play by the
same rules. Yet a fast gun and the willingness to kill were not
enough. Operating alone, a lawman first had to outwit his
prey, somehow gain an edge. That required developing
sources of intelligence, unsavory alliances with informants
who were themselves windward of the law. Over his years in
the Nations, Clint had cultivated many such contacts. But

the one he valued the most was the Bandit Queen, Belle Starr. Her one allegiance in life was to herself.

Myra Belle Shirley was a native of Jasper County, Missouri. In 1865, her family resettled in Texas on a hardscrabble farm. There, at the age of nineteen, she married a young horse thief named Jim Reed. Several years were spent on the run, with the law always one step behind. At last, with no place to turn, Reed sought refuge in Indian Territory. Belle shortly joined him, and her career as a lady bandit began in earnest.

The Reeds were given sanctuary by Tom Starr, a full-blood Cherokee. Starr and his eight sons were considered the principal hell-raisers of the Cherokee Nation. Belle, the only white woman present, was accorded royal treatment by the Starrs. Then, in the summer of 1874, she abruptly became a widow. Jim Reed was trapped following a stagecoach robbery and slain by lawmen. Never daunted, Belle soon shed her widow's weeds and married Sam Starr.

The eldest son of Old Tom Starr, Sam owned a parcel of land on Younger's Bend. From there, he and his gang of misfits rustled livestock and occasionally ran illegal whiskey. Belle, who was a dominant woman, shortly became the brains of the outfit. She planned their jobs and shrewdly brought the men together only when a raid was imminent. Afterward, the gang members scattered to Gibson and other railroad towns to squander their loot.

For years, Belle and Sam were virtually immune to arrest. Younger's Bend was surrounded by wilderness and mountains, and the only known approach was along a canyon trail rising steeply from the river. So inaccessible was the stronghold that lawmen—both Light Horse Police and federal marshals—gave it a wide berth. Myra Belle Starr gloried in her notoriety and flaunted her reputation as a lady bandit. She believed herself beyond the law.

In 1883, Clint proved her wrong. He lured Belle and Sam out of Younger's Bend and arrested them for horse theft. Convicted in Judge Parker's court, the Starrs served five months in federal prison at Detroit. After being released, they returned to the Nations and once more attempted to form a gang. But Sam gradually lost his battle with alcohol, and in 1886, he was killed in a gunfight. Belle, who believed in short mourning periods, wasted no time in finding another man. She took Jim July as her common-law husband.

These days Belle and her Creek paramour dabbled in stolen horses. Still, almost four years had passed since she'd last been arrested. Some attributed her good fortune to the remote location of Younger's Bend. Others assumed she had grown smarter with age. A few men, all of them deputy marshals, knew that she was protected by Clint Brannock. He allowed her to steal horses, and thereby maintain her coveted reputation as the Bandit Queen. She, in turn, acted as his personal informant.

In the lowering dusk, Clint emerged from the canyon trail. He visited Younger's Bend only at night, and in secret. Before him, surrounded by dense woods, lay a stretch of level ground. Not fifty yards away, a log house stood like a wilderness fort where the trail ended. A flock of crows cawed and took wing as he rode forward. From the house a pack of dogs joined in the chorus.

One window was lighted by a lamp. The door of the house opened and a woman stepped onto the porch. She hushed the dogs with a sharp command and stood waiting with her hands on her hips. Clint reined to a halt in the yard, mindful of their agreement. She would abide no lawman in her house, and on his nocturnal visits, he never dismounted. He nodded pleasantly.

"'Evenin', Belle."

"'Evening, marshal."

From the corner of the house a man materialized out of the shadows. He moved forward, holding a double-barrel shotgun cradled in his arms. As he crossed the porch, Clint recognized him as the half-breed Creek, Jim July. He was lithely built, with bark-dark skin and muddy eyes. His face was pinched in an oxlike expression.

"How's tricks, Jim?"

Clint's question drew a sour grunt. July moved through the doorway and disappeared inside the cabin. He detested any lawman, and in particular, he disliked Clint. His resentment stemmed from the fact that his woman was forced to play songbird for a *tibo* marshal. Still, for all his rough ways, he'd never once voiced an objection. He was allowed to stay on at Younger's Bend only so long as he behaved himself.

Belle waited until he was out of earshot. In the spill of lamplight, she was revealed as a singularly unattractive woman. She was horse-faced, with a lantern jaw and bloodless lips and beady close-set eyes. Her figure was somehow mannish, with wide hips and shoulders, and almost no breasts beneath her drab woolen dress. Her hold over men was all the more puzzling in broad daylight. She looked vaguely like a prune wearing a wig.

"Lemme guess," she said at last. "You stopped by for supper."

"Not tonight," Clint said in a neutral voice. "I'm looking for somebody."

Belle gave him the fisheye. "Who you after now?"

"Rafe Dixon."

"Figures the Judge would've sent you. Word's around that Dixon killed a marshal."

Clint's stare revealed nothing. "What else do you hear?"

"Just talk," Belle said hesitantly. "Dixon's stayin' out of sight."

"Any idea where he went to ground?"

"No, not just exactly."

"Like hell," Clint said with a measured smile. "C'mon, stop dancing me around. What've you heard?"

Belle opened her hands, shrugged. "There's talk he crossed paths with a Light Horse patrol. Way I got the story, they turned stone-blind. Just kept on riding."

"Whereabouts did they cross paths?"

"Nobody's sayin'."

"Then how'd you hear about it?"

"From a friend in Tahlequah."

Clint looked at her with narrow suspicion. "Are you telling me it's common knowledge?"

"Yeah, I suppose," Belle said cautiously. "Leastways, it's no secret."

A moment elapsed while Clint weighed her statement. Tahlequah was the capital of the Cherokee Nation. Major D. W. Lipe, head of the Light Horse Police, was headquartered there. Yet no word of sighting Dixon had been forwarded to Fort Smith.

"Hard to believe," he said finally. "Why would the Light Horse protect Dixon? He's a white man."

"So what?" Belle said with a lopsided smile. "Just because he killed a marshal doesn't change anything. The Light Horse figure it's one *tibo* against another."

"You might have a point there."

Belle laughed without humor. "No maybe about it. The Light Horse aren't no different than the rest of the Cherokees. They all hate your guts."

"I reckon they do at that. Anyway, thanks for the tip, Belle."

"Keep it in mind the next time me and Jim steal some horses."

Belle watched him ride out of the yard. Unlike other lawmen she'd known, she harbored a grudging admiration for Clint. He was hard as nails, but he always stuck to his word. For the past four years, he had kept her out of Judge Parker's courtroom. And that in itself gave her the best of the bargain.

She silently wished him luck with Rafe Dixon.

Late the next afternoon Clint rode into Tahlequah. While he'd been there many times before, he always felt himself the foreigner. White men were tolerated but never welcomed in the Cherokee capital. Federal marshals were viewed with even greater distrust.

However unwelcome, Clint was nonetheless impressed by the Cherokee people. In the old tribal language, the word for Cherokee was *Tsalagi*. The ancient emblem of bravery was the color red, and courage was believed to originate from the east, where the sun rose. Freely translated, *Tsalagi* meant "Red Fire Men" or "Brave Men." While most Cherokees had been converted to the Christian faith, tribal lore had not disappeared entirely from everyday life. Even today, the people still thought of themselves as the *Tsalagi*.

The Cherokees' ancestral homeland originally encompassed Alabama, Georgia, and Tennessee. In 1830, under pressure from white frontiersmen, Congress passed the Indian Removal Bill. Enacted despite the Cherokees' protests, the legislation granted Western lands to the Five Civilized Tribes in exchange for their ancestral birthright. A total of eighteen thousand Cherokees was herded westward over what became known as the Trail of Tears. Of that number, more than four thousand perished before reaching Indian Territory. The Cherokees still honored their memory by resisting white domination.

For all that, Clint thought it ironic that they had adopted the white man's form of government. The Cherokee Nation was virtually an independent republic, with a tribal chief who acted as head of state. The tribal council, similar in structure to Congress, comprised two houses, and there were two political parties. Yet, unlike the Western Plains tribes, the Cherokees accepted no annuities or financial assistance from Washington. Nor were white men allowed to own property except through intermarriage.

The Cherokee economy was founded on an agrarian base. As with the white world, some people were farmers, and others, clearly, were gentleman farmers. Outside Tahlequah there were baronial estates, with colonnaded homes and sweeping lawns. The setting was one of antebellum plantations transplanted from a more gracious era; before the Civil War many Cherokees were slave owners as large as any in the South. Still, the lavish estates were outnumbered manyfold by log cabins and unpretentious frame houses. Wealthy Cherokees, like wealthy whites, simply lived on a scale befitting their position.

Tahlequah itself was considered the hub of progress in

Indian Territory. The capitol building, which was a two-story
brick structure, dominated the town square. Nearby was the
supreme court building, and around the square were several
prosperous business establishments. One of these was the
Cherokee Advocate, a newspaper printed in both Cherokee
and English. Of all Indians, the Cherokees were the only
ones with an alphabet, and therefore a written language. No
other tribe was able to preserve its culture so completely in
the ancient tongue.

Clint dismounted in front of the capitol building. All government offices, as well as the tribal council chambers, were
housed there. The building was only slightly less stately than
the capitol in Arkansas, and there was an air of bustling efficiency about the place. As he went through the broad entryway, Clint marked again that the men who governed here
wore swallowtail coats and conducted themselves like seasoned diplomats. It occurred to him that they were no less
dignified than their counterparts in other frontier capitals.

On the second floor, Clint was ushered into the office of
Major D. W. Lipe. As a deputy marshal, he'd had previous
dealings with the Light Horse Police. He knew that Lipe, who
was an astute politician, wielded considerable power within
the Cherokee Nation. He reminded himself to watch his
mouth, and his temper. Nothing would be gained by accusa-
tions and harsh words. His purpose was to gather information.

Lipe was swarthy, somewhat darker than the usual
Cherokee, with marblelike eyes. He made no attempt to
shake hands, greeting Clint instead with a curt nod. Nor did
he extend the courtesy of offering Clint a chair. His mouth
was razored in a faint smile.

"Marshal Brannock," he said civilly. "What brings you to
Tahlequah?"

"Rafe Dixon," Clint told him.

"Of course," Lipe said matter-of-factly. "I understand he
killed one of your marshals."

"We have reason to believe he's holed up somewhere in
the Cherokee Nation."

"Do you, indeed?"

"For a fact," Clint said, no timbre in his voice. "I've been told your Light Horse know the location of Dixon's hideout."

Lipe sat perfectly still for a moment. "Are you accusing me of harboring a fugitive?"

"Not yet," Clint said equably. "I'm requesting your assistance in a criminal matter."

"And if I choose to decline the request?"

"Judge Parker would likely get his bowels in an uproar. Knowin' him, he'd probably file a formal protest with Washington."

For an instant their eyes locked. Then, as though unperturbed, Lipe made an offhand gesture. "One good turn deserves another," he said. "Are you open to a trade?"

Clint held his gaze. "Try me."

"A federal warrant has been issued on a young Cherokee. He's charged with operating a whiskey still."

"And—"

Lipe smiled. "His father is an influential member of the tribal council."

"Dixon for the boy," Clint said stolidly. "Is that the deal?"

"Exactly."

Clint nodded. "I'll arrange to have the charges dropped."

"In that event," Lipe said, "I suggest you confine your search to White Oak Creek. Perhaps three or four miles west of Vinita."

Vinita was a small settlement northwest of Tahlequah. Clint considered a moment, thoughtful. "When I get there," he asked, "what will I find?"

"Dixon and two of his men. At last report, they were living in an old cabin."

"What happened to the rest of his gang?"

"I presume they're scattered until the next job."

"Your turn now," Clint said, apparently satisfied. "What's the boy's name—the whiskey peddler?"

"Bluejacket," Lipe replied. "Joe Bluejacket."

"I'll attend to it when I get back to Fort Smith."

Clint turned away from the desk. He went out the door without a parting word or a backward glance. On his way

down the stairs, he silently cursed Lipe for demanding a
trade-off. But then, on second thought, he figured he'd come
out ahead on the deal. A whiskey peddler for a killer.

Judge Parker would have approved.

A crude but stoutly built log cabin stood in the center of the
clearing. Smoke drifted skyward from the mud chimney,
silty against an early-morning sun. There was no other sign
of activity.

Clint was seated in a stand of trees on the opposite side of
the creek. Shortly before dawn, he'd hidden his horse farther
downstream. Then, ghosting through the woods, he had
taken a position across from the cabin door. He waited now
for the door to open.

Across his knees was a Colt rifle chambered for .50–95
caliber. A pump-action repeater, it was a shade faster than a
Winchester carbine. Spent shells were ejected by a backward stroke of the foregrip, and a fresh round was chambered on the forward stroke. Beneath the octagon barrel was
a cartridge magazine that held ten rounds. The massive fifty-
caliber slug would down man or beast with a single shot.

The rifle typified Clint's approach to his work. A seasoned manhunter always sought any advantage possible.
One way to gain an edge was to be better armed, assured of a
knock-down shot every time the trigger was pulled. Another
way was to get the drop on a man and permit him only an instant's warning. Anyone fool enough to ignore the warning
was then shot without hesitation. By adhering to such pre-
cepts a bold lawman often lived to be an old lawman.

Today, Clint had all those factors working in his favor.
His position gave him a wide field of fire, allowing him to
cover the cabin and the clearing. He knew Rafe Dixon on
sight and he intended to wait until the element of surprise
gave him a decided edge. The speed of the pump-action repeater whittled the odds down even further, and thus he had
no qualms about tangling with three men. Nor was he concerned with taking prisoners. A coldblooded murderer deserved nothing. . . .

The door opened. Clint got to his feet, still concealed behind a tree. He thumbed the hammer on the rifle, watching as a man emerged from the cabin. Three horses were penned in a corral out back and the man walked in that direction. Clint lost sight of him but heard him talking to the horses. Through the open door the interior of the cabin was black as a cave.

Several minutes passed in silence. Abruptly, leading a saddled horse, the man reappeared around the corner of the cabin. Halting, he stepped into the saddle as a second man moved through the doorway. A moment elapsed before a third man emerged from the cabin. He was lean and stringy, with dark matted hair and a handlebar mustache. His face decorated wanted dodgers throughout the territory. His name was Rafe Dixon.

Clint barked a sharp command. "Don't move! You're covered!"

The mounted man spurred his horse. Dixon clawed at a holstered pistol and the other man was only a beat behind. Still framed in the doorway, Dixon cleared leather and looked toward the treeline. Clint shot him in the chest.

The impact of the slug dropped Dixon in his tracks. As he went down, the other man got off a hurried snapshot and whirled toward the corner of the cabin. The bullet whanged through the trees directly over Clint's head. He drew a bead and fired.

Stumbling forward, the man slowed, then suddenly buckled at the knees. His eyes rolled back in his head and the pistol fell from his hand. He slumped at the waist and toppled facedown in the dirt. His right leg twitched in a spasm of afterdeath.

Clint pumped another round into the chamber and turned upstream. He got a last glimpse of the man on horseback disappearing around a bend in the shoreline. His finger eased off the trigger and he looked back toward the cabin. Neither of the men had moved.

Quitting the treeline, Clint waded across the creek. He approached the fallen men with the rifle held at hip level.

Dixon was sprawled in the doorway, his shirtfront splattered with blood. The other man lay puddled in gore, half his rib cage blown away. A quick check revealed that the cabin was empty.

Clint felt neither elation nor remorse. He'd done his job, killing swiftly and cleanly when his warning was ignored. He thought Ernie Wilson would rest easier knowing that Dixon was dead. Still, he regretted having allowed the third man to escape. He disliked unfinished business.

No job was done until all accounts were settled.

FOUR

On March 10 Morg arrived in Kansas. He stepped off the train in Caldwell, a town three miles north of Indian Territory. Directly across the line was the Cherokee Outlet.

From New Mexico, Morg had traveled north to Colorado and then eastward across the Kansas plains. It was his first extended trip away from Spur and the Hondo Valley. He tended to think of it as a pilgrimage, one meant to broaden his horizons. He was being exposed to a world beyond the sphere of his youth.

Morg never questioned the purpose of the trip. His mother was grooming him to assume the reins of Spur. While she was a shrewd businesswoman, her principal interest lay in politics. She foresaw a time when she would relinquish control of the family enterprises to her son. The first step in that long-range plan was his inspection of the Outlet ranch.

One day he would be expected to fill his father's boots. The idea was at once a stimulus and a matter of some trepidation. His father was a figure of mythical proportions, larger than life. People still spoke of Virgil Brannock's vision and his almost godlike force of character. Dead six years, he even now haunted the minds of those who had known him.

To a degree, Morg walked in his father's shadow. He'd been there the day his father was killed, and the memory was still sharp, still painful. Yet the experience had aged

him, thrust him abruptly into manhood. Overnight his outlook had changed, and he'd stopped thinking like a fourteen-
year-old. His formative years became instead a time of early
maturity.

During those years, Morg had discovered something
about himself. He was a quick learner, mentally sharp, and
often given to insights beyond his experience. He found himself comfortable in the company of older men, unfazed by
the difference in age. He felt himself their equal and he'd seldom been proved wrong. What they saw in him was what he
had finally seen in himself. He was, in many respects, the
very incarnation of his father.

Floyd Dunn saw it too. As foreman and general manager
of the Outlet ranch, he was a man of some position. Until
Morg stepped off the train they had never met, and he might
well have viewed the youngster as an upstart. But from the
moment they shook hands, they got along famously. Dunn
was immediately impressed by Morg's physical similarity to
his father. Even more, he was impressed by the young man's
knowledge of cows.

At twenty, Morg was already a veteran cattleman. He'd
begun working roundup as a boy, and by age sixteen he was
considered a top hand. He was a skilled roper, a passable
broncbuster, and no stranger to the rigors of a trail drive. All
the more important, he understood bloodlines and herd management and possessed a keen eye for horseflesh. Far from a
wealthy young tyro, he was a product of the bunkhouse.
Whipcord tough, and savvy to the ways of cowhands, he
knew his business.

Dunn was a graduate of the same school. A whiskery
Texican, he was bowlegged from a lifetime spent in the saddle. In 1876, after ramrodding a trail herd to Kansas, he'd
been hired to run the Outlet spread. He had no family, and at
the age of fifty, he considered the ranch his only home. He
revered the memory of Virgil Brannock and looked upon
Elizabeth as a natural phenomenon. He took their son to be
one of his own.

The ranch was located on the Cimarron River, some forty miles inside Indian Territory. Aside from Dunn's ramshackle log cabin, there were a bunkhouse and corral and several outbuildings. The outfit carried ten full-time hands on the payroll and hired a dozen more during roundup. Every fall, upwards of four thousand shorthorn beeves were trailed to railhead at Caldwell. There the cows were sold to Eastern cattle buyers.

Morg moved into the cabin with Dunn. For the next few days, the old Texican showed him around the spread. The land was lush with graze, and tributaries branching off the river provided abundant water. The operation was tightly run and the books indicated that Dunn was a stickler for details. Every year for the past eleven years he had managed to turn a profit that any cattleman would envy. His word was law with the hands and he brooked no nonsense from anyone. He ran the ranch like a hardnosed drill sergeant.

The inspection left Morg suitably impressed. He saw nothing out of order and found little that might be improved. What intrigued him most was the Texican's garrulous recollections of days past. At night, seated at the cabin table, Dunn invariably turned talkative. Unlike other old-timers, he spoke not of trail drives and stampedes and fabled cowtowns. His ruminations were about the man who had hired him long ago, Virgil Brannock. And a dream centered on the Cherokee Outlet.

Virgil Brannock first saw the Outlet in the summer of 1876. By then Spur was already one of the largest spreads in New Mexico. What he sought was a similar operation, closer to the Kansas railheads. His goal was expansion, and like any true visionary, he saw potential often overlooked by lesser men. His search that summer ended on a dogleg bend in the Cimarron. Within the space of a year, he founded the ranch and formed an alliance with the Cherokee tribe. A short while later he took on the federal government.

The Outlet was a bizarre creation spawned earlier in the century. When the Five Civilized Tribes were resettled in

Indian Territory, the Cherokees were granted seven million
acres bordering southern Kansas. As a further concession,
they were granted a corridor extending westward, which
comprised another six million acres. Designated the Cherokee Outlet, the legal status of this strip was forever in question. By treaty, the tribe was forbidden to dispose of it in any
manner.

For nearly a half-century, the Outlet remained unoccu-
pied and forgotten. The Cherokees rarely ventured into the
western grant, for their lands to the east were sufficient for
the entire tribe. Then, in the early 1870s, the Chisholm Trail
was blazed through the heart of Indian Territory. Texas cattlemen were quick to discover the rolling plains watered by
the Canadian and the Cimarron. A perfect holding ground
for trail-weary longhorns, the Outlet was within a short distance of the Kansas border. Herds were halted and allowed
to fatten out before the final drive to a railhead.

By late spring of 1881 some twenty ranchers had staked
out permanent cowcamps in the Outlet. Among them was
Virgil Brannock, and he possessed a foresight the others
lacked. Envisioning problems from the federal government,
he organized the Cherokee Cattlemen's Association. The
ranchers elected him president and he promptly negotiated a
ten-year lease with the Cherokee tribal council. The lease
covered more than a million acres and enriched the tribal
treasury by $100,000 a year. Everyone involved benefited by
the arrangement.

From time to time, the bureaucrats in Washington attempted to overturn the lease agreement. But Virgil Brannock had formed a lasting alliance with the Cherokee
Nation. After his death, other men stepped forward to head
the Cattlemen's Association. The Cherokees proved to be
tolerant landlords and staunch allies, working to preserve
their annual lease payment. For the past six years, every effort by the government to create discord had been turned
aside. Harmony still prevailed between the Cherokees and
the ranchers.

"Folks don't forget," Dunn remarked late one night.

"Your pa wrote his own epitaph when he formed the Association. He was a helluva man."

"Yeah, he was," Morg said with a note of pride. "When I was a kid, he used to talk to me about the future. He opened my eyes plenty."

"Know what you mean," Dunn said breezily. "Gawd-almighty, he was a regular bearcat when it come to plannin' ahead. Always saw that rainbow out there in the distance."

Morg nodded vigorously. "And the rainbow was just as important as the pot of gold. I remember him saying the money's only a yardstick. It's what you build that counts."

"By jiggers!" Dunn hooted. "You sound just like him. Damn me if you don't."

A sudden grin cracked Morg's face. "I've got a ways to go, but I figure to make my mark. He taught me to aim high."

Dunn looked at him thoughtfully. "Your ma ain't no slouch either. Got a real head on her shoulders."

"Tell me about it," Morg said, laughing. "Back home they call her the Iron Butterfly. Nobody's got the best of her yet."

"Speakin' of which," Dunn observed. "The government's nippin' at our heels again. Looks to be a lulu of a fight."

"What's the problem?"

"Boomers," Dunn said angrily. "Gawddamn sodbusters lookin' to gobble up Injun land."

"You sound like it's serious."

"Liable to be the ruination of us all!"

Morg looked puzzled. "Are you saying they've got their eye on the Outlet?"

"Not just exactly," Dunn grumped. "You'll hear all about it tomorrow night. We're set to attend an Association meeting."

"Why not tell me now?"

"'Cause it's got more twists than a barrel of snakes. Ain't no way I could explain it."

On that somber note the conversation ended. Dunn snuffed the lamp and peeled down to his longjohns. Morg undressed in the dark, then crawled into his own bunk. His last waking thought was a word he'd never before heard.

He wondered what "Boomers" were.

• • •

Caldwell was the last of the cowtowns. With the railroads spreading throughout Texas, even Dodge City was slowly withering away. The era of the great trail drives was gradually fading into history.

Herds from the Outlet ranchers were now the mainstay of Caldwell's continued prosperity. The Cherokee Cattlemen's Association maintained offices on Chisholm Street, and the members regularly met there once a month. Tonight's meeting had been convened on short notice and the ranchers were in a sober mood. There was talk of trouble emanating out of Washington.

Joe Pardee was the current president of the Association. His beard was dappled with gray and his hair was thinning above a craggy forehead. He was a plain-spoken man who gave the impression of wisdom garnered through age. Like most of the other members, he was a Texan who had invested heavily in the Outlet. The only spread not owned by a Texan was Spur's operation on the Cimarron. Nobody held it against Floyd Dunn that he worked for a New Mexican outfit.

Upon arriving, Dunn introduced Morg to the various members. He was readily accepted, for the men there remembered his father with great admiration. Joe Pardee wrung his hand with genuine warmth, welcoming him to the gathering. Then, as the ranchers got themselves seated, Pardee called the meeting to order. He stood at the front of the room, staring them into silence.

"Glad you could make it," he said, nodding around the group. "We've got a pisspot full of things to discuss and none of it good news. So bear with me while I bring you up-to-date."

For all his rough edges, Pardee was an articulate speaker. He began by sketching a broad outline of the situation and the origin of the problem. At root was the fact that so many people coveted Indian lands. A flood of immigrants and settlers had already claimed the choice homesteads. The clamor to open all public lands to settlement intensified as

the westward migration gained strength. In the forefront of
the movement were the Boomers, an army of some ten thousand settlers. Too late to claim homesteads in Kansas, they
were encamped along the border of Indian Territory.

One of the prime targets of the Boomers was the Unassigned Lands. Ceded by the Creeks and the Seminoles as a
home for tribes yet to be resettled, the Unassigned Lands
embraced some two million acres of well-watered, fertile
plains. White settlers were also eyeing the Cherokee Outlet,
a vast landmass roughly 150 miles in length. Word of this
grassy paradise had drawn the attention of the Boomers as
well as vengeful politicians. Washington had never forgiven
the cattlemen, or the Cherokees, for circumventing the edict
against leasing agreements.

In short order, a public outcry arose over both the Unassigned Lands and the Outlet. The Boomers were backed by
several influential factions, all of which had a vested interest
in the western expansion. Politicians and merchant princes
and railroads, all looking to feather their own nests, rallied to
the cause. Alone in their opposition to settlement were the
Five Civilized Tribes. Their dealings with the government
formed a chain of broken pledges and unfulfilled treaties.
They saw settlement as a device for the enrichment of white
businessmen and greedy politicians.

In Washington these same politicians were holding out a
wide array of enticements. Efforts were under way to convince the Five Civilized Tribes that their best interests would
be served by abolishing tribal government. They were told
that full citizenship within the Republic would afford them
voting rights and equality before the law. Still, based on their
experiences with *tibo*'s promises, they had good reason to
doubt the faith of the government. Indian leaders, as well as
the lowliest tribesmen, were unwilling to exchange independence for the dubious privilege of citizenship.

For all their resistance, however, the Indians were
weighed down by a sense of fatalism. Thoughtful men knew
that the Nations were in the process of slow but certain ab-
sorption into the white culture. The Five Civilized Tribes

numbered less than fifty thousand people, and much of their land lay untilled. The movement to gain control of the Nations—23,000,000 acres—would ultimately put the tribes in an untenable position. For no one seriously doubted that the true goal was the dissolution of all of Indian Territory.

Over the past two years the pressure to open Indian lands to settlement had steadily mounted. Legislation enacted by Congress in 1885 paved the way for purchase of all unused land from the Five Civilized Tribes. Only a month ago the Severalty Act was passed, which made settlement of Indian Territory a virtual certainty. Negotiations were even now underway to bring about the allotment of lands in the Nations, forcing each tribesman to accept the same 160 acres awarded to white settlers under the Homestead Act. Worse, there was talk in Congress of creating from Indian lands what would be called Oklahoma Territory. The future was there for all to see.

"No doubt about it," Joe Pardee concluded. "We're between a rock and a hard place. Unless something happens fast, we're gonna lose the Outlet."

"So what'd we do?" one of the ranchers asked. "Damned if I'll give up without a fight."

"There's more'n one way to fight," Pardee noted slyly. "What we've gotta do is take a trick out of their own book— outfox the bastards."

"How you plan to pull that off?"

Pardee launched into an explanation. His scheme was to purchase their Outlet holdings directly from the Cherokee Nation. Now was the time to act, while they still had the leverage of a lease agreement, and before Indian lands were opened to white settlement. Once ownership was in private hands, the Outlet would be immune to the threat from Washington. Yet the price had to be right, so generous that the government couldn't claim they were hoodwinking the Cherokees. He proposed that the Association offer three dollars an acre for title to the Outlet lands under lease.

"Jesus Crucified Christ!" another Texan yelped. "You're

talkin' about three million dollars. Where're we gonna get that kind of money?"

"We'll borrow it," Pardee informed him. "We'll mortgage our herds and throw in the land as extra collateral. There's plenty of bankers that would cotton to the idea."

"And foreclose muy damn pronto if we couldn't meet the payments. Where'd we be then?"

"Where we are now," Pardee countered. "Up shit creek without a paddle. What choice do we have?"

The Association members bitched and grumbled. When it became clear that no one had a better idea, they finally put it to a vote. There were a few dissenters, but the majority agreed it was worth a try. Joe Pardee was authorized to approach bankers in Caldwell and Wichita.

Morg was unsettled by what he'd heard. Some vague premonition told him that it would never work. The federal government was clearly determined to do away with all of Indian Territory, including the Nations. And Washington would view a ragtag bunch of ranchers as an obstacle to that goal. He thought the Association members were living on borrowed time, a year or two at best. In the end, they would all be ousted from the Outlet.

The meeting adjourned a short time later. Morg and Floyd Dunn, along with the other members, trooped upstreet to a saloon. Standing at the bar, they were approached by a sturdy, thick-set man with a badge on his chest. Dunn introduced him as Jack Selman, Caldwell's town marshal.

"Brannock," Selman repeated, staring at Morg. "You any relation to Clint Brannock?"

"Sure am," Morg said. "He's my uncle."

"Small world," Selman said, pulling an envelope from his pocket. "A wire come in for Clint tonight. Figured I'd pass it along to Floyd."

Morg studied the telegraph envelope. The message was from the U.S. marshal in Fort Smith. Addressed to Clint, it had been sent in care of the Spur Ranch, Cherokee Outlet. He looked up at Selman. "Any idea what it's about?"

"Only a hunch," Selman said. "Week or so ago your uncle killed a couple of wanted men down in the Nations. A third one got away."

"And they think he's headed toward the Outlet?"

"That'd be my guess," Selman allowed. "More'n likely they figured Clint would stop by the ranch. So they sent the wire here."

Morg invited the lawman to join them for a drink. The barkeep brought another glass and poured. Selman and Dunn began talking, but Morg listened with only half an ear. His mind was on other matters.

He tried to remember how many men his uncle had killed.

Late the next afternoon Clint forded the Cimarron. Sundown was only an hour away and he hoped to make the ranch by nightfall. A warm bed and a hot meal sounded inviting. For the past week, he'd been tracking the third gang member. While the trail zigzagged and backtracked, the general direction was northwest. The man clearly believed he was being pursued and had resorted to evasive tactics. So far none of his dodges had worked.

Unconcerned, Clint doggedly stuck to the trail. His years as a cavalry scout enabled him to follow sign over the roughest ground. His one concern was that the man would quit the wilderness and head for a town. Where people congregated, a trail could be lost in an instant. Wooded terrain, even the open plains, was far more suitable to a manhunt.

With onrushing darkness the hoofprints began drifting off to the north. Clint studied them a moment, aware that he might lose the trail if he tracked any farther. He calculated he was no more than a mile from the ranch and a hot meal. Whether or not the man made a run for Caldwell was something he could better determine at first light. He turned west along the river.

Stars dotted the sky by the time he sighted the ranch. When he stepped down from the saddle, the cabin door opened.

Framed in a shaft of lamplight, he saw Morg standing behind Floyd Dunn. His surprised look was replaced by a wide grin as the youngster hurried forward and pumped his hand. They hadn't seen each other in almost a year and he'd hardly expected to find Morg in the Outlet. His detour suddenly took on the overtones of a reunion.

Oddly enough, Morg evidenced no surprise that their paths had crossed. The reason became apparent when they entered the cabin and he produced the telegram. He explained how he'd come by it the night before, while in Caldwell. In passing, he mentioned that Jack Selman, the town marshal, thought it had to do with law business. His instructions were to hand it over at the first opportunity.

Clint tore open the envelope. There were two message slips inside, one from John Carroll, the U.S. marshal. He stated that he was forwarding a wire from the Indian agent at the Comanche reservation. The second slip was a duplicate of the agent's message. It was dated March 14, two days past.

The message was short. Clint's eyes narrowed as he scanned it quickly, then read it again. His mouth went tight and his expression turned curiously stoic. He silently handed the message slip to Morg.

CLINT BRANNOCK
U.S. MARSHAL'S OFFICE
FT. SMITH, ARKANSAS

> YOUR SISTER-IN-LAW GRAVELY ILL.
> URGENT YOU COME AT ONCE.

GEORGE HAZEN
AGENT, FORT SILL
INDIAN TERRITORY

"Sounds bad," Morg said, glancing up. "Are you going?"
"Wouldn't think of doing otherwise."

"What about the man you're after?"

"To hell with him," Clint said shortly. His gaze shifted to Dunn. "Floyd, will you loan me a fresh horse?"

"Shore will," Dunn replied. "But gawddamn, Clint, you ain't plannin' on leaving tonight, are you?"

"Yeah, I am," Clint said. "Just as soon as you rustle up some hot grub. I travel better on a full belly."

Ten minutes later Clint swung aboard a roan gelding. His hat was pulled low and the collar of his mackinaw was turned high against the chill night air. A short distance from the cabin he again forded the Cimarron.

He rode south under pale starlight.

FIVE

A routine day at the clinic began early. The first patients started arriving shortly after breakfast. By midmorning the waiting room was usually crowded, with more gathered on the walkway outside. Seldom was the last patient attended until sometime after sundown.

Unlike most frontier doctors, Jennifer never traveled the backcountry circuit. The distances involved would have required her to be out of the office at least two days a week. She responded only to emergency calls, driving her own buggy and team. The balance of the time she kept regular office hours.

The system proved to be immensely practical. Her practice covered hundreds of square miles and Lincoln was centrally located. The patients came into town for treatment rather than relying on infrequent medical visits to their homes. The end result was that she saw more people and cured far more illnesses.

Some problems required a departure from her routine. There was no hospital in Lincoln and therefore no facilities for extended medical care. A childbirth, or any condition that left a patient bedridden, was attended in the home. Friends and family were depended upon to provide nursing care for prolonged illnesses. Hardly the perfect situation, it was nonetheless accepted by people accustomed to fending for themselves.

Jennifer's staff consisted of two *mexicano* women. Rosa, the nurse and surgical assistant, had been inherited from Dr. Chester Wood. She was capable and levelheaded, with an accumulated storehouse of practical medical knowledge. The other woman, Lupe, was younger and still somewhat inexperienced. Her duties revolved around sterilizing instruments and dressings, and maintaining the clinic in a state of cleanliness. Winter and summer, she kept caldrons of water boiling on an old woodburner stove.

The patients today were a representative lot. Jennifer had lanced an inflamed boil, treated a woman for blinding headaches, and examined an elderly man suffering from cystitis. The latter condition was a bladder infection, resulting in a burning sensation during urination. A sample of the man's urine was cloudy in color and showed traces of blood. He was running a slight fever.

By necessity, Jennifer was her own pharmacist. From supply houses back East, she ordered roots, herbs, and other natural materials. Using these base elements, she then mashed and pounded with mortar and pestle until the desired prescription was formulated. Once mixed, the compounded powders were packaged in squares of heavy paper. For all the advances in science, pharmacology offered few miracles. Some illnesses were still treated with rudimentary medicine.

The woman with a headache was ordered to take an enema with strong black coffee, cooled and undiluted. Afterward, she was to rest in a darkened room and avoid spicy foods for twenty-four hours. For the man with cystitis, Jennifer prescribed a potion of baking soda and water every two hours for three days. To flush out the bladder, he was required to drink five quarts of water daily. Should the symptoms persist, he was to return on the fourth day.

The elderly man typified one of Jennifer's major problems. All too many men were reluctant to consult a woman physician about personal ailments. Anything that required an examination of their private parts brought on an attack of male modesty. She chided them, remarking that she'd been raised on a ranch where bulls displayed no modesty whatever. Despite her casual attitude, the situation had improved only by degree. Some men still traveled fifty miles to see a male doctor.

Jennifer was keenly aware of the underlying prejudice. However enlightened the times, a female physician was severely stigmatized because of her sex. Following the Civil War, in the face of public disapproval, women began to invade the medical profession. At first they tended to specialize in the treatment of women and children, practicing gynecology and obstetrics. Even so, male physicians attempted to exclude them from all educational institutions. Johns Hopkins and Harvard, the two most prestigious medical schools, routinely denied entrance to women.

Harvard medical students protested with a resolution that stated: "No woman of true delicacy would be willing in the presence of men to listen to the discussions of subjects that necessarily come under consideration." Boston was nonetheless a hotbed of feminist activity, and the location of the first medical college for women. A unique institution, the New England Hospital for Women and Children was owned and operated exclusively by women. There the internship training denied by other hospitals was provided to aspiring lady physicians.

By 1884, when Jennifer entered medical school, less than three percent of all doctors were women. She chose one of the few coeducational institutions in the country, Tufts College. Her courses included anatomy, pathology, physiology, and pharmacology. She attended advanced lectures at City Hospital, where female students were allowed to observe operations in the hospital amphitheater. She interned there as well, working the charity wards with both male and female patients.

Female students were also allowed to witness autopsies conducted by the county coroner. The experience proved invaluable when students were later required to dissect cadavers. The old days, when "resurrectionists" raided cemeteries for bodies, were long since passed. Jennifer worked on cadavers excavated from potter's field for use in medical colleges. There again she was fortunate, for the dissections were performed on both men and women. She graduated with a knowledge of anatomy essential to the practice of general surgery.

After returning to Lincoln, she gained even wider experience. Dr. Chester Wood permitted her to assist in operations and quickly came to trust her ability. On occasion, she managed to enlighten him on new techniques developed in Boston and in European medical centers. By the time he died, Wood looked upon her as a colleague, a worthy successor. Her skill at the operating table was no less persuasive with the townspeople. Anglos and *mexicanos* alike accepted her despite the fact that she was a woman. Only some of the stodgier men still resented her because she wore skirts.

Late that afternoon her surgical skills were put to the test. A wagon rolled to a halt in front of the clinic. The driver owned a ranch on the Rio Bonito, west of Lincoln. One of his cowhands was stretched out on a pallet of blankets in the wagonbed. Several townsmen were summoned from upstreet and they assisted in unloading the cowhand. While the rancher supported his head, they carried him into the clinic.

The rancher told a familiar story. Working a bunch of cattle, the cowhand's horse had spooked and thrown him from the saddle. Cowhands were dumped all the time and generally managed to walk away. But this time the man had tumbled backward out of the saddle, arms and legs akimbo. As he fell, the horse lashed out with its hind hooves and kicked him in the head. His skull was crushed.

Jennifer had him placed on the operating table. Rosa brusquely waved the men out of the inner office and closed the door. The cowhand was unconscious, the crown of his head matted with blood. A quick examination revealed an ugly wound approximately two inches in diameter. Underneath the tangled hair and bone fragments, a section of the brain was exposed. His breathing was shallow and his features were ashen.

Unfastening his shirt, Jennifer checked his heartbeat with

a stethoscope. His pulse was feeble and his skin was cold to the touch. She then checked the pupils of his eyes, noting that they reacted to the overhead reflective lamp. With a needle, she pricked his finger and watched his hand retract. Finally, she inspected the crotch of his trousers and found he'd passed a small amount of urine.

The signs were better than Jennifer had dared expect. While the injury was serious, there was no indication of compression of the brain. The absence of paralysis, combined with the other favorable symptoms, gave her hope. Yet there was still the matter of the gaping hole and the exposed brain tissue. Staring down at the man, she suddenly recalled a lecture from medical school. Her professor had spoken of an ancient surgical procedure, reportedly traced to Egyptian times. No physician outside Boston was known to have attempted the operation.

Jennifer moved through the door to the waiting room. She ordered the rancher to take a silver dollar and hurry downstreet to the town blacksmith. She wanted the coin placed on an anvil and hammered into a thin disk, at least three inches in diameter. Lupe was then instructed to await his return and sterilize the disk. Time was the enemy and she told the rancher to run all the way. His eyes clouded with a question, but her stern look dampened his curiosity. He rushed out the door.

Lupe brought hot water and soap and Jennifer scrubbed for the operation. With a straight razor, she then shaved the cowhand's head, leaving the crown bald. Rosa fetched a bottle of carbolic solution and used the antiseptic to cleanse the bare spot. When she finished, Rosa moved to the side of the operating table. She waited with a sponge and a vial of ether, should the injured man regain consciousness.

Working with a probe and forceps, Jennifer gently removed splinters of bone from the wound. Several minutes passed before she satisfied herself that no foreign matter endangered the brain. As she straightened up, Lupe entered the room holding a wad of sterile dressing. She commented that the blacksmith had obligingly dropped everything else and rushed the job along. Within the folds of the cloth lay a shiny wafer of silver, slightly convex in shape. It was still warm from being sterilized.

Scalpel in hand, Jennifer quickly incised four lines radiating outward from the wound. She next peeled the flaps aside and gingerly implanted the silver disk over the exposed brain tissue. From the instrument tray she took a surgical needle and threaded it with catgut. A stitch at a time, she sutured the scalp closed with meticulous care. When she tied off the last suture, a spot of silver the size of a quarter was all that remained visible. She stepped back to admire her handiwork.

The cowhand groaned. His eyes fluttered open and he stared up at the overhead lamp with a groggy expression. He licked his lips and blinked into the harsh light. His voice sounded parched. "What happened?"

"You're fine," Jennifer said, moving to the side of the table. "You'll be up and around in no time."

"I don't—" His eyes focused and he stared at her. "That you, Doc?"

"Yes, it's me."

Jennifer smiled and took his hand. So far as she could recall, she had never seen him before. Which made the operation a milestone in more ways than one.

Today was the first time anybody had called her Doc.

Jennifer's living quarters were at the rear of the clinic. The furnishings were an eclectic blend of chintz and patterned slipcovers and dark hardwood. A broad window looked westward toward the mountains.

Early that evening Blake Hazlett found her seated in the parlor. After supper, he usually stopped by for an hour or so. Over a brandy, they shared the day's experiences and remarked on the state of things in Lincoln. He was as intrigued by her clinic as he was by his own law practice.

Blake was a stocky, amiable man with an even disposition and a contagious laugh. His hair was dark and curly and his mustache was the color of lampblack. Three years ago he'd opened an office in Lincoln and he now handled most of the legal work for Spur. Through Elizabeth, he had met Jennifer upon her return from medical school. They had been keeping steady company for the past nine months.

Tonight Jennifer was in a pensive mood. Her face appeared drained and her eyes were oddly vacant. She stared off into some thoughtful distance. Blake settled into an overstuffed chair and pulled out a tobacco pouch. He loaded his pipe, then fired up in a cloud of smoke. He looked at her inquisitively.

"Thought you'd be ready to celebrate," he said. "The whole town's talking about your operation. They say you brought that cowhand back from the dead."

"Hardly." Jennifer's voice was troubled. "We can't even provide him with proper medical care. He's been moved to a room in the hotel."

"I recall we've had this discussion before. You're talking about a hospital, aren't you?"

"Yes," Jennifer said quietly. "It's like practicing medicine in the Dark Ages. Any civilized town would have built a hospital years ago."

Blake laughed good-humoredly. "People around here pride themselves on being tough. A hospital sounds like some sissified Eastern notion."

Jennifer gave him a tired smile. "Perhaps we need an asylum more than a hospital. Anyone who thinks like that should be committed."

"What we need is a drink."

Blake got to his feet. He moved to an ornately carved cabinet and poured from a brandy decanter. When he returned with her glass, he stooped down and brushed her lips with a kiss. She looked at him strangely.

Their relationship was curiously unemotional. Jennifer was comfortable with him and she preferred his company to that of other men she'd met. Still, her feelings about him veered wildly, and she often reflected on the absence of passion between them. She sometimes wished he would sweep her off her feet.

Blake lifted his glass. "To the lady Doc," he said with a waggish grin. "The toast of Lincolntown."

Jennifer laughed deep in her throat. His sunny nature was irresistible and he never failed to lighten her mood. She wondered now whether her mother was right, after all. Perhaps there was more between a man and woman than fervid passion.

Perhaps, in the end, simple affection was enough.

Hondo Valley was bordered on the south by a low line of foothills. Some ten miles beyond the hogback ridges lay the Rio Felix, with its headwaters in the westward mountains. The river snaked through a land of broken plains and sparse graze.

Brad rode there once a week. He had homesteaded a quarter-section on the Rio Felix and built a crude log cabin. Farther downstream was the ranch of Homer Stockton, Morg's father-in-law. Upstream were the *jacales* and patchy farmlands of several *mexicano* families.

North of the river, a good part of the land was public domain. Over the last year, Brad had put together a herd of some fifty cows. Crossbred stock, longhorn cows topped by shorthorn bulls, they were able to forage for themselves and required little care. He generally rode over late on Saturday and stayed through Sunday.

The operation was financed on a shoestring. Apart from his wages as Spur's foreman, Brad had no money of his own. Nor was he willing to approach Elizabeth for a loan, even though she considered him family. While she never spoke of it, she looked upon his outside venture as a threat. She feared the small spread might grow into something larger, and lure him away from Spur. Her concern was justified, for his attitude had undergone a gradual turnaround. He was tired of working for someone else.

Elizabeth had returned from Santa Fe earlier in the week. A letter was waiting for her from Morg, who was still at the Cherokee Outlet ranch. When she read it aloud at the supper table, her pride was all too evident. Brad sensed she was grooming the youngster for greater things, and rightfully so. But the fact that Morg would one day take over Spur did nothing to improve his lot in life. He would still be a hired hand.

Cottonwoods and willows bordered the Rio Felix. Brad reined to a halt beneath the trees and sat staring at his cabin. Hardly more than a shanty, it was a one-room affair with furnishings as Spartan as a monk's cell. Off in the distance he saw the cattle cropping bunch-grass and spotted several new calves. He grunted sharply, reminded that roundup time was fast approaching. For him, it would be a one-man roundup.

A vague unease settled over Brad. He was no longer content with his job at Spur, where he often felt like the poor relation. Nor was he wildly enthused by the idea of his own pinch-penny spread, merely grubbing out an existence. Late at night, he sometimes wondered why the hell he'd staked the land and built the cabin. He seemed to itch with something that couldn't be scratched. He felt restless and bored and oddly trapped. His life was dull as dirt.

Glum as a sore-tailed bear, he turned his horse west along the river. Some three miles upstream he rode into the yard of Alfredo Ramírez. One of the many *mexicano* farmers on the upper Rio Felix, Ramírez worked a harsh plot of ground and ran a few head of sheep.

He was a small man, with seamed leathery features and a wizened expression. His wife was a happy dumpling of a woman who had given him a brood of seven children. The oldest, scarcely nineteen, was a girl named Juanita.

Ramírez welcomed Brad into his humble adobe. A peaceful man by nature, he held no particular animosity toward *gringos*. He was honored that the foreman of Spur showed such an interest in his eldest daughter. Every Saturday night Brad took supper with the family, and by now it had assumed the aspects of a courting ritual. Even the younger children were aware that Juanita had her eye set on marriage. They waited expectantly for her to spring the snare.

Señora Ramírez was also favorably inclined toward the match. While the men sipped *tequila,* she and Juanita bustled around setting the table. Supper consisted of roast kid, *frijoles* and *tortillas,* and coffee laced with goat's milk. The children stuffed their mouths, one eye on the wealthy Anglo, and maintained a respectful silence. Alfredo Ramírez, as the man of the house, set the tone of the conversation. He spoke with Brad of sheep and cows and the prospects of a long, dry summer. The women listened with rapt attentiveness.

After supper, Juanita threw a *rebozo* over her shoulders. As though on signal, the children began helping their mother clear the table. Ramírez rolled himself a cornhusk cigarette and settled into a chair before the fireplace. No one seemed particularly interested when Juanita opened the door and stepped outside. Brad collected his hat, all too aware that he was the subject of intense, carefully concealed scrutiny. He mumbled a hurried good night as he went through the door.

Juanita strolled off toward the river. She moved with sinuous grace, lithe and youthful, her breasts jutting from beneath the shawl. Her features were delicate, with high cheekbones and an olive complexion. There was a smoldering sensuality about her, some combination of innocence and earthiness that Brad found strangely beguiling. He thought she had the most provocative eyes he'd ever seen in a woman.

On the riverbank, she paused beneath a tall cottonwood. Starlight filtered through the leaves overhead and bathed her face in a shimmering glow. She turned and looked at him with a catlike smile. He met her gaze, found something merry lurking there.

"What is it, *querido*?" she said lightly. "You seem so thoughtful tonight."

"*Nada,*" Brad replied. "I've just got things on my mind, that's all. Not long now till roundup."

"*Madre mía!*" she said in a wounded voice. "We have only one night a week together. You should be thinking of me—not your cows!"

Brad smiled broadly. "When I'm with you nothing else occupies my mind for long. I would be a *manso* otherwise."

"No, not you," she said with an indrawn breath. "I

have reason to know you are not a tame bull. *Verdad?*"

"You are a small, wicked *bruja*. You try to put a spell on me with such talk."

Her eyes gleamed with mischief. "And do I succeed?"

"Sometimes," Brad said, deadpan.

"Sometimes!" she repeated with mock outrage. "You sound like a man who has had his way too often."

Brad beamed at her with genuine affection. "However often would never be often enough."

She laughed and tossed her head. Brad held out his arms and she stepped eagerly into his embrace. Her hands went behind his neck, pulling his mouth down, and she kissed him with a fierce, passionate urgency. The taste of her lips was a honeyed sweetness, at once intoxicating and warm. His arms tightened, strong and demanding, holding her closer still. When at last they separated, her voice was breathless, soft and husky.

"Oh, *caro mío,* how I've missed you."

The *rebozo* fell from her shoulders. They stood for a moment, words forgotten, entwined together like wisps of smoke. Then her mouth opened and she kissed him feverishly. Her nails taloned his back.

He slowly lowered her to the ground.

SIX

Fort Sill was located deep in Indian Territory. The cavalry regiment stationed there had not fought an engagement in almost twelve years. The army was now reduced to the role of benign watchdog.

Three miles south of the fort was the agency headquarters for the Comanche and the Kiowa. Once the scourge of the Southern Plains, the horseback tribes were now wards of the government. Hounded into submission in 1875, the last of the warlike bands had been driven onto the reservation. There they undertook a hard journey along the white man's road.

The reservation spread westward toward the Texas Panhandle, bounded on the north by the Washita River and on the south by the Red. West and north of the agency, the Wichita Mountains jutted skyward, the red granite slopes wrapped in a smoky haze. Sweeping eastward from the foothills were rolling prairies crisscrossed by lowland streams.

By treaty, some three million acres had been ceded to the hostile tribes. The Bureau of Indian Affairs, though somewhat misguided in its efforts, sought to transform horseback warriors into farmers. Over the past decade many of the younger men had adapted and begun to till the soil. Others took jobs in the sawmill and the blacksmith shop operated by the agency. A smaller number, fluent in English, hauled freight bound for the reservation from distant railheads.

Few of the older men were willing to labor in the fields. Hunters and warriors, still tied to the ancient ways, they were unimpressed by the wonders of modern agriculture. With their families, they congregated along Cache Creek, west of the agency. Their existence revolved around annuity goods, food and clothing doled out by the government. Yet they refused the offer of lumber and nails, unwilling to live in the white man's boarded structures. They clung to the hide lodges of their ancestors.

One lodge along the wooded stream was the home of Little Raven and her sons. Long ago she had married a white Comanchero, a renegade who traded with the warlike tribes. A widower, previously married to a white woman, his name was Earl Brannock. To their wedding lodge he brought a son by that marriage, a boy called Lon. She had adopted the youngster as her own, and in time she gave birth to another son. In the Comanche tongue he was known as Bull Calf. His Christian name was Hank.

Late in 1874, Earl Brannock had been killed at the Battle of Palo Duro Canyon. Little Raven, with Lon and Hank, fled onto the Staked Plains with the Comanche survivors. Some months later, pressed relentlessly by cavalry units, the band surrendered at Fort Sill. While Little Raven converted to the white man's religion, she followed the old ways in all other things. Her home for the past twelve winters had been the lodge on Cache Creek.

Grievously ill, Little Raven was now confined to her bedrobes. A persistent cough had worsened over the last few months, steadily sapping her energy. Her features grew wan and her breathing gradually deteriorated into a hoarse rasp. Finally, when she began coughing blood, the post surgeon was summoned from Fort Sill. By then, the disease had spread throughout her lungs, and there was nothing to be done. Her condition was diagnosed as consumption, and the surgeon's prognosis was grim. He gave her less than two weeks.

Today, as he had for the past ten days, Major Perry Traber stopped by to check on his patient. He was a short, bespectacled man, with metal-framed glasses perched on the bridge of his nose. His compassion toward the Indians was widely known, and yet he bitterly resented those who clung to the ancient ways. While there was no cure for consumption of the lungs, he felt Little Raven should have sent for him earlier. He was now able to do scarcely more than relieve her agony. He kept her dosed with laudanum, an opiate sedative.

Lon and Hank waited outside the lodge. The elder, Lon, was twenty-one and bore an uncanny resemblance to his father. He was a strapping six-footer, full-spanned through the shoulders, his hair bleached copper by the sun. His eyes were striking, yet cold, a peculiar shade of blue. There was a quiet confidence about him, and his manner was deceptive. Other men crossed him at their own peril.

By contrast, Hank had inherited his mother's broad features and dark hair. Yet like his half-brother, his eyes were blue, and his light-bronze skin immediately pegged him as a half-breed. He was almost fifteen, tall for his age, with the lithe, muscular build of his father. A prankster of sorts, he smiled easily and viewed life with sportive good humor. He was a steady, carefree youngster, slow to anger.

Neither of them was talkative today. They stood locked in glum silence, their features wooden. Overnight their mother had taken a turn for the worse, lapsing into periods of delirium. The end was near, and though it was unspoken, they both wished her suffering would quickly cease. Waiting now for the doctor, they stared morosely toward the spires of the distant mountains. There was nothing either of them could say that would console the other.

Major Traber emerged from the lodge. He gave them a hopeless shrug and a dark empty look. "She's holding on," he said dolefully. "God knows what's keeping her alive. I certainly don't."

"She's not ready," Hank said half-aloud. "Not yet."

Traber squinted at him. "What do you mean—not ready?"

"I told her our uncle was on the way. She's waiting until he gets here."

"Hardly likely." Traber's headshake was slow and emphatic. "In her condition, the next breath might be the last. Willpower alone wouldn't keep her alive."

"So you say," Lon muttered roughly. "Why else would she hang on?"

Traber avoided a direct reply. He knew Lon to be a hardcase and a troublemaker, and he saw no reason to provoke an argument. He nodded tersely. "Let me know if there's any change. Otherwise, I'll come by again tomorrow."

When Traber drove off in his buckboard, Hank went back inside the lodge. Lon walked down to the creek and seated himself at the base of a tree. A short-barreled Colt, carried in a crossdraw holster, protruded from beneath his coat. He adjusted the pistol to a more comfortable position, then lit a slim black cheroot. He exhaled smoke, staring vacantly out across the stream. Unbidden, his mind drifted backward in time.

A good part of his life had been spent on the reservation. Though white by birth, he had chosen to live among his adopted people, the Comanche. He had taken their ways and become a disciple of their last great war chief, Quanah Parker. He'd practiced the peyote religion and acquired a reputation as a rebellious hell-raiser. For a time, seeking independence, he had retreated to the fastness of the Wichita Mountains. On his own, answerable to no one, he had lived the simple life of a woodsman and hunter.

In the summer of 1881, all that had changed. With Quanah Parker, he'd traveled to Doan's Crossing, a waystation for trail herds on the Red River. There, after goading a surly Texan into drawing, he had killed his first man. The following summer, the cowhand's four brothers had come looking for him. Alerted by Comanche friends, Lon had ambushed the brothers on the trail to his wilderness cabin. When the shooting ended, two brothers lay dead and the other two retreated to Texas. At seventeen, Lon had already gunned down three men.

The Fort Sill commander ordered him off the reservation. Stubborn proud, he'd refused to join his lawman uncle in

Fort Smith. Instead, he had turned to his father's original
trade, that of a professional gambler. Enduring the lean
times, he had slowly learned the craft, developing into a
skilled poker player. For the last four years he'd worked the
gambling circuit throughout Texas, following a wide swing
that took him as far south as the Rio Grande. Wiser now, and
warier, he kept a sharp lookout wherever he traveled. Word
was out that he was still being hunted by the last two Jarrott
brothers.

Every six months or so Lon returned to the reservation.
These days he was generally in the chips, for he had acquired the knack of reading men across a poker table. He always brought presents for his mother and Hank, and the
visits were something of a homecoming. Even now, he continued to think of himself as a Comanche rather than a *tahboy-boh*. On this trip, however, the presents had gone
unopened. He'd arrived to find his mother frail and wasted,
near death. Another week and he would have been too late.

Lon was seldom given to emotion. As a boy, he had been
inducted into the Comanche ways, where stoicism to pain
was expected of men. Later, approaching manhood, he'd
killed the three Texicans with no lingering aftereffects. Four
years on the gambling circuit, where death was every man's
companion, had further hardened him. In large degree, the
life he'd led had brutalized him, turned him dispassionate
and cold. Other men read that in his flat stare and his cool
display of nerve. He would not hesitate to kill when provoked. Nor would he lose any sleep after the fact.

Yet now, staring across the creek, he felt his eyes mist. A
lump formed in his throat and his vision blurred as he
blinked back the tears. The woman who had been like his
mother lay dying, one quick step from the grave. She was
the only thing he revered in all the world, and her passing
seemed to him beyond comprehension. He felt helpless,
somehow broken by the prospect of having her taken from
his life. Death suddenly seemed all too personal, a thing of
dread and unleashed emotions. He grieved for her, and with

her, the loss of something inside himself. When she died, the best part of his life would go with her.

The sound of hoofbeats broke his spell. He turned and saw a horseman rein to a halt before the lodge. He blinked again, clearing his vision, and abruptly recognized the rider. Tossing his cheroot into the stream, he climbed to his feet and walked forward. His features were once more a mask, revealing nothing.

Clint stepped down from the saddle. His eyes were blood-shot and his jawline was covered with stubble. He hadn't slept in nearly three days and he felt tired to the bone. His horse was spent and he took a moment to loosen the cinch. As he straightened up, he heard a footstep to his rear. He looked around.

"Hullo," Lon said, stopping a pace away. "Where'd you come from?"

"The Outlet," Clint said without elaboration. "How's your mother?"

"Tomorrow would've been too late. She won't last out the night."

Clint's features went stony. He looked down, studying the ground for a long moment. When he glanced up, his mouth was set in a tight line. "What's wrong with her?"

"Consumption," Lon told him. "The doc says her lungs are plumb shot. She can't hardly draw a decent breath."

"No way to pull her through?"

"No," Lon said, averting his eyes. "No way."

The flap on the doorhole swung open. Hank stepped outside and stopped, momentarily taken aback. Then he crossed to where they stood, gamely trying for a smile, and nodded to Clint. He extended his hand.

Handshaking was a solemn affair among the Plains tribes. Though a white custom, the Indians had adopted it as a universal sign of peaceful intent. The Comanche, once the most feared warriors on the Southern Plains, placed great importance on gestures of friendship. Between blood relatives, the ritual assumed even more significance.

Clint clasped the boy's hand in both his own. He saw pain and sadness in the youngster's eyes, a deep inner sorrow. "Lon told me everything," he said. "Your mother was always a brave woman and she would want you to be brave. Knowing her, she has no fear of the shadow land."

"She goes gladly," Hank said in a hushed voice. "She believes she will join my father in the *tahboy-boh*'s heaven."

A mental image flashed before Clint's eyes. He saw his long-dead brother, grinning and proud, as though frozen in a moment of time. He cleared his throat. "We must be happy for her, then. She and your father were always of one spirit."

Lon put his hand on the boy's shoulder. There was a prolonged silence while the three of them stood searching for words. At last, as though by unspoken agreement, they walked toward the lodge. The youngsters moved aside at the doorhole, and Hank pulled back the flap. Clint ducked through the opening.

Little Raven lay motionless on her bedrobes. A trade blanket covered her, folded neatly beneath her chin. Her hair, cropped short according to Comanche custom, was streaked with gray. Her features were ravaged, taut and emaciated, blanched by a deadly pallor. She labored for breath, the sound ragged and harsh.

Clint knelt down beside her. Their relationship was warm and close, and he was genuinely fond of her. He thought of her as a good woman and a good mother, and he'd always admired her sense of family. Her life had been devoted to the boys, and he knew her to be a woman of fierce loyalty. He gently brushed a stray lock of hair off her forehead.

The touch of his hand was like a curative. Little Raven shuddered and her eyes slowly rolled open. She struggled back through the threshold of consciousness, fighting the hold of the laudanum. The haze lifted and her eyes focused on him. A faint smile softened her features.

"I've waited for you," she whispered. "I knew you would not fail me."

"No, little sister," Clint said, his voice clogged. "I would never fail you."

"Then you must do something for me . . . a vow."

"Whatever you ask," Clint said. "You have my oath on it."

Her hand appeared from beneath the blanket. She took hold of his arm and squeezed it with all her strength. "I give you my sons. They are in your lodge now . . . your blood . . ."

"Our blood," Clint said hollowly. "From the time you cross over, they will be as my own."

Little Raven nodded, her features serene and without pain. Her gaze went past him, settling on Lon and Hank. She stared at them, still smiling, as though burning their faces into memory for all time. Then, like a falling leaf, her hand dropped from Clint's arm.

A long sigh claimed her last breath. The light went out in her eyes and she slumped back on her bedrobes. Her features relaxed in a restful, faraway look, a look of final peace. Her mouth was still etched with a faint smile.

She crossed over to the shadow land.

A drenching, windswept downpour had fallen throughout the night. By morning, the wind dropped off and the rain squall drifted southward. The sky remained metallic and cold, suffused with dark clouds.

The cemetery was located on a grassy knoll beyond the agency buildings. A picket fence enclosed the burial ground, and wooden crosses stood stark and solitary under the overcast skies. It was the final resting place for Comanches who had followed the Jesus Road. Converts to the Christian faith were interred there with appropriate ceremony.

Late that afternoon family and mourners gathered for the services. The coffin bearing Little Raven rested on boards laid across the open grave. Clint, with Lon and Hank at his side, stood before the coffin. Quanah Parker, surrounded by his wives and children, was immediately behind them. Of the other mourners, almost a hundred in number, at least half of them still practiced the old tribal religion. They congregated nonetheless out of respect for a woman who had befriended them all.

The rites of burial were performed by a Methodist minister. He was a shambling, unkempt man attired in a black broadcloth coat and rumpled trousers. His mission was to convert the heathens into God-fearing Christians and every Sunday he preached hellfire and brimstone. Today he delivered a stirring eulogy to Little Raven Brannock, praising her as a mother and a woman of Christian charity. That she had been summoned in the flower of life he could only attribute to the will of the Lord God Jehovah. The mourners bowed their heads as he concluded with the Twenty-third Psalm.

After the services, Quanah Parker approached Clint. There was mutual respect between them, even though neither considered the other a friend. Clint had served as a civilian scout for the Fourth Cavalry Regiment, the unit that had driven the Comanche onto the reservation. Quanah held no grudges about the past, but his memory was sharp for those long-ago battles. He still thought of Clint as a scout.

"*Hao*," he said, shaking hands with a hard up-and-down pump. "Death brings us together again. But then, we are not strangers to such things, are we, scout?"

"No," Clint agreed. "We've both seen our share."

Quanah nodded owlishly. "What will become of Bull Calf? Will you leave him with his people?"

"I am his people," Clint said. "We are of the same blood."

"Think on it," Quanah replied formally. "Among the *tahboy-boh*, blood does not count. He will be a half-breed, still a Comanche."

Quanah was a half-breed himself. His mother, a white girl named Cynthia Ann Parker, had been taken captive during a Comanche raid on Texas. Shortly after being forced onto the reservation, he had assumed the family name as his own. He told his people it was a gesture of his willingness to follow the white man's road. Still, as all would attest, it made him no less a Comanche.

Before Clint could reply, the minister stopped to offer his condolences. Quanah's seven wives, not to mention a rowdy pack of children, were the preacher's great embarrassment in life. All the more so since the Comanche chief had been baptized into the Christian faith. The three of them chatted for a few minutes, then Quanah and the minister wandered off.

Clint turned back to join the boys. They were standing by themselves, just outside the gate to the graveyard. As he approached, they exchanged a glance and suddenly fell silent. Their look was oddly conspiratorial, and he caught an undercurrent of tension. Some visceral instinct warned him that trouble was afoot. His gaze fixed on Lon.

"What's the problem?"

"We've talked it out," Lon said with a half-smile. "Hank figures Fort Smith doesn't suit his style. He'd prefer to ride with me."

"With you?" Clint looked surprised, then suddenly irritated. "Hell, you follow the gambler's circuit. That's no life for a boy."

"It beats Fort Smith," Lon countered. "You're always off in the Nations somewhere. That'd leave him to fend for himself."

"Not by a damnsight," Clint said gruffly. "I room in a boardinghouse and the landlady's like an old mother hen. She'll see to it he goes to school and does his lessons."

"Yeah, I'll bet," Lon scoffed. "And he'll wind up the town 'breed. What sort of life is that?"

"The subject's closed," Clint said with strained patience. "Hank goes with me and that's final."

"Maybe you ought to ask him what he thinks."

Clint turned to the boy. "What do you say, son? Wouldn't you like to give Fort Smith a try?"

Hank fidgeted uncomfortably. "Tell you the truth, I'd sooner stay here. Either I go with Lon or I don't go nowhere."

Clint's tone was severe. "Lon runs with a rough crowd. You're a little young for that, aren't you?"

"I'm near fifteen," Hank said stoutly. "I can take care of myself just fine. Besides, brothers ought to stick together."

Before Clint could reply, he was distracted by an approaching horseman. A trooper from the garrison reined to a halt and saluted smartly. "Got a wire for you, marshal," he

said, extending an envelope. "The colonel told me to find
you lickety-split."

"Tell him I'm obliged."

The trooper touched his cap and rode off. Clint tore open
the envelope and scanned the telegraph message. The date-
line was Fort Smith and it was signed by John Carroll, the
U.S. marshal. His face registered blank astonishment.

GOVERNOR OF NEW MEXICO REQUESTS YOUR
IMMEDIATE TRANSFER. YOU ARE FORTHWITH
ASSIGNED TO U.S. MARSHAL'S OFFICE, SANTA FE.
TRANSFER APPROVED BY PRESIDENT GROVER
CLEVELAND. REPORT SANTA FE SOONEST.

Clint wagged his head back and forth. He looked up with
a wry smile. "How'd you boys like to see New Mexico?"

Lon eyed him with narrow suspicion. "What are you
talkin' about?"

"I've just been reassigned," Clint said. "I'm ordered to report to Santa Fe pronto."

"So?"

"So there's lots of mining camps in New Mexico. And I
hear it's hog-heaven for gamblers. Feel like a change of
luck?"

Lon examined the notion. "What about Hank?"

"We'll all go together," Clint said, spreading his hands.
"Until I get settled, Hank can stick with you. How's that
sound?"

A moment elapsed while they stared at one another. At
length, Lon glanced at the boy. "What d'you say, sport? Got
a yen to see New Mexico?"

Hank shrugged. "I'm game if you are."

"Hell, why not?" Lon said. "I've worn out my welcome in
Texas anyway."

"It's settled then," Clint said, nodding at them. "We'll
leave tomorrow."

On the way back to the lodge, the boys were curiously
silent. Clint looked like a cat spitting feathers, and tried to

hide it. By a stroke of luck, he'd been granted what seemed a timely reprieve. For New Mexico represented a whole new game where Hank was concerned.

One way or another he meant to see the youngster wind up where he belonged. On the Rio Hondo, with the Brannocks. The sound of it gave his spirits a sudden boost.

He'd been away too long himself.

SEVEN

The train chuffed to a halt before the Santa Fe depot. Hooked onto a long string of boxcars was a lone passenger coach. The conductor opened the door and stepped outside.

Elizabeth emerged from the coach, followed by John Taylor. He walked ahead, her leather carryall in one hand and his warbag in the other. At the end of the stationhouse, he signaled one of the horse-drawn cabs waiting on the street. The driver hopped down to assist with the luggage.

All the other passengers were men. They rushed past Elizabeth, hurrying toward the line of cabs. By the time she crossed the platform, Taylor was waiting beside the open door. He assisted her inside and ordered the driver to take them to the Exchange Hotel. They settled back for the short ride uptown.

Santa Fe lay in the shadow of the Sangre de Cristos. At an altitude of seven thousand feet, the town was surrounded by mountain ranges. Across the river from the train station was a broad plaza dominated by the governor's palace. The architecture was mostly adobe and the plaza was crowded with shops and businesses.

The date was April Fool's Day. Approaching the plaza, Elizabeth thought there would be few practical jokes exchanged today. An urgent wire from Ira Hecht had summoned her to Santa Fe. Though somewhat cryptic in nature, the message hinted at a political emergency. Hecht was the coordinator and chief strategist of her reform coalition.

Elizabeth's association with Hecht went back to 1881. As a stepping-stone into politics, she had organized a legal-assistance service for poor *mexicanos*. Her purpose was to combat widespread land frauds by Anglo speculators. Hecht, an idealistic young attorney, had been selected as head of the operation. Working together, they had assembled a network of lawyers throughout the territory. Their efforts in the courts had brought about judgments favoring small landowners.

Opposition to reform was centered around the Santa Fe Ring, an unsavory alliance. The Ring members were principally influential Republicans who controlled the economic lifeblood of the territory. At the time, the mastermind behind the Ring was a man named Stephen Benton. He commonly resorted to violence and assassination as a means of enforcing his will. Finally he'd gone too far by ordering the murder of Virgil Brannock. A week later, Clint had killed him in a shootout on the plaza.

With Benton's death, the Santa Fe Ring had fallen into temporary disarray. Elizabeth and Hecht, working swiftly, had created a coalition of *mexicanos* and progressive Anglos. Since then, they had managed to elect roughly half the members of the territorial legislature. But the Ring still controlled the other half, and a new leader had emerged in the person of Thomas Canby. Wiser than his predecessor, Canby refrained from violence and relied instead on racial animosity. He masterfully pitted the Anglos against the native New Mexicans.

Unlike other border regions, New Mexico was never a melting pot of cultures. An influx of Anglos into Texas and Arizona had swamped the *mexicano* population. But the descendants of the colonial Spaniards still constituted a majority in New Mexico Territory. Stubbornly resistant to change, they held to their language and their traditional way of life. In effect, they refused to adapt, even in their attitude toward politics. They clung to the customs of another time, their Old World values.

The problem was a constant source of friction within Elizabeth's coalition. At the top of the social order were the *ricos,* men with large holdings in livestock and land. By tradition, they provided the leadership at the local level, and their wealth enabled them to exert a great deal of influence. For the most part, the native political bosses—the *jefes políticos*—were the tools of the *ricos.*

The *mexicanos,* by and large, tended to support the system. Their principal concern was sufficient land to farm and adequate pasture for their stock. Tradition dictated that the common man had no interest in politics beyond the local level. By custom, the larger affairs of government were left to men of position and wealth, the *ricos.* So it was that a small group of men determined the results of any election. County offices, as well as seats in the territorial legislature, were controlled by an old and established order.

Elizabeth's goal was to forge a coalition of Anglos and *mexicanos* that would work to everyone's benefit. Yet the *ricos* were jealous of their power and evidenced little interest in social change. The *jefes políticos,* who were ambitious and interested in feathering their own nests, were often more susceptible to the idea of a coalition. Still another group, known as the young *políticos,* was opposed to both the *ricos* and the old-line *jefes.* A new order of *mexicano* politicians, they were pragmatic and not bound by ancient customs. Any alliance, even with an Anglo, was worthy of consideration.

All the factional bickering weakened the coalition. Elizabeth urged unity for the common good, and spent half her time refereeing disputes. A running climate of intrigue kept the *ricos,* the *jefes,* and the young *políticos* jockeying for position. Added to all that was the attitude of many progressive Anglos who supported her efforts. They saw the *mexicanos* as politically naive, unable to grasp the larger concept of solidarity. The coalition, in no small measure, survived in spite of itself.

On the ride uptown, Elizabeth wondered what new emergency awaited her. After checking into the hotel, she took a few minutes to freshen up and change her dress. Then she met Taylor in the lobby and they walked to the corner, skirting the plaza on the north side. West of the business area, they proceeded along a sidestreet and turned into a storefront office. The interior was sparsely furnished with a rolltop desk, several wooden armchairs, and a row of file cabinets. A faded picture of Abraham Lincoln hung over the desk.

Hecht greeted them with obvious relief. He was small and slightly built, his eyes magnified by thick-lensed glasses. His mild, unobtrusive appearance belied both his zealousness and a brilliant legal mind. He fought oppression as though ordained for the task.

"Glad you're here," he said, motioning them to chairs. "Sorry if my wire sounded a bit vague. I couldn't afford to put the information over the telegraph."

"What information?" Elizabeth asked. "I hope it's nothing to do with the coalition."

"Yes and no," Hecht said, his eyes grave. "You'll recall I've developed various sources of intelligence. One of them is a *mexicano* servant in the governor's palace."

"And?"

"There's a strong rumor circulating among the governor's staff. So far, it hasn't gone past that stage. It's all very hush-hush."

Elizabeth looked at him seriously. "What sort of rumor?"

"From what I gather," Hecht said hastily, "Governor Ross has gone off the deep end. He intends to declare war on *Las Gorras Blancas*."

"That's insane," Elizabeth said, clearly alarmed. "Any official move against the White Caps would merely enhance their cause. He'll make martyrs of them."

"It gets worse," Hecht said, his voice low and troubled. "I understand the governor plans to issue a dead-or-alive warrant on Miguel Ortega."

"Oh, my God!"

Elizabeth appeared stunned. Miguel Ortega was the leader of a secret organization known as *Las Gorras Blancas,* or White Caps. The name stemmed from the fact that they wore masks to conceal their identity. Ortega and his night riders, all *mexicanos,* employed organized violence as a means of intimidation. Their avowed enemies were large Anglo landholders.

The animosity was an outgrowth of disputes over the land. Anglo cattlemen were drawn to New Mexico by the lure of old Spanish land grants. The grants were mired in a tangled body of law and imprecise boundaries, which provided loopholes for the stockgrowers. Their purpose was to acquire title to grazeland by right of possession. The instrument of their landgrabbing scheme was barbed wire.

The *mexicanos* were bitterly opposed. Under Spanish rule, and later under the Mexican government, land grants were awarded to groups of settlers. By tradition, as well as official decree, ownership of the land was communal. House plots and patches of farmland were considered the personal property of individuals. But pasturelands and watering holes, the bulk of any grant, were shared by all. Grant boundaries were vague and unimportant, for use of the land was determined by ancient custom.

Nothing in the *mexicanos'* culture prepared them for the concept of "owning" water. Nor were they able to accept the idea of communal pastureland being deeded to a single individual. Anglo cattlemen, on the other hand, were insistent on private ownership. Their method was to acquire title to land along streams and rivers, filing claim under the Homestead Act. By agreement among themselves, cattlemen declared that a rancher's range covered all grazeland served by his water rights. *Mexicano* farmers were effectively displaced from their ancient Spanish grants.

Still another dodge was employed by large cattlemen. They obtained ownership to land within a grant by purchasing title from the original holder. Afterward, they argued that title to house lots and cultivated fields also included an interest in the communal lands. The *mexicanos* contended that common lands could never pass into absolute ownership. Without the consent of all grant holders, they asserted, the land could not be divided into parcels.

The stockgrowers' response was barbed wire. After

purchasing a tract, they would often string fences across vast sections of the communal land. Along streams and rivers, where homesteads had been filed, they would fence in all land bordering the waterways. Further, without the shadow of a title, the cattlemen proceeded to erect fences on great stretches of public domain. Their attitude was that possession represented nine points of the law. Barbed wire made it a reality.

To Elizabeth, it was like a recurrent nightmare. During the early 1880s, she had battled land fraud throughout the territory. With Ira Hecht, and the lawyers of the legal-assistance service, she had won the fight in the courts. Land speculators, who relied on phony surveys and political bribes, were effectively routed. Legal precedents were established which protected *mexicanos'* rights under the old Spanish grants. Wholesale land fraud became a thing of the past.

Then, not quite two years ago, barbed wire found its way to New Mexico. Promptly dubbed "the devil's hatband," its prickly spikes enabled a rancher to contain vast herds of cattle. No less significant, it made anyone who crossed the fenceline a trespasser on private property. Streams and rivers were fenced off, and *mexicano* shepherds were denied access to traditional grazelands. Barbed wire, in large degree, replaced the shady land speculators of years past. The Spanish grants were once again under siege.

As before, Elizabeth championed the cause of the common man. Her reform movement was composed of small ranchers and hardscrabble Anglo farmers as well as *mexicanos*. Yet these were poor people, and apart from the sums she contributed, the coalition was always strapped for funds. Her opposition, headed by Thomas Canby, suffered under no such limitations. The Santa Fe Ring, and its political apparatus, was generously funded by large cattlemen. Their donations ensured the ranchers a strong voice in the legislature.

The embittered *mexicanos* saw their way of life being destroyed. For them, a return to the traditional use of common land represented survival itself. By custom, however, they had never sought redress of wrongs through legislative assemblies or the vote. Nor were they willing to trust *gringo* courts for an equitable settlement of their grievances. Their choice was sullen acceptance or direct action, and they were a people who placed great honor on a man's defense of his rights. Barbed wire finally pushed them over the edge.

Miguel Ortega was a phantom. Little was known about him before he formed the original cadre of *Las Gorras Blancas*. But the movement spread rapidly, gaining strength and members, operating under a tight code of silence. Their targets were the landgrabbers, the complex of bankers, ranchers, and railroads, those who profited at the expense of the people. They stampeded cattle herds, ripped out railroad tracks, and burned Anglo businesses to the ground. The unifying symbol of their hatred was barbed wire.

Within the past year the White Caps had destroyed untold miles of fenceline. Tangled bales of wire were heaped atop a pile of fenceposts and turned into a bonfire. Anglo ranchers found threatening notes tacked to their doors, ordering them off the land. In several instances, when cattlemen fought back, their barns and outbuildings had been razed. Earlier in the year, the home of the Surveyor General had been torched within sight of the territorial capitol. No one had yet been killed, but the level of violence steadily increased.

"There's more bad news," Hecht said now. "Thomas Canby and his cronies have submitted a petition to Congress. They want a special court established to settle the land disputes."

Elizabeth regarded him thoughtfully. "I assume their own judges would be appointed to the court. And rule against the *mexicanos*."

"Exactly," Hecht said, then shrugged. "It's larceny on a grand scale. Millions upon millions of acres."

"What position has the governor taken?"

"Complete cooperation," Hecht replied. "He added his official endorsement to the request."

"Well—" Elizabeth said after a long pause. "It appears the governor no longer represents the people. He's joined forces with Canby and the Santa Fe Ring."

Hecht nodded solemnly. "That's how I assess it."

"I daresay two can play at the game. Contact our friends in Washington and let them know we oppose the plan. Ask them to lobby against its passage."

"I can try," Hecht said with no inward conviction. "Frankly, I think it's a waste of time and energy. Canby has the resources to bribe every politician in Washington."

"In that event," Elizabeth remarked, "perhaps I should have a talk with the governor. If nothing else, I might persuade him to change his mind about Miguel Ortega."

Hecht shook his head wonderingly. "I could sell tickets to that little dust-up. He hates outside interference worse than the devil hates holy water."

"Then he shouldn't have sold his soul to the Santa Fe Ring."

The meeting ended on that note. Taylor, who hadn't said a word throughout the conversation, exchanged a knowing smile with Hecht. Neither of them doubted that Elizabeth would beard the governor in his own den. Around Santa Fe, she was spoken of as "a woman with starch in her corset." She never took no for an answer.

The governor's palace occupied the entire west side of the plaza. A vast sprawl of adobe, it had been built in 1609 by the first Spanish viceroy. At various times it had flown the flags of Spain, Mexico, and the Confederacy. Following the Mexican War, it became the official capitol of New Mexico Territory. The governor's offices and living quarters occupied the central portion of the building.

Outside the main entrance, Elizabeth stumbled onto Thomas Canby. He was emerging as she and Taylor approached, and he quickly tipped his hat. A man of intellect and charm, he was of medium stature with agatelike eyes and tufts of snowy hair. He exuded the bearing and presence that comes with power.

"Mrs. Brannock," he said, scrupulously polite. "I heard you were in town."

Elizabeth forced a smile. "I must say you're well-informed, Mr. Canby. I've only just arrived."

"And here you are," Canby said genially. "I hope you have an appointment with the governor. He's somewhat pressed for time today."

"I presume you would know better than most. I understand you have his ear these days."

"Shifting tides," Canby said with a dry, scornful chuckle. "The ebb and flow of politics, Mrs. Brannock."

"No doubt," Elizabeth replied with perfect civility. "Although I would have thought 'strange bedfellows' the more appropriate axiom."

Canby laughed and again tipped his hat. Elizabeth moved past him into a central hallway, trailed closely by Taylor. She entered an anteroom and announced herself to the governor's appointments secretary. The man asked her to wait, then slipped through the door of an inner office. Taylor took a seat on a wide leather sofa.

A few moments later Elizabeth was ushered through the door. Governor Edmund Ross greeted her with feigned good humor. He was a huge man, with muttonchop sideburns and sweeping mustaches. As a political appointee, he owed allegiance to no one except the president. Still, he'd learned to respect Elizabeth's pragmatic approach to a man's game. He motioned her to a chair.

"Good of you to drop by," he said expansively. "Compared to my usual visitors, you're like a breath of fresh air."

"I know," Elizabeth said, smiling sweetly. "I just ran into Tom Canby on his way out."

Ross chose to ignore the gibe. "Well, now," he said pleasantly, "what brings you to see me, Mrs. Brannock? Nothing serious, I trust."

"I believe 'crisis' would be the better word."

"What seems to be the problem?"

Elizabeth looked at him without expression. "I understand you've endorsed Canby's scheme. The petition requesting a land-claims court."

Ross nodded sagely. "It's hardly a scheme, Mrs. Brannock. Such a court will resolve one of the most critical issues of our time."

"On the contrary," Elizabeth corrected him. "Canby and his crowd will handpick the judges. Every decision rendered will favor Anglo business interests and large ranchers."

"Aren't you being a tad too cynical?"

"Aren't you supposed to be the governor of *all* the people? You've endorsed a scheme that will deliberately discriminate against *mexicano* landowners."

"Don't presume to lecture me," Ross said with a flare of annoyance. "Until you have a better idea, I suggest you reserve judgment."

"By tomorrow, a bill will be introduced on the floor of the legislature. And it will be far more equitable for everyone concerned."

Elizabeth went on to explain. She proposed an act that would allow landholders within a grant to file for incorporation. An elected board of trustees would then determine the legitimate landowners and the extent of their holdings. All communal lands would be administered by the trustees.

"In effect," she concluded, "it would allow the people to resolve their own differences—with no outsiders involved."

Ross angled his head critically. "What it would do is guarantee a *mexicano* board of trustees. And those trustees would in turn rule against the cattlemen. I could never sign such a bill."

Elizabeth returned his gaze steadily. "Your veto would have grave political consequences, Governor. It would publicly brand you a tool of the Santa Fe Ring."

"Pure tripe," Ross said, his voice tight. "I do my duty as I see it, Mrs. Brannock. I'm certainly not accountable to you."

"Just between us . . ." Elizabeth paused, looked him directly in the eyes. "If you were an elected official—accountable to all the people—that *would* change your mind. Don't you agree?"

"No, I do not," Ross said curtly. "Now, unless you have something further to discuss . . ."

"One more thing," Elizabeth informed him. "I hear you're planning some sort of action against *Las Gorras Blancas*. Is that true?"

Ross's tone turned cold. "I will not allow a gang of thugs to terrorize the countryside. I intend to stop them."

"Governor, I've never for a moment condoned their methods. However, they have widespread support within the *mexicano* community. Any aggressive act on your part might very well incite more violence."

"I accept the risk," Ross retorted. "New Mexico will not be held hostage to a ragtag band of revolutionaries."

Elizabeth forced herself to stay calm. "I also heard you plan to issue a warrant for Miguel Ortega—dead or alive."

Ross strummed the tip of his nose. "You'll be interested to know I've arranged the transfer of your brother-in-law. He's en route to Santa Fe at this very moment."

"Clint?" Elizabeth looked at him, astounded. "You're assigning Clint to catch Ortega?"

"I can think of no one better qualified for the job. He's the most respected manhunter of our day. I suspect he'll make short work of Señor Ortega."

"Then it's true," Elizabeth said, openly concerned. "You want Ortega dead."

"I want law restored," Ross said with chilling simplicity. "Whatever measures I take are meant for the common good."

"Don't be absurd! You and Tom Canby have already rendered a verdict. And you've selected Clint as your executioner."

"Your words, Mrs. Brannock, not mine."

Elizabeth stormed out of the office. Taylor jumped to his feet and fell in beside her as she swept through the hallway. On the street, she abruptly stopped, staring blankly across the plaza. She seemed overwhelmed by the irony of the situation.

For years she'd wanted nothing more than to have Clint home again. And now, for all the wrong reasons, he was returning to New Mexico. She thought God had a warped sense of humor.

EIGHT

A midday sun stood fixed in the sky. Lincoln's three saloons were serving the noontime crowd and several loafers were congregated on the courthouse porch. Horses lined the hitch racks along the street.

Morg dismounted outside the clinic. He was riding a blood-red bay with a blaze face and four white stockings. He left the gelding at the hitch post and turned toward the walkway. He was whistling softly to himself.

Scarcely ten days past, Morg had returned from the Cherokee Outlet. His head was buzzing with ideas, some good and some not so good. Foremost among them was the conviction that the Outlet ranch was operating on borrowed time. He remained convinced that all of Indian Territory would be opened to settlement. Pressure from homesteaders would merely speed the federal government's agenda.

Upon arriving at Spur, Morg hadn't paused to catch his breath. Louise had greeted him with teary-eyed happiness, demanding attention. But his thoughts were elsewhere, and he'd put her off with the press of other matters. Shortly after walking into the house, he had drawn his mother into her office and closed the door. Their discussion lasted until long past midnight.

The gist of Morg's argument centered on the Outlet. Like a swami, he'd peered into a crystal ball and seen the future. Sooner or later, it was inevitable that they would lose the ranch on Cherokee lands. The subsequent loss in revenue would represent a severe blow to their overall operation. He was convinced that they should diversify now, expanding into areas unrelated to cattle. He suggested a move into the timber business.

Elizabeth was taken aback. She'd never before considered a venture outside ranching. Yet Morg's assessment of the Outlet was grounded in solid logic, a blunt truth. Then too, he was his father's son and possessed that rare gift of foresight. While she knew nothing of the timber business, she saw the wisdom of spreading their interests into other fields. She asked for details.

The idea was no overnight bombshell. Morg was a keen observer of people and events. When it suited his purpose, he was also a good listener. Nor was his vision limited to the Hondo Valley and Spur. There was a questing quality about him, and it fed what amounted to an innate curiosity. The whys and wherefores were more interesting to him than the happening itself. He always looked for the reason.

Developments of the last few years intrigued him. One lay to the west of Lincoln, in the high-country mining camps. There, principally in the towns of Nogal and White Oaks, new discoveries had brought about a resurgence of boom times. Old mines were being reopened and new shafts were being sunk to previously unimagined depths. Quartz mining, conducted far underground, required substantial tunnels. And every tunnel required loads of stout timbers.

To the east lay the Pecos Valley. Formerly the domain of John "Jinglebob" Chisum, it was now populated by swarms of homesteaders and small farmers. Until the early 1880s, the land was thought to be unsuitable for anything except grazing cattle. But the area was riddled with artesian springs as well as tributaries branching off the Pecos River. Some men thought it might be transformed into bountiful farmland, with long growing seasons. The climate was temperate and the soil was rich with minerals.

On a ranch northeast of Roswell, Pat Garrett installed the first irrigation project. The former sheriff of Lincoln County, Garrett was better known as the man who had shot Billy the

Kid. But his irrigation ditches, drawing on the Berrendo River, brought him newfound celebrity. Other farmers began irrigating from exposed artesian springs and there was talk of drilling wells to tap the underground reservoirs. By 1886, the Pecos Valley was dotted with farms, and land values had soared. Irrigation was proceeding at a feverish pace.

Field crops of wheat, corn, and oats thrived in the moderate climate. Alfalfa grew like wildweed and provided six cuttings over the season. Apple trees held the promise of vast orchards, and some farmers were experimenting with cotton. The town of Roswell expanded by leaps and bounds, with new businesses opening their doors every day. A building boom had been under way for the past year, and the population had swelled beyond all expectations. The Pecos Valley was reveling in a time of prosperity.

The growth of Roswell, added to the resurgence of the mining camps, produced a steady demand for lumber. The source of that timber lay in the Capitan Mountains, roughly north and west of Lincoln. At the lower elevations, below six thousand feet, the most common trees were cedar, piñon, and juniper. Far above, on the windswept slopes, were firs and aspen and spruces. In between, there was a vast forest of ponderosa pine, the prime source of commercial lumber. These stately giants were there for the taking.

Oddly enough, the demand for lumber far outstripped the supply. And that inconsistency, uncovered by Morg in his travels, had caused him to investigate further. He found several sawmills scattered throughout the mountains; but there was only one timber operator of any size. His name was Ralph McQuade and he carried less than twenty lumberjacks on his payroll. In effect, McQuade had a captive market and no competition. The door was wide open.

Morg proposed the organization of a timber company. He explained how it could be financed, using only a portion of the profits from the Outlet ranch. In his opinion, that made more sense than plowing money back into a cattle spread they would eventually lose. Lumberjacks could be found, and he estimated the initial investment at something less than $50,000. He believed the operation could turn a profit in six months, certainly no more than a year. From there on, the potential appeared to him virtually unlimited.

Elizabeth agreed. As with the ranch, the timber project would be a family enterprise. She arranged for funds to be shifted into a new bank account designated the Brannock Timber Company. The project was Morg's creation and she wisely gave him a free hand. Her one condition was that he not ignore his duties at Spur, which would remain the foundation of all they might achieve in the future. Other than that, she asked nothing more than to be kept abreast of events.

For the next week, Morg was like a perpetual-motion machine. West of Lincoln, he leased a thousand acres of mountainous timberland. He then journeyed north, touring logging camps in the Sangre de Cristos range. Higher wages, abetted by a case of whiskey, enabled him to pirate a crew of lumberjacks, complete with foreman. On his way home, he stopped off in Albuquerque, ordering various pieces of equipment. All the basic supplies for a camp were ordered at the general store in Lincoln.

By the end of the week, his personal life was a wreck. Louise hardly spoke to him when he returned home, greeting him with cool indifference. She walked around in a snit, as though punishing him with her silence. While the tactic got his attention, his mind was still diverted by the timber project. For the first time in his life, he had complete control of a business enterprise, absolute authority. The prospect proved to be heady stuff, and his energy was boundless.

Today marked an end to the planning phase of the operation. His new foreman, along with five lumberjacks and the camp cook, were due to arrive on the east-bound stage. Tomorrow, the balance of the crew, another half-dozen lumberjacks, was scheduled to arrive. Four wagonloads of equipment and supplies were parked behind the store, and teams of draft horses were stalled in the livery stable. He'd left nothing undone on a checklist that ran to several pages.

The Brannock Timber Company was ready to commence operations.

Entering the clinic, he found Jennifer taking lunch with her assistants. He accepted a cup of coffee, but excitement stilled his appetite. When he refused anything to eat, Jennifer walked him from the kitchen to the privacy of her office. She thought he looked like a man who had discovered the secret of winged flight. His nervous energy was disconcerting to watch, and she wondered when he'd last slept. He kept pacing to the window, darting glances upstreet.

"Calm down," Jennifer admonished. "You know the stage never runs on time. It's always late."

"Helluva note," Morg grumped. "Today of all days."

Jennifer tried to distract him. "How's Louise? Any change in her condition?"

"Not that you'd notice. She's her usual self—snippy and out of sorts."

"That's not uncommon with pregnant women. They feel bloated and unattractive, particularly with their first child. Quite often their personalities undergo a pronounced change."

"Tell me about it," Morg said peevishly. "She acts like I got her in a family way out of spite. Hell, she's the one that wanted a baby!"

Jennifer sniffed. "I suppose you never gave it a thought. Or don't you know how babies are made?"

"C'mon, sis," Morg groaned. "I've got enough worries without that. If you have to lecture somebody, lecture Louise."

"Well, you might try paying more attention to her. I mean, after all, she's only nineteen! She needs reassurance."

"Yeah, and I've been busier than a one-legged man in a kicking contest. I could use a little appreciation myself."

"Fiddlesticks," Jennifer chided him. "You've never needed reassurance in your entire life. I wonder that you haven't gotten chapped lips from kissing cold mirrors."

"Think I'm sold on myself, do you?"

"You're cocky as a barnyard rooster. You always have been."

Morg mugged, hands outstretched. "Guess that's what makes me a prince of a fellow. And you don't have to take my word on it. Everybody says so."

"God, you're impossible," Jennifer said, suppressing a smile. "Not to change the subject, but I had a wire from Mother. She's coming home tomorrow."

"Wonder what happened in Santa Fe. She lit out of here like her skirts were on fire."

"I haven't the vaguest idea. Of course, she thrives on all that political skulduggery. I think she'd really like to be governor."

"No, you're wrong," Morg said, a grin plastered on his face. "She'd rather pull the strings and watch everybody dance. She's got the knack for it, too."

"Perhaps," Jennifer said in a musing tone. "But it's a shame women don't have the vote. She could be elected to any office she wanted."

Full of himself, Morg laughed. "Speaking of women and babies . . . when are you gonna get married?"

"None of your business," Jennifer said airily. "I rarely give it a thought."

"Who're you kidding?" Morg joked. "Even lady doctors get the hankering now and then. You're still human."

Jennifer enjoyed the bantering. She was reminded that Morg was her closest friend as well as her brother. While she was away at medical school, she'd feared all that might change. Yet, upon returning, she found that Morg harbored no resentment about her education. He admired her accomplishment, but he had no desire himself to attend college. He valued instead the lessons won from experience. What he called "the school of hard knocks."

When Jennifer looked at him, she often saw a younger version of her father. A man of limited education, her father had possessed a steel-trap mind and the courage to dare greatly. He was the product of an era when bold men challenged a raw frontier with gritty determination. Before his death, he had achieved the aura of legend, one of the rough-hewn pioneer visionaries. She saw those same characteristics in Morg, coupled with fierce ambition. She thought their father would have been proud.

A tingling sensation swept over her. While she'd never considered it in just that light, she saw it now as a full-blown revelation. Her mother was the most powerful woman in New Mexico, commanding the respect of friends and enemies alike. Her brother was a burgeoning timber baron, smart and resourceful, capable of one day assuming the mantle of Spur. And she herself was the first, not to mention the only woman doctor in the whole of the territory. So her father's legacy had been borne out just as he'd intended. Nobody in the Brannock family rested on his laurels.

"Here they come!"

Morg whooped and turned toward the door. From the window, Jennifer watched as he hurried up the street. She saw a gang of tough-looking men climb out of the stagecoach and gather before the express office. Then Morg burst into their midst, shaking hands and talking a mile a minute. His face was split in a nutcracker grin.

She thought the timber business would never again be the same.

The Capitan Mountains towered against the skyline. Sierra Blanca rose twelve thousand feet in the air, the summit still capped with snow. A westering sun limned the craggy battlements in a coppery glow.

By midafternoon the wagons were approaching timber country. Morg rode out front on his bay gelding, blazing a trail where no roads existed. The campsite he'd selected was on the southern slope of a forested mountain. A stream, cascading over jumbled rocks, swept past a natural clearing. With water for men and animals, it seemed made to order for a logging camp.

Ponderosa pines, like tall sentinels, marched onward beyond sight. The thousand acres leased by Morg were strategically located. Abutted on three sides by public domain, the parcel provided access to a limitless sea of timber. Having done his homework, he was aware that the federal government placed little value on remote wilderness lands. There was no watchdog agency to regulate, or hinder, the timber companies.

Loopholes in the Homestead Act permitted timber outfits to harvest millions of acres originally intended for settlement. In mountainous areas, where the land was unsuited for farming, the logging companies became squatters on public domain. The Timber and Stone Act of 1878 provided a loophole of even greater proportions. Under the law, an individual was allowed to buy 160 acres of land "unfit for cultivation" at a price of $2.50 per acre. Land speculators and timber operators hired front men to file on thousands of quarter-sections, and thereby created sprawling domains of virgin forest. Great Lakes timber barons had used the ploy to reap untold millions in profits.

After careful consideration, Morg had added a new wrinkle. The leased parcel gave him a legitimate base, and from there he would expand the operation onto public domain. At some later time, he planned to recruit "dummy" applicants and file on quarter-sections at a cost of only $400 apiece. But for now, unfettered by government restrictions, he was content to harvest public-domain lands. The timber, in effect, was free for the taking.

Halting in the center of the clearing, he left the gelding ground-reined. Chunk Devlin, his new foreman, hopped down from the lead wagon. A burly man, Devlin was heavily built, with a bull neck and a square, thick-jowled face. He was a veteran of the Wisconsin logging camps, and more recently, the timber boss for an outfit supplying roadbed ties to the railroad. He looked like a cross between a pugilist and a circus strongman.

"What do you think?" Morg asked, gesturing around the clearing. "Good spot to set up camp?"

"I've seen worse," Devlin said in a stilled rumble. "'Course, my boys ain't persnickety. We'll make do."

"How long till we get into operation?"

"Well, as to that, it's first things first. We've gotta build ourselves a bunkhouse and a privy and a corral for the animals. I'd say no more'n a week at the outside."

"Sounds good," Morg said, nodding. "I've got teamsters and wagons ready whenever you are. All we need is timber."

"And timber you'll have!" Devlin said with a wide peg-toothed grin. "All you want and all you can haul."

Some while later Morg rode out of the clearing. At the edge of the treeline, he paused and looked back. Devlin was already barking orders like a Prussian sergeant major. The lumberjacks and the cook jumped every time he yelled.

San Patricio was a small village near the juncture of the Rio Bonito and the Rio Hondo. Deep in the foothills, it was some five miles southeast of Lincoln. The sole industry, supporting fully half the villagers, was lumber.

Tipton's Sawmill was located on the banks of the Rio Hondo. Harry Tipton was lean and weathered, bald as a tonsured monk, with a mouthful of teeth like old yellowed dice. He operated the mill with the benign manner of an indulgent *patrón*. The villagers affectionately called him *ancianito*.

Shortly before sundown Morg dismounted outside the mill. The building was essentially a long open-sided shed, roofed with shingles and ankle-deep in sawdust. Huge circular saws occupied one side and board planers were arrayed along the other. The equipment was operated by *mexicano* workers and powered by a wood-burning steam engine. A cubbyhole office was tacked on to one end of the structure.

At the far end of the building, four men were unloading the last log from a heavy-duty lumber wagon. Morg recognized one of them as his chief competitor, Ralph McQuade. A face appeared at the window of the office; then the door opened and Tipton hurried outside. His face was wreathed in a troubled frown and his manner was curiously edgy. His palm was damp when he shook hands with Morg.

"Hello, Harry," Morg said affably. "Thought I'd stop by and give you the news. I got my men started working on the camp today. Ought to have the first load of timber in a couple of weeks."

"You've come at a bad time," Tipton informed him. "I've just had words with McQuade."

"What's the problem?"

"You," Tipton said simply. "Until now, McQuade's had a lock on the timber business. He's hopping mad."

Morg laughed shortly. "Don't let it worry you, Harry. He'll get used to the idea."

"Maybe, maybe not." Tipton paused, shook his head ruefully. "McQuade's a rough customer. He's liable to cause trouble."

"For you," Morg asked, "or for me?"

"Hard to say one way or the other. I just know I don't trust him."

"Well, let's not jump at shadows. He'll most likely cool down."

"Here he comes!" Tipton hissed. "Watch your step."

Morg turned, thumbs hooked in his belt. He'd heard that McQuade had a reputation as a brawler, and his first impression confirmed the stories. A gnarled, lynx-eyed man, McQuade was beefy through the shoulders and padded with muscle from a lifetime of physical labor. He lumbered to a halt, glowering at Morg.

"You and me need to have a talk."

"All right by me," Morg said lazily. "What's on your mind?"

"You're crowding me," McQuade said, his voice brittle with hostility. "I don't like people horning in on my business."

"Last I heard, it was a free country. Nobody needs permission to cut timber."

"Yeah, you do," McQuade bristled. "Around here, I'm bull-o'-the-woods. I aim to keep it that way."

"Bull-o'-the-woods?" Morg repeated, as though mildly entertained. "What happens when you meet cock-o'-the-walk?"

"You sayin' you're not gonna back off?"

"Sounds that way, don't it?"

"I'm warnin' you," McQuade said churlishly, "don't crowd me no further. You do and you'll wish you hadn't."

Morg laughed in his face. "Whenever you get the urge, wade right in. I enjoy a good scrap, myself."

McQuade's hands hardened into fists. His features mottled with anger and he seemed on the verge of swinging. Morg stared him straight in the eye, challenging him. At last, with an unintelligible oath, the logger wheeled away. Morg let out a slow breath, looked at Tipton.

"Harry, I think you're right. One of these days he's gonna try to haul my ashes."

"Stay away from him," Tipton cautioned. "I've seen him work men over something awful. He fights dirty, no holds barred."

"What the hell," Morg said lightly. "I've been in some knock-down-drag-outs myself. Half the boys on Spur were weaned on tiger spit."

"You just remember what I said. He's loco mean when he comes unwound."

"I'll keep it in mind."

From San Patricio, Morg followed a rutted wagon road along the Rio Hondo. Darkness fell as he crossed onto Spur land and rode toward the headquarters compound. His first day in the timber business had been more eventful than expected. What concerned him most was that McQuade had picked an argument and then backed off. It seemed somehow out of character, and therefore suspicious.

He decided to keep a sharp lookout.

NINE

Three days before Easter, Clint rode into Santa Fe. On the west side of the plaza, he reined to a halt before the governor's palace and dismounted. He left his horse tethered to the hitch rack.

The U.S. marshal's office was at the south end of the plaza. His gaze fixed on the tall granite monument commemorating the Civil War dead. Erected in the center of the plaza, the monument was a local landmark.

Some six years ago Clint had killed two men at the base of the monument. One was Stephen Benton, the man responsible for his brother's murder. The other was Benton's bodyguard, a hired gun and sometime assassin. In the aftermath of the shootout, a political deal had been struck, and all charges were dropped. The one condition was that Clint get out of New Mexico.

Today, staring at the monument, he smiled with sardonic amusement. One Brannock had been exiled from New Mexico and three had returned. From Indian Territory, he'd crossed the Staked Plains with Lon and Hank. Late yesterday they had parted company at Lamy, a town southeast of Santa Fe. There, the boys had sold their horses and hopped a southbound train. Their destination was Lordsburg.

The choice had been made at Clint's suggestion. Lon wanted fast action and a crack at the high rollers. Lordsburg, which was one of the richest mining camps in New Mexico, seemed a likely prospect. Apart from that, Clint intended to keep track of them, and a larger camp made the chore easier. At the first opportunity, he planned to contact the Lordsburg town marshal and request a professional courtesy. One way or another, he meant to keep an eye on the boys.

U.S. Marshal Fred Mather was expecting him. While they'd never met, Mather was aware of Clint's long record in law enforcement. Before being exiled from New Mexico, Clint had served for seven years as a special investigator for the army. The intervening years with Judge Parker's court had merely enhanced his reputation as a manhunter. Among peace officers, his name alone commanded respect.

Mather was a ruddy-faced man with a walrus mustache and a quiet voice. Like most U.S. marshals, he was an administrator rather than a seasoned lawman. He reported directly to the governor and had only eight deputy marshals to cover all of New Mexico Territory. His greeting was somewhat taciturn and his manner was decidedly enigmatic. He refused to answer any questions about the transfer until Clint had spoken with Governor Ross. His choice of words indicated he was merely following orders.

Ten minutes later Clint found himself standing in the governor's office. Mather performed the introductions, then unobtrusively slipped out the door. Edmund Ross shook hands with a firm grasp and motioned to one of the leather armchairs before his desk. Clint took a seat and began rolling himself a smoke. All the secrecy seemed to him a bit overdone.

"First off," Ross said in an orotund voice, "let me say I personally requested your transfer. I advised the president that you're the only man for the job."

Clint struck a match, lit up in a cloud of smoke. "What job is that?"

"*Las Gorras Blancas,*" Ross replied crisply. "Otherwise known as the White Caps. Have you heard of them?"

"Not that I recollect."

"Well, then, allow me to inform you that they are a threat to the very existence of New Mexico Territory. *Las Gorras Blancas* are nothing less than armed revolutionaries."

"I take it they're *mexicanos*?"

"Precisely," Ross intoned. "A large, well-organized conspiracy composed solely of *mexicanos*. Their leader is a fanatic by the name of Miguel Ortega."

"Never heard of him either," Clint said. "What are they revolting against, just exactly?"

Ross jackknifed to his feet. He paced back and forth behind his desk, his features florid. His voice rose an octave and he punctuated his speech with vigorous gestures. He briefly explained the *mexicanos'* hostility to Anglo business interests in general, and barbed wire in particular. He went on to recount a litany of violence and terror.

Earlier in the year, a San Miguel County grand jury had been convened. After the hearings, indictments were returned against twenty-three *mexicanos* for fence-cutting. That night, sixty masked horsemen brandishing firearms and torches galloped into town. They surrounded first the home of the county prosecutor, and then the courthouse. Their leader spoke of harsh retaliation should the fence-cutters be convicted. Following a quick trial, the jury voted acquittal.

A week later six thousand railroad ties had been destroyed in a mammoth bonfire. Three Anglo teamsters who witnessed the incident testified before a grand jury. When the case came to trial, the teamsters failed to appear, and hadn't been seen since. All charges were dismissed and the accused night riders were allowed to go free. Afterward, a crowd of nearly a thousand *mexicanos* gathered before the courthouse. The celebration was marked by fiery speeches and a fusillade of gunshots.

The sphere of violent outbreaks expanded. The night riders struck throughout Santa Fe County, Bernalillo County, and farther north, Colfax County. Business ground to a standstill, and the tide of homesteaders into New Mexico virtually ceased. *Las Gorras Blancas,* operating in secret, had all but defeated the justice system. Witnesses to the acts were now intimidated, and unwilling to testify. Juries, which were composed largely of *mexicanos,* were sympathetic to the night riders. Conviction, even with strong evidence, was no longer possible.

The governor returned to his chair. Unrest was spreading, he noted, and there was reason to believe the White Caps could forge a movement that would sweep all of New Mexico. President Cleveland was now convinced that the uprisings were part of an organized conspiracy. The goal was to achieve *mexicano* independence by forcing Anglos to flee the territory. *Las Gorras Blancas* would then move to reunite their homeland with Old Mexico.

"We're confronted with war," Ross concluded hotly. "A war we're certain to lose unless we somehow stop Miguel Ortega."

Clint mulled it over a moment. "What makes you think Ortega's that dangerous?"

"We have certain influential friends among the *mexicanos*. They tell us that Ortega patterns himself after Mexico's greatest revolutionary, Benito Juárez. You may recall that Juárez defeated the French emperor Maximilian—and won independence for Mexico."

"Why not call in the military? Sounds like it's a job for the army."

Ross shook his head. "The army's far too cumbersome to catch one man. We need a specialist for this job—someone like you."

Clint's eyes were impersonal. "What do you know about Ortega?"

"Not much," Ross admitted. "I understand he was a farmer before he turned revolutionary. As we've seen, however, he has a natural gift for leadership. His movement has increased a thousandfold in one year."

"Any idea where he might be found?"

"None," Ross confessed. "He's a will-o'-the-wisp, impossible to predict. However, we have reliable information as to his next objective. He plans to organize the White Caps in Lincoln County."

"Is that why you sent for me?"

"Who else knows Lincoln County better? Your family lives there and you've hunted outlaws all throughout that country. I'd say you're eminently qualified."

Clint took a long drag on his cigarette. He blew a perfect smoke ring toward the ceiling, watching it widen. "I'm not a *pistolero*," he said evenly. "I don't kill men on order. Not for you or anybody else."

Ross appraised him through narrowed eyes. "I'm not ordering you to kill Ortega. I want you to track him down and bring him to justice."

"And if he resists arrest?"

"I trust you to use your discretion, Marshal Brannock."

Clint just looked at him.

"One other thing," Ross went on. "Your sister-in-law is opposed to any move against Ortega or the White Caps. Do you have a problem with that?"

"You're saying she doesn't want Ortega killed."

"I believe that represents her main concern."

"Off the record"—Clint hesitated, staring across the desk—"what's your preference?"

"A speedy resolution," Ross said in a measured tone. "Without Ortega, the revolt will wither away. I want it handled in an expeditious manner."

Clint laughed harshly. "I'll do my damndest where Ortega's concerned. As for Elizabeth, I figure she's your problem. I never get involved in politics."

"A commendable attitude."

Ross stood, signaling an end to the interview. They shook hands and Clint walked from the room. Outside he turned downstreet and proceeded to the marshal's office. He found Mather seated behind a battered desk, shuffling papers. There was a moment of stiff silence.

"I passed muster," Clint said dryly. "From the way the governor talks, I've been appointed a one-man fire brigade."

"Quite a compliment," Mather observed neutrally. "Let's hope you can stop it from spreading any further."

Clint flipped a hand back and forth. "What's the latest on these White Caps?"

Mather let his gaze drift out the window. Speaking quietly, he underscored the theory that a revolution was building. The number of *mexicanos* involved in the raids indicated well-planned organization and central command. Within the various counties, no single village could provide the large forces of men engaged in such attacks. The similarity of tactics and targets also pointed to a highly coordinated campaign of terror. All the evidence led to an inescapable conclusion.

"No doubt about it," Mather said, turning from the window. "*Las Gorras Blancas* are actively trying to overthrow the government. Their goal is anarchy—open rebellion."

Clint examined a fingernail. "What was the last report on Ortega?"

"Lincoln County," Mather stated firmly. "We know he's meeting secretly with the *mexicano* leaders. Word's out that he's moving from village to village."

Clint nodded, thoughtful. "The governor stopped just short of ordering me to kill Ortega. How do you feel about it?"

Mather grinned unpleasantly. "I think you'll never take Ortega alive. He's shrewd and he's tough, a real bad hombre. He won't quit without a fight."

Clint accepted the statement at face value. Something told him he'd heard the straight goods, even though no one wanted to say it out loud. A warrant for Miguel Ortega's arrest amounted to a death sentence. A one-way ticket to hell.

And he'd been selected to "expedite" the journey.

On Good Friday the villagers of San Patricio began gathering outside the church. Evening services were scheduled on this holiest of holy days, two nights before Easter Sunday. By ancient custom, the rites were in commemoration of the Crucifixion.

The mood of the villagers was solemn. Congregated out front were the women and children. The men were simply dressed and the women and young girls wore black mantillas draped over their heads. An air of hushed expectancy seemed to permeate the gathering.

Elizabeth stood at the rear of the crowd. She was accompanied by John Taylor and Félix Montoya, the local *jefe político*. At Montoya's insistence, she had finally agreed to attend the services. His reasons were vague, but over the past few days Montoya had persisted in his arguments. There seemed no way to decline without offending him.

The villagers, like almost all *mexicanos,* worshiped Elizabeth. Her efforts on their behalf, whether in land frauds or the free medical clinic, elevated her to a position approaching sainthood. Even more, her long battle with the *gringo* bosses in Santa Fe was considered a mark of rare courage. Her charitable works throughout the Hondo Valley were equally well known, and she never flaunted her wealth. She was thought to be a true woman of the people.

For all that, Elizabeth still had no idea why she'd been invited to the services. Montoya, who was a short, rotund man with sagging jowls, had deftly evaded her questions. His position as *jefe político,* more than his badgering attitude, had finally persuaded her. A loyal member of her coalition, he had aided her in the past and would do so in future elections. Whatever his reason, he was calling in the debt for services rendered. She felt she had no choice but to accept.

A bell tolled from the church tower. For an instant, a low murmur swept through the crowd. Then the tolling stopped and the villagers abruptly went silent. Dusk turned to darkness, and an inky quiet settled over San Patricio. Off in the distance, the voice of a man, raised in an eerie chant, drifted down from the foothills. In the next instant, a column of fiery torches appeared out of the night. The chant grew louder.

Arrayed in single file, a column of some twenty men descended a rocky path from the westward hills. Half of them were dressed in monks' habits, wooden crucifixes suspended from their necks. The other half wore white cotton trousers and black hoods, their upper bodies bare. An elderly man, carrying a large silver cross, led the procession. Behind him, a cowled monk chanted prayers in a keening voice.

The men dressed in habits carried torches. Of the others,

those naked above the waist, eight were soaked with blood. As they trudged into the village, they lashed themselves across the back and chest with short whips fashioned from sharp-thorned cactus spines. Still another man pulled a heavy wooden cart, a coarse horsehair harness strapped around his shoulders. Seated in the cart was a skeleton, cloaked in black, obsidian eyes set deep in the bleached skull. A drawn bow, with the arrow fixed for flight, was wired onto the skeleton's outstretched arms.

The last of the ten half-naked men wore a crown of thorns. He lurched forward, dripping blood, bowed beneath the weight of a cross constructed of hewn timbers. Outside the church he staggered to a halt and dropped to his knees, still supporting the cross on his shoulders. His back was scourged from repeated lashings, latticed with ugly welts and torn flesh. Unable to raise his head, he stared down at the stone steps with a hollow expression.

Elizabeth stood transfixed. Over the years she had heard of a mysterious order of Franciscan monks. Known as the Brotherhood of Penitents, they lived in the remote mountains of New Mexico and southern Colorado. Their order descended from St. Francis of Assisi and their mission was to care for the sick and the dying. Nearly five centuries ago the Roman Catholic Church had outlawed their rites of self-flagellation and scourging. Yet, after all that time, small bands still followed the ancient religious practices.

On Good Friday night, a procession of monks made their way to the church. The *penitentes* were brothers who vowed to flagellate themselves as the Roman soldiers had lashed Jesus. Their whips were yucca cactus, soaked in salt water, and drew blood with every stroke. They were led by the *hermano mayor,* the head brother, and prayers were recited from a religious text passed down from generation to generation. The cart was called the *carreta del muerto,* and the skeleton represented the figure of Death.

To Elizabeth's knowledge, no Anglo had been permitted to witness the Good Friday ritual. Even Harry Tipton, who owned the sawmill, was instructed to remain indoors. She watched now as the brothers made their way inside the church and stopped before the altar. Prayers were offered and their voices were raised in doleful *alabados,* accompanied by the wail of a flute. At last, the candles were snuffed and the church went dark. The brothers slowly filed out the door.

Once more the *penitentes* began whipping themselves. The brother honored with the role of Jesus again shouldered his cross. Their chant resumed and the procession turned back toward the foothills. The villagers of San Patricio dutifully trailed along behind. Félix Montoya, urging Elizabeth to follow, assisted her on the rocky pathway. Taylor brought up the rear, the last man in line.

A short time later the procession halted on a barren hillside. The villagers fell to their knees, heads bowed, and began muttering prayers. The brothers gathered in a torchlit circle around the man burdened with the cross. Several *penitentes* removed it from his shoulders and laid it flat on the ground. His eyes vacant, the man lowered himself onto the cross, his arms outstretched and his ankles locked together. Other *penitentes* approached with hammers and spikes, and knelt at opposite ends of the crossbeam. Working quickly, they spread his hands wide and positioned spikes over the open palms. Their hammers flashed in the glow of torchlight.

Elizabeth's breath caught in her throat. The night echoed with a metallic ring as the spikes were driven through the man's hands. His mouth opened in a strangled scream and blood spurted with every stroke of the hammers. Elizabeth stared at him with wide-eyed horror and willed herself not to gag. Then the hammers fell silent and the *penitentes* raised the cross for all to see, holding the man aloft. His gaze was fixed, blind with pain, his hands studded to the wooden beam. The head brother led the onlookers in a murmured incantation.

A monk appeared at Elizabeth's side. He spoke her name and she looked around. Then, pushing the cowl off his head, he revealed himself in the torchlight. His features were hawklike, stark and strong, with deep-set onyx eyes and a thick black mustache. He was wiry, somewhat taller than the usual *mexicano,* and his gaze seemed oddly piercing. He nodded, a slight smile at the corners of his mouth.

"Permit me to introduce myself, *señora.* I am Miguel Ortega."

A startled expression crossed Elizabeth's face. She sensed movement as Taylor took a step forward, and motioned him away. "We meet at last," she said, collecting herself. "Was I brought here at your instructions, Señor Ortega?"

"A thousand pardons," Ortega apologized. "Here with the brotherhood seemed the safest place. As you know, I am a hunted man."

"I learned of it only this week. Governor Ross has branded you a revolutionary."

"The governor honors me," Ortega said, smiling broadly. "I am but a humble man working to protect my people. In fact, you and I are much alike, *señora.*"

"Yes, perhaps we are," Elizabeth conceded. "Certain men in Santa Fe probably think of me as an *insurrecta.*"

"I would not otherwise have arranged this meeting. Your sense of justice is without question."

"What is it you wish of me, Señor Ortega?"

"Your support," Ortega informed her. "Among my people you are known as *La Mariposa de Hierro.* Your name would do much to further our cause."

Elizabeth sounded uncertain. "How would my name benefit you?"

"Lincoln County will be our next battleground. I have come here to organize the people for the fight ahead. Were you to support my efforts, they would rush to join *Las Gorras Blancas.*"

"I endorse your cause," Elizabeth temporized, "but I cannot condone your methods. Violence merely breeds more violence, and resolves nothing. I believe your goals will be won at the ballot box—not with guns."

Ortega's expression became immobile and dark. His mouth tightened and his eyes flashed with a formidable glitter. He stared at her with a strange, unsettling look.

"You are wrong, *señora*," he said in a low, intense voice. "For forty years, we tried peaceful means, and where has it gotten us? We are still *peones,* serving under a different master. The time for talk and reason is long past."

Elizabeth felt mesmerized. A messianic quality seemed to emanate from his eyes, and his voice burned with fervor. She understood now why the *mexicanos* were drawn to his cause, spoke his name with reverence. He was like a prophet of olden times, preaching liberty and freedom.

"We will fight," he went on confidently, "and we will win. No longer will we endure the oppression of *ladrones americanos*."

"I must tell you something," Elizabeth said, her voice soft and troubled. "Governor Ross has brought in a new lawman and ordered him to hunt you down. His name is Clint Brannock."

"Ai, caramba," Ortega muttered. "Your brother-in-law, *verdad*? I remember the name from long ago. A *pistolero,* very dangerous."

"Yes," Elizabeth said dismally. "Very dangerous and very determined. He won't stop until he finds you."

Ortega laughed. "I am not easily found."

"I am concerned as much for him as for you. He is very dear to me."

"Have no fear, *señora.* I will see to it that we never meet. In the meantime, consider yourself under my protection. *Las Gorras Blancas* will avoid the Hondo Valley. We do not harm our friends."

Elizabeth merely nodded. "I wish you well . . . *buena suerte*."

"Vaya con Dios."

With that, Ortega turned away. Elizabeth watched as he skirted the villagers and melted into the darkness. A moment later her attention was drawn to the torchlit circle. She saw the *penitentes* gently lower the crucified monk to the ground. She thought it somehow symbolic, and fearful.

Miguel Ortega might be martyred to yet another cause.

TEN

Lordsburg lay at the foot of the Pyramid Mountains. Some twenty miles from the Arizona border, the town was located in the southwestern corner of New Mexico. The earth in every direction was a vast repository of copper.

Lon and Hank stepped off the train on Easter Sunday. Their trip had taken them south from the Sangre de Cristo range and along the valley of the upper Rio Grande. After changing trains at Rincon, they had turned westward into a bleak wasteland of rock and sand. The sight of forested mountains brought a welcome end to their long journey.

For Hank, the trip had been a time of wonder. His entire life had been spent on the reservation, far removed from the white man's world. In three short weeks he'd crossed the fabled *Llano Estacado* and traveled through the better part of New Mexico Territory. What seemed the greater marvel, however, was his first train ride. The speeds attained by the locomotive still left him somewhat stupefied.

Even his physical appearance had been altered. At Lamy, the town where they'd parted company with Clint, Lon had introduced him to the wonders of the local tonsorial parlor. First, he'd soaped and scrubbed himself in the steamy waters of a great wooden bathtub. Then the barber trimmed his hair short and slicked it back with sweet-smelling pomade. The next stop was a mercantile, where Lon outfitted him from hat to boots, with extra underdrawers and two extra shirts. Their last purchase was a used .44-40 Colt, with belt and holster.

The pistol still seemed strange. Crossing the depot platform, Hank was all too aware of the weight on his hip. On the reservation, he'd sometimes practiced shooting with Lon, and he remembered being amazed at his brother's speed and accuracy. Yet he was uncomfortable carrying a gun, and he had accepted it only at Lon's insistence. The Colt, like the new clothes and his scalped haircut, were merely outward signs of change. On the inside, he was still Bull Calf, a Quahadi Comanche. And he felt himself an intruder in the land of the *tahboy-boh*.

From the depot, Lon led the way uptown. Lordsburg seemed to Hank a carnival in motion, and he could hardly keep from gawking. The main street was a hurdy-gurdy assortment of saloons and gaming parlors and raucous dance halls. A mining camp was open seven days a week, and Easter Sunday was no exception. The boardwalks were crowded with miners, and ruby-lipped girls, decked out in spangles, were visible through the doorways. Despite himself, Hank found his mouth dropping open every few paces.

Lordsburg was originally a silver camp. In the late 1860s, a discovery lode had drawn prospectors from all across the West. Over the next decade the town had prospered in a boom-time atmosphere. Then the silver began petering out and the emphasis shifted to copper. By 1881, when the Southern Pacific laid tracks through the mountains, another boom was already under way. Within a short ride from downtown, there were eighty-five copper mines.

In large degree, Lordsburg was typical of Western mining camps. For more than three decades, gold and silver were the mainstays of the mining industry. During the 1880s, however, the age of electricity ushered in an era that made copper a profitable venture. Thomas Edison's remarkable invention—the electric light—was spreading westward across the nation. A growing number of cities and towns were also installing telephones, as well as electric street-lamps and streetcars.

The advent of this new source of energy transformed the mining industry. Copper was previously a metal for which there was no market, and thus it had remained virtually untouched. But the demand mushroomed overnight when it was discovered that copper acted as a conductor for electricity. No less important was the expansion of the railroads into the remote, and sometimes isolated, mountainous camps. The ore could be brought to the surface, freighted to the smelters, and then transported eastward by rail. Exploitation of the West's vast copper deposits began in earnest.

At that point, prospectors and placer miners moved on to other diggings. Large corporations bought up the claims and undertook a search for minerals locked deep within the bowels of the earth. By 1887, copper was king, and Lordsburg was controlled by bankers and financiers. Absentee owners, generally a consortium of wealthy businessmen, pulled the strings from Denver and San Francisco. A thousand or more miners worked the underground shafts, and the monthly payroll exceeded a quarter-million dollars. The town entered still another era of boom-time prosperity.

Technology was the key to the financiers' takeover. A new invention—dynamite—was used to blast through the rock and excavate tunnels. Underground drilling, formerly done by hand, was now accomplished by power drills operating on compressed air. Working in tandem, dynamite and power drills made it possible to burrow far beneath the earth's surface. Some operations were a thousand feet below the ground and extended through a labyrinth of tunnels.

As the mines probed ever deeper, the danger to workers multiplied at an alarming rate. Safety measures were virtually nonexistent, and accidents became commonplace. Men were killed and maimed by cave-ins, sometimes drowned when subterranean springs flooded the tunnels, and frequently incinerated when fire swept through the timbered mine shafts. Yet there was no shortage of men willing to risk their lives, and most of the mines worked double shifts. The wages, compared with other lines of work, were almost munificent. A cowhand's earnings were generally a third of those paid to the lowliest miner.

For Lon, it represented an El Dorado. On the Texas circuit,

he'd been lucky to find a five-dollar-limit game. By comparison, Lordsburg was a town of high rollers, with table stakes more common than not. The gaming parlors operated around the clock, and on any given night a tidy fortune changed hands. He was anxious to test his skills in a cutthroat check-and-bet game. He doubted that miners understood poker any better than Texican cattlemen.

Uptown, Lon paused and surveyed Lordsburg's three hotels. They were all within a block of one another, but only one had a veranda. Early on, he'd learned that a gambling man had a certain reputation to maintain. Word got around, and high rollers preferred to pit themselves against a gambler who displayed a taste for the good life. Appearances counted among the sporting crowd, and nowhere more than within the gambling fraternity. A solid front invariably attracted well-heeled players.

The hotel lobby confirmed Lon's judgment. Several men, chatting and reading newspapers, were seated in easy chairs and a lone horsehair sofa. The conversation ceased as Lon, trailed closely by Hank, came through the door. The men seemed particularly interested in the youngster, and their appraisal was somehow severe. Lon was aware of their scrutiny, but he chose to ignore it. He moved across the lobby, halting at the registration desk. He nodded to the clerk behind the counter.

"The name's Brannock," he said amiably. "I'd like the best room in the house."

The desk clerk was a gangling man with bony features. He gave Lon a quick once-over; then his gaze shifted to Hank. He subjected the boy to a slow up-and-down inspection, and his expression turned frosty. At length, he looked back at Lon.

"No offense," he said, "but we don't accommodate Indians. Our clientele wouldn't stand for it."

"We'll fix that," Lon said confidently. "Let me talk with the owner."

"I am the owner," the man replied. "You have to understand,

there's still a lotta hard feeling in these parts. We lost some good men to the Apache."

"Well, you're in luck," Lon said, motioning to the boy. "Any fool could see he's not Apache."

"Still doesn't change anything. It's a policy of the house—no Indians."

"C'mon, Lon," Hank said, shuffling uneasily. "We'll go somewheres else."

Lon shook his head. He smiled without warmth, staring at the hotel owner. "Here's the story," he said in a faintly ominous tone. "Either I get a room or you better start packin' a gun. I won't be insulted."

"You can't threaten me! I'll have the law down on you."

"Go ahead," Lon told him. "You'll still wind up in the bone orchard. I give you my personal guarantee."

A tense silence settled over the lobby. The hotel owner saw something cold and implacable in Lon's gaze. His Adam's apple bobbed and he swallowed hard. After a moment, he produced a key and slapped it down on the counter. "You're in room two-o-one."

"Much obliged."

Lon grinned, nodding at Hank, then walked to the stairway. In their room, he seemed to dismiss the incident from mind. Unpacking his bag, he laid out a fresh shirt and his shaving gear. At the washstand, he poured water into a porcelain bowl and tested the edge on his straight razor. He glanced up and found Hank watching him in the mirror. He winked and began soaping his face.

"I think I'm gonna like this town, sport. Folks seem real friendly."

"Were you bluffin'," Hank asked, "or would you've shot him?"

"I only bluff at poker," Lon said jovially. "Anything else, I'm as good as my word. You oughta know that by now."

Somewhile later they emerged from the hotel. Lon stopped on the veranda and lit a cheroot. Exhaling smoke, he once again surveyed the string of saloons and gaming parlors. A sign across the street caught his eye and he nodded to himself. He led Hank toward the Tivoli Palace.

The batwing doors opened onto a combination saloon and gaming dive. The backbar was a gaudy clutch of bottles centered around a huge French mirror. On the opposite wall were three faro layouts, a chuck-a-luck game, and a twenty-one spread. Toward the rear, several tables with overhead coal-oil lamps were set aside for poker. There was no piano, no dance floor, and the atmosphere was subdued, almost businesslike. From all appearances, it was a place devoted to serious gambling.

Lon thought he'd picked a likely spot. What appeared to be a high-stakes game was under way at one of the poker tables. He noted a shotgun guard perched on a tall chair just past the twenty-one spread. Throwing an arm over Hank's shoulders, he walked to the bar. A nearby drinker grumped something under his breath, then turned away. The bartender strolled over, arms folded across his chest.

"Whiskey for me," Lon said, "and a sarsaparilla for my partner."

The barkeep frowned. "You'll have to take your trade elsewhere. Injuns ain't allowed in here."

Lon grunted sharply. "Set 'em up and be damn fast about it. I'm not gonna tell you again."

"And I'm tellin' you to waltz the hell outta here."

A man at the end of the bar hurried forward. His features were coarse and an ugly scar traced a welt along his jawbone. From beneath his jacket the bulge of a short-barreled pistol was visible. He squinted querulously at Lon.

"What's the problem?"

Lon turned from the bar. "Who're you?"

"Ace McMasters. I own the joint."

"Then tell your barkeep to watch his mouth. I ordered a drink and I mean to have it."

"You heard him," McMasters growled. "We don't serve gut-eaters."

Lon gave him a slow go-to-hell smile. "You got a smart mouth yourself."

"Don't push it," McMasters said in a loud, hectoring voice. "Get moving before I bust you upside the head."

"You try it," Lon warned with cold menace, "and I'll make your asshole wink."

McMasters stepped clear, widening the space between them. The shotgun guard rose from his perch, thumbing the hammer on his sawed-off scattergun. All thought suspended, Lon acted on reflex alone. His hand dipped inside his coat and reappeared with a cocked pistol. He leveled the Colt and fired in one fluid motion.

The slug took the guard in the throat. His mouth opened in a breathless whoofing sound and the shotgun dropped from his hands. He teetered on the edge of his chair, then pitched forward and slammed facedown on the floor. A noxious stench filled the room as his bowels voided in death.

Lon wagged his pistol at the bar owner. McMasters froze, his belly-gun halfway out of the holster. A thick silence descended on the room and they stared at each other for a long moment. At last, avoiding any sudden movement, McMasters lowered his arm to his side.

"I call it self-defense," Lon said pointedly. "What do you call it?"

McMasters shrugged. "Guess I shouldn't've sicced him on you."

"Suppose you send for the marshal, Ace. I think he oughta hear you say that."

The bartender went to fetch Lordsburg's town marshal. Lon holstered his pistol, then glanced around, motioning to Hank. They moved past McMasters and walked to the poker table at the rear of the room. There were five players seated at the table and they watched silently as Lon stopped behind an empty chair. He looked from man to man, his mouth curled in a smile.

"Anybody object if I take a seat?"

Nobody objected.

Easter services always drew large crowds. There were two churches in Lincoln, one Catholic and one Methodist.

Mexicanos had traveled long distances to attend early-morning Mass. The Protestant congregation, comprising only Anglos, began filing into church shortly before eleven.

Elizabeth was there with the entire family. In all, they were six, including Brad and Blake Hazlett. Seated in a front pew, they listened as the pastor delivered a stirring sermon on the Resurrection. Afterward, the organ wheezed to life and everyone joined in a final hymn. Services concluded on the stroke of twelve.

The pastor stationed himself just outside the front door. As the congregation filed past, he shook hands with the men and exchanged pleasantries with the women. Elizabeth, as the matriarch of the town's most prominent family, was greeted with unusual warmth. Her generous contributions, which represented fully a third of the annual budget, made her presence all the more noteworthy. Had she been a man, the church elders would have unanimously elected her a deacon.

Following custom, the women were attired in their Easter Sunday finery. Elizabeth and Jennifer and Louise drew admiring glances as they moved along the walkway. Blake looked dashing, while Morg and Brad appeared singularly uncomfortable. Neither of them was a regular churchgoer, and their serge suits smelled vaguely of mothballs. Twice a year, Easter and Christmas, they were dragooned into attending services.

A family gathering was planned at Spur. Jennifer and Blake would follow in a buckboard, while the others rode in a large phaeton carriage. Elizabeth believed in celebrating holidays and she always insisted that the family be together. At her direction, a festive dinner was even now being prepared back at the ranch. Like the church services, attendance was considered mandatory.

Morg assisted Louise into the carriage. He heard a faint gasp and turned back just as his mother put a hand to her throat. Elizabeth was staring uptown, her gaze fixed on a tall rider astride a roan gelding. One by one the others recognized the horseman, and suddenly everybody started talking at once. They stood waiting in a tableau of grinning faces.

Clint reined to a halt behind the carriage. When he swung down from the saddle, Morg and Brad swarmed him with whooped laughter and arm-pumping handshakes. Jennifer kissed him soundly and performed the introductions with Blake. Louise waved from her seat in the carriage, and the church congregation stared en masse. Those who remembered him agreed it was a resurrection of sorts for the Brannock family. The exile to a far land had at last returned.

Clint finally made his way to Elizabeth. Her eyes shone, glistening with tears, and her face radiated happiness. She took a tentative step forward, then moved into his arms and embraced him with a great hug. He held her close for a moment, and when they separated, she looked up at him with warm affection. Her mouth trembled with a smile.

"Welcome home," she said softly. "I've missed you."

"You're a sight for sore eyes yourself."

"Honestly, your timing couldn't have been better. We're having a family get-together."

Clint laughed. "Sounds mighty good to me. I rode a long way to get here."

"Oh, I just can't tell you! I'm so happy to see you."

The dinner was transformed into a homecoming celebration. With Clint the guest of honor, the family gathered around a table loaded with food. They ate and talked, uncorking three bottles of wine, and peppered him with questions. Clint kept his answers short and turned the conversation instead to events in their lives. By the end of the meal, he'd been brought up-to-date on the entire family.

Sated with food, everyone retired to the parlor after dinner. Elizabeth and Clint left the others conversing among themselves and stepped out onto the veranda. There, at last, Elizabeth got him to talk. Seated on the porch swing, he told her of his trip to the reservation, and Little Raven's death. His voice was detached, but she nonetheless saw the hurt in his eyes. Not for the first time, she realized he was a man of deep-felt emotions and intense loyalty. She sensed as well that he would speak of such things to no one but her.

Under her gentle questioning, Clint went on to relate his parting with Lon and Hank. His voice was now troubled, and he seemed somehow at a loss. He held out no great hope that Lon would ever lead a normal life. Yet, however slim, he thought there was still a chance for young Hank. The major obstacle was to separate them, and remove the boy from Lon's influence. Listening to him, Elizabeth understood that he'd now assumed the role of their father. He was talking about his sons.

To the west, the sun dropped lower beyond the mountains. They fell silent, watching the faraway slopes silhouetted against a fiery sky. For Clint, her nearness and the light scent of her perfume suddenly stirred old memories. Even now, after a long year apart, her presence still kindled a starstruck feeling. He knew she was the reason he'd never married, and yet he suppressed the thought. While men sometimes wed their brothers' widows, it would never happen with them. Her affection for him was that of a loving and concerned sister. And he'd always known it wouldn't change.

"I have something to tell you," Elizabeth said in the deepening twilight. "Something you won't like."

Clint looked at her. "Sounds serious."

"Yes, it is," she said with a broken smile. "Two nights ago, Miguel Ortega arranged a meeting with me. He asked me to come out in support of *Las Gorras Blancas*."

"And?"

"I refused," she said, lowering her eyes. "I won't be a party to violence, even for a good cause."

"Glad to hear it," Clint said, still watching her. "Guess you know I've been sent here to run him down."

"Yes, I know."

"Would you consider telling me where this meeting took place?"

"I've already thought it through very thoroughly. I won't help him and I won't help you."

"Hard to stay neutral in a thing like this."

"Be honest," she asked directly. "You intend to kill him, don't you?"

Clint grunted, shook his head. "I've never killed a man who wasn't trying to kill me. Ortega's no different."

"Yes, he is different," she insisted. "He's fighting for a cause, his people! He's not an outlaw."

Clint subscribed to no particular ideology. Nor was he a man of strong political convictions. Yet he held to the belief that no man was above the law. What he saw as his life's work was founded on a single tenet. Those who broke the rules must be made to pay the penalty.

"Ortega's dangerous," he said now. "One way or another, he's got to be stopped. The law don't make exceptions."

"And when you catch him—if he refuses to surrender—what then?"

"I reckon that'll be his choice, not mine."

The statement foreshadowed what Elizabeth feared most. A cold premonition swept over her and she felt a sudden seesaw of emotions. Somehow she had to ensure that Miguel Ortega was not killed. And that put her at odds with the one man she treasured above all others.

She took Clint's hand and squeezed it tightly. He nodded, merely looking at her, as though reading her mind. Neither of them spoke of it again.

ELEVEN

The calf bawled in protest. Hair sizzled as Brad pressed down on the red-hot iron, holding it there several seconds. When he pulled it away, the calf's flank was marked with his ⫞D brand.

Stepping back, he dropped the iron on the ground and shook his lariat free of the calf's neck. Then he moved forward, stooping down, and jerked the piggin' string loose. The hog-tied calf scrambled to its feet and took off at a wobbly lope. Some distance away the mama cow stood watching with flared eyes and lowered head. The calf lumbered into her and immediately began suckling.

Brad kicked dirt onto the small fire he'd built. With the coals smothered, and the branding iron cooled, he walked to his horse. After strapping the iron behind the cantle, he mounted and began recoiling his lariat. His eyes roved out across the land, where his herd of longhorns slowly grazed toward the river. Working by himself, he'd managed to brand three calves within the last hour. By rough count, there were another thirty-one yet to be chased down.

Late that afternoon he had ridden over to the Rio Felix. Sometime next week, barring bad weather, he planned to commence roundup on Spur. Once the gather started, there would be little time left for his own affairs. So he'd decided to get the calves branded rather than put it off until later. But now, with the sun dropping toward the mountains, he was forced to call it quits. He would have to work straight through Sunday to get the job finished.

Unlike other Saturdays, he wouldn't be taking dinner with the Ramírez family tonight. Earlier, upon approaching his cabin, he'd noted smoke coming from the chimney. To his amazement, he found Juanita busily preparing a meal for that evening. She'd already tidied up the cabin, and an earthen vase of wildflowers was centered on the table. She blithely remarked that she was tired of sharing him with her family. She had decided to fix their supper herself.

Something about her manner troubled Brad. Her presence there wasn't peculiar, for she had been to the cabin many times before. But she'd never offered to cook supper, or shown the least interest in cleaning the cabin. She'd even walked the three miles from her father's place, lugging a sackful of food all the way. When he rode out to start the branding, it occurred to him that she was acting strangely like a wife. He wondered if she was in the family way.

Juanita was waiting when he returned. She watched from the door while he unsaddled and turned his horse into the corral. Laughing happily, she kissed him as he entered the cabin and made him wash up before supper. At the table, she heaped his plate with several savory dishes, clearly proud of her cooking. Through the meal she chattered on about inconsequential things, merely picking at her own food. Afterward, when they were finished, she shooed him outside. Humming to herself, she began washing the dishes.

Brad took a seat in the doorway. The night was dark and stars were scattered like flecks of ice through a sky of purest indigo. His gaze roved back and forth, searching the patchwork heavens, as though some immutable truth were to be found in the stars. He found instead the quandary of his own thoughts, and deepening concern. Until tonight, their arrangement had been pleasant and informal, no strings attached. But now he sensed a change, some vague domestic undertone that left him disturbed. He had a hunch he was about to get an earful.

A short time later Juanita joined him in the doorway. She leaned back, her head against his shoulder, pulling his arm tight around her waist. She smelled sweet and alluring, and Brad was all too aware of her rounded hips and high full breasts. She seemed content with the silence and several minutes passed while they stared off into the night. Then, wriggling closer, she arched her head and slowly scanned the sky.

"The old ones," she said softly, "believe the stars foretell the future. Do you think it's true?"

"I dunno," Brad replied. "I've never been much on superstition."

"No, no," she said quickly. "It's not superstition. They believe some things are destined . . . meant to be."

"What do you believe?"

She clamped a hand over her mouth and giggled. "Are you sure you want me to tell you?"

Brad had a feeling he couldn't stop her. "Go ahead," he said. "I'd like to hear it."

"Well—" She laughed her sensuous little laugh. "I believe the stars were meant for lovers. Why else would God put them there?"

"Maybe he just wanted to light up the sky."

"Oh!" she scolded. "Why aren't you more romantic? You never say nice things."

Brad looked at her blankly. "What would you have me say?"

"For one thing," she said with innocent directness, "you might speak to me of *amor*. Just once, tell me what I mean to you."

"What would you like to mean to me?"

"Tu corazón," she murmured, *"tu vida*—everything."

Brad felt a powerful tug of emotion toward her. Yet he was not a man who revealed his innermost thoughts easily. Nor was he all that ready to admit them to himself. His restlessness had grown worse, not better, and he seemed saddled with discontent. He wasn't sure what the hell he wanted.

"Are you talking about marriage?" he asked now. "If you are, let's get it out in the open."

There was something brazen in her eyes. *"Sí,"* she said without hesitation. "I have been your woman many months now. I came to you a *virgen* and you knew—I thought you understood."

"Understood what?"

"How it is with my people! A girl does not surrender herself casually. She waits and saves herself . . . for one man."

A moment elapsed while she waited for some response. "I have to know," he said finally. "Are you with child?"

"No!"

She recoiled as though slapped. Shoulders squared, she pulled back and held his gaze with a steadfast look. "I am no fool," she informed him. "I watch the moon and I attend to myself. I would never disgrace myself with a *bastardo.*"

Brad stared at her, his face very earnest. "Our child would never be born without a name—my name."

"What are you saying?"

An instant of weighing and deliberation slipped past. Brad realized he was about to say the one thing he'd never allowed himself to consider. Still, though he failed to comprehend the reason, it was what he wanted to say.

"We will be married," he promised. "But it must wait until after the fall roundup. I have obligations to satisfy."

"Are you talking about Señora Brannock?"

"Don't ask me to explain. Just tell me you're willing to wait."

A vixen look touched her eyes and she moistened her bottom lip with her tongue. Her voice turned silky. "I would wait forever, *caro mío.*"

She smiled and her arms encircled his neck. Brad suddenly stiffened, staring past her with a puzzled frown. Her arms fell away and she turned, following the direction of his gaze. Far in the distance, a flare of light split the darkness.

"What is it?" she asked.

"Fire," Brad said, rising to his feet. "Homer Stockton's place."

"Where are you going?"

"Way it looks, he's bound to need help. Stay here till I get back."

Brad hurried off to the corral. He quickly saddled his horse, then opened the gate and swung aboard. Juanita watched from the doorway as he spurred the gelding into a lope.

He rode east along the Rio Felix.

The main house was unharmed. Several outbuildings had been doused with coal oil and burned to the ground. All that remained was a smoky pile of embers.

Homer Stockton stood in the middle of the compound. He looked on without expression as cowhands carried water buckets from the river and soaked down the rubble. His eyes were empty, and cold.

Brad dismounted and left his horse ground-reined. He'd covered the five miles downstream at a steady lope, negotiating the rough terrain by starlight. Along the way, he had spotted tangled knots of fenceposts and barbed wire, and bunches of cattle far off their home range. Someone had methodically stampeded Stockton's herds.

"Hard luck, Homer," Brad said, halting beside the rancher. "Any idea who did it?"

"Who else?" Stockton said in a dead monotone. *"Las Gorras Blancas."*

"How do you know for sure?"

"Last night the sonsabitches snuck in here and tacked a warning on the door. Told me to clear out."

Stockton paused, shook his head dumbly. "Helluva thing, when a man gets posted off his own land. Never figured it'd happen to me."

Brad was silent a moment, thoughtful. Last week, while Clint was at the ranch, they had spoken at length about the White Caps. Clint was confident that *mexicanos* were being organized into bands of night riders. He believed they would strike soon, hitting targets selected as a warning to all Anglos. Upon departing Spur, Clint had taken a room at the hotel in town. From there, he planned to conduct an investigation throughout Lincoln County.

Something else stuck in Brad's mind. After swearing him to secrecy, Clint had told him about Elizabeth's meeting with Miguel Ortega. Apparently she'd taken a neutral stance in the matter, refusing to support or denounce Ortega's movement. And now, Homer Stockton was the first rancher to be hit by *Las Gorras Blancas*. Which raised the question of Stockton's ties to the Brannocks. His daughter was married to Morg, and that made him a relative of sorts. So perhaps the raid was a message meant for Elizabeth. A warning about the prospects of remaining neutral.

Whether coincidence or not, Brad thought the raid was a well-designed object lesson. Stockton was a hard man, and no friend of the *mexicanos*. He'd strung barbed wire across a large stretch of public domain, as well as a chunk of communal pastureland from an old Spanish grant. Worse, he had fenced off parts of the Rio Felix, denying water to nomadic *mexicano* shepherds. All that made him a prime target for *Las Gorras Blancas*. He typified Anglo cattlemen who rode roughshod over the native people and their customs.

"Guess you ought to know," Brad said now. "Your fences are down between here and my place. From what I saw, your cows are scattered to hell and gone."

Stockton's eyes glazed with rage. "Goddamn greasers! Hit me just before I was fixin' to start roundup. How's that for a kick in the balls?"

"Pretty smart thinkin'," Brad muttered out loud. "Looks like they aimed to put you in a squeeze."

"I'll fight 'em!" Stockton punched a fist into the palm of his hand. "Any peppergut I catch on my land will wish he hadn't been born. Nobody runs me out."

Brad took a deep breath, blew it out heavily. "Only one problem, Homer. Fast as you string fence, they'll tear it down again. You can't patrol your whole spread."

"What's that mean?" Stockton said tightly. "Are you tellin' me I shouldn't string fence?"

"We do all right without it on Spur."

"Hell, yes, you do. Every greaser on the Hondo would kiss Elizabeth Brannock's ass if she'd lift her skirts."

"You watch your mouth where Miz Brannock's concerned. Otherwise you'll have to deal with me."

Stockton eyed him warily. "No need to get your nose out of joint. I didn't mean it personal."

"Just remember what I said, Homer."

Brad walked to his horse. He stepped into the saddle and reined out of the yard. Fording the river, it occurred to him that he'd never particularly liked Stockton. But then, from the looks of things, he wasn't alone. Lots of people knew a sonovabitch when they saw one.

At the head of the line was Miguel Ortega and *Las Gorras Blancas*.

Weekends were a special time for Jennifer. For reasons she'd never fathomed, people tended to nurse their ailments through Saturday night and Sunday. Whatever the cause, she was thankful for the respite.

After closing her office, her Saturday-night ritual seldom varied. She took a long luxurious bath, soaking away the week's aches and strains. Then she selected something frilly and feminine from her wardrobe, and tried to do something special with her hair. The result, when she finally inspected herself in the mirror, was always a pleasant surprise. Underneath the doctor there was a woman of passable good looks.

While she was attending to her toilette, her cook prepared dinner. A *mexicano* woman, the cook worked only on weekends, spoiling Jennifer with pastries and fresh-baked bread and all manner of special dishes. In part, the cook was also a concession to Jennifer's need for relaxation and entertainment. One aspect of the Saturday-night ritual was that she always invited Blake for supper. He was what the townspeople discreetly referred to as her "gentleman friend."

Tonight, Jennifer was in an unusually zestful mood. She'd lost no patients during the past week, and cheating death seemed to her a cause for celebration. At the dinner table, some of her old vivacity returned, and she joined with Blake in animated conversation. He enjoyed telling anecdotes, generally woven around some courtroom experience, and she found herself laughing gaily at his dry wit. By the time coffee was served, she felt curiously giddy and carefree.

All that abruptly changed. A loud knock at the front door brought her back to reality. She excused herself with an apologetic smile and hurried through the waiting room. When she opened the door, she recognized Morg's timber foreman, Chunk Devlin. Behind him were four lumberjacks carrying a man on a stretcher rigged from blankets. Devlin's features were shrouded with concern.

"Sorry to bother you, ma'am," he said, jerking a thumb over his shoulder. "We've got a man who's hurt bad."

"Bring him inside."

Jennifer quickly lighted the lamps in her office. Devlin explained that one of the chains on a logging wagon had snapped. The load shifted, and a log weighing upwards of a thousand pounds rolled onto the man, crushing his leg. A war veteran himself, Devlin had the presence of mind to apply a tourniquet. The accident had occurred at quitting time, just before sundown. Three hours had been required to transport the man into town.

A brief examination confirmed Jennifer's worst fears. After placing the lumberjack on the operating table, she cut away his trouser leg with scissors. His lower leg and foot, still encased in a heavy workboot, had been crushed to a pulp. His upper leg, from a point four inches above the knee, was horribly mangled. The femur bone, broken and jagged, protruded through his lower thigh. The extent of the injuries left Jennifer no alternative. She would have to amputate.

The logger was still conscious. His teeth were gritted against the pain and beads of sweat glistened on his forehead. Jennifer moved to the head of the table and placed a reassuring hand on his shoulder. He licked his parched lips, searching her face.

"I'm sorry," she said gently. "Unless I operate immediately, you'll develop gangrene. I have to remove the leg."

A pinpoint of terror surfaced in his eyes. "Godamight—" his voice cracked. "Ain't there no other way, Doc?"

"Your injuries are too severe. Without an operation, you'll die. We have to do it now."

The logger mustered a feeble smile. "Never thought I'd wind up a pegleg. Guess you just never know."

"Lie back and rest. I'll give you something to ease the pain."

Jennifer dosed him with laudanum, a mild sedative. She then sent Blake to fetch Rosa, her surgical assistant. The cook was hastily drafted to sterilize instruments and prepare bandages. Devlin and his men, under Jennifer's direction, gingerly undressed the lumberjack. When they finished, she ushered them out into the waiting room.

Alone with her patient, Jennifer briskly scrubbed her hands. She used a sterile towel to dry off and then set about cleansing the leg with a carbolic solution. The antiseptic vastly reduced the chances of infection, and death, following surgery. Jennifer was no less thankful for the development of modern-day anesthetics. Before the discovery of ether, surgeons prided themselves on performing amputations in under three minutes. Tonight, mercifully, the logger would be spared such agony.

Within the hour, all the preparations were complete. A sponge soaked with ether had been used to render the lumberjack unconscious. On Jennifer's command, Rosa stretched the skin tight on his pelvis and applied pressure to shut off the femoral artery. Jennifer selected a scalpel from the instrument tray and leaned forward over the man's thigh. Her incision was made through healthy tissue some four inches above the compound fracture. One circular cut of the scalpel opened the leg from the inner thigh to the outer thigh.

Working swiftly, Jennifer separated the tissue and cut through the outer leg muscles. She performed retraction and then incised the deeper muscles attached to the large femur bone. With the scalpel, she carefully separated muscle from bone, to a point three inches above the incision.

After applying a linen retractor, she sliced through the tough membrane surrounding the bone. Grasping the leg in one hand, she next sawed through the bone with a small surgical saw. A stroke of the scalpel at last detached the mangled leg.

Jennifer quickly tied off the arteries with thread ligature. She then cut the nerves, allowing them to retract, and sponged the surgical wound with sterilized water. Drying her hands, she delicately quilted the large muscle flaps over the truncated bone. The skin flaps were cut long and sutured loosely, forming a bag to allow for postoperative swelling and drainage. Stepping back, she reviewed the procedure and found nothing left undone. She concluded by wrapping the stump with sterile bandage.

The logger's breathing and pulse were normal. Jennifer instructed Rosa to bundle the severed leg and prepare it for burial. After removing her surgical apron, she moved through the door to the waiting room. Devlin and his men jumped to their feet.

"Everything went fine," Jennifer said. "I prefer to keep him here overnight. We'll move him to the hotel tomorrow."

Devlin nodded somberly. "How long will he be laid up?"

"At least a month, perhaps longer. After that, he'll be able to get around on crutches."

"Tough luck, him gettin' caught that way. Things can sure go haywire fast."

"Actually, he's quite fortunate, Mr. Devlin. Any man who cheats death can afford to lose a leg."

"You're right there, ma'am. Six feet under would've made a poor second choice."

Devlin and his men departed, thanking her profusely. Jennifer dismissed the cook for the night and proceeded toward the rear of the house. She found Blake seated in the parlor, the aroma of his pipe a relief from the smells of the operating room. He poured her a brandy and she dropped wearily into a chair. Surgery always left her depleted but strangely exhilarated. Her face was flushed with excitement.

"Quite a night," Blake commented. "Although not exactly what I'd planned."

"Oh?" Jennifer said, sipping her brandy. "What was that?"

"Maybe you're not up to another surprise so soon."

"You really are terrible. Don't be a tease—tell me!"

"You insist?"

"Yes, for goodness' sake. I insist."

Blake pulled a small box from his jacket pocket. He presented it to her without ceremony or explanation. A slight smile played at the corner of his mouth as he watched her open the lid. Inside, nestled in cotton, was a simple gold wedding band.

Jennifer thought the gesture was so like him. No words of endearment or glowing speeches. Nothing of the impassioned declaration considered to be customary when a man proposed marriage. And his timing, only minutes after she'd finished surgery, was exquisitely unromantic. All in all, it seemed rather informal, almost mundane.

Staring at the ring, Jennifer realized that some hours weigh against a whole lifetime. With Blake, there would be nothing of the great love shared by her mother and father. He was warm and comfortable, infinitely gentle, but he would kindle no fires. Still, he was a professional man, educated and intelligent, at ease with her devotion to medicine. While it was not the stuff of dreams, it was nonetheless a practical match. Nowhere was it written that husband and wife had to be lovers.

She looked up with a melancholy smile. "Am I to assume you're proposing marriage?"

"Nothing less," Blake said with a graveled chuckle. "You'd honor me by becoming my wife."

"Since I'm hardly the coy type—I accept."

Blake set his pipe in an ashtray. He rose, taking her hand, and lifted her from her chair. He tilted her chin and kissed her with considerably more ardor than she expected. His gaze was warm with affection.

"I'll make you a good husband, Jen. You won't regret it."

She merely nodded, somehow touched by his sincerity. Her eyes misted with what she hoped was happiness.

TWELVE

On the last day of April, Elizabeth arrived in Santa Fe. She was accompanied by John Taylor, who had long ago learned to interpret the warning signs. Her mood was anything but cordial.

Their train ride north had been spent in glum silence. Elizabeth was carrying a letter from Ira Hecht, and the contents had cast a cloud over her normally sunny disposition. She was upset and angry, and clearly spoiling for a fight. Her eyes blazed with quiet fury.

Apart from Hecht's letter, she was burdened with personal problems. Her concern for Clint's safety had mounted alarmingly over the past three weeks. He was working alone and reportedly scouring the countryside for Miguel Ortega. She feared some harm might befall him in the *mexicano* villages, for Ortega's followers were now everywhere. Fanatics all too often justified unconscionable deeds in the name of a cause. And a lawman, traveling alone, was easily killed.

Ortega, though hardly a personal concern, was nonetheless a constant worry. Never in her wildest dreams could she have imagined how easily he would inflame the *mexicanos*. Starting with the raid on Homer Stockton's ranch, *Las Gorras Blancas* had swept through Lincoln County like a marauding horde. From the Rio Felix in the south, to the Rio Bonito in the north, scarcely a night passed without some act of violence. A guerrilla campaign, directed at Anglos, recalled the days of the Apache wars.

True to his word, Ortega had not ventured into the Hondo Valley. So far as Elizabeth knew, he'd made no effort to organize the *mexicanos* who lived there. A curious peace, as though centered in the eye of the storm, had settled over the basin. Yet people talked, and there were widespread rumors about her meeting with Ortega. The gossip troubled her, for embattled Anglos were certain to believe the worst. However false, it was being whispered that she had made a pact with the leader of *Las Gorras Blancas*. A secretive deal to spare the ranchlands of Spur from retribution.

Uptown, Elizabeth ordered the hack driver to stop at the hotel. Taylor took their bags into the lobby and left them with the desk clerk. Normally, upon arriving in Santa Fe, Elizabeth insisted on freshening up and changing her clothes. Her departure from routine merely confirmed Taylor's earlier appraisal. She was definitely on the warpath.

From the hotel, they drove directly to Hecht's office. Elizabeth stepped down hardly before the coach rolled to a stop. While Taylor settled with the driver, she marched through the door like a gunnery sergeant on parade. Hecht looked up and seemed to wince as she approached his desk. She pulled his letter from her pocketbook.

"I'd like an explanation of this, Ira."

"Elizabeth, please," Hecht said mildly. "Have a seat and we'll discuss it. There's no need to get yourself exercised."

"No need!" she echoed. "I demand to know what's behind it. And don't you dare try to placate me."

Hecht glanced past her as Taylor entered the office. He lifted his hands in a bemused shrug. "John, would you ask her to calm down? We need our wits about us."

Taylor dropped into a chair. "She's been building up a head of steam ever since we left Lincoln. You might as well let her sound off."

"Stop it!" Elizabeth demanded. "I won't be treated like some dithering female."

Hecht waved a hand. "Then I suggest you get hold of your temper. We'll never get anywhere shouting at one another."

Elizabeth sat down. She tossed the letter on his desk. "Very well," she said, "no more shouting. Now, I'll have an explanation."

"We lost," Hecht said simply. "Our lobbyist ran into a stone wall. The mood in Washington has turned pro-American."

"*Mexicanos* are American. The Treaty of Guadalupe Hidalgo awarded them unconditional citizenship. Any fool knows that!"

"I have to disagree. First off, the *mexicanos* have never considered themselves American. They still look upon Anglos as an occupying army."

"And rightly so," Elizabeth said indignantly. "They've been cheated and hoodwinked for the last thirty years."

"No argument there," Hecht agreed. "But the fact remains, they've refused to assimilate, work within the system. *Las Gorras Blancas* merely underscores their resistance to change."

"Perhaps it reflects the shoddy treatment they've received. By and large, they haven't been made to feel like equals."

"Look at it from the other side. Washington sees them as troublemakers, an obstacle to progress."

"Are you defending that attitude?"

"No," Hecht said quickly. "I'm trying to explain why we lost. A speech President Cleveland made last week was widely reported in the newspapers. He said, and I quote, 'We will not allow anarchists to prevail in New Mexico Territory.'"

"Anarchists?" Elizabeth repeated in a low voice. "Does anyone seriously believe they're trying to overthrow the government?"

"Apparently so," Hecht said in disgust. "The bill has been introduced to establish a land-claims court. Our lobbyist informs me Congress will pass it by an overwhelming margin."

"Legalized larceny," Elizabeth said hotly. "By court order, the *mexicanos* will be robbed of their land."

"Not necessarily," Hecht advised her. "Since I wrote you, I've been doing a lot of thinking. I believe there's a way to stymie the landgrabbers."

"Well, don't just sit there—tell me!"

Hecht proposed a masterful gambit. By law, a settler who homesteaded land was granted valid title after five years. His plan was to petition the federal district court on behalf of the *mexicanos*. The court would be asked to rule that a native New Mexican was entitled to equal protection under the law. He would request that a *mexicano* with ten years' occupancy be awarded clear and unencumbered title to the land. The key to the petition was in doubling the customary five-year time requirement. No court would casually reject such a reasonable request.

"Ira"—Elizabeth laughed aloud—"that's brilliant!"

"Thank you," Hecht said modestly. "I believe it might just work. The court would be under heavy pressure to grant a favorable ruling. To do otherwise would smack of outright prejudice."

Elizabeth stared at him a moment, her expression pensive. When she spoke, her tone was crisp and incisive. "As it happens, I've had my thinking cap on too. I've devised a plan that could—and I stress 'could'—give us control of the legislature."

"Good God," Hecht moaned. "I'm almost afraid to ask. What've you concocted now?"

"I intend to call a convention of all the *mexicano* leaders."

"You're joking."

"I never joke about politics."

Elizabeth went on to explain her idea. She would summon the *ricos,* the *jefes,* and the young *políticos* to a convention on neutral ground. There, with all the warring factions in one room, she would hammer out an accord based on mutual self-interest. The goal would be to win control of the legislature in the upcoming fall elections. By defeating the Santa Fe Ring at the polls, her coalition would then dominate affairs in New Mexico. Central to the success of the plan was the abrasive attitude of Governor Edmund Ross. His hostility toward *Las Gorras Blancas* represented an opportunity to mobilize the *mexicano* vote throughout the territory.

"Sounds good," Hecht said tentatively, "but you'll have a deuce of a time getting them together in one room. Nobody trusts anybody in that bunch."

"Oh, they'll show up," Elizabeth assured him. "Anyone who doesn't would risk being cut out of the arrangement. I guarantee a packed house."

Hecht nodded, reflective a moment. "Assuming you pull it off, I foresee two problems. One has to do with Miguel Ortega."

"What about him?"

"A rumor is circulating, and it's taken on vicious overtones. You're accused of forming an alliance with Ortega to further your own political goals."

"That's a despicable lie!"

"I'm sorry to say, it gets worse."

"How could it possibly get worse?"

Hecht took off his glasses. He wiped them with a handkerchief, avoiding her eyes. "People are whispering that it's more than a political alliance. They say you and Ortega are personally involved—a liaison . . . lovers."

Elizabeth flushed angrily. "How dare anyone say that? I've only met the man one time! I hardly know him."

"I don't have to tell you"—Hecht paused, fixed the spectacles on his nose—"politics is a dirty game. Canby and his crowd started the rumor to smear you and destroy your credibility. A *gringa* involved with a *mexicano* makes for juicy gossip."

"And if I deny it, that merely lends credence to the lie. I can't win either way."

Taylor cleared his throat. "I could always pay a call on Mr. Canby. That'd stop it muy damn pronto."

"No," Hecht said sharply. "We can't afford even a hint of violence. If anything, that would fuel the rumor."

Elizabeth nodded agreement. "You mentioned two problems. What's the other one?"

"A *mexicano* convention," Hecht pointed out, "will play

right into Canby's hands. For openers, he'll use it as a fright tactic with Anglos. People will be led to believe it's a show of support for *Las Gorras Blancas*."

"And—?" Elizabeth arched an eyebrow in question. "There's something more, isn't there?"

"I'm afraid so," Hecht said dolefully. "Canby will use the convention to buttress the story about you and Ortega. He'll claim it's proof positive that you've fallen for a *mexicano* revolutionary."

Elizabeth shook her head. "Hold the convention and sully my reputation forever. Is that what you're saying?"

"Something along those lines."

"Or forget the convention and abandon any hope of a true coalition. Isn't that the alternative?"

"Yes, I suppose it is."

"Then the choice is really quite simple. We'll proceed with plans for the convention."

Until today, Elizabeth had kept her personal life separated from politics. But now, forced to confront a harsh truth, she saw that the rules had been altered. Dirty innuendo, and character assassination, were the new order of things.

She vowed Thomas Canby would pay dearly for resorting to gutter tactics.

"Get the lead outta your pants!"

Chunk Devlin glowered fearsomely. The lumberjacks working to fell a tree put more muscle behind their axes. Wood chips flew as the thunk of steel on timber increased to a drumlike tattoo. The sound echoed distantly through the forest.

Morg was a tolerated observer. Twice a week he visited the logging camp, ostensibly to inspect the operation. But there was unspoken agreement between himself and his timber boss. Devlin brooked no interference, and he allowed no one, not even the owner, to tell him his business. He ran the camp with the autocratic manner of a feudal lord.

All things considered, Morg found no reason to object. The logging camp had been in operation exactly one month.

In that time, Devlin and his men had already cut a wide swath through the forest of ponderosa pines. The amount of timber delivered to the sawmill far exceeded anything Morg might have expected. He estimated the investment would begin to show a profit by early September, months ahead of schedule. His judgment of Chunk Devlin thus far seemed faultless.

Adding further to the profits was the lumber operation. Morg had contracted with freighters to haul the finished lumber from the sawmill. Working through brokers and lumberyards, he'd arranged to market his own timber. A swing through Lincoln County had resulted in steady orders from the mining camps, as well as the Pecos Valley settlements. By contracting for the freighting, he had eliminated the investment in payroll and equipment. The profit was quick and substantial, nearly forty cents on the dollar.

Apart from the financial aspects of the business, Morg was intrigued by life in a logging camp. He found the lumberjacks similar in many ways to cowhands. Their home was a crude bunkhouse, with rough tables, benches, and a potbellied stove. Every morning at five o'clock they were rousted out of their bunks, and by sunup they were in the woods. Their workday was sunrise to sundown.

The actual logging seemed to Morg a form of organized chaos. The men who chopped down the trees were called "fallers." Working in two-man teams, the fallers first sliced into a towering ponderosa with a long crosscut saw. Then, using double-bitted axes, they chopped away at a forty-five-degree angle to create the undercut. Essentially the undercut weakened a tree at the base and determined which direction it would fall. The crosscut saw was then used to cut through the trunk from the opposite side. Heavy metal wedges, pounded home with wooden mallets, were next driven into the back cut. When the tree began to topple, the cry of *"Timber!"* rang out through the forest.

Once on the ground, a ponderosa was sawed into sixteen-foot lengths by the "buckers." A heavy chain, known as a choker, was then worked under and around the log, and hooked tight. The next step was to fasten the choker to steel cables which ran to a donkey engine. Mounted on a platform, the wood-burning engine was geared to a winchlike drum and created herculean power. Hissing and belching cinders, the donkey engine reeled in the cables and snaked the log out of the woods. At the loading platform, usually situated on a downslope, the logs were rolled onto the bed of a wagon. From there, the teamsters hauled the logs to the sawmill at San Patricio.

The work was grueling and dangerous, hard on men and animals. The lumberjack who had lost his leg was by no means an isolated case. Yet the logging crew willingly accepted the risks, for they were paid double the wages earned by a cowhand. By day's end, when they trudged back to the bunkhouse, scarcely a man among them had escaped without some sort of injury. After supper, they gathered around the stove, smoking and drinking coffee, for stronger stimulants were barred from a logging camp. On the stroke of ten, the lamps were doused and the men crawled into their bunks. At the crack of dawn, the brutal grind started all over again.

Today, standing at the loading platform, Morg watched as the last log was rolled onto a wagon. Heavy chains were cinched around the load, securing the logs for the bone-jarring trip out of the mountains. Devlin approached as the teamster popped the reins and the massive draft horses strained into the traces. He halted beside Morg.

"Well, now," he said in his booming voice. "Are you satisfied with what you've seen?"

"No complaints," Morg said, a pleased look on his face. "You run a tight operation."

Devlin's rumbling laugh sounded like distant artillery. "God's blood!" he said in high good humor. "We're not slackers, me and my timber monkeys. We aim to earn the bonus you promised."

"From the looks of things, that won't be any problem. You're already ahead of schedule."

"And gaining speed," Devlin bragged. "We gonna cost you a pisspot full of money. You mark my word."

Morg smiled, his judgment again reaffirmed. At the outset, he'd allowed Devlin to establish a production quota for the first six months. Then, increasing that figure by half, he had promised foreman and crew a month's extra wages if the new goal were met. The upshot was a gang of lumberjacks who worked like they owned part of the company.

Thinking on it now, he decided to let Devlin gloat on the deal. A pisspot full of money seemed a small price to pay.

Far in the distance, thunderheads roiled over the mountains. Bolts of lightning crackled across the sky, then flashed down to strike the earth. There was a smell of rain in the air.

Morg rode into San Patricio through the gathering dusk. The sawmill was closed for the night and he dismounted outside Harry Tipton's house. Through the window, he saw the movement of shadows against lamplight. He rapped on the door.

Tipton greeted him warmly. "Well, Morg, where'd you drop from? We unloaded your last wagon just before quitting time."

"Yeah, I know," Morg said, moving into the parlor. "I met them on the road headed back to camp."

"Have you had supper? The missus oughta have it on the table any minute now. We'd be proud to have you stay."

"Thanks anyway, Harry. I just stopped by on my way home. You got a minute to talk?"

"Why, sure," Tipton said, motioning him to a chair. "What's on your mind?"

Morg took a seat, his hat hooked over one knee. "Saw Chunk today," he said. "Way it looks, I'll have to put on another wagon. They're dropping timber like there's no tomorrow."

"I'll vouch for that. Your boys keep me hoppin'."

"Guess that's why I'm here. I figure we'll double our output by the end of September. You reckon you'll be able to handle the extra work?"

A sudden frown creased Tipton's brow. "I dunno about that, Morg. Not that I wouldn't like the business, you understand . . ."

His voice trailed off and Morg studied his downcast features. "What's the trouble, Harry?"

"Ralph McQuade," Tipton said in an aggrieved tone. "We had ourselves a few choice words. He wants me to stop milling your timber."

Morg laughed shortly. "I hope you told him where to shove it."

"I didn't tell him yea or nay. McQuade's not the sort of man you wanna cross."

"Hell, he's all wind," Morg said with a bluff air of assurance. "Lots of talk and no action."

Tipton's eyes narrowed. "You don't know him like I do. I told you before, he's got a mean streak."

"If he's so tough, why doesn't he pay me a call? I'm the one taking his business."

"'Cause he knows I scare easier. And I have to tell you, I'm plenty goddamn worried. He put me on warning."

"What's that supposed to mean?"

"Told me all kinds of accidents could happen around a sawmill. Laughed and called 'em 'manmade' accidents."

"Maybe I ought to have a talk—"

Morg suddenly stopped. He cocked one ear, as though listening, and quieted Tipton with an upraised palm. The thud of hoofbeats swelled until the sound seemed to fill the room. Before either of them could move, a solid wedge of horsemen pounded across the yard and rode toward the sawmill. One of the riders carried a blazing torch.

Tipton bounded from his chair, followed closely by Morg. At the window, they watched as some thirty horsemen reined to a halt before the sawmill. One of the riders rapped out a muffled command and several others rode forward with corked bottles. Arms drawn back, they hurled the bottles at a mountainous stack of timbers and piles of finished lumber. The bottles shattered in a *pop-pop-pop* of glistening liquid.

"Jesus Christ!" Tipton yelped. "That's kerosene in them bottles. They're gonna burn me out."

Morg stepped to the door and jerked it open. He started outside, drawing his pistol as he moved through the doorway. In the flare of torchlight, he dimly registered that all the riders were masked with strips of white cloth. The leader spotted him and barked an order. He realized the man had spoken in Spanish.

Wheeling their horses, several riders opened fire with pistols. Slugs pocked the walls of the house and splintered the doorframe all around Morg. Even as he ducked and spun back inside the house, it crossed his mind that they weren't trying to kill him. The shots had bracketed him instead, warning him off. He kicked the door shut.

The rider with the torch tossed it onto the timbers. A roaring *whoosh* of light illuminated the night with fiery brilliance. The flames spread from the timbers to the piles of lumber and the storage yard was abruptly transformed into a crackling inferno. Spurring his horse, the leader motioned to his men. His voice was raised in a jubilant shout.

"Vámonos, muchachos! Vámonos!"

The horsemen formed into a broad phalanx and thundered off into the night. Morg eased the door open as the hoofbeats faded into the distance. Staring at the towering flames, it occurred to him that the raiders hadn't attempted to torch the sawmill itself. Their objective, instead, was the finished lumber and timbers for the mining companies. A blow directed at Anglo business interests rather than Harry Tipton.

Who they were, and what they called themselves, was never in question. Morg silently repeated the name to himself.

Las Gorras Blancas.

THIRTEEN

*L*as Gorras Blancas struck again the following night. At a ranch east of Lincoln, the raiders destroyed a stretch of barbed-wire fence and stampeded nearly a thousand cows. When they rode off, two men were left dead.

The ranch was located on the Rio Bonito, not far from the juncture with the Rio Hondo. After the fences were cut, and the cattle stampeded, the night raiders swept into the main compound. Their intent, as in previous raids was to burn down the outbuildings. For the first time, they met with armed resistance.

A wakeful cowhand rushed out of the bunkhouse. He opened fire with a saddle carbine just as an equipment shed went up in flames. One of the raiders pitched to the ground and the others instantly returned fire. The cowhand was blown off his feet, riddled with slugs. Before the White Caps could recover their fallen comrade, they came under general fire from the men in the bunkhouse. Their leader ordered retreat rather than fight a pitched battle.

Early next morning, the dead men were brought into Lincoln. The cowhand and the *mexicano* raider were laid out side-by-side in the back of a wagon. A crowd gathered around as the wagon rolled to a halt in front of the courthouse. Summoned from his office, Sheriff Will Grant pulled back the tarpaulin covering the bodies. Several onlookers recognized the *mexicano* and made positive identification. The dead men were then taken to the funeral parlor.

An hour or so later Clint rode into Lincoln. About the same time yesterday, he'd been notified of the raid on Tipton's Sawmill. On the chance he might uncover a lead, he had ridden out to San Patricio. There, after a long talk with Harry Tipton, he had remarked that it was the old story of "same song, second verse." The raiders were masked, and always struck at night, and no one had yet been able to identify a member of *Las Gorras Blancas*. He saw no reason to waste time questioning Morg.

One thing, however, left him intrigued. According to Tipton, the raiders could have easily killed Morg. Instead, they had peppered the doorway with gunfire and driven him back into the house. Clint wondered whether they had known it was Elizabeth Brannock's son. That would have accounted for their actions, for Miguel Ortega had promised her no harm would come to Spur. Still, even if it were true, it raised yet another question. How had they known Morg was inside Tipton's house at the precise moment of the raid? Since Morg had dropped by unannounced, it hardly made sense.

From San Patricio, Clint had attempted to track the raiders. Their trail led west along the Rio Hondo for a distance of some four miles. At that point, the riders had scattered to the winds, hoofprints leading in every direction. On a hunch, Clint had followed the trail of two men headed deeper into the mountains. But then, shortly before dark, the tracks had disappeared along a rocky stretch of terrain. Far from town, he had made camp near the headwaters of the river. He'd spent the night huddled in his rain slicker, waking often to feed a small fire.

The ride back to Lincoln had been a time of sober reflection. Almost four weeks had passed since he'd undertaken the investigation. Searching for a lead, he had visited half a dozen villages, questioning the local *jefes*. To a man, they had proved disinclined to talk about *Las Gorras Blancas*. Whether from fear or loyalty, their answers were politely evasive, revealing nothing. Nor had his luck improved when he'd broadened the search to the scene of the raids. By the time he arrived at the far-flung ranches, the trail was cold and the night riders had vanished into the hills. To date, he hadn't uncovered so much as a trace of Miguel Ortega.

In town, Clint rode directly to the livery stable. Hardly before he'd stepped off his horse, the livery owner began regaling him with the news of last night's raid. His interest quickened when he heard that one of the dead men was a White Cap, a local *mexicano*. He cut short the stable owner's windy report and hurried downstreet toward the courthouse. In his opinion, Will Grant was a poor excuse for a lawman, and practically worthless as an investigator. But the dead *mexicano* gave him a quick lift in spirits. A corpse sometimes told a tale that led elsewhere.

Grant was on his way out the door. "Well, I'll be jiggered," he said, spotting Clint. "I was hopin' you'd show up. Have you heard the news?"

"Just now," Clint replied. "Who's the dead Mexican?"

"A no-account by the name of Bonifacio Pérez. I'm not surprised he got himself killed."

"And you're sure he's a member of *Las Gorras Blancas*?"

"No question a'tall," Grant said jovially. "Sorry bastard got shot right off his horse. Wearin' a white mask, too."

Clint nodded. "What do you know about him?"

"Nothin' special," Grant allowed. "I arrested him a couple of times for drunk-and-disorderly, and once for startin' a knife fight. Him and his family farmed a little plot just outside town."

"Was he married?"

"Nope," Grant said. "Got a brother and sister, though. All of 'em lived with the mother."

"What happened to his father?"

"Passed away a year or so ago."

"Where's their house?" Clint asked. "I'd like to talk with his family."

"Just come on with me," Grant said. "I sent word for 'em to meet me at the undertaker's."

Grant was a tall ferret of a man, loose and rangy. He strode down the street looking rather pleased with himself. Since Clint had arrived in town, he'd been playing second fiddle in the *Las Gorras Blancas* investigation. Today his shoulders were squared and his stride was almost military. He acted like a man who had resumed charge of important matters.

The undertaker greeted them with glum reserve. They were shown into the viewing parlor, where two coffins were arranged on low platforms. The bodies were covered to the chin with blankets, for neither of them had yet been prepared for burial. The cowhand looked somehow surprised, as though he'd met death without sufficient warning. The *mexicano* looked curiously stern, almost angry.

Señora Pérez stood beside the coffin of her son. With her was her daughter, a young girl no more than sixteen. They both wore black *rebozos* over their heads, and the girl's eyes were red from crying. The mother appeared stoic, her features drained of emotion. Her lips moved in silent prayer as she fingered a rosary.

Grant and Clint removed their hats. They exchanged a glance and Clint nodded toward the women. Señora Pérez continued fingering her beads as the lawmen moved closer. The girl kept her eyes on the floor.

"Excuse the intrusion," Grant said in halting Spanish. "We're here on official business, *señora*. We have to ask you some questions about your son."

The woman's fingers stopped. She clutched the rosary in both hands, her expression resigned. When she made no reply, Grant went on. "Were you aware your son was a member of *Las Gorras Blancas*?"

"*No,*" Señora Pérez said without inflection. "Bonifacio kept such matters to himself."

"He never explained where he went?"

"Never."

"How many times was he away at night?"

"Often," Señora Pérez said vaguely. "I did not count the times."

Grant studied her with a calm judicial gaze. "The truth, *señora*. You knew he was attending meetings, didn't you?"

"He told me nothing and I knew nothing."

"Did he mention any names? Other men who were involved?"

Señora Pérez shook her head. "Bonifacio never spoke of his affairs, and I did not ask. I preferred not to know."

With an unpleasant grunt, the sheriff motioned at the coffin. "Your son was killed in a raid on *americanos*. Do you deny any knowledge of the men he rode with?"

"I have already denied it, *señor*. I know nothing."

Clint edged a step closer. His features were sphinxlike, but he spoke with steady authority, iron sureness. "A final question, *señora*," he said. "I believe you have another son, *verdad*?"

"*Sí.*"

"What is his name?"

"Florentino."

"Why isn't he here to honor his dead brother? Doesn't that seem strange?"

Señora Pérez fidgeted, suddenly uncomfortable. "I cannot answer for Florentino."

"Where is he today?"

"I do not know."

Clint fixed her with a pale stare. "Was he with his brother last night?"

"*Sí.*"

"And he returned home, told you of Bonifacio's death. Isn't that true?"

Her eyes puddled with tears. Clint waited a moment, then resumed the questioning. "I am an officer of the law, *señora*. You must not lie, even to protect your son. Where is he now?"

Señora Pérez looked down at the rosary in her hands. Her voice dropped to a whisper. "After we talked, he took a few clothes and some food. He rode away."

"Where?" Clint demanded. "He wouldn't leave home without telling you."

There was a beat of oppressive silence. Señora Pérez finally lifted her head, met his gaze. "I have nothing more to say, *señor*. I will not betray my son."

"None of that," Grant blustered. "You speak up or I'll have to arrest you. We're conducting a murder investigation."

"Let it go," Clint said, turning toward the door. "She's told us all we're likely to hear."

Grant sputtered something under his breath. He glowered at the woman, then reluctantly followed Clint through the door. Outside they paused on the street and Grant crammed his hat on his head. He shot Clint a dirty look.

"You shouldn't've cut me off like that. I'm supposed to be the law around here."

Clint ignored the remark. "Any idea where the Pérez boy might've gone?"

"Why, hell, yes!" Grant flung an arm in a wild gesture. "He's off hidin' somewheres with Miguel Ortega. Find one and you'll find the other."

"I don't think so," Clint said slowly. "Ortega wouldn't keep anybody around who's been identified. I figure he sent Pérez packing for parts unknown."

Grant beamed like a trained bear. "By God, you just gimme the answer. I know where he's at!"

"Where?"

"Socorro," Grant said importantly. "One of their cousins moved over there last fall. Heard he went to work in the mines."

"Would he stick his neck out for a wanted man?"

"Jee—rusalem, would he ever! Them boys was always thicker'n fleas."

"What's the cousin's name?"

"Ummm—" Grant concentrated hard, suddenly laughed. "Aguilar. Luis Aguilar!"

Clint quickly assessed the situation. His one solid lead thus far was Florentino Pérez. And through Pérez, he might yet untangle the web of secrecy surrounding Miguel Ortega. The option was to hang around Lincoln and continue to hope for a break. Which seemed to him no option at all. He looked at Grant.

"I'll need descriptions of both men—Pérez and Aguilar."

Grant bobbed his head. "I take it you're headed for Socorro."

"Yeah," Clint said with a clenched smile. "Maybe it'll
change my luck."

"What d'you want me to do while you're away?"

"Just what you've been doing, Will."

Grant wasn't sure how to take the remark. Up till now he'd
done nothing, and that made it sound like an insult. On the
other hand, he had just provided a hot lead to the whereabouts
of Florentino Pérez. He decided the latter version made the
better story. One he would quietly spread around town.

A sheriff always had to keep one eye trained on the next
election.

Socorro was located on the banks of the upper Rio Grande.
An established mining town, it was the county seat and a
widely renowned hellhole. Local boosters proudly claimed
forty-four saloons and a dozen round-the-clock cathouses.
The sporting crowd, much like the miners, worked double
shifts.

Clint rode into town in the early forenoon. His trip had
consumed three days, covering more than a hundred miles.
A good part of that time had been spent in crossing the Jor-
nada del Muerto. Aptly named, it was a wasteland of alka-
line waterholes and slow death for the unwary traveler.
Fording the Rio Grande seemed a deliverance of sorts.

Oscar Packard was the county sheriff. When Clint entered his office, the rawboned lawman jackknifed to his feet.
He pumped Clint's arm vigorously, genuinely delighted to
see him. In the old days, when Clint was a special agent for
the army, they had often worked together. Packard was still
sheriff, and that fact alone commanded respect. A lesser
man wouldn't have lasted in Socorro's rough, and sometimes deadly, sporting district.

After lighting a cigarette, Clint told his story straight
through. He had a warrant for Florentino Pérez; but he first
had to find the cousin, Luis Aguilar. Packard listened without interruption or comment, nodding to himself. While the

White Caps had not yet organized in Socorro, he kept abreast of their activities elsewhere. He was eager to assist a fellow lawman.

When Clint finished, there was a moment's silence. Packard tilted back in his chair, hands steepled, and tapped his forefingers together. Finally he leaned forward, elbows on the desk.

"Lots of Mexicans in Socorro," he said, "and they stick to themselves. We need somebody who knows his way around."

Clint flicked an ash off his cigarette. "You got someone in mind?"

"Just the man." Packard swiveled toward the door. "Baca! Elfego Baca. C'mon in here."

A *mexicano* appeared from the outer office. He was a stocky, broad-shouldered man with quick eyes and a neatly trimmed mustache. He paused in the doorway, the badge of a deputy sheriff pinned to his shirt. Packard waved him forward and performed introductions. Baca shook Clint's hand with a firm strong grasp.

"An honor," he said, smiling. "Your name is known to all lawmen."

"A pleasure to meet you," Clint said. "I recollect your name's not unknown either."

The offhand compliment was an understatement. In 1884, Baca had arrested a drunken cowhand in a village west of Socorro. Taken before a justice of the peace, the prisoner was fined five dollars and released. When Baca emerged from the courtroom, he was met by a rowdy bunch of cowhands, angered that a *mexicano* had arrested their friend. A shot was fired, and Baca ducked into an alley.

With the crowd on his heels, Baca took refuge in a *jacal* constructed of mud and posts. Led by two ranchers, the mob quickly swelled to eighty armed cowhands. They opened fire and Baca hugged the floor, which was slightly below ground level. He held them off for a day and a half, popping up to return their fire with deadly accuracy. When the siege finally ended, he had killed four men and wounded several others.

Since then, Baca's reputation had proved a deterrent in itself. No one cared to tangle with a man who would dare any odds.

"Got a job for you," Packard said now. "Clint's after a member of *Las Gorras Blancas*. The charge is murder."

"Those *bastardos*," Baca cursed. "They dirty the name of all *mexicanos*. I'm at your service, Señor Brannock."

Clint briefly outlined the situation. When he mentioned the men's names, there was no reaction. But then, after remarking that Aguilar worked in the mines, he noted a change in Baca's expression. The *mexicano* deputy looked thoughtful.

"I know that *hombre*," he said. "I've seen him around the *cantinas*. He works the day shift at one of the mines."

"Any idea which one?"

"No," Baca said, then chuckled slyly. "But he has an adobe just outside town. I've heard he's married, three or four children."

Clint considered a moment. "Have you heard anything about Pérez?"

"Nothing."

"Guess we don't have a helluva lot of choice. We'll have to sit on Aguilar's house and hope we get lucky."

Baca laughed, spread his hands. "We wait like the spider, eh? Let him come to us."

"Yeah," Clint said with a hard grin. "Except we have to trap him, not kill him. I want him alive."

"What if he decides to fight?"

"We'll just have to talk him out of it, Elfego. He's no good to me dead."

"*Sangre de Cristo*! I think it will be an interesting night."

A livid moon hung suspended in a black sky. The landscape appeared ghostly, flooded in a bluish, spectral light. Somewhere in the distance an owl hooted faintly.

Clint and Baca were posted on top a hogback ridge. Soon after dark they had left their horses in a gully beyond the reverse slope. For the past hour, seated in the shadow of an outcropping, neither of them had spoken. Their eyes were fixed on an adobe at the bottom of the hill.

The house was located three miles north of Socorro. Cottonwoods lined the banks of the Rio Grande, and a short distance upstream there was a stand of willows. The voices of children carried distinctly in the still night air. From time to time, the voice of a woman, loud and scolding, could be heard. So far, there had been nothing to indicate the presence of a man.

Clint suddenly tensed. He nudged Baca and pointed downstream. A shadowy figure appeared in the wash of moonlight, walking toward the house. As they watched, the figure took the shape of a man dressed in rough workclothes. Words were unnecessary, for they each read the other's thoughts. The man was Luis Aguilar, returning from a day in the mines.

The squeals of laughing children erupted as Aguilar entered the adobe. For a short while the sounds of excited voices carried to the top of the hill. Then the commotion dropped off and things inside the house gradually returned to normal. Some minutes later Aguilar appeared in the doorway. He put his fingers to his mouth and whistled a single sharp blast.

Upstream, a man emerged from the stand of willows. He walked swiftly toward the house, dimly visible in the dappled moonglow. As he approached closer, he was revealed in a shaft of lamplight spilling through the door. His head was bare, but he wore the *vaquero* garb favored by *mexicano* horsemen. Aguilar waved him inside and closed the door.

Clint felt certain there was a horse picketed in the willows. He was equally confident as to the identity of the man. From all appearances, Florentino Pérez hid out along the riverbank during the day. After dark, when his cousin signaled the all-clear, he came out for supper. Whether or not he spent the night in the house seemed a moot point. He was there now.

Quiet as drifting hawks, Clint and Baca made their way down the hill. Cautiously, their guns drawn, they approached a small window at the front of the house. A quick look confirmed that the entire family was seated around the supper table. Clint flattened himself against the wall directly beside the door. He nodded and Baca kicked it open.

There was an instant of dumbstruck silence. The woman sat at the far end of the table, a fork halfway to her mouth. Aguilar was at the head of the table, his back to the door, and Pérez was seated to his immediate right. Abruptly, the woman screamed and the three children shrieked in terror. Pérez bolted to his feet, his eyes glittering with a look of trapped desperation. He fumbled at the gun holstered on his hip, wheeling away from the table.

Clint crossed the room in two quick strides. His arm rose and fell as Pérez cleared leather. The pistol barrel struck Pérez high on the forehead with a mushy whump. His mouth opened in a soundless grunt and the gun fell from his hand. For a moment he stood rigid; then his eyes went blank and his knees buckled. He dropped like a stone.

From the door, Baca covered the room. His sights were trained on Aguilar, who had risen from his chair. Baca grinned and slowly motioned with his pistol. Aguilar obeyed the unspoken command, resuming his seat. Against the far wall, his wife was huddled with the children, holding them clutched in her arms. Their eyes gleamed dark and wide in the sallow lamplight.

Kneeling down, Clint scooped the gun off the floor and stuck it in his waistband. He then holstered his pistol and pulled a set of manacles from his hip pocket. A moment later he had Pérez's wrists secured, hands locked at the small of the back. He climbed to his feet glancing around at Baca.

"Gracias," he said. "You can back my play anytime."

"De nada," Baca said casually. "What will you do with him now?"

Clint smiled. "Teach him to sing the right tune."

"Perdón?"

"A songbird, *compadre*. Otherwise known as a turncoat."

FOURTEEN

The afternoon stage arrived late. Dusk had fallen over Lincoln as the driver sawed back on the reins. He brought his six-horse hitch to a stop outside the express office.

John Taylor hopped out of the coach. He assisted Elizabeth down and then collected their bags from the luggage boot. The other passengers, most of them bound for Roswell, stepped out to stretch their legs. Upstreet, the sound of laughter drifted from a saloon.

Elizabeth asked Taylor to meet her at the clinic. She knew he wanted a drink and felt reasonably certain he would stop by the saloon. Having fortified himself, he would then retrieve the buckboard and team from the livery stable. She allowed herself at least a half-hour before he would return.

The trip to Santa Fe had been exhaustive. Apart from the travel itself, Elizabeth hadn't rested properly. Her mind was like a whirligig, spinning round and round with too many projects. The *mexicano* convention, in particular, preoccupied her thoughts. Announcements had gone out to the *políticos,* but their response was still an unknown factor. She worried that some of them would refuse to attend.

The clinic was closed for the night. Elizabeth walked along a pathway to the rear, noting that lamps were lighted in the living quarters. Jennifer answered her knock with a look of surprise and a pleased laugh. They hugged, kissing

each other on the cheek, and moved into the parlor. When
Jennifer offered her supper, Elizabeth asked instead for a
cup of tea. The jouncing stagecoach had robbed her of her
appetite.

Jennifer put a pot of tea to steeping. She returned from
the kitchen and found her mother slumped in an armchair.
Neither of them spoke as she seated herself on the sofa. Her
eyebrows lifted in a slight frown.

"You look tired," she said. "You really should eat something."

"Oh, I will," Elizabeth said evasively. "I'll have a bit of
something when we get home."

"Why not spend the night here? From the way you act,
you could certainly use the rest."

"I prefer to sleep in my own bed. Besides, I've been away
almost a week. I have things to do at the ranch."

"I might as well tell you myself," Jennifer said after a moment. "You'll find out when you get home, anyway. There's
been a good deal of trouble while you were gone."

"What kind of trouble?"

Jennifer recounted the raid on Tipton's Sawmill. She
touched briefly on the shooting, commenting that *Las Gorras Blancas* had deliberately spared Morg's life. There
seemed no other explanation.

"And Morg's all right?" Elizabeth asked in a concerned
voice. "You're not hiding anything from me?"

"No, he's fine," Jennifer said. "Nothing bruised but his
pride."

"I—" Elizabeth hesitated, shook her head. "Apparently
Miguel Ortega is a man of his word. He said no harm would
come to anyone on Spur."

"Too bad the truce doesn't extend to everyone. There was
another raid the following night, and more shooting . . . two
men were killed."

Jennifer went on to relate the details. The cowhand and
the *mexicano,* Bonifacio Pérez, had been buried on the same
day. After securing a murder warrant, Clint had ridden off in

search of Pérez's brother. A rumor was circulating that his investigation centered on Socorro.

"Socorro?" Elizabeth repeated. "John and I came through there last night. We caught the morning stage."

Jennifer nodded. "Uncle Clint might have been staying in the same hotel. It's possible you missed him coming and going."

A troubled look settled over Elizabeth's face. "I worry about him more than you know. He's too old to be chasing around after outlaws."

"Well, it certainly doesn't show. He's been here, there, and yon the past month or so."

"That worries me too," Elizabeth said quietly. "Your Uncle Clint won't stop till he catches Miguel Ortega. Nothing good will come of it."

"Tell me, Mother—" Jennifer paused, one eyebrow raised. "Which do you worry about most?"

"Ortega," Elizabeth said with more truth than she intended. "Despite everything, he's a decent man. All he really wants is justice for his people."

"You admire him, don't you?"

"Yes, I do! And I'm not ashamed to admit it. He could have been a great leader . . ."

"But, instead, he's a wanted man," Jennifer finished the thought. "And you're afraid Uncle Clint will kill him."

"How else can it end?" Elizabeth said. "Ortega will never be taken alive. I saw it in his eyes the night we met."

Jennifer could think of nothing reassuring to say. She went to the kitchen and returned with an enameled teapot. Elizabeth accepted a steaming cup and took several quick sips. The hot tea seemed to revive her and she sat straighter in her chair. Her mood suddenly brightened.

"I've had enough depressing talk for one night. What's happening in your life?"

Jennifer shrugged. "Nothing all that extraordinary."

"You know very well I'm talking about Blake. Have you set a date?"

"As a matter of fact, we've decided on June twenty-first."

"Good!" Elizabeth said happily. "I've never believed in long betrothals. Your father and I were married a month after he proposed."

On the verge of replying, Jennifer's features clouded with a shadow of anxiety. Her expression was oddly unsettled, as though pulled back from a distant thought. A thought she couldn't bring herself to confront.

"When you married," she said softly, "were you in love with Father?"

"What a strange question." Elizabeth stared at her over the rim of the teacup. "Yes, I was very much in love. Why do you ask?"

Her reply was so quiet that Elizabeth had to strain to hear. "I don't love Blake," she said. "I respect him, and I'm terribly fond of him. But it isn't the way I always imagined . . ."

"Few things are," Elizabeth said calmly. "Our schoolgirl notions seldom live up to reality. We learn to compromise."

"Was Father a compromise?"

"No, not in the beginning. Quite soon, though, I discovered that marriage fell short of the dream. Hardly a day went by that I didn't compromise in some fashion."

Jennifer smiled wanly. "Perhaps it's easier to compromise when you love someone."

"Are you having second thoughts about marrying Blake?"

"I suppose I am. Wouldn't you, in my position?"

Elizabeth sighed inwardly. "Maybe you ought to call it off. You're still young and there'll be other men. You might even find one you love."

"Do you really believe that?"

"To be perfectly honest, I think you're already married. Your grand love affair is with medicine—not men."

"I know," Jennifer said. "That's why I accepted Blake's proposal."

"What are you saying?"

"Being a doctor will always come first in my life. I think Blake resigned himself to that a long time ago. Not many men could."

"Well then," Elizabeth remarked, "it seems you have a choice between love and an understanding husband. Which do you prefer?"

"Both," Jennifer said with a sudden sad grin. "But as you pointed out, life is a matter of compromise. So I guess I'll marry Blake."

"Why are we talking about it, then? You sound like your mind was made up all along."

"I just needed to hear myself say it out loud. Sometimes it's hard to accept until you actually admit it."

Elizabeth sensed a deeper conflict. Her daughter was a complex woman, and emotional problems were never resolved with oblique reasoning. Still, there was nothing to be gained in pressing beyond certain limits.

She decided to leave well enough alone.

The day began early on Spur. Spring roundup was underway and the hands rode out shortly after sunrise. By seven o'clock the compound was virtually deserted.

Elizabeth slept late. She awoke refreshed, her mind uncluttered with worries. Simply returning to Spur infused her with energy, for the ranch was her touchstone in life. She somehow drew strength from the land, an inner reservoir of certainty. All things seemed possible on the Hondo.

After fixing her hair, she laid out her clothes for the day. She planned to inspect the roundup and have a talk with Brad. Accordingly she selected a *charro* outfit with a short jacket and split skirt. She'd long ago put aside feminine modesty, as well as her old side saddle, when she mounted a horse. She often marveled that she hadn't done it sooner.

Entering the dining room, she found Morg and Louise still seated at the breakfast table. Morg leapt up, full of restless vitality, and kissed her on the cheek. She then exchanged kisses with Louise, who greeted her with considerably less warmth. Her daughter-in-law resented her, and she'd never been able to establish a comfortable relationship. She supposed it was the natural order of things when two women lived under the same roof. However inequitable, there was only one mistress of the house.

Elizabeth took her seat at the head of the table. A serving girl brought her usual breakfast of coffee, dry toast, and canned fruit. She noted that Morg and Louise had already eaten and appeared to be dawdling over a final cup of coffee. Her intuition told her that something was afoot, something that required her presence. She glanced down the table at Morg.

"Aren't you off to a late start this morning?"

"Figured you'd want a report," Morg said easily. "Lots of things have happened while you were away."

"So I heard," Elizabeth commented. "Jen told me you almost got yourself shot."

"I guess it was a close call. But like they say, close only counts in horseshoes."

"You're being awfully casual about it."

Louise sniffed and Morg darted her a look. When she dropped her eyes, he turned back to Elizabeth. "Got some good news," he said. "We'll turn a profit on the timber company by the end of September."

"That's marvelous," Elizabeth said, clearly impressed. "I never thought you'd do it so quickly."

"Tell you the truth, I'm a little surprised myself. 'Course, now that it's a going concern, we've got ourselves a real opportunity."

"How do you mean?"

"Way I see it," Morg said, "the timber business proves my point. It's time we branched out in a big way."

Elizabeth sipped her coffee. "Are you hinting at another venture of some sort?"

"Nothing else," Morg announced. "I'd like to take a crack at the mining game."

For a moment, Elizabeth was speechless. "Why mining?" she said finally. "Whatever put that idea in your head?"

"Things are booming over at White Oaks. I figure it's the chance of a lifetime."

Morg went on with mounting enthusiasm. His timber business had taken him to the towns of Nogal and White

Oaks. Located west of Lincoln, these were the principal mining camps in the distant mountains. Gold had been discovered there in the late 1870s; but the boom had faded as placer mines slowly played out. Technical advances now made it possible to follow the rich veins deep underground.

"The gold's there," Morg concluded, "but hard-rock mining costs money. Tunnels and equipment don't come cheap."

Elizabeth smiled gently. "What do you know about the mining business?"

"Not a whole lot," Morg conceded. "'Course, I was a greenhorn at the timber business too. It's a matter of finding the right man."

"Are you talking about a foreman?"

"What I had in mind was more on the order of a partner."

Morg quickly outlined his plan. There were many small mine owners around White Oaks who lacked capital. Constantly strapped for funds, they were unable to exploit the true value of their claims. He proposed to search out such an individual and offer to finance the operation. To bind the deal, a corporation would then be formed.

"We'll insist on control," Morg observed. "Divvy the stock fifty-one percent in our favor."

"Even so," Elizabeth said, "how would we know the money was being spent wisely? We've had no experience at mining."

A crafty look came over Morg's face. "Our partner will have to convince me day-by-day, nickel-by-nickel. Otherwise I'll hire an outside mining engineer."

"All that will take time," Elizabeth reminded him. "With the timber company, and the new mining venture, you'll have your hands full. Who's to look after things here at Spur?"

"Brad doesn't need any help. Let him run the ranch and I'll go on to other prospects. That way we've got our bets hedged all the way round."

Elizabeth shook her head wonderingly. She marked again that Morg was hauntingly like his father. As though an echo from the past, she recalled Virgil saying that a man's reach should always exceed his grasp. At length, she let out a deep breath.

"How much money do you need?"

Morg laughed. "Forty thousand ought to turn the trick. Fifty would guarantee it."

For a while longer they talked about the project. Elizabeth finally agreed, on condition that she be kept apprised of the details. After a final cup of coffee, she excused herself, all the more aware of the need to talk with Brad. She left the house and walked toward the stables.

When the front door closed, an uneasy quiet descended on the dining room. Louise suddenly looked wretched, her features pale and drawn. She stared across the table at Morg with an expression of disgust. There was a harried sharpness in her words.

"You were right after all," she said. "Your mother couldn't say no—she never says no!"

Morg was determined not to quibble. "She just knows a good deal when she hears one. Nothin' wrong with that."

"Wrong?" Her voice quivered with anger. "What's wrong is that you're always off tending to business. And this gold mine will just make it worse. I'm sick of it!"

"C'mon, Lou, don't get yourself upset. You knew I wasn't a homebody when we got married."

"I did not! I thought I married a rancher, not a businessman. Why can't you be like everyone else?"

"You always told me I was different from everyone else. I thought that's why you were sweet on me."

"Stop it!" Her eyes flooded with tears. "I won't be fobbed off with your silly jokes. It's not funny."

Morg heard the pain in her voice. He silently wished she'd hurry up and have the baby. But then, on quick reflection, he admitted she had a point. For the last few months his every waking thought had been devoted to business. He knew he hadn't been much of a husband.

On sudden impulse, Morg told her something he'd never told anyone else. His father had believed that nothing extraordinary was ever achieved without the ambition to dare

greatly. As a boy, he had watched his father transform a remote valley into a ranch envied by all cattlemen. Spur was
his father's legacy, the result of ambition and daring and
hard work. He felt honor-bound to build on that legacy,
rather than loaf along on what he'd inherited. Otherwise he
would be something less than his father's son.

"Don't you see, Lou," he said earnestly, "the ranch was Pa's
doing, his dream. I've got to make my mark my own way."

Louise dashed tears from her face with the back of her
hand. She knew he had revealed a secret part of himself,
something he'd kept locked inside since his father's death.
Even more, she realized he had told her out of feeling, a
sense of something shared. It was important to him that she
understand.

"Yes, I do see," she said in a hushed voice. "In a way, I
wish I didn't. It would be easier to stay mad at you."

Morg studied her a moment. "Does that mean you're not
mad anymore?"

She smiled an upside-down smile. "What good would it
do me? You aren't about to change, are you?"

"Would you want me to change?"

"Yes," she said with a bright little nod. "But I married you
for better or worse. I guess I'm stuck."

Morg grinned, rising from his chair. He moved around
the table and walked to her side. Tilting her chin, he kissed
her full on the mouth and held her close in his arms. When
they parted, his hand dropped from her face and playfully
rubbed the mound of her stomach. He chuckled softly, his
mouth brushing her ear.

"Tell the kid he'd better hurry. His daddy wasn't meant to
be a monk."

Four cowhands worked the branding fire. Off in the distance,
outriders circled a herd of shorthorns being held on a grassy
swale. Bawling calves were lassoed and dragged to the fire,
where they were thrown to the ground. The men on foot
quickly branded them and castrated the bull calves.

Elizabeth and Brad watched from a nearby knoll. She

was mounted on a *grulla* mare and Brad rode a sorrel cow-pony. Her inspection of the roundup had brought her to a holding ground not far from the southern foothills. There she'd found Brad checking one of the many branding operations on Spur.

For a time they discussed routine affairs. Brad planned to start the gather for trail herds within the week. Extra men, who drifted from one outfit to another during trailing season, had already been hired. By the end of the month, the first herd would be driven north toward the railhead. From there, the cows would be shipped to eastern slaughterhouses.

Brad foresaw no problems with the trail drives. While attentive to his report, Elizabeth was preoccupied with other thoughts. She'd known for some time that he might quit Spur to build his own outfit on the Rio Felix. Yet now, more than ever, she needed him to stay on as foreman. With Morg distracted by other business interests, she simply couldn't afford to lose Brad. She somehow had to ensure his loyalty to Spur.

"Not to change the subject," she said now, "but I had a talk with Morg this morning. He has his mind set on starting a mining venture."

"Yeah, I know," Brad said, smiling. "He's been bending my ear about it for the past week."

"I've decided to go along with the idea. It sounds promising."

"Well, Morg's got a good head for business. I just suspect he'll pull it off."

Elizabeth tried to keep her voice casual. "With Morg gone so much, that means added responsibility for you. I was thinking we might work out a new arrangement."

"Oh," Brad said without much interest. "What's that?"

"As a matter of fact, I was considering a bonus of some sort. Say ten percent on the increase over last year. How does that strike you?"

"Wouldn't hurt my feelings," Brad said absently. "I could always use the extra money."

"What I'm asking—" Elizabeth hesitated, searching for

words. "I need some assurance from you, Brad. I want to know you'll stay on as foreman."

Brad stared stonily ahead, his face blank. "I'll stay on till the end of trailing season. I can't promise anything after that."

Elizabeth looked at him for a long moment. "Would more money change your mind? I'm agreeable to anything within reason."

"It's not the money," Brad said in a faraway voice. "Tell you the truth, I'm sort of betwixt and between. I don't know what I'm gonna do."

"While you're trying to decide, remember that we think of you as family. Spur wouldn't be the same without you."

"I'm not likely to forget."

Elizabeth nodded, all too aware of his quandary. She reined her mare around and rode off. Fording the river, it occurred to her that the conversation had resolved nothing. Yet she couldn't fault Brad anymore than she could take issue with Morg. Nor could she stand in their way.

A young man was entitled to try his wings, wherever it might lead. She wouldn't deny either of them the chance.

FIFTEEN

The passenger coach was crowded. Sante Fe appeared in the distance as the train rounded a curve at the base of a hill. The engineer tooted his whistle with three sharp blasts.

Clint was seated at the rear of the coach. Beside him, hands manacled, was Florentino Pérez. All the other seats were occupied by men whose affairs brought them to the territorial capital. Their curiosity regarding the prisoner was confined to speculative stares. None of them had mustered the nerve to start a conversation.

Early that morning Clint and Pérez had boarded the train at Socorro. The trip to Santa Fe was quicker by rail and Clint had left his horse stalled at a livery stable. Pérez, who was a study in abject resignation, looked somewhat the worse for wear. A large goose egg swelled his forehead where he'd been struck with the pistol barrel.

The long ride from Socorro had passed in silence. Clint hadn't attempted to question his prisoner about the activities of *Las Gorras Blancas*. Instead, he had let Pérez sweat, allowing the tension to build as they neared Santa Fe. He thought a formal interrogation, conducted at the territorial prison, would make a greater impression. The gallows was only a short walk away.

A wire had been sent ahead from Socorro. U.S. Marshal Fred Mather was waiting at the train station. Pérez was hustled into an enclosed buggy and they drove directly to the governor's palace. There the prisoner was handed over to the jailer and lodged in a cell at the rear of the building. Clint then made his report and explained what he had in mind. Mather agreed it was worth a try.

Vance Traver, the attorney general, was summoned from his office at the opposite end of the building. A bloodless man in his early fifties, Traver was stoop-shouldered with skin the texture of parchment. When he entered the office, he appeared surprised to see Clint. After they were seated, Mather briefly outlined the situation. He ended on a positive note.

"We've got a chance to bust the White Caps wide open. All we have to do is make Pérez talk."

Traver looked skeptical. "How do you propose to do that?"

"Offer him a deal," Mather replied. "In exchange for cooperation, we'll reduce the murder charge to manslaughter. He'll serve time but he won't hang."

"I see." Traver paused, then glanced around at Clint. "Was this your idea, marshal?"

"Yessir," Clint said impassively. "Pérez is one of the small fry in *Las Gorras Blancas*. I'd like to use him to get Miguel Ortega."

"The governor would certainly endorse that sentiment. But you still haven't answered my question. Why should Pérez talk?"

"I don't take your meaning."

"It was my understanding," Traver said, "that these people are fanatics. Wouldn't he prefer to hang rather than betray Ortega?"

Clint's face was dispassionate. "You'd be surprised what a man will do to avoid the gallows. You follow my lead and we might just loosen his tongue."

"What is it you want me to do?"

At some length, Clint detailed his plan. Afterward, Florentino Pérez was brought from the lockup, his hands still manacled, and ushered into the office. Traver sat behind the desk, flanked by Clint and Mather. Clint nodded to the prisoner, addressing him in Spanish.

"This man," he said, indicating Traver, "will decide whether you live or die. He is the *jefe* of the courts here and the judges do his bidding. *Comprende*?"

"*Sí*," Pérez said, his eyes cast downward. "I understand."

"You are charged with taking part in a murder. Under the law, you are as guilty as the man who actually pulled the trigger. Is that clear?"

A muscle twitched in Pérez's cheek. "*Sí.*"

"Listen closely." Clint's tone was harsh, roughly insistent. "Your life will be spared on one condition. We want information on Miguel Ortega."

Pérez might have been deaf, for all the change in his expression. When he made no reply, Clint went on. "Either you help us or we will have no choice. A court will order your execution by hanging."

"Do what you must, *señor*. I have nothing to say."

Clint interpreted his answer. Traver abruptly stood and fixed the prisoner with a baleful stare. His voice was vindictive and he jabbed a blunt forefinger at Pérez. After he finished speaking, Clint translated into Spanish.

"You have angered the *jefe*. He orders that your mother and sister be taken into custody and brought to Sante Fe. They will be forced to watch you hanged."

All the color drained from Pérez's features. He appeared petrified by the prospect, and his voice sounded parched. "Why would you make them suffer? They have done nothing wrong."

"The choice is yours," Clint said sternly. "Your mother has already lost one son, and justice requires that she witness your death. Her grief will be on your head."

Clint had taken a calculated risk. He waited, allowing silence to exert its own pressure. Family loyalty now hung in the balance against loyalty to Miguel Ortega. At last Pérez looked at him with dulled eyes.

"What is it you wish, *señor*?"

"Tell me where I can find Ortega."

"No one can tell you that. Ortega never spends two nights in the same place."

"Are you saying he doesn't have a hideout?"

"*Sí, señor*. Sometimes he stays overnight with a *mexicano* family. Other times he camps somewhere in the mountains. Even his followers never know."

"When he plans a raid," Clint asked, "how does he get word to *Las Gorras Blancas*?"

Pérez shrugged. "One man passes the message along to another and it spreads rapidly. Within a few hours all the members have been notified."

"Does Ortega travel alone?"

"*No*," Pérez said. "A *pistolero* is always at his side, night and day. He guards Ortega with his life."

"What is the *pistolero*'s name?"

"I do not know. I have never heard Ortega address him by name."

"Aside from your brother," Clint said deliberately, "who are the other members—their names?"

Pérez managed a smile. "All *mexicanos* belong to *Las Gorras Blancas*. None would dare to do otherwise."

"Even the *políticos*?"

"As to that, I cannot say. I have never seen a *político* at the meetings."

"But they support Ortega, *verdad*?"

"No *mexicano* would oppose Ortega, *señor*. To do so would be to forfeit your life."

The interrogation continued for a while longer. Yet it was evident to Clint that nothing of immediate value would be uncovered. *Las Gorras Blancas* was operated under a mantle of secrecy designed to protect its leader. However forthcoming, Pérez made only one significant contribution to the investigation. His testimony implicated Miguel Ortega in the death of the Rio Bonito cowhand.

Pérez was finally returned to his cell. Afterward the attorney general complimented Clint on his skill as an interrogator. The threat involving Pérez's mother had proved to be a masterful gambit. Still, Traver expressed disappointment with the outcome. In his view, they were no closer to catching Ortega than before.

Clint strongly disagreed. "Until now," he said, "the only charges we had against Ortega were fence-cutting and destruction of property. As of today, we've got a witness who can put his head in a noose."

"Quite true," Traver conceded. "We'll have no problem obtaining a murder warrant against Ortega. Unless it's served, of course, it's just another piece of paper. You first have to apprehend him."

Clint's mouth set in a hard line. "Ortega doesn't walk on water. Sooner or later he'll make a mistake. When he does, I'll be there."

"Let's hope it's sooner," Mather interjected. "So far, he's made a laughingstock out of the law."

"Way I see it," Clint said, "it's the last laugh that counts. We'll just have to make sure the joke's on Ortega."

Traver nodded solemnly. "Amen to that."

Within the hour a court hearing was convened. The attorney general presented Florentino Pérez as the territory's chief witness. His testimony, backed by Clint's account, proved to be conclusive. The judge rendered an immediate decision.

A murder warrant was issued on Miguel Ortega.

Late that afternoon Clint was called to the governor's office. He found Edmund Ross in a chatty mood, almost jocular. Their handshake was firm and cordial.

When they were seated, Clint rolled himself a cigarette. He lit it and then took a deep drag, exhaling little spurts of smoke. Ross was talking all the while, reviewing the day's events. His manner was at once benign and magnanimous, somehow lordly.

"You're to be congratulated," he remarked. "You've accomplished a great deal under adverse circumstances."

Clint shrugged off the compliment. "We've still got a ways to go. Ortega's plenty slick."

"Don't be modest," Ross admonished. "I knew from the start you were the man for the job. You'll run him down."

"I aim to do my damnedest, governor."

"Bring him to justice and you'll have my everlasting gratitude, Mr. Brannock. Not to mention the esteem of President Cleveland."

Clint looked at him for a long moment. "Governor, I've talked to a lot of Mexicans in the past month or so. Would you like to hear what I found out?"

"Indeed I would."

"Well, just for openers, Ortega's not preachin' revolution. From what I gather, he's never called for an uprising against the government."

"Tommyrot," Ross said crossly. "Everyone knows he wants a realignment with Old Mexico. His goal is to drive all Anglos from the territory."

"Funny thing," Clint said. "The only ones talkin' about revolution are the Anglos. As near as I can pinpoint it, the talk got its start here in Santa Fe."

"What are you driving at, Mr. Brannock?"

"Way it looks to me, Ortega's preachin' reform, not revolution. He just wants an end to all these land-grabbing schemes."

Ross's voice was clipped, incisive. "Are you saying he's been unjustly branded as a revolutionary?"

"Lots of folks," Clint reminded him, "don't like the sound of reform. Goes against their business interests."

"And you believe they would slander Ortega to further their own interests?"

"Nothing easier, what with him and the White Caps raising so much hell. A murder warrant tends to make it even worse."

"What makes it worse," Ross said shortly, "is your sister-in-law's poor judgment. I understand she's allied herself with Ortega."

"You understand wrong," Clint informed him stiffly. "Ortega asked her to support *Las Gorras Blancas* and she refused. Anybody who says different is a goddamn liar."

"How does that square with her coalition? Not even Elizabeth Brannock would deny that the *mexicanos* support Ortega."

A stony look settled on Clint's face. "Her coalition was

around long before Ortega. There wouldn't be any White Caps if she'd got the reforms she wanted."

"Tell me," Ross said heavily, "does your loyalty to Mrs. Brannock affect your attitude as a peace officer? We can't allow anything of a personal nature to influence your investigation."

Clint kept his gaze level and cool. "When I pinned on a badge, I took an oath to uphold the law. Nothing's happened to change that, governor."

Ross studied him a moment, finally nodded. "I want an end written to the matter of Miguel Ortega. Don't disappoint me, Mr. Brannock."

"Anytime you're not satisfied . . ."

Ross dismissed him with a brusque gesture. Clint stubbed out his cigarette in an ashtray and rose, walking to the door. As he turned the knob, the governor's voice stopped him. "Mr. Brannock."

"Yessir?"

"One last piece of advice. A lawman should never take sides in politics. I suggest you bear that in mind."

"Governor, so far as I'm concerned, the only difference between politics and a bucket of horse apples is the bucket. I wouldn't dirty my hands."

The door opened and closed. Far from being offended, Edmund Ross was amused by the rebuff. A wintry smile lighted his eyes and he slowly nodded to himself. He still thought he'd picked the right man for the job.

Miguel Ortega now had one foot in the grave.

That evening Clint took supper at the hotel. The food was passable, and since he'd engaged a room for the night, he saw no reason to go elsewhere. He ordered the house special, a charred steak and fried potatoes.

After a second cup of coffee, he wandered into the hotel barroom. He planned to be in bed by ten and up by sunrise, in time to catch the morning train. A couple of drinks, on top of a big meal, would ensure a good night's sleep. He seated himself at an empty table opposite the bar.

The first drink went down smoothly. He signaled the barkeep for a refill and began rolling a smoke. As he struck a match, he saw Thomas Canby come through the door. Their eyes met and Canby walked in his direction. He waited without expression.

" 'Evening," Canby said, halting beside the table. "Heard you were in town and thought we might have a talk. Mind if I join you?"

"Suit yourself."

Canby settled into a chair. The barkeep appeared with a bottle and another glass, and poured. When he moved away, neither of the men touched their whiskey. Clint looked across the table.

"What have we got to talk about?"

"Your sister-in-law," Canby said. "I'd be obliged if you would deliver a message."

Clint tapped an ash off his cigarette. "I'm willing to listen."

"Are you aware Mrs. Brannock plans to hold a *mexicano* political convention?"

"I read the papers."

Canby inclined his head. "Then you know she's playing with fire. The only one who will benefit is Miguel Ortega."

"None of my concern," Clint said, meeting his gaze. "Why don't you get to the point?"

"I'll be quite frank," Canby said. "New Mexico is on the verge of a revolution. We want that convention canceled."

"By 'we,' " Clint asked, "do you mean the Santa Fe Ring?"

Canby forced a smile. "I represent men who control the legislature and the territory's major business interests. We're willing to make peace with Mrs. Brannock."

"In exchange for what?"

"We'll wipe the slate clean. An invitation will be extended to Mrs. Brannock, asking her to join with us in forming one political party. In effect, we would then control the destiny of New Mexico."

Clint stared at him. "You still haven't told me the price."

"Let's call it a condition," Canby said. "We would insist

that she cancel the convention and sever all ties with the *mexicanos*. We want her coalition disbanded."

"Suppose she met your condition," Clint replied. "What's to stop Ira Hecht from taking over the coalition?"

Canby's mouth went tight, scornful. "We'll take care of Hecht in our own way. He's no problem."

"Sounds to me like you're running scared."

"I beg your pardon?"

"You're afraid you'll lose the fall elections. You figure Elizabeth's finally gonna unite the Mexican vote. And if she does, your boys will get tossed out of office."

Canby looked at him with a kind of contempt. "I assure you we won't lose, Mr. Brannock. We'll take whatever steps are necessary to ensure a victory."

"Is that meant to be a threat?"

"It's a statement of fact. Forced to the wall, we'll have no choice but to play rough. The stakes are just too big."

Clint's voice was suddenly edged. "Here's another statement of fact. Take care that no harm comes to anybody in my family. One misstep and I'll kill you."

"The governor wouldn't care for that at all. I suspect he'd hang you."

"Wouldn't matter," Clint observed. "You'd still be dead."

Canby appeared unconcerned. "I suggest you deliver my message to Mrs. Brannock. Perhaps she'll accept and save us all some grief."

"Just remember what I said . . . no rough stuff."

Canby got to his feet, his drink untouched. He nodded curtly and walked to the door. Clint took a pull on his cigarette, exhaling a thin streamer of smoke. His expression was stoic, somehow faraway.

He thought he'd got a glimpse of the future. And he didn't like what he saw.

A mealy, weblike darkness cloaked the room. Clint awoke to a muffled sound and his every sense alerted. He lay perfectly still, feigning sleep.

His room was on the ground floor at the rear of the hotel.

While the nights were generally cool in Santa Fe, he always opened a window. Something about the mountain air made him sleep better.

Hardly moving, he slowly turned his head on the pillow. Starlight dimly illuminated the window in a fuzzy glow. He saw a man halfway through the lower portion of the window, one leg in and one leg out. A glint of light reflected off a pistol in the man's hand.

Still frozen, Clint gingerly slid his hand under the pillow. He found the butt of his Colt and hooked his thumb over the hammer. As the intruder stepped through the window, he rolled out of bed and dropped onto the floor. A gunshot limned the room with fiery brilliance, followed instantly by another. The slugs tore ragged furrows in the mattress.

Clint bobbed up at the foot of the bed. He extended the Colt at arm's length, thumbing the hammer. Within the space of a few heartbeats, he touched off five shots, emptying the gun. Across the room, the man stiffened, arms windmilling, driven backward by the impact of the slugs. His head slammed into the upper windowpane and it exploded in a shower of glass. He slumped forward onto the floor.

As the man fell, Clint jerked his gunbelt off a nearby chair. He dropped behind the bed, ejecting spent shells, and reloaded the Colt by feel. Then, alert to any sound, he cautiously rose and circled the bed. At the window, he hugged the wall and took a quick look outside. Satisfied there was no one else, he finally turned to the man on the floor. The body lay crumpled in a welter of blood, visible in the pale starlight. His would-be assassin was *mexicano*.

Some thirty minutes later, Fred Mather walked into the room. Notified of the shooting, he had hurried from his home on the west side of town. He stared down at the dead man, shaking his head from side to side. At last he looked around at Clint.

"Kee-rist," he said. "You cut him to ribbons."

Clint shrugged. "If a man's worth shooting, he's worth killing. I figure he deserved what he got."

"You ever seen him before?"

"Not that I recollect."

Mather massaged his jaw. "Something about it doesn't make sense. Why would Ortega send a man to kill you?"

"Good question," Clint said. "Pérez would've been a more likely candidate. He's the one who talked."

"So where's that leave us?"

"At this point, I haven't got an inkling."

"Anybody else have a reason to kill you?"

Clint was silent for a time. He thought back to his conversation with Tom Canby. He'd threatened the leader of the Santa Fe Ring and that alone might have provoked the attack. Still, something about it didn't ring true. Canby was a meticulous planner, given to details. He wouldn't have sanctioned such a sloppy job. Nor would he have sent just one man.

"You're awful quiet," Mather said. "You know something I don't?"

"Nothing worth repeating."

"Then what the hell are you stewing on so hard?"

Clint smiled. "I reckon it's time I had a talk with Señor Ortega."

"Talk?" Mather echoed. "Don't you have to find him first?"

"I'll find him," Clint said without irony. "It's in the cards."

"Which cards are those?"

"The one's I'm fixin' to deal."

SIXTEEN

White Oaks was located in the foothills of the Jicarilla Mountains. Some thirty miles northwest of Lincoln, the town was rough even by mining-camp standards. In days past, it had been a favorite haunt of Billy the Kid.

On the first Thursday in May, Morg dismounted outside the assayer's office. He was known in White Oaks, for he'd become the principal supplier of timbers to the mines. Today, he meant to capitalize on contacts made in the course of his business affairs. His inside coat pocket was stuffed with hundred-dollar bills.

The town was scattered along a rutted street hardly a half-mile long. Overshadowed by mountains, the frame buildings were wedged side by side, most of them topped with false fronts. Saloons and dance halls were liberally sprinkled among more legitimate forms of enterprise. One of the mainstays of the economy was the girls who worked the whorehouses and backroom cribs. Miners, by nature, were a randy breed.

Morg left his horse tethered at the hitch rail. He crossed the boardwalk and entered a small one-room building. The interior smelled of grit and dust, and bags of ore samples were stacked along the walls. A counter bisected the room, with assayer's scales and other paraphernalia prominently displayed. To the rear were a lone desk and a workbench crowded with beakers and vials. Beyond that was a huge standing safe, the massive doors locked tight.

"'Afternoon, Elmer," Morg said, stopping before the counter. "How's things?"

"Well, by golly, Morg Brannock."

Elmer Westfall rose from behind his desk. He was a slender man of medium height, his hairline receding into a widow's peak. He had a warm smile and an affable manner, and innocent brown eyes. Those who knew him well were not deceived by his mild appearance. He was shrewd and quick, a hardnosed businessman.

Morg was scarcely more than an acquaintance. On occasion, when their paths crossed, he'd bought Westfall a drink. The assayer was a loquacious man and overly impressed with his own opinions. What he talked about most was mining, and Morg had proved to be an attentive audience. Their conversations invariably centered on prospects around White Oaks.

From these casual meetings, Morg's idea for a mining venture had ultimately taken shape. He knew nothing of Westfall's personal or professional ethics, though the assayer was widely respected. Still, he'd always operated on the theory that any man was susceptible to temptation. In business dealings, he had discovered early on that money talks loudest. He planned to test that premise on Westfall.

"You're looking fit," he said now. "Business must be good."

"Never better," Westfall said in a reedy voice. "I'm busier than a one-armed paper hanger."

"You and me both. I can't hardly keep the mines supplied with timbers."

"Doesn't surprise me in the least. Everywhere you look, somebody's sinking a new shaft."

"Tell you the truth," Morg said in a conspiratorial tone, "that's why I dropped by. Thought we might have ourselves a talk."

Westfall regarded him with a keen sidewise scrutiny. "What's on your mind?"

"I'm interested in making an investment. Figured you're the man to give me some advice."

"Always happy to oblige a friend. How can I help?"

"I've got the gold bug," Morg explained. "Last month or so, I've developed a real itch for the mining game. Finally decided there's no time like the present."

Westfall was not unaware of the Brannock name. He was Morg's senior by some twenty years, but age and experience were relative. What counted most in the world of mining was a man's financial resources. Without adequate funds, the most promising claims were little more than a plot of dirt. The wealth of the Brannock family, he told himself, placed them in the same league as Eastern financiers. His interest suddenly took a sharp upturn.

"Lots of people get the itch," he said amiably. "You could throw a rock in any direction and hit a dozen prospectors. There's no end to them."

"You're right," Morg said with cheery vigor. "And most of them never get within sniffin' distance of the mother lode. That's why I've come to you."

"I'm not sure I understand."

"Way I see it," Morg said cautiously, "nobody knows more about the mining game than an assayer. You get an inside peek before anyone else."

Westfall looked at him questioningly. "You'll have to be a little more specific. What is it you're after?"

"Information," Morg said with a faint smile. "You know who's sitting on a bonanza and who's not. I thought you might steer me in the right direction. All hush-hush, of course."

"Are you aware you're asking me to violate a confidence? After all, I have a professional responsibility to my clients."

"For the right tip, I'd be willing to pay handsomely."

"That sounds vaguely like a bribe."

Morg grinned. "Elmer, a bribe would be beneath a man of your position. Let's call it a finder's fee."

Westfall gave the matter some thought. "Suppose I agree," he said finally. "What kind of fee are we talking about?"

Morg pulled a wad of bills from his inside coat pocket. He fanned them out on the counter, and smiled. "A thousand now for a topnotch recommendation. Another thousand when I actually buy into the property."

There was a prolonged silence. Westfall lightly drummed his fingers on the counter, staring down at the bills. At length he scooped them up and tucked them into his vest pocket. His mouth twisted in a cynical grin.

"You've got a deal," he said. "Now, what sort of property are you after?"

"Something undeveloped," Morg told him. "A claim with good potential but still unworked. I'm looking for an owner who's lean and hungry."

"Do you want to steal it from him or take him on as a partner?"

"Elmer, I've got fifty thousand dollars to invest. For that, I want a partner who knows his stuff, an experienced mining man. I'll have to rely on him to run the operation."

Westfall's eyes narrowed in thought. "The wrong man could rob you blind. What you need is somebody who's honest and got himself a whiz-bang of a claim. Not many of them around."

"Don't forget," Morg added, "he has to be damn near dead broke. Otherwise he won't need me to develop the property."

Westfall nodded, mulling it over. "Goddurn!" he said abruptly. "I've got just the man. His name's Dave Todd."

"Where's his claim?"

"Couple of miles south of town. He's strictly a one-man outfit, poor as a church mouse. But the way he talks, he's a demon for work. Told me he'd excavated a hundred feet of tunnel all by himself."

"You've had a look at his ore samples?"

"Oh, you betcha," Westfall said. "Assays out to two hundred dollars a ton. He's onto something big."

"In that case," Morg said doubtfully, "how come he's still operating on a shoestring? Why hasn't he found a backer?"

"Because he's snake-bit about outsiders. Anybody who's approached him tried to buy the claim for peanuts. They wanted the whole kit and caboodle, all or nothing."

"So you think he'd be interested in a partner?"

"Only if he trusts you," Westfall cautioned. "Dave's just bullheaded enough that he won't be cheated out of his claim. He figures he's finally struck Eldorado."

Morg deliberated a moment. "Has he got the experience to run a large operation? I'm talking about quartz mining done right."

"Yes, I'd say he does. First time he brought ore samples in, he told me he'd been a foreman at some mine up in Colorado. Way he talks, he's spent half his life underground."

"Elmer, I might just owe you another thousand dollars. He sounds made-to-order."

"Well, make sure you don't mention my name. I've got a reputation to protect."

"Wild horses couldn't drag it out of me. You've got my word on it."

Westfall drew him a map. Morg studied it a moment, satisfying himself as to the mine's location. On the way out the door, he suppressed the urge to laugh out loud. What he'd learned would have been cheap at any price. For a thousand dollars it was a genuine bargain.

He silently gave himself a pat on the back.

South of White Oaks the terrain gradually steepened. Off in the distance the summit of Carrizo Peak towered almost ten thousand feet into the sky. A dusty washboard road snaked through the rocky foothills.

Morg held his horse to a walk. He was embarked on an undertaking of no small proportions, and his mood had turned reflective. He'd already weighed the risk against the potential gain, and the odds favored the project. Yet he readily admitted he was a tyro at the game, and that in itself dictated a certain caution. He mentally cataloged all he knew about hard-rock mining.

Any gold rush began with traces of yellow metal being located in streambeds. In mountainous terrain, erosion due to weather slowly loosened subsurface pockets of ore from rock formations. Seasonal rains then carried the gold from the vein and deposited it somewhere downstream, usually in the form of flakes or fine dust. These runoff deposits were the discoveries originally uncovered by prospectors.

By panning the streams, which was known as placer mining, the prospector was able to work his claim. Before long, however, these surface deposits played out and more elaborate methods were needed to dredge the streams. In the end, when the placers failed altogether, there was no choice but to undertake quartz mining. The first step, and one that defeated most prospectors, was to trace the vein to its origin. Once the lode was located, mine shafts were excavated and the job of transporting the ore to the surface was begun.

Often called hard-rock mining, a quartz operation required freeing the ore from lodes buried deep within the earth. Extracting the gold from a quartz vein was a herculean task that demanded men and machinery, and a heavy investment of capital. The mined ore was first crushed in a stamp mill and then passed over shelves of quicksilver. The process was laborious and time-consuming, but gold in pure form was eventually distilled from the crushed rock. Such an operation required a knowledge of mining techniques and the ability to manage a venture of some magnitude. In short, it was no game for greenhorns.

The thought was foremost in Morg's mind. As he rode into the campsite, he warned himself to take nothing for granted. A crude shack, constructed of rough-sawn lumber, stood on a stretch of open ground. Beyond, on the slope of a hill, he spotted the mouth of the tunnel. No one answered his call as he dismounted in front of the shack. Then, from upslope, he heard a muffled voice. He saw a man emerge from the mine shaft.

"What d'ya want?" the man shouted.

"Are you Dave Todd?"

"Who's askin'?"

"The name's Brannock," Morg called out. "I'd like to talk to you."

"Just stay where you are. I'll be there directly."

Todd started down a trail along the face of the slope. His attitude indicated he was suspicious of strangers. A pistol was strapped to his side, and from his rough tone, he allowed no one near his diggings. Heavy through the shoulders, he was short and muscular and looked to be in his early thirties. His features were hidden behind a full beard.

Halting at the corner of the shack, he subjected Morg to a quick once-over. "You said you wanted to talk."

Morg ignored the abrasive manner. Yet his assessment of the man told him a roundabout approach wouldn't work. He decided to come straight to the point.

"Got a proposition for you," he said. "Hear me out before you get your bowels in an uproar."

"I ain't interested in no proposition."

"Won't cost you nothing to listen."

"Get to it, then," Todd said sourly. "I got no time to lolly-gag around."

Morg stated his case in brisk, no-nonsense terms. While he mentioned no source, he spoke knowledgeably of Todd's claim. Completely aboveboard, he admitted the mine's potential for uncovering a rich lode. Then, hammering home the point, he declared that potential by itself meant nothing until the ore was brought to the surface. He offered to bankroll the operation to the tune of fifty thousand dollars.

When he paused, Todd eyed him skeptically. "Who told you about my claim?"

"The word's around," Morg said reasonably. "Not many secrets in a mining camp."

"You're not trying to buy me out? You'd actually want me to run the operation?"

"I don't know beans from buckshot about mining. Unless you agree to stay on, I'm not interested."

Todd gave him a long, searching stare. "What d'ya want for your fifty thousand?"

"Fifty-one percent," Morg said flatly, "and it's not negotiable. I'll give you a free hand running things, but I control the purse strings. It's my money."

Todd examined the notion. "Where'd a young feller like you get such a bankroll?"

"I own a timber company and I'm partners with my

family in a cattle spread. Anybody in Lincoln will vouch for the Brannocks."

"Wondered about the name when you mentioned it. You any relation to a gambler name of Lon Brannock?"

Morg looked dumbstruck. "Where the devil do you know Lon from? He's my first cousin."

Todd flashed a yellow-toothed smile. "Him and his half-breed brother drifted into town last week. I seen 'em in the gaming dives."

"White Oaks?" Morg said, astounded. "Last I heard, they were in Lordsburg."

"Well, he's here now. Way I got the story, he killed a man over at Lordsburg. Finally wore out his welcome."

"I'll be damned."

Todd chortled aloud. "Lots of folks don't take to a 'breed livin' in town. 'Course, they keep their traps shut on that score. Your cousin's sorta handy with a gun."

"They're both my cousins," Morg said. "Different mothers but the same father."

"Figured as much," Todd noted. "Maybe you and me can do business after all. Anybody with an honest gambler in the family couldn't be no crook."

"How do you know he's honest?"

" 'Cause a tinhorn wouldn't be travelin' with a 'breed kid. Tends to draw attention to a man's gamblin' habits."

Their conversation turned again to the mining venture. On the basis of a handshake, the deal was struck along the terms outlined by Morg. A formal contract would be drawn, but for now each of them was willing to accept the other's word. As Morg mounted his horse, he was reminded that life sometimes took a strange twist. He'd clinched the deal today because he was related to an honest gambler. It seemed to him a curious recommendation, almost laughable.

He rode back toward White Oaks.

The Lady Gay saloon was packed with miners. A banjo and an upright piano provided the entertainment, and the gaming tables were positioned opposite the bar. Girls with kewpie-doll faces drifted through the crowd.

Shortly after sundown, Lon and Hank emerged from a café across the street. By now they were a familiar sight and no one bothered to stare. From Lordsburg, they had traveled a circuitous route, never stopping long in one place. White Oaks' proximity to the Hondo Valley, and their kinfolk, was a matter of small interest. To them it was simply one more stopover on the gamblers' circuit. When the urge struck them, they would move on to still another mining camp.

Entering the Lady Gay, they started toward the poker tables at the rear of the saloon. One of the barkeeps spotted them and gave Lon the high sign. Followed by Hank, Lon moved to the end of the bar. After waiting on another customer, the barkeep strolled over. He leaned across the counter, lowering his voice.

"A fellow's been askin' about you."

"Who is he?"

"Search me." The barkeep jerked his head toward a table near the front window. "That's him, the one sittin' by hisself. Wandered in about an hour ago."

"Much obliged."

Lon inspected the man at the table. Something about him was familiar, but he couldn't place the face. He noted in passing that the man was about his own age and carried a pistol in a belt holster. He exchanged a glance with Hank, who shrugged. They crossed to the table, halting as the man looked up from a half-empty schooner of beer. Lon gave him an impersonal nod.

"Understand you've been askin' for me. I'm Lon Brannock."

"Hello, cousin," Morg said, grinning broadly. "You don't recognize me, do you?"

"Cousin—?"

"Morg Brannock. Virgil Brannock's boy."

"Well, I'll be a son-of-a-bitch."

Neither of them had seen the other in almost fourteen

years. Their last meeting had been in Colorado Springs, where Morg's parents lived at the time. Afterward their paths had diverged, with no mutual contact except their lawman uncle, Clint. But now, caught up in a spirit of reunion, they shook hands warmly. Lon took hold of Hank's elbow and pulled him forward.

"Meet your other cousin," he said to Morg. "This here's my brother, Hank."

"I'm proud to make your acquaintance, Hank. Heard a lot about you."

"Likewise," Hank said, shaking his hand. "Uncle Clint always bragged on you and your family."

"C'mon, sit down." Morg motioned them to take chairs. "We've got a lot of catchin' up to do."

"How's your mom?" Lon asked.

"She's fine," Morg said. "Her and Jen both. They'll expect you to come by for a visit."

Lon made an empty gesture. "Hard to say where we'll light next. We keep on the move."

Morg gave him a quizzical side glance. "You're not worried about Clint, are you?"

"What's he got to do with anything?"

"Way I heard the story, he'd like Hank to move in at Spur. Leastways that's what he told Mom."

"Fat chance," Lon said indifferently. "We thrashed that out once before. Hank stays with me."

Morg laughed. "Then you've got no reason to hold off. Hell, I'm married and about to become a daddy. I want you to meet my wife."

"We'll see," Lon said, deliberately noncommittal. "All depends on how things go."

Morg let it drop there. He turned the conversation to Lon's trade as a gambler and listened with rapt attention. Yet, as they talked, he watched Hank out of the corner of his eye. He saw that the boy idolized his older brother, hanging on his every word. Some inner voice told him that the bond between them was too strong to be broken. A gradual realization came over him, and he recognized it for a sad, but undeniable truth.

Hank Brannock would never set foot on Spur. He was a boy who walked in his brother's shadow, and there he would stay.

SEVENTEEN

The convention was held in Albuquerque. Situated on the upper Río Grande, the town was positioned roughly in the middle of New Mexico. From virtually anywhere in the territory, it was the central location for such a meeting.

All the more important, Albuquerque represented neutral ground. A major railhead, with commerce in timber, farm produce, and livestock, it was fast developing into a city. Because of its rapid growth, the influence of the Sante Fe ring was not a pervasive factor in local issues. Nor were the divisions between Anglo and Mexican so sharply drawn.

In total, Elizabeth had extended invitations to fifty-seven *políticos*. Topping the list were the wealthy *ricos,* who dominated affairs in their districts. Below them were the *jefes,* the men responsible for daily operation of the political apparatus. Lower still were the *jóvenes políticos,* aspiring young politicians who challenged the old order. Of those invited, fifty-one arrived in Albuquerque on May 14.

The convention began the following morning. Elizabeth had rented the banquet hall in a hotel and transformed it into a meeting room. Tables were arranged in rows, five men to a table, with an aisle down the center. There were no seating assignments, which made the affair somewhat more democratic. People sat where they pleased and with whom they pleased. No special consideration was extended to anyone.

An air of animosity and mistrust filled the room. The *ricos* and the *jóvenes políticos* were separated by an ideological chasm. The old order, who thought of themselves as aristocrats, jealously guarded their power. The younger faction, ambitious men from the lower classes, championed reforms for the people. Caught in the middle were the *jefes,* who attempted to appease everyone while offending no one. The overall sense of discord was palpable.

There were only three Anglos in attendance. At the front of the room, Elizabeth and Ira Hecht were seated behind a speaker's table, with a lectern between them. Their principal support was from the *jóvenes políticos* and a handful of *jefes*. On that foundation, their shaky coalition between *mexicanos* and Anglo reformers remained intact. The *ricos,* by and large, viewed the coalition as a menace to the established order. Fearful of losing power, they had given only spotty cooperation in the past.

The third Anglo was John Taylor. Stationed at the rear of the room, he stood beside the wide double doors leading to the hall. He appeared unusually vigilant, not unlike a watchdog alert to danger. Scarcely a week ago, Elizabeth had received a letter from Clint. In it, he'd outlined Thomas Canby's offer of an alliance, as well as the veiled threat should the offer be refused. Without explanation, he went on to state that the governor had ordered him to expand his investigation into San Miguel County. He cautioned Elizabeth to beware at the convention.

Elizabeth found Canby's offer to be revealing. Clearly, he was concerned that the convention would broaden her coalition among the *mexicano* leaders. His concern, quite obviously, was that a groundswell movement would cost him the fall elections. As for the threat, she simply ignored it, evidencing no fear for her own safety. John Taylor, on the other hand, was openly concerned for her welfare. Like Clint, he got deadly serious whenever Elizabeth put herself in harm's way. He'd kept a sharp lookout since their arrival in Albuquerque.

The convention had gotten off to a bad start. Elizabeth was all too aware that the *ricos,* in particular, resented a woman involving herself in men's affairs. They respected the power she wielded, but they were bitterly affronted by the fact that she wore skirts. To allay their resentment, she had limited her remarks to a brief opening statement. Forcefully, she had addressed the need for cohesion and harmony in pursuit of a common goal. Afterward, Ira Hecht had acted as moderator of the meeting.

The squabbling commenced almost immediately. One of the *jóvenes políticos* took the floor to denounce the *ricos* in scathing terms. Outraged, the *ricos,* supported by loyal *jefes,* shouted him down. Time and again, Hecht restored order by pounding his gavel and urging them to seek some common ground. No sooner would the next speaker take the floor than tempers flared anew and the bickering resumed at a hotter pitch. The convention slowly degenerated into a running skirmish between factions.

Watching them fight, Elizabeth despaired of bringing about a truce. Their animosity evolved from one generation attempting to wrest power from another. Her conciliatory remarks at the beginning had done nothing to dampen their antagonism. Hoping to further placate the *ricos,* she'd even worn a tailored suit of navy serge with a high-necked white blouse. Her thought was to remove any hint of feminine influence and conduct the meeting in a businesslike fashion. She saw now that her efforts had been largely wasted.

On the verge of speaking out, her attention was distracted. The door at the rear of the room opened and three *mexicanos* in white jackets wheeled in a serving trolley. Looking closer, she noted that the trolley was loaded with coffee cups and a large coffee urn. She hadn't ordered refreshments and the appearance of the waiters left her momentarily confused. Then, jolted into acute awareness, she fixed her gaze on one of the men. His features were unmistakable.

Miguel Ortega.

John Taylor walked over to the serving trolley. One of the waiters was whipcord lean, with a face that looked adzed from hard dark wood. He smiled, pulling a pistol from beneath his jacket, and stuck it in Taylor's ribs. A moment later

Taylor was disarmed and forced to take a seat at the rearmost table. The third *mexicano* stepped from behind the trolley and produced a nickel-plated six-gun. The dark-skinned man rapped out a sharp order.

"Silencio!"

A sudden hush fell over the room. The convention members turned in their chairs, spotting the men with drawn pistols. They sat immobilized, as though frozen in place, a uniform look of astonishment on their faces. As Miguel Ortega walked down the aisle, they watched with the spellbound expression normally reserved for sword-swallowers and magicians. One of them whispered his name and a buzz of conversation swept through the crowd.

Ortega moved around the speaker's table. Elizabeth looked at him, certain now that something momentous was about to happen. He smiled pleasantly, nodding to her. *"Con su permiso, señora,"* he said formally. "With your permission, *señora.*"

Halting behind the lectern, Ortega stared out at the *políticos.* He customarily spoke in quiet commands that others unquestioningly obeyed. Today his voice crackled with authority.

"Buenos días, caballeros," he said. "For those of you I have not met personally, I am Miguel Ortega. I bring you greetings from *Las Gorras Blancas.*"

The crowd sat mesmerized, reduced to absolute silence. Ortega launched into a fiery speech, gesturing to underscore his points. His tone of voice alternated between sardonic mockery and outright contempt. He railed at the politicians, addressing his remarks directly to the *ricos* and the *jefes.* In harsh terms, he upbraided them for placing greed and self-interest before the welfare of the people. His eyes were alive with a light akin to madness.

Toward the end, he gestured at Elizabeth. He told the crowd she was a woman of goodwill, a friend to all *mexicanos.* He praised her selfless devotion to reform and her long struggle to bring about equality under the law. Then, abruptly, his tone turned ominous and his voice took on a soft, menacing lilt. There was a distant, prophetic look in his eyes, and he seemed to stare at the men one by one. He warned them to settle their differences and join with Señora Brannock in forging a true alliance. To remove any vestige of doubt, he concluded with a bald-faced threat.

"Anyone who withholds his support will be marked as a traitor. And all such men will be dealt with by *Las Gorras Blancas*. Heed my words or we shall meet again."

A turgid silence settled over the crowd. Ortega bowed to Elizabeth, then walked away from the speaker's table. She realized that this was one of those rare moments that alter one's life irrevocably. Her coalition, even she herself, was now linked to the man who led *Las Gorras Blancas*. On sudden impulse, she rose and followed him up the aisle.

Ortega's men waited beside the door. The dark-skinned *pistolero* placed John Taylor's six-gun on the floor. Taylor started to rise from his chair, but Elizabeth waved him down. The third man opened the door, motioning the *pistolero* through, and they preceded Ortega into the hallway. Elizabeth was only a step behind and she caught up with Ortega outside. His men moved off to a discreet distance.

"Thank you," Elizabeth said gratefully. "You risked your life by coming here today."

Ortega smiled with satisfaction. "Perhaps I have been of some small assistance, *señora*. Those fools would have argued among themselves and accomplished nothing."

"I must say you've speeded things along. You're a very persuasive speaker."

"Some men cannot be dealt with in a reasonable manner. I felt sterner measures were required."

Elizabeth appeared bemused. "Why is it so important to you that we win the elections? I thought you had lost faith in the ballot box."

"I have faith in you," Ortega said, then shrugged. "Besides, a wise man always prepares for the unforeseen. Should anything happen to me, you and your coalition can continue the fight."

"You once told me you would never be captured. Has that somehow changed?"

"No, señora," Ortega replied. "I will never be captured."

"Are you—" Elizabeth hesitated, searched his eyes. "You believe you might be killed, don't you?"

Ortega's mouth lifted in a tight grin. "There are powerful men who wish me dead. Who knows where it will lead?"

"Is there no other way?"

"De seguro," Ortega said. "No way whatever. God willing, you may yet win at the ballot box. In the meantime, I will fight on."

Elizabeth smiled warmly. "You are a brave and honorable man, and your people need you. I wish you well."

"Hasta luego, señora."

Ortega turned toward his men. As they hurried along the hallway, Elizabeth was struck by yet another realization. A moment ago, in a quicksilver splinter of time, she had seen revealed a new aspect of Miguel Ortega. He was not suffering from messianic delusions. Nor was there any sense of his own immortality.

He saw himself, instead, as the most mortal of men. He believed he would be killed.

Glorieta Pass was at the southern tail of the Sangre de Cristo range. First discovered by the Spaniards in the 1590s, it had been an ancient byway through the mountains. In more recent times it had served as an artery on the Santa Fe Trail.

The pass itself was surrounded by lofty mountains. A quarter of a mile wide, it sliced through rugged heights almost eight thousand feet in elevation. The slopes on either flank were steep and rocky, studded with cedar and stunted pines. At the western end of the pass there was a deep gorge, carved through the aeons by a winding stream.

Some years past, the railroad had spanned the gorge with a bridge. The wooden trestles were like an intricate latticework rising high above the streambed. On the far side of the bridge, the tracks extended through the pass and gradually curved off toward the southwest. At the town of Lamy, a spur line turned northwest into the mountains, terminating at Santa Fe. The main line descended on a southerly arc into the Rio Grande valley.

Clint stood at the edge of the gorge, looking westward. Before him, where the bridge had traversed the deep crevasse, there was now a yawning chasm. Far below, the streambed was littered with timbers and charred rubble. Sometime last night, an explosion heard twenty miles away had blown the bridge to smithereens. Staring down at the debris, he idly wondered how much dynamite had been required for the job. He had no doubt whatever as to who had lit the fuse.

Not quite two weeks ago a freight train had been derailed along the Gallinas River. The incident had occurred the same night he'd shot the *mexicano* in his hotel room. Early next morning, the governor had ordered him into San Miguel County, where the sabotage had taken place. While none of the crew had been killed, railroad officials had apparently put a bee in the governor's ear. Unless checked, the derailment of trains could bring commerce to a standstill throughout the territory.

Clint had traveled by rail from Santa Fe. Headed east through the mountains, he'd toyed with an intriguing notion. Until now, *Las Gorras Blancas* had been content to pester the railroad. But derailing trains was serious business and indicated a high degree of planning. Which raised the possibility that Ortega had returned to San Miguel County. Nothing was known of Ortega's lieutenants or their ability to carry out such an act of sabotage. So the idea hadn't seemed all that farfetched.

Quickly enough, Clint had been disabused of his optimism. San Miguel County was where Ortega had organized the first bands of masked night riders. The northern *mexicanos,* if anything, were more secretive than those Clint had encountered in Lincoln County. He'd spent the last ten days trying to uncover a lead, with nothing to show for his efforts. *Las Gorras Blancas* openly claimed credit for the derailment, but the trail ended there. No one would talk to a *gringo* lawman, particularly an outsider. Any mention of Ortega's name drew blank stares, and silence.

Early that morning, Clint had ridden out to Glorieta Pass. Work crews, supervised by bridge engineers, were already busy assessing the damage. The magnitude of the destruction once again raised the specter of Miguel Ortega. Staring down the gorge, Clint asked himself who else could have planned and executed such a feat. But today, like so many days in the past, he was stumped for an explanation. There were no answers, only tough questions.

A handcar, pumped by two brawny workmen, rolled to a halt a short distance uptrack. Boyce Thompson, sheriff of San Miguel County, hopped down and walked forward. His experience with *Las Gorras Blancas* made him an expert on the subject, though he'd yet to obtain a conviction. He stopped beside Clint, looking out across the gorge.

"Helluva mess," he said. "Somebody shore has a way with dynamite."

Clint made an offhand gesture. "I was thinkin' that same thing myself. You reckon it might've been Ortega?"

"Not unless he's got wings."

"What's that mean?"

"Nothin' you're gonna like," Thompson said with a mirthless laugh. "Wire come in on the telegraph a while ago. Ortega was reported in Albuquerque yesterday mornin'."

"Albuquerque?"

Thompson took a hitch at his pants, cleared his throat. "You know that Mex confab your sister-in-law's holdin'? Word leaked out that Ortega dropped by unannounced. Albuquerque paper reports he made a piss-cutter of a speech."

"Goddamnit," Clint said stolidly. "The bastard's always one jump ahead."

"What d'you aim to do now?"

"Go on back to Lincoln County. I've got a hunch that's where he'll pop up next."

"Why so?"

Clint sidestepped the question. His hunch was part supposition and part fact. Ortega was using Elizabeth and her coalition to his own ends. What stymied Clint was that Elizabeth had nothing to gain. She could only lose by being linked to *Las Gorras Blancas*.

He thought it was time they had another talk.

Homer Stockton rode into Spur three days later. He was accompanied by Aaron Kimble, whose ranch was located on the Rio Bonito. They dismounted outside the main house.

Kimble was a large man, with a broad hard face and close-cropped hair. Scarcely three weeks past he'd buried a cowhand killed during the raid on his ranch. He took small solace from the fact that one of the White Caps had also been killed. A life for a life seemed to him a poor trade.

Elizabeth received them in her office. She had never cared for Stockton, who was a blustering, overbearing man. By virtue of his daughter being her daughter-in-law, she worked hard at maintaining cordial relations. Today, however, there was nothing cordial about either man. Stockton wasted no time on greetings.

"I'll come to the point," he said. "We've been appointed spokesmen for the ranchers on the Rio Bonito and the Rio Felix. We'd like some straight answers."

"Very well," Elizabeth said with icy courtesy. "How can I help you?"

"We're here about that meeting you held over at Albuquerque. Way we got the story, Miguel Ortega showed up and made a speech."

"That's correct," Elizabeth acknowledged. "He urged the *mexicano* leaders to adopt a position of unity in the fall elections."

"Do tell?" Stockton's tone bordered on sarcasm. "I'd say it's a case of one hand washin' the other. Question is, what does Ortega get for helping you whip the greasers into line?"

"I beg your pardon?"

"Let's get down to brass tacks. Folks are sayin' you've thrown your support behind Ortega. There's even talk you let him hide out here."

Elizabeth regarded him evenly. "Whoever says such a thing is a liar. I do not harbor fugitives."

Kimble's face was pinched in an oxlike expression. "If that's so," he demanded roughly, "how come Spur hasn't been raided? Why haven't the White Caps hit you?"

"For one thing," Elizabeth informed him, "I don't believe in barbed wire. For another, the *mexicanos* on the Hondo have always been treated fairly. You would do well to follow the example."

"Bullfeathers!" Kimble said, almost shouting. "We're not talkin' about better treatment for the pepperguts. We're talkin' about you gettin' cozy with Ortega."

"Aaron's right," Stockton said, his face darkening. "We wanna know what kind of game you're playin'. And by God, we mean to have an answer!"

Elizabeth rose from her chair. "Good day, gentlemen," she said with chilly smile. "You're no longer welcome in my home."

"You can't toss us out like that."

"I just have," she corrected him. "Please show yourselves the door."

Stockton and Kimble stormed out of the house. Elizabeth resumed her seat and went back to work. Some while later footsteps sounded in the hallway and Clint appeared in the door. His clothes were covered with trail dust and his face was gaunt with fatigue. On the road, he'd met the two ranchers and heard their side of the story. He asked for an explanation.

Elizabeth was wounded by his abrupt manner. She hadn't seen him in nearly six weeks, and she knew he'd been avoiding Spur. Their last meeting had ended with harsh words about Ortega, and she suspected that was the reason. Even now, as she explained the latest allegations, she realized nothing had changed. She was still on the defensive.

When she finished, Clint just stared at her. "You're dead wrong," he said after a long pause. "You've lost the governor's support and pushed him over into Canby's camp. And now the other cattlemen have turned against you. Where do you draw the line?"

"I have nothing to apologize for," Elizabeth said patiently. "Miguel Ortega forced his way into the meeting at gunpoint. I didn't invite him."

"You didn't ask him to leave, either. Hell, wake up, Beth! You're playing patty-cake with an outlaw—a murderer."

"I've told you before and I'll tell you again: I do not condone his methods. I've told him the same thing."

"So what?" Clint growled, half under his breath. "You're sympathetic to his cause and everybody knows it. Way it looks, you're aiding and abetting."

A veil seemed to drop over Elizabeth's eyes. "Nothing outweighs the importance of the fall elections. With Miguel Ortega's backing, I intend to take control of the legislature."

"Christ, it's not worth selling your soul."

"Contrary to what you may think, I've made no pact with the devil."

"Haven't you?" Clint asked sharply. "For your information, Ortega tried to have me killed in Santa Fe. I got his man instead."

"I don't believe that for an instant. He promised me no harm would come to any member of this family—you included."

"One way or another, I aim to see he delivers on the promise."

"By killing him?"

"I'd judge that's his choice, not mine."

Clint declined an invitation to stay the night. When he walked from the office, Elizabeth slumped back in her chair. She felt drained, no longer certain what was right and what was wrong. A bargain with the devil seemed to her an outlandish charge. And yet . . .

She asked herself the question Clint had posed only moments ago. Where should she draw the line?

EIGHTEEN

The examining room was awash in sunlight. Jennifer sat at her desk, entering notes on her last patient in a medical journal. She looked around as the door opened.

Rosa, her surgical assistant, motioned a man into the room. His name was Hubert Wallace, which the townspeople had shortened to "Wally." A clerk at the dry-goods store, he was short and chubby with a moonlike face. He appeared to be in considerable pain.

Jennifer finished the entry in her journal. Then, returning the pen to the inkstand, she gestured to a chair beside her desk. Wallace seated himself as Rosa closed the door. He was clutching his left arm tightly against his portly waistline.

"What seems to be the problem, Wally?"

"Goldanged if I know," Wallace said uncertainly. "Got something bad wrong with my wrist."

"Let me have a look."

Wallace reluctantly surrendered his arm. Jennifer laid his hand, palm down, on the edge of the desk. A large bulge was visible on the back of his wrist, just below the cuff on his shirt. She gently touched it with her fingertips.

"Ouch!" Wallace yelped.

"Tender?"

"Sore as a boil, Miss Brannock."

Wallace, like many of the townsmen, still found it difficult to address her as "Doctor." Jennifer ignored the oversight, by now resigned to their unintentional prejudice. She lifted his hand from the desk, holding the forearm straight out. Without warning, she bent his wrist down at a sharp angle.

"Gawdalmightybingo!"

"I take it that hurt?"

"Yes, ma'am," Wallace croaked. "You like to brought me plumb offen this chair."

Jennifer nodded. "Have you noticed any unusual weakness in your wrist?"

"Now that you mention it, I surely have. Last couple of days I can't hardly lift a fork."

From the size of his potbelly, Jennifer doubted he'd missed any meals. She studied his wrist closer and noted that the bulge had popped up, stretching the skin taut with a prominent knot. She examined it a moment longer, satisfying herself of the diagnosis.

"You have a ganglion, Wally."

"Ganglion?" Wallace echoed, his eyes widening. "What the blue blazes is that?"

Jennifer explained it in layman's terms. A lubricated sheath encased every tendon found in the body. While the reason was unknown, a painful bulge sometimes developed in the sheath. The bulge was thought to be a cystic tumor, an abnormal saclike growth filled with fluid. "Ganglion" was the medical term for such growths, most commonly found in the wrist.

The old-fashioned cure for ganglions was a wallop with a heavy book. The blow popped the saclike growth and dispersed the fluid through surrounding tissues. Too often, however, an overenthusiastic walloper also broke the patient's wrist. Advances in medicine now allowed for the reduction of a ganglion through surgery. A quicker method, always tried first, was manual reduction by a physician.

"The procedure's quite simple," Jennifer concluded. "With your help, I can do it right now."

Wallace looked dubious. "Will it hurt much?"

"Not all that badly," Jennifer said. "The alternative is to put you to sleep and operate."

The thought of a scalpel gave Wallace a queasy sensation.

"I guess it's okay," he said skittishly. "What d'you want me to do?"

"Take hold of your knuckles with your right hand and keep your wrist bent down over the edge of the desk. And once I start, Wally, you can't move. I want you to remain perfectly still."

"Cripes, I sure hope you know what you're doing."

"Trust me."

Wallace bent his wrist over the desk. Unable to watch, he closed his eyes and turned his head away. Jennifer centered the bulge between her thumbs and firmly squeezed inward. She steadily increased the pressure, her arms straining as the growth was pinched tighter in the viselike action of her thumbs. The ganglion suddenly burst with an almost inaudible popping sound.

Wallace winced and slowly opened one eye. Jennifer grasped his left hand and flexed the wrist up and down. The bulge had disappeared completely, and with it the pain. When she released his hand, Wallace somewhat tentatively rotated his wrist. A relieved grin spread over his face.

"By golly," he said bouyantly, "that's some trick. You're a regular wizard."

"Nothing to it," Jennifer said, smiling. "Especially when you have a cooperative patient."

"Well, I surely do thank you, Miss Brannock. How much do I owe you?"

"Three dollars ought to cover it, Wally."

"I'll bring it around on payday. That okay?"

"Of course."

Jennifer walked him to the door. When she opened it, she heard voices from the waiting room. As Wallace crossed to the outer door, she saw Rosa engaged in conversation with two men. The noon hour was approaching, and except for the men, the waiting room was empty. She nodded to them.

"May I help you?"

"Yes, ma'am," one of them replied. "Leastways if you're the doctor lady."

"Are you ill?"

"Oh, no, ma'am, nothin' like that. We're just lookin' for information."

Jennifer's appraisal was deliberate. The men were tall and rawboned, with hands gnarled from a lifetime of hard work. One appeared to be in his late thirties and the other was perhaps ten years younger. Their clothes, particularly their tall-crowned hats and spurs, identified them as cattlemen. She noted that the younger one wore crossed gunbelts with a brace of holstered pistols.

"Do I know you?" she asked. "I don't recall seeing you around town."

"We're new to the territory, ma'am. We just pulled into town this mornin'."

The older man apparently did all the talking. She caught a drawl in his voice, vaguely reminiscent of Texans she'd met. But the dictates of Western custom prohibited asking where they were from. She smiled pleasantly.

"What sort of information were you looking for?"

"We stopped off at the livery stable jest now. Feller told us you was some relation to Lon Brannock."

Jennifer had the immediate impression he was lying. She recalled Morg mentioning Lon and Hank, and their chance meeting in White Oaks. Yet, apart from family members, no one was aware of the Brannocks' kinfolk. She knew for a certainty that the livery owner had never heard of Lon.

"I'm Lon's cousin," she said. "Why do you ask?"

"We was hopin' to run acrost him. Heard he'd put down stakes somewhere in New Mexico."

"Are you friends of Lon's?"

The older man laughed. "Yes, ma'am, we're pards from way back. Him and us had some high old times together."

"I suppose that was when Lon lived in Texas?"

The man shuffled uneasily. "I don't know as you could say he lived there. His home was mostly up in the Injun Nations."

"Then you must know his brother."

"Uh—" The man faltered, clearly taken aback. "I do recollect him mentionin' it. 'Course, he never talked much about his kin."

"Oh?" Jennifer said innocently. "But you knew he had family here?"

"Well, that there's a different story altogether. He used to brag a heap on you folks. Told us you got a big ranch hereabouts."

Jennifer knew he was lying now. Everyone in the family was aware that Lon considered himself a Brannock in name only. To think that he would brag on them was patently absurd. "Quite honestly, I've never concerned myself with Lon's affairs. Have you inquired at the ranch?"

"C'mon, Bob," the younger man cut in gruffly. "She don't know nothin'."

"Do try at the ranch," Jennifer said helpfully. "Perhaps my mother could tell you something."

"Yes, ma'am," the older man said, bobbing his head. "We'll ride out first chance we get. Obliged for your time."

Jennifer realized the men hadn't volunteered their names. As they went out the door, she was struck by their similarity in build and features. The thought suddenly occurred that they were quite probably brothers. She turned back into her office.

From the corner window she watched them amble up the street. The younger one was talking now, gesturing angrily with his hands. Some dark premonition told her that they were hunting Lon, meant him harm. She waited until they were out of sight.

After removing her medical apron, she ordered Rosa to close the clinic. She then walked uptown to the hotel and asked for Clint. The desk clerk informed her the marshal had ridden out of town early that morning. She stood there a moment, indecisive as to her next move. Abruptly, she decided to ask Blake's advice.

Outside she angled across the street. Blake's law office was in a small frame building beside the courthouse. As she entered the door, she saw the two men leading their horses from the livery stable. She quickly stepped inside, closing the door, and watched from the window. The men halted before a saloon a short distance upstreet.

"What's so interesting?"

She turned at the sound of Blake's voice. He was seated behind a broad desk strewn with papers and open lawbooks. His expression was quizzical, and she hurriedly motioned him forward. He gave her an indulgent look, then rose from his chair and circled the desk. He stopped beside her at the window.

"I don't get it," he said. "What's the big mystery?"

"See those men?"

Blake followed the direction of her gaze. He saw two men, dressed in range clothes, hitching their horses outside the saloon. The bartender and owner, Dutch Fredericks, was sweeping the boardwalk with a straw broom. The older of the two men greeted him and Fredericks paused, leaning on the broomstick. They began talking.

"You mean the cowhands?" Blake asked. "What about them?"

Jennifer frowned. "Do you think they could be peace officers?"

Blake took a closer look. "From their appearance, I'd have to say no. They're a little too scruffy for lawmen. Why do you ask?"

"They're looking for Lon," she said. "A few minutes ago, they came by the clinic. They tried to pass themselves off as Lon's friends."

"What makes you think they're not?"

"Because every other word was a lie."

Jennifer quickly recounted the conversation. She stressed the older man's uneasy manner and the implausible story he'd told. Proud of herself, she explained how she'd tripped him up with leading questions.

"I have a bad feeling," she said at length. "Something about them just doesn't seem right."

Blake considered a moment. "On the face of it, I suspect you have a point. No one lies without a reason."

"Well, anyway, Lon's in no immediate danger. They'd never think to look for him in White Oaks."

"On the contrary, I have an idea that's their next stop."

"What—?"

"See for yourself."

Jennifer stared out the window. She saw the older man and the saloonkeeper with their heads together. As she watched, they turned and disappeared into the saloon, followed by the younger man. She glanced back at Blake.

"I don't understand what that has to do with Lon."

"Dutch Fredericks is the town gadfly. He's sure to let the cat out of the bag."

"Will you please make sense?"

"Jen, I just assumed you'd heard it too. Word's around that a gambler relative of the Brannocks has set up shop in White Oaks. No one has mentioned him by name, but those men—"

"Will worm it out of Dutch Fredericks."

"—and put two and two together."

"Omigod!" Jennifer cried. "We have to get to the ranch!"

"What good will that do?"

"Uncle Clint might be there. Or if he's not, Mother will think of something. Hurry up, go get your buckboard!"

Blake obediently got his hat and rushed out the door. Jennifer stood at the window, fidgeting nervously as he walked toward the livery stable. Her eyes strayed to the saloon and her mouth compressed in a tight line.

She suddenly wished Dutch Fredericks would be struck dumb.

A midafternoon sun heeled over toward the mountains. Blake hauled back on the reins and brought his sweat-lathered team to a halt. Jennifer jumped down and ran inside the house.

She found her mother and Morg seated in the office. Only a step behind, Blake followed her down the hallway. Louise emerged from her bedroom, startled by the commotion, and gave him a strange look. She joined him in the doorway.

Jennifer began talking the instant she entered the office. Elizabeth appeared disconcerted, and then, as the story unfolded her expression turned to open concern. Morg listened impassively, trying to follow his sister's scrambled account of the morning's events. She finally paused to catch her breath.

"Way it sounds," Morg said lightly, "you're jumping at shadows. Maybe those fellows have got personal business with Lon."

"Very personal," Elizabeth said in a troubled voice. "Unless I'm mistaken, they are the last of the Jarrott brothers. They've come here to kill Lon."

Jennifer stared at her, aghast. "Why would they want to kill him?"

Until now, none of the family had been told of Lon's past. Elizabeth knew the details, for Clint had kept her informed over the years. But he had sworn her to secrecy and she'd never betrayed his trust. Today there seemed no way around an explanation.

Elizabeth briefly sketched a tale of violence and death. As a youngster, Lon had killed a cowhand in a barroom argument. Later, the dead man's four brothers crossed over from Texas onto the Comanche reservation. Their family name was Jarrott, and their purpose was retribution. They wanted an eye for an eye.

Warned by his Comanche friends, Lon ambushed the Texans on a mountain trail. He killed two and sent the other two scurrying back across the Red River. Yet the last of the Jarrott brothers had never relented, vowing to avenge the deaths of their kinsmen. For years, they had tracked Lon unsuccessfully when he worked the gambling circuit in Texas. And now, still intent on vengeance, they had tracked him to New Mexico.

"We have to warn Lon," Elizabeth said at last. "The Jarrotts are certain to find him this time."

"I'll do it," Morg volunteered. "There's a back trail through the mountains to White Oaks. I can be there before dark."

Elizabeth nodded in approval. "Clint has to be alerted as well. It's possible he might somehow stop the Jarrotts."

"Leave that to me," Blake said briskly. "One way or another, I'll locate him. Someone's bound to know where he's gone."

"Thank you, Blake," Elizabeth said graciously. "When you find him, send him directly to White Oaks. In the meantime, Morg will have advised Lon of the situation."

"No!" Louise said in a shrill voice. "Why should Morgan risk getting himself killed? He won't just warn Lon—he'll try to help!"

"For Chrissake," Morg grumbled. "Would you button your lip for once? We'll talk about it later."

Louise started to protest, but Morg brushed past her and went through the doorway. A moment later Jennifer and Blake followed him along the hall. The front door slammed and a sudden stillness fell over the house. Louise burst into tears.

Elizabeth went to her. The girl tried to pull away, but Elizabeth firmly sat her down in one of the chairs before the desk. She then seated herself in the other chair and waited for the tears to subside. Louise slowly got control of herself and pulled a hanky from her sleeve. She blew her nose loudly.

"We need to have a talk," Elizabeth said. "I think it's time you became part of the family."

Louise stared daggers at her. "You kicked my father out of this house and you'd like to be rid of me too. Don't you think I know that?"

"Whatever differences I have with your father, it doesn't affect how I feel about you. I've always hoped we could be friends."

Louise tossed her head. "You've resented me from the day I walked into this house. You never wanted me to marry Morg."

"You're so very wrong," Elizabeth said with some dignity. "What you haven't realized is that you didn't marry Morg alone. You married the entire Brannock family."

Surprise washed over the girl's face. "I don't understand what you're talking about."

"Yes, I know," Elizabeth said. "When I married into the family, it all seemed very strange to me too. I couldn't understand why my husband loved his brothers at least as much as he loved me."

"Are you serious?" Louise asked with a confused little laugh. "You really felt that way?"

"Oh, yes, indeed," Elizabeth observed. "And that's how I know what you're going through right now."

"No, you don't," Louise said in an injured voice. "Your husband didn't go running off when you were pregnant and leave you to wonder if he'll come back alive. I'll never forgive Morg!"

"When I was twenty-one," Elizabeth said quietly, "I was pregnant with Jennifer. Virgil, my husband, walked out of the house with his brothers on a cold October morning. An hour later they killed four men who were trying to kill them."

"How could you let him go?"

"How could I stop him? He had a responsibility to his brothers which overshadowed all my tears and agonizing. Morg feels that same responsibility toward Lon."

"Yes, but that was different. Lon's just a cousin—not a brother."

"Family is family," Elizabeth said, an observant look on her face. "You have to understand how it is with the Brannocks. We stand by one another, whatever the cost to us personally. We simply couldn't do less."

Louise's voice was thoughtful. "You're saying I have to feel that way too. Or else I'll never be a Brannock."

"You are a Brannock," Elizabeth said firmly. "To every member of the family, you're not just Morg's wife. You are one of us, one of our own."

"I . . ." Louise stopped, her eyes suddenly misty. "I'm just so scared. So terrified I'll lose him."

"Before he was your husband, he was my son. I know exactly how you feel."

"But you let him go anyway."

"And so must you."

Louise looked down at her hands. She sat there for a long moment, twisting the handkerchief between her fingers. Then she straightened, wiping her eyes, and forced herself to smile. She tried to sound strong.

"It's not easy, being a Brannock."

"I'll help you. I've spent a lifetime learning how."

Elizabeth extended her hands, clasping the girl's in her own. Neither of them spoke, but some silent communion passed between them. What they shared was what all the Brannock women somehow came to know.

The family, however cruel the adversity, would endure.

NINETEEN

In the lowering dusk Bob and Charley Jarrott rode into White Oaks. Nightfall was fast approaching and the town's streetlamps were already lighted. They reined to a halt outside a saloon.

Dutch Fredericks, the Lincoln saloonkeeper, had proved to be a repository of information. At Bob Jarrott's prompting, he'd revealed every scrap of gossip, past and present, about the Brannocks. One item, related with a sly wink, had to do with the latest rumor.

The Brannocks, according to Dutch Fredericks, had a "family skeleton." For all their high-and-mighty airs, it appeared that one of their relatives ran with the sporting crowd. The man in question was a gambler and he'd been reported in White Oaks. His game was poker, and word had it that he was something of a cardsharp.

Bob Jarrott had done all the talking. His younger brother, Charley, was surly and short-tempered and hadn't joined in the conversation. After a final drink they'd parted with Fredericks, who took them to be saddle tramps in search of work. Their ride from Lincoln to White Oaks had consumed the balance of the afternoon.

Neither of the Jarrotts had ever seen a mining camp. But they had driven herds up the Western Trail to Dodge City, largest of the Kansas cowtowns. Their first impression of White Oaks was favorable, for like the cowtowns, it was wide open and populated by rough men. They began their search with a tour of the saloons and gaming dives.

The Jarrotts didn't know Lon on sight. Yet, over the years, they had put together a fairly accurate physical description. Tonight, as they'd done on the gamblers' circuit in Texas, they engaged bartenders in conversation. After inquiring about the hottest poker game in town, they turned the talk to gamblers. One way or another, they managed to raise the name of Lon Brannock.

The Jarrotts were a stubborn lot, and proud. Though largely uneducated, they practiced a rigid code of honor. Any man who wronged a member of their family wronged them as well. And it made no difference that Lon had killed their brothers in defense of his own life. For six years, whenever they could spare the time from their ranch, they had resumed the hunt. Never before had they been so close, so confident it would end. White Oaks seemed to them the last stop on a long and tortuous trail.

After hitting three saloons, they wandered into the Lady Gay. One of the barkeeps, in response to Bob Jarrott's question, jerked his thumb toward the rear of the room. He indicated a poker table and identified one of the players as the gambler named Brannock. The other players included two businessmen, attired in conservative suits, and three rough-clad miners. The barkeep remarked that it was a table-stakes game.

Bob Jarrott nodded to his brother. They moved through the crowd, skirting the faro layouts on the opposite side of the room. At the rear of the saloon, beyond the three poker tables, there was a lone pool table. They idly noted a half-breed kid and a grungy miner with cue sticks, playing a game of eight ball. Their attention centered on the poker table positioned near the left-hand wall. Lon Brannock was seated on the far side of the table, facing them.

The Jarrotts separated. Charley moved off to the left and Bob halted to the right of the table. Even in a personal dispute, the law demanded that a certain code be observed. A man could be called out and killed so long as he was given an even break. To shoot a man in coldblood was considered

unsporting, and inevitably resulted in a murder trial. Or
worse, since they were strangers in town, they might find
themselves lynched from the nearest tree. For appearances'
sake, they somehow had to provoke their man.

Bob Jarrott took the lead. He stood a pace away from the
table, staring directly at Lon. "I'm lookin' for a sorry sonovabitch name of Brannock. Somebody told me you was him."

The challenge froze the other players in a stilled tableau.
Except for a startled glance, none of them moved, and they
kept their hands on top the table. Lon looked up from his
cards, assessing the man who had spoken. His gaze shifted
to the younger man, noting the crossed gunbelts and the
tense stance. Some instinct told him the younger man was
faster and therefore more dangerous. He directed his attention to the older one.

"I'm Lon Brannock," he said. "What's that to you?"

"Name's Jarrott," Bob Jarrott grated out. "You put three
of my brothers in their graves. Ambushed two of them and
gunned 'em down without warnin'."

An ironic smile touched the corner of Lon's mouth. He
understood that the speech was for the benefit of the onlookers. Jarrott was laying the groundwork for what later might
be ruled justifiable homicide. It was a smart move, well
thought out.

"Tell the whole story," Lon said in a flat voice. "You and
your brothers were out to nail my hide. Four to one wasn't
exactly a fair fight."

"We was within our rights! You'd already killed one of
my brothers."

"Mister, you've got things catty-wampus. I seem to recollect your brother drew first."

A brittle silence had now settled over the other poker tables. Toward the rear, Hank stood behind the pool table, listening intently. While he'd never seen the Jarrotts, he was
aware of their past efforts at killing Lon. His eyes moved
from one brother to the next, studying them carefully. He
thought Lon would take the younger one first.

Hank suddenly stiffened. He saw Morg rush through the front door and look wildly around the saloon. It flashed through his mind that Morg's unexpected appearance was somehow tied to the Jarrotts. Then, spotting Lon at the poker table, Morg bulled a path through the crowd. From his expression, he hadn't yet grasped the situation. There was nothing to indicate he'd recognized the Jarrott brothers.

"You gonna fight?" Bob Jarrott flared, glowering at Lon. "Or you gonna show your yellow streak?"

A cold tinsel glitter surfaced in Lon's eyes. "You've got me at a disadvantage, Jarrott. Two to one and I'm still in my chair."

"Then get on your gawddamn feet."

"Lon—!" Morg called out, hurrying forward.

The Jarrotts were momentarily distracted. They half-turned toward the sound of the voice, then recovered. In that instant, Lon kicked back his chair and stood erect. The other players hit the floor as his Colt appeared from the crossdraw holster. His arm leveled at the exact moment Charley Jarrott pulled both guns.

Lon fired across the table. Charley Jarrott stood perfectly still, a great splotch of red covering his breastbone. He fired his right-hand gun into the floor, dropping the other one, and then he wilted at the middle. As he toppled forward, Bob Jarrott got off a hurried snapshot. The bullet ripped through Lon's left thigh and his leg went dead. He collapsed sideways onto the floor.

Jarrott started around the table. He raised his gun, intent on finishing the job with a second shot. From the rear of the room, Hank extended his pistol at arm's length. He fired over the pool table, triggering two rounds a split-second apart. The slugs jolted Bob Jarrott back a step at a time, splattering his shirtfront with blood. He went down like a puppet with its strings gone haywire.

A dense cloud of gunsmoke hung over the poker table. For a long moment everyone in the saloon stared at the three men on the floor. The Jarrotts lay motionless, their eyes fixed

blankly on nothing. Lon slowly raised himself up on one elbow, his features waxen, teeth gritted against the pain. His
pants leg was soaked with blood.

Morg abruptly broke the spell. He circled the poker table
and dropped to one knee beside Lon. A quick inspection revealed that the bullet had struck Lon in the upper thigh. After ripping the pants leg apart, Morg saw that the wound was
still pumping blood. He jerked a kerchief from his pocket
and began fashioning a tourniquet. The men around him
watched with morbid curiosity.

Hank walked forward from the pool table. He appeared
shaken and studiously avoided looking at the man he'd shot.
The pistol was still clutched tightly in his hand, as though he
had forgotten to holster it. He seemed unaware of the poker
players and other nearby onlookers, who were watching him
strangely. At the table, he knelt down as Morg tied off the
tourniquet.

Lon's forehead was beaded with sweat. He took hold of
Morg's arm, pulled him closer. "Get me out of town," he
said. "I'll never get a fair shake here."

"Sure, you will," Morg said earnestly. "Hell, they're the
ones that started the fight. You just defended yourself."

"Won't matter," Lon told him. "Hank and me aren't liked
around here. Nobody'll take my side."

Hank nodded agreement. "Lon's right," he said in a low
voice. "Folks tagged him an Injun lover 'cause of me.
They'd like to make trouble for him."

"So what?" Morg said, turning back to Lon. "You're liable to bleed to death if we don't get you to a doctor. You're
wounded bad."

Lon shook his head. "I'm likely to get my neck stretched
before I bleed to death. Take a look around."

Morg glanced up at the men gathered nearby. Their faces
were cold and implacable, somehow unfriendly. He recalled
the resentment against Lon for forcing the town to accept a
half-breed. Until now, fearful of offending Lon, no one had
dared to speak out. But a wounded man no longer posed a
threat.

A sudden murmur swept through the crowd. George Watson, the town marshal, eased past the front rank of onlookers. As he approached the poker table, he quickly surveyed the carnage, taking note of Lon's bloody leg. He stooped down, checking both the Jarrotts in turn for a pulsebeat. Satisfied they were dead, he looked across at Lon.

"What happened here, Brannock?"

"Old business," Lon said, grimacing against the throb in his leg. "They trailed me into town . . . picked a fight."

Watson stared at him. "You kill both of them?"

"Hell, no!" one of the crowd yelled. "He pulled first and got the younger one. The 'breed potshot the older fellow from over at the pool table."

"That right?" Watson asked, still looking at Lon. "You draw first?"

"I beat 'em to it," Lon said in a weak voice. "They were fixin' to throw down on me."

Watson grunted something unintelligible. His gaze flicked to Hank, spotted the pistol in the boy's hand. "How about it?" he said roughly. "You shoot the older one before he saw you?"

"I didn't do nothin' till after he'd shot Lon."

"Guess that's for a coroner's jury to decide. I'm placing you both under arrest."

"What for?" Hank protested. "You got no right."

'None of your lip." Watson advanced another step, extended his hand. "I'll take that gun."

Hank reacted on impulse. He raised the pistol, thumbing the hammer, and pointed it at the lawman. "Just stay back."

Lon struggled to push himself erect. His strength failed him, and he grabbed Morg's arm. "Don't let 'em take us," he said. "They'll lynch Hank, too."

An instant of leaden silence slipped past. Morg looked at the marshal, then scanned the faces of the crowd. He saw it in their eyes and the feral set to their mouths. They wouldn't hesitate to hang a 'breed kid.

Morg climbed to his feet. He drew his pistol from the holster, glancing at Hank. "We'll need a buckboard or a wagon.

Lon wouldn't last any time on a horse. Go see what you can round up on the street."

Hank moved through the crowd, waving his pistol. A path opened before him and he hurried out the door. Morg nodded to the lawman. "Don't get brave, marshal. We're not looking for trouble."

Watson glowered at him. "You think I don't know you? Your name's Morgan Brannock."

"What of it?"

"You're supposed to be a respectable businessman. Why get yourself involved in a sucker's game? You'll never get away with it."

"I'm gonna make a damn good try."

Hank returned within minutes. He'd commandeered a wagon and team and had it waiting on the street. With his assistance, Lon was able to hobble outside on his good leg. Morg followed close behind, brandishing the pistol as he backed away. At the door he paused, looking at the crowd.

"Everybody stay put till we're long gone. Anybody pokes his head outside will wish he hadn't."

The door swung open and Morg stepped into the night. Hank popped the reins as he scrambled aboard the wagon. They drove south out of White Oaks.

No one attempted to follow them in the darkness.

Jennifer was awakened shortly after midnight. She threw on a housecoat and hurried from her bedroom through the clinic. The pounding at the front door grew louder.

After lighting a lamp in the waiting room, she opened the door. Her breath caught in her throat and she quickly moved aside. Morg and Hank edged through the door, carrying Lon in their arms. His left pants leg was dark with blood.

Holding the lamp for them, Jennifer lighted the way into her office. She ordered Lon placed on the operating table and then lit the overhead reflector lamp. As she turned to the instrument cabinet, Morg told her that he had periodically loosened the tourniquet. She deftly snipped open the trouser leg with medical scissors.

While she worked, Morg explained what had transpired in White Oaks. She let him talk, but her attention was focused on Lon. His breathing was shallow, and though he'd lost a great deal of blood, his pulse rate was still strong. She satisfied herself that he was unconscious before turning to the wound itself. The flesh around the entry hole was puffy and bruised, caked with dried blood. From all outward appearances, the femoral artery had not been severed.

With Morg's help, she got Lon undressed. Hank stood by, gathering the blood-soaked clothing as it was tossed aside. Jennifer next examined the backside of the leg, determining that the slug had not exited. She felt reasonably confident that the thigh bone hadn't been shattered, but the track of the bullet remained a mystery. She wouldn't know for certain until she operated.

Jennifer scrubbed her hands with strong soap and cold water. As she finished, she caught Hank watching her with an awestruck expression. It occurred to her that she and her Comanche cousin had never met until tonight. Nor had she seen Lon since she was a small girl, some fourteen years ago. Wondering on it, she suddenly realized she'd never before operated on one of her relatives. She quickly pushed the thought aside.

There was always a chance that Lon would regain consciousness. She accordingly instructed Morg on the proper method of administering ether. While she talked, she put together a tray of surgical dressings and sterilized instruments. She then cleansed the wound with a carbolic solution and prepared to operate. Morg took his place at the head of the table, ready with a sponge and a small can of ether.

The operation proceeded without complications. Jennifer located the bullet with a probe and gingerly extracted it from the wound channel. There was no excess bleeding and she found no evidence of foreign matter in the wound. In the process, she reaffirmed her belief that the femur bone had not been damaged. She completed the procedure by applying a loose bandage to permit drainage. Stepping back, she told herself Lon had drawn heavily on his gambler's luck. The bullet had missed the femoral artery by only a few centimeters.

The front door banged open. A moment later Clint appeared in the entrance to the operating room. He looked from one to the other and his gaze finally came to rest on Lon. His expression darkened.

"What the hell's going on here?"

"Where have you been?" Jennifer demanded. "Blake's out trying to find you."

"I just got back from Fort Stanton. I saw a light on and thought I'd better check."

"You missed the party," Morg said, moving away from the operating table. "Lon and Hank bagged the last of the Jarrott brothers. Killed 'em stone dead."

"The Jarrotts?" Clint repeated hollowly. "Where'd they come from?"

"Showed up out of the blue. Started asking questions here and finally tracked Lon down at White Oaks."

"Looks like Lon caught one himself."

Jennifer held up the bullet. "So far as I can tell, there's no permanent damage. He should recover nicely."

Clint nodded. "How'd it come to a shooting?"

Morg started at the beginning and told the story straight through. His one reservation was that he'd arrived too late to warn Lon. He credited Hank with quick thinking and quick shooting, which was all that had saved Lon's life. When he finished, there was a moment of profound silence. Clint's features congealed into a tight scowl.

"Jesus Christ," he said slowly. "You actually put a gun on George Watson?"

"No choice," Morg countered. "It was that or a lynching bee. Watson couldn't have stopped that crowd."

"What's the difference?" Clint grumbled. "Lon and Hank both will be charged with murder. In case you forgot, that's a hanging offense."

"Yeah, but they have to be caught first. We'll hide 'em someplace on Spur."

"Don't be a fool," Clint said, annoyed. "Watson's probably

putting a posse together right now. You think you're gonna fight him off with your cowhands?"

Morg waved his hand, as though dusting away the problem. "There's always the ranch in the Outlet. Nobody would look for them there."

"What about yourself?" Clint persisted. "You'll be charged with obstructing the law and harboring fugitives. You figure to ride the owlhoot too?"

Morg smiled uneasily, "I never thought of that."

Clint pondered it a moment, and then, almost as though he was thinking out loud, he glanced at Jennifer. "How long before Lon can be moved?"

"In an emergency," she said, "he could be moved now. Of course, it would have to be done carefully. We can't risk reopening his wound."

"Here's what I want," Clint said, nodding to Morg. "Load Lon in that wagon and take him out to Spur. Your mother's a pretty fair nurse. She'll tend to him proper."

Morg appeared puzzled. "You sound like you've got something up your sleeve."

"Let's just hope it works. I'm gonna try to talk turkey with George Watson."

"You mean, get him to drop the charges?"

Clint shrugged, then turned away. His gaze fell on Hank and his features softened. "Don't blame yourself for what happened. Anybody worth his salt would've done the same thing. Your brother's lucky you were there."

The boy gave him a hangdog look. "I wish't them Jarrotts hadn't never showed up."

"Some men are bound to get themselves killed. You couldn't have stopped it."

Clint patted the youngster on the shoulder. Then, looking around at Morg, he made a short, emphatic nod. "Get Lon out of town before daylight. I'll see you at the ranch."

Without waiting for a reply, he walked from the room. The front door opened and closed and there was a moment's silence. At length, Morg turned to the boy. His expression was bemused.

"I've been wonderin'," he said. "Where'd you learn to shoot like that?"

Hank smiled sheepishly. "Lon and me practice just about every mornin'. I got to where I generally hit the mark."

"By God, you hit it dead center tonight! Lon oughta thank his lucky stars he taught you so good."

Jennifer couldn't bear to listen. By rough calculation she placed Hank's age at fifteen. She thought him far too young to have killed his first man. But then, on quick reflection, she realized there was no good age for such things. In the end, whether young or old, killing left its mark.

She wondered how it would end for Hank.

TWENTY

A faint blush of dawn lighted the sky. Clint slowed his horse to a walk as he rode into White Oaks. Upstreet, his gaze was drawn to a knot of men outside the marshal's office.

George Watson stood on the boardwalk. Before him was grouped a motley collection of miners and townspeople. The men were grim-eyed, their features cold and hard in the sallow overcast.

The posse was composed of volunteers. Their love of a good fight, rather than civic pride, had enabled Watson to recruit them from the town's saloons. The greater incentive, however, was the likelihood that they would hang the 'breed kid along with his smartass brother. No one believed the fugitives would be brought back alive.

All the men were armed and leading horses. Watson had delayed pursuit until first light, though he had no intention of tracking his quarry. He felt reasonably confident that they would have taken refuge at Spur, with a brief stopover in Lincoln for medical attention. His plan was to arrive at the ranch in force and demand their surrender from Elizabeth Brannock. He doubted she would let it come to a fight.

Watson was still counting heads. Fourteen men had volunteered, but so far only ten had shown up. He was debating whether to roust them out of bed when he spotted Clint. The posse members caught his startled expression and craned for a better look. They saw a tall, broad-shouldered rider with a badge pinned to his shirt. None of them knew him, but the shape of the badge was distinctive. The murmured words "U.S. marshal" swept through their ranks.

Clint dismounted at the hitch rack. He looped the reins around the crossbar and moved to the boardwalk.

"'Mornin', George," he said. "I'd like a word with you."

Before Watson could reply, Clint brushed past him and entered the office. The men were staring at him curiously and Watson tried to put the best face on it. "Don't you boys wander off," he ordered. "I'll be with you in a jiffy."

Turning away, he hurried inside the office. Clint stood beside a wood-burning stove, pouring himself a mug of coffee from a smoke-blackened galvanized pot. He replaced the pot and took a long swig from the steaming mug.

"Tastes damn good," he said. "I've been on the road all night."

Watson smiled without humor. "You could've saved yourself a trip. I was just about to head over your way."

"Yeah, I know," Clint said pointedly. "I saw the boys at my niece's place. You'll recollect she's the lady doctor."

"Figured as much when you rode up. Guess they must've told you about the fracas last night."

"That's what I wanted to talk to you about."

"Won't do no good," Watson said in a raspy voice. "Nobody pulls a gun on me and gets away with it. Not even your kinfolk."

Clint's features were impassive. "Let's understand one another. Are you saying they're charged with evading arrest . . . nothing else?"

"Hell, no." Watson paused, regarding him with a dour look. "Way the witnesses tell it, Lon drew first. That makes it murder."

"You ever play suppose, George?"

"I dunno what you mean."

"Well, just for example, let's suppose Hank wasn't a half-breed. Then we'll suppose Lon never forced everybody to tread light around his Injun brother. Supposin' all that, you reckon anybody would give a goddamn that they killed the Jarrotts?"

"Suppose whatever you want," Watson said balefully. "How's that change anything?"

Clint's eyes were pale and very direct. "You're gonna drop all the charges, George. Otherwise, you'll end up with egg on your face."

"Maybe you'd like to spell that out."

"Glad to."

Clint stuck to the salient details. He recounted the Jarrott brothers' six-year vendetta against Lon. In passing, he observed that the Jarrotts had ridden all the way from Texas for the sole purpose of revenge. Lon, on the other hand, had sought to avoid trouble at every turn.

"You force me to it," he concluded, "and I'll bring 'em before the judge at Lincoln. How do you think he'd rule?"

"So what?" Watson muttered lamely. "They still resisted arrest and took off in a stolen wagon."

"That's what I meant about egg on your face. You could have prevented all that just by listening to their side of the story. Instead, you took the word of a bunch of rumdum barflies."

Watson let out his breath in a low whistle. "Thunderation, Clint, I can't just call it off. I've got a posse waitin' out there! I'd look like the town idiot."

Clint shrugged. "You press charges and you'll come off like a real dimdot. C'mon, admit it, you've got no case."

"Goddamnit, they stuck a gun in my face! How'd it look if I just let that drop? I've got to uphold the law in this town."

"All right," Clint allowed. "We'll have the judge stick 'em with a stiff fine for resisting arrest. Will that get you off the hook?"

"What about the wagon and team they stole?"

"I'll have it returned with a hundred dollars for the owner's trouble. That ought to satisfy everybody."

"Still not enough," Watson grouched. "I want 'em posted out of White Oaks—permanent."

Clint was silent a moment, thoughtful. "Where Lon and the boy are concerned, that's no problem. Morg's an altogether different matter. He's got business affairs over here."

"Have it your way," Watson conceded glumly. "But you tell them other two to stay the hell outta my town. I've had a bellyful."

"George, I'll tend to it personal. You've got my word on it."

Watson appeared somewhat mollified. They shook hands and Clint placed his coffee mug on a table beside the stove. Then, as they turned toward the door, Watson abruptly stopped. He gave Clint a sidelong look.

"Your kinfolk got me so pissed-off I almost forgot I'm a lawman. I come damn close to not tellin' you what I stumbled across."

"What's that?"

"Well, like I said," Watson remarked, "this here's my town. I keep my ear to the ground."

"So?"

"So we've got a fair number of greasers that live hereabouts. I got wind somebody's been recruitin' for *Las Gorras Blancas*."

"Miguel Ortega?" Clint asked.

Watson shook his head. "Nobody mentioned any names. What I heard was, they're plannin' another raid on the Rio Bonito."

"Any idea which rancher they aim to hit?"

"Nope," Watson said, then shrugged. "I only heard it night before last. For all I know, it's so much hot air."

"Who's your source?" Clint said, looking at him. "You wouldn't get something like that on the grapevine."

Watson ducked his head. "I see a little Mex gal now and then. We was workin' on a bottle of tequila and—" He hesitated, lifted his hands. "What with one thing and another, she let it slip."

"What makes you believe her?"

"Hell, she was drunker'n a hoot owl! Had no notion what she was sayin'."

Clint considered briefly. "You think she might talk to me?"

"Not sober," Watson said, chuckling. "Let me work on her my own way. Anything turns up, I'll send you word."

"I'd be obliged, George."

Outside the office, Clint walked directly to the hitch rack. He mounted, reining the gelding around, and rode off at a trot. Behind, as Watson ordered the posse disbanded, he heard catcalls and heated curses from the men. He smiled to himself, amused by their anger.

In a manner of speaking, George Watson had just spoiled their fun. Nobody would be hanged today.

Shortly after sunrise, the wagon lumbered to a halt outside the main house. Morg wrapped the reins around the brake lever and jumped down to the ground. He waved to several hands walking toward the corral.

Lon was stretched out in the back of the wagon. A pallet of blankets had cushioned him on the bumpy road from town. Hank sat beside him, ready with a bottle of laudanum provided by Jennifer. So far, Lon had refused to take any of the sedative. He was alert and thoroughly irritated.

Halfway from Lincoln, Lon had finally regained consciousness. When informed he was being taken to Spur, he'd flatly rejected the idea. Between them, Morg and Hank had finally convinced him that there was no choice. For the moment, the ranch was the one place where he could recuperate while being looked after properly. With grudging reluctance, he had at last agreed. Yet he was still in a grumpy mood.

Elizabeth appeared on the veranda. A moment later Brad approached the wagon, followed by several cowhands. Lon was unloaded, with the pallet of blankets serving as a stretcher, and they carried him into the house. Leading the way, Elizabeth showed them to one of the spare bedrooms at the end of the hall. There Lon was transferred from the blankets to a wide brass-knobbed bed.

After the hands trooped out of the house, Elizabeth demanded an explanation. Morg wearily recounted the story, ending with Clint's decision to ride to White Oaks. At that point, Louise appeared in the doorway, rubbing sleep from her eyes, a housecoat thrown on over her nightgown. She shrieked with a mixture of happiness and relief and rushed into Morg's arms. He looked oddly embarrassed by her teary welcome.

Elizabeth finally shooed everyone out of the room. Louise led Morg away, peppering him with questions. Brad volunteered to get Hank some breakfast and they walked toward the kitchen. When Elizabeth closed the door, she found Lon watching her from the bed. His expression was unreadable, although she suspected he was in considerable pain. She moved to the side of the bed, mustering her warmest smile.

"Are you comfortable?" she asked. "Anything I can get you?"

"No, I'm fine," Lon said. "Don't go to any trouble on my account."

"It's no trouble," Elizabeth assured him. "We're really very pleased to have you here. I just wish it could have been under happier circumstances."

"Well, I'll try not to be a bother. Soon's I can ride, Hank and me will be on our way."

"Nonsense," Elizabeth said cheerily. "You're both welcome as long as you care to stay. I want you to think of this as your home."

Lon just stared at her. When he didn't reply, Elizabeth turned back the sheet and bent to examine his wound. He wore only his undershorts and he looked vaguely uncomfortable at her attentions. The bandage on his thigh was lightly spotted with blood but otherwise unsoiled. She lifted the edge, checking for drainage, and nodded to herself. He appeared visibly relieved when she draped the sheet back over his chest.

"Aren't you fortunate?" she said, smiling. "Not everyone has a doctor in the family. Jennifer took care of you very nicely."

"Funny thing," Lon said slowly. "I never even saw her. I was passed out the whole time she was workin' on me."

"I shouldn't wonder," Elizabeth commented. "You lost a good deal of blood. Anyone would pass out."

"Except for Hank, I would've lost a lot more blood. He saved my bacon just in the nick of time."

"How does Hank feel about that? I mean—apart from saving you—does he regret having killed a man?"

Lon looked faintly amused. "Why would he regret killin' a no-account like Jarrott? I'd say he deserves a medal."

A thought tugged at the corner of Elizabeth's mind. Because of Lon, young Hank had been subjected to a harrowing experience. Yet Lon seemed impervious to even the simplest emotion. On the face of it, he had no concept that the boy might suffer some lingering aftereffect. Thinking about it, a strange sadness came over her. She actually felt sorry for Lon.

"I don't know about medals," she said, trying to treat it lightly, "but you must be in some pain. Would you like a spoonful of laudanum?"

Lon's smile was cryptic. "I'd sooner keep my wits about me. I'm not hurtin' all that bad."

"Are you hungry, then? I could ask the cook to fix you something special."

"Whatever you got will suit me just fine. I'm not hard to please."

Elizabeth excused herself. When she went out the door, Lon slumped back against his pillow. He stared up at the ceiling and silently cursed whatever fate had brought him to Spur. He'd sworn never to set foot on the place or to get himself involved with the family. He felt somehow like a charity case. Or worse, a poor relation.

Some while later there was a knock at the door. John Taylor stepped into the room, balancing a serving tray on one hand. After closing the door, he crossed to the bed, nodding to Lon. His smile was inquisitive.

"How you feelin'?" he said. "I brought you some eats."

"No complaints," Lon said evenly. "Who're you?"

"John Taylor. I work for Miz Brannock."

Lon pushed himself to a sitting position. His leg throbbed with the effort, and he winced, swearing softly. Taylor watched without comment, then placed the tray across his lap. On it was a bowl of beef broth and a pot of tea.

"What's this?" Lon asked. "You'd think I was an invalid."

Taylor chuckled. "Miz Brannock figured you oughta stick to liquids. Go ahead, it'll do you good."

Lon spooned the broth, slurping loudly. He glanced up at Taylor. "I heard about you from my uncle. Aren't you the one from Texas?"

"I'm the one," Taylor said with a wry smile. "Some folks used to call me a hired gun. 'Course, I'm retired now."

"Why's that?" Lon said. "Way I heard it, you're still pretty fast."

"Well, there's always somebody a little faster. You might say it's a temporary occupation."

"Temporary?"

A ghost of a grin touched Taylor's mouth. "I've never yet seen a man that couldn't be beat. That includes yours truly."

Lon took a sip of tea. "So you just quit?"

"Anybody with a lick of sense knows when to fold his cards. I reckon that goes for gunhands the same way it does gamblers."

Lon gave him a quick, guarded glance. "Why do I get the feelin' you're trying to tell me something?"

"What's to tell?" Taylor said equably. "You win some and you lose some. 'Course, when you lose with a gun, it's a mite different than cards. You cash out for good."

There was the merest beat of hesitation. "When the time comes," Lon scoffed, "maybe I'll fold my cards too. Just now, I'm still playin' into luck."

Taylor walked to the door. He turned, looking back with a sardonic smile. "You should've kept that slug your cousin dug outta you. You'll never see the one that kills you."

The door opened and closed before Lon could frame a reply. He told himself he'd been sandbagged, and by his aunt no less. She wanted a message delivered, but she knew he wouldn't listen to a woman. So she hadn't returned with the tray herself.

She'd sent John Taylor instead.

Clint arrived late that afternoon. He hadn't slept in thirty-six hours and his eyes felt lead-weighted. Outside the corral he dismounted and turned his horse over to a wrangler. As he walked toward the house, his boot heels seemed to drag the ground.

Elizabeth was relieved to see him. She listened attentively to the account of his meeting with George Watson. Her relief was all the more evident when he told her Morg would not be posted from White Oaks. After talking awhile, he left her and moved down the hallway to Lon's room. He knew he wouldn't rest until he'd spoken his piece.

Lon was propped up in bed. His leg was hurting, but he steadfastly refused to be dosed with laudanum. He expressed neither surprise nor gratitude when informed that the charges had been dropped. Yet his anger flared when Clint told him he was no longer welcome in White Oaks. His tone was hotly indignant.

"I go where I please," he said. "Damned if I'll be posted out of town when I've done nothin' wrong. Hell, I've got my rights!"

Clint gave him a straight hard look. "I made the deal and you'll stick by it. I don't want any argument."

"Some deal!" Lon bridled. "Christ, it was the Jarrotts that come hunting me. You talk like it was the other way round."

"Lemme tell you something," Clint said with a lightning frown. "Trouble hunts those who look for it, and you've got a chip on your shoulder. You're too goddamned cocky for your own good."

Lon eyed him with a steady, uncompromising gaze. "What's got your nose out of joint? You're not that mad over the Jarrotts, are you?"

A vein pulsed in Clint's forehead. "I don't know any way to say it except straight-out. You've made a killer of Hank."

"Jesus, that's rich!" Lon laughed harshly. "Where do you come off lecturing me? You're not exactly a shining example yourself."

"I never encouraged a kid to pack a gun. You ought to be real proud of what you've done for your brother."

"Tough titty makes strong baby. Hank's a half-breed in a white man's world. He's gotta learn how to hold his own."

Clint fixed him with a terrible look. "All your life you've had a crosswise attitude about things. I won't have Hank infected with your brand of poison."

"Won't you?" Lon said sullenly. "You might recollect what happened the last time we had this discussion. Hank decided to tag along with me."

"Maybe shooting somebody has brought him to his senses."

"Nobody's stoppin' you from asking him."

"I damn sure don't need your permission, Lon. I never did."

Clint turned and walked from the room. Outside he found Elizabeth waiting in the hallway. Her features were clouded with concern.

"What happened?" she said. "Your voices carried throughout the house."

"Beth, he's just no goddamn good. I've got to separate him and Hank somehow."

"I'm afraid that's easier said than done. Like it or not, you're just an uncle. Lon is his brother."

"Where's Hank now?"

"Out with Brad," Elizabeth replied. "I thought he'd like to see the ranch."

Clint's jawline tightened. "When he gets back, we'll have ourselves a talk. I aim to settle this once and for all."

"Would you listen to a suggestion?"

"Try me."

"You'll accomplish nothing by putting Hank in the middle. Until now, he's been forced to choose between you and Lon. Why not allow him to choose a different way of life?"

"I don't follow you."

"Time is on your side," Elizabeth said. "Lon won't be

able to ride for at least a week, perhaps longer. While he's recuperating, let Hank see what we have here on Spur." She paused, nodding wisely. "He might just decide it's the life for him."

Clint looked impressed. "You've gotten shifty with age, Beth. That's not a half-bad idea."

"I'll even enlist Brad's help. He and Hank seem to have hit it off."

"By God, I like it! I like it a lot."

"Good," Elizabeth said, taking his arm. "Because that's the end of the conversation. I'm going to insist that you get some sleep."

"I think maybe you're right. I'm plumb tuckered out."

Elizabeth walked him to one of the spare bedrooms. At the door, she kissed him on the cheek and gently shoved him inside. As she turned back up the hallway, it occurred to her that they hadn't once spoken of Miguel Ortega. Instead, family matters had again brought them together, perhaps healed the wound. She wanted desperately to believe that all the bad times were past.

One silver lining in a world of storms seemed little enough to ask.

TWENTY-ONE

Early the next morning the compound was a flurry of activity. Various crews, bossed by *segundos,* were assigned the day's work. They rode out shortly after sunrise.

Brad's routine seldom varied. He met with the *segundos* following breakfast and reviewed their instructions for the day. Some were assigned to work roundup, while others were responsible for putting together trail herds. A select few were permanently assigned to the horse-breeding operation.

The balance of Brad's day was spent in the saddle. He relied on the *segundos* to carry out his orders and complete their separate tasks. His job was to inspect the various operations and ensure that everything went according to plan. He generally managed to check out four or five work crews in the course of a day.

Usually, Brad rode alone. Overnight, however, he'd had a long discussion with Elizabeth. Their talk had centered on Hank, and how the youngster might be encouraged to stay on at Spur. The first step, Elizabeth stressed, was to intrigue the boy with life on a ranch. Only then could they contend with the influence of his older brother.

Brad readily volunteered his services. Yesterday he had shown the boy around the compound, as well as visiting one of the roundup camps. He'd found Hank to be an intelligent youngster, filled with curiosity. He also sensed that the boy felt somewhat out of place, an interloper of sorts. Hank seemed overly sensitive about the fact that he was a half-breed.

Today, the boy eagerly accepted Brad's invitation. Their first stop was at the eastern end of the valley, where the next trail herd was being gathered. Hank was fascinated by every aspect of the operation, asking an endless stream of questions. Apart from his time in the mining camps, he knew virtually nothing of the white man's world. He evidenced a willingness to learn that belied his youth.

From the cow camp, they turned northwest. By midmorning they arrived at the breaking corrals, known among the hands as the "riding academy." There they watched bronc busters in the initial stages of working raw range stock. The horses were green four-year-olds, tough and fiery-tempered. Within the month, they would be converted into well-schooled cowponies.

Encouraged by Hank's questions, Brad explained the operation in some detail. Virgil Brannock, the founder of Spur, had begun a crossbreeding program in the late 1870s. At first, mustang brood mares were topped by a thoroughbred stallion imported from Kentucky. By culling the mares, and continually breeding up, the offspring soon possessed the best traits of both strains.

Colts sired by the original stallion further extended the bloodline. The horses were now known for their stamina and catlike agility, and their blazing speed over the short stretch. In recent times, the term "quarter-mile horse" had been coined, denoting an animal capable of bursting speed from a standing start. A decade of selective crossbreeding had resulted in the ultimate cowpony.

Within the cattle industry, these barrel-chested quarter-mile horses were highly prized for cutting and roping. Throughout the summer, horse buyers from across the West traveled to Spur to look over the stock. At peak season, the herds totaled more than a thousand head, and annual sales exceeded $250,000. Livestock dealers who traded in blooded saddle mounts provided still another market.

Hank was visibly impressed. His ancestors, the Comanche, had been the most superb horsemen of all the Plains tribes. No less a personage than General Phil Sheridan had dubbed them "the finest light cavalry in the world." Their herds numbered in the thousands, and their ancient term for the horse was the "god-dog." Even on the reservation, a man's wealth was still measured in horses.

"My people bred horses too," Hank said now, watching a broncbuster fork a snorty cowpony. "Long ago, the Comanche stole pure-blood stock from Mexican *rancheros*. They were then mixed with our own herds."

Brad eyed him in silence for a moment. "You ever think of raisin' horses yourself?"

"Sure," Hank said with a gee-whiz grin. "What Comanche wouldn't?"

"Lookit here," Brad said. "You mind if I ask you a personal question?"

"No—I guess not."

"Well, you're just as much white as you are Indian. So why do you keep callin' yourself a Comanche?"

Hank looked at him with some surprise. "A half-breed don't have much choice. Way most folks figure, the white part don't count."

"On Spur," Brad ventured, "we're pretty much color-blind. Around here, you're just another Brannock."

"You tryin' to tell me nobody thinks of me as a 'breed?"

"I'm sayin' everybody looks on you as one of the family. The fact that you're half Comanche doesn't change a thing."

Hank beamed happily. "I'd sure like to believe that. You reckon the others think the same way?"

"Hell, yes," Brad said reasonably. "Your Aunt Elizabeth heads the list. Her and Morg talked it over last night."

"Talked what over?"

"How they'd like you to stay on at Spur. There's more dangblasted work than we can handle. We need another Brannock to help run things."

"No kiddin'?" Hank said with soft wonder. "They actually told you that?"

"Like I said, you're family. We tend to stick together."

Hank thought for a moment. "I haven't heard you mention Lon. How do they feel about him?"

"No different," Brad said with a vague wave of his hand. "You and Lon both are welcome to make your home here. Your Uncle Clint figures it's where you belong, anyhow."

"Yeah, I know," Hank said, his face serious. "Trouble is, Lon's got other ideas. He's dead set against it."

"How about your ownself? Would you like to stay on?"

"I dunno," Hank said slowly. "What would I do on a ranch?"

"For openers, you could lend a hand with the horse-breeding operation. You said yourself a Comanche has an eye for blooded horseflesh."

"I gotta admit it sounds good."

"Why not try it?" Brad asked carefully. "You could do lots worse."

"All depends on what Lon says. I don't wanna get on the outs with him."

"Maybe you ought to have a talk with him. Unless I'm wide of the mark, you're not too keen on a gambler's life."

"You won't get no argument there. I just tagged along because of Lon."

"So talk to him," Brad persisted. "You're old enough to know your own mind."

Hank smiled manfully, nodded. "I suppose it wouldn't hurt nothin'. All he could do is blow his cork."

Brad regarded him somberly. "Lemme ask you something straight out. You got any particular itch to kill people?"

"I'd sooner raise horses."

"Then cut the knot with Lon before it's too late. You stick with him and you're bound to kill somebody else. He draws trouble like a lightning rod."

Hank shrugged. "He's still my brother."

"That don't make him your keeper. Or vice versa, either."

There was an awkward silence. After a time they reined away from the breaking corral and rode south. Brad sensed that his last remark had struck a nerve. He could almost hear the boy thinking out loud. And loyalty was no longer the issue.

Hank was considering instead the *price* of loyalty.

Late-afternoon shadows played across the bedroom wall. Lon lay with his hands locked behind his head, staring at the ceiling. His mood was testy.

Earlier, Clint had dropped by to check on him. For Lon, their conversation had all the overtones of an old sermon. He'd listened with one ear, indifferent to the admonition that he mend his ways. The good news was that Clint was leaving for Lincoln, presumably on law business. Lon was happy to see him go.

Shortly before suppertime the door opened. Hank stepped into the room, smiling tentatively, and crossed to the bed. Lon perked up noticeably, pushing himself upright against the pillows. So far as he was concerned, the youngster's was the first friendly face he'd seen all day. He felt trapped in a household of people intent on converting the family heathen.

"How you feeling?" Hank asked. "Your leg still hurtin'?"

"Only when I smile," Lon replied, deadpan. "Which ain't too often around here."

"What happened now?"

"The usual," Lon said. "Old stick-in-the-mud popped in to give me another lecture."

"Uncle Clint?"

"Nobody else."

"What'd he have to say?"

"Nothin' worth repeating," Lon observed. "Lucky for me, he was on his way into town. I got off light."

"Guess you can't blame him too much. He just figures he knows what's best."

The boy's reply was overdrawn, a little too guileless. Lon was silent a moment, watching him intently. Never before had the youngster defended their uncle, and that bothered Lon. Finally, he decided to let the remark pass.

"How was the grand tour?" he said. "Brad show you around the place?"

Hank smiled broadly. "I never seen nothin' like it. All them stories Uncle Clint told us . . ."

"Yeah?"

"Well, he wasn't fibbin'," Hank went on. "They've got more goldurn horses and cows than you could shake a stick at. Lots bigger'n I expected."

Lon frowned. "Sounds like you had yourself quite a looksee."

"Brad says we only just got started. He's gonna show me the rest of it tomorrow."

"What else did he have to say?"

"I don't follow you."

Lon squinted at him. "They're not givin' you the royal treatment without a reason. You must've got a clue of some sort."

The boy squirmed under Lon's ugly stare. "No need to lie about it," he said with a lame grin. "Brad offered me a job workin' horses. Him and the family want me to stay on."

"'Course, they do!" Lon said, his face pale and furious. "The whole connivin' bunch aims to split us up. They're tryin' to drive a wedge between you and me."

"No such thing," Hank protested. "Brad says the family wants you to stay on too. He says we could make ourselves a good home here."

"Quit tellin' me what Brad says! He's just a polly-parrot for Clint and the rest of 'em. You think I'm not wise to their game?"

Hank shook his head vigorously. "We're family and they're tryin' to look out for us. What's wrong with that?"

"Plenty," Lon said, his voice tight with rage. "Jesus Christ, you wanna be a shitkicker the rest of your life—a hired hand?"

"Brad's done all right for himself."

Lon's laugh was scratchy, abrasive. "A foreman takes orders too. Family or not, he's still workin' for wages."

"Mebbe so," Hank said, averting his eyes, "but leastways it's honest work."

Lon gave him a dirty look. "You sayin' there's something crooked about gambling?"

"I'm sayin' we could make a place for ourselves here. Hard work never hurt nobody."

"Suit yourself," Lon said with chilly finality. "I'm leavin' as soon as I can ride a horse. You mark my word on it."

A moment elapsed while they stared at one another. Hank stood as though nailed to the floor, his expression faintly stricken. At length, he flushed and bobbed his head.

"Guess you're right," he said. "We ought to stick together."

"Now you're talkin' sense."

Lon permitted himself a thin smile. Yet he seethed with bitter anger toward all the Brannocks. After today, he knew they would stop at nothing to separate him from the boy. He vowed to himself that it would never happen.

One way or another, he and Hank would leave Spur together. The sooner the better for all concerned.

Clint took supper that night with Jennifer and Blake. The meal was simple fare, served at the small dining table in Jennifer's living quarters. Their conversation centered principally on family matters.

Late that afternoon Clint had stopped by the sheriff's office. Without revealing his source, he'd informed Will Grant that *Las Gorras Blancas* were planning another raid. The tip seemed to him reliable and some hunch told him it would happen fairly soon. He asked to be contacted the minute the attack was reported.

Tonight, however, he made no mention of the White Caps. Whenever possible, he kept his law duties separate from private affairs. The talk turned instead on Lon and Hank, and the deal he'd struck on their behalf. Apart from being posted out of White Oaks, he explained, they would be fined for resisting arrest. All other charges would be dropped.

"Way it worked out," he concluded, "they'll just get a rap

on the knuckles. I doubt the judge will fine 'em more than fifty dollars apiece."

Blake speared a bite of steak with his fork. He popped it into his mouth and chewed thoughtfully. "I wonder if they know how lucky they are. Except for your intervention, they could have been in serious trouble."

"Hank knows," Clint said solemnly. "Lon wouldn't admit it come hell or high water. He don't like to be in my debt."

"Why is that?" Jennifer asked. "You're practically the only father he's ever known."

"Maybe that's the problem," Clint replied. "Lon always resented me trying to keep him on the straight and narrow. He's bound to go his own way."

"It's an unfortunate situation," Jennifer said rather sadly. "All the more so because of his influence over Hank. I hate to think what might happen."

"Yeah, me too." Clint suddenly laughed, spread his hands. "Let's talk about something a little more pleasant. How's your wedding plans comin' along?"

"Quite well," Jennifer said, smiling brightly. "We'll be married on a Sunday and back to work on Monday. We've both agreed a honeymoon will have to wait."

"Never thought to ask," Clint said, "but maybe you just answered the question. You aim to keep on practicin' medicine?"

"Of course," Jennifer said, lifting her chin slightly. "A woman is no less entitled to a career than a man."

Blake grunted, smothering a laugh. "Given a choice, I'd keep her barefoot and pregnant. But she's too much the suffragist to play housewife." He paused, gave Jennifer an affectionate look. "I'm afraid we're stuck with a doctor in the family."

Jennifer wrinkled her nose. "You wouldn't have it any other way. Admit it."

"I certainly will not," Blake said with great relish. "Every woman a pot-walloper, that's my motto."

"Good Lord," Jennifer said, rolling her eyes. "You really are impossible."

Clint watched their byplay with a bemused expression.

Age had made him more tolerant, but some ideas died hard. He often thought the suffragists would benefit by the old "barefoot-and-pregnant" theory. The notion of a petticoat politician and a lady doctor in the same family still seemed to him an oddity of nature. He sometimes wondered if he'd outlived his time.

After coffee and dessert, he decided to call it a night. Jennifer walked him to the door and kissed him good night on the cheek. Outside, he turned uptown and strolled off in a thoughtful mood. Beyond the hotel, the lights of a saloon beckoned, casting a tallowed glow onto the street. He stepped inside for a drink.

Several men stood at the bar. Clint moved past them, nodding, and took a seat at an empty table. The barmaid drifted over with his usual nightcap, a tumbler of rye whiskey. Her name was Molly O'Day and she was a rarity in Lincoln. She hustled drinks but she never sold herself. Her favors were dispensed only to a select few.

"'Evening, marshal," she said, placing his drink on the table. "How goes the battle?"

Clint looked up at her. "So far, it's just another day. How're things with you?"

"Why complain?" she said, laughing softly. "God has a tin ear when it comes to whiners."

"You talk to God, do you?"

Molly O'Day caught his bantering tone. She was an impressive woman, short and buxom, with dark auburn hair. Her green eyes held a certain bawdy wisdom and her voice was low and throaty. She gave him a slow once-over.

"When I was younger," she said, "I used to talk with God all the time. Then I found out he's just like other men."

"How so?"

"All promises," she said lightly. "He never answers a girl's prayers."

"Are you praying for something special?"

A vixen look touched her eyes. She moistened her lips with the tip of her tongue and her voice turned silky. "Why don't we talk about it when I get off work?"

Clint smiled. "What makes you think I'll answer your prayers?"

"Well . . ." She paused, batted her eyes. "You didn't do so bad last time."

"You still get off at twelve?"

She nodded, her laughter somehow musical. As she walked away, Clint watched the wig-wag of her hips with an appreciative look. Over the past month she had invited him into her bed at least once a week. She made no secret of the fact that she saw other men, and he'd never raised the subject. Their arrangement was casual, no strings attached, and he was content to keep it that way. He wanted no ties.

All his life Clint had avoided entanglements. He preferred romping women of zest and laughter who made no demands on him. Such women were easily forgotten, for there was no emotional attachment, no lasting bond. While he seldom reflected on it, he was aware he purposely sought out women like Molly O'Day. With them, when the good times faded, there were no regrets, no reason for hard feelings. They invariably parted friends, no one the worse for the experience.

As he sipped his whiskey, Clint's mind suddenly leapfrogged. For no discernible reason, his thoughts jumped to Elizabeth. He pondered what her life had been like since Virgil's death. To all appearances, she was not involved with a man, preferring the privacy of her memories. Yet she was a good-looking woman and far too young for the self-imposed abstinence of a nun. It occurred to him that he'd never allowed himself to think of her in that way. Instead, treating her like an icon of sorts, he had always suppressed such thoughts.

The realization jarred him. He wondered how she would react if, after all these years, he were to make his feelings known. For a moment, he turned the idea this way and that, studying it like a multifaceted prism. Then, on sudden impulse, he ruthlessly suppressed the notion. What mattered most was how she felt, and he already knew the answer to that. She saw him as a brother and a friend, an old and trusted confidant. The odds on her ever feeling more were too dismal to calculate. No better, certainly, than a snowball in hell.

Clint downed his drink. He turned, about to signal Molly for a refill, when the front door slammed open. Will Grant rushed into the saloon, looking around wildly. Upon spotting Clint, he waved and hurried toward the table. His features were grim.

"Word just come in," he said, halting beside the table. "The White Caps hit Joe Hobson tonight."

"Hobson?" Clint repeated in a remote voice. "I recollect his place is west of here."

"Yep," Grant affirmed. "On the Rio Bonito, maybe ten miles out."

"That gives us plenty of time. We can't start trackin' till dawn anyway."

"We?" Grant repeated. "You want me to go along?"

"You and your deputies," Clint told him. "Any objections?"

"No, I don't suppose so."

"Then you'd better get a move on. We'll meet at your office in an hour."

Grant nodded, turning back toward the door. Clint rose from his chair and crossed to the far end of the bar. He stopped beside Molly.

"Something's come up," he said. "We'll have to make it another night."

"Trouble?" she asked.

"Nothing out of the ordinary."

"Look after yourself, anyhow. I figure you owe me one."

Clint chuckled. "I always square accounts with a lady."

Molly O'Day watched him out the door. She'd always thought him a curious man, prodded by strange devils. But of all her gentlemen friends, he was the most considerate of the lot. Which made him stranger still.

No one expected kindness of a man who traded in sudden death.

TWENTY-TWO

A dingy haze lighted the sky at false dawn. The riders were like warm ghosts, caught in that moment when night turns to day. None of them spoke as they forded the Rio Bonito.

Clint rode in the lead. Strung out behind him were Will Grant and three deputies. Since leaving Lincoln, they had followed the stage road on a westerly track. But now, where the river made a dogleg to the north, they dropped off the road and crossed at a shallow ford. Farther on, the mountains rose in dim silhouette against a gray horizon.

Signs of the raid were immediately evident. Where a fence line had once intersected the stream, there was now a great tangle of barbed wire and splintered posts. From all appearances, horsemen had roped the posts and rolled sections of fence into spiked masses of wire. The process had been repeated at intervals, leaving the rangeland dotted with balls of downed fence. None of it looked salvageable.

A short while later Clint and the lawmen spotted the ranch compound. Smoke drifted lazily from the embers of a large barn that had burned to the ground. The main house and several nearby outbuildings appeared undamaged. Outside the bunkhouse a group of cowhands stood bunched in a tight knot. Their clothes were singed and their faces streaked from having vainly fought the barn fire. They looked like soot-blackened scarecrows.

The door of the main house banged open. A stocky man with a nose the color of rotten plums stalked outside and halted in the yard. His eyes were bloodshot and his eyebrows were singed off, clearly lost in battling the fire. He planted himself, waiting as the lawmen reined to a halt. He glared angrily at Will Grant.

"By Christ!" he said dourly. "You took your own sweet time. I sent a man to fetch you last night."

"C'mon now, Joe," Grant said with a pained expression. "Wasn't nothin' we could've done last night. You know that."

"I don't know no such thing."

Hobson glowered at them. Clint and the sheriff dismounted and left their horses ground-reined. As they moved forward, Clint dug out the makings and began rolling himself a smoke. He nodded to the rancher.

"Don't blame Will," he said. "I'm the one that decided to wait for first light. You can't track anybody in the dark."

Hobson snorted. "Way I hear it, you can't track anybody a'tall—night or day."

Clint popped a match on his thumbnail. He lit his cigarette, then dropped the match and ground it underfoot. He glanced up, exhaling a streamer of smoke. "You heard wrong."

"Says you." Hobson flipped a hand in scorn. "We've never met, but folks talk. I know all about you."

"Yeah?" Clint said levelly. "Such as?"

"You're no closer to catchin' Ortega than you was the day you hit town. There's them that says you don't wanna catch him . . . never did."

"Any of these big talkers got a name?"

"Damn right!" Hobson said in a voice webby with phlegm. "How about Homer Stockton? That ring any bells?"

Clint shrugged. "His daughter married my nephew. What's that got to do with me?"

"Way Stockton tells it, you've got personal reasons for not catchin' Ortega."

"What personal reasons?"

"Elizabeth Brannock," Hobson said flatly. "Everybody knows her and Ortega are thick as thieves. Only makes sense you'd try to protect your sister-in-law."

"Homer Stockton said that?"

"Him and lots of others. If you don't believe me, ask the sheriff."

Clint glanced sideways at Grant. "I'd like a straight answer, Will. Any truth to it?"

Grant avoided his eyes. "Hell, talk's cheap, Clint. Why bother you with it?"

"You should've let me decide that."

"I figured you'd just as soon not hear it."

Clint took a drag on his cigarette. He let out a thread of smoke and his gaze shifted back to Hobson. "Next time I see Stockton," he said in a flinty voice, "I'll tell him what I'm gonna tell you now. He's a goddamn liar, plain and simple."

Hobson's face twisted in a prunelike mask of skepticism. "Why should I take your word over Stockton's?"

"Would you believe Miguel Ortega instead?"

"Come again?"

"Ortega tried to have me killed," Clint said. "Check with the U.S. marshal in Santa Fe. He'll verify the story."

Hobson gave him a short look. "I don't get it. Unless you were breathin' down his neck, why would Ortega want you dead?"

Clint smiled with hard irony. "I think you just answered your own question."

"I'll be damned," Hobson muttered. "How come nobody ever heard about it?"

"The man Ortega sent after me wasn't able to testify. He got himself killed."

"All the same," Grant interjected, "you should've told me. I thought we was workin' together on this thing."

"Slipped my mind," Clint noted dryly. "Next time you'll be the first to know."

When Grant mumbled an inaudible reply, Clint turned back to the rancher. "I'd like the particulars on what

happened last night. How many men were in the raiding
party?"

"Three, maybe four," Hobson said uncertainly. "Nobody
suspicioned anything till they'd already fired the barn. After
that, they skedaddled pretty quick."

"So they just went after the barn? None of the other
buildings?"

"Yeah, now that you mention it, that's right. They could've
fired every building on the place before we woke up."

"Any shooting?" Clint asked.

"Not a helluva lot," Hobson replied. "One of my boys got
off a couple of shots, but it was wasted lead. They were high-
tailin' it by then."

"And they didn't fire back?"

"Like I said, they were lookin' to be long gone."

"Which way were they headed?"

"Off to the southwest," Hobson said, motioning with his
arm. "That would've put 'em on a direct line with the river."

Clint took a final pull on his cigarette. He hesitated a
moment, as though considering a matter of weighty importance. At length, after grinding the cigarette underfoot, he
nodded to Hobson.

"Guess that ought to do it," he said. "We'll pick up their
trail and see where it leads."

"You want some help?" Hobson offered. "I could send
along four or five of my boys."

"We'll manage," Clint assured him. "From the looks of
your fences, you'll need all your hands anyway. I'd wager
your cows are scattered to hell and gone by now."

"Sonsabitches!" Hobson cursed savagely. "I'd like to be
there when you catch Ortega and his greasers."

"We'll let you know how it works out."

Clint turned away, followed closely by the sheriff. On
foot, they led their horses past the ruins of the barn. The
three deputies, still mounted, tagged along behind. Some
distance from the house, Grant finally looked around at
Clint. His brow puckered in a frown.

"I'm curious," he said. "Why'd you ask Hobson all them questions about the raid?"

"Just satisfying myself," Clint informed him. "There's a pattern to the way the White Caps operate. I wanted to see if they stuck with it."

"What d'you mean—pattern?"

"Well, first off, they never set fire to a building with people in it. Everything they've torched has been a shed or a barn, some sort of outbuilding."

Grant looked puzzled. "What's that tell you?"

"By itself, nothing," Clint said. "But there's more to it. You'll recall they never shoot at anybody. Leastways not till they're fired on first."

"Judas Priest," Grant groaned. "Are you sayin' they're not out to kill anybody?"

"That's how it tallies in my book."

"How about that cowhand they killed east of town?"

"Proves my point," Clint said. "He dropped one of their men before they opened fire on him."

"Even so, it don't make a nickel's worth of difference. The law still calls it murder."

"No argument there, Will."

"What about yourself?" Grant demanded. "You said Ortega tried to have you killed. Don't that blow your theory all to hell?"

Clint cracked a smile. "Señor Ortega made an exception in my case. He probably figures lawdogs are fair game."

"Especially when you're hot on his trail."

"Speakin' of which, look what we've got here."

Their position was perhaps fifty yards past the smoldering barn. Clint motioned for Grant and the others to remain where they were. He walked forward a step at a time, slowly scanning the ground. Every three or four paces, his gaze swept an arc off to either side.

For an old cavalry scout, the sign was readily apparent. Hoofprints indicated that four riders had converged together some distance from the compound. Studying on it, Clint saw

that they had spread out upon riding away from the barn.
The tactic made them less likely targets while they were still
visible in the blazing firelight. After gaining the safety of
darkness, they had joined up in a rough formation. Their direction was almost due southwest.

Clint noted that the horses had been driven at a hard gallop. His assessment was quick but certain, based on the
length of the stride and the depth of the tracks. He thought it
quite probable that neither the men nor their mounts had
been wounded by gunfire. There were no traces of blood and
the hoofprints were hammered into the ground at an unbro-
ken pace. From all indications, the night riders had escaped
in good order.

Turning back, Clint walked toward the waiting lawmen.
He was reminded of the old days, when a cavalry patrol
waited for him to scout the trail ahead. At various times, before the horseback tribes were defeated, he'd campaigned
against the Comanche as well as the Apache. Tracking *Las
Gorras Blancas* seemed to him little different from pursuing
bands of hostiles. In the end, it was a game of hide-and-seek
with a deadly twist. The loser, more often than not, got
killed.

Will Grant was already mounted. Clint stepped aboard
his horse, gesturing off into the distance. "Four men," he
said. "I'd judge they were on a beeline for the river. Not
wastin' any time, either."

"Four here," Grant said carefully, "means there were
probably twice that many tearin' down fence and scattering
cattle. All told, we're talkin' about twelve men, maybe
more."

Clint nodded agreement. "I've got an idea they planned a
rendezvous somewhere along the river. From what I've seen
before, Ortega likes to regroup after a raid."

"What makes you think he led it himself?"

"Ortega's still building an organization in Lincoln
County. Takes time to train farmers and teach 'em tactics. I
doubt he's found himself a lieutenant just yet."

Grant raised an uncertain eyebrow. "Way it looks, we're

outnumbered better'n two to one. Ortega leadin' them only makes it worse."

"What's your point, Will?"

"Maybe we ought to accept Hobson's offer. Four or five of his boys would sorta balance the odds."

"No." Clint's voice was hard and determined. "A bunch of trigger-happy cowhands wouldn't solve anything. We'll tend to it ourselves."

"Lemme ask you something." Grant hesitated, gave him an odd look. "Up till now, you've always played a lone hand. Why'd you bring us along this time?"

Clint was aware of the three deputies watching him intently. He returned Grant's stare with a cryptic expression. "So far," he said, "Ortega has stuck to that pattern I mentioned. I've got a hunch we can make it work to our advantage."

Grant appeared confused. Before he could frame a reply, Clint rode off at a sharp trot. The sheriff glanced back at his men, then motioned them onward. The trail they followed led once more toward the Rio Bonito.

The river was molten with sunlight. Overhead a hawk floated past on smothered wings, scanning for prey. Nothing moved along a shoreline studded with cottonwoods.

To the west, the mountains rose against a backdrop of limitless sky. The Rio Bonito curved in a graceful, southwesterly bend toward its headwaters in the high country. The rushing waters tumbled beneath a bridge on the stage road, which sliced east to west through the mountainous terrain. Far in the distance, the majestic spire of Sierra Blanca was rimmed with cottony clouds.

Clint called a halt just north of the stage road. He shaded his eyes against the noonday sun and stared at the bridge for a long moment. Then he dismounted, leaving his horse with Grant and the deputies, and walked along the riverbank. Upstream he angled off to the right and stopped beneath a copse of trees. After a time, he slowly quartered the shoreline, his gaze fastened to the ground. He paused where the treeline ended, staring again at the bridge.

The expression on Clint's face was abstracted. He hauled out the makings, his movements somehow mechanical, and rolled himself a cigarette. He cupped his hands around the flare of a match and lit up in a wreath of smoke. For what seemed an interminable time, he stood puffing on the cigarette, apparently lost in thought. Finally, he turned back downstream.

Grant and the deputies waited where he'd left them. Clint flipped the cigarette into the river, then swung aboard his horse. He jerked his chin toward the copse of trees.

"That's where they met," he said. "The four we were trailin' joined up with the rest of the bunch. By their tracks, I put the count at eleven."

"Eleven," Grant repeated without inflection. "Any idea where they headed?"

"You'll recollect I talked about a pattern."

"Yeah?"

"Well, nothing's changed," Clint observed. "They regrouped, then they scattered like jackstraws. Five took off crosscountry toward White Oaks. Four more headed in the direction of Lincoln. The last two turned upstream."

"Damned odd," Grant said, staring past the bridge. "Up that way, the river skirts around Fort Stanton. You'd think they'd steer clear of the military."

"Maybe not," Clint said thoughtfully. "For anybody with the nerve, it'd make a fine hideout. Lots of rough country up there."

Grant studied him quizzically. "Are you talkin' about Ortega?"

"Not much question he's nervy enough to give it a try."

"How long have you suspected?"

"A week or so," Clint replied. "I paid a call on the post commander just a couple of days ago. Asked him to have the troops keep a sharp lookout. So far, I haven't heard anything."

Grant was silent a moment. "Let's assume it was Ortega that went upstream. Who would he have ridin' with him?"

"His *pistolero*," Clint said. "I've been told he always travels with a bodyguard. Appears I got the straight goods."

"What're we waitin' for, then? We oughta be sniffin' out his trail."

Clint smiled. "No offense, but it's like you said back at Hobson's ranch. I prefer to work alone."

"Jesus H. Christ!" Grant fumed. "You mean to say you're cuttin' us out of it?"

"What I had in mind was splittin' up."

Clint quickly sketched the plan. Grant and one of his deputies would follow the White Caps in the direction of Lincoln. The other two deputies would take the trail leading toward White Oaks. By splitting forces, the odds of capturing at least one raider were greatly increased.

"Hell's bells," Grant retorted. "Somewhere down the line they're gonna scatter to the winds. We'll end up with trails headed ever' whichaway."

Clint shrugged. "Stick with the one that looks the most promising. You might get lucky."

"And meantime, you're takin' Ortega for yourself!"

Grant was still grumbling when they parted at the bridge. With one of his deputies, the sheriff rode eastward on the stage road. The other deputies followed the tracks angling off toward the northwest. Clint watched until the four lawmen were out of sight.

He then turned upstream along the Rio Bonito.

A brooding loneliness hung over the mountains. Somewhere in the distance a squirrel chattered, and a bluejay, sounding a scolding cry, took flight. Within moments, an empty silence once again settled across the timbered slopes.

By late afternoon Clint was some eight miles upstream. The terrain was rugged and steep, ascending steadily into the high country. Weathered boulders and rocky outcroppings jutted from a ridge overlooking the river. A game trail, beaten into the hard earth by deer, bordered the streambed.

Fresh hoofprints covered the deer tracks. The game trail had begun a short way past Fort Stanton, where the Rio Bonito skirted the garrison. At that point, Clint had lost any lingering doubt about the men he trailed. The riders had swung sharply east, detouring around the army post. A mile farther on their tracks had merged once again with the river.

Halting now, Clint studied the trail ahead. The stream curved westward, dropping below a craggy bluff. There was nothing out of the ordinary, but suddenly, for no apparent reason, his scalp tingled. Years of living on the razor edge of death had honed in him a sixth sense for danger. He'd learned to trust his instincts, and he sat for a moment staring at the jagged outcropping. His hand moved to the butt of the rifle in his saddle scabbard.

A flicker of sunlight on metal caught Clint's eye. He vaulted out of the saddle, grabbing the pump-action repeater as he kicked free of the stirrups. The report of a carbine reverberated through the mountains and a slug sizzled past his head. He hit the ground and rolled, heaving himself over the edge of the riverbank. His horse spooked and bolted back down the trail.

The carbine barked twice in rapid succession. Dirt showered him as the shots plowed furrows across the top of the bank. From high on the outcropping, he spotted puffs of smoke beside a stunted juniper. Quickly, acting almost on reflex, he removed his hat and flung it into the air. Then, crouching lower still, he scuttled several yards upstream. He paused to catch his breath, slowly counted to ten.

The carbine remained silent. Clint waited a moment longer, reasonably confident his assailant had been distracted by the hat. He got to his knees, the pump-action rifle at the ready, and cautiously peeked over the riverbank. High above, he saw a man rise from behind the juniper, gripping a saddle carbine. As he watched, the man edged forward, straining for a better look into the streambed.

Clint jammed the butt of the rifle into his shoulder. The big .50-95 boomed and he instantly jacked another shell into the chamber, triggering a second shot. The man on the bluff jerked upright, his mouth open in a strangled scream. His hands splayed, dropping the carbine, and he clawed at empty air. He pitched forward and tumbled end-over-end down the face of the outcropping. His body slammed to a halt on the game trail.

Still watchful, Clint held his position for several minutes. He carefully inspected the bluff, alert to any sign of movement. At last, he scrambled over the riverbank and walked forward. The dead man was a *mexicano,* sprawled on his back with blood plastered across his chest. A Remington revolver was cinched around his waist and cartridge bandoliers were crisscrossed over his shoulders. Staring down at him, Clint felt any vestige of doubt drain away. He'd just killed Miguel Ortega's *pistolero.*

Some three hours later Clint located the campsite. High in the mountains, near the headwaters of the Rio Bonito, the hideout was situated in a grove of trees. Supplies and assorted gear were piled beneath a lean-to, but the clearing itself was deserted. There were no signs of recent activity and ashes in the campfire were at least two days old. A picket line for horses showed no fresh droppings.

Standing there, Clint felt a keen sense of disappointment. Yet, even though he'd come up short, he was moved to a grudging admiration. For the first time, he understood fully the hold that Ortega exerted over the *mexicanos.* The *pistolero,* far from a hired gun, was a martyr to a cause. Thinking back, Clint saw now that the man had sacrificed his own life so that his leader might escape. No greater act of loyalty could be asked, or rendered.

Still, where Clint was personally concerned, it was an altogether different matter. Twice now, Miguel Ortega had tried to have him killed. He resolved to end it before there was a third time.

TWENTY-THREE

How are we doing, now?" "Terrible," Louise said. "My backbone feels like it's going to snap."

"Unfortunately, you'll have to grin and bear it. That's all part of having a baby."

Elizabeth pulled the bedsheet aside. She placed her hand on the girl's rounded abdomen and waited for the next contraction. Louise turned her head into the pillow, still embarrassed at being examined by her mother-in-law. The fact that Elizabeth was an experienced midwife hardly relieved her discomfort.

Early that morning Louise had gone into labor. An initial examination convinced Elizabeth that it would be a slow birth. Years ago, when she'd been active at the clinic, she had assisted in dozens of deliveries. On her own she had acted as midwife for countless *mexicano* women throughout the Hondo Valley. She recalled that first babies were often difficult, and seldom born quickly.

Fearful of complications, she had sent John Taylor to fetch Jennifer. By modern standards, the old midwifery methods were hopelessly outdated. She wanted a doctor in attendance, and Louise's condition allowed some leeway in time. The round trip into town would consume the better part of the day; but she wasn't worried. At the latest, she expected Jennifer to arrive well before nightfall.

Louise moaned softly when the contraction hit. By silent count, Elizabeth determined that the spasms were now occurring some three minutes apart. She lifted the girl's nightgown and saw a light spotting of blood on the bottom sheet. Her concern suddenly mounted, for she realized the birthing time was fast approaching. A quick glance out the window alarmed her even more; sundown was slowly fading to dusk. She stepped back, draping the top sheet over Louise.

"Everything's fine," she said. "You're progressing right on schedule."

"How much longer?" Louise asked. "It seems like it's taking forever."

Elizabeth forced herself to smile. "No complaints, young lady. You're actually having an easy time of it. I've seen women in labor for two days, sometimes longer."

Louise groaned. "I'll never have another one. Not after this."

"You'll change your mind," Elizabeth said lightly. "One baby just never seems enough. They're so sweet and cuddly, you always want more."

"Was that how you felt?"

"I remember it just like yesterday. After I had Jennifer, I couldn't wait to get pregnant again. Morgan was born scarcely a year later."

"I hope it's a boy," Louise said dreamily. "Morg wants a son so much."

"All men say that," Elizabeth remarked. "But you needn't worry yourself about it. He'll be perfectly satisfied with a daughter."

"Are you sure?"

"Positive," Elizabeth said with conviction. "Morgan is very much like his father, more than he realizes. And Virgil was too proud for words when Jennifer was born."

Louise suddenly appeared pensive. "Do you think Jen will get here in time?"

"Why, of course," Elizabeth assured her. "After all, she's about to become an aunt. She wouldn't miss that for anything."

"I hope not," Louise said, averting her eyes. "To tell you the truth, I'm a little scared."

"Why don't I send Morg in to keep you company. I'm sure Jennifer will be here any moment now."

Elizabeth smiled confidently, patting her hand. Turning from the bed, she crossed to the door and stepped into the hallway. Morg was waiting outside.

"How's Louise?" he said anxiously. "Everything all right?"

"She's fine," Elizabeth noted. "I want you to stay with her for a while. And smile for heaven's sake—act cheerful!"

Morg appeared troubled rather than nervous. Like many first-time fathers, he'd thought having a baby was a routine affair. He was clearly concerned that it was taking so long.

"What'll I say to her?" he wondered aloud. "Last time I was in there, she seemed pretty upset."

"She has more spunk than you give her credit for. Hold her hand and tell her you love her—and smile!"

Elizabeth waited until he entered the bedroom. She then walked to the vestibule and opened the front door. A moment passed while she searched the quickening darkness, straining for any sign of the buckboard. She finally turned and proceeded to the dining room.

Supper was being served. Brad sat on one side of the long table, and seated opposite him were Lon and Hank. Elizabeth greeted them quietly, taking her place at the head of the table. She wasn't particularly hungry, and when Brad offered a platter of beefsteak, she declined. She had a cup of coffee instead.

Brad inquired about Louise. Sparing the details, Elizabeth commented that her condition was unchanged. The talk then turned general, with Brad and Hank carrying the conversation. Lon ate in silence, like a man performing a necessary, if somewhat tedious, chore. Sipping her coffee, Elizabeth watched them with a thoughtful look.

She found little hope for Lon. His leg wound was mending and he'd recently begun hobbling around on a crutch. He wasn't yet strong enough to leave the house, but he now took his meals at the table. Still, his recovery was slow and his mood was one of sullen impatience. He was clearly champing to be gone from Spur.

Hank was an entirely different matter. On occasion, Elizabeth thought he showed signs of wavering. He spent his days working with the horse herd and he seemed drawn to life on a ranch. All the more important, he'd been influenced by the strong sense of unity among the family. He was by no means distanced from Lon, but something about him had changed. He appeared in no rush to leave the Hondo.

Any reflection on the boy inevitably led to Clint. Yet Elizabeth was far less sanguine where her old friend was concerned. Some two weeks had passed since the gunfight in the mountains and Miguel Ortega's narrow escape. A few days afterward, Clint had stopped overnight at the ranch. He was headed south, following a lead that Ortega was recruiting in the Seven Rivers district. From his attitude, the manhunt had now become a personal matter.

Elizabeth worried about him constantly. Seven Rivers was a remote stretch of backcountry located some ninety miles southeast of Lincoln. Far removed from the county seat, it was isolated and lawless, a stronghold of hard-bitten Anglo ranchers. An outbreak of violence by *Las Gorras Blancas* would almost certainly result in reprisals against the local *mexicanos*. Whether or not Clint could maintain order in such a climate was an arguable point. He might easily find himself caught in the middle.

The passage of time merely aggravated Elizabeth's concern. The date was June 2 and she'd heard nothing from Clint in almost ten days. She still found it hard to believe that Miguel Ortega had tried to take his life. Yet the evidence seemed insurmountable, particularly after the ambush in the mountains. Even worse, in the remote Seven Rivers country a man could be bushwhacked and never heard from again. She'd always thought Clint invincible, like the proverbial cat with nine lives. And yet there were limits beyond which . . .

Jennifer suddenly appeared in the doorway. John Taylor was only a step behind, carrying her medical bag. She advanced into the dining room, nodding to her mother. "Sorry I'm so late," she said. "I was in the middle of an operation when John arrived. I had to finish."

"You're here now," Elizabeth said, pushing back her chair. "That's all that matters."

"Louise hasn't had the baby?"

"I think you've come just in time. She's very close."

Jennifer ordered hot water brought to the bedroom. Morg was ushered into the hallway and told to wait outside. In separate washbasins, Jennifer and her mother both scrubbed their hands. Then while Elizabeth laid out instruments and sterile gauze, Jennifer took a stethoscope from her medical bag. She approached the bed, smiling at Louise.

"Well, now, suppose we have a look."

Louise smiled bravely. "The way I feel, you'd better make it quick."

After turning back the sheet, Jennifer placed the stethoscope on her swollen abdomen. The fetal heartbeat was loud and rapid, gratifyingly strong. Laying the stethoscope aside, Jennifer then timed the contractions. She found them occurring regularly, one after another, hardly a minute apart.

With Elizabeth assisting, Jennifer helped the girl slip out of her nightgown. She next spread Louise's legs and performed an internal examination. The cervix was dilated sufficiently to allow the insertion of three fingers. She withdrew her hand, smiling brightly.

"Louise, you're about to become a mother. Take deep breaths and do exactly what I tell you."

The contractions abruptly quickened. Louise uttered a stifled shriek, her forehead dotted with perspiration. She gulped a shuddering breath as the pain mounted in intensity. Elizabeth moved behind her, standing between the wall and the head of the bed. She leaned forward, grasping Louise beneath the knees with her hands. When she pulled back, the girl's straining buttocks were lifted slightly off the mattress.

Jennifer positioned herself at the foot of the bed. She crouched on her knees and began massaging the girl's widened vulva. She kneaded the flesh, drawing it outward, gently forcing it to stretch without tearing. She commanded Louise to bear down, and the girl puffed, gasping air, and strained harder. The baby's forehead appeared and Jennifer stretched the folds of the vulva wider still. Then, with a sudden rush, the head emerged cradled in Jennifer's hand. She gingerly worked the shoulders free and a moment later lifted the newborn infant from the bed.

"It's a boy," she said, laughing. "A perfect baby boy."

Louise strained for a better look, tears flooding her eyes. Unable to speak, she slumped back on the bed, utterly exhausted. Jennifer slapped the baby on the rump and he squawled a loud cry of outrage. She then cut the umbilical cord, deftly tying it off, and turned the baby over to Elizabeth. When the afterbirth emerged, she wrapped it in a cloth and set it aside. Finally, with gauze and warm water, she began cleaning Louise.

A short time later Jennifer stepped into the hall. Her eyes were bright with happiness and she nodded to Morg. "Congratulations," she said. "You have a son."

"A son." Morg beamed. "I'll be damned."

"And I'm happy to report, mother and child are both doing fine."

"I'll be double damned."

Jennifer smiled. "You may be triple damned before you get him away from Mama. So far, she refuses to let go of her grandson."

Morg threw back his head and roared laughter.

Louise slept the night through. Her energy was spent from the long hours of labor and the ordeal of birthing. She awoke only to nurse the baby.

At dawn, Jennifer entered the bedroom. She aroused Louise only long enough to perform a final examination. All the bleeding had stopped the evening before and there was nothing to indicate unforeseen complications. The baby was in perfect health, strong and lusty, with bright blue eyes. Jennifer thought the only danger he faced was in being spoiled by a doting grandmother.

The household was already stirring with activity. Elizabeth walked Jennifer to the door, embracing her with a warm hug. Outside, Taylor waited with a buckboard and team, prepared to drive Jennifer back to town. She had no qualms about leaving Louise and the baby in her mother's care. Elizabeth was like a dowager empress at last assured that the bloodline would be extended. A male child ensured still another generation of Brannocks.

Shortly before sunrise Morg slipped into the bedroom. Following the delivery, he and Louise had talked briefly. While she was lucid, she kept dropping off to sleep and he'd finally let her rest. To afford her some degree of privacy, he had bunked last night with Brad. Today, he returned hoping to find her restored. There were things he felt compelled to say.

The baby was asleep, swaddled in a crib beside the bed. Morg stood there, looking down at the tiny, peaceful face, his throat dry with emotion. He was suffused with pride, the almost overwhelming realization that he'd fathered a son. His ears buzzed and he felt curiously light-headed. A dopy, moonlike grin wreathed his features.

"Do you like him?"

Her voice startled Morg. Louise was sleepy-eyed but awake, radiant with happiness. She held out her hand and he took it, seating himself on the edge of the bed. He suddenly seemed at a loss for words.

"I had a speech all prepared," he said, "but now I've forgot it. I'm just so damn proud I can't hardly stand myself."

"I'm glad," she said softly. "I prayed it would be a boy."

"Well, somebody up there must've been listenin'. We've got ourselves a son, Lou."

"Have you given any thought to a name?"

"Yeah, I have," Morg acknowledged. "Unless you're dead set against it, I'd like to call him Lucas."

"Lucas." She repeated it to herself. "Lucas Brannock. I think it's a fine name."

"Took it after my great-great-grandfather. He's the one that founded the family way back when."

"Then it's settled," she said. "And we'll call him Luke, for short."

Morg squeezed her hand. "Glad you approve, Mrs.

Brannock. Now, you lay back and get yourself some rest. I'll see you later."

"Where are you going?"

"San Patricio," Morg replied. "But don't get yourself upset. I'll be back tonight."

She frowned prettily. "Promise?"

"On my oath. You and Luke look for me about dark."

"We'll be waiting."

Morg kissed her gently on the mouth. He walked to the door, still grinning, then waved and stepped into the hall. When the door closed, Louise leaned over the bed and looked into the crib. She touched the baby's face, her fingers like the caress of a snowflake. Her eyes misted and she tenderly spoke his name. Lucas Brannock.

She thought it was a good name, a proud name. A fitting name for her son. *Luke.*

A brassy sun stood high in the sky. Summer had come at last to the Hondo, and the foothills west of the valley were splotched with wildflowers. Borne on gentle winds, the scent of their fragrance was like a heady nectar.

As Morg approached San Patricio, his spirits still soared. He was intoxicated with himself and his world, drunk with the wonder of the day. The birth of his son somehow expanded his horizons and all things seemed possible. Nothing was beyond his reach.

Nor was it simply a matter of cockeyed optimism. His business ventures had prospered far beyond what he'd originally anticipated. Dave Todd, his mining partner, had proved to be an engineering marvel. In less than a month, Todd had organized an operation to rival anything in White Oaks. A stamping mill was under construction, and raw ore, rich in gold, would start pouring through within the week. On the mountainside, another crew of workers had extended the mine shaft almost a quarter-mile. The vein was wider than even Todd had suspected, with no end in sight. By late fall, perhaps sooner, the operation would begin to show a profit.

Expectations for the logging company were even brighter.

Under Chunk Devlin's able management, production had doubled over the original estimates. To keep pace, Morg had expanded his sales efforts throughout the mountains and across the Pecos Valley. Earlier in the week he'd been awarded a lumber contract for proposed construction at Fort Stanton. Devlin was after him to increase the size of the timber crew and thereby double production again. The idea was sound and Morg had decided to go along. Given time, he might very well corner the timber market.

The prospect of expansion had prompted his trip to San Patricio. The capacity of the lumber mill was a critical factor in his plans, and he wanted to talk with Harry Tipton. Devlin was scheduled to deliver a load of timber today and the timing would never be better. The three of them could hash it out in detail and determine a course of action for the future. If pressed, Morg was willing to invest a sizable sum for part-ownership of the mill. One way or another, he meant to ensure that his timber got converted into lumber.

When he arrived at the mill, Devlin and the timber crew were already there. Every Saturday, when the last delivery was made, the loggers accompanied the teamsters and helped with the off-loading. Afterward, with a week's wages in their pockets, they backtracked to Lincoln for a night on the town. By the next morning, most of them were broke and they were all suffering gargantuan hangovers. The return trip to camp was inevitably an agonizing experience.

Morg dismounted outside the mill office. Devlin jumped down from one of the wagons as Harry Tipton appeared in the office doorway. After a round of handshakes, they stood talking for a moment. A sudden commotion from the road attracted their attention and they turned in unison. Three timber wagons, loaded with Ralph McQuade's logging crew, rolled into the yard. McQuade stepped down from the lead wagon.

"I was gonna warn you," Tipton whispered to Morg. "He's spoiling for trouble. Watch yourself."

McQuade halted a pace away. "Brannock, I wanna talk with you."

"Nothin' stopping you," Morg said equably. "What's on your mind?"

"You undercut me on that Fort Stanton job. Everywhere I go anymore, it turns out you're the low bidder. I'm not gonna stand for it."

"Way it looks to me, you haven't got a lot of choice. It's a matter of like it or lump it."

"In a pig's ass!" McQuade snarled. "I'll be gawddamned if I'll let you drive me into the poorhouse."

"Try lowering your prices," Morg told him. "There's contracts enough to go around."

"I got a better idea."

"What's that?"

McQuade glowered at him. "You're gonna get the hell outta the timber business. 'Cause if you don't, I'm fixin' to haul your ashes."

"You're sure you won't have it any other way?"

"I just finished tellin' you—get out or get whipped."

Morg hit him. The blow caught McQuade flush between the eyes, staggered him backward. A roar went up as McQuade's timber crew jumped off the wagons and advanced in a burly wedge. Several of them carried lengths of logging chain and their eyes glinted with cold ferocity. From the opposite end of the mill, Devlin's men hurried forward to join the fray. Harry Tipton darted into his office and slammed the door.

McQuade somehow recovered his balance. Uncommonly agile for his size, he feinted with his left and threw a murderous roundhouse right. Morg slipped inside the blow and exploded two splintering punches on the other man's jaw. Knocked off his feet, McQuade went down like a wet sack of oats, out cold. Devlin waded in at the forefront, almost shoulder to shoulder with Morg. Together, their fists flying, they clubbed and hammered in a blurred flurry.

The men on both sides battered their way into the center of the action, hurling themselves at one another. Their struggle quickly became a contest of brute strength. Over the grunts and curses, men fell in increasing numbers, trampled and crushed underfoot. The momentum of the battle slowly shifted as Devlin's loggers surged forward, arms flailing, and forced the other side to give ground. McQuade's men gradually broke ranks before the onslaught, and then, with abrupt suddenness, those still on their feet scattered across the yard. The melee ended as they retreated toward their wagons.

Blood oozed down over Morg's cheekbone and an ugly cut split his lower lip. Beside him, Chunk Devlin stood with his shirt ripped loose at the shoulder and his scalp laid open along the hairline. Their men were grouped around them, bloodied and mauled, breathing hard. On Morg's signal, they backed away and allowed the other crew to load their fallen comrades onto the wagons. The last man to be lifted aboard was Ralph McQuade, his jaw broken and three teeth missing. A moment later the wagons turned away from the mill and rumbled onto the road.

Not far behind were the wagons of Devlin's loggers. Early that afternoon they roared into Lincoln like a band of conquering warriors. Laughing and shouting, they invaded one of the saloons and took it over. Morg, flush with victory, ordered the bartender to keep the drinks coming.

He arrived home late that night, drunk as a lord.

TWENTY-FOUR

The *mexicano* was a wizened man with a face like a walnut. He wore a tattered *jorongo,* a sort of sleeveless jacket, and white cotton pants now faded with grime. A floppy sombrero covered his head and his feet were encased in bullhide sandals. His name was Jesús Mantanzas.

Outside the house Mantanzas dismounted from a prancing coal-black stallion. The horse seemed at odds with a man who looked the part of a humble *peón.* Had anyone asked, he would have denied ownership of the fiery-eyed stud. Yet, even on threat of death, he would have admitted nothing more. The *hombre* who owned the horse had sworn him to silence.

At the door, he asked for Señora Brannock. The serving girl, herself a *mexicana,* gave him a distasteful look. She left him standing on the veranda and disappeared into the house. Several moments elapsed while he waited, shifting from one foot to the other. Then the door swung open and Elizabeth paused in the entryway. She smiled pleasantly.

"Buenos días," she said. "You wished to see me?"

Jesús Mantanzas doffed his sombrero. *"Buenos días, señora.* I have been sent by a friend."

"Does your friend have a name?"

"No," Mantanzas said quickly. "He told me you would know him by what I say now. He last saw you with the *políticos,* in Albuquerque."

A sudden foreboding crept over Elizabeth. She asked

herself why Miguel Ortega would contact her in such an oblique manner. She was almost afraid to ask.

"What does your friend want of me?"

Mantanzas' voice dropped. "He needs your assistance, *señora*. He is *muy enfermo*."

"Sick?" Elizabeth said, taken aback. "What's wrong?"

"We do not know, *señora*. My woman has tended him, but nothing helps. He grows worse."

"Tell me of his condition. How is he sick?"

Mantanzas patted his belly. "He has a terrible hurt here. He cannot hold his food and he is hot to the touch."

"Fiebre?" Elizabeth asked. "You're certain he has fever?"

"Sí, señora. My woman has given him herbs and bathed him with cold water. And still he burns with sickness."

"Why has he sent you to me?"

"La doctora," Mantanzas said. "He asks that you bring your daughter, *señora*."

"You could have asked her yourself. Why come to me?"

"Our friend does not know your daughter, *señora*. He trusts you to do this thing in secret—*sin hablar*."

"In other words," Elizabeth said, "he believes I will not inform the law. *Verdad*?"

Mantanzas bobbed his head. "Unless you help, he will not live, *señora*. Even now, *muerte* is written on his face."

Elizabeth took an instant to collect herself. She appeared calm, but inwardly she was torn with mixed emotions. How could she help Ortega without betraying Clint? Yet, even as she asked herself the question, she knew she couldn't refuse. Miguel Ortega would never have sent for her unless his situation was desperate.

Whatever happened, she realized she had no choice. An outlaw, no less than other men, could not be denied medical attention. The decision made, her thoughts quickly turned to Louise and her grandson. The baby was only three days old and she was reluctant to leave the ranch. Still, mother and child were in perfect health and she saw no reason for concern. Should anything serious develop . . .

She looked at Mantanzas. "Where is your friend now? How far away?"

"Not too far, *señora*. I have a small flock of sheep on the Rio Bonito, outside Lincoln. He took refuge in my home."

"When was this?"

"Yesterday, before dark," Mantanzas said uneasily. "When he stopped, I thought he wanted only a meal. But he was too sick to ride on and we made room for him. I gave him my own bed."

"Was he alone?"

"I saw no one else."

"Wait for me here," Elizabeth told him. "We will leave in a few minutes."

"Sí, señora."

Inside the house, Elizabeth proceeded to the office. Morg was seated at a small worktable opposite her desk. He glanced up from an accounting ledger as she moved through the door. His gaze was mildly interested.

"What was that all about?"

"Someone's sick," Elizabeth said. "I have to go out."

"Anyone I know?"

Elizabeth sidestepped the question. "I may be gone overnight. If Louise or the baby needs any help, I want you to send for Rosa."

"Rosa?" Morg repeated. "Jennifer's assistant?"

"Yes."

"Why wouldn't I send for Jen?"

"She's going with me."

"With you?" Morg said, faintly mystified. "What's the big emergency?"

"I told you," Elizabeth said vaguely. "Someone needs medical attention."

"C'mon now, Mom, you haven't told me anything. Who's this *someone*?"

"Oh, honestly, stop asking so many questions."

Morg stared at her, baffled. "I don't like the idea of you and Jen traipsing off somewhere. Who's the man at the door?"

"You needn't worry," Elizabeth said. "John will drive me in the buckboard. I'll be perfectly fine."

"And you won't tell me where you're going?"

Elizabeth gave him an enigmatic look. "I'll tell you when I get back. Let's not discuss it any further."

A short while later the buckboard pulled out of the yard. John Taylor held the reins and Elizabeth sat beside him, staring straight ahead. Jesús Mantanzas, mounted on the stallion, brought up the rear.

Morg stood on the veranda watching them. He felt oddly disturbed by his mother's evasive manner. Even more, he was troubled by the *mexicano* on the barrel-chested stud. The horse looked far too grand for the man.

For no apparent reason a name came into his mind. And he somehow knew he'd guessed right. His mother was on her way to Miguel Ortega.

A midafternoon sun blazed down on Lincoln. The buckboard rolled to a halt in a swirl of dust. Elizabeth stepped down before Taylor could move to assist her. She hurried toward the clinic.

Jesús Mantanzas had parted with them east of town. He thought it unwise to draw attention to himself, or the stallion, by parading through Lincoln. Instead, he'd arranged to meet them on the stage road, a mile or so to the west. From there, he would lead them to his adobe.

Entering the door, Elizabeth was surprised to find the waiting room empty. Then she remembered that it was a Monday, not one of the regular clinic days. She crossed to the open door of the inner office and stepped inside. Jennifer looked up from her desk.

"Mother!" she said happily. "What a surprise."

"I wish it weren't," Elizabeth remarked. "Would it be possible for you to close the office?"

"Is anything wrong with Louise or the baby?"

"No, they're fine," Elizabeth said promptly. "It's someone else."

"Who?"

"Miguel Ortega."

Jennifer stared at her with shocked round eyes. "You're not serious," she said slowly. "You want me to treat Miguel Ortega?"

"Does your physician's oath exclude wanted men?"

"I was thinking of you. After all, people are already talking about your involvement with *Las Gorras Blancas*. Why compromise yourself further?"

"I've no choice," Elizabeth said resolutely. "Without Ortega's help, my coalition would have fallen apart. I won't refuse him now."

Jennifer looked at her curiously. "Are you thinking of bringing him here?"

Elizabeth quickly explained the situation. She outlined everything she'd been told by Jesús Mantanzas. He was waiting now, she noted, to act as their guide.

"From what he said," she concluded, "Ortega can't be moved. We have to go there."

Jennifer was thoughtful a moment. "The symptoms he described could be any number of things. How can I be certain until I examine Ortega?"

"Prepare for the worst," Elizabeth said, her voice low and urgent. "Take everything you might need."

Working swiftly, Jennifer began gathering items from the medical cabinet. She included ether and surgical instruments as well as a portable stomach pump and various pharmaceutical powders. Elizabeth helped her pack the equipment in an oversize leather storage case. Her normal paraphernalia was carried in her black medical bag.

Jennifer advised Rosa that the office would be closed for the remainder of the day. She and her mother then hurried outside and secured the bags in the back of the buckboard. When they were seated, Taylor popped the reins and drove off upstreet. As they approached the courthouse, Blake Hazlett came down the stairs. He hailed them with a wave.

Taylor reined the team to a halt. Blake smiled, tipping his hat to Elizabeth, then looked at Jennifer. "What's wrong?" he asked. "Someone ill?"

"Yes," Jennifer said hesitantly. "A *mexicano* family sent word to Mother."

"Why would they . . . ?"

Blake paused, glancing at Elizabeth. Her expression was unreadable, and his gaze shifted back to Jennifer. "What's going on here?" he demanded. "You're not telling me something."

"I—" Jennifer faltered, reluctant to lie. "There's no reason to concern yourself. We'll talk about it later."

"I'd prefer to talk about it now."

"We haven't time. You'll just have to trust me."

"Trust you?" Blake echoed. "Look here—"

"I'm sorry," Jennifer cut him off. "We have to go."

Taylor snapped the reins. The team lurched into a startled trot and the buckboard pulled away. Blake was left standing in the middle of the road staring after them. His features dissolved into a bewildered frown.

Somehow he felt patronized, even belittled. He promised himself it wouldn't end there. A man deserved more from the woman he intended to marry.

And a lady doctor was no exception.

Something over an hour later the buckboard forded the Rio Bonito. Jesús Mantanzas led them northwest, toward a line of sawtoothed foothills. The trail they followed was narrow and rutted, hardly more than a wilderness trace.

A mile or so from the river they pulled into a clearing. From the rough countryside the Mantanzas family had hacked and hoed a small plot of land. Beyond the house was a well-tended garden, and a flock of some thirty sheep grazed on sparse grasses. A belled milk goat, udders swaying, ran with the sheep.

The adobe was stoutly built, situated near a shallow mountain stream. Three young children, two boys and a girl, were weeding the garden. Off in the distance, an older boy stood watch over the sheep. A woman, aged before her time, waited in the doorway. Her features were expressionless as the buckboard rolled to a halt.

Mantanzas greeted his wife with a somber nod. She stepped aside as he led Jennifer and Elizabeth into the house. Taylor unloaded the case of medical gear and followed them inside. The interior was crude, with a dirt floor and a few pieces of rough furniture. A beehive fireplace provided heat for cooking and warmth.

Ortega lay on a rickety bed. He was stripped to his undershorts, motionless on a mattress of coarse ticking stuffed with straw. His features were pallid and his eyes seemed clouded with pain. His forehead glistened with perspiration and he had the blotchy coloring of a seriously ill man. He smiled weakly, focusing on Elizabeth.

"Gracias, señora," he said in a parched voice. "I knew you would not fail me."

Elizabeth forced herself to smile. "We came as soon as we could. I'm sorry it took so long."

"Do not apologize, *señora*. It is I who am in your debt."

"This is my daughter," Elizabeth said, indicating Jennifer. "She is the one you asked for, the physician. You can have faith in her power to heal."

Ortega coughed raggedly. "I am in need of healing. A *bruja* tears at my insides."

Jennifer moved to the side of the bed. "Señor Ortega, I want you to forget I'm a woman. A doctor cannot afford modesty. Show me where you hurt."

Ortega placed a shaky hand on his abdomen. "All across here. I have never known such pain."

"Are you queasy, sick to your stomach?"

"Sí."

"Have you experienced vomiting, loose bowels?"

Ortega appeared embarrassed by the question. He nodded his head with a clenched smile. Jennifer sat down on the edge of the bed, opened her medical bag. She took out a thermometer and popped it into his mouth. While she waited, she gripped his wrist, her forefinger on the artery. His pulsebeat was abnormally rapid, hammering against her fingertip.

After a short time, she removed the thermometer and held it to the light of a nearby window. The reading was dangerously high, confirming a raging fever. Her expression betrayed nothing as she returned the thermometer to its wooden case. She smiled in apology and lowered his undershorts down over his groin. Gingerly, her hands centered on his belly, she palpated the stomach wall. Ortega's face twisted in a grimace.

Jennifer noted that the stomach wall was rigid. She lightly touched a spot between his bellybutton and his right side. "Does it hurt most here or somewhere else?"

"There," Ortega rasped. "Your finger is like a nail driven through my soul."

"Tell me how this sickness came on you. Was the pain gradual or did it start all at once?"

Ortega described a punishing ordeal. A week past, he'd been in the Seven Rivers district. At first, his stomach had been only slightly tender to the touch. He had experienced nausea and diarrhea; but he attributed it to some digestive disorder. Then, as he rode north toward Lincoln, the pain had intensified, centering to the right of his navel. By the time he happened upon Mantanzas' home, he could barely sit a horse. Since yesterday, he'd been unable to hold down food.

Jennifer nodded. "Your symptoms lead to only one diagnosis. You have appendicitis."

Ortega looked at her blankly. "I do not know that word."

"The appendix," Jennifer explained, "is an outgrowth off the large intestine. Yours is inflamed and badly swollen. I can feel it through your stomach."

"What is the cure?"

"We must remove it."

"You intend to cut me open?"

"There's no alternative," Jennifer said. "Should your appendix rupture and burst, your insides would be flooded with poison. The medical term for it is peritonitis."

"And then?" Ortega asked. "What would happen?"

"I wouldn't be able to save you. Death would occur within a matter of hours."

"So I have no choice but the knife?"

"I'm afraid not."

"Suerte del cielo baja," Ortega said with a faint smile. "Fortune comes from above. God will guide your hand."

"Then I suggest we proceed, Señor Ortega. We haven't a moment to lose."

Jennifer asked Señora Mantanzas to boil a pot of water. With the help of Taylor and Jesús Mantanzas, she then moved Ortega to the rough-hewn dining table. When the water boiled, Elizabeth joined her at a stone basin beside the fireplace. They began scrubbing for the operation.

"Be honest," Elizabeth whispered. "How dangerous is it?"

"God only knows," Jennifer said gravely. "It's a surgical procedure of last resort. In medical school, I saw it performed just once."

The concern in her voice was justified. The first recorded appendectomy had been performed in 1736 at St. George's Hospital in London. The physician was Claudius Amyand, surgeon to the royal family, and thereafter a name known to medical students around the world. Over the next century, however, the procedure had remained largely ignored. Considered risky, it had been relegated to a position of obscurity in surgical textbooks.

Still another fifty years passed before an appendectomy was performed in the United States. In early 1886, a surgeon at New York's Roosevelt Hospital had successfully undertaken the operation. Only then was the procedure introduced into the classrooms of medical institutions; not one doctor in ten had ever seen it performed. An exception to the rule, Jennifer had observed an appendectomy during her last week in medical school.

Yet she was hardly an expert on the subject. Standing beside the improvised operating table, she waited while her mother administered ether to Ortega. In those final moments, she mentally reviewed the steps in the procedure. Her one small comfort was in the statement she'd made earlier. Without the operation Miguel Ortega would never see another sunrise.

Jennifer took a scalpel in hand. She made a vertical

incision three inches long over the right side. Her next cut
separated the deeper muscles and exposed the pouch of the
large intestine. Slipping her fingers into the wound, she followed one of the longitudinal bands downward to the base of
the appendix. Where the appendix was attached to the bowel,
she tied it off to preclude bleeding from arteries. She then
severed the appendix from the bowel.

Thus far there were no complications. Jennifer paused a
moment to catalog the remaining steps, each one crucial to
the survival of her patient. Working to a large extent by feel,
she isolated the base of the appendix and wound it tightly
with catgut. At last, the scalpel once more in hand, she cut
the appendix loose from the large intestine. After removing
it, she laid the scalpel aside and slipped the stump of the appendix beneath the intestinal pouch. Finally, with a surgical
needle, she stitched the membrane lining of the pouch over
the invaginated stump.

The procedure ended in reverse order. Working outward,
she sutured first the abdominal muscles and then closed the
surface incision. When she stepped back, she felt reasonably
confident that the operation had been performed without
mishap. Her gaze was drawn to the severed appendix, where
she'd dropped it on the table. Shaped like a lumpy grub-
worm, it was swollen to twice normal size. Another hour, she
told herself, and it would have ruptured. So perhaps Miguel
Ortega had been right after all.

Suerte del cielo baja.

The sun sank lower, smothering in a bed of copper beyond
the mountains. Elizabeth and Jennifer stood outside the
adobe, talking quietly. Across the yard, Taylor waited beside
the buckboard.

Ortega was still sedated. Following the operation, he'd
been lifted from the table and moved back to bed. There was
nothing more to be done, and now, with nightfall approaching, Jennifer was preparing to leave. Taylor was reluctant to
chance the winding trail in the dark.

Tomorrow was clinic day and Jennifer felt obligated to

return to town. Elizabeth had elected to stay the night, concerned that Ortega was not yet out of danger. Apart from infection, which was always a threat, Jennifer foresaw no complications. She thought all the signs pointed to a full recovery.

"Unless I hear from you," she said now, "I'll be back late tomorrow afternoon. We'll know by then whether or not there's any infection."

"Except for you," Elizabeth said, smiling warmly, "he would never have pulled through. I want you to know I'm very proud of you."

Jennifer laughed. "Modesty aside, I'm rather proud of myself. Not many sawbones could have snipped an appendix."

Elizabeth enfolded her in an affectionate hug. When they parted, Jennifer walked to the buckboard, turning back to wave. A moment later Taylor snapped the reins and they drove out of the yard. Not far down the trail they disappeared from sight.

For a time Elizabeth stood motionless in the waning light. Somewhat reflective, her thoughts went back to a comment made earlier by Ortega. Before the operation, he'd mentioned his torturous ride from Seven Rivers. She wondered now whether or not Clint was on his backtrail. All the more, she felt a sudden rush of guilt.

Clint would never understand what she'd done today. She wasn't sure she understood it herself.

TWENTY-FIVE

The sky was sprinkled with stars. A crescent moon, tilted at an angle, advanced slowly across the eastern foothills. From the mountains, a cool evening breeze rustled through the treetops.

Clint was seated on the veranda of the hotel. Upstreet the sound of male laughter racketed from a saloon. He felt no urge for a drink and the idea of other men's company appealed to him even less. His mood was withdrawn, oddly embittered.

Fireflies darted though the dusky night. He watched them without interest, slouched back in a cane-bottomed rocker. His cigarette glowed as he took a long drag, exhaling smoke. After supper in the hotel dining room he had retired to the veranda. For the past hour he'd sat there brooding, mired in disgust.

Late that afternoon Clint had ridden into Lincoln. His journey to the Seven Rivers country had proved to be a washout. He'd found the ranchers cooperative but wary, mistrustful of outside lawmen. Their attitude toward *Las Gorras Blancas* was one of low contempt. Any raids, they told him, would bring harsh reprisals against all *mexicanos*. They prided themselves on keeping the greasers in line.

Quickly enough, Clint discovered that their bragging contained an element of truth. There were rumors that Miguel Ortega had been sighted in the Seven Rivers district. Yet his efforts to incite violence had come to nothing. The *mexicanos* wanted no part of an uprising against Anglo cattlemen. Nor were they moved by Oretega's exhortations about land fraud and the spread of barbed wire. Life was unjust, but they feared retribution by the *gringos* even more. They refused to join *Las Gorras Blancas*.

In Clint's mind, the decisive factor was dread. Seven Rivers was remote and sparsely populated, a land where might made right. Over the years the ranchers had intimidated and terrorized the *mexicanos*. However brutal, the force of Anglo rule was a fact of life. So the call to revolution, unlike in other parts of New Mexico, had fallen on deaf ears. Peace at any price was preferable to the wrath of the cattlemen. Where horse thieves were routinely hanged, no man would risk the fate of a night rider.

For all that, Clint had been unable to turn up a lead. He'd covered lots of ground, but he always seemed to be a day behind. Not quite a week ago, word began circulating that Ortega had quit the Seven Rivers country. Logic dictated that the White Cap leader would turn north, toward Lincoln. Having failed at Seven Rivers, Ortega would almost certainly resume raiding elsewhere. A quick show of force was needed to counter the Seven Rivers setback and embolden partisan *mexicanos*. Lincoln seemed the most likely spot.

To Clint, it was like starting over again. The manhunt was now entering its third month, and he'd been euchred at every turn. Yet, while he was disgruntled, he was no less determined. A wily fugitive somehow chaffed his stubborn streak, made him bow his neck. In the past, he had prevailed, running down wanted men, through sheer tenacity. Ortega was a smooth article, devilishly clever; but Clint operated on the theory that every dog had his day. All he needed was a fresh lead.

Along those lines, his mind turned to Elizabeth. On his way into town he had stopped by at Spur. To his surprise, he discovered he'd become a great-uncle. Morg and Louise proudly displayed the baby, and he had made all the obligatory remarks. But later, when he inquired after Elizabeth, he'd got a strange story. According to Morg, she had gone off with a *mexicano* on some unexplained mission of mercy. Though Morg hadn't stated it outright, he had dropped several broad hints. The sick man might well be Miguel Ortega.

Clint's first stop upon arriving in town had been the clinic. When he found it closed, he had then paid a call on Blake Hazlett. The story he got tended to support everything he'd heard from Morg. Elizabeth and Jennifer, accompanied by John Taylor, had driven westward out of Lincoln. Blake knew nothing of the *mexicano* horseman, and that in itself made Clint all the more suspicious. A Mexican riding a blooded stallion would have drawn a crowd outside the clinic. Clearly, all those involved were reluctant to attract attention to themselves. Which meant they had something to hide.

On reflection, Clint thought it all dovetailed. Elizabeth and Jennifer were by nature the most forthright of women. Their secretive manner today was uncharacteristic of either of them, and led to a troubling conclusion. The *mexicano* was known in Lincoln, probably lived somewhere nearby. Whether he was a member of *Las Gorras Blancas* was a moot point. The fact remained that he was a go-between as well as a guide. And while the destination was unknown, Elizabeth and Jennifer had gone along willingly. There seemed little question that they had been summoned by Miguel Ortega.

The belief served to darken Clint's mood. That Elizabeth would act as an angel of mercy for Ortega left him hurt and stunned. She knew beyond doubt that Ortega had twice tried to have him killed. Yet she'd still rushed off to provide aid for the man. He felt betrayed, somehow double-crossed, for she was family. Even more, she was the one woman who had won his trust and his lifelong devotion. His world suddenly seemed smaller, strangely empty.

A buckboard passed by the hotel. Clint stiffened, straining for a better look. In the pale moonlight, he saw Taylor at the reins and Jennifer's unmistakable profile. He searched for some sign of Elizabeth, baffled that she wasn't with them. Then, as though struck a hard blow, it hit him. She was still with Ortega.

Clint slammed out of the rocker. He stepped off the veranda and hurried downstreet. Ahead, he saw the buckboard roll to a halt before the clinic. Taylor jumped down, then assisted Jennifer from her seat. She stood waiting while he unloaded what seemed to be a box of some sort. Neither of them was aware of Clint until he rounded the tail of the buckboard.

"Uncle Clint!" Jennifer gasped. "What are you doing here?"

"Waiting for you," Clint said, frowning heavily. "Where's your mother?"

"Why?" Jennifer stalled. "Are you looking for her?"

Clint's voice was reproachful. "Suppose we quit beating around the bush. I'd like a straight answer to my question. Where is she?"

"You needn't be so gruff. What gave you the idea she was with me?"

"Stop trying my patience, missy. You drove out of town with her and you've come back without her. So I'll have an answer—right now."

"I'm sorry," Jennifer said softly. "I can't tell you."

"You mean you won't tell me."

"Either way, it amounts to the same thing."

"Then I'll tell you," Clint said angrily. "She's with Ortega, isn't she?"

A smile froze on Jennifer's face. "I really couldn't say."

There was a moment of deadened silence. Clint's features took on a sudden hard cast. "All right, let's forget family. I'm talking to you as a law officer now." He paused, glaring at her. "Ortega's a killer and I have a warrant for his arrest. Where is he?"

Jennifer's lingering smile faded. "I save lives," she said. "Enforcing the law isn't my concern."

"You're gonna leave it like that?"

"Yes, I am."

Clint eyed her, considering. "I reckon there's other ways. For instance"—his gaze shifted to Taylor—"I'll just trail along behind you."

Taylor shrugged indifferently. "What makes you think I'm headed anywhere?"

"Because I know you," Clint announced. "You wouldn't leave Beth alone with Ortega overnight. You're fixin' to turn right around, aren't you?"

"Whatever I do," Taylor said casually, "it's not gonna change anything. You still won't find her."

"Why the hell not?"

"You're right when you said I wouldn't leave her alone. But I won't let you follow me, either."

Clint squinted at him. "How do you propose to stop me?"

Taylor met his gaze levelly. "I'm still pretty handy with a gun. You try to follow me and I'll use it."

"You're not that good," Clint said tightly. "You never were. You'd just get yourself killed."

"Yeah, probably so," Taylor agreed. "'Course, that wouldn't help you none. You still wouldn't find her."

Clint shook his head. "I never took you for a damn fool. Maybe I was wrong."

Taylor spread his open-palmed hands. "Miz Brannock kept me on the payroll all these years and I never once had to earn my keep. Let's just say I owe her."

Clint accepted the statement for what it was, a blunt truth. John Taylor had signed on as a hired gun some seven years past. In that time, he'd lived an easy life and never been forced to draw his gun. He felt an obligation, a certain debt of honor. He wouldn't back off now.

"Tell you the truth," Clint said finally, "Ortega's not worth it. I won't have your blood on my hands."

Taylor stared at him for a moment. "Have I got your word you won't follow me?"

"On one condition," Clint muttered. "You make goddamn sure Beth doesn't come to any harm. Savvy?"

"Don't give it another thought. I'll get her back safe and sound."

Taylor climbed into the buckboard. He hauled on the reins and brought the team around in the road. Jennifer and Clint watched as he drove west out of town. At length, Clint hefted the medical case and turned up the walkway. Jennifer hurried along to open the door.

Inside the waiting room, Clint lowered the case onto the floor. Jennifer placed her medical bag on a chair, then lighted a lamp. When she turned around, Clint was standing at the door staring out into the night. He didn't look at her.

"Sorry I got rough," he said. "It's got nothing to do with you."

"I know," Jennifer said quietly. "You're worried about Mother."

Clint was silent so long she wasn't sure he would respond. At last, he turned from the door. "What's wrong with Ortega?"

"Appendicitis," Jennifer replied. "One of his internal organs became poisoned. I had to operate and remove it."

"Will he recover?"

"Yes, I believe so."

"Good." Clint's voice hardened. "Wouldn't want him to miss his date with the hangman."

Jennifer was pensive a moment. "I hope you don't blame Mother too much. She felt she had to stay with him, at least for tonight."

"Why?" Clint asked sharply. "What's Ortega to her?"

"I'm afraid you wouldn't like my answer."

"Try me and see."

"Well—" Jennifer paused, searching for words. "To be perfectly honest, I think she's attracted to him. And I suspect she doesn't even know it."

Clint looked at her with disbelief. "How in Christ's name could she be attracted to somebody like him?"

"Have you ever met him?"

"No."

"Until today, I hadn't either. I have to admit it was something of a shock."

"I don't follow you."

Jennifer smiled. "Speaking as a woman, I found him very handsome. But that's only part of it." She hesitated, uncertain what she wanted to say. "There's a mystery about him, something almost indefinable. He's a compelling man . . . forceful . . ."

"He's a man with a price on his head—an outlaw!"

"Aren't you really saying something else?"

"Such as?"

"He's a *mexicano*," Jennifer remarked. "And no white woman—especially Mother—should be attracted to a Mexican. Isn't that it?"

"You're putting words in my mouth."

"Am I?"

"For your mother's sake," Clint said, ignoring the question, "let's hope she isn't attracted to him. Señor Ortega's not long for this world."

"How ironic," Jennifer observed. "I save him and you hang him. Somehow it doesn't seem fair."

"Maybe not," Clint said, "but it's a damnsight more than he deserves. Lots of people are dead on his account."

Blake stepped through the door. "I saw a light," he said, nodding to Jennifer. "Have you been here long?"

"Only a few minutes."

"Where's your mother?"

Clint cleared his throat. "I think I'll call it a night. Let me know if you hear anything."

Before Jennifer could reply, he turned and walked from the clinic. When the door closed, Blake looked at her strangely. His expression was at once critical and concerned.

"I take it you and Clint had words?"

"Yes, we did," Jennifer acknowledged. "He's upset because Mother stayed behind . . ."

"With Ortega," Blake finished it for her. "Is that what you were going to say?"

"I see you already know."

Blake shrugged. "Clint and I figured it out for ourselves this afternoon."

Jennifer laughed without humor. "Apparently it wasn't much of a secret."

"No, not much," Blake said in a carefully measured voice. "Why did you feel it was necessary to lie to me?"

"I didn't lie to you."

"On the contrary," Blake corrected her, "you lied by omission. You let me believe something that wasn't true."

Jennifer looked down at the floor. "I merely honored Mother's request. She thought it was better that way."

"Then I'm doubly disappointed. I expected a little more in the way of trust."

"Oh, for God's sake, Blake! Don't be such a stuffed shirt."

Blake shook his head in stern disapproval. "There's nothing stuffed-shirt about honesty. I have every right to be offended."

"Do you?" Jennifer said crossly. "Well, don't expect an apology. You won't get one from me."

"What I expect," Blake informed her, "is that it won't happen again. I have no secrets from you and I demand the same in return. I won't settle for less."

"And I won't be dictated to!"

"Listen closely," Blake said in a solemn tone. "I'm stating an unalterable condition for our marriage. The matter isn't open to debate, now or in the future."

A cone of silence enveloped them. Jennifer saw an aspect of him she'd never seen before. Beneath the gentleness, there was a deliberate and very forceful man. He would indulge her in many things, but he would not be deceived. She suddenly realized her next words would decide their marriage.

"One mistake doesn't affect a lifetime, does it?"

"So far as I'm concerned," Blake allowed, "we can forget it right now."

"Then let's kiss and make up . . . agreed?"

Blake took her in his arms. He kissed her soundly on the mouth and squeezed her so tight she came up on tiptoe. She seemed to melt within his embrace, and for the first time she didn't want it to end. His kiss was ardent and curiously demanding.

She thought making up might be fun.

· · ·

Elizabeth awoke at dawn. She had slept fitfully, seated beside the bed with her back to the wall. She was wrapped in a tattered blanket that smelled faintly of woodsmoke.

The Mantanzas family was still asleep. John Taylor, with a blanket pulled around him, was snoring lightly. He lay curled on the floor near the fireplace, one arm tucked under his head. No one stirred as Elizabeth got stiffly to her feet.

She felt brittle and unrested. During the night she had awakened periodically to check on Ortega. His fever had abated and his pulse rate was steady. From all indications, there was no sign of postoperative infection. A single dose of laudanum had kept him quiet throughout the night.

In the chilly dawn, Elizabeth almost wished she'd taken a dose herself. Taylor had returned from town shortly before midnight. His recounting of the encounter with Clint had left her shaken. She was relieved that Clint hadn't attempted to follow the buckboard. But she was now all the more concerned that he felt betrayed, and deeply hurt. She worried that the breach between them might be irreparable.

She worried as well that the truce was only temporary. Clint was personally affronted, and the greater part of his anger would be directed toward Ortega. Once the search resumed, his efforts would be redoubled, with the ugly overtones of a vendetta. The surgery, performed to prolong life, was in reality a fleeting reprieve. Ortega, more than at any time in the past, was now doomed. Given the slightest excuse, Clint would kill him.

"Buenos días, señora."

Startled, Elizabeth turned toward the bed. She found Ortega awake and alert, watching her. "How do you feel?" she asked. "Are you in pain?"

Ortega smiled. "I am much better now, *gracias.* You are a good nurse."

"Thank my daughter," Elizabeth said. "Her skill is what saved you."

Ortega nodded, silent a moment. "You seem troubled, *señora.* Am I still in danger?"

"No, I don't believe so."

"Then why do I see concern in your eyes?"

Elizabeth hesitated, choosing her words carefully. She told him of Clint's return to Lincoln, and the shaky agreement with Taylor. She expressed the belief that it wouldn't last.

"I'll have to leave today," she said. "Once I'm gone, Clint won't delay much longer. His search will begin again."

"I expect no less," Ortega said matter-of-factly. "But do not alarm yourself, *señora*. Nothing will stop me from completing my work."

"We both know that isn't true. Your only hope is to take refuge in Mexico. Otherwise he will find you . . . and kill you."

"I cannot desert my people when they need me most. There is no one to take my place."

"Would your death serve them any better?"

Ortega scrutinized her closely. "Why do you fear for my life, *señora*? What importance does it have for you?"

Elizabeth's heart suddenly pounded. His eyes were darkly intense and she saw mirrored there her own confusion. She felt drawn to him in ways that disturbed her, almost an emotional attachment. Yet she'd fought it from the outset, and all the more so because of Clint. In the end, she'd somehow known it would come down to this moment. A choice between one or the other, with no turning back. Which made it no choice at all.

She took a deep breath to steady herself. "I must ask you something," she said. "Is it true you tried to have Clint killed?"

"*Sí,*" Ortega readily admitted. "But it has nothing to do with you, *señora*. One of us must kill the other." He paused, staring at her. "You cannot change what will be."

Elizabeth was quiet for a long moment. When she spoke, there was an echoing sadness in her voice. "Without your help, the reform coalition would have fallen apart. You rendered a great service and I will always be thankful. But now, I feel I have repaid the debt."

"You and your daughter saved my life, *señora*. It is I who am in your debt."

"Then I release you," Elizabeth said quickly. "Neither of us owes the other anything. As of today, we are even."

"I understand," Ortega said in wistful agreement. "It will be as though we had never met. *Verdad*?"

"Yes."

Elizabeth let it end there. She checked his temperature and his pulse and found his condition stable. By then the others were awake and she instructed Señora Mantanzas on the care he would need. Sometime that afternoon, she advised, Jennifer would return to examine him. Ortega merely listened, his expression stoic.

Their parting was formal, a brief handshake. As the sun crested the horizon, Elizabeth and Taylor drove out of the yard. She suppressed the urge to look back, and instead stared straight ahead. Her eyes glistened in the brilliant flare of sunrise.

She told herself it could have ended no other way. She suddenly hated the sound of the truth.

TWENTY-SIX

Lon stepped onto the veranda. His leg was still bothersome, but he was walking now with a cane. He moved to a rocker and seated himself.

A midmorning sun blazed down on the valley. The Rio Hondo meandered off in the distance like a silvery ribbon. The day was already sweltering, and shimmering heat waves obscured the western foothills. Along the river a listless breeze rippled through the treetops.

From his shirt pocket Lon removed a slim black cheroot. He struck a match and lit up in a lazy cloud of smoke. Settling back, he puffed on the cheroot, his cane hooked over the arm of the rocker. His gaze wandered out across the compound, settling on the corral. He stared at the horses with a faraway look.

To his great disgust, Lon found himself involved in a petty subterfuge. He mentally calculated the date as June 12, marking his third week at Spur. His leg was stiff, still somewhat weak, but the bullet wound was completely healed. In the secrecy of his room, he'd tested his leg without the cane, experiencing little difficulty. He walked with only a slight limp.

In effect, the cane was a stage prop. As he puffed the cheroot, his gaze remained fixed on the corral. He knew he could saddle one of the horses and ride away anytime it suited his purpose. Yet he continued the pretense of favoring his leg, hobbling about on the cane. His reason for acting the

invalid centered on a nagging uncertainty about Hank. He
was no longer confident of his hold over the boy.

The nub of the problem was Brad. As foreman of the
ranch, he struck a bold figure. On a daily basis he commanded the respect of a crew of roughshod cowhands and
their *segundos*. All the more significant, he was responsible
for thousands of head of livestock, both cattle and horses. To
an impressionable youngster like Hank, it was heady stuff.
He hung on Brad's every word, eager as a puppy. His awe
was apparent even to the casual observer.

For Lon, it was a source of festering hostility. With each
passing day he saw Brad's influence growing stronger. He
was all too aware that he'd lost ground in the fight for Hank.
The boy was starstruck by the ranch and increasingly drawn
to the life of a stockgrower. His greater interest was in the
horse herds and the breeding program. But he listened like
an acolyte when Brad talked of Durham cows and blooded
bulls. He was slowly being won over.

Today, as he sat brooding on it, Lon had a sense of time
slipping away. He still felt reasonably certain of Hank's loyalty, for the bond between brothers exerted a strong pull. But
he was reluctant to put it to the test, force a showdown between himself and Brad. Instead, he continued to hobble
around on the cane and delay any mention of leaving Spur.
He wasn't at all sure the boy would follow him when he
rode out.

The one bright spot was that he no longer had to worry
about Clint. From what he gathered, Clint and Elizabeth
were at loggerheads over the *mexicano* troublemaker Miguel
Ortega. Clint hadn't visited the ranch in more than a week,
and so far as Lon was concerned it was good riddance. In
fact, he hoped the squabble might last indefinitely, or at least
until he'd resolved his more immediate problem. With Clint
out of his hair, he had only to contend with Brad, and he
meant to somehow force the issue. He'd already let it go too
long.

Off in the distance he spotted two riders approaching from
the south. As they forded the river, he saw that one was Brad

and the other was Hank. He took a thoughtful pull on his che-root, considering how he might turn the moment to advan-tage. It crossed his mind that he had nothing to gain by acting in a roundabout manner. He decided to call a spade a spade.

Brad and Hank dismounted at the corral. They left their horses hitched to the fence and walked toward the house. Lon rose from his chair as they stepped onto the veranda. He stuck the cheroot in his mouth and limped forward, leaning on the cane. Hank grinned, veering off in his direction. Brad merely nodded and started into the house.

"Hold on, Brad," Lon called out. "You and me need to have a talk."

Brad turned at the door. "I've got to see Mrs. Brannock. Will it wait?"

"Hell, no," Lon said with a corrosive glare. "We're way past overdue."

For a moment they stared at one another in silent assess-ment. Hank appeared confused, uncertain which way to turn. At length, Brad crossed the veranda.

"Awright," he said. "What's so important it won't keep?"

Lon's voice was edged. "I don't like people trying to put one over on me. You think you've got me hoodwinked, but you don't."

"Hoodwinked about what?"

"You know damn well I'm talkin' about Hank."

A look of puzzlement crossed Brad's face. "You just lost me."

"C'mon," Lon taunted, "why act so innocent? I know what you've been sayin' behind my back."

"Wait a minute," Hank broke in quickly. "Nobody's been talkin' behind your back."

"Stay out of it," Lon ordered. "This here's between me and Brad."

"Whatever it is," Brad told him, "you're gonna have to give me a clue. I still haven't got your drift."

Lon let go a mocking humorless laugh. "Hell's bells and little fishes," he said loudly, "you're tryin' to turn Hank against me. Any fool could see that."

"You're way off the mark, Lon. I never tried any such thing."

"Are you callin' me a liar?"

"Nope," Brad said carefully. "I'm just sayin' you're wrong."

"Am I now?" Lon muttered with a cold smile. "I suppose you haven't been workin' on Hank to keep him here at the ranch? Go ahead, let's hear you deny it."

"Nothin' to deny," Brad said. "I've told him he's welcome to stay on."

"Sure you have," Lon said sarcastically. "And you told him nobody'd think the worse because he's a half-breed. Just one big family, wasn't that how you put it?"

"What of it?"

"You're full of hot air, that's what! He'd spend his life workin' for wages . . . the same as you."

Brad's face went chalky. "I haven't done so bad."

"Yeah?" Lon needled him. "Then how come you're runnin' cows over on the Rio Felix? Way it looks, you're fixin' to quit the Brannocks yourself."

"Lay off," Hank interrupted, stealing a glance at Brad. "You got no call to put him on the spot like that. What's between him and the family is his business."

"Family, my ass!" Lon crowed. "Why do you think he's all set to quit Spur? Christ, he's not family, no more'n you would be. He's a hired hand."

Brad shook his head. "I never said nothin' about leaving Spur."

Lon's smile grew broader. "Well, now's your chance to set the record straight. Are you movin' on or not?"

Too late Brad saw the trap. Whatever he said, it would sound as though he'd misled Hank. How could he recommend Spur to the boy when he was thinking of leaving himself? No reasonable answer occurred to him.

"Whatever I do," he said finally, "I've got no complaints about the family. They've treated me square from the day I rode onto Spur."

Lon knew when to keep silent. He had planted a seed of doubt in the youngster's mind, and Brad's lame reply merely reinforced his argument. He lightly punched Hank on the shoulder.

"C'mon, sport," he said, grinning. "Let's have ourselves a little target practice. Never pays to let yourself get rusty."

"I dunno," Hank said hesitantly. "We were gonna talk to Miz Brannock about some colts. I saw one that sorta took my fancy."

"I'll sound her out," Brad assured him. "You go ahead and enjoy yourself. I'll catch up with you later."

An evil light began to dance in Lon's eyes. "What the hell," he said to Brad, "the more the merrier. You're welcome to come along."

"Not today," Brad replied. "I've got other business with Mrs. Brannock."

"Sure, you go on," Lon said with an offhand gesture. "It'll save you some embarrassment, anyway. Never yet saw a cowhand worth his salt with a gun."

The words were a direct challenge. Brad saw no way to refuse and still retain Hank's respect. Even now, he sensed the youngster watching him closely. He motioned casually to Lon.

"Tell you what," he drawled, "a dollar says I don't miss. You interested?"

Lon feigned indifference. "Low stakes don't make much of a game. How about a dollar a shot?"

"You've got yourself a bet."

Hank collected an armload of airtights from the trash heap behind the cookhouse. They walked down to the river and Brad indicated a spot upstream where the bank rose sharply from the river. The empty tin cans were arranged in a line, with the riverbank serving as a backstop. They stepped off ten paces.

The toss of a coin decided who went first. Lon won and he turned to face the riverbank, leaning slightly on the cane. His arm moved in a shadowy blur and the Colt appeared in his hand. The shots blended into a staccato roar and four cans leapt into the air. On the fifth shot, a spurt of sand kicked up beside a tomato can.

"Damn!" he swore under his breath. "I singed the label on that sonovabitch."

Brad smiled. "Close don't count when there's money on the line."

"Four outta five's nothin' to sneeze at. Let's see you beat it."

Brad squared off against the riverbank. His draw was deliberate, without waste motion, and he brought the Peacemaker to shoulder level. He concentrated on the front sight, feathering the trigger and thumbing the hammer with practiced ease. While he was a shade slower than Lon, he emptied the pistol in a matter of seconds. Every shot sent a can flying.

"Hello, down there."

A man's voice brought them around. John Taylor appeared downstream, drawn by the sound of gunfire. He walked toward them, looking from one to the other. His expression was inquisitive.

"What's all the shootin' about?"

"Just poppin' some cans," Brad said. "Had a wager of a dollar a shot."

"Who won?"

"Not me," Lon grouched. "I touched one off a mite too quick."

Taylor sensed the antagonism between them. He'd been a distant observer of their struggle for Hank's loyalty. The shooting match, he decided now, was all part of the same contest. Still, it worried him, for he had an instinctive mistrust of Lon. Shooting cans was only a step away from shooting people.

"Wanna try your hand?" Lon inquired. "I've heard you're pretty fair with a gun."

"I'll pass," Taylor said pleasantly. "You boys are too good for me."

"Go ahead," Brad urged him. "We could both use a lesson in fast and fancy."

"Yeah, why not?" Lon added with a go-to-hell smile. "Old dogs are supposed to know all the tricks."

Taylor ignored the gibe. He directed Hank to stack five tin cans one atop the other. The boy looked puzzled, but obediently followed instructions. When the airtights were arranged in a wobbly stack, he rejoined the men.

Facing the riverbank, Taylor pulled and fired, too quick for the eye. The bottom can jumped backward and the other four came tumbling down. There was scarcely a pulsebeat between shots as Taylor blasted the cans while they were still in midair. The last one went spinning crazily an instant before it touched the ground.

Without a word, Taylor shucked the empty shells and began reloading. The others watched him in silence, like an audience witnessing a magician perform some staggering sleight-of-hand. At last, Hank let out a low whistle between his teeth.

"Goddurn," he said huskily. "I never seen nuthin' like that."

Taylor smiled. "Your Uncle Clint showed me that stunt. 'Course, he does it a hair faster'n me."

"Faster?" Hank repeated. "You mean he could beat you?"

"Six days a week and all day on Sunday. I'm plumb slow up beside him."

Lon laughed out loud. "All that trick shootin' don't mean a hill of beans. Tin cans don't shoot back."

Taylor fixed him with an austere look. "What's your point?"

"I'm just sayin' Clint's past his prime. A younger man could take him easy."

"Well, as for that," Taylor said in a dry cold manner, "there's been a few young squirts that tried it. He put 'em all in the bone orchard."

Lon snorted. "You talk like he's got you buffaloed."

Taylor's eyes narrowed, and a smile appeared at the corner of his mouth. "When the Lord was handin' out nerves, Clint didn't take none. I'd sooner tangle with a grizzly bear."

"Well, I still say he's round the bend. Hell, he can't even catch that asshole greaser—Ortega."

Taylor wagged his head. "Sonny, if I was you, I wouldn't say that to Clint's face. He's liable to box your ears."

Lon appeared on the verge of saying something more. But then he evidently thought it over and changed his mind. Taylor waited, studying him with a look of amused contempt. After a marked silence, the older man holstered his gun and walked away.

Brad followed him up the riverbank. Neither Lon nor Hank said anything for a long while. Yet the boy easily read his brother's thoughts. A choice to go or stay would have to be made soon.

Lon was the odd man out at Spur.

The sound of footsteps echoed through the hallway. Elizabeth looked up from her desk as Brad appeared in the door of the office. She beckoned him inside.

"I heard shooting," she said. "What's going on?"

Brad dropped into a chair. "That was Lon and me havin' a little target practice. He's pretty handy with a gun."

"Too much so," Elizabeth said in a firm voice. "I take it he's feeling better. Or doesn't a cane inhibit his shooting?"

"Not so's you'd notice."

"Well, anyway, I'm glad you're here. I wanted to ask you about the next trail herd."

"Everything looks good," Brad said. "I figure to get 'em headed out by the first of the week."

"Just in time," Elizabeth sighed. "We're running short on operating funds."

"Anything wrong?"

"Nothing besides Morg. I've authorized more money to expand his business ventures. Not that it won't return a profit, of course. It just takes time."

"Where's he at now?" Brad asked. "I hardly ever see him anymore."

"Roswell," Elizabeth said uncertainly. "Or maybe it's White Oaks. I lose track myself."

"Well, there's no two ways about it. He's a whizbang once he gets started."

"Which reminds me," Elizabeth commented. "Have you given any thought to our last discussion? I'm afraid we've lost Morg to the ranch entirely."

Brad had thought of little else. Whether or not to stay on at Spur preoccupied his mind. All the more so since Juanita was pressing him to get married. He seemed bogged down in indecision.

"Wish I had an answer," he said. "I'm just not sure what's best."

Elizabeth saw the troubled look in his eyes. "You'll recall I offered you a bonus. What if we increased it another two or three percent? Would that influence your thinking?"

Brad leaned forward, elbows resting on his knees. He stared down at the floor. "I'm not holdin' out for more money. Tell you the God's honest truth, I'm not even sure I want my own ranch." He paused, his expression bemused. "Things just don't seem so cut-and-dried anymore."

"I understand," Elizabeth said gently. "At one time or another, we all go through a period of soul-searching. Such things are never easy."

"Trouble is, I've got no idea what I'm searchin' for. It's like I want to be movin' on, start fresh somewheres. Only I don't know where."

"Whatever you decide, you'll always be a part of the family. Nothing could change that."

"I'm obliged," Brad said, uncoiling from his chair. "I'll try not to let you down."

"I know you too well to worry about that."

"One other thing . . ."

"Yes?"

An indirection came into Brad's eyes. "I heard you're on the outs with Ortega. Any truth to it?"

Elizabeth smiled stiffly. "Apparently there are no secrets on Spur."

"One of the serving girls heard you and Morg talkin'. Word got around."

"I see," Elizabeth said, looking at him. "What interest do you have in Miguel Ortega?"

Brad shrugged noncommittally. "Just wondered whether I'd heard the straight goods."

"In a word—yes."

"Sorry if it sounds like I'm pryin' into your business. Never meant it that way."

"I'm sure you didn't. Anything else?"

"No," Brad said. "I'll get on back to work."

Elizabeth watched him out the door. His curiosity about Ortega reminded her of deeper concerns. She hadn't seen Clint since the operation on the *mexicano* leader. She'd sent him a note, trying to explain, but there had been no response. By now, it was apparent he was avoiding her, punishing her with his silence. She felt miserable about the whole affair.

For the first time in memory, her life seemed weighted down with problems. Aside from Clint, there was Morg's increasing involvement in other businesses. Someone needed to visit the Cherokee Outlet ranch; but Morg was too busy, and with the uncertainty about Brad, she was reluctant to absent herself from Spur. Then too, there were the upcoming fall elections and the never-ending burden of holding her coalition together. Sometimes it all seemed too much.

John Taylor rapped on the door of the office. She blinked, jarred from her reverie, and quickly regained her composure. As he halted before the desk, she began shuffling through a stack of correspondence.

"Yes, John," she said busily. "What is it?"

"Something you oughta know," Taylor commenced in a sandy voice. "'Course, it's not rightly any of my affair. So if you figure I'm out of line . . ."

Elizabeth smiled. "That's never stopped you before."

"Well, howsomever," Taylor said, suddenly flustered, "it's about Lon. He's fixin' to make trouble."

"Why do you say that?"

Taylor recounted his part in the shooting match. He went on to relate his general impression of Lon's attitude. Finally, he told how he'd walked back from the river with Brad. In that short time, he had learned of the earlier argument between Brad and Lon.

"Way it looks to me," he concluded, "Lon's not gonna let it drop. Chances are he'll try to goad Brad into a fight."

"Over Hank?" Elizabeth asked, somewhat surprised. "Do you really think the boy means that much to him?"

"Miz Brannock," Taylor said seriously, "that kid's all the family Lon's got. Leastways, that's how he sees it."

"Well, something has to be done right away. We can't have Lon and Brad fighting."

"No, ma'am, you can't," Taylor agreed. "Specially since Lon would pull a gun. He's mean as a snake."

"I'll have a talk with him," Elizabeth said. "If he wants to blame someone, he can blame me. It was my idea that Hank stay on here."

"If it was me," Taylor said with studied calm, "I'd run him off the place today. You gimme the go-ahead and I'll do it for you."

Elizabeth seemed to look at him and past him at the same time. Lon was intractable and abrasive, probably immune to reason. But she felt compelled to give it one last try. He was, after all, family.

"Thank you, John," she said at length. "I really prefer to settle it without any ill will. Of course, should that fail . . ."

"All you gotta do is say the word, Miz Brannock."

"I'll keep that in mind."

Taylor turned back into the hallway. Elizabeth heaved a sigh that would have blown out a candle. The one thing she didn't need was still another problem. Yet it was there and she could hardly shunt it aside. Nor could she allow reason to fail.

The alternative was John Taylor.

TWENTY-SEVEN

A vagrant breeze stirred the window curtain. Clint lay with his hands locked behind his head, staring at the ceiling. His gunbelt was hooked over the bedpost.

The room was sparsely furnished. A washstand, with a faded mirror dangling from the wall, was positioned opposite the bed. Wedged into the corner near the window was a battered dresser, and beside it, a johnny pot. Apart from a small bedside table, the remaining furniture consisted of a single straight-back chair.

Clint was only vaguely aware of his surroundings. A good part of his life had been spent in hotel rooms or monastic quarters assigned to him on army posts. One was like another, impersonal and utilitarian, with little to mark a man's passage. He never thought of them as home or associated them in any way with comfort. It was a place where he slept.

Tonight, he was in a reflective mood. After supper, he had returned to the room and lit the bedside lamp. The desk clerk had given him a day-old Santa Fe newspaper and he'd scanned that with no great interest. Then, stretching out on the bed, he had smoked several cigarettes, dropping the butts into a glass of water on the table. The room was so quiet he could hear the tick of his pocket watch.

What preoccupied him most was Miguel Ortega. For all intents and purposes, the man had vanished from the face of the earth. No one had reported sighting him and there was little or no talk about him among the *mexicanos*. Nor was there any activity on the part of *Las Gorras Blancas,* either in the form of raids or clandestine meetings. Over the past fortnight it was as though Ortega had ceased to exist.

At first, Clint thought he might have died. Any operation, even one performed by Jennifer, was a risky proposition. But the death of Miguel Ortega would have been widely reported. He was a heroic figure to *mexicanos* and word of his passing would have surfaced almost instantly. So the odds dictated that he was alive and well. His whereabouts was another question entirely.

Though tempted, Clint hadn't spoken with Jennifer. He knew she had visited Ortega the evening following the operation. Yet he had honored his word and made no effort at trailing her. Since then, insofar as he could determine, she'd had no contact with her patient. His reason for not interrogating her was of a personal nature. Any conversation would inevitably lead to talk of Elizabeth. And he wasn't ready to broach the matter.

Elizabeth's note hadn't swayed him. In it, she had attempted to justify her actions with respect to Ortega. Her arguments were filled with compassion for the sick, and the belief that anyone, even an outlaw, should not be denied medical attention. She assured Clint that she hadn't meant to betray his trust, or to choose sides. Nor was there any intent to hamper his investigation. She asked for understanding and faith in her sincerity. She wanted nothing to come between them.

Clint felt stung by her tone. However persuasive her arguments, the facts were undeniable. She had given aid to a man who tried to kill him. Worse, she excused her actions on humane grounds rather than offering an apology. Her choice of words, at least in Clint's reading, somehow made it seem he was at fault. She expected understanding and faith, but ignored what was really at issue. By assisting Ortega, she herself had broken faith.

From Clint's viewpoint there was still another factor involved. The day after the operation he'd waited for Elizabeth to contact him. He fully expected her to come forward, volunteer to lead him to Ortega. In good conscience, having saved the *mexicano*'s life, she could have assisted in his capture. Instead, she had passed through town without stopping and returned to the ranch. She had deliberately chosen to shield Ortega from the law.

Her note, delivered by a cowhand, had arrived the following day. Upon reading it, Clint's worst doubts had been confirmed. She had stepped over the line and she meant to stay there. By her continued silence, she was protecting a fugitive, thwarting his apprehension. Jennifer, by virtue of her physician's oath, avoided any charge of culpability. Elizabeth, on the other hand, had no plausible excuse for her actions. She had simply elected to stand with Ortega.

For Clint, the law itself was a matter of secondary importance. His anger stemmed from what he saw as a breach of trust, a personal slap in the face. Tonight, as he had for the past week, he tried to fathom Elizabeth's behavior. His mind kept returning to Jennifer's remark, that her mother was somehow attracted to Ortega. If true, then it seemed to Clint the cruelest blow of all. Everything he felt for Elizabeth was now tinged by the thought. He searched for another reason, wanting not to believe. And yet . . .

A knock at the door brought him bolt upright out of bed. He pulled the Colt from its holster and moved quietly to the door. It passed through his mind that he was being overly cautious. Still, Ortega had tried once before in a hotel room and he saw no reason to take chances. He flattened himself against the wall.

"Who is it?"

"Brad," a voice replied.

Clint turned the key. When he opened the door, Brad saw the pistol and gave him a strange look. Stepping aside, Clint motioned him into the room.

"Expecting company?" Brad asked. "Or do you always answer the door with a gun?"

"Old habits are hard to break. Where'd you spring from?"

"Wanted to have a word with you. Figured I'd take a chance on catching you in town."

Clint twisted the key in the lock. He turned from the door, his eyes questioning. "Anything wrong at the ranch?"

"No, not a thing," Brad said. "Everybody's fine."

"Have a seat."

Brad took the straight-back chair. Clint holstered his pistol and sat down on the edge of the bed. He began rolling himself a smoke.

"Long ride into town," he said. "What's so important?"

"Well, first off," Brad replied, "I wanted to tell you I'm leavin' Spur. I decided this afternoon."

Clint lit his cigarette. He snuffed the match, nodding. "Elizabeth told me about it sometime ago. She hoped you'd agree to stay on."

"I had a talk with her this mornin'. Guess that's what finally decided me. Just wasn't fair to drag it out any longer."

"You think they can manage without you?"

"A good foreman won't be hard to find. Lots of men will jump at the job."

"How about you?" Clint said, exhaling smoke. "Got any plans?"

"For openers," Brad said, grinning, "I'm gonna get married. Decided that this afternoon too."

"The girl over on the Rio Felix?"

Brad's grin faded. "Some folks think white and Mexican shouldn't mix. Way I see it, that's nobody's business but my own."

"No argument there," Clint agreed. "A man can't let other people run his life."

"'Course, there's them that might try. All the more so if a man was lookin' for work."

"I thought you'd started your own cattle spread."

"Yeah, in a half-assed way," Brad said hollowly. "Trouble is, I'm wore out with raisin' cows. I finally admitted it to myself today."

Clint stared at him in puzzlement. "Sounds like you've been doing some serious thinking."

"Guess that's one of the reasons I wanted to talk to you. I'd like your advice on something."

"What sort of advice?"

"You know me about as well as anybody. How do you think I'd stack up as a law officer?"

"Law officer?" Clint said, taken aback. "Where'd you get a notion like that?"

"Watchin' you," Brad said with a vague gesture. "Looks to be a line of work where a man wouldn't get bored. I've got an idea it'd be just the ticket."

"Maybe so, except you're plannin' on getting married. How would your woman feel about you wearing a badge? It's not the safest occupation in the world."

"Juanita's not the worryin' type. Besides, I don't aim to make her a young widow. I figure to live a long time."

"Way you talk, you've already made up your mind."

"In a manner of speaking," Brad said, "I've taken the first step. That's the other reason I'm here."

"How so?"

"I've got information on Miguel Ortega."

Clint looked at him quick, fully alert. "What sort of information?"

Brad wormed around in his chair. "Before we get into that, I have to explain something. I wouldn't want you to think I'd sold out Mrs. Brannock."

"I don't take your meaning."

"When I talked to her this mornin', she said her and Ortega are quits. She's washed her hands of him."

Clint studied him thoughtfully. "She told you that?"

"In so many words," Brad noted. "Otherwise I wouldn't be here now. She's been too good to me."

Clint's expression revealed nothing. Yet he felt an overwhelming sense of relief. Elizabeth's break with Ortega eliminated his greatest personal concern. Something told him that her decision had been prompted by the attempts on his life. Her loyalty, in the end, had remained constant.

"One thing bothers me," he said now, looking at Brad. "Elizabeth knew how I felt about her and Ortega. Why wouldn't she tell me they're quits?"

"No mystery there," Brad remarked. "She's too proud to admit she was wrong. You and her are a lot alike."

Clint reviewed her note in his mind. It occurred to him that she had tried to say something without actually saying it. He thought Brad's point was well taken. Pride ran strong in the Brannocks.

"Let's get back to Ortega," he said. "What've you got?"

"A rumor," Brad informed him. "But I'd lay money it's more'n idle talk. Juanita told me about it herself."

"Why would she spill the beans on Ortega?"

"Her and her folks don't support him. I convinced 'em he'll do *mexicanos* more harm than good."

Clint appeared satisfied. "What's the rumor?"

"Ortega's in Roswell," Brad said. "Word's out he's gonna hold a meeting tomorrow night. He aims to recruit new members for *Las Gorras Blancas*."

"Any idea where the meeting will be held?"

"All Juanita heard was somewhere outside Roswell. Details were pretty sketchy by the time the news drifted over to the Rio Felix."

Clint accepted the statement. From Brad's place on the Rio Felix to Roswell was a distance of some twenty-five miles. Few *mexicanos* would travel that far to attend a meeting. On the other hand, it made sense that Ortega would attempt to organize *Las Gorras Blancas* along the upper Pecos. The area around Roswell was fast being overrun by Anglos.

"No question, though?" Clint said. "You're sure the meeting's set for tomorrow night?"

"That's the word."

Clint doused his cigarette. He rose from the bed and motioned Brad to his feet. "Raise your right hand."

Brad looked startled. "What's the idea?"

"You said you wanted to be a lawman, didn't you?"

"Yeah . . ."

"Then we'll make it official. Repeat after me."

Clint issued the oath and swore him in as a deputy.

Afterward, as though thinking out loud, Clint debated whether to notify Sheriff Grant. He finally rejected the thought of a force so large it would draw unwanted attention. He and Brad would handle the matter themselves.

They decided to leave at first light.

Roswell was situated near the juncture of the Pecos and the Rio Hondo. The land was relatively flat, a valley stretching north and south along the Pecos. *Llano Estacado,* the fabled Staked Plains, wandered off northeast into a vast emptiness.

Formerly a crossroads trading post, Roswell had been a supply point for cattle drives. The Goodnight-Loving Trail, which began in Texas, had passed through on its way to the High Plains of Wyoming. At one time, the valley had been the private domain of John "Jinglebob" Chisum, largest of all the Western cattle barons.

Following Chisum's death, homesteaders flooded into the valley. The water from rivers, and natural artesian springs, eventually led to irrigation and widespread farming. Yet the upper Pecos remained a stronghold of Anglo cattlemen. While the farmers were irrigating, the ranchers were stringing barbed wire.

The town itself doubled and redoubled in size. As the population swelled, the business district expanded and residential areas sprang up in every direction. A progressive atmosphere, bustling with commerce, centered on what was once a wayside trading post. The sound of hammers on fresh-sawed lumber rang out across the valley.

Morg emerged from the office of Goddard's Lumber Yard. He halted on the boardwalk as a late-afternoon sun slowly retreated westward. Thumbs hooked in his vest, he congratulated himself on a nifty piece of business. After some minor haggling, he had just clinched a deal with Alex Goddard. Starting immediately, the lumber yard's weekly orders would be increased by half.

For Morg, the deal was a harbinger of the future. In the growth of Roswell he saw an affirmation of everything he'd originally envisioned. The Pecos Valley, like other parts of

Lincoln County, was entering an era of unimaginable prosperity. He intended to share in those boom times, expanding from timber and mining into other businesses. These days he often reminded himself of his father's favorite axiom: A man's reach should always exceed his grasp.

Still, for all Morg's confidence, there were obstacles to progress. Chief among them was *Las Gorras Blancas,* and the spread of unrest among *mexicanos.* He thought it timely that his mother had broken with Miguel Ortega. By whatever means, the budding revolt would have to be crushed, and Ortega brought to justice. Otherwise an era of growth and prosperity might be transformed into anarchy, a racial bloodletting. Something he'd heard today added a note of urgency to his concern.

"Look who we got here! The prodigal son himself."

Brad's voice jarred him from his woolgathering. Somewhat dumbstruck, he saw Brad and Clint rein to a halt at the hitch rack. They stepped down from the saddle before he could collect his wits. Brad inspected him with a wry grin.

"What's the matter, cat got your tongue?"

"Damn near it," Morg confessed. "Where'd you two come from?"

"Lincoln," Brad said. "We've been on the trail since sunup."

"What brings you all the way over here?"

Clint edged forward. "Keep it under your hat," he said in a low voice. "We got word Ortega's holding a meeting hereabouts. I deputized Brad to lend a hand."

"I'll be dipped," Morg said, astounded. "Alex Goddard just told me the same thing."

"How'd Goddard find out?"

"One of the Mexicans that works for him let it slip."

Clint fixed him with a speculative look. "Goddard say anything about where the meeting's taking place?"

"Nooo," Morg said slowly. "But I'll bet the Mexican knows. Why don't we ask him?"

"Tell you what," Clint said. "You just introduce me to Goddard and I'll take it from there. I don't want you involved."

"What the devil's that supposed to mean?"

Clint's genial face toughened. "It means I want you to go on about your business. Leave Ortega to me."

"Nosiree," Morg declared. "You deputized Brad and you can deputize me. You're liable to need an extra gun, anyway."

"Save your breath," Clint said flatly. "You're out of it and that's that. Savvy?"

"Savvy what?" Morg persisted. "Why don't you want me along?"

Clint hesitated, considering. "I'll give it to you straight. Your mother would scald me good if anything happened to you. I won't have you on my conscience."

Morg burst out laughing. "You're not gonna brush me off that easy. Like it or not, I'm going along."

"Goddamnit," Clint said stolidly, "you'll do what you're told to do. I don't want any more argument about it."

"Won't wash," Morg said with a devil-may-care grin. "Whether you deputize me or not, I plan to tag along. There's no way you can stop me."

Clint smiled in spite of himself. "I could toss your butt in the local pokey. How's that sound?"

Morg squared himself up. "It'll take you and Brad both to do it. Why not save your fight for Ortega?"

"How the hell'd you get so pigheaded?"

"Guess it runs in the family."

"You're sure you won't listen to reason?"

Morg's grin widened. "We could jawbone all day and it wouldn't change nothin'. You've got yourself a volunteer."

"Lucky me," Clint growled, half under his breath. "All right, we've wasted enough time. Let's go talk to that Mexican."

Brad and Morg exchanged a quick smile. Clint moved around the hitch rack and started across the boardwalk. Sober as three judges, they went through the lumber-yard door. A few minutes later, in the privacy of Alex Goddard's office, they began grilling the Mexican.

He told them everything they wanted to know.

· · ·

A copse of trees stood in dark silhouette against a starswept sky. Beneath the cottonwoods, the deepening indigo of nightfall was broken by torches jammed into the ground. The shadowed figures of men, apparitions in the flickering light, were visible in a small clearing.

The grove was some four miles north of Roswell. Situated on the west bank of the Pecos, the clearing overlooked a lazy bend in the river. A short distance downstream Clint lay hidden in the shelterbelt of the woods. Beside him were Brad and Morg, bellied down on the ground. Their attention was fixed on Miguel Ortega.

Ortega's voice rang out across the clearing. He stood with his back to the riverbank, limned in the flare of torchlight. For the past hour, he had spoken with impassioned eloquence. A mesmerizing figure, he addressed the injustice of land frauds and the evil of those who governed in Santa Fe. When he spoke of *gringo* cattlemen, his eyes became black pinpoints of hate. He called for war without quarter on any *americano* who defiled the land with barbed wire.

A gathering of perhaps thirty *mexicanos* listened in spellbound silence. Some of them nodded, their faces mirroring bitterness and anger. Others appeared stoic, torn between caution and a simmering urge for vengeance. At last, when Ortega sounded a final call to action, their voices were raised in a sharp unleashing of rage. They crowded forward, a clotted mass of men, pledging themselves to *Las Gorras Blancas.* Then, one by one, they moved past Ortega, their sombreros clutched in their hands. To a man, they vowed to ride with him in the days ahead.

From downstream, Clint watched as the meeting drew to a close. He thought the *mexicanos* here tonight were unlike those he'd met in the Seven Rivers district. These men were being pressed on all sides by an invasion of Anglos, and they would fight to protect their land. Which was all the more reason to remain hidden and await developments. Until the crowd thinned out, any attempt to arrest Ortega would be nothing less than suicide. Yet, even as he cautioned himself to patience, he was gripped by a sense of newfound respect. After what he'd just witnessed, he finally understood why men were drawn to *Las Gorras Blancas*. Ortega was like a prophet of old, preaching deliverance from bondage. A stark figure seemingly ordained for greatness.

The *mexicanos* slowly scattered into the night. Within a short time only three men were left with Ortega. One of them carried a rifle cradled in his arms and the other two wore holstered pistols. They stood huddled together, listening intently while Ortega spoke of future raids. To all appearances, they had been selected as his lieutenants on the upper Pecos.

Clint motioned to Brad and Morg. Quietly, careful of betraying their presence, they got to their feet. Fanning out, their guns drawn, they ghosted through the woods. As they stepped into the circle of torchlight, Ortega suddenly stopped talking. The other *mexicanos* turned in the direction of his gaze and Ortega hissed a warning out of the side of his mouth. An eerie stillness settled over the clearing.

"Don't move," Clint commanded. "I'll shoot the first man that tries anything."

Ortega flicked a glance at Brad and Morg, assessing the situation. His gaze shifted back to Clint. *"Buenas noches, hombre,"* he said coolly. "We meet at last."

"No funny business," Clint said evenly. "I have a warrant for your arrest."

Ortega laughed. "Are you asking me to surrender?"

"That's about the size of it."

"And then you will put me on trial and hang me. *Verdad*?"

"You'll get your day in court. After that, it's up to a judge and jury."

"No, my friend," Ortega said, shaking his head. "I have no taste for hanging. I prefer to settle it here."

Clint's jawline tightened. "You force me to it and I'll kill you. Why do it the hard way?"

"Why not?" Ortega said with wintry malice. "You would prefer it that way yourself. We will oblige one another, agreed?"

"What about your men?" Clint asked. "Will they stay out of it?"

Ortega spoke to the *mexicanos*. They hesitated, reluctant to accept the order, then moved aside. When they were safely out of the way, he looked back at Clint. "Have no fear, *hombre*. They will honor my request."

Clint holstered his pistol. "Brad," he said, still staring at Ortega, "you and Morg watch yourselves. Anybody so much as blinks, start shooting."

"Hold on, now," Brad demanded. "What if he beats you?"

"Not likely," Clint said with a faint smile. "But if he does, he's a free man. Understood?"

"You're sure that's the way you want it?"

"I'm sure."

A peculiar glitter surfaced in Clint's eyes. He nodded to Ortega. "Whenever you're ready."

For a sliver of eternity they stared at each other. Ortega's mouth curled an instant before his hand moved. The telltale giveaway was all the edge Clint needed. He pulled and fired just as Ortega cleared leather. A starburst of blood darkened Ortega's chest and a surprised look came over his face. His gun roared, kicking up dirt at his feet. Then he sagged at the knees and slumped limply to the ground. One leg kicked in a spastic jerk of afterdeath.

Clint stared at the body only a moment. Without a flicker of emotion, his gaze swung to Ortega's men. *"Vaynase,"* he ordered. "Tell your people it's over. Miguel Ortega *está muerto.*"

The *mexicanos* slowly backed out of the clearing. At the edge of the treeline, they mounted their horses and vanished into the darkness. Clint stood listening until the hoofbeats faded off into the distance. At last he turned to Brad and Morg. His features were grim in the sallow torchlight.

"Helluva note," he said. "I've got a hunch Ortega had the last laugh."

"What d'you mean?" Morg blurted. "He's dead."

"Some dead men live a long time. Ortega's liable to live forever."

There was a sobering truth to the statement. Clint saw now that it wasn't a matter of cheating the hangman. Ortega had chosen to die with honor, a *guerrero* to the end. The story would be told and retold, the stuff of legend.

Las Gorras Blancas would stand as testament to the man and the legend. Miguel Ortega in death would emerge larger than life.

TWENTY-EIGHT

A funeral Mass was held three days later. People began filing into the Catholic church in Lincoln shortly after sunrise. By ten o'clock that morning the crowd spilled out into the street.

An open casket rested on a bier garlanded with mounds of wildflowers. The body of Miguel Ortega was laid out with an amethyst rosary draped over his hands. He was dressed in peasant clothes, with his mustache trimmed and his hair neatly combed. He looked like he might awaken at any moment.

The mourners gathered there were principally *mexicano*. They had traveled from San Patricio and White Oaks and remote villages scattered across the county. Drawn by the news of Ortega's death, they had come to witness his burial. Their presence honored his passage and memorialized him in the minds of their children. In life, he had been the champion of their cause, their defender. He was now a figure of reverence.

The front pews were occupied by prominent *políticos*. Félix Montoya, the *jefe* of San Patricio, was there with his family. Across the aisle were Roberto Díaz from Lincoln, and Juan Herrera from White Oaks. In the pew directly behind them, Elizabeth was seated with Ira Hecht, who had traveled all the way from Santa Fe. The story of Elizabeth's alliance with Ortega was by now part of the growing legend. The people spoke of her not by name but as *La Mariposa de Hierro*—the Iron Butterfly.

Following the Mass, Father Narváez, the local priest, delivered a stirring eulogy. He praised Miguel Ortega as a man of the people, one of *los pobres*. In a solemn voice, he spoke of the deceased as a paladin of liberty, a martyr to the cause of justice. He declared that *Las Gorras Blancas* would stand as the dead man's epitaph, a symbol of sacrifice and valor. The fight would go forward, he prophesied, until *mexicanos* enjoyed the rights of all free men. Miguel Ortega, even in death, would continue to lead his people.

A low murmur swept through the church as the priest finished his eulogy. The *jefes políticos* nodded their heads, and those in the packed congregation muttered approval. Watching them, Elizabeth knew that the priest's words would spread from village to village, gathering force as the message was repeated by *los pobres* throughout New Mexico. She doubted that a man of Ortega's stature would emerge to lead the fight. Yet she was certain that the struggle had only just begun. No *mexicano* would ever again stand alone in the face of injustice.

From the church, a funeral cortege formed on the street. Six stout men hefted the casket onto their shoulders, and the mourners, some three hundred strong, fell in behind. The procession, led by Father Narváez, slowly made its way to the Mexican cemetery on the outskirts of town. There, over a freshly dug grave, the priest delivered a final prayer. The pallbearers, holding the casket suspended on ropes, then lowered Miguel Ortega into the ground. A granite headstone would later be set into place.

When the graveside service ended, the *jefes políticos* made a point of paying homage to Elizabeth. Their deference left no question that she would continue to command their allegiance. To the throng of *mexicanos* it was obvious that her coalition would not suffer by Ortega's death. No one spoke of her brother-in-law, the *bárbaro americano* who hunted men. Instead, they whispered of how she and her daughter, the lady doctor, had once saved Ortega's life. As she walked from the cemetery, the men doffed their sombreros and the women bowed their heads. She smiled, holding firmly to Ira Hecht's arm, trying not to betray her discomfort. She felt deeply humbled by their adulation.

Uptown, Elizabeth and Hecht stopped outside the express office. There were pressing matters in Santa Fe and he planned to catch the noon stage. Last night, upon arriving in town, he had presented Elizabeth with a letter from Thomas Canby. In it, the leader of the Santa Fe Ring outlined a sweeping proposal. He offered to support her fight for land reform, as well as an end to corruption in the territorial legislature. From her, he asked only the assurance that certain business legislation would not be opposed. He guaranteed cooperation with respect to her struggle on behalf of the *mexicanos*.

Because the funeral was scheduled for midmorning, Elizabeth had spent the night with Jennifer. But she'd gotten little sleep, for Canby's letter left her with great misgivings. She roamed the clinic like a distracted ghost, weighing all the possible ramifications. At breakfast, she hadn't mentioned the letter and Hecht had tactfully avoided the subject. However, he could scarcely fail to notice that her features were drawn and tired. She looked somehow burdened.

Outside the express office, they stood wrapped in silence. Hecht thought she was preoccupied with the funeral and he had no wish to intrude. Still, there were affairs to be discussed, and the stage was due shortly. He decided on an oblique approach.

"Quite a turnout," he said. "Were you surprised by the number of people who showed up?"

"No, not at all," Elizabeth commented. "For them, Miguel Ortega was like a saint on horseback. He restored their faith in themselves."

"Speaking of faith," Hecht observed, "you're not doing so badly yourself. The *jefes* were at some pains to exhibit their respect. I got the feeling they're anxious to climb aboard the bandwagon."

Elizabeth nodded, then smiled a little. "I suppose it's only natural. We're almost certain to carry the fall elections, and they know it. Everyone loves a winner."

"Everyone including Tom Canby. He's convinced we'll win by a landslide."

"Yes, his letter indicates as much."

Hecht looked at her. "Have you given his proposal any thought?"

"Before I answer," Elizabeth said, "I'd prefer to hear your assessment. How do you see it?"

"Essentially, Canby's trying to cut his losses. His crystal ball tells him we'll wind up with a majority in the legislature. He thinks it's time to strike a deal."

"What about the business legislation he mentions? Should we just look the other way?"

"Well, let's evaluate it," Hecht suggested. "He's talking about legislation that affects banks and railroads and various tariffs. He and his cronies want to protect their financial base."

Elizabeth's face was troubled. "In other words, an under-the-table tradeoff. He supports land reform and we pretend to overlook the vested interests. Is that it?"

"Quid pro quo," Hecht temporized. "One hand washes the other. Nothing unusual about that."

"Except for the fact that we've associated ourselves with a gang of thieves. Doesn't that dirty us in the process?"

"At some point, I suppose pragmatism becomes unavoidable. Government operates on the principle of give-and-take. No one ever gets it all his own way."

Elizabeth couldn't dispute the argument. Compromise, in the end, was the lifeblood of politics. The system was by no means perfect, but it was the way things worked. Nothing of consequence was achieved without some form of quid pro quo.

"So then?" she said. "Are you advising me to accept his offer?"

Hecht's gaze did not waver. "A majority doesn't necessarily mean we *control* the legislature. Tom Canby could still buy the votes to deadlock us on reform. I believe the wiser course would be to accept."

"Magnanimous in victory, is that it?"

"Something along those lines."

A note of concern came into Elizabeth's voice. "What guarantees do we have that Canby will honor his word? You've said yourself he's totally without scruples."

"Our motto," Hecht quipped, "will be eternal vigilance. We'll have to watch him like a hawk."

"I prefer something a bit more concrete. Suppose we attach a condition to the arrangement."

"What sort of condition?"

Elizabeth smiled. "Your appointment as attorney general should do it rather nicely. Don't you agree?"

Behind his wire-rimmed glasses, Hecht's eyes did a slow roll. "We certainly wouldn't have to worry about any shenanigans. Canby's only road would be the straight and narrow."

"Exactly," Elizabeth said with calm assurance. "And if he strays, we won't be quite so magnanimous. I think Tom Canby would look rather dapper in a prison uniform."

Hecht chuckled softly. "You've learned to play a rough game."

"On the contrary, I simply play to win. And win we will, Ira. I won't settle for less."

"The Mexicans got it right when they nicknamed you the Iron Butterfly. You're a true-blue original."

"Why, thank you, Mr. Attorney General."

"God save us." Hecht beamed. "Wait till Canby hears that!"

A short while later Hecht boarded the west-bound stage. He took a seat by the window and gave Elizabeth an offhand salute. She waved as the driver popped his whip and the six-horse hitch pulled away. She watched until the stagecoach was out of sight.

Elizabeth started toward the clinic. John Taylor was waiting for her there and she still had to talk with Jennifer. The wedding was Sunday and all the arrangements weren't yet complete. She made a mental note to have a word with the preacher.

One thought prompted another. Elizabeth was suddenly struck by the incongruity of life. Today she had attended a funeral and on Sunday her daughter would be married. She recalled a line she'd read somewhere: a season of endings and beginnings. She felt it was perfect to the moment, worth remembering. Whatever the circumstances, life went on in the midst of death.

As she turned downstreet, her gaze was drawn to the courthouse. She saw Clint and Will Grant emerge from the sheriff's office. For almost three weeks, she hadn't spoken with Clint. At first, he had avoided her because he felt betrayed. He was avoiding her now because he'd killed Miguel Ortega. Alive or dead, the *mexicano* leader seemed to stand between them.

Clint spotted her outside the express office. She looked straight at him, her head high, and waited. After a moment, he said something to Grant, who turned back into the courthouse. She experienced a tremulous sensation as he came down the steps and started across the street. She was all too aware that there would never be another chance. Unless their differences were reconciled now, there was no hope for the future.

"Hello, Beth," Clint said, halting in front of her. "How're things with you?"

"Fine," Elizabeth said agreeably. "I just saw Ira Hecht off on the stage. He asked me to give you his regards."

"Yeah, I heard he was in town. Guess you had a lot of political matters to talk over?"

"Well, that wasn't the real reason for his trip. He actually came down for the funeral."

"Ortega was a popular fellow," Clint said uneasily. "I suppose some folks felt obliged to pay their respects."

"I was one of them," Elizabeth said in a low voice. "Do you hold that against me?"

Clint shook his head. "Brad gave me the lowdown on how you busted off with Ortega. I stopped being sore the minute he told me."

"Then why haven't you come by the ranch?"

"Figured I wasn't welcome."

"Not welcome?" Elizabeth echoed. "Whatever gave you that idea?"

"Beth . . ." Clint hesitated, his eyes dwelling on her. "Whether you believe it or not, I tried my damnedest to take Ortega alive. He all but forced me to kill him."

"Yes, I know," Elizabeth acknowledged. "Morg told me everything."

Clint studied her. "Are you sayin' you don't fault me for what happened?"

"How could I? You gave him every chance."

"In that case, what's been holdin' you back? How come I haven't got an invite out to the ranch?"

"Stubborn pride," Elizabeth said honestly. "We're alike in that respect."

"I reckon we are," Clint admitted. "Even Brad's of the same opinion. He told me so straight out."

Elizabeth smiled warmly. "Perhaps we're too stubborn for our own good."

A slow grin tugged at the corner of Clint's mouth. "Tell you the truth, I was thinkin' the same thing. What say we just forget the whole mess?"

"Oh, we have to! Otherwise Jennifer would disown us both."

"Jennifer?"

"Of course." Elizabeth's eyes suddenly shone, and she laughed. "Had you forgotten she's being married Sunday? She expects you to give her away."

Clint's grin broadened. "Tell her I'd count it an honor."

"I have a better idea." Elizabeth took his arm. "Let's both tell her."

Arm in arm, they walked off toward the clinic. As though by mutual accord, neither of them again made reference to the past. They spoke instead of the future.

The marriage of a Brannock was considered the social event of the year. By half-past twelve on Sunday, the street outside the Methodist Church was clogged with buckboards and wagons. The ceremony was scheduled for one o'clock, and shortly before the hour the steeple bell began to peal.

Every pew in the church was packed. Elizabeth and the

family, which included John Taylor, occupied the entire front row. Juanita Ramírez, with a black mantilla covering her head, was seated beside Brad. The congregation, both townspeople and ranchers, had stayed over after the regular Sunday-morning services. No one wanted to miss the most talked about wedding in recent memory.

A few latecomers hurried through the vestibule. Off to one side, Jennifer stood with her hand tucked in Clint's arm. She was a vision in white, her wedding gown molded to her like the curves in melting ivory. Her hair was upswept, with curls fluffed high on her forehead, and the train of her veil brushing the floor. Her cheeks were flushed with color and her eyes sparkled with excitement. She looked radiantly beautiful.

Clint was attired in a black broadcloth coat and striped trousers. A pearl stickpin gleamed from the cravat cinched around his stiff winged collar. The outfit was spanking new, bought especially for the occasion. On his left side, the coat bulged where he'd jammed his pistol in the waistband. Over all protests, he had refused to come without it. Even his niece's wedding was no reason to go unarmed.

As the last of the guests filed through the doorway, he patted Jennifer's hand. "I never told you before," he said, "but I'm mighty proud of you. Just thought I'd mention it."

"Thank you, Uncle Clint." She gave his arm an affectionate squeeze. "You being here makes today extra special."

"My sentiments exactly."

The organ rumbled to life. As the strains of the wedding march filled the church, Clint led her down the aisle. The congregation turned in their seats, craning for a better view of the bride. Elizabeth, who wore a dress of teal-blue cambric, looked marvelously elegant. Watching Jennifer, she thought her heart would burst. She dabbed at her eyes with a lace hanky.

Blake waited at the altar. His gaze fixed on Jennifer and their eyes remained locked the entire time she moved down the aisle. Clint paused, placing her hand in Blake's, as the organ mounted to a crescendo. Then he turned, stepping back from the altar, and took his seat beside Elizabeth. She managed a teary smile.

The preacher moved forward with an open Bible. He wore a hammertail coat and his hair looked buttered to his head. Smiling down at the bride and groom, he let the last strains of the organ fade away. At last, with the church gone silent, he stared out over the congregation.

"Dearly beloved," he intoned, "we are gathered together in the sight of God to join this man and this woman in holy wedlock."

The ceremony lasted not quite ten minutes. When they were pronounced man and wife, Blake lifted Jennifer's veil and kissed her gently on the mouth. Her eyes glistened with happiness as the organ once again wheezed to life. They turned up the aisle and slowly made their way from the church. Outside, a crowd of well-wishers pelted them with rice and shouted congratulations. A buggy festooned with colored streamers was waiting on the street.

Jennifer had finally relented and agreed to a brief honeymoon. She and Blake would spend two days in Roswell, the nearest town of any size. But now, under a downpour of rice, they retreated to the clinic and changed into traveling clothes. When they emerged, Jennifer exchanged a teary-eyed hug with her mother before stepping into the buggy. At the last instant, she took deliberate aim and tossed her bridal bouquet to Juanita. Blake snapped the reins and they took off in a fresh barrage of rice.

The crowd began departing by the time the buggy was out of sight. Some of the ranchers and a few of the more prominent townspeople stopped off to pay their respects to Elizabeth. Within minutes, the last hand had been shaken and the immediate family was left by themselves outside the clinic. Clint excused himself and walked toward the hitch rack, where Lon and Hank stood with their horses. They appeared anxious to be on their way.

Clint had resigned himself to the inevitable. Hank was determined to follow his brother, rather than remain on at Spur. In the end, loyalty had decided the matter, and there was no way to force the youngster against his will. While Clint was concerned, he saw nothing to be gained by further argument. Some things, however grudgingly, could only be accepted.

"All set?" he asked, halting beside the hitch rail. "Got everything you need?"

Lon shrugged lazily. "We're fixed just fine."

"Whereabouts are you headed?"

"Anywhere they play poker," Lon said. "One of the mining camps most likely."

Clint nodded, glancing at Hank. "I'll expect a letter every now and then. That was our deal."

Hank bobbed his head. "Don't worry, we're gonna be all right. I'll keep you posted."

"And you," Clint said, frowning at Lon, "make damn sure you take care of your brother. Otherwise you'll answer to me."

Lon grinned crookedly. "I'll teach him everything I know."

"Yeah, that's what worries me."

After a round of handshakes, the brothers climbed aboard their horses. Lon tugged his hat low and Hank waved as they reined about from the hitch rack. Clint watched them ride off, a leaden feeling in his chest. He finally turned away when they disappeared along the westward road.

Brad and Juanita waited nearby. As Clint approached them, the girl smiled shyly and Brad extended his hand. "Wanted to thank you," he said, pumping Clint's arm. "Your talk with Will Grant turned the trick. I'll sign on as a deputy right after fall roundup."

"Save your thanks till later," Clint advised. "You're liable to change your mind about wearin' a badge."

"Not much chance of that."

Clint looked at the girl. "I understand you're getting married. How do you feel about a lawman for a husband?"

Juanita laughed. "A woman follows where her man leads, *señor*. I trust him to know what is best."

"Well, I wish you both all the luck. I'll try to get back for your wedding."

Brad shook hands again, then walked with Juanita to their buckboard. Morg and Louise, along with John Taylor, were standing beside the phaeton carriage. Elizabeth, as though biding her time, waited on the clinic pathway. Clint joined her, his features suddenly sober. She smiled, nodding to the younger couples.

"All these Brannocks," she said. "We've done well, haven't we?"

"Yeah, we have," Clint agreed. "Some of us tend to scatter out, but that doesn't change anything. Family's still family."

There was a look of deep sadness in Elizabeth's features. "Won't you reconsider?" she asked. "You could retire with honor and leave the law to younger men. You've earned it."

"Not just yet," Clint said, avoiding her gaze. "Got a wire from the governor ordering me back to Santa Fe. Guess there's always plenty of work for men like me."

"There's work here," Elizabeth said, her voice husky. "You could stay on and help me run Spur. You know that's what I want . . . don't you?"

A mad jumble of images and recollections flashed through Clint's mind. He'd often lain awake brooding on the road not taken, the words not spoken. Years ago he might have told her what he felt, what she meant to him. How she would have reacted was something he would never know. The time for asking had long since passed and would never return. Neither of them could recapture what they were, or what might have been. It was too late.

"One of these days—" He paused, cleared his throat of a sudden tightness. "Well, you never know, I might just take you up on your offer. There's worse places than the Rio Hondo."

Elizabeth's eyes filled with emotion. She cupped his face in her hands and brushed his mouth with a soft kiss. "I'll miss you terribly," she said, her voice curiously vibrant. "Don't stay away too long."

"I won't," Clint promised. "That's one thing you can always count on."

Elizabeth smiled, unable to speak. She whirled quickly away and walked to the carriage. John Taylor assisted her into the front seat while Morg and Louise seated themselves in the rear. A moment later they drove off toward the Hondo Valley.

Clint waited even though he knew she wouldn't look back. Their partings were always bittersweet and neither of them prolonged it beyond certain limits. At last, when the carriage passed the outskirts of town, he turned upstreet. Hands jammed in his pockets, he ambled off in the direction of the hotel.

Somewhile later Clint led his horse from the livery stable. He'd changed from the suit to range clothes, and the Colt was once again strapped around his waist. He stepped into the saddle and reined the gelding onto the road. His thoughts were no longer inward, but rather somewhere ahead. He too refused to look back.

Outside town, he heeled the gelding into a smooth, ground-eating trot. He squinted against the late-afternoon sun, content once more to be on the trail. One day he would return to the Hondo, and the Brannocks. But for now his gaze was faraway, fixed on a distant land. A land that still called him on beyond.

He rode west toward the mountains.